D1569596

George Borrow

from the picture in the possession of John Murray.

LAVENGRO

The Classic Account of Gypsy Life in Nineteenth-Century England

George Borrow

DOVER PUBLICATIONS, INC.
New York

Published in Canada by General Publishing Company, Ltd., 30 Lesmill Road, Don Mills, Toronto, Ontario.

Published in the United Kingdom by Constable and Company, Ltd., 3 The Lanchesters, 162–164 Fulham Palace Road, London W6 9ER.

This Dover edition, first published in 1991, is an unabridged republication of the edition of *Lavengro* originally published in 1900 by G. P. Putnam's Sons, New York, and John Murray, London, "containing the unaltered text of the original issue; some suppressed episodes now printed for the first time; ms.variorum, vocabulary and notes by the author of *The Life of George Borrow*." (The first edition of the book was by John Murray, London, 1851.) The placement of the illustrations has been slightly altered for this edition.

Manufactured in the United States of America
Dover Publications, Inc., 31 East 2nd Street, Mineola, N.Y. 11501

Library of Congress Cataloging-in-Publication Data

Borrow, George Henry, 1803–1881.
    Lavengro : the classic account of gypsy life in nineteenth-century England / George Borrow.
        p.   cm.
    Reprint. Originally published: New York : Putnam, 1900.
    ISBN 0-486-26915-9
    1. Gypsies—England—History—19th century—Fiction.   I. Title.
PR4154.L3   1991
823'.8—dc20   91-23990
                                            CIP

LAVENGRO;

THE SCHOLAR—THE GYPSY—THE PRIEST.

By GEORGE BORROW,

AUTHOR OF "THE BIBLE IN SPAIN" AND "THE GYPSIES OF SPAIN"

IN THREE VOLUMES—VOL. I.

LONDON:

JOHN MURRAY, ALBEMARLE STREET.

1851.

ADVERTISEMENT.

(1851.)

IN compliance with the advice of certain friends who are desirous that it may not be supposed that the following work has been written expressly for the present times, the author begs leave to state that it was planned in the year 1842, and all the characters sketched before the conclusion of the year 1843. The contents of the volumes here offered to the public have, with the exception of the Preface, existed in manuscript for a very considerable time.

PREFACE TO THE FIRST EDITION.

(1851.)

In the following pages I have endeavoured to describe a dream, partly of study, partly of adventure, in which will be found copious notices of books, and many descriptions of life and manners, some in a very unusual form.

The scenes of action lie in the British Islands. Pray be not displeased, gentle reader, if perchance thou hast imagined that I was about to conduct thee to distant lands, and didst promise thyself much instruction and entertainment from what I might tell thee of them. I do assure thee that thou hast no reason to be displeased, inasmuch as there are no countries in the world less known by the British than these selfsame British Islands, or where more strange things are every day occurring, whether in road or street, house or dingle.

The time embraces nearly the first quarter of the present century. This information, again, may perhaps be anything but agreeable to thee; it is a long time to revert to—but fret not thyself, many matters which at present much occupy the public mind originated in some degree towards the latter end of that period, and some of them will be treated of.

The principal actors in this dream, or drama, are, as you will have gathered from the title-page, a Scholar, a Gypsy, and a Priest. Should you imagine that these three form one, permit me to assure you that you are very much mistaken. Should there be something of the Gypsy manifest in the Scholar, there is certainly nothing of the Priest. With respect to the Gypsy—decidedly the most entertaining character of the three—there is certainly nothing of the Scholar or the Priest in him; and as for the

Priest, though there may be something in him both of scholarship and gypsyism, neither the Scholar nor the Gypsy would feel at all flattered by being confounded with him.

Many characters which may be called subordinate will be found, and it is probable that some of these characters will afford much more interest to the reader than those styled the principal. The favourites with the writer are a brave old soldier and his helpmate, an ancient gentlewoman who sold apples, and a strange kind of wandering man and his wife.

Amongst the many things attempted in this book is the encouragement of charity, and free and genial manners, and the exposure of humbug, of which there are various kinds, but of which the most perfidious, the most debasing, and the most cruel, is the humbug of the Priest.

Yet let no one think that irreligion is advocated in this book. With respect to religious tenets, I wish to observe that I am a member of the Church of England, into whose communion I was baptised, and to which my forefathers belonged. Its being the religion in which I was baptised, and of my forefathers, would be a strong inducement to me to cling to it; for I do not happen to be one of those choice spirits " who turn from their banner when the battle bears strongly against it, and go over to the enemy," and who receive at first a hug and a " viva," and in the sequel contempt and spittle in the face ; but my chief reason for belonging to it is, because, of all Churches calling themselves Christian ones, I believe there is none so good, so well founded upon Scripture, or whose ministers are, upon the whole, so exemplary in their lives and conversation, so well read in the Book from which they preach, or so versed in general learning, so useful in their immediate neighbourhoods, or so unwilling to persecute people of other denominations for matters of doctrine.

In the communion of this Church, and with the religious consolation of its ministers, I wish and hope to live and die, and in its and their defence will at all times be ready, if required, to speak, though humbly, and to fight, though feebly, against enemies, whether carnal or spiritual.

And is there no priestcraft in the Church of England ? There is certainly, or rather there was, a modicum of priest-craft in the Church of England, but I have generally found that those who are most vehement against the Church of England are chiefly dissatisfied with her because there is only a modicum of that article in her. . Were she stuffed to the very cupola with it, like a certain other Church, they would have much less to say against the Church of England.

By the other Church I mean Rome. Its system was once prevalent in England, and, during the period that it prevailed there, was more prolific of debasement and crime than all other causes united. The people and the govern-ment at last becoming enlightened by means of the Scripture, spurned it from the island with disgust and horror, the land instantly after its disappearance becoming a fair field, in which arts, sciences, and all the amiable virtues flourished, instead of being a pestilent marsh where swine-like ignorance wallowed, and artful hypocrites, like so many wills-o'-the-wisp, played antic gambols about, around and above debased humanity.

But Popery still wished to play her old part, to regain her lost dominion, to reconvert the smiling land into the pestilential morass, where she could play again her old antics. From the period of the Reformation in England up to the present time, she has kept her emissaries here— individuals contemptible in intellect, it is true, but cat-like and gliding, who, at her bidding, have endeavoured, as much as in their power has lain, to damp and stifle every genial, honest, loyal and independent thought, and to reduce minds to such a state of dotage as would enable their old Popish mother to do what she pleased with them.

And in every country, however enlightened, there are always minds inclined to grovelling superstition—minds fond of eating dust and swallowing clay—minds never at rest, save when prostrate before some fellow in a surplice ; and these Popish emissaries found always some weak enough to bow down before them, astounded by their dreadful denunciations of eternal woe and damnation to any who should refuse to believe their Romania ; but they played a poor game—the law protected the servants of Scripture, and the priest with his beads seldom ventured to approach any but the remnant of those of the eikono-latry—representatives of worm-eaten houses, their debased dependants and a few poor crazy creatures among the middle classes—he played a poor game, and the labour was about to prove almost entirely in vain, when the English Legislature, in compassion or contempt, or, yet more pro-bably, influenced by that spirit of toleration and kindness which is so mixed up with Protestantism, removed almost entirely the disabilities under which Popery laboured, and enabled it to raise its head and to speak out almost without fear.

And it did raise its head, and, though it spoke with some little fear at first, soon discarded every relic of it; went about the land uttering its damnation cry, gathering around it—and for doing so many thanks to it—the favourers of priestcraft who lurked within the walls of the Church of England; frightening with the loudness of its voice the weak, the timid and the ailing; perpetrating, whenever it had an opportunity, that species of crime to which it has ever been most partial—*deathbed robbery;* for as it is cruel, so is it dastardly. Yes, it went on enlist-ing, plundering and uttering its terrible threats till—till it became, as it always does when left to itself, a fool, a very fool. Its plunderings might have been overlooked, and so might its insolence, had it been common insolence, but it—, and then the roar of indignation which arose from outraged England against the viper, the frozen viper which it had permitted to warm itself upon its bosom.

But thanks, Popery, you have done all that the friends of enlightenment and religious liberty could wish; but if ever there were a set of foolish ones to be found under Heaven, surely it is the priestly rabble who came over from Rome to direct the grand movement, so long in its getting up.

But now again the damnation cry is withdrawn, there is a subdued meekness in your demeanour, you are now once more harmless as a lamb. Well, we shall see how the trick —" the old trick "—will serve you.

PREFACE TO THE SECOND EDITION.

(1872.)

Lavengro made its first appearance more than one and twenty years ago. It was treated in anything but a courteous manner. Indeed, abuse ran riot, and many said that the book was killed. If by killed was meant knocked down and stunned, which is the Irish acceptation of the word—there is a great deal about Ireland in the book—they were right enough. It was not dead, however, oh dear no! as is tolerably well shown by the present edition, which has been long called for.

The chief assailants of the book were the friends of Popery in England. They were enraged because the author stood up for the religion of his fathers, his country, and the Bible, against the mythology of a foreign priest. As for the Pope—but the Pope has of late had his misfortunes, so no harsh language. To another subject! From the Pope to the Gypsies! From the Roman Pontiff to the Romany Chals!

A very remarkable set of people are the Gypsies; frequent mention is made of them in *Lavengro*, and from their peculiar language the word "Lavengro" is taken. They first attracted notice in Germany, where they appeared in immense numbers in the early part of the fifteenth century, a period fraught with extraordinary events: the coming of the Black Death; the fortunes and misfortunes of the Emperor Sigismund; the quarrels of the Three Popes—the idea of three Popes at one time!—the burning alive of John Huss; the advance of the Crescent, and the battle of Agincourt. They were of dark complexion, some of them of nearly negro blackness, and spoke a language of their own, though many could converse in German and

other tongues.   They called themselves Zingary and
Romany Chals, and the account they gave of themselves
was that they were from Lower Egypt, and were doing
penance, by a seven years' wandering, for the sin of their
forefathers, who of old had refused hospitality to the Virgin
and Child.   They did not speak truth, however ; the name
they bore, Zingary, and which, slightly modified, is still
borne by their descendants in various countries, shows that
they were not from Egypt, but from a much more distant
land, Hindostan ; for Zingaro is Sanscrit, and signifies
a man of mixed race, a mongrel ; whilst their conduct was
evidently not that of people engaged in expiatory pilgrim-
age ; for the women told the kosko bokht, the good luck,
the *buena ventura ;* kaured, that is, filched money and
valuables from shop-boards and counters by a curious
motion of the hands, and poisoned pigs and hogs by means
of a certain drug, and then begged, and generally obtained,
the carcases, which cut up served their families for food ;
the children begged and stole ; whilst the men, who it is
true professed horse-clipping, farriery and fiddling, not
unfrequently knocked down travellers and plundered them.
The hand of justice of course soon fell heavily upon them ;
men of Egypt, as they were called, were seized, hung, or
maimed ; women scourged or branded ; children whipped ;
but no severity appeared to have any effect upon the
Zingary ; wherever they went (and they soon found their
way to almost every country in Europe), they adhered to
their evil practices.   Before the expiration of the fifteenth
century bands of them appeared in England with their
horses, donkeys and tilted carts.   How did they contrive
to cross the sea with their carts and other property ?   By
means very easy to people with money in their pockets,
which the Gypsies always have, by paying for their passage ; just as the Hungarian tribe did, who a few years ago
came to England with their horses and vehicles, and who,
whilst encamping with their English brethren in the love-
liest of all forests, Epping Wesh, exclaimed " Sore si mensar
si men ".*

The meaning of Zingary, one of the names by which

* We are all relations, all alike ; all who are with us are ourselves.

the pseudo-penitents from Lower Egypt called themselves, has been given above. Now for that of the other, Romany Chals, a name in which the English Gypsies delight, who have entirely dropped that of Zingary. The meaning of Romany Chals is lads of Rome or Rama; Romany signifying that which belongs to Rama or Rome, and Chal a son or lad, being a Zingaric word connected with the *Shilo* of Scripture, the meaning of which may be found in the Lexicon of the brave old Westphalian Hebraist, Johannes Buxtorf.[1]

The Gypsies of England, the Zigany, Zigeuner, and other tribes of the Continent, descendants of the old Zingary and Romany Chals, retain many of the characteristics of their forefathers, and, though differing from each other in some respects, resemble each other in many. They are much alike in hue and feature; speak amongst themselves much the same tongue; exercise much the same trades, and are addicted to the same evil practices. There is a little English Gypsy gillie, or song, of which the following quatrain is a translation, containing four queries, to all of which the English Romanó might respond by Ava, and the foreign Chal by the same affirmative to the three first, if not to the last :—

> Can you speak the Roman tongue?
> Can you make the fiddle ring?
> Can you poison a jolly hog?
> And split the stick for the linen string?

So much for the Gypsies. There are many other things in the book to which perhaps the writer ought to advert; but he is weary, and, moreover, is afraid of wearying others. He will, therefore, merely add that every book must eventually stand or fall by its deserts; that praise, however abundant, will not keep a bad book alive for any considerable time, nor abuse, however virulent, a good one for ever in the dust; and he thinks himself justified in saying, that were there not some good in *Lavengro*, it would not again be raising its head, notwithstanding all it underwent one and twenty years ago.

---

[1] *Chal* is simply the contraction of *chavál*, a form cognate with *chavoró* the diminutive of *chavó*, a lad. *Chavál* is still common in Spain, both among the Gypsies and the lower orders of Spaniards.—ED.

CONTENTS.

CHAPTER I.

PAGE

Birth—My Father—Tamerlane—Ben Brain—French Protestants—East Anglia—Sorrow and Troubles—True Peace—A Beautiful Child—Foreign Grave—Mirrors—Alpine Country—Emblems—Slow of Speech—The Jew —Strange Gestures 1

CHAPTER II.

Barracks and Lodgings—A Camp—The Viper—A Delicate Child—Black-berry Time—Meum and Tuum—Hythe—The Golgotha—Daneman's Skull—Superhuman Stature—Stirring Times—The Sea-Bord . . 9

CHAPTER III.

Pretty D . . .—The Venerable Church—The Stricken Heart—Dormant Energies—The Small Packet—Nerves—The Books—A Picture—Moun-tain-like Billows—The Foot-Print—Spirit of De Foe—Reasoning Powers —Terrors of God—Heads of the Dragons—High-Church Clerk—A Journey—The Drowned Country 15

CHAPTER IV.

Norman Cross—Wide Expanse—Vive l'Empereur—Unpruned Woods—Man with the Bag—Froth and Conceit—I beg your Pardon—Growing Timid —About Three o'Clock—Taking One's Ease—Cheek on the Ground—King of the Vipers—French King—Frenchmen and Water . . . 23

CHAPTER V.

The Tent—Man and Woman—Dark and Swarthy—Manner of Speaking—Bad Money—Transfixed—Faltering Tone—Little Basket—High Opinion —Plenty of Good—Keeping Guard—Tilted Cart—Rubricals—Jasper—The Right Sort—The Horseman of the Lane—John Newton—The Alarm —Gentle Brothers 29

CHAPTER VI.

Three Years—Lilly's Grammar—Proficiency—Ignorant of Figures—The School Bell—Order of Succession—Persecution—What are we to do?—Northward—A Goodly Scene—Haunted Ground—Feats of Chivalry—Rivers—Over the Brig 38

CHAPTER VII.

The Castle—A Father's Inquiries—Scotch Language—A Determination—Bui hin Digri—Good Scotchman—Difference of Races—Ne'er a Haggis—Pugnacious People—What are ye, Man?—The Nor Loch—Gestures Wild—The Bicker—New Town Champion—Wild Looking Figure—Headlong 45

CHAPTER VIII.

Expert Climbers—The Crags—Something Red—The Horrible Edge—David Haggart—Fine Materials—The Greatest Victory—Extraordinary Robber —The Ruling Passion 52

CHAPTER IX.

Napoleon—The Storm—The Cove—Up the Country—The Trembling Hand —Irish—Tough Battle—Tipperary Hills—Elegant Lodgings—A Speech —Fair Specimen—Orangemen 56

CHAPTER X.

Protestant Young Gentlemen—The Greek Letters—Open Chimney—Murtagh —Paris and Salamanca—Nothing to Do—To Whit, to Whoo!—The Pack of Cards—Before Christmas 62

CHAPTER XI.

Templemore—Devil's Mountain—No Companion—Force of Circumstance— Way of the World—Ruined Castle—Grim and Desolate—The Donjon— Old Woman—My own House. 66

CHAPTER XII.

A Visit—Figure of a Man—The Dog of Peace—The Raw Wound—The Guard-Room—Boy Soldier—Person in Authority—Never Solitary— Clergyman and Family—Still Hunting—Fairy Man—Near Sunset— Bagg—Left-Handed Hitter—Irish and Supernatural—At Swanton Morley . . . . , ... 71 .

CHAPTER XIII.

Groom and Cob—Strength and Symmetry—Where's the Saddle?—The First Ride—No more Fatigue—Love for Horses—Pursuit of Words—Philologist and Pegasus—The Smith—What more, Agrah?—Sassanach Ten Pence 78

CHAPTER XIV.

A fine old City—Norman Master-Work—Lollards' Hole—Good Blood—The Spaniard's Sword—Old Retired Officer—Writing to a Duke—God Help the Child—Nothing like Jacob—Irish Brigades—Old Sergeant Meredith —I have been Young—Idleness—Only Course Open—The Bookstall— A Portrait—A Banished Priest 84

CHAPTER XV.

Monsieur Dante—Condemned Musket—Sporting—Sweet Rivulet—The Earl's Home—The Pool—The Sonorous Voice—What dost thou Read?—Man of Peace—Zohar and Mishna—Money Changers 91

CHAPTER XVI.

Fair of Horses—Looks of Respect—The Fast Trotter—Pair of Eyes—Strange Men—Jasper, Your Pal—Force of Blood—Young Lady with Diamonds —Not quite so Beautiful , ... 97

CHAPTER XVII.

PAGE

The Tents—Pleasant Discourse—I am Pharaoh—Shifting for One's Self—Horse-Shoes—This is Wonderful—Bless your Wisdom—A Pretty Manœuvre—Ill Day to the Romans—My Name is Herne—Singular People—An Original Speech—Word Master—Speaking Romanly . 102

CHAPTER XVIII.

What Profession?—Not Fitted for a Churchman—Erratic Course—The Bitter Draught—Principle of Woe—Thou Wouldst be Joyous—What Ails You?—Poor Child of Clay 109

CHAPTER XIX.

Agreeable Delusions—Youth—A Profession—Ab Gwilym—Glorious English Law—There They Pass—My Dear Old Master—The Deal Desk—Language of the Tents—Where is Morfydd?—Go To—Only Once—[Physiognomy—The Poet Parkinson] 113

CHAPTER XX.

Silver Grey—Good Word for Everybody—A Remarkable Youth—Clients—Grades in Society—The Archdeacon—[The Wake of Freya]—Reading the Bible 126

CHAPTER XXI.

The Eldest Son—Saying of Wild Finland—The Critical Time—Vaunting Polls—One Thing Wanted—A Father's Blessing—Miracle of Art—The Pope's House—Young Enthusiast—Pictures of England—Persist and Wrestle—The Little Dark Man 134

CHAPTER XXII.

Desire for Novelty—Lives of the Lawless—Countenances—Old Yeoman and Dame—We Live Near the Sea—Uncouth-looking Volume—The Other Condition—Draoitheac—A Dilemma—The Antinomian—Lodowick Muggleton—Almost Blind—Anders Vedel 139

CHAPTER XXIII.

The Two Individuals—The Long Pipe—The Germans—Werther—The Female Quaker—Suicide—Gibbon—Jesus of Bethlehem—Fill Your Glass—Shakespeare—English at Minden—Melancholy Swayne Vonved—The Fifth Dinner—Strange Doctrines—Are You Happy?—Improve Yourself in German 146

CHAPTER XXIV.

The Alehouse Keeper—Compassion for the Rich—Old English Gentleman—How is this?—Madeira—The Greek Parr—Twenty Languages—Whiter's Health—About the Fight—A Sporting Gentleman—The Flattened Nose—Lend us that Pightle—The Surly Nod. 153

CHAPTER XXV.

Doubts—Wise King of Jerusalem—Let Me See—A Thousand Years—Nothing New—The Crowd—The Hymn—Faith—Charles Wesley—There He Stood—Farewell, Brother—Death—Sun, Moon and Stars—Wind on the Heath. 159

CHAPTER XXVI.

PAGE

The Flower of the Grass—Days of Pugilism—The Rendezvous—Jews-Bruisers of England—Winter, Spring—Well-earned Bays—The Fight—Huge Black Cloud—Frame of Adamant—The Storm—Dukkeripens—The Barouche—The Rain-Gushes 166

CHAPTER XXVII.

My Father—Premature Decay—The Easy Chair—A Few Questions—So You Told Me—A Difficult Language—They Call it Haik—Misused Opportunities—Saul—Want of Candour—Don't Weep—Heaven Forgive Me—Dated from Paris—I Wish He Were Here—A Father's Reminiscences—Farewell to Vanities 172

CHAPTER XXVIII.

My Brother's Arrival—The Interview—Night—A Dying Father—Christ . 179

CHAPTER XXIX.

The Greeting—Queer Figure—Cheer Up—The Cheerful Fire—It Will Do—The Sally Forth—Trepidation—Let Him Come in 181

CHAPTER XXX.

The Sinister Glance—Excellent Correspondent—Quite Original—My System—A Losing Trade—Merit—Starting a Review—What Have You Got?—Stop!—*Dairyman's Daughter*—Oxford Principles—More Conversation—How is This? 185

CHAPTER XXXI.

The Walk—London's Cheape—Street of the Lombards—Strange Bridge—Main Arch—The Roaring Gulf—The Boat—Cly-Faking—A Comfort—The Book—The Blessed Woman—No Trap 191

CHAPTER XXXII.

The Tanner—[Cromwell—The *Dairyman's Daughter*]—The Hotel—Drinking Claret—London Journal—New Field—Commonplaceness—The Three Individuals—Botheration—Frank and Ardent 196

CHAPTER XXXIII.

Dine with the Publisher—Religions—No Animal Food—Unprofitable Discussions—Principles of Criticism—The Book Market—Newgate Lives—Goethe a Drug—German Acquirements—Moral Dignity . . . 202

CHAPTER XXXIV.

The Two Volumes—A Young Author—Intended Editor—Quintilian—Loose Money 207

CHAPTER XXXV.

Francis Ardry—Certain Sharpers—Brave and Eloquent—Opposites—Flinging the Bones—Strange Places—Dog Fighting—Learning and Letters—Batch of Dogs—Redoubled Application 209

CHAPTER XXXVI.

PAGE

Occupations—Traduttore Traditore—Ode to the Mist—Apple and Pear—
Reviewing—Current Literature—Oxford-like Manner—A Plain Story—
Ill-regulated Mind—Unsnuffed Candle—Strange Dreams . . . 214

CHAPTER XXXVII.

My Brother—Fits of Crying—Mayor Elect—The Committee—The Norman
Arch—A Word of Greek—Church and State—At My Own Expense—If
You Please 219

CHAPTER XXXVIII.

Painter of the Heroic—I'll Go!—A Modest Peep—Who is This?—A
Capital Pharaoh — Disproportionably Short — Imaginary Picture —
English Figures 223

CHAPTER XXXIX.

No Authority Whatever—Interference—Wondrous Farrago—Brandt and
Struensee—What a Life!—The Hearse—Mortal Relics—Great Poet—
Fashion and Fame—What a Difference!—[Portobello] 227

CHAPTER XL.

London Bridge—Why Not?—Every Heart has its Bitters—Wicked Boys—
Give me my Book—Such a Fright—Honour Bright 240

CHAPTER XLI.

Decease of the Review—Homer Himself—Bread and Cheese—Finger and
Thumb—Impossible to Find—Something Grand—Universal Mixture—
Some Other Publisher 244

CHAPTER XLII.

Francis Ardry—That Won't do, Sir—Observe my Gestures—I Think You
Improve—Better than Politics—Delightful Young Frenchwoman—A
Burning Shame—Magnificent Impudence—Paunch—Voltaire—Lump of
Sugar 248

CHAPTER XLIII.

Progress—Glorious John—Utterly Unintelligible—What a Difference! . 253

CHAPTER XLIV.

The Old Spot—A Long History—Thou Shalt Not Steal—No Harm—Education—Necessity—Foam on Your Lip—Apples and Pears—What Will
You Read—Metaphor - The Fur Cap—I Don't Know Him . . . 255

CHAPTER XLV.

Bought and Exchanged—Quite Empty—A New Firm—Bibles—Countenance
of a Lion—Clap of Thunder—A Truce with This—I Have Lost It—
Clearly a Right—Goddess of the Mint 260

CHAPTER XLVI.

The Pickpocket—Strange Rencounter—Drag Him Along—A Great Service
—Things of Importance—Philological Matters—Mother of Languages—
Zhats 265

CHAPTER XLVII.

PAGE

New Acquaintance—Wired Cases—Bread and Wine—Armenian Colonies—
Learning Without Money—What a Language—The Tide—Your Foible
—Learning of the Haiks—Old Proverb—Pressing Invitation .   .   . 269

CHAPTER XLVIII.

What to do—Strong Enough—Fame and Profit—Alliterative Euphony—
Excellent Fellow—Listen to Me—A Plan—Bagnigge Wells .   .   . 274

CHAPTER XLIX.

Singular Personage—A Large Sum—Papa of Rome—We are Christians—
Degenerate Armenians—Roots of Ararat—Regular Features .   .   . 278

CHAPTER L.

Wish Fulfilled—Extraordinary Figure—Bueno—Noah—The Two Faces—I
Don't Blame Him—Too Fond of Money—Were I an Armenian   .   . 281

CHAPTER LI.

The One Half-Crown—Merit in Patience—Cementer of Friendship—Dreadful Perplexity—The Usual Guttural—Armenian Letters—Much Indebted
to You—Pure Helplessness—Dumb People   284

CHAPTER LII.

Kind of Stupor—Peace of God—Divine Hand—Farewell, Child—The Fair—
Massive Edifice—Battered Tars—Lost! Lost!—Good Day, Gentlemen 288

CHAPTER LIII.

Singular Table—No Money—Out of Employ—My Bonnet—We of the
Thimble—Good Wages—Wisely Resolved—Strangest Way in the World
—Fat Gentleman—Not Such Another—First Edition—Not Very Fast—
Won't Close—Avella Gorgio—Alarmed Look   292

CHAPTER LIV.

Mr. Petulengro—Rommany Rye—Lil Writers—One's Own Horn—Lawfully
Earnt Money—The Wooded Hill—A Great Favourite—The Shop
Window—Much Wanted   299

CHAPTER LV.

Bread and Water—Fair Play—Fashionable Life—Colonel B——Joseph Sell
—The Kindly Glow—Easiest Manner Imaginable 303

CHAPTER LVI.

Considerably Sobered—Power of Writing—The Tempter—Hungry Talent—
Work Concluded   306

CHAPTER LVII.

Nervous Look—The Bookseller's Wife—The Last Stake—Terms—God
Forbid!—Will You Come to Tea?—A Light Heart   309

CHAPTER LVIII.

PAGE

Indisposition—A Resolution—Poor Equivalents—The Piece of Gold—Flashing Eyes—How Beautiful!—Bonjour, Monsieur 312

CHAPTER LIX.

The Milestone—The Meditation—Want to Get Up?—The Off-hand Leader—Sixteen Shillings—The Near-hand Wheeler—All Right . . . 315

CHAPTER LX.

The Still Hour—A Thrill—The Wondrous Circle—The Shepherd—Heaps and Barrows—What do you Mean?—Milk of the Plains—Hengist spared it—No Presents 318

CHAPTER LXI.

The River—Arid Downs—A Prospect 322

CHAPTER LXII.

The Hostelry—Life Uncertain—Open Countenance—The Grand Point—Thank you, Master—A Hard Mother—Poor Dear!—Considerable Odds—The Better Country—English Fashion—Landlord-looking Person . 324

CHAPTER LXIII.

Primitive Habits—Rosy-faced Damsel—A Pleasant Moment—Suit of Black—The Furtive Glance—The Mighty Round—Degenerate Times—The Newspaper—The Evil Chance—I Congratulate You 329

CHAPTER LXIV.

New Acquaintance—Old French Style—The Portrait—Taciturnity—The Evergreen Tree—The Dark Hour—The Flash—Ancestors—A Fortunate Man—A Posthumous Child—Antagonistic Ideas—The Hawks—Flaws—The Pony—Irresistible Impulse—Favourable Crisis—The Topmost Branch—Twenty Feet—Heartily Ashamed 334

CHAPTER LXV.

Maternal Anxiety—The Baronet—Little Zest—Country Life—Mr. Speaker!—The Craving—Spirited Address—An Author 342

CHAPTER LXVI.

Trepidations—Subtle Principle—Perverse Imagination—Are they Mine?—Another Book—How Hard!—Agricultural Dinner—Incomprehensible Actions—Inmost Bosom—Give it Up—Chance Resemblance—Rascally Newspaper 346

CHAPTER LXVII.

Disturbed Slumbers—The Bed-Post—Two Wizards—What can I Do?—Real Library—The Rev. Mr. Platitude—Toleration to Dissenters—Paradox—Sword of St. Peter—Enemy to Humbug—High Principles—False Concord—The Damsel—What Religion?—Further Conversation—That would never Do!—May You Prosper! 351

CHAPTER LXVIII.

PAGE

Elastic Step—Disconsolate Party—Not the Season—Mend Your Draught—Good Ale—Crotchet—Hammer and Tongs—Schoolmaster—True Eden Life—Flaming Tinman—Twice my Size—Hard at Work—My Poor Wife—Grey Moll—A Bible—Half and Half—What to do—Half Inclined —In No Time—On One Condition—Don't Stare—Like the Wind . . 359

CHAPTER LXIX.

Effects of Corn—One Night Longer—The Hoofs—A Stumble—Are You Hurt?—What a Difference—Drowsy—Maze of Bushes—Housekeeping —Sticks and Furze—The Drift-way—Account of Stock—Anvil and Bellows—Twenty Years 369

CHAPTER LXX.

New Profession—Beautiful Night—Jupiter—Sharp and Shrill—The Rommany Chi—All Alone—Three and Sixpence—What is Rommany?—Be Civil—Parraco Tute—Slight Start—She Will Be Grateful—The Rustling 375

CHAPTER LXXI.

Friend of Slingsby—All Quiet—Danger—The Two Cakes—Children in the Wood—Don't be Angry—In Deep Thought—Temples Throbbing—Deadly Sick—Another Blow—No Answer—How Old are You?—Play and Sacrament—Heavy Heart—Song of Poison—Drow of Gypsies—The Dog—Ely's Church—Get Up, Bebee—The Vehicle—Can you Speak !—The Oil 381

CHAPTER LXXII.

Desired Effect—The Three Oaks—Winifred—Things of Time—With God's Will—The Preacher—Creature Comforts—Croesaw—Welsh and English —Mayor of Chester 391

CHAPTER LXXIII.

Morning Hymn—Much Alone—John Bunyan—Beholden to Nobody—Sixty-five—Sober Greeting—Early Sabbaths—Finny Brood—The Porch—No Fortune-telling—The Master's Niece—Doing Good—Two or Three Things—Groans and Voices—Pechod Ysprydd Glan 396

CHAPTER LXXIV.

The Following Day—Pride—Thriving Trade—Tylwyth Teg—Ellis Wyn—Sleeping Bard—Incalculable Good—Fearful Agony—The Tale . . 403

CHAPTER LXXV.

Taking a Cup—Getting to Heaven—After Breakfast—Wooden Gallery—Mechanical Habit—Reserved and Gloomy—Last Words—A Long Time —From the Clouds—Ray of Hope—Momentary Chill—Pleasing Anticipation 407

CHAPTER LXXVI.

Hasty Farewell—Lofty Rock—Wrestlings of Jacob—No Rest—Ways of Providence—Two Females—Foot of the Cross—Enemy of Souls—Perplexed—Lucky Hour—Valetudinarian—Methodists—Fervent in Prayer —You Saxons—Weak Creatures—Very Agreeable—Almost Happy—Kindness and Solicitude 413

CHAPTER LXXVII.

PAGE

Getting Late—Seven Years Old—Chastening—Go Forth—London Bridge—
Same Eyes—Common Occurrence—Very Sleepy 421

CHAPTER LXXVIII.

Low and Calm—Much Better—Blessed Effect—No Answer—Such a Sermon 424

CHAPTER LXXIX.

Deep Interest—Goodly Country—Two Mansions—Welshman's Candle—
Beautiful Universe—Godly Discourse—Fine Church—Points of Doctrine
—Strange Adventures—Paltry Cause—Roman Pontiff—Evil Spirit . 426

CHAPTER LXXX.

The Border—Thank You Both—Pipe and Fiddle—Taliesin 431

CHAPTER LXXXI.

At a Funeral—Two Days Ago—Very Coolly—Roman Woman—Well and
Hearty--Somewhat Dreary--Plum Pudding—Roman Fashion—Quite
Different—The Dark Lane—Beyond the Time—Fine Fellow—Such a
Struggle—Like a Wild Cat—Fair Play—Pleasant Enough Spot—No
Gloves 433

CHAPTER LXXXII.

Offence and Defence—I'm Satisfied—Fond of Solitude—Possession of Property
—Chal Devlehi—Winding Path 441

CHAPTER LXXXIII.

Highly Poetical—Volundr—Grecian Mythology—Making a Petul—Tongues
of Flame—Hammering—Spite of Dukkerin—Heaviness 444

CHAPTER LXXXIV.

Several Causes—Frogs and Eftes—Gloom and Twilight—What Should I Do?
—Our Father—Fellow Men—What a Mercy!—Almost Calm—Fresh
Store—History of Saul—Pitch Dark 448

CHAPTER LXXXV.

Free and Independent—I Don't See Why—Oats—A Noise—Unwelcome
Visitors—What's the Matter?—Good Day to Ye—The Tall Girl—Dovre-
field—Blow on the Face—Civil Enough—What's This?—Vulgar Woman
—Hands Off—Gasping for Breath—Long Melford—A Pretty Manœuvre
—A Long Draught—Signs of Animation—It Won't Do—No Malice—
Bad People 453

CHAPTER LXXXVI.

At Tea—Vapours—Isopel Berners—Softly and Kindly—Sweet Pretty
Creature—Bread and Water—Two Sailors—Truth and Constancy—
Very Strangely 463

CHAPTER LXXXVII.

Hubbub of Voices—No Offence—Nodding—The Guests 467

CHAPTER LXXXVIII.

PAGE

A Radical—Simple-Looking Man—Church of England—The President—Aristocracy — Gin and Water — Mending the Roads — Persecuting Church—Simon de Montfort—Broken Bells—Get Up—Not for the Pope —Quay of New York—Mumpers' Dingle—No wish to Fight—First Draught—A Poor Pipe—Half a crown Broke 469

CHAPTER LXXXIX.

The Dingle—Give them Ale—Not over Complimentary—America—Goodly Land—Washington—Promiscuous Company—Language of the Roads —The Old Women—Numerals—The Man in Black 477

CHAPTER XC.

Buona Sera—Rather Apprehensive—The Steep Bank—Lovely Virgin—Hospitality—Tory Minister—Custom of the Country—Sneering Smile—Wandering Zigan—Gypsies' Cloaks—Certain Faculty—Acute Answer —Various Ways—Addio—Best Hollands 482

CHAPTER XCI.

Excursions—Adventurous English—Opaque Forests—The Greatest Patience 489

CHAPTER XCII.

The Landlord—Rather Too Old—Without a Shilling—Reputation—A Fortnight Ago—Liquids—The Main Chance—Respectability—Irrational Beings—Parliament Cove—My Brewer 491

CHAPTER XCIII.

Another Visit—A la Margutte—Clever Man—Napoleon's Estimate—Another Statue 496

CHAPTER XCIV.

Prerogative—Feeling of Gratitude—A Long History—Alliterative Style—Advantageous Specimen—Jesuit Benefice—Not Sufficient—Queen Stork's Tragedy — Good Sense — Grandeur and Gentility — Ironmonger's Daughter—Clan Mac-Sycophant—Lick-Spittles—A Curiosity—Newspaper Editors—Charles the Simple—High-flying Ditty—Dissenters—Lower Classes—Priestley's House—Horseflesh—Austin—Renovating Glass—Money—Quite Original 499

CHAPTER XCV.

Wooded Retreat—Fresh Shoes—Wood Fire—Ash, when Green—Queen of China—Cleverest People—What's a Declension?—The First Noun—Thunder—Deep Olive—What Do You Mean?—Koul Adonai—The Thick Bushes—Wood Pigeon—Old Goethe 510

CHAPTER XCVI.

A Shout—A Fire Ball—See to the Horses—Passing Away—Gap in the Hedge—On Three Wheels—Why Do You Stop?—No Craven Heart—The Cordial—Across the Country—Small Bags 517

CHAPTER XCVII.

PAGE

Fire of Charcoal—The New Comer—No Wonder !—Not a Blacksmith—A Love Affair—Gretna Green—A Cool Thousand—Family Estates—Borough Interest—Grand Education—Let us Hear—Already Quarrelling—Honourable Parents—Most Heroically—Not Common People—Fresh Charcoal 522

CHAPTER XCVIII.

An Exordium—Fine Ships—High Barbary Captains—Free-Born Englishmen —Monstrous Figure—Swash-Buckler—The Grand Coaches—The Footmen—A Travelling Expedition—Black Jack—Nelson's Cannon—Pharaoh's Butler—A Diligence—Two Passengers—Sharking Priest—Virgilio —Lessons in Italian—Two Opinions—Holy Mary—Priestly Confederates—Methodist Chapel—Eternal City—Foaming at the Mouth—Like a Sepulchre—All for Themselves 529

CHAPTER XCIX.

A Cloister—Half-English—New Acquaintance—Fits of Absence—Turning Papist—Purposes of Charity—Foreign Religion—Melancholy—Elbowing and Pushing—Outlandish Sight—The Figure—I Don't Care for You—Rosy-faced Rascal—One Good—Religion of my Country—Fellow of Spirit—A Dispute—The Next Morning—Female Doll—Proper Dignity —Fetish Country 540

CHAPTER C.

Nothing but Gloom—Sporting Character—Gouty Tory—Servant's Club—Politics—Reformado Footman—Peroration—Good-Night . . . 549

Editor's Postscript 553

Notes 555

Gypsy List 568

LIST OF ILLUSTRATIONS.

GEORGE BORROW (*photogravure*), FROM THE PORTRAIT BY
PHILLIPS, R.A., IN THE POSSESSION OF JOHN MURRAY   *Frontispiece*

EDINBURGH CASTLE . . . .   *Facing page*   44

A TYPICAL IRISH CASTLE (CASHEL) . . . . .   ,,   45

ENTRANCE TO GRAMMAR SCHOOL, NORWICH . . .   ,,   84

THE ERPINGHAM GATE, NORWICH, FROM THE CATHEDRAL
CLOSE . . . .   ,,   85

EARLHAM HALL, NEAR NORWICH . . . . .   ,,   92

"MARSHLAND SHALES" . . . .   ,,   93

RACKHAM'S OFFICES, TUCK'S COURT, ST. GILES', NORWICH   ,,   114

WILLIAM TAYLOR OF NORWICH (B. 1765, D. 1836) . .   ,,   115

STONEHENGE . . . .   ,,   318

MUMPERS' DINGLE . . . .   ,,   319

LAVENGRO.

(1851.)

CHAPTER I.

On an evening of July, in the year 18—, at East D——, a beautiful little town in a certain district of East Anglia, I first saw the light.[1]

My father was a Cornish man, the youngest, as I have heard him say, of seven brothers. He sprang from a family of gentlemen, or, as some people would call them, *gentillâtres*, for they were not very wealthy; they had a coat of arms, however, and lived on their own property at a place called Tredinnock, which being interpreted means *the house on the hill*, which house and the neighbouring acres had been from time immemorial in their possession. I mention these particulars that the reader may see at once that I am not altogether of low and plebeian origin; the present age is highly aristocratic, and I am convinced that the public will read my pages with more zest from being told that I am a *gentillâtre* by birth with Cornish blood * in my veins, of a family who lived on their own property at a place bearing a Celtic name, signifying the house on the hill, or more strictly the house on the *hillock*.

My father was what is generally termed a posthumous child —in other words, the *gentillâtre* who begot him never had the satisfaction of invoking the blessing of the Father of All upon his head, having departed this life some months before the birth of his youngest son. The boy, therefore, never knew a father's care; he was, however, well tended by his mother, whose favourite he was; so much so, indeed, that his brethren, the youngest of whom was considerably older than himself, were rather jealous of

---

[1] *MS.*, " On the fifth day of July, 1803, at East D——, a beautiful little town in the western division of Norfolk, I first saw the light ".

* " In Cornwall are the best gentlemen."—*Corn. Prov.*

I

him. I never heard, however, that they treated him with any marked unkindness; and it will be as well to observe here that I am by no means well acquainted with his early history, of which, indeed, as I am not writing his life, it is not necessary to say much. Shortly after his mother's death, which occurred when he was eighteen, he adopted the profession of arms, which he followed during the remainder of his life, and in which, had circumstances permitted, he would probably have shone amongst the best. By nature he was cool and collected, slow to anger, though perfectly fearless, patient of control, of great strength, and, to crown all, a proper man with his hands.

With far inferior qualifications many a man has become a field-marshal or general; similar ones made Tamerlane, who was not a *gentillâtre*, but the son of a blacksmith, emperor of one-third of the world; but the race is not always for the swift, nor the battle for the strong, indeed I ought rather to say very seldom; certain it is, that my father, with all his high military qualifications, never became emperor, field-marshal, or even general; indeed, he had never an opportunity of distinguishing himself save in one battle, and that took place neither in Flanders, Egypt, nor on the banks of the Indus or Oxus, but in Hyde Park.

Smile not, gentle reader, many a battle has been fought in Hyde Park, in which as much skill, science and bravery have been displayed as ever achieved a victory in Flanders or by the Indus. In such a combat as that to which I allude, I opine that even Wellington or Napoleon would have been heartily glad to cry for quarter ere the lapse of five minutes, and even the Blacksmith Tartar would, perhaps, have shrunk from the opponent with whom, after having had a dispute with him,[1] my father engaged in single combat for one hour, at the end of which time the champions shook hands and retired, each having experienced quite enough of the other's prowess. The name of my father's antagonist was Brain.

What! still a smile? did you never hear that name before? I cannot help it! Honour to Brain, who four months after the event which I have now narrated was champion of England, having conquered the heroic Johnson. Honour to Brain, who at the end of other four months, worn out by the dreadful blows which he had received in his many [2] combats, expired in the arms of my father, who read the Bible to him in his latter moments— Big Ben Brain.

[1] *MS.*, "after being insulted by him".
[2] So in *MSS.*; "manly," an erratum.

You no longer smile, even *you* have heard of Big Ben.

I have already hinted that my father never rose to any very ex-
alted rank in his profession, notwithstanding his prowess and other
qualifications. After serving for many years in the line, he at last
entered as captain in the militia regiment of the Earl of ——,[1]
at that period just raised, and to which he was sent by the Duke
of York to instruct the young levies in military manœuvres and
discipline; and in this mission I believe he perfectly succeeded,
competent judges having assured me that the regiment in question
soon came by his means to be considered as one of the most
brilliant in the service, and inferior to no regiment of the line in
appearance or discipline.

As the head-quarters of this corps were at D——, the duties
of my father not unfrequently carried him to that place, and it was
on one of these occasions that he became acquainted with a
young person of the neighbourhood, for whom he formed an
attachment, which was returned; and this young person was my
mother.

She was descended from a family of French Protestants, natives
of Caen, who were obliged to leave their native country when old
Louis, at the instigation of the Pope, thought fit to revoke the
Edict of Nantes. Their name was Petrement, and I have reason
for believing that they were people of some consideration; that
they were noble hearts and good Christians they gave sufficient
proof in scorning to bow the knee to the tyranny of Rome. So
they left beautiful Normandy for their faith's sake, and with a few
louis d'ors in their purse, a Bible in the vulgar tongue, and a
couple of old swords, which, if report be true, had done service
in the Huguenot wars, they crossed the sea to the isle of civil
peace and religious liberty, and established themselves in East
Anglia.

And many other Huguenot families bent their steps thither,
and devoted themselves to agriculture or the mechanical arts;
and in the venerable old city, the capital of the province, in the
northern shadow of the Castle of De Burgh, the exiles built for
themselves a church where they praised God in the French tongue,
and to which, at particular seasons of the year, they were in the
habit of flocking from country and from town to sing—

"Thou hast provided for us a goodly earth; Thou waterest
her furrows, Thou sendest rain into the little valleys thereof,
Thou makest it soft with the drops of rain, and blessest the
increase of it".

[1] *MS.,* "Orford".

I have been told that in her younger days my mother was strikingly handsome; this I can easily believe. I never knew her in her youth, for though she was very young when she married my father (who was her senior by many years) she had attained the middle age before I was born, no children having been vouchsafed to my parents in the early stages of their union. Yet even at the present day, now that years threescore and ten have passed over her head, attended with sorrow and troubles manifold, poorly chequered with scanty joys, can I look on that countenance and doubt that at one time beauty decked it as with a glorious garment? Hail to thee, my parent! as thou sittest there, in thy widow's weeds, in the dusky parlour in the house overgrown with the lustrous ivy of the sister isle, the solitary house at the end of the retired court shaded by lofty poplars. Hail to thee, dame of the oval face, olive complexion, and Grecian forehead; by thy table seated with the mighty volume of the good Bishop Hopkins spread out before thee; there is peace in thy countenance, my mother; it is not worldly peace, however, not the deceitful peace which lulls to bewitching slumbers, and from which, let us pray, humbly pray, that every sinner may be roused in time to implore mercy not in vain! Thine is the peace of the righteous, my mother, of those to whom no sin can be imputed, the score of whose misdeeds has been long since washed away by the blood of atonement, which imputeth righteousness to those who trust in it. It was not always thus, my mother; a time was, when the cares, pomps and vanities of this world agitated thee too much; but that time is gone by, another and a better has succeeded, there is peace now on thy countenance, the true peace; peace around thee, too, in thy solitary dwelling, sounds of peace, the cheerful hum of the kettle and the purring of the immense Angola, which stares up at thee from its settle with its almost human eyes.

No more earthly cares and affections now, my mother? Yes, one. Why dost thou suddenly raise thy dark and still brilliant eye from the volume with a somewhat startled glance? What noise is that in the distant street? Merely the noise of a hoof— a sound common enough; it draws nearer, nearer, and now it stops before thy gate. Singular! And now there is a pause, a long pause. Ha! thou hearest something—a footstep, a swift but heavy footstep! thou risest, thou tremblest; there is a hand on the pin of the outer door; there is some one in the vestibule; and now the door of thy apartment opens; there is a reflection on the mirror behind thee—a travelling hat, a grey head and sunburnt face. " My dearest Son ! "   " My darling Mother ! "

Yes, mother, thou didst recognise in the distant street the hoof-tramp of the wanderer's horse.

I was not the only child of my parents ; I had a brother some three years older than myself.   He was a beautiful child ; one of those occasionally seen in England, and in England alone ; a rosy, angelic face, blue eyes, and light chestnut hair.   It was not exactly an Anglo-Saxon countenance, in which, by-the-bye, there is generally a cast of loutishness and stupidity ; it partook, to a certain extent, of the Celtic character, particularly in the fire and vivacity which illumined it ; his face was the mirror of his mind ; perhaps no disposition more amiable was ever found amongst the children of Adam, united, however, with no inconsiderable portion of high and dauntless spirit.   So great was his beauty in infancy, that people, especially those of the poorer classes, would follow the nurse who carried him about in order to look at and bless his lovely face.   At the age of three months an attempt was made to snatch him from his mother's arms in the streets of London, at the moment she was about to enter a coach ; indeed, his appearance seemed to operate so powerfully upon every person who beheld him, that my parents were under continual apprehension of losing him ; his beauty, however, was perhaps surpassed by the quickness of his parts.   He mastered his letters in a few hours, and in a day or two could decipher the names of people on the doors of houses and over the shop windows.

As he grew up, his personal appearance became less prepossessing, his quickness and cleverness, however, rather increased ; and I may say of him, that with respect to everything which he took in hand he did it better and more speedily than any other person.   Perhaps it will be asked here, what became of him ? Alas ! alas ! his was an early and a foreign grave.   As I have said before, the race is not always for the swift, nor the battle for the strong.

And now, doubtless, after the above portrait of my brother, painted in the very best style of Rubens, the reader will conceive himself justified in expecting a full-length one of myself, as a child, for as to my present appearance, I suppose he will be tolerably content with that flitting glimpse in the mirror. But he must excuse me ; I have no intention of drawing a portrait of myself in childhood ; indeed it would be difficult, for at that time I never looked into mirrors. No attempts, however, were

___

ever made to steal me in my infancy, and I never heard that my
parents entertained the slightest apprehension of losing me by
the hands of kidnappers, though I remember perfectly well that
people were in the habit of standing still to look at me, ay, more
than at my brother; from which premises the reader may form any
conclusion with respect to my appearance which seemeth good
unto him and reasonable.   Should he, being a good-natured
person and always inclined to adopt the charitable side in any
doubtful point, be willing to suppose that I, too, was eminently
endowed by nature with personal graces, I tell him frankly that
I have no objection whatever to his entertaining that idea;
moreover, that I heartily thank him, and shall at all times be
disposed, under similar circumstances, to exercise the same
species of charity towards himself.

With respect to my mind and its qualities I shall be more
explicit; for, were I to maintain much reserve on this point, many
things which appear in these memoirs would be highly mysterious
to the reader, indeed incomprehensible.   Perhaps no two individuals were ever more unlike in mind and disposition than my
brother and myself.   As light is opposed to darkness, so was that
happy, brilliant, cheerful child to the sad and melancholy being
who sprang from the same stock as himself, and was nurtured by
the same milk.

Once, when travelling in an Alpine country, I arrived at a
considerable elevation; I saw in the distance, far below, a
beautiful stream hastening to the ocean, its rapid waters here
sparkling in the sunshine, and there tumbling merrily in cascades.
On its banks were vineyards and cheerful villages; close to where
I stood, in a granite basin with steep and precipitous sides,
slumbered a deep, dark lagoon, shaded by black pines, cypresses
and yews.   It was a wild, savage spot, strange and singular;
ravens hovered above the pines, filling the air with their uncouth
notes, pies chattered, and I heard the cry of an eagle from a
neighbouring peak; there lay the lake, the dark, solitary and
almost inaccessible lake; gloomy shadows were upon it, which,
strangely modified as gusts of wind agitated the surface, occasionally assumed the shape of monsters.   So I stood on the Alpine
elevation, and looked now on the gay distant river, and now at
the dark granite-encircled lake close beside me in the lone
solitude, and I thought of my brother and myself.   I am no
moraliser; but the gay and rapid river and the dark and silent
lake, were, of a verity, no bad emblems of us two.

So far from being quick and clever like my brother, and able to rival the literary feat which I have recorded of him, many years elapsed before I was able to understand the nature of letters, or to connect them. A lover of nooks and retired corners, I was as a child in the habit of fleeing from society, and of sitting for hours together with my head on my breast. What I was thinking about, it would be difficult to say at this distance of time ; I remember perfectly well, however, being ever conscious of a peculiar heaviness within me, and at times of a strange sensation of fear, which occasionally amounted to horror, and for which I could assign no real cause whatever.

By nature slow of speech, I took no pleasure in conversation, nor in hearing the voices of my fellow-creatures. When people addressed me I not unfrequently, especially if they were strangers, turned away my head from them, and if they persisted in their notice burst into tears, which singularity of behaviour by no means tended to dispose people in my favour. I was as much disliked as my brother was deservedly beloved and admired. My parents, it is true, were always kind to me ; and my brother, who was good nature itself, was continually lavishing upon me every mark of affection.

There was, however, one individual who, in the days of my childhood, was disposed to form a favourable opinion of me. One day, a Jew—I had quite forgotten the circumstance, but I was long subsequently informed of it—one day a travelling Jew knocked at the door of a farmhouse in which we had taken apartments. I was near at hand, sitting in the bright sunshine, drawing strange lines on the dust with my fingers, an ape and dog were my companions. The Jew looked at me and asked me some questions, to which, though I was quite able to speak, I returned no answer. On the door being opened, the Jew, after a few words, probably relating to pedlary, demanded who the child was, sitting in the sun ; the maid replied that I was her mistress's youngest son, a child weak *here*, pointing to her forehead. The Jew looked at me again, and then said : "'Pon my conscience, my dear, I believe that you must be troubled there yourself to tell me any such thing. It is not my habit to speak to children, inasmuch as I hate them, because they often follow me and fling stones after me ; but I no sooner looked at that child than I was forced to speak to it. His not answering me shows his sense, for it has never been the custom of the wise to fling away their words in indifferent talk and conversation. The child is a sweet child, and has all the look of one of our people's children. Fool, indeed ! did I not see his eyes sparkle just now when the monkey seized the dog by the

ear? they shone like my own diamonds—does your good lady
want any, real and fine? Were it not for what you tell me, I
should say it was a prophet's child. Fool, indeed! he can write
already, or I'll forfeit the box which I carry on my back, and for
which I should be loth to take two hundred pounds!" He then
leaned forward to inspect the lines which I had traced. All of a
sudden he started back, and grew white as a sheet; then, taking off
his hat, he made some strange gestures to me, cringing, chattering,
and showing his teeth, and shortly departed, muttering something
about "holy letters," and talking to himself in a strange tongue.
The words of the Jew were in due course of time reported to my
mother, who treasured them in her heart, and from that moment
began to entertain brighter hopes of her youngest-born than she
had ever before ventured to foster.

CHAPTER II.

I HAVE been a wanderer the greater part of my life; indeed I
remember only two periods, and these by no means lengthy, when
I was, strictly speaking, stationary. I was a soldier's son, and as
the means of my father were by no means sufficient to support
two establishments, his family invariably attended him wherever
he went, so that from my infancy I was accustomed to travelling
and wandering, and looked upon a monthly change of scene and
residence as a matter of course. Sometimes we lived in barracks,
sometimes in lodgings, but generally in the former, always eschew-
ing the latter from motives of economy, save when the barracks
were inconvenient and uncomfortable; and they must have been
highly so indeed to have discouraged us from entering them; for
though we were gentry (pray bear that in mind, gentle reader),
gentry by birth, and incontestably so by my father's bearing the
commission of good old George the Third, we were not *fine gentry*,
but people who could put up with as much as any genteel Scotch
family who find it convenient to live on a third floor in London,
or on a sixth at Edinburgh or Glasgow. It was not a little that
could discourage us. We once lived within the canvas walls of a
camp, at a place called Pett, in Sussex; and I believe it was at
this place that occurred the first circumstance, or adventure, call
it which you will, that I can remember in connection with myself. It was a strange one, and I will relate it.

It happened that my brother and myself were playing one
evening in a sandy lane, in the neighbourhood of this Pett camp;
our mother was at a slight distance. All of a sudden, a bright
yellow, and, to my infantine eye, beautiful and glorious object
made its appearance at the top of the bank from between the
thick quickset, and, gliding down, began to move across the lane
to the other side, like a line of golden light. Uttering a cry of
pleasure, I sprang forward, and seized it nearly by the middle.
A strange sensation of numbing coldness seemed to pervade my
whole arm, which surprised me the more as the object to the eye
appeared so warm and sunlike. I did not drop it, however, but,
holding it up, looked at it intently, as its head dangled about a

(9)

foot from my hand. It made no resistance; I felt not even the slightest struggle; but now my brother began to scream and shriek like one possessed. "O mother, mother!" said he, "the viper! my brother has a viper in his hand!" He then, like one frantic, made an effort to snatch the creature away from me. The viper now hissed amain, and raised its head, in which were eyes like hot coals, menacing, not myself, but my brother. I dropped my captive, for I saw my mother running towards me; and the reptile, after standing for a moment nearly erect, and still hissing furiously, made off, and disappeared. The whole scene is now before me, as vividly as if it occurred yesterday—the gorgeous viper, my poor dear frantic brother, my agitated parent, and a frightened hen clucking under the bushes; and yet I was not three years old.

It is my firm belief that certain individuals possess an inherent power, or fascination, over certain creatures, otherwise I should be unable to account for many feats which I have witnessed, and, indeed, borne a share in, connected with the taming of brutes and reptiles. I have known a savage and vicious mare, whose stall it was dangerous to approach, even when bearing provender, welcome, nevertheless, with every appearance of pleasure, an uncouth, wiry-headed man, with a frightfully seamed face, and an iron hook supplying the place of his right hand, one whom the animal had never seen before, playfully bite his hair and cover his face with gentle and endearing kisses; and I have already stated how a viper would permit, without resentment, one child to take it up in his hand, whilst it showed its dislike to the approach of another by the fiercest hissings. Philosophy can explain many strange things, but there are some which are a far pitch above her, and this is one.

I should scarcely relate another circumstance which occurred about this time but for a singular effect which it produced upon my constitution. Up to this period I had been rather a delicate child; whereas, almost immediately after the occurrence to which I allude, I became both hale and vigorous, to the great astonishment of my parents, who naturally enough expected that it would produce quite a contrary effect.

It happened that my brother and myself were disporting ourselves in certain fields near the good town of Canterbury. A female servant had attended us, in order to take care that we came to no mischief. She, however, it seems, had matters of her own to attend to, and, allowing us to go where we listed, remained in one corner of a field, in earnest conversation with

a red-coated dragoon. Now it chanced to be blackberry time,
and the two children wandered under the hedges, peering
anxiously among them in quest of that trash so grateful to
urchins of their degree. We did not find much of it, however,
and were soon separated in the pursuit. All at once I stood
still, and could scarcely believe my eyes. I had come to a spot
where, almost covering the hedge, hung clusters of what seemed
fruit, deliciously-tempting fruit—something resembling grapes of
various colours, green, red and purple. Dear me, thought I,
how fortunate! yet have I a right to gather it? is it mine? for
the observance of the law of *meum* and *tuum* had early been
impressed upon my mind, and I entertained, even at that tender
age, the utmost horror for theft; so I stood staring at the varie-
gated clusters, in doubt as to what I should do. I know not how
I argued the matter in my mind; the temptation, however, was
at last too strong for me, so I stretched forth my hand and ate.
I remember perfectly well, that the taste of this strange fruit was
by no means so pleasant as the appearance; but the idea of eating
fruit was sufficient for a child, and, after all, the flavour was much
superior to that of sour apples, so I ate voraciously. How long
I continued eating I scarcely know. One thing is certain, that I
never left the field as I entered it, being carried home in the arms
of the dragoon in strong convulsions, in which I continued for
several hours. About midnight I awoke, as if from a troubled
sleep, and beheld my parents bending over my couch, whilst the
regimental surgeon, with a candle in his hand, stood nigh, the
light feebly reflected on the whitewashed walls of the barrack-
room.

Another circumstance connected with my infancy, and I have
done. I need offer no apology for relating it, as it subsequently
exercised considerable influence over my pursuits. We were, if
I remember right, in the vicinity of a place called Hythe, in Kent.
One sweet evening, in the latter part of summer, our mother took
her two little boys by the hand, for a wander about the fields.
In the course of our stroll we came to the village church; an old
grey-headed sexton stood in the porch, who, perceiving that we
were strangers, invited us to enter. We were presently in the
interior, wandering about the aisles, looking on the walls, and
inspecting the monuments of the notable dead. I can scarcely
state what we saw; how should I? I was a child not yet four
years old, and yet I think I remember the evening sun streaming
in through a stained window upon the dingy mahogany pulpit,
and flinging a rich lustre upon the faded tints of an ancient

banner. And now once more we were outside the building, where, against the wall, stood a low-eaved pent-house, into which we looked. It was half-filled with substances of some kind, which at first looked like large grey stones. The greater part were lying in layers; some, however, were seen in confused and mouldering heaps, and two or three, which had perhaps rolled down from the rest, lay separately on the floor. " Skulls, madam," said the sexton; "skulls of the old Danes! Long ago they came pirating into these parts; and then there chanced a mighty shipwreck, for God was angry with them, and He sunk them; and their skulls, as they came ashore, were placed here as a memorial. There were many more when I was young, but now they are fast dis-- appearing. Some of them must have belonged to strange fellows, madam. Only see that one; why, the two young gentry can scarcely lift it!" And, indeed, my brother and myself had entered the Golgotha, and commenced handling these grim relics of mortality. One enormous skull, lying in a corner, had fixed our attention, and we had drawn it forth. Spirit of eld, what a skull was yon!

I still seem to see it, the huge grim thing; many of the others were large, strikingly so, and appeared fully to justify the old man's conclusion that their owners must have been strange fellows; but, compared with this mighty mass of bone, they looked small and diminutive, like those of pigmies; it must have belonged to a giant, one of those red-haired warriors of whose strength and stature such wondrous tales are told in the ancient chronicles of the north, and whose grave-hills, when ransacked, occasionally reveal secrets which fill the minds of puny moderns with astonish- ment and awe. Reader, have you ever pored days and nights over the pages of Snorro? probably not, for he wrote in a language which few of the present day understand, and few would be tempted to read him tamed down by Latin dragomans. A brave old book is that of Snorro, containing the histories and adventures of old northern kings and champions, who seemed to have been quite different men, if we may judge from the feats which they performed, from those of these days. One of the best of his histories is that which describes the life of Harald Haardraade, who, after manifold adventures by land and sea, now a pirate, now a mercenary of the Greek emperor, became King of Norway, and eventually perished at the battle of Stanford Bridge, whilst engaged in a gallant onslaught upon England. Now, I have often thought that the old Kemp, whose mouldering skull in the golgotha of Hythe my brother and myself could scarcely lift, must have resembled in one respect at least this Harald, whom Snorro describes as a great and wise ruler and a determined leader, dangerous in battle, of fair presence, and measuring in height just *five ells*,* neither more nor less.

I never forgot the Daneman's skull; like the apparition of the viper in the sandy lane, it dwelt in the mind of the boy, affording copious food for the exercise of imagination. From that moment with the name of Dane were associated strange ideas of strength, daring, and superhuman stature; and an undefinable curiosity for all that is connected with the Danish race began to pervade me; and if, long after, when I became a student, I devoted myself with peculiar zest to Danish lore and the acquirement of the old Norse tongue and its dialects, I can only explain the matter by the early impression received at Hythe from the tale of the old sexton, beneath the pent-house, and the sight of the Danish skull.

And thus we went on straying from place to place, at Hythe to-day, and perhaps within a week looking out from our hostel-window upon the streets of old Winchester, our motions ever in accordance with the "route" of the regiment, so habituated to change of scene that it had become almost necessary to our existence. Pleasant were those days of my early boyhood; and a melancholy pleasure steals over me as I recall them. Those were stirring times of which I am speaking, and there was much passing around me calculated to captivate the imagination. The dreadful struggle which so long convulsed Europe, and in which England bore so prominent a part, was then at its hottest; we were at war, and determination and enthusiasm shone in every face; man, woman and child were eager to fight the Frank, the hereditary, but, thank God, never dreaded enemy of the Anglo-Saxon race. "Love your country and beat the French, and then never mind what happens," was the cry of entire England. Oh, those were days of power, gallant days, bustling days, worth the bravest days of chivalry, at least; tall battalions of native warriors were marching through the land; there was the glitter of the bayonet and the gleam of the sabre; the shrill squeak of the fife and loud rattling of the drum were heard in the streets of country towns, and the loyal shouts of the inhabitants greeted the soldiery on their arrival, or cheered them at their departure. And now let us leave the upland, and descend to the sea-bord; there is a sight for you upon the billows! A dozen men-of-war are gliding majestically out of port, their long buntings streaming

* Norwegian ells—about eight feet.

from the top-gallant masts, calling on the skulking Frenchman to come forth from his bights and bays ; and what looms upon us yonder from the fog-bank in the east ? a gallant frigate towing behind her the long low hull of a crippled privateer, which but three short days ago had left Dieppe to skim the sea, and whose crew of ferocious hearts are now cursing their imprudence in an English hold.   Stirring times those, which I love to recall, for they were days of gallantry and enthusiasm, and were moreover the days of my boyhood.

CHAPTER III.

AND when I was between six and seven years of age we were once more at D——, the place of my birth, whither my father had been despatched on the recruiting service. I have already said that it was a beautiful little town—at least it was at the time of which I am speaking; what it is at present I know not, for thirty years and more have elapsed since I last trod its streets. It will scarcely have improved, for how could it be better than it then was? I love to think on thee, pretty, quiet D——, thou pattern of an English country town, with thy clean but narrow streets branching out from thy modest market-place, with thine old-fashioned houses, with here and there a roof of venerable thatch, with thy one half-aristocratic mansion, where resided thy Lady Bountiful—she, the generous and kind, who loved to visit the sick, leaning on her golden-headed cane, whilst the sleek old footman walked at a respectful distance behind. Pretty, quiet D——, with thy venerable church, in which moulder the mortal remains of England's sweetest and most pious bard.

Yes, pretty D——, I could always love thee, were it but for the sake of him who sleeps beneath the marble slab in yonder quiet chancel. It was within thee that the long-oppressed bosom heaved its last sigh, and the crushed and gentle spirit escaped from a world in which it had known nought but sorrow. Sorrow! do I say? How faint a word to express the misery of that bruised reed; misery so dark that a blind worm like myself is occasionally tempted to exclaim, Better had the world never been created than that one so kind, so harmless, and so mild, should have undergone such intolerable woe! But it is over now, for, as there is an end of joy, so has affliction its termination. Doubtless the All-wise did not afflict him without a cause. Who knows but within that unhappy frame lurked vicious seeds which the sunbeams of joy and prosperity might have called into life and vigour? Perhaps the withering blasts of misery nipped that which otherwise might have terminated in fruit noxious and lamentable. But peace to the unhappy one, he is gone to his rest; the deathlike face is no longer occasionally seen timidly

(15)

and mournfully looking for a moment through the window-pane
upon thy market-place, quiet and pretty D——; the hind in thy
neighbourhood no longer at evening-fall views, and starts as he
views, the dark lathy figure moving beneath the hazels and alders
of shadowy lanes, or by the side of murmuring trout streams;
and no longer at early dawn does the sexton of the old church
reverently doff his hat, as, supported by some kind friend, the
death-stricken creature totters along the church-path to that
mouldering edifice with the low roof, inclosing a spring of
sanatory waters, built and devoted to some saint—if the legend
over the door be true, by the daughter of an East Anglian
king.

But to return to my own history. I had now attained the
age of six. Shall I state what intellectual progress I had been
making up to this period? Alas! upon this point I have little to
say calculated to afford either pleasure or edification. I had
increased rapidly in size and in strength; the growth of the mind,
however, had by no means corresponded with that of the body.
It is true, I had acquired my letters, and was by this time able to
read imperfectly, but this was all; and even this poor triumph
over absolute ignorance would never have been effected but for
the unremitting attention of my parents, who, sometimes by threats,
sometimes by entreaties, endeavoured to rouse the dormant energies
of my nature, and to bend my wishes to the acquisition of the
rudiments of knowledge; but in influencing the wish lay the
difficulty. Let but the will of a human being be turned to any
particular object, and it is ten to one that sooner or later he
achieves it. At this time I may safely say that I harboured
neither wishes nor hopes; I had as yet seen no object calculated
to call them forth, and yet I took pleasure in many things which
perhaps unfortunately were all within my sphere of enjoyment. I
loved to look upon the heavens, and to bask in the rays of the
sun, or to sit beneath hedgerows and listen to the chirping of
the birds, indulging the while in musing and meditation as far
as my very limited circle of ideas would permit; but, unlike my
brother, who was at this time at school, and whose rapid progress
in every branch of instruction astonished and delighted his pre-
ceptors, I took no pleasure in books, whose use, indeed, I could
scarcely comprehend, and bade fair to be as arrant a dunce as
ever brought the blush of shame into the cheeks of anxious and
affectionate parents.

But the time was now at hand when the ice which had hitherto
bound the mind of the child with its benumbing power was to

be thawed, and a world of sensations and ideas awakened to which it had hitherto been an entire stranger.   One day a young lady, an intimate acquaintance of our family, and godmother to my brother, drove up to the house in which we dwelt; she staid some time conversing with my mother, and on rising to depart she put down on the table a small packet, exclaiming: "I have brought a little present for each of the boys: the one is a History of England, which I intend for my godson when he returns from school, the other is——" and here she said something which escaped my ear, as I sat at some distance, moping in a corner: "I intend it for the youngster yonder," pointing to myself; she then departed, and, my mother going out shortly after, I was left alone.

I remember for some time sitting motionless in my corner, with my eyes bent upon the ground; at last I lifted my head and looked upon the packet as it lay on the table.   All at once a strange sensation came over me, such as I had never experienced before—a singular blending of curiosity, awe and pleasure, the remembrance of which, even at this distance of time, produces a remarkable effect upon my nervous system.   What strange things are the nerves—I mean those more secret and mysterious ones in which I have some notion that the mind or soul, call it which you will, has its habitation; how they occasionally tingle and vibrate before any coming event closely connected with the future weal or woe of the human being.   Such a feeling was now within me, certainly independent of what the eye had seen or the ear had heard.   A book of some description had been brought for me, a present by no means calculated to interest me; what cared I for books?   I had already many into which I never looked but from compulsion; friends, moreover, had presented me with similar things before, which I had entirely disregarded, and what was there in this particular book, whose very title I did not know, calculated to attract me more than the rest? yet something within told me that my fate was connected with the book which had been last brought; so, after looking on the packet from my corner for a considerable time, I got up and went to the table.

The packet was lying where it had been left—I took it up; had the envelope, which consisted of whitish brown paper, been secured by a string or a seal, I should not have opened it, as I should have considered such an act almost in the light of a crime; the books, however, had been merely folded up, and I therefore considered that there could be no possible harm in inspecting them, more especially as I had received no injunction to the contrary. Perhaps there was something unsound in this reasoning, something sophistical ; but a child is sometimes as ready as a grown-up person in finding excuses for doing that which he is inclined to. But whether the action was right or wrong, and I am afraid it was not altogether right, I undid the packet. It contained three books, two from their similarity seemed to be separate parts of one and the same work ; they were handsomely bound, and to them I first turned my attention. I opened them successively and endeavoured to make out their meaning ; their contents, however, as far as I was able to understand them, were by no means interesting : whoever pleases may read these books for me, and keep them too, into the bargain, said I to myself.

I now took up the third book. It did not resemble the others, being longer and considerably thicker ; the binding was of dingy calf-skin. I opened it, and as I did so another strange thrill of pleasure shot through my frame. The first object on which my eyes rested was a picture ; it was exceedingly well executed, at least the scene which it represented made a vivid impression upon me, which would hardly have been the case had the artist not been faithful to nature. A wild scene it was—a heavy sea and rocky shore, with mountains in the background, above which the moon was peering. Not far from the shore, upon the water, was a boat with two figures in it, one of which stood at the bow, pointing with what I knew to be a gun at a dreadful shape in the water ; fire was flashing from the muzzle of the gun, and the monster appeared to be transfixed. I almost thought I heard its cry. I remained motionless, gazing upon the picture, scarcely daring to draw my breath, lest the new and wondrous world should vanish of which I had now obtained a glimpse. " Who are those people, and what could have brought them into that strange situation ? " I asked of myself ; and now the seed of curiosity, which had so long lain dormant, began to expand, and I vowed to myself to become speedily acquainted with the whole history of the people in the boat. After looking on the picture till every mark and line in it were familiar to me, I turned over various leaves till I came to another engraving ; a new source of wonder—a low sandy beach on which the furious sea was breaking in mountain-like billows ; cloud and rack deformed the firmament, which wore a dull and leaden-like hue ; gulls and other aquatic fowls were toppling upon the blast, or skimming over the tops of the maddening waves—" Mercy upon him ! he must be drowned ! " I exclaimed, as my eyes fell upon a poor wretch who appeared to be striving to reach the shore ; he was upon his legs, but was evidently half-smothered with the brine; high above his head curled a horrible billow, as if to engulf him for ever. "He must be drowned! he must be drowned!" I almost shrieked, and dropped the book. I soon snatched it up again, and now my eye lighted on a third picture: again a shore, but what a sweet and lovely one, and how I wished to be treading it; there were beautiful shells lying on the smooth white sand, some were empty like those I had occasionally seen on marble mantelpieces, but out of others peered the heads and bodies of wondrous crayfish; a wood of thick green trees skirted the beach and partly shaded it from the rays of the sun, which shone hot above, while blue waves slightly crested with foam were gently curling against it; there was a human figure upon the beach, wild and uncouth, clad in the skins of animals, with a huge cap on his head, a hatchet at his girdle, and in his hand a gun; his feet and legs were bare; he stood in an attitude of horror and surprise; his body was bent far back, and his eyes, which seemed starting out of his head, were fixed upon a mark on the sand—a large distinct mark—a human footprint!

Reader, is it necessary to name the book which now stood open in my hand, and whose very prints, feeble expounders of its wondrous lines, had produced within me emotions strange and novel? Scarcely, for it was a book which has exerted over the minds of Englishmen an influence certainly greater than any other of modern times, which has been in most people's hands, and with the contents of which even those who cannot read are to a certain extent acquainted; a book from which the most luxuriant and fertile of our modern prose writers have drunk inspiration; a book, moreover, to which, from the hardy deeds which it narrates, and the spirit of strange and romantic enterprise which it tends to awaken, England owes many of her astonishing discoveries both by sea and land, and no inconsiderable part of her naval glory.

Hail to thee, spirit of De Foe! What does not my own poor self owe to thee? England has better bards than either Greece or Rome, yet I could spare them easier far than De Foe, "unabashed De Foe," as the hunchbacked rhymer styled him.

The true chord had now been touched. A raging curiosity with respect to the contents of the volume, whose engravings had fascinated my eye, burned within me, and I never rested until I had fully satisfied it. Weeks succeeded weeks, months followed months, and the wondrous volume was my only study and principal source of amusement. For hours together I would sit poring over a page till I had become acquainted with the import of every line,

My progress, slow enough at first, became by degrees more rapid, till at last, under "a shoulder of mutton sail," I found myself cantering before a steady breeze over an ocean of enchantment, so well pleased with my voyage that I cared not how long it might be ere it reached its termination.

And it was in this manner that I first took to the paths of knowledge.

About this time I began to be somewhat impressed with religious feelings. My parents were, to a certain extent, religious people; but, though they had done their best to afford me instruction on religious points, I had either paid no attention to what they endeavoured to communicate, or had listened with an ear far too obtuse to derive any benefit. But my mind had now become awakened from the drowsy torpor in which it had lain so long, and the reasoning powers which I possessed were no longer inactive. Hitherto I had entertained no conception whatever of the nature and properties of God, and with the most perfect indifference had heard the Divine name proceeding from the mouths of the people—frequently, alas! on occasions when it ought not to be employed; but I now never heard it without a tremor, for I now knew that God was an awful and inscrutable being, the maker of all things; that we were His children, and that we by our sins, had justly offended Him; that we were in very great peril from His anger, not so much in this life, as in another and far stranger state of being yet to come; that we had a Saviour withal to whom it was necessary to look for help: upon this point, however, I was yet very much in the dark, as, indeed, were most of those with whom I was connected. The power and terrors of God were uppermost in my thoughts; they fascinated though they astounded me. Twice every Sunday I was regularly taken to the church, where from a corner of the large, spacious pew, lined with black leather, I would fix my eyes on the dignified high-church rector, and the dignified high-church clerk, and watch the movement of their lips, from which, as they read their respective portions of the venerable liturgy, would roll many a portentous word descriptive of the wondrous works of the Most High.

Rector. "Thou didst divide the sea, through Thy power: Thou brakest the heads of the dragons in the waters."

Philoh. "Thou smotest the heads of Leviathan in pieces: and gavest him to be meat for the people in the wilderness."

Rector. "Thou broughtest out fountains and waters out of the hard rocks: Thou driedst up mighty waters."

Philoh. " The day is Thine, and the night is Thine : Thou hast prepared the light and the sun."

Peace to your memories dignified rector and yet more dignified clerk ! by this time ye are probably gone to your long homes, and your voices are no longer heard sounding down the aisles of the venerable church ; nay, doubtless, this has already long since been the fate of him of the sonorous " Amen ! "—the one of the two who, with all due respect to the rector, principally engrossed my boyish admiration—he, at least, is scarcely now among the living ! Living ! why, I have heard say that he blew a fife—for he was a musical as well as a Christian professor—a bold fife, to cheer the Guards and the brave Marines as they marched with measured step, obeying an insane command, up Bunker's height, whilst the rifles of the sturdy Yankees were sending the leaden hail sharp and thick amidst the red-coated ranks ; for Philoh had not always been a man of peace, nor an exhorter to turn the other cheek to the smiter, but had even arrived at the dignity of a halberd in his country's service before his six-foot form required rest, and the grey-haired veteran retired, after a long peregrination, to his native town, to enjoy ease and respectability on a pension of " eighteen-pence a day " ; and well did his fellow-townsmen act when, to increase that ease and respectability, and with a thoughtful regard for the dignity of the good church service, they made him clerk and precentor—the man of the tall form and of the audible voice, which sounded loud and clear as his own Bunker fife. Well, peace to thee, thou fine old chap, despiser of dissenters, and hater of papists, as became a dignified and high-church clerk ; if thou art in thy grave the better for thee ; thou wert fitted to adore a bygone time, when loyalty was in vogue, and smiling content lay like a sunbeam upon the land, but thou wouldst be sadly out of place in these days of cold philosophic latitudinarian doctrine, universal tolerism, and half-concealed rebellion—rare times, no doubt, for papists and dissenters, but which would assuredly have broken the heart of the loyal soldier of George the Third, and the dignified high-church clerk of pretty D——.

We passed many months at this place. Nothing, however, occurred requiring any particular notice, relating to myself, beyond what I have already stated, and I am not writing the history of others. At length my father was recalled to his regiment, which at that time was stationed at a place called Norman Cross, in Lincolnshire, or rather Huntingdonshire, at some distance from the old town of Peterborough. For this place he departed, leaving my mother and myself to follow in a few days. Our journey was a singular one. On the second day we reached a marshy and fenny country, which owing to immense quantities of rain which had lately fallen, was completely submerged. At a large town we got on board a kind of passage-boat, crowded with people ; it had neither sails nor oars, and those were not the days of steam-vessels ; it was a treck-schuyt, and was drawn by horses.

Young as I was, there was much connected with this journey which highly surprised me, and which brought to my remembrance particular scenes described in the book which I now generally carried in my bosom. The country was, as I have already said, submerged—entirely drowned—no land was visible; the trees were growing bolt upright in the flood, whilst farmhouses and cottages were standing insulated ; the horses which drew us were up to the knees in water, and, on coming to blind pools and " greedy depths," were not unfrequently swimming, in which case the boys or urchins who mounted them sometimes stood, some-times knelt, upon the saddle and pillions. No accident, however, occurred either to the quadrupeds or bipeds, who appeared respectively to be quite *au fait* in their business, and extricated themselves with the greatest ease from places in which Pharaoh and all his host would have gone to the bottom. Nightfall brought us to Peterborough, and from thence we were not slow in reaching the place of our destination.

CHAPTER IV.

AND a strange place it was, this Norman Cross, and, at the time of which I am speaking, a sad cross to many a Norman, being what was then styled a French prison, that is, a receptacle for captives made in the French war. It consisted, if I remember right, of some five or six casernes, very long, and immensely high; each standing isolated from the rest, upon a spot of ground which might average ten acres, and which was fenced round with lofty palisades, the whole being compassed about by a towering wall, beneath which, at intervals, on both sides sentinels were stationed, whilst, outside, upon the field, stood commodious wooden barracks, capable of containing two regiments of infantry, intended to serve as guards upon the captives. Such was the station or prison at Norman Cross, where some six thousand French and other foreigners, followers of the grand Corsican, were now immured.

What a strange appearance had those mighty casernes, with their blank blind walls, without windows or grating, and their slanting roofs, out of which, through orifices where the tiles had been removed, would be protruded dozens of grim heads, feasting their prison-sick eyes on the wide expanse of country unfolded from that airy height. Ah! there was much misery in those casernes; and from those roofs, doubtless, many a wistful look was turned in the direction of lovely France. Much had the poor inmates to endure, and much to complain of, to the disgrace of England be it said—of England, in general so kind and bountiful. Rations of carrion meat, and bread from which I have seen the very hounds occasionally turn away, were unworthy entertainment even for the most ruffian enemy, when helpless and a captive; and such, alas! was the fare in those casernes. And then, those visits, or rather ruthless inroads, called in the slang of the place [1] "straw-plait hunts," when, in pursuit of a contraband article, which the prisoners, in order to procure themselves a few of the necessaries and comforts of existence, were in the habit of making,

---

[1] *MS.*, "in regimental slang".

red-coated battalions were marched into the prisons, who, with
the bayonet's point, carried havoc and ruin into every poor
convenience which ingenious wretchedness had been endeavouring to raise around it ; and then the triumphant exit with the
miserable booty ; and, worst of all, the accursed bonfire, on the
barrack parade, of the plait contraband, beneath the view of the
glaring eyeballs from those lofty roofs, amidst the hurrahs of the
troops, frequently drowned in the curses poured down from above
like a tempest-shower, or in the terrific war-whoop of " *Vive
l'Empereur !* "

It was midsummer when we arrived at this place, and the
weather, which had for a long time been wet and gloomy, now
became bright and glorious.   I was subjected to but little control,
and passed my time pleasantly enough, principally in wandering
about the neighbouring country.   It was flat and somewhat fenny,
a district more of pasture than agriculture, and not very thickly
inhabited.   I soon became well acquainted with it.   At the
distance of two miles from the station was a large lake, styled in
the dialect of the country a " mere," about whose borders tall
reeds were growing in abundance.   This was a frequent haunt of
mine ; but my favourite place of resort was a wild sequestered
spot at a somewhat greater distance.   Here, surrounded with
woods, and thick groves, was the seat of some ancient family,
deserted by the proprietor, and only inhabited by a rustic servant
or two.   A place more solitary and wild could scarcely be
imagined ; the garden and walks were overgrown with weeds and
briars, and the unpruned woods were so tankled as to be almost
impervious.   About this domain I would wander till overtaken
by fatigue, and then I would sit down with my back against some
beech, elm or stately alder tree, and, taking out my book, would
pass hours in a state of unmixed enjoyment, my eyes now fixed
on the wondrous pages, now glancing at the sylvan scene around ;
and sometimes I would drop the book and listen to the voice of
the rooks and wild pigeons, and not unfrequently to the croaking
of multitudes of frogs from the neighbouring swamps and fens.

In going to and from this place I frequently passed a tall,
elderly individual, dressed in rather a quaint fashion, with a skin
cap on his head and stout gaiters on his legs ; on his shoulders
hung a moderate sized leathern sack ; he seemed fond of loitering
near sunny banks, and of groping amidst furze and low scrubby
bramble bushes, of which there were plenty in the neighbourhood
of Norman Cross.   Once I saw him standing in the middle of a
dusty road, looking intently at a large mark which seemed to have

been drawn across it, as if by a walking-stick. "He must have been a large one," the old man muttered half to himself, "or he would not have left such a trail, I wonder if he is near; he seems to have moved this way." He then went behind some bushes which grew on the right side of the road, and appeared to be in quest of something, moving behind the bushes with his head downwards, and occasionally striking their roots with his foot. At length he exclaimed, "Here he is!" and forthwith I saw him dart amongst the bushes. There was a kind of scuffling noise, the rustling of branches, and the crackling of dry sticks. "I have him!" said the man at last; "I have got him!" and presently he made his appearance about twenty yards down the road, holding a large viper in his hand. "What do you think of that, my boy?" said he, as I went up to him; "what do you think of catching such a thing as that with the naked hand?" "What do I think?" said I. "Why, that I could do as much myself." "You do," said the man, "do you? Lord! how the young people in these days are given to conceit; it did not use to be so in my time; when I was a child, childer knew how to behave themselves; but the childer of these days are full of conceit, full of froth, like the mouth of this viper"; and with his forefinger and thumb he squeezed a considerable quantity of foam from the jaws of the viper down upon the road. "The childer of these days are a generation of—God forgive me, what was I about to say!" said the old man; and opening his bag he thrust the reptile into it, which appeared far from empty. I passed on. As I was returning, towards the evening, I overtook the old man, who was wending in the same direction. "Good-evening to you, sir," said I, taking off a cap which I wore on my head. "Good-evening," said the old man; and then, looking at me, "How's this?" said he, "you ar'n't, sure, the child I met in the morning?" "Yes," said I, "I am; what makes you doubt it?" "Why, you were then all froth and conceit," said the old man, "and now you take off your cap to me." "I beg your pardon," said I, "if I was frothy and conceited; it ill becomes a child like me to be so." "That's true, dear," said the old man; "well, as you have begged my pardon, I truly forgive you." "Thank you," said I; "have you caught any more of those things?" "Only four or five," said the old man; "they are getting scarce, though this used to be a great neighbourhood for them." "And what do you do with them?" said I; "do you carry them home and play with them!" "I sometimes play with one or two that I tame," said the old man; "but I hunt them mostly for the fat which they contain, out of which I make unguents which are good for various sore troubles, especially for the rheumatism." "And do you get your living by hunting these creatures?" I demanded. "Not altogether," said the old man; "besides being a viper-hunter, I am what they call a herbalist, one who knows the virtue of particular herbs; I gather them at the proper season, to make medicines with for the sick." "And do you live in the neighbourhood?" I demanded. "You seem very fond of asking questions, child. No, I do not live in this neighbourhood in particular, I travel about; I have not been in this neighbourhood till lately for some years."

From this time the old man and myself formed an acquaintance; I often accompanied him in his wanderings about the neighbourhood, and on two or three occasions assisted him in catching the reptiles which he hunted. He generally carried a viper with him which he had made quite tame, and from which he had extracted the poisonous fangs; it would dance and perform various kinds of tricks. He was fond of telling me anecdotes connected with his adventures with the reptile species. "But," said he one day, sighing, "I must shortly give up this business, I am no longer the man I was, I am become timid, and when a person is timid in viper-hunting he had better leave off, as it is quite clear his virtue is leaving him. I got a fright some years ago, which I am quite sure I shall never get the better of; my hand has been shaky more or less ever since." "What frightened you?" said I. "I had better not tell you," said the old man, "or you may be frightened too, lose your virtue, and be no longer good for the business." "I don't care," said I; "I don't intend to follow the business; I dare say I shall be an officer, like my father." "Well," said the old man, "I once saw the king of the vipers, and since then ——" "The king of the vipers!" said I, interrupting him; "have the vipers a king?" "As sure as we have," said the old man, "as sure as we have King George to rule over us, have these reptiles a king to rule over them." "And where did you see him?" said I. "I will tell you," said the old man, "though I don't like talking about the matter. It may be about seven years ago that I happened to be far down yonder to the west, on the other side of England, nearly two hundred miles from here, following my business. It was a very sultry day, I remember, and I had been out several hours catching creatures. It might be about three o'clock in the afternoon, when I found myself on some heathy land near the sea, on the ridge of a hill, the side of which, nearly as far down as the sea,

was heath; but on the top there was arable ground, which had
been planted, and from which the harvest had been gathered—
oats or barley, I know not which—but I remember that the
ground was covered with stubble.   Well, about three o'clock, as
I told you before, what with the heat of the day and from having
walked about for hours in a lazy way, I felt very tired; so I
determined to have a sleep, and I laid myself down, my head just
on the ridge of the hill, towards the field, and my body over the
side down amongst the heath; my bag, which was nearly filled
with creatures, lay at a little distance from my face; the creatures
were struggling in it, I remember, and I thought to myself, how
much more comfortably off I was than they; I was taking my ease
on the nice open hill, cooled with the breezes, whilst they were in
the nasty close bag, coiling about one another, and breaking their
very hearts, all to no purpose; and I felt quite comfortable and
happy in the thought, and little by little closed my eyes, and fell
into the sweetest snooze that ever I was in in all my life; and
there I lay over the hill's side, with my head half in the field, I
don't know how long, all dead asleep.   At last it seemed to me
that I heard a noise in my sleep, something like a thing moving,
very faint, however, far away; then it died, and then it came again
upon my ear as I slept, and now it appeared almost as if I heard
crackle, crackle; then it died again, or I became yet more dead
asleep than before, I know not which, but I certainly lay some
time without hearing it.   All of a sudden I became awake, and
there was I, on the ridge of the hill, with my cheek on the ground
towards the stubble, with a noise in my ear like that of something
moving towards me, amongst the stubble of the field; well, I lay
a moment or two listening to the noise, and then I became
frightened, for I did not like the noise at all, it sounded so odd;
so I rolled myself on my belly, and looked towards the stubble.
Mercy upon us! there was a huge snake, or rather a dreadful
viper, for it was all yellow and gold, moving towards me, bearing
its head about a foot and a half above the ground, the dry stubble
crackling beneath its outrageous belly.   It might be about five
yards off when I first saw it, making straight towards me, child,
as if it would devour me.   I lay quite still, for I was stupefied
with horror, whilst the creature came still nearer; and now it was
nearly upon me, when it suddenly drew back a little, and then—
what do you think?—it lifted its head and chest high in the air,
and high over my face as I looked up, flickering at me with its
tongue as if it would fly at my face.   Child, what I felt at that
moment I can scarcely say, but it was a sufficient punishment for
all the sins I ever committed; and there we two were, I looking

up at the viper, and the viper looking down upon me, flickering
at me with its tongue.   It was only the kindness of God that
saved me : all at once there was a loud noise, the report of a gun,
for a fowler was shooting at a covey of birds, a little way off in the
stubble.   Whereupon the viper sunk its head, and immediately
made off over the ridge of the hill, down in the direction of the
sea.   As it passed by me, however—and it passed close by me—
it hesitated a moment, as if it was doubtful whether it should not
seize me ; it did not, however, but made off down the hill.   It has
often struck me that he was angry with me, and came upon me
unawares for presuming to meddle with his people, as I have always
been in the habit of doing."

"But," said I, "how do you know that it was the king of the
vipers ? "

"How do I know?" said the old man, "who else should it
be ?   There was as much difference between it and other reptiles
as between King George and other people."

"Is King George, then, different from other people?" I
demanded.

"Of course," said the old man ; "I have never seen him
myself, but I have heard people say that he is a ten times greater
man than other folks ; indeed, it stands to reason that he must be
different from the rest, else people would not be so eager to see
him.   Do you think, child, that people would be fools enough to
run a matter of twenty or thirty miles to see the king, provided
King George——"

"Haven't the French a king?" I demanded.

"Yes," said the old man, "or something much the same, and
a queer one he is ; not quite so big as King George, they say, but
quite as terrible a fellow.   What of him ? "

"Suppose he should come to Norman Cross ! "

"What should he do at Norman Cross, child ? "

"Why, you were talking about the vipers in your bag breaking
their hearts, and so on, and their king coming to help them.
Now, suppose the French king should hear of his people being in
trouble at Norman Cross, and——"

"He can't come, child," said the old man, rubbing his hands,
"the water lies between.   The French don't like the water;
neither vipers nor Frenchmen take kindly to the water, child."

When the old man left the country, which he did a few days
after the conversation which I have just related, he left me the
reptile which he had tamed and rendered quite harmless by
removing the fangs.   I was in the habit of feeding it with milk,
and frequently carried it abroad with me in my walks.

CHAPTER V.

ONE day it happened that, being on my rambles, I entered a green lane which I had never seen before; at first it was rather narrow, but as I advanced it became considerably wider; in the middle was a drift-way with deep ruts, but right and left was a space carpeted with a sward of trefoil and clover; there was no lack of trees, chiefly ancient oaks, which, flinging out their arms from either side, nearly formed a canopy, and afforded a pleasing shelter from the rays of the sun, which was burning fiercely above. Suddenly a group of objects attracted my attention. Beneath one of the largest of the trees, upon the grass, was a kind of low tent or booth, from the top of which a thin smoke was curling; beside it stood a couple of light carts, whilst two or three lean horses or ponies were cropping the herbage which was growing nigh. Wondering to whom this odd tent could belong, I advanced till I was close before it, when I found that it consisted of two tilts, like those of waggons, placed upon the ground and fronting each other, connected behind by a sail or large piece of canvas, which was but partially drawn across the top; upon the ground, in the intervening space, was a fire, over which, supported by a kind of iron crowbar, hung a caldron. My advance had been so noiseless as not to alarm the inmates, who consisted of a man and woman, who sat apart, one on each side of the fire; they were both busily employed—the man was carding plaited straw, whilst the woman seemed to be rubbing something with a white powder, some of which lay on a plate beside her. Suddenly the man looked up, and, perceiving me, uttered a strange kind of cry, and the next moment both the woman and himself were on their feet and rushing upon me.

I retreated a few steps, yet without turning to flee. I was not, however, without apprehension, which, indeed, the appearance of these two people was well calculated to inspire. The woman was a stout figure, seemingly between thirty and forty; she wore no cap, and her long hair fell on either side of her head, like horse-tails, half-way down her waist; her skin was dark and swarthy, like that of a toad, and the expression of her countenance was particularly evil; her arms were bare, and her

(29)

bosom was but half-concealed by a slight bodice, below which she wore a coarse petticoat, her only other article of dress. The man was somewhat younger, but of a figure equally wild; his frame was long and lathy, but his arms were remarkably short, his neck was rather bent, he squinted slightly, and his mouth was much awry; his complexion was dark, but, unlike that of the woman, was more ruddy than livid; there was a deep scar on his cheek, something like the impression of a halfpenny. The dress was quite in keeping with the figure: in his hat, which was slightly peaked, was stuck a peacock's feather; over a waistcoat of hide, untanned and with the hair upon it, he wore a rough jerkin of russet hue; smallclothes of leather, which had probably once belonged to a soldier, but with which pipeclay did not seem to have come in contact for many a year, protected his lower man as far as the knee; his legs were cased in long stockings of blue worsted, and on his shoes he wore immense old-fashioned buckles.

Such were the two beings who now came rushing upon me; the man was rather in advance, brandishing a ladle in his hand.

"So I have caught you at last," said he; "I'll teach ye, you young highwayman, to come skulking about my properties!"

Young as I was, I remarked that his manner of speaking was different from that of any people with whom I had been in the habit of associating. It was quite as strange as his appearance, and yet it nothing resembled the foreign English which I had been in the habit of hearing through the palisades of the prison; he could scarcely be a foreigner.

"Your properties!" said I; "I am in the King's Lane. Why did you put them there, if you did not wish them to be seen?"

"On the spy," said the woman, "hey? I'll drown him in the sludge in the toad-pond over the hedge."

"So we will," said the man, "drown him anon in the mud!"

"Drown me, will you?" said I; "I should like to see you! What's all this about? Was it because I saw you with your hands full of straw plait, and my mother there ——"

"Yes," said the woman; "what was I about?"

Myself. How should I know? Making bad money, perhaps!

And it will be as well here to observe, that at this time there was much bad money in circulation in the neighbourhood, generally supposed to be fabricated by the prisoners, so that this false coin and straw plait formed the standard subjects of conversation at Norman Cross.

"I'll strangle thee," said the beldame, dashing at me. "Bad money, is it?"

"Leave him to me, wifelkin," said the man, interposing; "you shall now see how I'll baste him down the lane."

Myself. I tell you what, my chap, you had better put down that thing of yours; my father lies concealed within my tepid breast, and if to me you offer any harm or wrong, I'll call him forth to help me with his forked tongue.

Man. What do you mean, ye Bengui's bantling? I never heard such discourse in all my life; playman's speech or French-man's talk—which, I wonder? Your father! tell the mumping villain that if he comes near my fire I'll serve him out as I will you. Take that—Tiny Jesus! what have we got here? Oh, delicate Jesus! what is the matter with the child?

I had made a motion which the viper understood; and now, partly disengaging itself from my bosom, where it had lain perdu, it raised its head to a level with my face, and stared upon my enemy with its glittering eyes.

The man stood like one transfixed, and the ladle with which he had aimed a blow at me, now hung in the air like the hand which held it; his mouth was extended, and his cheeks became of a pale yellow, save alone that place which bore the mark which I have already described, and this shone now portentously, like fire. He stood in this manner for some time; at last the ladle fell from his hand, and its falling appeared to rouse him from his stupor.

"I say, wifelkin," said he in a faltering tone, "did you ever see the like of this here?"

But the woman had retreated to the tent, from the entrance of which her loathly face was now thrust, with an expression partly of terror and partly of curiosity. After gazing some time longer at the viper and myself, the man stooped down and took up the ladle; then, as if somewhat more assured, he moved to the tent, where he entered into conversation with the beldame in a low voice. Of their discourse, though I could hear the greater part of it, I understood not a single word; and I wondered what it could be, for I knew by the sound that it was not French. At last the man, in a somewhat louder tone, appeared to put a question to the woman, who nodded her head affirmatively, and in a moment or two produced a small stool, which she delivered to him. He placed it on the ground, close by the door of the tent, first rubbing it with his sleeve, as if for the purpose of polishing its surface.

Man. Now, my precious little gentleman, do sit down here by the poor people's tent; we wish to be civil in our slight way. Don't be angry, and say no; but look kindly upon us, and satisfied, my precious little God Almighty.

Woman. Yes, my gorgious angel, sit down by the poor bodies'
fire, and eat a sweetmeat. We want to ask you a question or two ;
only first put that serpent away.

Myself. I can sit down, and bid the serpent go to sleep, that's
easy enough ; but as for eating a sweetmeat, how can I do that ?
I have not got one, and where am I to get it ?

Woman. Never fear, my tiny tawny, we can give you one,
such as you never ate, I dare say, however far you may have come
from.

The serpent sunk into its usual resting-place, and I sat down
on the stool. The woman opened a box, and took out a strange
little basket or hamper, not much larger than a man's fist, and
formed of a delicate kind of matting. It was sewed at the top ;
but, ripping it open with a knife, she held it to me, and I saw, to
my surprise, that it contained candied fruits of a dark green hue,
tempting enough to one of my age. "There, my tiny," said she ;
" taste, and tell me how you like them."

" Very much," said I ; " where did you get them ? "

The beldame leered upon me for a moment, then, nodding
her head thrice, with a knowing look, said : " Who knows better
than yourself, my tawny ? "

Now, I knew nothing about the matter ; but I saw that these
strange people had conceived a very high opinion of the abilities
of their visitor, which I was nothing loath to encourage. I therefore answered boldly, " Ah ! who indeed ! "

" Certainly," said the man ; " who should know better than
yourself, or who so well ? And now my tiny one, let me ask you
one thing—you didn't come to do us any harm ? "

" No," said I, " I had no dislike to you ; though, if you were
to meddle with me——"

Man. Of course, my gorgious, of course you would ; and
quite right too. Meddle with you !—what right have we ? I
should say it would not be quite safe. I see how it is ; you
are one of them there ;—and he bent his head towards his left
shoulder.

Myself. Yes, I am one of them—for I thought he was alluding
to the soldiers,—you had best mind what you are about, I can
tell you.

Man. Don't doubt we will for our own sake ; Lord bless you,
wifelkin, only think that we should see one of them there when
we least thought about it. Well, I have heard of such things,
though I never thought to see one ; however, seeing is believing. Well ! now you are come, and are not going to do

us any mischief, I hope you will stay; you can do us plenty of good if you will.

Myself. What good can I do you?

Man. What good? plenty! Would you not bring us luck? I have heard say, that one of them there always does, if it will but settle down. Stay with us, you shall have a tilted cart all to yourself if you like. We'll make you our little God Almighty, and say our prayers to you every morning!

Myself. That would be nice; and if you were to give me plenty of these things, I should have no objection. But what would my father say? I think he would hardly let me.

Man. Why not? he would be with you; and kindly would we treat him. Indeed, without your father you would be nothing at all.

Myself. That's true; but I do not think he could be spared from his regiment. I have heard him say that they could do nothing without him.

Man. His regiment! What are you talking about?—what does the child mean?

Myself. What do I mean! why, that my father is an officer-man at the barracks yonder, keeping guard over the French prisoners.

Man. Oh! then that sap is not your father!

Myself. What, the snake? Why, no! Did you think he was?

Man. To be sure we did. Didn't you tell me so?

Myself. Why, yes; but who would have thought you would have believed it? It is a tame one. I hunt vipers and tame them.

Man. O—h!

" O—h!" grunted the woman, "that's it, is it?"

The man and woman, who during this conversation had resumed their former positions within the tent, looked at each other with a queer look of surprise, as if somewhat disconcerted at what they now heard. They then entered into discourse with each other in the same strange tongue which had already puzzled me. At length the man looked me in the face, and said, some-what hesitatingly, "so you are not one of them there, after all?"

Myself. One of them there? I don't know what you mean.

Man. Why, we have been thinking you were a goblin—a devilkin! However, I see how it is: you are a sap-engro, a chap who catches snakes, and plays tricks with them! Well, it comes very nearly to the same thing; and if you please to list

with us, and bear us pleasant company, we shall be glad of you.
I'd take my oath upon it that we might make a mort of money by
you and that sap, and the tricks it could do; and, as you seem
fly to everything, I shouldn't wonder if you would make a prime
hand at telling fortunes.

"I shouldn't wonder," said I.

Man. Of course. And you might still be our God Almighty,
or at any rate our clergyman, so you should live in a tilted cart
by yourself and say prayers to us night and morning—to wifelkin
here, and all our family; there's plenty of us when we are all
together; as I said before, you seem fly, I shouldn't wonder if
you could read.

"Oh, yes!" said I, "I can read;" and, eager to display my
accomplishments, I took my book out of my pocket, and opening
it at random, proceeded to read how a certain man whilst
wandering about a certain solitary island, entered a cave, the
mouth of which was overgrown with brushwood, and how he
was nearly frightened to death in that cave by something which
he saw.

"That will do," said the man; "that's the kind of prayers for
me and my family, ar'n't they, wifelkin? I never heard more delicate prayers in all my life! Why, they beat the rubricals hollow!
—and here comes my son Jasper.[1] I say, Jasper, here's a
young sap-engro that can read, and is more fly than yourself.
Shake hands with him; I wish ye to be two brothers."

With a swift but stealthy pace Jasper came towards us from
the farther part of the lane; on reaching the tent he stood still,
and looked fixedly upon me as I sat upon the stool; I looked
fixedly upon him. A queer look had Jasper; he was a lad of some
twelve or thirteen years, with long arms, unlike the singular being
who called himself his father; his complexion was ruddy, but his
face was seamed, though it did not bear the peculiar scar which
disfigured the countenance of the other; nor, though roguish
enough, a certain evil expression which that of the other bore,
and which the face of the woman possessed in a yet more remarkable degree. For the rest, he wore drab breeches, with certain
strings at the knee, a rather gay waistcoat, and tolerably white
shirt; under his arm he bore a mighty whip of whalebone with
a brass knob, and upon his head was a hat without either top
or brim.

"There, Jasper! shake hands, with the sap-engro."

---

[1] *MS.,* "Ambrose" throughout the book.

"Can he box, father?" said Jasper, surveying me rather contemptuously. "I should think not, he looks so puny and small."

"Hold your peace, fool!" said the man; "he can do more than that—I tell you he's fly; he carries a sap about, which would sting a ninny like you to dead."

"What, a sap-engro!" said the boy, with a singular whine, and, stooping down, he leered curiously in my face, kindly, however, and then patted me on the head. "A sap-engro," he ejaculated; "lor!"

"Yes, and one of the right sort," said the man; "I am glad we have met with him; he is going to list with us, and be our clergyman and God Almighty, a'n't you, my tawny?"

"I don't know," said I; "I must see what my father will say."

"Your father; bah!"—— but here he stopped, for a sound was heard like the rapid galloping of a horse, not loud and distinct as on a road, but dull and heavy as if upon a grass sward; nearer and nearer it came, and the man, starting up, rushed out of the tent, and looked around anxiously. I arose from the stool upon which I had been seated, and just at that moment, amidst a crashing of boughs and sticks, a man on horseback bounded over the hedge into the lane at a few yards' distance from where we were; from the impetus of the leap the horse was nearly down on his knees; the rider, however, by dint of vigorous handling of the reins, prevented him from falling, and then rode up to the tent. "'Tis Nat," said the man; "what brings him here?" The new comer was a stout, burly fellow, about the middle age; he had a savage, determined look, and his face was nearly covered over with carbuncles; he wore a broad slouching hat, and was dressed in a grey coat, cut in a fashion which I afterwards learnt to be the genuine Newmarket cut, the skirts being exceedingly short; his waistcoat was of red plush, and he wore broad corduroy breeches and white top-boots. The steed which carried him was of iron grey, spirited and powerful, but covered with sweat and foam. The fellow glanced fiercely and suspiciously around, and said something to the man of the tent in a harsh and rapid voice. A short and hurried conversation ensued in the strange tongue. I could not take my eyes off this new comer. Oh, that half-jockey half-bruiser countenance, I never forgot it! More than fifteen years afterwards I found myself amidst a crowd before Newgate; a gallows was erected, and beneath it stood a criminal, a notorious malefactor. I recognised him at once; the horseman of the lane is now beneath the fatal tree, but nothing altered; still the same man; jerking his head to the right and left with the same fierce and under glance, just as if the affairs of this world had the same kind of interest to the last; grey coat of Newmarket cut, plush waistcoat, corduroys, and boots, nothing altered; but the head, alas! is bare and so is the neck. Oh, crime and virtue, virtue and crime!—it was old John Newton, I think, who, when he saw a man going to be hanged, said: "There goes John Newton, but for the grace of God!"

But the lane, the lane, all was now in confusion in the lane; the man and woman were employed in striking the tents and in making hurried preparations for departure; the boy Jasper was putting the harness upon the ponies and attaching them to the carts; and, to increase the singularity of the scene, two or three wild-looking women and girls, in red cloaks and immense black beaver bonnets, came from I know not what direction, and, after exchanging a few words with the others, commenced with fierce and agitated gestures to assist them in their occupation. The rider meanwhile sat upon his horse, but evidently in a state of great impatience; he muttered curses between his teeth, spurred the animal furiously, and then reigned it in, causing it to rear itself up nearly perpendicular. At last he said: "Curse ye, for Romans, how slow ye are! well, it is no business of mine, stay here all day if you like; I have given ye warning, I am off to the big north road. However, before I go, you had better give me all you have of that."

"Truly spoken, Nat, my pal," said the man; "give it him, mother. There it is; now be off as soon as you please, and rid us of evil company."

The woman had handed him two bags formed of stocking, half full of something heavy, which looked through them for all the world like money of some kind. The fellow, on receiving them, thrust them without ceremony into the pockets of his coat, and then, without a word of farewell salutation, departed at a tremendous rate, the hoofs of his horse thundering for a long time on the hard soil of the neighbouring road, till the sound finally died away in the distance. The strange people were not slow in completing their preparations, and then, flogging their animals terrifically, hurried away seemingly in the same direction.

The boy Jasper was last of the band. As he was following the rest, he stopped suddenly, and looked on the ground appearing to muse; then, turning round, he came up to me where I was standing, leered in my face, and then, thrusting out his hand, he said, "Good-bye, Sap, I dare say we shall meet again, remember we are brothers, two gentle brothers."

Then whining forth, "What a sap-engro, lor!" he gave me a parting leer, and hastened away.

I remained standing in the lane gazing after the retreating company. "A strange set of people," said I at last, "I wonder who they can be."

CHAPTER VI.

YEARS passed on, even three years; during this period I had increased considerably in stature and in strength, and, let us hope, improved in mind; for I had entered on the study of the Latin language. The very first person to whose care I was entrusted for the acquisition of Latin was an old friend of my father's, a clergyman who kept a seminary at a town the very next we visited after our departure from "the Cross". Under his instruction, however, I continued only a few weeks, as we speedily left the place. "Captain," said this divine, when my father came to take leave of him on the eve of our departure, "I have a friendship for you, and therefore wish to give you a piece of advice concerning this son of yours. You are now removing him from my care; you do wrong, but we will let that pass. Listen to me: there is but one good school book in the world— the one I use in my seminary—Lilly's Latin Grammar, in which your son has already made some progress. If you are anxious for the success of your son in life, for the correctness of his conduct and the soundness of his principles, keep him to Lilly's Grammar. If you can by any means, either fair or foul, induce him to get by heart Lilly's Latin Grammar, you may set your heart at rest with respect to him; I, myself, will be his warrant. I never yet knew a boy that was induced, either by fair means or foul, to learn Lilly's Latin Grammar by heart, who did not turn out a man, provided he lived long enough.

My father, who did not understand the classical languages, received with respect the advice of his old friend, and from that moment conceived the highest opinion of Lilly's Latin Grammar. During three years I studied Lilly's Latin Grammar under the tuition of various schoolmasters, for I travelled with the regiment, and in every town in which we were stationary I was invariably (God bless my father!) sent to the classical academy of the place. It chanced, by good fortune, that in the generality of these schools the grammar of Lilly was in use; when, however, that was not the case, it made no difference in my educational course, my father always stipulating with the masters that I should be daily examined

in Lilly.   At the end of the three years I had the whole by heart ;
you had only to repeat the first two or three words of any sentence
in any part of the book, and forthwith I would open cry, commencing without blundering and hesitation, and continue till you
were glad to beg me to leave off, with many expressions of
admiration at my proficiency in the Latin language.   Sometimes,
however, to convince you how well I merited these encomiums, I
would follow you to the bottom of the stair, and even into the
street, repeating in a kind of sing-song measure the sonorous lines
of the golden schoolmaster.   If I am here asked whether I understood anything of what I had got by heart, I reply—" Never mind,
I understand it all now, and believe that no one ever yet got Lilly's
Latin Grammar by heart when young, who repented of the feat at
a mature age ".

And when my father saw that I had accomplished my task,
he opened his mouth, and said, " Truly this is more than I
expected.   I did not think that there had been so much in you,
either of application or capacity ; you have now learnt all that is
necessary, if my friend Dr. B——'s opinion was sterling, as I
have no doubt it was.   You are still a child, however, and must
yet go to school, in order that you may be kept out of evil company.   Perhaps you may still contrive, now you have exhausted
the barn, to pick up a grain or two in the barnyard.   You are still
ignorant of figures, I believe, not that I would mention figures in
the same day with Lilly's Grammar."

These words were uttered in a place called ——, in the north,
or in the road to the north, to which, for some time past, our
corps had been slowly advancing.   I was sent to the school of the
place, which chanced to be a day school.   It was a somewhat
extraordinary one, and a somewhat extraordinary event occurred to
me within its walls.

It occupied part of the farther end of a small plain, or square,
at the outskirts of the town, close to some extensive bleaching
fields.   It was a long low building of one room, with no upper
storey ; on the top was a kind of wooden box, or sconce, which I
at first mistook for a pigeon-house, but which in reality contained a
bell, to which was attached a rope, which, passing through the
ceiling, hung dangling in the middle of the school-room.   I am
the more particular in mentioning this appurtenance, as I had
soon occasion to scrape acquaintance with it in a manner not
very agreeable to my feelings.   The master was very proud of his
bell, if I might judge from the fact of his eyes being frequently
turned to that part of the ceiling from which the rope depended.

Twice every day, namely, after the morning and evening tasks had been gone through, were the boys rung out of school by the monotonous jingle of this bell. This ringing out was rather a lengthy affair, for, as the master was a man of order and method, the boys were only permitted to go out of the room one by one ; and as they were rather numerous, amounting, at least, to one hundred, and were taught to move at a pace of suitable decorum, at least a quarter of an hour elapsed from the commencement of the march before the last boy could make his exit. The office of bell-ringer was performed by every boy successively ; and it so happened that, the very first day of my attendance at the school, the turn to ring the bell had, by order of succession, arrived at the place which had been allotted to me ; for the master, as I have already observed, was a man of method and order, and every boy had a particular seat, to which he became a fixture as long as he continued at the school.

So, upon this day, when the tasks were done and completed, and the boys sat with their hats and caps in their hands, anxiously expecting the moment of dismissal, it was suddenly notified to me, by the urchins who sat nearest to me, that I must get up and ring the bell. Now, as this was the first time that I had been at the school, I was totally unacquainted with the process, which I had never seen, and, indeed, had never heard of till that moment. I therefore sat still, not imagining it possible that any such duty could be required of me. But now, with not a little confusion, I perceived that the eyes of all the boys in the school were fixed upon me. Presently there were nods and winks in the direction of the bell-rope ; and, as these produced no effect, uncouth visages were made, like those of monkeys when enraged ; teeth were gnashed, tongues thrust out, and even fists were bent at me. The master, who stood at the end of the room, with a huge ferule under his arm, bent full upon me a look of stern appeal ; and the ushers, of whom there were four, glared upon me, each from his own particular corner, as I vainly turned, in one direction and another, in search of one reassuring look.

But now, probably in obedience to a sign from the master, the boys in my immediate neighbourhood began to maltreat me. Some pinched me with their fingers, some buffeted me, whilst others pricked me with pins or the points of compasses. These arguments were not without effect. I sprang from my seat, and endeavoured to escape along a double line of benches, thronged with boys of all ages, from the urchin of six or seven, to the nondescript of sixteen or seventeen. It was like running the

gauntlet; every one, great or small, pinching, kicking, or otherwise maltreating me as I passed by.

Goaded on in this manner, I at length reached the middle of
the room, where dangled the bell-rope, the cause of all my
sufferings.   I should have passed it—for my confusion was so
great, that I was quite at a loss to comprehend what all this could
mean, and almost believed myself under the influence of an ugly
dream—but now the boys who were seated in advance in the
row, arose with one accord, and barred my farther progress; and
one, doubtless more sensible that the rest, seizing the rope, thrust
it into my hand.   I now began to perceive that the dismissal of
the school, and my own release from torment, depended upon this
self same rope.   I therefore in a fit of desperation, pulled it once
or twice, and then left off, naturally supposing that I had done
quite enough.   The boys who sat next the door, no sooner heard
the bell, than, rising from their seats, they moved out at the door.
The bell, however, had no sooner ceased to jingle, than they
stopped short, and, turning round, stared at the master, as much
as to say, "What are we to do now?"   This was too much
for the patience of the man of method, which my previous
stupidity had already nearly exhausted.   Dashing forward into
the middle of the room, he struck me violently on the shoulders
with his ferule, and snatching the rope out of my hand, exclaimed,
with a stentorian voice, and genuine Yorkshire accent, "Prodigy
of ignorance! dost not even know how to ring a bell?   Must I
myself instruct thee?"   He then commenced pulling at the bell
with such violence, that long before half the school was dismissed
the rope broke, and the rest of the boys had to depart without
their accustomed music.

But I must not linger here, though I could say much about
the school and the pedagogue highly amusing and diverting,
which, however, I suppress, in order to make way for matters of
yet greater interest.   On we went, northwards, northwards! and,
as we advanced, I saw that the country was becoming widely
different from those parts of merry England in which we had
previously travelled.   It was wilder and less cultivated, and more
broken with hills and hillocks.   The people, too, of these regions
appeared to partake of something of the character of their country.
They were coarsely dressed; tall and sturdy in frame; their voices
were deep and guttural; and the half of the dialect which they
spoke was unintelligible to my ears.

I often wondered where we could be going, for I was at this
time about as ignorant of geography as I was of most other things,

However, I held my peace, asked no questions, and patiently awaited the issue.

Northward, northward, still!   And it came to pass that, one morning, I found myself extended on the bank of a river.   It was a beautiful morning of early spring; small white clouds were floating in the heaven, occasionally veiling the countenance of the sun, whose light, as they retired, would again burst forth, coursing like a race-horse over the scene—and a goodly scene it was! Before me, across the water, on an eminence, stood a white old city, surrounded with lofty walls, above which rose the tops of tall houses, with here and there a church or steeple.   To my right hand was a long and massive bridge, with many arches and of antique architecture, which traversed the river.   The river was a noble one, the broadest that I had hitherto seen.   Its waters, of a greenish tinge, poured with impetuosity beneath the narrow arches to meet the sea, close at hand, as the boom of the billows breaking distinctly upon a beach declared.   There were songs upon the river from the fisher-barks; and occasionally a chorus, plaintive and wild, such as I had never heard before, the words of which I did not understand, but which, at the present time, down the long avenue of years, seem in memory's ear to sound like "Horam, coram, dago".   Several robust fellows were near me, some knee-deep in water, employed in hauling the seine upon the strand.   Huge fish were struggling amidst the meshes—princely salmon,—their brilliant mail of blue and silver flashing in the morning beam; so goodly and gay a scene, in truth, had never greeted my boyish eye.

And, as I gazed upon the prospect, my bosom began to heave, and my tears to trickle.   Was it the beauty of the scene which gave rise to these emotions?   Possibly; for though a poor ignorant child—a half-wild creature—I was not insensible to the loveliness of nature, and took pleasure in the happiness and handiworks of my fellow-creatures.   Yet, perhaps, in something more deep and mysterious the feelings which then pervaded me might originate.   Who can lie down on Elvir Hill without experiencing something of the sorcery of the place?   Flee from Elvir Hill, young swain, or the maids of Elle will have power over you, and you will go elf-wild!—so say the Danes.   I had unconsciously laid myself down upon haunted ground; and I am willing to imagine that what I then experienced was rather connected with the world of spirits and dreams than with what I actually saw and heard around me.   Surely the elves and genii of the place were conversing, by some inscrutable means, with the principle of intelligence lurking within the poor uncultivated clod! Perhaps to that ethereal principle, the wonders of the past, as connected with that stream, the glories of the present, and even the history of the future, were at that moment being revealed. Of how many feats of chivalry had those old walls been witness, when hostile kings contended for their possession?—how many an army from the south and from the north had trod that old bridge?—what red and noble blood had crimsoned those rushing waters?—what strains had been sung, ay, were yet being sung, on its banks?—some soft as Doric reed; some fierce and sharp as those of Norwegian Skaldaglam; some as replete with wild and wizard force as Finland's runes, singing of Kalevala's moors, and the deeds of Woinomoinen! Honour to thee, thou island stream! Onward may thou ever roll, fresh and green, rejoicing in thy bright past, thy glorious present, and in vivid hope of a triumphant future! Flow on, beautiful one!—which of the world's streams canst thou envy, with thy beauty and renown? Stately is the Danube, rolling in its might through lands romantic with the wild exploits of Turk, Polak, and Magyar! Lovely is the Rhine! on its shelvy banks grows the racy grape; and strange old keeps of robber-knights of yore are reflected in its waters, from picturesque crags and airy headlands!—yet neither the stately Danube, nor the beauteous Rhine, with all their fame, though abundant, needst thou envy, thou pure island stream!—and far less yon turbid river of old, not modern, renown, gurgling beneath the walls of what was once proud Rome, towering Rome, Jupiter's town, but now vile Rome, crumbling Rome, Batuscha's town, far less needst thou envy the turbid Tiber of bygone fame, creeping sadly to the sea, surcharged with the abominations of modern Rome—how unlike to thee, thou pure island stream!

And, as I lay on the bank and wept, there drew nigh to me a man in the habiliments of a fisher. He was bare-legged, of a weather beaten countenance, and of stature approaching to the gigantic. "What is the callant greeting for?" said he, as he stopped and surveyed me. "Has ony body wrought ye ony harm?"

"Not that I know of," I replied, rather guessing at than understanding his question; "I was crying because I could not help it! I say, old one, what is the name of this river?"

"Hout! I now see what you was greeting at—at your ain ignorance, nae doubt—'tis very great! Weel, I will na fash you with reproaches, but even enlighten ye, since you seem a decent man's bairn, and you speir a civil question. Yon river is called the Tweed; and yonder, over the brig, is Scotland. Did ye never hear of the Tweed, my bonny man?"

" No," said I, as I rose from the grass, and proceeded to cross the bridge to the town at which we had arrived the preceding night; " I never heard of it; but now I have seen it, I shall not soon forget it ! "

The Southern Side of Edinburgh Castle

EDINBURGH CASTLE.

[See page 45.

A Typical Irish Castle (Cashel).

[See page 68.

CHAPTER VII.

It was not long before we found ourselves at Edinburgh, or rather in the Castle, into which the regiment marched with drums beating, colours flying, and a long train of baggage-waggons behind. The Castle was, as I suppose it is now, a garrison for soldiers. Two other regiments were already there; the one an Irish, if I remember right, the other a small Highland corps.

It is hardly necessary to say much about this Castle, which everybody has seen; on which account, doubtless, nobody has ever yet thought fit to describe it—at least that I am aware. Be this as it may, I have no intention of describing it, and shall content myself with observing, that we took up our abode in that immense building, or caserne, of modern erection, which occupies the entire eastern side of the bold rock on which the Castle stands. A gallant caserne it was—the best and roomiest that I had hitherto seen—rather cold and windy, it is true, especially in the winter, but commanding a noble prospect of a range of distant hills, which I was told were "the hieland hills," and of a broad arm of the sea, which I heard somebody say was the Firth of Forth.

My brother, who, for some years past, had been receiving his education in a certain celebrated school in England, was now with us; and it came to pass, that one day my father, as he sat at table, looked steadfastly on my brother and myself, and then addressed my mother: "During my journey down hither I have lost no opportunity of making inquiries about these people, the Scotch, amongst whom we now are, and since I have been here I have observed them attentively. From what I have heard and seen, I should say that upon the whole they are a very decent set of people; they seem acute and intelligent, and I am told that their system of education is so excellent, that every person is learned—more or less acquainted with Greek and Latin. There is one thing, however, connected with them, which is a great drawback—the horrid jargon which they speak. However learned they may be in Greek and Latin, their English is execrable; and yet I'm told it is not so bad as it was. I was in company the

(45)

other day with an Englishman who has resided here many years. We were talking about the country and its people. 'I should like both very well,' said I, ' were it not for the language. I wish sincerely our Parliament, which is passing so many foolish acts every year, would pass one to force these Scotch to speak English.' ' I wish so too,' said he. ' The language is a disgrace to the British Government; but, if you had heard it twenty years ago, captain!—if you had heard it as it was spoken when I first came to Edinburgh!'"

" Only custom," said my mother. " I dare say the language is now what it was then."

" I don't know," said my father; "though I dare say you are right; it could never have been worse than it is at present. But now to the point. Were it not for the language, which, if the boys were to pick it up, might ruin their prospects in life,—were it not for that, I should very much like to send them to a school there is in this place, which everybody talks about—the High School, I think they call it. 'Tis said to be the best school in the whole island; but the idea of one's children speaking Scotch —broad Scotch! I must think the matter over."

And he did think the matter over; and the result of his deliberation was a determination to send us to the school. Let me call thee up before my mind's eye, High School, to which, every morning, the two English brothers took their way from the proud old Castle through the lofty streets of the Old Town. High School!—called so, I scarcely know why; neither lofty in thyself, nor by position, being situated in a flat bottom; oblong structure of tawny stone, with many windows fenced with iron netting—with thy long hall below, and thy five chambers above, for the reception of the five classes, into which the eight hundred urchins, who styled thee instructress, were divided. Thy learned rector and his four subordinate dominies; thy strange old porter of the tall form and grizzled hair, hight Boee, and doubtless of Norse ancestry, as his name declares; perhaps of the blood of Bui hin Digri, the hero of northern song—the Jomsborg Viking who clove Thorsteinn Midlangr asunder in the dread sea battle of Horunga Vog, and who, when the fight was lost and his own two hands smitten off, seized two chests of gold with his bloody stumps, and, springing with them into the sea, cried to the scanty relics of his crew, " Overboard now, all Bui's lads!" Yes, I remember all about thee, and how at eight of every morn we were all gathered together with one accord in the long hall, from which, after the litanies had been read (for so I will call them, being an

Episcopalian), the five classes from the five sets of benches trotted off in long files, one boy after the other, up the five spiral staircases of stone, each class to its destination; and well do I remember how we of the third sat hushed and still, watched by the eye of the dux, until the door opened, and in walked that model of a good Scotchman, the shrewd, intelligent, but warmhearted and kind dominie, the respectable Carson.

And in this school I began to construe the Latin language, which I had never done before, notwithstanding my long and diligent study of Lilly, which illustrious grammar was not used at Edinburgh, nor indeed known. Greek was only taught in the fifth or highest class, in which my brother was; as for myself, I never got beyond the third during the two years that I remained at this seminary. I certainly acquired here a considerable insight in the Latin tongue; and, to the scandal of my father and horror of my mother, a thorough proficiency in the Scotch, which, in less than two months, usurped the place of the English, and so obstinately maintained its ground, that I still can occasionally detect its lingering remains. I did not spend my time unpleasantly at this school, though, first of all, I had to pass through an ordeal.

"Scotland is a better country than England," said an ugly, blear-eyed lad, about a head and shoulders taller than myself, the leader of a gang of varlets who surrounded me in the play-ground, on the first day, as soon as the morning lesson was over. "Scotland is a far better country than England, in every respect."

"Is it?" said I. "Then you ought to be very thankful for not having been born in England."

"That's just what I am, ye loon; and every morning when I say my prayers, I thank God for not being an Englishman. The Scotch are a much better and braver people than the English."

"It may be so," said I, "for what I know—indeed, till I came here, I never heard a word either about the Scotch or their country."

"Are ye making fun of us, ye English puppy?" said the blear-eyed lad; "take that!" and I was presently beaten black and blue. And thus did I first become aware of the difference of races and their antipathy to each other.

"Bow to the storm, and it shall pass over you." I held my peace, and silently submitted to the superiority of the Scotch—*in numbers.* This was enough; from an object of persecution I soon became one of patronage, especially amongst the champions of the class. "The English," said the blear-eyed lad, "though a wee bit behind the Scotch in strength and fortitude, are nae to be sneezed at, being far ahead of the Irish, to say nothing of the French, a pack of cowardly scoundrels. And with regard to the English country, it is na Scotland, it is true, but it has its gude properties; and, though there is ne'er a haggis in a' the land, there's an unco deal o' gowd and siller. I respect England, for I have an auntie married there."

The Scotch are certainly a most pugnacious people; their whole history proves it. Witness their incessant wars with the English in the olden time, and their internal feuds, highland and lowland, clan with clan, family with family, Saxon with Gael. In my time, the school-boys, for want, perhaps, of English urchins to contend with, were continually fighting with each other; every noon there was at least one pugilistic encounter, and sometimes three. In one month I witnessed more of these encounters than I had ever previously seen under similar circumstances in England. After all, there was not much harm done. Harm! what harm could result from short chopping blows, a hug, and a tumble? I was witness to many a sounding whack, some blood shed, "a blue ee" now and then, but nothing more. In England, on the contrary, where the lads were comparatively mild, gentle, and pacific, I had been present at more than one death caused by blows in boyish combats, in which the oldest of the victors had scarcely reached thirteen years; but these blows were in the jugular, given with the full force of the arm shot out horizontally from the shoulder.

But, the Scotch—though by no means proficients in boxing (and how should they box, seeing that they have never had a teacher?)—are, I repeat, a most pugnacious people; at least they were in my time. Anything served them, that is, the urchins, as a pretence for a fray, or, Dorically speaking, a *bicker;* every street and close was at feud with its neighbour; the lads of the school were at feud with the young men of the college, whom they pelted in winter with snow, and in summer with stones; and then the feud between the Old and New Town!

One day I was standing on the ramparts of the castle on the south-western side which overhangs the green brae, where it slopes down into what was in those days the green swamp or morass, called by the natives of Auld Reekie the Nor Loch; it was a dark gloomy day, and a thin veil of mist was beginning to settle down upon the brae and the morass. I could perceive, however, that there was a skirmish taking place in the latter spot. I had an indistinct view of two parties—apparently of urchins—and I heard whoops and shrill cries. Eager to know the cause of this disturbance, I left the castle, and descending the brae reached the borders of the morass, where was a runnel of water and the remains of an old wall, on the other side of which a narrow path led across the swamp; upon this path at a little distance before me there was "a bicker". I pushed forward, but had scarcely crossed the ruined wall and runnel, when the party nearest to me gave way, and in great confusion came running in my direction. As they drew nigh, one of them shouted to me, "Wha are ye, mon? are ye o' the Auld Toon?" I made no answer. "Ha! ye are o' the New Toon; De'il tak ye, we'll moorder ye;" and the next moment a huge stone sung past my head. "Let me be, ye fule bodies," said I, "I'm no of either of ye, I live yonder aboon in the castle." "Ah! ye live in the castle; then ye're an auld tooner; come gie us your help, mon, and dinna stand there staring like a dunnot, we want help sair eneugh. Here are stanes."

For my own part I wished for nothing better, and, rushing forward, I placed myself at the head of my new associates, and commenced flinging stones fast and desperately. The other party now gave way in their turn, closely followed by ourselves; I was in the van and about to stretch out my hand to seize the hindermost boy of the enemy, when, not being acquainted with the miry and difficult paths of the Nor Loch, and in my eagerness taking no heed of my footing, I plunged into a quagmire, into which I sank as far as my shoulders. Our adversaries no sooner perceived this disaster, than, setting up a shout, they wheeled round and attacked us most vehemently. Had my comrades now deserted me, my life had not been worth a straw's purchase, I should either have been smothered in the quag, or, what is more probable, had my brains beaten out with stones; but they behaved like true Scots, and fought stoutly around their comrade, until I was extricated, whereupon both parties retired, the night being near at hand.

"Ye are na a bad hand at flinging stanes," said the lad who first addressed me, as we now returned up the brae; "your aim is right dangerous, mon, I saw how ye skelpit them, ye maun help us agin thae New Toon blackguards at our next bicker."

So to the next bicker I went, and to many more, which speedily followed as the summer advanced; the party to which I had given my help on the first occasion consisted merely of outlyers, posted about half way up the hill, for the purpose of overlooking the movements of the enemy.

Did the latter draw nigh in any considerable force, messengers were forthwith despatched to the "auld toon," especially to the filthy alleys and closes of the High Street, which forthwith would disgorge swarms of bare-headed and bare-footed "callants," who, with gestures wild and "eldrich screech and hollo," might frequently be seen pouring down the sides of the hill. I have seen upwards of a thousand engaged on either side in these frays, which I have no doubt were full as desperate as the fights described in the Iliad, and which were certainly much more bloody than the combats of modern Greece in the war of independence. The callants not only employed their hands in hurling stones, but not unfrequently slings; at the use of which they were very expert, and which occasionally dislodged teeth, shattered jaws, or knocked out an eye. Our opponents certainly laboured under considerable disadvantage, being compelled not only to wade across a deceitful bog, but likewise to clamber up part of a steep hill before they could attack us; nevertheless, their determination was such, and such their impetuosity, that we had sometimes difficulty enough to maintain our own. I shall never forget one bicker, the last indeed which occurred at that time, as the authorities of the town, alarmed by the desperation of its character, stationed forthwith a body of police on the hill side to prevent, in future, any such breaches of the peace.

It was a beautiful Sunday evening, the rays of the descending sun were reflected redly from the grey walls of the castle, and from the black rocks on which it was founded. The bicker had long since commenced, stones from sling and hand were flying; but the callants of the New Town were now carrying everything before them.

A full-grown baker's apprentice was at their head; he was foaming with rage, and had taken the field, as I was told, in order to avenge his brother, whose eye had been knocked out in one of the late bickers. He was no slinger, or flinger, but brandished in his right hand the spoke of a cart-wheel, like my countryman Tom Hickathrift of old in his encounter with the giant of the Lincolnshire fen. Protected by a piece of wicker-work attached to his left arm, he rushed on to the fray, disregarding the stones which were showered against him, and was ably seconded by his followers. Our own party was chased half way up the hill, where I was struck to the ground by the baker, after having been foiled in an attempt which I had made to fling a handful of earth into his eyes. All now appeared lost, the Auld Toon was in full retreat. I myself lay at the baker's feet, who had just raised his

spoke, probably to give me the *coup de grâce*,—it was an awful
moment.   Just then I heard a shout and a rushing sound.   A
wild-looking figure is descending the hill with terrible bounds ; it
is a lad of some fifteen years ; he is bare-headed, and his red
uncombed hair stands on end like hedgehogs' bristles ; his frame
is lithy, like that of an antelope, but he has prodigious breadth of
chest ; he wears a military undress, that of the regiment, even of
a drummer, for it is wild Davy, whom a month before I had seen
enlisted on Leith Links to serve King George with drum and
drumstick as long as his services might be required, and who,
ere a week had elapsed, had smitten with his fist Drum-Major
Elzigood, who, incensed at his own inaptitude, had threatened
him with the cane ; he has been in confinement for weeks, this is
the first day of his liberation, and he is now descending the hill
with horrid bounds and shoutings ; he is now about five yards
distant, and the baker, who apprehends that something dangerous
is at hand prepares himself for the encounter ; but what avails the
strength of a baker, even full grown ?—what avails the defence of
a wicker shield ? what avails the wheel-spoke, should there be an
opportunity of using it, against the impetus of an avalanche or a
cannon ball ?—for to either of these might that wild figure be
compared, which, at the distance of five yards, sprang at once with
head, hands, feet and body, all together, upon the champion of
the New Town, tumbling him to the earth amain.   And now it
was the turn of the Old Town to triumph.   Our late discomfited
host, returning on its steps, overwhelmed the fallen champion
with blows of every kind, and then, led on by his vanquisher who
had assumed his arms, namely, the wheelspoke and wicker shield,
fairly cleared the brae of their adversaries, whom they drove down
headlong into the morass.

CHAPTER VIII.

MEANWHILE I had become a daring cragsman, a character to which an English lad has seldom opportunities of aspiring; for in England there are neither crags nor mountains. Of these, however, as is well known, there is no lack in Scotland, and the habits of individuals are invariably in harmony with the country in which they dwell. The Scotch are expert climbers, and I was now a Scot in most things, particularly in language. The castle in which I dwelt stood upon a rock, a bold and craggy one, which, at first sight, would seem to bid defiance to any feet save those of goats and chamois; but patience and perseverance generally enable mankind to overcome things which, at first sight, appear impossible. Indeed, what is there above man's exertions? Unwearied determination will enable him to run with the horse, to swim with the fish, and assuredly to compete with the chamois and the goat in agility and sureness of foot. To scale the rock was merely child's play for the Edinbro' callants. It was my own favourite diversion. I soon found that the rock contained all manner of strange crypts, crannies, and recesses, where owls nestled, and the weasel brought forth her young; here and there were small natural platforms, overgrown with long grass and various kinds of plants, where the climber, if so disposed, could stretch himself, and either give his eyes to sleep or his mind to thought; for capital places were these same platforms either for repose or meditation. The boldest features of the rock are descried on the southern side, where, after shelving down gently from the wall for some distance, it terminates abruptly in a precipice, black and horrible, of some three hundred feet at least, as if the axe of nature had been here employed cutting sheer down, and leaving behind neither excrescence nor spur—a dizzy precipice it is, assimilating much to those so frequent in the flinty hills of Northern Africa, and exhibiting some distant resemblance to that of Gibraltar, towering in its horridness above the neutral ground.

It was now holiday time, and having nothing particular wherewith to occupy myself, I not unfrequently passed the greater part

of the day upon the rocks.   Once, after scaling the western crags,
and creeping round a sharp angle of the wall, overhung by a kind
of watch tower, I found myself on the southern side.   Still keeping
close to the wall, I was proceeding onward, for I was bent upon a
long excursion which should embrace half the circuit of the castle,
when suddenly my eye was attracted by the appearance of something red, far below me ; I stopped short, and, looking fixedly
upon it, perceived that it was a human being in a kind of red
jacket, seated on the extreme verge of the precipice, which I
have already made a faint attempt to describe.   Wondering who
it could be, I shouted; but it took not the slightest notice,
remaining as immovable as the rock on which it sat.   " I should
never have thought of going near that edge," said I to myself ;
"however, as you have done it, why should not I ?   And I
should like to know who you are."   So I commenced the
descent of the rock, but with great care, for I had as yet never
been in a situation so dangerous ; a slight moisture exuded from
the palms of my hands, my nerves were tingling, and my brain
was somewhat dizzy—and now I had arrived within a few yards
of the figure, and had recognised it : it was the wild drummer
who had turned the tide of battle in the bicker on the Castle
Brae.   A small stone which I dislodged now rolled down the
rock, and tumbled into the abyss close beside him.   He turned
his head, and after looking at me for a moment somewhat vacantly,
he resumed his former attitude.   I drew yet nearer to the horrible
edge ; not close, however, for fear was on me.

   "What are you thinking of, David?" said I, as I sat behind
him and trembled, for I repeat that I was afraid.

   David Haggart. I was thinking of Willie Wallace.

   Myself. You had better be thinking of yourself, man.   A
strange place this to come to and think of William Wallace.

   David Haggart. Why so ?   Is not his tower just beneath our
feet ?

   Myself. You mean the auld ruin by the side of the Nor Loch
—the ugly stane bulk, from the foot of which flows the spring
into the dyke, where the watercresses grow ?

   David Haggart. Just sae, Geordie.

   Myself. And why were ye thinking of him ?   The English
hanged him long since, as I have heard say.

   David Haggart. I was thinking that I should wish to be like him.

   Myself. Do ye mean that ye would wish to be hanged ?

   David Haggart. I wad na flinch from that, Geordie, if I
might be a great man first.

Myself. And wha kens, Davie, how great you may be, even
without hanging? Are ye not in the high road of preferment?
Are ye not a bauld drummer already? Wha kens how high ye
may rise? perhaps to be general, or drum-major.

David Haggart. I hae na wish to be drum-major; it were na
great things to be like the doited carle, Else-than-gude, as they
call him; and, troth, he has nae his name for naething. But I
should have nae objection to be a general, and to fight the
French and Americans, and win myself a name and a fame like
Willie Wallace, and do brave deeds, such as I have been reading
about in his story book.

Myself. Ye are a fule, Davie; the story book is full of lies.
Wallace, indeed! the wuddie rebel! I have heard my father
say that the Duke of Cumberland was worth twenty of Willie
Wallace.

David Haggart. Ye had better sae naething agin Willie
Wallace, Geordie, for, if ye do, De'il hae me, if I dinna tumble
ye doon the craig.

. . . .

Fine materials in that lad for a hero, you will say. Yes,
indeed, for a hero, or for what he afterwards became. In other
times, and under other circumstances, he might have made what
is generally termed a great man, a patriot, or a conqueror. As
it was, the very qualities which might then have pushed him on
to fortune and renown were the cause of his ruin. The war
over, he fell into evil courses; for his wild heart and ambitious
spirit could not brook the sober and quiet pursuits of honest
industry.

"Can an Arabian steed submit to be a vile drudge?" cries
the fatalist. Nonsense! A man is not an irrational creature, but
a reasoning being, and has something within him beyond mere
brutal instinct. The greatest victory which a man can achieve
is over himself, by which is meant those unruly passions which
are not convenient to the time and place. David did not do
this; he gave the reins to his wild heart, instead of curbing it,
and became a robber, and, alas! alas! he shed blood—under
peculiar circumstances, it is true, and without *malice prepense*
—and for that blood he eventually died, and justly; for it
was that of the warden of a prison from which he was escaping,
and whom he slew with one blow of his stalwart arm.

Tamerlane and Haggart! Haggart and Tamerlane! Both
these men were robbers, and of low birth, yet one perished on
an ignoble scaffold, and the other died emperor of the world.

Is this justice? The ends of the two men were widely dissimilar
—yet what is the intrinsic difference between them? Very great
indeed; the one acted according to his lights and his country,
not so the other. Tamerlane was a heathen, and acted according
to his lights; he was a robber where all around were robbers, but
he became the avenger of God—God's scourge on unjust kings,
on the cruel Bajazet, who had plucked out his own brothers'
eyes; he became to a certain extent the purifier of the East,
its regenerator; his equal never was before, nor has it since
been seen. Here the wild heart was profitably employed, the
wild strength, the teeming brain. Onward, Lame one! Onward,
Tamur—lank! Haggart. . . .

But peace to thee, poor David! why should a mortal worm be
sitting in judgment over thee? The Mighty and Just One has
already judged thee, and perhaps above thou hast received pardon
for thy crimes, which could not be pardoned here below; and
now that thy feverish existence has closed, and thy once active
form become inanimate dust, thy very memory all but forgotten,
I will say a few words about thee, a few words soon also to be
forgotten. Thou wast the most extraordinary robber that ever
lived within the belt of Britain; Scotland rang with thy exploits,
and England, too, north of the Humber; strange deeds also
didst thou achieve when, fleeing from justice, thou didst find
thyself in the Sister Isle; busy wast thou there in town and on
curragh, at fair and race-course, and also in the solitary place.
Ireland thought thee her child, for who spoke her brogue better
than thyself?—she felt proud of thee, and said, "Sure, O'Hanlon
is come again." What might not have been thy fate in the far
west in America, whither thou hadst turned thine eye, saying, "I
will go there, and become an honest man!" But thou wast not
to go there, David—the blood which thou hadst shed in Scotland
was to be required of thee; the avenger was at hand, the avenger
of blood. Seized, manacled, brought back to thy native land,
condemned to die, thou wast left in thy narrow cell and told to
make the most of thy time, for it was short: and there, in thy
narrow cell, and thy time so short, thou didst put the crowning
stone to thy strange deeds, by that strange history of thyself,
penned by thy own hand in the robber tongue. Thou mightest
have been better employed, David!—but the ruling passion was
strong with thee, even in the jaws of death. Thou mightest have
been better employed!—but peace be with thee, I repeat, and the
Almighty's grace and pardon.

CHAPTER IX.

ONWARD, onward! and after we had sojourned in Scotland nearly two years, the long continental war had been brought to an end; Napoleon was humbled for a time, and the Bourbons restored to a land which could have well have dispensed with them. We returned to England, where the corps was disbanded, and my parents with their family retired to private life. I shall pass over in silence the events of a year, which offer little of interest as far as connected with me and mine. Suddenly, however, the sound of war was heard again; Napoleon had broken forth from Elba, and everything was in confusion. Vast military preparations were again made, our own corps was levied anew, and my brother became an officer in it; but the danger was soon over, Napoleon was once more quelled and chained for ever, like Prometheus, to his rock. As the corps, however, though so recently levied, had already become a very fine one, thanks to my father's energetic drilling, the Government very properly determined to turn it to some account, and, as disturbances were apprehended in Ireland about this period, it occurred to them that they could do no better than despatch it to that country.

In the autumn of the year 1815 we set sail from a port in Essex; we were some eight hundred strong, and were embarked in two ships, very large, but old and crazy; a storm overtook us when off Beachy Head, in which we had nearly foundered. I was awakened early in the morning by the howling of the wind, and the uproar on deck. I kept myself close, however, as is still my constant practice on similar occasions, and waited the result with that apathy and indifference which violent sea-sickness is sure to produce. We shipped several seas, and once the vessel missing stays—which, to do it justice, it generally did at every third or fourth tack—we escaped almost by a miracle from being dashed upon the foreland. On the eighth day of our voyage we were in sight of Ireland. The weather was now calm and serene, the sun shone brightly on the sea and on certain green hills in the distance, on which I descried what at first sight I believed to be

two ladies gathering flowers, which, however, on our nearer
approach, proved to be two tall white towers, doubtless built for
some purpose or other, though I did not learn for what.

We entered a kind of bay, or cove, by a narrow inlet; it was
a beautiful and romantic place this cove, very spacious, and being
nearly land-locked, was sheltered from every wind. A small
island, every inch of which was covered with fortifications, appeared
to swim upon the waters, whose dark blue denoted their immense
depth; tall green hills, which ascended gradually from the shore,
formed the background to the west; they were carpeted to the
top with turf of the most vivid green, and studded here and there
with woods, seemingly of oak; there was a strange old castle
half-way up the ascent, a village on a crag—but the mists of
morning were half veiling the scene when I surveyed it, and
the mists of time are now hanging densely between it and
my no longer youthful eye; I may not describe it;—nor will I
try.

Leaving the ship in the cove, we passed up a wide river in
boats till we came to a city where we disembarked. It was a large
city, as large as Edinburgh to my eyes; there were plenty of fine
houses, but little neatness; the streets were full of impurities;
handsome equipages rolled along, but the greater part of the
population were in rags; beggars abounded; there was no lack
of merriment, however; boisterous shouts of laughter were heard
on every side. It appeared a city of contradictions. After a few
days' rest we marched from this place in two divisions. My father
commanded the second; I walked by his side.

Our route lay up the country; the country at first offered no
very remarkable feature; it was pretty, but tame. On the second
day, however, its appearance had altered, it had become more
wild; a range of distant mountains bounded the horizon. We
passed through several villages, as I suppose I may term them,
of low huts, the walls formed of rough stones without mortar,
the roof of flags laid over wattles and wicker-work; they seemed
to be inhabited solely by women and children; the latter were
naked, the former, in general, blear-eyed beldames, who sat beside
the doors on low stools, spinning. We saw, however, both men
and women working at a distance in the fields.

I was thirsty; and going up to an ancient crone, employed in
the manner which I have described, I asked her for water; she
looked me in the face, appeared to consider for a moment, then
tottering into her hut, presently reappeared with a small pipkin of
milk, which she offered to me with a trembling hand. I drank

---

the milk; it was sour, but I found it highly refreshing. I then took out a penny and offered it to her, whereupon she shook her head, smiled, and, patting my face with her skinny hand, murmured some words in a tongue which I had never heard before.

I walked on by my father's side, holding the stirrup-leather of his horse; presently several low uncouth cars passed by, drawn by starved cattle; the drivers were tall fellows, with dark features and athletic frames—they wore long loose blue cloaks with sleeves, which last, however, dangled unoccupied; these cloaks appeared in tolerably good condition, not so their under garments. On their heads were broad slouching hats; the generality of them were bare-footed. As they passed, the soldiers jested with them in the patois of East Anglia, whereupon the fellows laughed and appeared to jest with the soldiers; but what they said who knows, it being in a rough guttural language, strange and wild. The soldiers stared at each other, and were silent.

"A strange language that!" said a young officer to my father, "I don't understand a word of it; what can it be?"

"Irish," said my father, with a loud voice, "and a bad language it is; I have known it of old, that is, I have often heard it spoken when I was a guardsman in London. There's one part of London where all the Irish live—at least all the worst of them—and there they hatch their villanies and speak this tongue; it is that which keeps them together and makes them dangerous. I was once sent there to seize a couple of deserters—Irish—who had taken refuge among their companions; we found them in what was in my time called a *ken*, that is, a house where only thieves and desperadoes are to be found. Knowing on what kind of business I was bound, I had taken with me a sergeant's party; it was well I did so. We found the deserters in a large room, with at least thirty ruffians, horrid-looking fellows, seated about a long table, drinking, swearing, and talking Irish. Ah! we had a tough battle, I remember; the two fellows did nothing, but sat still, thinking it best to be quiet; but the rest, with an ubbubboo, like the blowing up of a powder-magazine, sprang up, brandishing their sticks; for these fellows always carry sticks with them, even to bed, and not unfrequently spring up in their sleep, striking left and right."

"And did you take the deserters?" said the officer.

"Yes," said my father; "for we formed at the end of the room, and charged with fixed bayonets, which compelled the others to yield notwithstanding their numbers; but the worst was when we got out into the street; the whole district had become alarmed, and hundreds came pouring down upon us—men, women, and children. Women, did I say!—they looked fiends, half naked, with their hair hanging down over their bosoms; they tore up the very pavement to hurl at us, sticks rang about our ears, stones, and Irish—I liked the Irish worst of all, it sounded so horrid, especially as I did not understand it. It's a bad language."

"A queer tongue," said I, "I wonder if I could learn it?"

"Learn it!" said my father; "what should you learn it for? —however, I am not afraid of that. It is not like Scotch; no person can learn it, save those who are born to it, and even in Ireland the respectable people do not speak it, only the wilder sort, like those we have passed."

Within a day or two we had reached a tall range of mountains running north and south, which I was told were those of Tipperary; along the skirts of these we proceeded till we came to a town, the principal one of these regions. It was on the bank of a beautiful river, which separated it from the mountains. It was rather an ancient place, and might contain some ten thousand inhabitants; I found that it was our destination; there were extensive barracks at the farther end, in which the corps took up its quarters; with respect to ourselves, we took lodgings in a house which stood in the principal street.

"You never saw more elegant lodgings than these, captain," said the master of the house, a tall, handsome, and athletic man, who came up whilst our little family were seated at dinner late in the afternoon of the day of our arrival; "they beat anything in this town of Clonmel. I do not let them for the sake of interest, and to none but gentlemen in the army, in order that myself and my wife, who is from Londonderry, may have the advantage of pleasant company, genteel company; ay, and Protestant company, captain. It did my heart good when I saw your honour ride in at the head of all those fine fellows, real Protestants, I'll engage, not a Papist among them—they are too good-looking and honest-looking for that. So I no sooner saw your honour at the head of your army, with that handsome young gentleman holding by your stirrup, than I said to my wife, Mistress Hyne, who is from Londonderry, 'God bless me,' said I, 'what a truly Protestant countenance, what a noble bearing, and what a sweet young gentleman. By the silver hairs of his honour—and sure enough I never saw hairs more regally silver than those of your honour— by his honour's gray silver hairs, and by my own soul, which is not worthy to be mentioned in the same day with one of them— it would be no more than decent and civil to run out and welcome

such a father and son coming in at the head of such a Protestant
military.' And then my wife, who is from Londonderry, Mistress
Hyne, looking me in the face like a fairy as she is, 'You may say
that,' says she. 'It would be but decent and civil, honey.' And
your honour knows how I ran out of my own door and welcomed
your honour riding, in company with your son who was walking;
how I welcomed ye both at the head of your royal regiment, and
how I shook your honour by the hand, saying, I am glad to see
your honour, and your honour's son, and your honour's royal
military Protestant regiment. And now I have you in the house,
and right proud I am to have ye one and all: one, two, three,
four, true Protestants every one, no Papists here; and I have
made bold to bring up a bottle of claret which is now waiting
behind the door; and, when your honour and your family have
dined, I will make bold too to bring up Mistress Hyne, from Londonderry, to introduce to your honour's lady, and then we'll drink
to the health of King George, God bless him; to the 'glorious and
immortal'—to Boyne water—to your honour's speedy promotion
to be Lord Lieutenant, and to the speedy downfall of the Pope
and Saint Anthony of Padua."

Such was the speech of the Irish Protestant addressed to my
father in the long lofty dining-room with three windows, looking
upon the High street of the good town of Clonmel, as he sat at
meat with his family, after saying grace like a true-hearted respectable soldier as he was.

"A bigot and an Orangeman!" Oh, yes! It is easier to
apply epithets of opprobrium to people than to make yourself
acquainted with their history and position. He was a specimen,
and a fair specimen, of a most remarkable body of men, who
during two centuries have fought a good fight in Ireland in the
cause of civilisation and religious truth; they were sent as colonists,
few in number, into a barbarous and unhappy country, where ever
since, though surrounded with difficulties of every kind, they have
maintained their ground; theirs has been no easy life, nor have
their lines fallen upon very pleasant places; amidst darkness they
have held up a lamp, and it would be well for Ireland were all her
children like these her adopted ones. "But they are fierce and
sanguinary," it is said. Ay, ay! they have not unfrequently
opposed the keen sword to the savage pike. "But they are
bigoted and narrow-minded." Ay, ay! they do not like idolatry,
and will not bow the knee before a stone! "But their language
is frequently indecorous." Go to, my dainty one, did ye ever
listen to the voice of Papist cursing?

The Irish Protestants have faults, numerous ones; but the greater number of these may be traced to the peculiar circumstances of their position.　But they have virtues, numerous ones; and their virtues are their own, their industry, their energy, and their undaunted resolution are their own.　They have been vilified and traduced—but what would Ireland be without them? I repeat, that it would be well for her were all her sons no worse than these much calumniated children of her adoption.

CHAPTER X.

WE continued at this place for some months, during which time
the soldiers performed their duties, whatever they were; and I,
having no duties to perform, was sent to school. I had been to
English schools, and to the celebrated one of Edinburgh; but
my education, at the present day, would not be what it is—
perfect, had I never had the honour of being *alumnus* in an Irish
seminary.

"Captain," said our kind host, "you would, no doubt, wish
that the young gentleman should enjoy every advantage which the
town may afford towards helping him on in the path of genteel
learning. It's a great pity that he should waste his time in idleness—doing nothing else than what he says he has been doing
for the last fortnight—fishing in the river for trouts which he
never catches, and wandering up the glen in the mountain in
search of the hips that grow there. Now, we have a school here,
where he can learn the most elegant Latin, and get an insight into
the Greek letters, which is desirable; and where, moreover, he
will have an opportunity of making acquaintance with all the
Protestant young gentlemen of the place, the handsome well-
dressed young persons whom your honour sees in the church on
the Sundays, when your honour goes there in the morning, with
the rest of the Protestant military; for it is no Papist school,
though there may be a Papist or two there—a few poor farmers'
sons from the country, with whom there is no necessity for your
honour's child to form any acquaintance at all, at all!"

And to the school I went, where I read the Latin tongue and
the Greek letters, with a nice old clergyman, who sat behind a
black oaken desk, with a huge Elzevir Flaccus before him, in a
long gloomy kind of hall, with a broken stone floor, the roof
festooned with cobwebs, the walls considerably dilapidated, and
covered over with strange figures and hieroglyphics, evidently
produced by the application of burnt stick; and there I made
acquaintance with the Protestant young gentlemen of the place,
who, with whatever *éclat* they might appear at church on a
Sunday, did assuredly not exhibit to much advantage in the

(62)

school-room on the week days, either with respect to clothes or
looks.   And there I was in the habit of sitting on a large stone,
before the roaring fire in the huge open chimney, and entertaining
certain of the Protestant young gentlemen of my own age, seated
on similar stones, with extraordinary accounts of my own adventures and those of the corps, with an occasional anecdote extracted
from the story-books of Hickathrift and Wight Wallace, pretending
to be conning the lesson all the while.

And there I made acquaintance, notwithstanding the hint of
the landlord, with the Papist "gasoons," as they were called, the
farmers' sons from the country; and of these gasoons, of which
there were three, two might be reckoned as nothing at all; in
the third, however, I soon discovered that there was something
extraordinary.

He was about sixteen years old, and above six feet high,
dressed in a gray suit; the coat, from its size, appeared to have
been made for him some ten years before.   He was remarkably
narrow-chested and round-shouldered, owing, perhaps, as much to
the tightness of his garment as to the hand of nature.   His face
was long, and his complexion swarthy, relieved, however, by certain
freckles, with which the skin was plentifully studded.   He had
strange wandering eyes, gray, and somewhat unequal in size; they
seldom rested on the book, but were generally wandering about
the room from one object to another.   Sometimes he would fix
them intently on the wall; and then suddenly starting, as if from
a reverie, he would commence making certain mysterious movements with his thumbs and forefingers, as if he were shuffling
something from him.

One morning, as he sat by himself on a bench, engaged in
this manner, I went up to him and said, "Good day, Murtagh;
you do not seem to have much to do."

"Faith, you may say that, Shorsha dear! it is seldom much to
do that I have."

"And what are you doing with your hands?"

"Faith, then, if I must tell you, I was e'en dealing with the
cards."

"Do you play much at cards?"

"Sorra a game, Shorsha, have I played with the cards since
my uncle Phelim, the thief, stole away the ould pack, when he
went to settle in the county Waterford!"

"But you have other things to do?"

"Sorra anything else has Murtagh to do that he cares about;
and that makes me dread so going home at nights."

"I should like to know all about you; where do you live, joy?"

"Faith, then, ye shall know all about me, and where I live. It is at a place called the Wilderness that I live, and they call it so, because it is a fearful wild place, without any house near it but my father's own ; and that's where I live when at home."

"And your father is a farmer, I suppose?"

"You may say that ; and it is a farmer I should have been, like my brother Denis, had not my uncle Phelim, the thief ! tould my father to send me to school, to learn Greek letters, that I might be made a saggart of and sent to Paris and Salamanca."

"And you would rather be a farmer than a priest?"

"You may say that ! for, were I a farmer, like the rest, I should have something to do, like the rest, something that I cared for, and I should come home tired at night and fall asleep, as the rest do, before the fire; but when I comes home at night I am not tired, for I have been doing nothing all day that I care for ; and then I sits down and stares about me, and at the fire, till I become frighted ; and then I shouts to my brother Denis, or to the gasoons, 'Get up, I say, and let's be doing something ; tell us a tale of Finn-ma-Coul, and how he lay down in the Shannon's bed and let the river flow down his jaws !' Arrah, Shorsha, I wish you would come and stay with us, and tell us some o' your sweet stories of your ownself and the snake ye carried about wid ye. Faith, Shorsha dear ! that snake bates anything about Finn-ma-Coul or Brian Boroo, the thieves two, bad luck to them !"

"And do they get up and tell you stories?"

"Sometimes they does, but oftenmost they curses me and bids me be quiet ! But I can't be quiet, either before the fire or abed ; so I runs out of the house, and stares at the rocks, at the trees, and sometimes at the clouds, as they run a race across the bright moon ; and the more I stares, the more frighted I grows, till I screeches and holloas. And last night I went into the barn and hid my face in the straw ; and there, as I lay and shivered in the straw, I heard a voice above my head singing out 'To whit, to whoo !' and then up I starts and runs into the house, and falls over my brother Denis, as he lies at the fire. 'What's that for?' says he. 'Get up, you thief !' says I, 'and be helping me. I have been out in the barn, and an owl has crow'd at me !'"

"And what has this to do with playing cards?"

"Little enough, Shorsha dear !—If there were card-playing, I should not be frighted."

" And why do you not play at cards ? "

" Did I not tell you that the thief, my uncle Phelim, stole away the pack ?   If we had the pack, my brother Denis and the gasoons would be ready enough to get up from their sleep before the fire, and play cards with me for ha'pence, or eggs, or nothing at all ; but the pack is gone—bad luck to the thief who took it ! "

" And why don't you buy another ? "

" Is it of buying you are speaking?   And where am I to get the money ? "

" Ah ! that's another thing ! "

" Faith it is, honey !—And now the Christmas holidays is coming, when I shall be at home by day as well as night, and then what am I to do?   Since I have been a saggarting, I have been good for nothing at all—neither for work nor Greek—only to play cards !   Faith, it's going mad I will be ! "

" I say, Murtagh ! "

" Yes, Shorsha dear ! "

" I have a pack of cards."

" You don't say so, Shorsha mavourneen ! you don't say that you have cards fifty-two ? "

" I do, though ; and they are quite new—never been once used."

" And you'll be lending them to me, I warrant ? "

" Don't think it !   But I'll sell them to you, joy, if you like."

" *Hanam mon Dioul !* am I not after telling you that I have no money at all ? "

" But you have as good as money, to me, at least ; and I'll take it in exchange."

" What's that, Shorsha dear ? "

" Irish ! "

" Irish ? "

" Yes, you speak Irish ; I heard you talking it the other day to the cripple.   You shall teach me Irish."

" And is it a language-master you'd be making of me ? "

" To be sure !—what better can you do ?—it would help you to pass your time at school.   You can't learn Greek, so you must teach Irish ! "

Before Christmas, Murtagh was playing at cards with his brother Denis, and I could speak a considerable quantity of broken Irish.

CHAPTER XI.

WHEN Christmas was over, and the new year commenced, we broke up our quarters, and marched away to Templemore. This was a large military station, situated in a wild and thinly inhabited country. Extensive bogs were in the neighbourhood, connected with the huge bog of Allan, the Palus Mæotis of Ireland. Here and there was seen a ruined castle looming through the mists of winter; whilst, at the distance of seven miles, rose a singular mountain, exhibiting in its brow a chasm, or vacuum, just, for all the world, as if a piece had been bitten out; a feat which, according to the tradition of the country, had actually been performed by his Satanic majesty, who, after flying for some leagues with the morsel in his mouth, becoming weary, dropped it in the vicinity of Cashel, where it may now be seen in the shape of a bold bluff hill, crowned with the ruins of a stately edifice, probably built by some ancient Irish king.

We had been here only a few days, when my brother, who, as I have before observed, had become one of his Majesty's officers, was sent on detachment to a village at about ten miles' distance. He was not sixteen, and, though three years older than myself, scarcely my equal in stature, for I had become tall and large-limbed for my age; but there was a spirit in him that would not have disgraced a general; and, nothing daunted at the considerable responsibility which he was about to incur, he marched sturdily out of the barrack-yard at the head of his party, consisting of twenty light-infantry men, and a tall grenadier sergeant, selected expressly by my father for the soldier-like qualities which he possessed, to accompany his son on this his first expedition. So out of the barrack-yard, with something of an air, marched my dear brother, his single drum and fife playing the inspiring old melody,

Marlbrouk is gone to the wars,
He'll never return no more!

I soon missed my brother, for I was now alone, with no being

at all assimilating in age, with whom I could exchange a word.
Of late years, from being almost constantly at school, I had cast
aside, in a great degree, my unsocial habits and natural reserve,
but in the desolate region in which we now were there was no
school; and I felt doubly the loss of my brother, whom, moreover,
I tenderly loved for his own sake.   Books I had none, at least
such "as I cared about;" and with respect to the old volume,
the wonders of which had first beguiled me into common reading,
I had so frequently pored over its pages, that I had almost got its
contents by heart.   I was therefore in danger of falling into the
same predicament as Murtagh, becoming "frighted" from having
nothing to do!   Nay, I had not even his resources; I cared not
for cards, even if I possessed them, and could find people disposed
to play with them.   However, I made the most of circumstances,
and roamed about the desolate fields and bogs in the neighbourhood, sometimes entering the cabins of the peasantry, with a
"God's blessing upon you, good people!" where I would take
my seat on the "stranger's stone" at the corner of the hearth,
and, looking them full in the face, would listen to the carles and
carlines talking Irish.

Ah, that Irish!   How frequently do circumstances, at first
sight the most trivial and unimportant, exercise a mighty and
permanent influence on our habits and pursuits!—how frequently
is a stream turned aside from its natural course by some little rock
or knoll, causing it to make an abrupt turn!   On a wild road in
Ireland I had heard Irish spoken for the first time; and I was
seized with a desire to learn Irish, the acquisition of which, in
my case, became the stepping-stone to other languages.   I had
previously learnt Latin, or rather Lilly; but neither Latin nor
Lilly made me a philologist.   I had frequently heard French and
other languages, but had felt little desire to become acquainted
with them; and what, it may be asked, was there connected with
the Irish calculated to recommend it to my attention?

First of all, and principally, I believe, the strangeness and
singularity of its tones; then there was something mysterious and
uncommon associated with its use.   It was not a school language,
to acquire which was considered an imperative duty; no, no; nor
was it a drawing-room language, drawled out occasionally, in
shreds and patches, by the ladies of generals and other great
dignitaries, to the ineffable dismay of poor officers' wives.
Nothing of the kind; but a speech spoken in out-of-the-way
desolate places, and in cut-throat kens, where thirty ruffians, at
the sight of the king's minions, would spring up with brandished

sticks and an " ubbubboo, like the blowing up of a powder-
magazine ". Such were the points connected with the Irish,
which first awakened in my mind the desire of acquiring it; and
by acquiring it I became, as I have already said, enamoured of
languages. Having learnt one by choice, I speedily, as the reader
will perceive, learnt others, some of which were widely different
from Irish.

Ah, that Irish! I am much indebted to it in more ways than
one. But I am afraid I have followed the way of the world,
which is very much wont to neglect original friends and benefactors. I frequently find myself, at present, turning up my nose
at Irish, when I hear it in the street; yet I have still a kind of
regard for it, the fine old language:

A labhair Padruic n'insefail nan riogh.

One of the most peculiar features of this part of Ireland is the
ruined castles, which are so thick and numerous that the face of
the country appears studded with them, it being difficult to choose
any situation from which one, at least, may not be descried.
They are of various ages and styles of architecture, some of great
antiquity, like the stately remains which crown the Crag of
Cashel; others built by the early English conquerors; others,
and probably the greater part, erections of the times of Elizabeth
and Cromwell. The whole, speaking monuments of the troubled
and insecure state of the country, from the most remote periods
to a comparatively modern time.

From the windows of the room where I slept I had a view of
one of these old places—an indistinct one, it is true, the distance
being too great to permit me to distinguish more than the general
outline. I had an anxious desire to explore it. It stood to the
south-east; in which direction, however, a black bog intervened,
which had more than once baffled all my attempts to cross it.
One morning, however, when the sun shone brightly upon the
old building, it appeared so near, that I felt ashamed at not being
able to accomplish a feat seemingly so easy; I determined, therefore, upon another trial. I reached the bog, and was about to
venture upon its black surface, and to pick my way amongst its
innumerable holes, yawning horribly, and half filled with water
black as soot, when it suddenly occurred to me that there was
a road to the south, by following which I might find a more
convenient route to the object of my wishes. The event justified
my expectations, for, after following the road for some three miles,

seemingly in the direction of the Devil's Mountain, I suddenly beheld the castle on my left.

I diverged from the road, and, crossing two or three fields, came to a small grassy plain, in the midst of which stood the castle. About a gun-shot to the south was a small village, which had, probably, in ancient days, sprung up beneath its protection. A kind of awe came over me as I approached the old building. The sun no longer shone upon it, and it looked so grim, so desolate and solitary; and here was I in that wild country, alone with that grim building before me. The village was within sight, it is true; but it might be a village of the dead for what I knew; no sound issued from it, no smoke was rising from its roofs, neither man nor beast was visible, no life, no motion—it looked as desolate as the castle itself. Yet I was bent on the adventure, and moved on towards the castle across the green plain, occasionally casting a startled glance around me; and now I was close to it.

It was surrounded by a quadrangular wall, about ten feet in height, with a square tower at each corner. At first I could discover no entrance; walking round, however, to the northern side, I found a wide and lofty gateway with a tower above it, similar to those at the angles of the wall; on this side the ground sloped gently down towards the bog, which was here skirted by an abundant growth of copsewood, and a few evergreen oaks. I passed through the gateway, and found myself within a square enclosure of about two acres. On one side rose a round and lofty keep, or donjon, with a conical roof, part of which had fallen down, strewing the square with its ruins. Close to the keep, on the other side, stood the remains of an oblong house, built something in the modern style, with various window-holes; nothing remained but the bare walls and a few projecting stumps of beams, which seemed to have been half burnt. The interior of the walls was blackened, as if by fire; fire also appeared at one time to have raged out of the window-holes, for the outside about them was black, portentously so.

" I wonder what has been going on here ! " I exclaimed.

There were echoes along the walls as I walked about the court. I entered the keep by a low and frowning doorway: the lower floor consisted of a large dungeon-like room, with a vaulted roof; on the left hand was a winding staircase in the thickness of the wall; it looked anything but inviting; yet I stole softly up, my heart beating. On the top of the first flight of stairs was an arched doorway; to the left was a dark passage; to the right, stairs leading still higher. I stepped under the arch and found myself in an apartment somewhat similar to the one below, but higher. There was an object at the farther end.

An old woman, at least eighty, was seated on a stone, cowering over a few sticks burning feebly on what had once been a right noble and cheerful hearth ; her side-glance was towards the doorway as I entered, for she had heard my footsteps. I stood suddenly still, and her haggard glance rested on my face.

" Is this your house, mother ? " I at length demanded, in the language which I thought she would best understand.

" Yes, my house, my own house ; the house of the broken-hearted."

" Any other person's house ? " I demanded.

" My own house, the beggar's house—the accursed house of Cromwell ! "

CHAPTER XII.

ONE morning I set out, designing to pay a visit to my brother at the place where he was detached; the distance was rather considerable, yet I hoped to be back by evening fall, for I was now a shrewd walker, thanks to constant practice. I set out early, and directing my course towards the north, I had in less than two hours accomplished considerably more than half of the journey. The weather had at first been propitious : a slight frost had rendered the ground firm to the tread, and the skies were clear ; but now a change came over the scene : the skies darkened and a heavy snow-storm came on ; the road then lay straight through a bog, and was bounded by a deep trench on both sides ; I was making the best of my way, keeping as nearly as I could in the middle of the road, lest, blinded by the snow which was frequently borne into my eyes by the wind, I might fall into the dyke, when all at once I heard a shout to windward, and turning my eyes I saw the figure of a man, and what appeared to be an animal of some kind, coming across the bog with great speed, in the direction of myself ; the nature of the ground seemed to offer but little impediment to these beings, both clearing the holes and abysses which lay in their way with surprising agility ; the animal was, however, some slight way in advance, and, bounding over the dyke, appeared on the road just before me. It was a dog, of what species I cannot tell, never having seen the like before or since ; the head was large and round, the ears so tiny as scarcely to be discernible, the eyes of a fiery red ; in size it was rather small than large, and the coat, which was remarkably smooth, as white as the falling flakes. It placed itself directly in my path, and showing its teeth, and bristling its coat, appeared determined to prevent my progress. I had an ashen stick in my hand, with which I threatened it ; this, however, only served to increase its fury ; it rushed upon me, and I had the utmost difficulty to preserve myself from its fangs.

"What are you doing with the dog, the fairy dog?" said a man, who at this time likewise cleared the dyke at a bound.

He was a very tall man, rather well-dressed as it should seem ; his garments, however, were like my own, so covered with snow that I could scarcely discern their quality.

"What are ye doing with the dog of peace ?"

"I wish he would show himself one," said I ; "I said nothing to him, but he placed himself in my road, and would not let me pass."

"Of course he would not be letting you till he knew where ye were going."

"He's not much of a fairy," said I, "or he would know that without asking ; tell him that I am going to see my brother."

"And who is your brother, little Sas ?"

"What my father is, a royal soldier."

"Oh, ye are going then to the detachment at —— ; by my shoul, I have a good mind to be spoiling your journey."

"You are doing that already," said I, "keeping me here talking about dogs and fairies ; you had better go home and get some salve to cure that place over your eye ; it's catching cold you'll be, in so much snow."

On one side of the man's forehead there was a raw and staring wound, as if from a recent and terrible blow.

"Faith, then I'll be going, but it's taking you wid me I will be."

"And where will you take me ?"

"Why, then, to Ryan's Castle, little Sas."

"You do not speak the language very correctly," said I ; "it is not *Sas* you should call me—'tis *Sassannach*," and forthwith I accompanied the word with a speech full of flowers of Irish rhetoric.

The man looked upon me for a moment, fixedly, then, bending his head towards his breast, he appeared to be undergoing a kind of convulsion, which was accompanied by a sound something resembling laughter ; presently he looked at me, and there was a broad grin on his features.

"By my shoul, it's a thing of peace I'm thinking ye."

But now with a whisking sound came running down the road a hare ; it was nearly upon us before it perceived us ; suddenly stopping short, however, it sprang into the bog on the right-hand side ; after it amain bounded the dog of peace, followed by the man, but not until he had nodded to me a farewell salutation. In a few moments I lost sight of him amidst the snow-flakes.

The weather was again clear and fine before I reached the place of detachment. It was a little wooden barrack, surrounded by a wall of the same material; a sentinel stood at the gate, I passed by him, and, entering the building, found myself in a rude kind of guard-room ; several soldiers were lying asleep on a wooden couch at one end, others lounged on benches by the side of a turf fire. The tall sergeant stood before the fire, holding a cooking utensil in his left hand ; on seeing me, he made the military salutation.

"Is my brother here?" said I, rather timidly, dreading to hear that he was out, perhaps for the day.

"The ensign is in his room, sir," said Bagg, "I am now preparing his meal, which will presently be ready ; you will find the ensign above stairs," and he pointed to a broken ladder which led to some place above.

And there I found him—the boy soldier—in a kind of upper loft, so low that I could touch with my hands the sooty rafters ; the floor was of rough boards, through the joints of which you could see the gleam of the soldiers' fire, and occasionally discern their figures as they moved about ; in one corner was a camp bedstead, by the side of which hung the child's sword, gorget, and sash ; a deal table stood in the proximity of the rusty grate, where smoked and smouldered a pile of black turf from the bog—a deal table without a piece of baize to cover it, yet fraught with things not devoid of interest : a Bible, given by a mother ; the Odyssey, the Greek Odyssey ; a flute, with broad silver keys ; crayons, moreover, and water colours, and a sketch of a wild prospect near, which, though but half finished, afforded ample proof of the excellence and skill of the boyish hand now occupied upon it.

Ah ! he was a sweet being, that boy soldier, a plant of early promise, bidding fair to become in after time all that is great, good, and admirable. I have read of a remarkable Welshman, of whom it was said, when the grave closed over him, that he could frame a harp, and play it ; build a ship, and sail it ; com pose an ode, and set it to music. A brave fellow that son of Wales—but I had once a brother who could do more and better than this, but the grave has closed over him, as over the gallant Welshman of yore ; there are now but two that remember him— the one who bore him, and the being who was nurtured at the same breast. He was taken, and I was left ! Truly, the ways of Providence are inscrutable.

"You seem to be very comfortable, John," said I, looking around the room and at the various objects which I have described above : "you have a good roof over your head, and have all your things about you,"

"Yes, I am very comfortable, George, in many respects; I am, moreover, independent, and feel myself a man for the first time in my life—independent did I say?—that's not the word, I am something much higher than that; here am I, not sixteen yet, a person in authority, like the centurion in the book there, with twenty Englishmen under me, worth a whole legion of , his men, and that fine fellow Bagg to wait upon me, and take my orders. Oh! these last six weeks have passed like hours of heaven."

"But your time must frequently hang heavy on your hands; this is a strange wild place, and you must be very solitary?"

"I am never solitary; I have, as you see, all my things about me, and there is plenty of company below stairs. Not that I mix with the soldiers; if I did, good-bye to my authority; but when I am alone I can hear all their discourse through the planks, and I often laugh to myself at the funny things they say."

"And have you any acquaintance here?"

"The very best; much better than the Colonel and the rest, at their grand Templemore; I had never so many in my whole life before. One has just left me, a gentleman who lives at a distance across the bog; he comes to talk with me about Greek, and the Odyssey, for he is a very learned man, and understands the old Irish and various other strange languages. He has had a dispute with Bagg. On hearing his name, he called him to him, and, after looking at him for some time with great curiosity, said that he was sure he was a Dane. Bagg, however, took the compliment in dudgeon, and said that he was no more a Dane than himself, but a true-born Englishman, and a sergeant of six years' standing."

"And what other acquaintance have you?"

"All kinds; the whole neighbourhood can't make enough of me. Amongst others there's the clergyman of the parish and his family; such a venerable old man, such fine sons and daughters! I am treated by them like a son and a brother—I might be always with them if I pleased; there's one drawback, however, in going to see them; there's a horrible creature in the house, a kind of tutor, whom they keep more from charity than anything else; he is a Papist and, they say, a priest; you should see him scowl sometimes at my red coat, for he hates the king, and not unfrequently, when the king's health is drunk, curses him between his teeth. I once got up to strike him, but the youngest of the sisters, who is the handsomest, caught my arm and pointed to her forehead."

" And what does your duty consist of?   Have you nothing
else to do than pay visits and receive them?"

" We do what is required of us : we guard this edifice, perform
our evolutions, and help the excise ; I am frequently called up in
the dead of night to go to some wild place or other in quest of an
illicit still ; this last part of our duty is poor mean work, I don't
like it, nor more does Bagg ; though without it, we should not see
much active service, for the neighbourhood is quiet ; save the
poor creatures with their stills, not a soul is stirring.   'Tis true,
there's Jerry Grant."

" And who is Jerry Grant?"

" Did you never hear of him? that's strange, the whole country
is talking about him ; he is a kind of outlaw, rebel, or robber,
all three, I daresay ; there's a hundred pounds offered for his
head."

" And where does he live?"

" His proper home, they say, is in the Queen's County, where
he has a band ; but he is a strange fellow, fond of wandering about
by himself amidst the bogs and mountains, and living in the old
castles ; occasionally he quarters himself in the peasants' houses,
who let him do just what he pleases ; he is free of his money, and
often does them good turns, and can be good-humoured enough,
so they don't dislike him.   Then he is what they call a fairy man,
a person in league with fairies and spirits, and able to work much
harm by supernatural means, on which account they hold him in
great awe ; he is, moreover, a mighty strong and tall fellow. Bagg
has seen him."

" Has he?"

" Yes! and felt him ; he too is a strange one. A few days
ago he was told that Grant had been seen hovering about an old
castle some two miles off in the bog ; so one afternoon what does
he do but, without saying a word to me—for which, by-the-bye,
I ought to put him under arrest, though what I should do without
Bagg I have no idea whatever—what does he do but walk off to
the castle, intending, as I suppose, to pay a visit to Jerry. He
had some difficulty in getting there on account of the turf-holes
in the bog, which he was not accustomed to ; however, thither at
last he got and went in. It was a strange lonesome place, he
says, and he did not much like the look of it ; however, in he
went, and searched about from the bottom to the top and down
again, but could find no one ; he shouted and hallooed, but
nobody answered, save the rooks and choughs, which started up
in great numbers. ' I have lost my trouble,' said Bagg, and left

the castle. It was now late in the afternoon, near sunset, when about half-way over the bog he met a man ——''

'' And that man was —— ''

'' Jerry Grant! there's no doubt of it. Bagg says it was the most sudden thing in the world. He was moving along, making the best of his way, thinking of nothing at all save a public-house at Swanton Morley, which he intends to take when he gets home and the regiment is disbanded—though I hope that will not be for some time yet : he had just leaped a turf-hole, and was moving on, when, at the distance of about six yards before him, he saw a fellow coming straight towards him. Bagg says that he stopped short, as suddenly as if he had heard the word halt, when marching at double-quick time. It was quite a surprise, he says, and he can't imagine how the fellow was so close upon him before he was aware. He was an immense tall fellow—Bagg thinks at least two inches taller than himself—very well dressed in a blue coat and buff breeches, for all the world like a squire when going out hunting. Bagg, however, saw at once that he had a roguish air, and he was on his guard in a moment. 'Good evening to ye, sodger,' says the fellow, stepping close up to Bagg, and staring him in the face. 'Good evening to you, sir! I hope you are well,' says Bagg. 'You are looking after some one?'' says the fellow. 'Just so, sir,' says Bagg, and forthwith seized him by the collar; the man laughed, Bagg says it was such a strange awkward laugh. 'Do you know whom you have got hold of, sodger?' said he. 'I believe I do, sir,' said Bagg, 'and in that belief will hold you fast in the name of King George, and the quarter sessions;' the next moment he was sprawling with his heels in the air. Bagg says there was nothing remarkable in that; he was only flung by a kind of wrestling trick, which he could easily have baffled, had he been aware of it. 'You will not do that again, sir,' said he, as he got up and put himself on his guard. The fellow laughed again more strangely and awkwardly than before ; then, bending his body and moving his head from one side to the other as a cat does before she springs, and crying out, ' Here's for ye, sodger!' he made a dart at Bagg, rushing in with his head foremost. 'That will do, sir,' says Bagg, and drawing himself back he put in a left-handed blow with all the force of his body and arm, just over the fellow's right eye—Bagg is a left-handed hitter, you must know—and it was a blow of that kind which won him his famous battle at Edinburgh with the big Highland sergeant. Bagg says that he was quite satisfied with the blow, more especially when he saw the fellow reel, fling out his arms, and fall to the ground.

'And now, sir,' said he, 'I'll make bold to hand you over to the quarter sessions, and, if there is a hundred pounds for taking you, who has more right to it than myself?' So he went forward, but ere he could lay hold of his man the other was again on his legs, and was prepared to renew the combat. They grappled each other—Bagg says he had not much fear of the result, as he now felt himself the best man, the other seeming half stunned with the blow—but just then there came on a blast, a horrible roaring wind bearing night upon its wings, snow, and sleet, and hail. Bagg says he had the fellow by the throat quite fast, as he thought, but suddenly he became bewildered, and knew not where he was; and the man seemed to melt away from his grasp, and the wind howled more and more, and the night poured down darker and darker, the snow and the sleet thicker and more blinding. 'Lord have mercy upon us!' said Bagg.

Myself. A strange adventure that; it is well that Bagg got home alive.

John. He says that the fight was a fair fight, and that the fling he got was a fair fling, the result of a common enough wrestling trick. But with respect to the storm, which rose up just in time to save the fellow, he is of opinion that it was not fair, but something Irish and supernatural.

Myself. I dare say he's right. I have read of withcraft in the Bible.

John. He wishes much to have one more encounter with the fellow; he says that on fair ground, and in fine weather, he has no doubt that he could master him, and hand him over to the quarter sessions. He says that a hundred pounds would be no bad thing to be disbanded upon; for he wishes to take an inn at Swanton Morley, keep a cock-pit, and live respectably.

Myself. He is quite right; and now kiss me, my darling brother, for I must go back through the bog to Templemore.

CHAPTER XIII.

AND it came to pass that, as I was standing by the door of the barrack stable, one of the grooms came out to me, saying, "I say, young gentleman, I wish you would give the cob a breathing this fine morning."

"Why do you wish me to mount him?" said I; "you know he is dangerous. I saw him fling you off his back only a few days ago."

"Why, that's the very thing, master. I'd rather see anybody on his back than myself; he does not like me; but, to them he does, he can be as gentle as a lamb."

"But suppose," said I, "that he should not like me?"

"We shall soon see that, master," said the groom; "and, if so be he shows temper, I will be the first to tell you to get down. But there's no fear of that; you have never angered or insulted him, and to such as you, I say again, he'll be as gentle as a lamb."

"And how came you to insult him," said I, "knowing his temper as you do?"

"Merely through forgetfulness, master. I was riding him about a month ago, and having a stick in my hand, I struck him, thinking I was on another horse, or rather thinking of nothing at all. He has never forgiven me, though before that time he was the only friend I had in the world; I should like to see you on him, master."

"I should soon be off him; I can't ride."

"Then you are all right, master; there's no fear. Trust him for not hurting a young gentleman, an officer's son who can't ride. If you were a blackguard dragoon, indeed, with long spurs, 'twere another thing; as it is, he'll treat you as if he were the elder brother that loves you. Ride! he'll soon teach you to ride, if you leave the matter with him. He's the best riding master in all Ireland, and the gentlest."

The cob was led forth; what a tremendous creature! I had frequently seen him before, and wondered at him; he was barely fifteen hands, but he had the girth of a metropolitan dray-horse;

his head was small in comparison with his immense neck, which curved down nobly to his wide back.   His chest was broad and fine, and his shoulders models of symmetry and strength; he stood well and powerfully upon his legs, which were somewhat short.   In a word, he was a gallant specimen of the genuine Irish cob, a species at one time not uncommon, but at the present day nearly extinct.

"There!" said the groom, as he looked at him, half-admiringly, half-sorrowfully, "with sixteen stone on his back, he'll trot fourteen miles in one hour; with your nine stone, some two and half more, ay, and clear a six-foot wall at the end of it."

"I'm half afraid," said I; "I had rather you would ride him."

"I'd rather so, too, if he would let me; but he remembers the blow.   Now, don't be afraid, young master, he's longing to go out himself.   He's been trampling with his feet these three days, and I know what that means; he'll let anybody ride him but myself, and thank them; but to me he says, 'No! you struck me'".

"But," said I, "where's the saddle?"

"Never mind the saddle; if you are ever to be a frank rider, you must begin without a saddle; besides, if he felt a saddle, he would think you don't trust him, and leave you to yourself. Now, before you mount, make his acquaintance—see there, how he kisses you and licks your face, and see how he lifts his foot, that's to shake hands.   You may trust him—now you are on his back at last; mind how you hold the bridle—gently, gently! I'ts not four pair of hands like yours can hold him if he wishes to be off.   Mind what I tell you—leave it all to him."

Off went the cob at a slow and gentle trot, too fast and rough, however, for so inexperienced a rider.   I soon felt myself sliding off, the animal perceived it too, and instantly stood stone still till I had righted myself; and now the groom came up: "When you feel yourself going," said he, "don't lay hold of the mane, that's no use; mane never yet saved man from falling, no more than straw from drowning; it's his sides you must cling to with your calves and feet, till you learn to balance yourself.   That's it, now abroad with you; I'll bet my comrade a pot of beer that you'll be a regular rough rider by the time you come back."

And so it proved; I followed the directions of the groom, and the cob gave me every assistance.   How easy is riding, after the first timidity is got over, to supple and youthful limbs; and there is no second fear.   The creature soon found that the nerves of his rider were in proper tone.   Turning his head half round he made a kind of whining noise, flung out a little foam, and set off.

In less than two hours I had made the circuit of the Devil's Mountain, and was returning along the road, bathed with perspiration, but screaming with delight; the cob laughing in his equine way, scattering foam and pebbles to the left and right, and trotting at the rate of sixteen miles an hour.

Oh, that ride! that first ride!—most truly it was an epoch in my existence; and I still look back to it with feelings of longing and regret.   People may talk of first love—it is a very agreeable event, I dare say—but give me the flush, and triumph, and glorious sweat of a first ride, like mine on the mighty cob!   My whole frame was shaken, it is true; and during one long week I could hardly move foot or hand; but what of that?   By that one trial I had become free, as I may say, of the whole equine species.   No more fatigue, no more stiffness of joints, after that first ride round the Devil's Hill on the cob.

Oh, that cob! that Irish cob!—may the sod lie lightly over the bones of the strongest, speediest, and most gallant of its kind!   Oh! the days when, issuing from the barrack-gate of Templemore, we commenced our hurry-skurry just as inclination led—now across the fields—direct over stone walls and running brooks—mere pastime for the cob!—sometimes along the road to Thurles and Holy Cross, even to distant Cahir!—what was distance to the cob?

It was thus that the passion for the equine race was first awakened within me—a passion which, up to the present time, has been rather on the increase than diminishing.   It is no blind passion; the horse being a noble and generous creature, intended by the All-Wise to be the helper and friend of man, to whom he stands next in the order of creation.   On many occasions of my life I have been much indebted to the horse, and have found in him a friend and coadjutor, when human help and sympathy were not to be obtained.   It is therefore natural enough that I should love the horse; but the love which I entertain for him has always been blended with respect; for I soon perceived that, though disposed to be the friend and helper of man, he is by no means inclined to be his slave; in which respect he differs from the dog, who will crouch when beaten; whereas the horse spurns, for he is aware of his own worth, and that he carries death within the horn of his heel.   If, therefore, I found it easy to love the horse, I found it equally natural to respect him.

I much question whether philology, or the passion for

languages, requires so little of an apology as the love for horses. It has been said, I believe, that the more languages a man speaks, the more a man is he; which is very true, provided he acquires languages as a medium for becoming acquainted with the thoughts and feelings of the various sections into which the human race is divided; but, in that case, he should rather be termed a philosopher than a philologist—between which two the difference is wide indeed! An individual may speak and read a dozen languages, and yet be an exceedingly poor creature, scarcely half a man; and the pursuit of tongues for their own sake, and the mere satisfaction of acquiring them, surely argues an intellect of a very low order; a mind disposed to be satisfied with mean and grovelling things; taking more pleasure in the trumpery casket than in the precious treasure which it contains, in the pursuit of words, than in the acquisition of ideas.

I cannot help thinking that it was fortunate for myself, who am, to a certain extent, a philologist, that with me the pursuit of languages has been always modified by the love of horses; for scarcely had I turned my mind to the former, when I also mounted the wild cob, and hurried forth in the direction of the Devil's Hill, scattering dust and flint-stones on every side; that ride, amongst other things, taught me that a lad with thews and sinews was intended by nature for something better than mere word-culling; and if I have accomplished anything in after life worthy of mentioning, I believe it may partly be attributed to the ideas which that ride, by setting my blood in a glow, infused into my brain. I might, otherwise, have become a mere philologist; one of those beings who toil night and day in culling useless words for some *opus magnum* which Murray will never publish, and nobody ever read—beings without enthusiasm, who, having never mounted a generous steed, cannot detect a good point in Pegasus himself; like a certain philologist, who, though acquainted with the exact value of every word in the Greek and Latin languages, could observe no particular beauty in one of the most glorious of Homer's rhapsodies.[1] What knew he of Pegasus? he had never mounted a generous steed; the merest jockey, had the strain been interpreted to him, would have called it a brave song!—I return to the brave cob.

On a certain day I had been out on an excursion. In a

---

[1] *MS.,* "like the philologist Scaliger, who, though acquainted with the exact value of every word in the Latin language, could see no beauty in the 'Enchantments of Canidia,' the master-piece of the prince of Roman poets. What knew he," etc.

cross-road, at some distance from the Satanic hill, the animal which I rode cast a shoe. By good luck a small village was at hand, at the entrance of which was a large shed, from which proceeded a most furious noise of hammering. Leading the cob by the bridle, I entered boldly. "Shoe this horse, and do it quickly, a gough, " said I to a wild grimy figure of a man, whom I found alone, fashioning a piece of iron.

"*Arrigod yuit?* " said the fellow, desisting from his work and staring at me.

"O yes, I have money," said I, "and of the best ; " and I pulled out an English shilling.

"*Tabhair chugam,*" said the smith, stretching out his grimy hand.

"No, I sha'n't," said I ; "some people are glad to get their money when their work is done."

The fellow hammered a little longer and then proceeded to shoe the cob, after having first surveyed it with attention. He performed his job rather roughly, and more than once appeared to give the animal unnecessary pain, frequently making use of loud and boisterous words. By the time the work was done, the creature was in a state of high excitement, and plunged and tore. The smith stood at a short distance, seeming to enjoy the irritation of the animal, and showing, in a remarkable manner, a huge fang, which projected from the under jaw of a very wry mouth.

"You deserve better handling," said I, as I went up to the cob and fondled it ; whereupon it whinnied, and attempted to touch my face with its nose.

"Are ye not afraid of that beast?" said the smith, showing his fang. "Arrah, it's vicious that he looks!"

"It's at you, then!—I don't fear him ; " and thereupon I passed under the horse, between his hind legs.

"And is that all you can do, agrah?" said the smith.

"No," said I, "I can ride him."

"Ye can ride him, and what else, agrah?"

"I can leap him over a six-foot wall," said I.

"Over a wall, and what more, agrah?"

"Nothing more," said I ; "what more would you have?"

"Can you do this, agrah?" said the smith, and he uttered a word which I had never heard before, in a sharp pungent tone. The effect upon myself was somewhat extraordinary, a strange thrill ran through me ; but with regard to the cob it was terrible ; the animal forthwith became like one mad, and reared and kicked with the utmost desperation.

" Can you do that, agrah ? " said the smith.

" What is it ? " said I, retreating, " I never saw the horse so before."

" Go between his legs, agrah," said the smith, " his hinder legs ; " and he again showed his fang.

" I dare not," said I, " he would kill me."

" He would kill ye ! and how do ye know that, agrah ?."

" I feel he would," said I, " something tells me so."

" And it tells ye truth, agrah ; but it's a fine beast, and it's a pity to see him in such a state : *Is agam an't leigeas* "—and here he uttered another word in a voice singularly modified, but sweet and almost plaintive ; the effect of it was as instantaneous as that of the other, but how different !—the animal lost all its fury and became at once calm and gentle.   The smith went up to it, coaxed and patted it, making use of various sounds of equal endearment ; then turning to me, and holding out once more the grimy hand, he said : " And now ye will be giving me the Sassanach tenpence, agrah ? "

CHAPTER XIV.

From the wild scenes which I have attempted to describe in the latter pages I must now transport the reader to others of a widely different character. He must suppose himself no longer in Ireland, but in the eastern corner of merry England. Bogs, ruins and mountains have disappeared amidst the vapours of the west: I have nothing more to say of them ; the region in which we are now is not famous for objects of that kind ; perhaps it flatters itself that it can produce fairer and better things, of some of which let me speak ; there is a fine old city before us, and first of that let me speak.

A fine old city, truly, is that, view it from whatever side you will ; but it shows best from the east, where the ground, bold and elevated, overlooks the fair and fertile valley in which it stands. Gazing from those heights, the eye beholds a scene which cannot fail to awaken, even in the least sensitive bosom, feelings of pleasure and admiration. At the foot of the heights flows a narrow and deep river, with an antique bridge communicating with a long and narrow suburb, flanked on either side by rich meadows of the brightest green, beyond which spreads the city, the fine old city, perhaps the most curious specimen at present extant of the genuine old English town. Yes, there it spreads from north to south, with its venerable houses, its numerous gardens, its thrice twelve churches, its mighty mound, which, if tradition speaks true, was raised by human hands to serve as the grave heap of an old heathen king, who sits deep within it, with his sword in his hand and his gold and silver treasures about him. There is a grey old castle upon the top of that mighty mound ; and yonder, rising three hundred feet above the soil, from among those noble forest trees, behold that old Norman master-work, that cloud-encircled cathedral spire, around which a garrulous army of rooks and choughs continually wheel their flight. Now, who can wonder that the children of that fine old city are proud of her, and offer up prayers for her prosperity ? I, myself, who was not born within her walls, offer up prayers for her prosperity, that want may never visit her cottages, vice her palaces, and that the abomination of idolatry

(84)

ENTRANCE TO GRAMMAR SCHOOL, NORWICH.

[See page 84.

THE ERPINGHAM GATE, NORWICH.

[See page 88.

may never pollute her temples. Ha, idolatry! the reign of
idolatry has been over there for many a long year, never more,
let us hope, to return; brave hearts in that old town have borne
witness against it and sealed their testimony with their hearts'
blood—most precious to the Lord is the blood of His saints! we
are not far from hallowed ground. Observe ye not yon chalky
precipice to the right of the Norman bridge? On this side of the
stream, upon its brow, is a piece of ruined wall, the last relic of
what was of old a stately pile, whilst at its foot is a place called
the Lollards' Hole; and with good reason, for many a saint of
God has breathed his last beneath that white precipice, bearing
witness against Popish idolatry, midst flame and pitch; many a
grisly procession has advanced along that suburb, across the old
bridge, towards the Lollards' Hole: furious priests in front, a
calm pale martyr in the midst, a pitying multitude behind. It
has had its martyrs, the venerable old town!

Ah! there is good blood in that old city, and in the whole
circumjacent region of which it is the capital. The Angles possessed the land at an early period, which, however, they were
eventually compelled to share with hordes of Danes and North-
men, who flocked thither across the sea to found hearthsteads on
its fertile soil. The present race, a mixture of Angles and Danes,
still preserve much which speaks strongly of their northern ancestry; amongst them ye will find the light-brown hair of the
north, the strong and burly forms of the north, many a wild
superstition, ay, and many a wild name connected with the ancient
history of the north and its sublime mythology; the warm heart
and the strong heart of the old Danes and Saxons still beats in
those regions, and there ye will find, if anywhere, old northern
hospitality and kindness of manner, united with energy, perseverance and dauntless intrepidity; better soldiers or mariners never
bled in their country's battles than those nurtured in those regions
and within those old walls. It was yonder, to the west, that the
great naval hero of Britain first saw the light; he who annihilated
the sea pride of Spain and dragged the humbled banner of France
in triumph at his stern. He was born yonder towards the west,
and of him there is a glorious relic in that old town; in its dark
flint guildhouse, the roof of which you can just descry rising above
that maze of buildings, in the upper hall of justice, is a species of
glass shrine, in which the relic is to be seen: a sword of curious
workmanship, the blade is of keen Toledan steel, the heft of
ivory and mother-of-pearl. 'Tis the sword of Cordova, won in
bloodiest fray off St. Vincent's promontory, and presented by

Nelson to the old capital of the much-loved land of his birth.
Yes, the proud Spaniard's sword is to be seen in yonder guildhouse, in the glass case affixed to the wall ; many other relics has
the good old town, but none prouder than the Spaniard's sword.

Such was the place to which, when the war was over, my
father retired : it was here that the old tired soldier set himself
down with his little family. He had passed the greater part of
his life in meritorious exertion in the service of his country, and
his chief wish now was to spend the remainder of his days in
quiet and respectability ; his means, it is true, were not very
ample ; fortunate it was that his desires corresponded with them :
with a small fortune of his own, and with his half-pay as a royal
soldier, he had no fears for himself or for his faithful partner and
helpmate ; but then his children ! how was he to provide for them ?
how launch them upon the wide ocean of the world ? This was,
perhaps, the only thought which gave him uneasiness, and I
believe that many an old retired officer at that time, and under
similar circumstances, experienced similar anxiety ; had the war
continued, their children would have been, of course, provided for
in the army, but peace now reigned, and the military career was
closed to all save the scions of the aristocracy, or those who were
in some degree connected with that privileged order, an advantage
which few of these old officers could boast of ; they had slight
influence with the great, who gave themselves very little trouble
either about them or their families.

" I have been writing to the Duke," said my father one day
to my excellent mother, after we had been at home somewhat
better than a year, " I have been writing to the Duke of York
about a commission for that eldest boy of ours. He, however,
affords me no hopes ; he says that his list is crammed with names,
and that the greater number of the candidates have better claims
than my son."

" I do not see how that can be," said my mother.

" Nor do I," replied my father. " I see the sons of bankers
and merchants gazetted every month, and I do not see what
claims they have to urge, unless they be golden ones. However,
I have not served my king fifty years to turn grumbler at this
time of life. I suppose that the people at the head of affairs
know what is most proper and convenient ; perhaps when the lad
sees how difficult, nay, how impossible it is that he should enter
the army, he will turn his mind to some other profession ; I
wish he may ! "

" I think he has already," said my mother ; " you see how

fond he is of the arts, of drawing and painting, and, as far as I can judge, what he has already done is very respectable; his mind seems quite turned that way, and I heard him say the other day that he would sooner be a Michael Angelo than a general officer. But you are always talking of him; what do you think of doing with the other child?"

"What, indeed!" said my father; "that is a consideration which gives me no little uneasiness. I am afraid it will be much more difficult to settle him in life than his brother. What is he fitted for, even were it in my power to provide for him? God help the child! I bear him no ill-will, on the contrary all love and affection; but I cannot shut my eyes; there is something so strange about him! How he behaved in Ireland! I sent him to school to learn Greek, and he picked up Irish!"

"And Greek as well," said my mother. "I heard him say the other day that he could read St. John in the original tongue."

"You will find excuses for him, I know," said my father. "You tell me I am always talking of my first-born; I might retort by saying you are always thinking of the other; but it is the way of women always to side with the second-born. There's what's-her-name in the Bible, by whose wiles the old blind man was induced to give to his second son the blessing which was the birthright of the other. I wish I had been in his place! I should not have been so easily deceived! no disguise would ever have caused me to mistake an impostor for my first-born. Though I must say for this boy that he is nothing like Jacob; he is neither smooth nor sleek, and, though my second-born, is already taller and larger than his brother."

"Just so," said my mother, "his brother would make a far better Jacob than he."

"I will hear nothing against my first-born," said my father, "even in the way of insinuation: he is my joy and pride—the very image of myself in my youthful days, long before I fought Big Ben, though perhaps not quite so tall or strong built. As for the other, God bless the child! I love him, I'm sure; but I must be blind not to see the difference between him and his brother. Why, he has neither my hair nor my eyes; and then his countenance! why, 'tis absolutely swarthy, God forgive me! I had almost said like that of a gypsy, but I have nothing to say against that; the boy is not to be blamed for the colour of his face, nor for his hair and eyes; but, then, his ways and manners! I confess I do not like them, and that they give me no little uneasiness. I know that he kept very strange company when he

was in Ireland; people of evil report, of whom terrible things
were said—horse-witches and the like. I questioned him once
or twice upon the matter, and even threatened him, but it was of no
use; he put on a look as if he did not understand me, a regular
Irish look, just such a one as those rascals assume when they wish
to appear all innocence and simplicity, and they full of malice and
deceit all the time. I don't like them; they are no friends to old
England, or its old king, God bless him! They are not good
subjects, and never were; always in league with foreign enemies.
When I was in the Coldstream, long before the Revolution, I
used to hear enough about the Irish brigades kept by the French
kings, to be a thorn in the side of the English whenever opportunity
served. Old Sergeant Meredith once told me, that in the time of
the Pretender there were always in London alone, a dozen of
fellows connected with these brigades, with the view of seducing
the king's soldiers from their allegiance, and persuading them to
desert to France to join the honest Irish, as they were called.
One of these traitors once accosted him and proposed the matter
to him, offering handfuls of gold if he could induce any of his
comrades to go over. Meredith appeared to consent, but secretly
gave information to his colonel; the fellow was seized, and certain
traitorous papers found upon him; he was hanged before Newgate,
and died exulting in his treason. His name was Michael Nowlan.
That ever son of mine should have been intimate with the Papist
Irish, and have learnt their language!"

"But he thinks of other things now," said my mother.

"Other languages, you mean," said my father. "It is strange
that he has conceived such a zest for the study of languages; no
sooner did he come home than he persuaded me to send him to
that old priest to learn French and Italian, and, if I remember
right, you abetted him; but, as I said before, it is in the nature
of women invariably to take the part of the second-born. Well,
there is no harm in learning French and Italian, perhaps much
good in his case, as they may drive the other tongue out of his
head. Irish! why, he might go to the university but for that;
but how would he look when, on being examined with respect to
his attainments, it was discovered that he understood Irish?
How did you learn it? they would ask him; how did you become
acquainted with the language of Papists and rebels? The boy
would be sent away in disgrace."

"Be under no apprehension, I have no doubt that he has long
since forgotten it."

"I am glad to hear it," said my father; "for, between our-

selves, I love the poor child ; ay, quite as well as my first-born.
I trust they will do well, and that God will be their shield and
guide ; I have no doubt He will, for I have read something in
the Bible to that effect.   What is that text about the young ravens
being fed ? "

"I know a better than that," said my mother; "one of
David's own words, 'I have been young and now am grown old,
yet never have I seen the righteous man forsaken, or his seed
begging their bread '."

I have heard talk of the pleasures of idleness, yet it is my own
firm belief that no one ever yet took pleasure in it.   Mere idleness is the most disagreeable state of existence, and both mind
and body are continually making efforts to escape from it.   It
has been said that idleness is the parent of mischief, which is
very true ; but mischief itself is merely an attempt to escape from
the dreary vacuum of idleness.   There are many tasks and
occupations which a man is unwilling to perform, but let no one
think that he is therefore in love with idleness ; he turns to something which is more agreeable to his inclination, and doubtless
more suited to his nature ; but he is not in love with idleness.
A boy may play the truant from school because he dislikes books
and study ; but, depend upon it, he intends doing something the
while—to go fishing, or perhaps to take a walk ; and who knows
but that from such excursions both his mind and body may derive
more benefit than from books and school ?   Many people go to
sleep to escape from idleness ; the Spaniards do ; and, according
to the French account, John Bull, the 'squire, hangs himself in
the month of November ; but the French, who are a very sensible
people, attribute the action, " *à une grande envie de se désennuyer ;* "
he wishes to be doing something, say they, and having nothing
better to do, he has recourse to the cord.

It was for want of something better to do that, shortly after
my return home, I applied myself to the study of languages.   By
the acquisition of Irish, with the first elements of which I had
become acquainted under the tuition of Murtagh, I had contracted a certain zest and inclination for the pursuit.   Yet it is
probable, that had I been launched about this time into some
agreeable career, that of arms, for example, for which, being the
son of a soldier, I had, as was natural, a sort of penchant, I
might have thought nothing more of the acquisition of tongues
of any kind ; but, having nothing to do, I followed the only
course suited to my genius which appeared open to me.

So it came to pass that one day, whilst wandering listlessly about the streets of the old town, I came to a small book-stall, and stopping, commenced turning over the books; I took up at least a dozen, and almost instantly flung them down. What were they to me? At last, coming to a thick volume, I opened it, and after inspecting its contents for a few minutes, I paid for it what was demanded, and forthwith carried it home.

It was a tessara-glot grammar—a strange old book, printed somewhere in Holland, which pretended to be an easy guide to the acquirement of the French, Italian, Low Dutch, and English tongues, by means of which any one conversant in any one of these languages could make himself master of the other three. I turned my attention to the French and Italian. The old book was not of much value; I derived some benefit from it, however, and, conning it intensely, at the end of a few weeks obtained some insight into the structure of these two languages. At length I had learnt all that the book was capable of informing me, yet was still far from the goal to which it had promised to conduct me. "I wish I had a master?" I exclaimed; and the master was at hand. In an old court of the old town lived a certain elderly personage, perhaps sixty, or thereabouts; he was rather tall, and something of a robust make, with a countenance in which bluffness was singularly blended with vivacity and grimace; and with a complexion which would have been ruddy, but for a yellow hue which rather predominated. His dress consisted of a snuff-coloured coat and drab pantaloons, the former evidently seldom subjected to the annoyance of a brush, and the latter exhibiting here and there spots of something which, if not grease, bore a strong resemblance to it; add to these articles an immense frill, seldom of the purest white, but invariably of the finest French cambric, and you have some idea of his dress. He had rather a remarkable stoop, but his step was rapid and vigorous, and as he hurried along the streets, he would glance to the right and left with a pair of big eyes like plums, and on recognising any one would exalt a pair of grizzled eyebrows, and slightly kiss a tawny and ungloved hand. At certain hours of the day he might be seen entering the doors of female boarding-schools, generally with a book in his hand, and perhaps another just peering from the orifice of a capacious back pocket; and at a certain season of the year he might be seen, dressed in white, before the altar of a certain small popish chapel, chanting from the breviary in very intelligible Latin, or perhaps reading from the desk in utterly unintelligible English. Such was my preceptor in the French and Italian tongues. "*Exul sacerdos;* vone banished priest. I came into England twenty-five years ago, ' my dear.' "

CHAPTER XV.

So I studied French and Italian under the tuition of the banished priest, to whose house I went regularly every evening to receive instruction. I made considerable progress in the acquisition of the two languages. I found the French by far the most difficult, chiefly on account of the accent, which my master himself possessed in no great purity, being a Norman by birth. The Italian was my favourite.

" *Vous serez un jour un grand philologue, mon cher,*" said the old man, on our arriving at the conclusion of Dante's Hell.

" I hope I shall be something better," said I, " before I die, or I shall have lived to little purpose."

" That's true, my dear ! philologist—one small poor dog. What would you wish to be ? "

" Many things sooner than that ; for example, I would rather be like him who wrote this book."

" *Quoi, Monsieur Dante ?* He was a vagabond, my dear, forced to fly from his country. No, my dear, if you would be like one poet, be like Monsieur Boileau ; he is the poet."

" I don't think so."

" How, not think so ! He wrote very respectable verses ; lived and died much respected by everybody. T'other, one bad dog, forced to fly from his country—died with not enough to pay his undertaker."

" Were you not forced to flee from your country ? "

" That very true ; but there is much difference between me and this Dante. He fled from country because he had one bad tongue which he shook at his betters. I fly because benefice gone, and head going ; not on account of the badness of my tongue."

" Well," said I, " you can return now ; the Bourbons are restored."

" I find myself very well here ; not bad country. *Il est vrai que la France sera toujours la France ;* but all are dead there who knew me. I find myself very well here. Preach in popish chapel, teach schismatic, that is Protestant, child tongues and literature. I find myself very well; and why? Because I know how to govern my tongue; never call people hard names. *Ma foi, il y a beaucoup de différence entre moi et ce sacré de Dante.*"

Under this old man, who was well versed in the southern languages, besides studying French and Italian, I acquired some knowledge of Spanish. But I did not devote my time entirely to philology; I had other pursuits. I had not forgotten the roving life I had led in former days, nor its delights; neither was I formed by Nature to be a pallid indoor student. No, no! I was fond of other and, I say it boldly, better things than study. I had an attachment to the angle, ay, and to the gun likewise. In our house was a condemned musket, bearing somewhere on its lock, in rather antique characters, "Tower, 1746"; with this weapon I had already, in Ireland, performed some execution among the rooks and choughs, and it was now again destined to be a source of solace and amusement to me, in the winter season, especially on occasions of severe frost when birds abounded. Sallying forth with it at these times, far into the country, I seldom returned at night without a string of bullfinches, blackbirds, and linnets hanging in triumph round my neck. When I reflect on the immense quantity of powder and shot which I crammed down the muzzle of my uncouth fowling-piece, I am less surprised at the number of birds which I slaughtered, than that I never blew my hands, face, and old honey-combed gun, at one and the same time, to pieces.

But the winter, alas! (I speak as a fowler) seldom lasts in England more than three or four months; so, during the rest of the year, when not occupied with my philological studies, I had to seek for other diversions. I have already given a hint that I was also addicted to the angle. Of course there is no comparison between the two pursuits, the rod and line seeming but very poor trumpery to one who has had the honour of carrying a noble firelock. There is a time, however, for all things; and we return to any favourite amusement with the greater zest, from being compelled to relinquish it for a season. So, if I shot birds in winter with my firelock, I caught fish in summer, or attempted so to do, with my angle. I was not quite so successful, it is true, with the latter as with the former—possibly because it afforded me less pleasure. It was, indeed, too much of a listless pastime to inspire me with any great interest. I not unfrequently fell into a doze whilst sitting on the bank, and more than once let my rod drop from my hands into the water.

Earlham Hall, near Norwich. "The Earl's Home."

[See page 93.

"MARSHLAND SHALES."

[See page 98.

At some distance from the city, behind a range of hilly ground which rises towards the south-west, is a small river, the waters of which, after many meanderings, eventually enter the principal river of the district, and assist to swell the tide which it rolls down to the ocean.   It is a sweet rivulet, and pleasant it is to trace its course from its spring-head, high up in the remote regions of Eastern Anglia, till it arrives in the valley behind yon rising ground ; and pleasant is that valley, truly a goodly spot, but most lovely .where yonder bridge crosses the little stream.   Beneath its arch the waters rush garrulously into a blue pool, and are there stilled for a time, for the pool is deep, and they appear to have sunk to sleep.   Farther on, however, you hear their voice again, where they ripple gaily over yon gravelly shallow.   On the left, the hill slopes gently down to the margin of the stream.   On the right is a green level, a smiling meadow, grass of the richest decks the side of the slope ; mighty trees also adorn it, giant elms, the nearest of which, when the sun is nigh its meridian, fling a broad shadow upon the face of the pool ; through yon vista you catch a glimpse of the ancient brick of an old English hall.   It has a stately look, that old building, indistinctly seen, as it is, among those umbrageous trees ; you might almost suppose it an earl's home ; and such it was, or rather upon its site stood an earl's home, in days of old, for there some old Kemp, some Sigurd, or Thorkild, roaming in quest of a hearthstead, settled down in the gray old time, when Thor and Freya were yet gods, and Odin was a portentous name.   Yon old hall is still called the Earl's Home, though the hearth of Sigurd is now no more, and the bones of the old Kemp, and of Sigrith his dame, have been mouldering for a thousand years in some neighbouring knoll—perhaps yonder, where those tall Norwegian pines shoot up so boldly into the air.   It is said that the old earl's galley was once moored where is now that blue pool, for the waters of that valley were not always sweet ; yon valley was once an arm of the sea, a salt lagoon, to which the war-barks of "Sigurd, in search of a home," found their way.

I was in the habit of spending many an hour on the banks of that rivulet, with my rod in my hand, and, when tired with angling, would stretch myself on the grass, and gaze upon the waters as they glided past ; and not unfrequently, divesting myself of my dress, I would plunge into the deep pool which I have already mentioned, for I had long since learned to swim.   And it came to pass, that on one hot summer's day, after bathing in the pool, I passed along the meadow till I came to a shallow part, and, wading over to the opposite side, I adjusted my dress, and commenced fishing in another pool, beside which was a small clump of hazels.

And there I sat upon the bank, at the bottom of the hill which slopes down from "the Earl's Home"; my float was on the waters, and my back was towards the old hall. I drew up many fish, small and great, which I took from off the hook mechanically and flung upon the bank, for I was almost unconscious of what I was about, for my mind was not with my fish. I was thinking of my earlier years—of the Scottish crags and the heaths of Ireland—and sometimes my mind would dwell on my studies—on the sonorous stanzas of Dante, rising and falling like the waves of the sea—or would strive to remember a couplet or two of poor Monsieur·Boileau.

"Canst thou answer to thy conscience for pulling all those fish out of the water, and leaving them to gasp in the sun?" said a voice, clear and sonorous as a bell.

I started, and looked round. Close behind me stood the tall figure of a man, dressed in raiment of quaint and singular fashion, but of goodly materials. He was in the prime and vigour of manhood; his features handsome and noble, but full of calmness and benevolence; at least I thought so, though they were somewhat shaded by a hat of finest beaver, with broad drooping eaves.

" Surely that is a very cruel diversion in which thou indulgest, my young friend," he continued.

"I am sorry for it, if it be, sir," said I, rising; "but I do not think it cruel to fish."

"What are thy reasons for not thinking so?"

"Fishing is mentioned frequently in Scripture. Simon Peter was a fisherman."

"True; and Andrew and his brother. But thou forgettest: they did not follow fishing as a diversion, as I fear thou doest. Thou readest the Scriptures?"

"Sometimes."

"Sometimes? not daily? that is to be regretted. What profession dost thou make? I mean to what religious denomination dost thou belong, my young friend?"

"Church."

"It is a very good profession—there is much of Scripture contained in its liturgy. Dost thou read aught besides the Scriptures?"

"Sometimes."

"What dost thou read besides?"

"Greek, and Dante."

"Indeed! then thou hast the advantage over myself; I can only read the former. Well, I am rejoiced to find that thou hast other pursuits besides thy fishing. Dost thou know Hebrew?"

"No."

"Thou shouldst study it. Why dost thou not undertake the study?"

"I have no books."

"I will lend thee books, if thou wish to undertake the study. I live yonder at the hall, as perhaps thou knowest. I have a library there, in which are many curious books, both in Greek and Hebrew, which I will show to thee, whenever thou mayest find it convenient to come and see me. Farewell! I am glad to find that thou hast pursuits more satisfactory than thy cruel fishing."

And the man of peace departed, and left me on the bank of the stream. Whether from the effect of his words, or from want of inclination to the sport, I know not, but from that day I became less and less a practitioner of that "cruel fishing". I rarely flung line and angle into the water, but I not unfrequently wandered by the banks of the pleasant rivulet. It seems singular to me, on reflection, that I never availed myself of his kind invitation. I say singular, for the extraordinary, under whatever form, had long had no slight interest for me; and I had discernment enough to perceive that yon was no common man. Yet I went not near him, certainly not from bashfulness, or timidity, feelings to which I had long been an entire stranger. Am I to regret this? perhaps, for I might have learned both wisdom and righteousness from those calm, quiet lips, and my after-course might have been widely different. As it was, I fell in with other guess companions, from whom I received widely different impressions than those I might have derived from him. When many years had rolled on, long after I had attained manhood, and had seen and suffered much, and when our first interview had long since been effaced from the mind of the man of peace, I visited him in his venerable hall, and partook of the hospitality of his hearth. And there I saw his gentle partner and his fair children, and on the morrow he showed me the books of which he had spoken years before, by the side of the stream. In the low quiet chamber, whose one window, shaded by a gigantic elm, looks down the slope towards the pleasant stream, he took from the shelf his learned books, Zohar and Mishna, Toldoth Jesu and Abarbenel.

"I am fond of these studies," said he, "which, perhaps, is not to be wondered at, seeing that our people have been compared

to the Jews.   In one respect I confess we are similiar to them :
we are fond of getting money.   I do not like this last author, this
Abarbenel, the worse for having been a money-changer.   I am a
banker myself, as thou knowest.''

And would there were many like him, amidst the money-
changers of princes !   The hall of many an earl lacks the bounty,
the palace of many a prelate the piety and learning, which adorn
the quiet Quaker's home !

CHAPTER XVI.

I was standing on the castle hill in the midst of a fair of horses.

I have already had occasion to mention this castle. It is the remains of what was once a Norman stronghold, and is perched upon a round mound or monticle, in the midst of the old city. Steep is this mound and scarped, evidently by the hand of man; a deep gorge, over which is flung a bridge, separates it, on the south, from a broad swell of open ground called "the hill;" of old the scene of many a tournament and feat of Norman chivalry, but now much used as a show-place for cattle, where those who buy and sell beeves and other beasts resort at stated periods.

So it came to pass that I stood upon this hill, observing a fair of horses.

The reader is already aware that I had long since conceived a passion for the equine race, a passion in which circumstances had of late not permitted me to indulge. I had no horses to ride, but I took pleasure in looking at them; and I had already attended more than one of these fairs: the present was lively enough, indeed, horse fairs are seldom dull. There was shouting and whooping, neighing and braying; there was galloping and trotting; fellows with highlows and white stockings, and with many a string dangling from the knees of their tight breeches, were running desperately, holding horses by the halter, and in some cases dragging them along; there were long-tailed steeds, and dock-tailed steeds of every degree and breed; there were droves of wild ponies, and long rows of sober cart horses; there were donkeys, and even mules: the last rare things to be seen in damp, misty England, for the mule pines in mud and rain, and thrives best with a hot sun above and a burning sand below. There were—oh, the gallant creatures! I hear their neigh upon the wind; there were—goodliest sight of all—certain enormous quadrupeds only seen to perfection in our native isle, led about by dapper grooms, their manes ribanded and their tails curiously clubbed and balled. Ha! ha!—how distinctly do they say, ha! ha!

An old man draws nigh, he is mounted on a lean pony, and he leads by the bridle one of these animals; nothing very remarkable about that creature, unless in being smaller than the rest and gentle, which they are not; he is not of the sightliest look; he is almost dun, and over one eye a thick film has gathered. But stay! there *is* something remarkable about that horse, there is something in his action in which he differs from all the rest. As he advances, the clamour is hushed! all eyes are turned upon him—what looks of interest—of respect—and, what is this? people are taking off their hats—surely not to that steed! Yes, verily! men, especially old men, are taking off their hats to that one-eyed steed, and I hear more than one deep-drawn ah!

"What horse is that?" said I to a very old fellow, the counterpart of the old man on the pony, save that the last wore a faded suit of velveteen, and this one was dressed in a white frock.

"The best in mother England," said the very old man, taking a knobbed stick from his mouth, and looking me in the face, at first carelessly, but presently with something like interest; "he is old like myself, but can still trot his twenty miles an hour. You won't live long, my swain; tall and overgrown ones like thee never does; yet, if you should chance to reach my years, you may boast to thy great grand boys, thou hast seen Marshland Shales."

Amain I did for the horse what I would neither do for earl or baron, doffed my hat; yes! I doffed my hat to the wondrous horse, the fast trotter, the best in mother England; and I, too, drew a deep ah! and repeated the words of the old fellows around. "Such a horse as this we shall never see again; a pity that he is so old."

Now during all this time I had a kind of consciousness that I had been the object of some person's observation; that eyes were fastened upon me from somewhere in the crowd. Sometimes I thought myself watched from before, sometimes from behind; and occasionally methought that, if I just turned my head to the right or left, I should meet a peering and inquiring glance; and, indeed, once or twice I did turn, expecting to see somebody whom I knew, yet always without success; though it appeared to me that I was but a moment too late, and that some one had just slipped away from the direction to which I turned, like the figure in a magic lanthorn. Once I was quite sure that there were a pair of eyes glaring over my right shoulder; my attention, however, was so fully occupied with the objects which I have attempted to describe, that I thought very little of this

coming and going, this flitting and dodging of I knew not whom
or what. It was, after all, a matter of sheer indifference to me
who was looking at me. I could only wish, whomsoever it might
be, to be more profitably employed; so I continued enjoying
what I saw; and now there was a change in the scene, the
wondrous old horse departed with his aged guardian; other
objects of interest are at hand; two or three men on horseback
are hurrying through the crowd, they are widely different in their
appearance from the other people of the fair; not so much in
dress, for they are clad something after the fashion of rustic
jockeys, but in their look—no light brown hair have they, no
ruddy cheeks, no blue quiet glances belong to them; their
features are dark, their locks long, black and shining, and their
eyes are wild; they are admirable horsemen, but they do not sit
the saddle in the manner of common jockeys, they seem to float
or hover upon it, like gulls upon the waves; two of them are
mere striplings, but the third is a very tall man with a countenance
heroically beautiful, but wild, wild, wild. As they rush along,
the crowd give way on all sides, and now a kind of ring or circus
is formed, within which the strange men exhibit their horseman-
ship, rushing past each other, in and out, after the manner of a
reel, the tall man occasionally balancing himself upon the saddle,
and standing erect on one foot. He had just regained his seat
after the latter feat, and was about to push his horse to a gallop,
when a figure started forward close from beside me, and laying
his hand on his neck, and pulling him gently downward, appeared
to whisper something into his ear; presently the tall man raised
his head, and, scanning the crowd for a moment in the direction
in which I was standing, fixed his eyes full upon me, and anon the
countenance of the whisperer was turned, but only in part, and
the side-glance of another pair of wild eyes was directed towards
my face, but the entire visage of the big black man half stooping
as he was, was turned full upon mine.

But now, with a nod to the figure who had stopped him, and
with another inquiring glance at myself, the big man once more
put his steed into motion, and after riding round the ring a few
more times darted through a lane in the crowd, and followed by
his two companions disappeared, whereupon the figure who had
whispered to him and had subsequently remained in the middle
of the space, came towards me, and cracking a whip which he
held in his hand so loudly that the report was nearly equal to that
of a pocket pistol, he cried in a strange tone :—

" What ! the sap-engro ? Lor ! the sap-engro upon the hill ! "

"I remember that word," said I, "and I almost think I remember you. You can't be—— "

"Jasper, your pal! Truth, and no lie, brother."

"It is strange that you should have known me," said I. "I am certain, but for the word you used, I should never have recognised you."

"Not so strange as you may think, brother; there is something in your face which would prevent people from forgetting you, even though they might wish it; and your face is not much altered since the·time you wot of, though you are so much grown. I thought it was you, but to make sure I dodged about, inspecting you. I believe you felt me, though I never touched you; a sign, brother, that we are akin, that we are dui palor—two relations. Your blood beat when mine was near, as mine always does at the coming of a brother; and we became brothers in that lane."

"And where are you staying?" said I; "in this town?"

"Not in the town; the like of us don't find it exactly wholesome to stay in towns; we keep abroad. But I have little to do here—come with me and I'll show you where we stay."

We descended the hill in the direction of the north, and passing along the suburb reached the old Norman bridge, which we crossed; the chalk precipice, with the ruin on its top, was now before us; but turning to the left we walked swiftly along, and presently came to some rising ground, which ascending, we found ourselves upon a wild moor or heath.

"You are one of them," said I, "whom people call—— "

"Just so," said Jasper; "but never mind what people call us."

"And that tall handsome man on the hill, whom you whispered? I suppose he's one of ye. What is his name?"

"Tawno Chikno," said Jasper, "which means the small one; we call him such because he is the biggest man of all our nation. You say he is handsome, that is not the word, brother; he's the beauty of the world. Women run wild at the sight of Tawno. An earl's daughter, near London—a fine young lady with diamonds round her neck—fell in love with Tawno. I have seen that lass on a heath, as this may be, kneel down to Tawno, clasp his feet, begging to be his wife—or anything else—if she might go with him. But Tawno would have nothing to do with her. 'I have a wife of my own,' said he, 'a lawful Rommany wife, whom I love better than the whole world, jealous though she sometimes be'."

" And is she very beautiful ? " said I.

" Why, you know, brother, beauty is frequently a matter of taste ; however, as you ask my opinion, I should say not quite so beautiful as himself."

We had now arrived at a small valley between two hills or downs, the sides of which were covered with furze. In the midst of this valley were various carts and low tents forming a rude kind of encampment ; several dark children were playing about, who took no manner of notice of us. As we passed one of the tents, however, a canvas screen was lifted up, and a woman supported upon a crutch hobbled out. She was about the middle age, and, besides being lame, was bitterly ugly ; she was very slovenly dressed, and on her swarthy features ill nature was most visibly stamped. She did not deign me a look, but addressing Jasper in a tongue which I did not understand, appeared to put some eager questions to him.

" He's coming," said Jasper, and passed on. " Poor fellow," said he to me, " he has scarcely been gone an hour and she's jealous already. Well," he continued, " what do you think of her ? you have seen her now and can judge for yourself—that 'ere woman is Tawno Chikno's wife ! "

CHAPTER XVII.

WE went to the farthest of the tents, which stood at a slight distance from the rest, and which exactly resembled the one which I have described on a former occasion ; we went in and sat down, one on each side of a small fire which was smouldering on the ground, there was no one else in the tent but a tall tawny woman of middle age, who was busily knitting. " Brother," said Jasper, " I wish to hold some pleasant discourse with you."

" As much as you please," said I, " provided you can find anything pleasant to talk about."

" Never fear," said Jasper; " and first of all we will talk of yourself. Where have you been all this long time ? "

" Here and there," said I, " and far and near, going about with the soldiers ; but there is no soldiering now, so we have sat down, father and family, in the town there."

" And do you still hunt snakes ? " said Jasper.

" No," said I, " I have given up that long ago ; I do better now : read books and learn languages."

" Well, I am sorry you have given up your snake-hunting ; many's the strange talk I have had with our people about your snake and yourself, and how you frightened my father and mother in the lane."

" And where are your father and mother ? "

" Where I shall never see them, brother ; at least, I hope so."

" Not dead ? "

" No, not dead ; they are bitchadey pawdel."

" What's that ? "

" Sent across—banished."

" Ah ! I understand ; I am sorry for them. And so you are here alone ? "

" Not quite alone, brother ! "

" No, not alone ; but with the rest—Tawno Chikno takes care of you."

" Takes care of me, brother ! "

" Yes, stands to you in the place of a father—keeps you out of harm's way."

" What do you take me for, brother ? "

" For about three years older than myself."

" Perhaps ; but you are of the Gorgios, and I am a Rommany Chal.   Tawno Chikno take care of Jasper Petulengro ! "

" Is that your name ? "

" Don't you like it ? "

" Very much, I never heard a sweeter ; it is something like what you call me."

" The horse-shoe master and the snake-fellow, I am the first."

"Who gave you that name ? "

" Ask Pharaoh."

" I would, if he were here, but I do not see him."

" I am Pharaoh."

" Then you are a king."

" Chachipen, pal."

" I do not understand you."

" Where are your languages ?   You want two things, brother : mother sense and gentle Rommany."

" What makes you think that I want sense ? "

" That, being so old, you can't yet guide yourself ! "

" I can read Dante, Jasper."

" Anan, brother."

" I can charm snakes, Jasper."

" I know you can, brother."

" Yes, and horses too ; bring me the most vicious in the land, if I whisper he'll be tame."

" Then the more shame for you—a snake-fellow—a horse-witch—and a lil-reader—yet you can't shift for yourself.   I laugh at you, brother ! "

" Then you can shift for yourself? "

" For myself and for others, brother."

" And what does Chikno ? "

" Sells me horses, when I bid him.   Those horses on the chong were mine."

" And has he none of his own ? "

" Sometimes he has ; but he is not so well off as myself. When my father and mother were bitchadey pawdel, which, to tell you the truth, they were, for chiving wafodo dloovu, they left me all they had, which was not a little, and I became the head of our family, which was not a small one.   I was not older than you when that happened ; yet our people said they had never a better krallis to contrive and plan for them and to keep them in order.   And this is so well known, that many Rommany Chals, not of our family, come and join themselves to us, living with us for a time, in order to better themselves, more especially those of the poorer sort, who have little of their own. Tawno is one of these."

" Is that fine fellow poor ? "

" One of the poorest, brother. Handsome as he is, he has not a horse of his own to ride on. Perhaps we may put it down to his wife, who cannot move about, being a cripple, as you saw."

" And you are what is called a Gypsy King ? "

" Ay, ay ; a Rommany Kral."

" Are there other kings ? "

" Those who call themselves so ; but the true Pharaoh is Petulengro."

" Did Pharaoh make horse-shoes ? "

" The first who ever did, brother."

" Pharaoh lived in Egypt."

" So did we once, brother."

" And you left it ? "

" My fathers did, brother."

" And why did they come here ? "

" They had their reasons, brother."

" And you are not English ? "

" We are not Gorgios."

" And you have a language of your own ? "

" Avali."

" This is wonderful."

" Ha, ha ! " cried the woman, who had hitherto sat knitting at the farther end of the tent, without saying a word, though not inattentive to our conversation, as I could perceive by certain glances which she occasionally cast upon us both. " Ha, ha ! " she screamed, fixing upon me two eyes, which shone like burning coals, and which were filled with an expression both of scorn and malignity, " It is wonderful, is it, that we should have a language of our own ? What, you grudge the poor people the speech they talk among themselves? That's just like you Gorgios, you would have everybody stupid, single-tongued idiots, like yourselves. We are taken before the Poknees of the gav, myself and sister, to give an account of ourselves. So I says to my sister's little boy, speaking Rommany, I says to the little boy who is with us, ' Run to my son Jasper, and the rest, and tell them to be off, there are hawks abroad '. So the Poknees questions us, and lets us go, not being able to make anything of us ; but, as we are going, he calls us back. ' Good woman,' says the Poknees, ' what was that I heard you say just now to the little boy?' 'I was telling him, your worship, to go and see the time of day, and, to save trouble, I said it in our own language.' 'Where did you get that language?' says the Poknees. ' 'Tis our own language, sir,' I tells him, 'we did not steal it.' ' Shall I tell you what it is, my good woman?' says the Poknees. ' I would thank you, sir,' says I, ' for 'tis often we are asked about it.' ' Well, then,' says the Poknees, ' it is no language at all, merely a made-up gibberish.' ' Oh, bless your wisdom,' says I, with a curtsey, ' you can tell us what our language is without understanding it!' Another time we meet a parson. ' Good woman,' says he, ' what's that you are talking? Is it broken language?' ' Of course, your reverence,' says I, ' we are broken people ; give a shilling, your reverence, to the poor broken woman.' Oh, these Gorgios! they grudge us our very language!"

"She called you her son, Jasper?"

"I am her son, brother."

"I thought you said your parents were——"

"Bitchadey pawdel ; you thought right, brother. This is my wife's mother."

"Then you are married, Jasper?"

"Ay, truly ; I am husband and father. You will see wife and chabo anon."

"Where are they now?"

"In the gav, penning dukkerin."

"We were talking of language, Jasper?"

"True, brother."

"Yours must be a rum one?"

" 'Tis called Rommany."

"I would gladly know it."

"You need it sorely."

"Would you teach it me?"

"None sooner."

"Suppose we begin now."

"Suppose we do, brother."

"Not whilst I am here," said the woman, flinging her knitting down, and starting upon her feet ; "not whilst I am here shall this Gorgio learn Rommany. A pretty manœuvre, truly ; and what would be the end of it? I goes to the farmingǀker with my sister, to tell a fortune, and earn a few sixpences for the chabes. I sees a jolly pig in the yard, and I says to my sister, speaking Rommany, ' Do so and so,' says I ; which the farming man hearing, asks what we are talking about. ' Nothing at all, master,' says I ; ' something about the weather' ; when who should start up from behind a pale, where he has been listening, but this ugly gorgio, crying out, 'They are after poisoning your pigs, neighbour!' so that we are glad to run, I and my sister, with perhaps the farm-engro shouting after us.   Says my sister to me, when we have got fairly off, 'How came that ugly one to know what you said to me?'   Whereupon I answers, 'It all comes of my son Jasper, who brings the gorgio to our fire, and must needs be teaching him'. 'Who was fool there?' says my sister.   'Who, indeed, but my son Jasper,' I answers.   And here should I be a greater fool to sit still and suffer it; which I will not do.   I do not like the look of him; he looks over-gorgious.   An ill day to the Romans when he masters Rommany; and when I says that, I pens a true dukkerin."

"What do you call God, Jasper?"

"You had better be jawing," said the woman, raising her voice to a terrible scream; "you had better be moving off, my Gorgio; hang you for a keen one, sitting there by the fire, and stealing my language before my face.   Do you know whom you have to deal with?   Do you know that I am dangerous?   My name is Herne, and I comes of the hairy ones!"

And a hairy one she looked!   She wore her hair clubbed upon her head, fastened with many strings and ligatures; but now, tearing these off, her locks, originally jet black, but now partially grizzled with age, fell down on every side of her, covering her face and back as far down as her knees.   No she-bear of Lapland ever looked more fierce and hairy than did that woman, as, standing in the open part of the tent, with her head bent down, and her shoulders drawn up, seemingly about to precipitate herself upon me, she repeated, again and again,—

"My name is Herne, and I comes of the hairy ones!—— "

"I call God Duvel, brother."

"It sounds very like Devil."

"It doth, brother, it doth."

"And what do you call divine, I mean godly?"

"Oh! I call that duvelskoe."

"I am thinking of something, Jasper."

"What are you thinking of, brother?"

"Would it not be a rum thing if divine and devilish were originally one and the same word?"

"It would, brother, it would—— "

.   .   .   .

From this time I had frequent interviews with Jasper, some-times in his tent, sometimes on the heath, about which we would roam for hours, discoursing on various matters.   Sometimes mounted on one of his horses, of which he had several, I would accompany him to various fairs and markets in the neighbourhood, to which he went on his own affairs, or those of his tribe. I soon found that I had become acquainted with a most singular people, whose habits and pursuits awakened within me the highest interest. Of all connected with them, however, their language was doubtless that which exercised the greatest influence over my imagination. I had at first some suspicion that it would prove a mere made-up gibberish. But I was soon undeceived. Broken, corrupted, and half in ruins as it was, it was not long before I found that it was an original speech, far more so, indeed, than one or two others of high name and celebrity, which, up to that time, I had been in the habit of regarding with respect and veneration. Indeed, many obscure points connected with the vocabulary of these languages, and to which neither classic nor modern lore afforded any clue, I thought I could now clear up by means of this strange broken tongue, spoken by people who dwelt among thickets and furze bushes, in tents as tawny as their faces, and whom the generality of mankind designated, and with much semblance of justice, as thieves and vagabonds. But where did this speech come from, and who were they who spoke it? These were questions which I could not solve, and which Jasper himself, when pressed, confessed his inability to answer. " But, whoever we be, brother," said he, " we are an old people, and not what folks in general imagine, broken gorgios; and, if we are not Egyptians, we are at any rate Rommany chals ! "

" Rommany chals ! I should not wonder after all," said I, " that these people had something to do with the founding of Rome. Rome, it is said, was built by vagabonds; who knows but that some tribe of the kind settled down thereabouts, and called the town which they built after their name; but whence did they come originally ? ah ! there is the difficulty."

But abandoning these questions, which at that time were far too profound for me, I went on studying the language, and at the same time the characters and manners of these strange people. My rapid progress in the former astonished, while it delighted, Jasper. "We'll no longer call you Sap-engro, brother," said he; " but rather Lav-engro, which in the language of the gorgios meaneth Word Master." " Nay, brother," said Tawno Chikno, with whom I had become very intimate, " you had better call him Cooro-mengro, I have put on *the gloves* with him, and find him a pure fist master; I like him for that, for I am a Cooro-mengro myself, and was born at Brummagem."

"I likes him for his modesty," said Mrs. Chikno; "I never hears any ill words come from his mouth, but, on the contrary, much sweet language. His talk is golden, and he has taught my eldest to say his prayers in Rommany, which my rover had never the grace to do." "He is the pal of my rom," said Mrs. Petulengro, who was a very handsome woman, "and therefore I likes him, and not less for his being a rye; folks calls me high-minded, and perhaps I have reason to be so; before I married Pharaoh I had an offer from a lord—I likes the young rye, and, if he chooses to follow us, he shall have my sister. What say you, mother? should not the young rye have my sister Ursula?"

"I am going to my people," said Mrs. Herne, placing a bundle upon a donkey, which was her own peculiar property; "I am going to Yorkshire, for I can stand this no longer. You say you like him; in that we differs: I hates the gorgio, and would like, speaking Romanly, to mix a little poison with his waters. And now go to Lundra, my children, I goes to Yorkshire. Take my blessing with ye, and a little bit of a gillie to cheer your hearts with when ye are weary. In all kinds of weather have we lived together; but now we are parted, I goes broken-hearted. I can't keep you company; ye are no longer Rommany. To gain a bad brother, ye have lost a good mother."

CHAPTER XVIII.

So the gypsies departed: Mrs. Herne to Yorkshire, and the rest to London. As for myself, I continued in the house of my parents, passing my time in much the same manner as I have already described, principally in philological pursuits. But I was now sixteen, and it was highly necessary that I should adopt some profession, unless I intended to fritter away my existence, and to be a useless burden to those who had given me birth. But what profession was I to choose? there being none in the wide world perhaps for which I was suited; nor was there any one for which I felt any decided inclination, though perhaps there existed within me a lurking penchant for the profession of arms, which was natural enough, as, from my earliest infancy, I had been accustomed to military sights and sounds; but this profession was then closed, as I have already hinted, and, as I believe, it has since continued, to those who, like myself, had no better claims to urge than the services of a father.

My father, who, for certain reasons of his own, had no very high opinion of the advantages resulting from this career, would have gladly seen me enter the Church. His desire was, however, considerably abated by one or two passages of my life, which occurred to his recollection. He particularly dwelt on the unheard-of manner in which I had picked up the Irish language, and drew from thence the conclusion that I was not fitted by nature to cut a respectable figure at an English university. "He will fly off in a tangent," said he, "and, when called upon to exhibit his skill in Greek, will be found proficient in Irish; I have observed the poor lad attentively, and really do not know what to make of him; but I am afraid he will never make a churchman!" And I have no doubt that my excellent father was right, both in his premises and the conclusion at which he arrived. I had undoubtedly, at one period of my life, forsaken Greek for Irish, and the instructions of a learned Protestant divine for those of a Papist gassoon, the card-fancying Murtagh; and of late, though I kept it a strict secret, I had abandoned in a

(109)

great measure the study of the beautiful Italian, and the recitation of the sonorous terzets of the Divine Comedy, in which at one time I took the greatest delight, in order to become acquainted with the broken speech, and yet more broken songs, of certain houseless wanderers whom I had met at a horse fair. Such an erratic course was certainly by no means in consonance with the sober and unvarying routine of college study. And my father, who was a man of excellent common sense, displayed it, in not pressing me to adopt a profession which required qualities of mind which he saw I did not possess.

Other professions were talked of, amongst which the law; but now an event occurred which had nearly stopped my career, and merged all minor points of solicitude in anxiety for my life. My strength and appetite suddenly deserted me, and I began to pine and droop. Some said that I had overgrown myself, and that these were the symptoms of a rapid decline ; I grew worse and worse, and was soon stretched upon my bed, from which it seemed scarcely probable that I should ever more rise, the physicians themselves giving but slight hopes of my recovery ; as for myself, I made up my mind to die, and felt quite resigned. I was sadly ignorant at that time, and, when I thought of death, it appeared to me little else than a pleasant sleep, and I wished for sleep, of which I got but little. It was well that I did not die that time, for I repeat that I was sadly ignorant of many important things. I did not die, for somebody coming, gave me a strange, bitter draught ; a decoction, I believe, of a bitter root which grows on commons and desolate places ; and the person who gave it me was an ancient female, a kind of doctress, who had been my nurse in my infancy, and who, hearing of my state, had come to see me ; so I drank the draught, and became a little better, and I continued taking draughts made from the bitter root till I manifested symptoms of convalescence.

But how much more quickly does strength desert the human frame than return to it ! I had become convalescent, it is true, but my state of feebleness was truly pitiable. I believe it is in that state that the most remarkable feature of human physiology frequently exhibits itself. Oh, how dare I mention the dark feeling of mysterious dread which comes over the mind, and which the lamp of reason, though burning bright the while, is unable to dispel ! Art thou, as leeches say, the concomitant of disease— the result of shattered nerves ? Nay, rather the principle of woe itself, the fountain head of all sorrow co-existent with man, whose influence he feels when yet unborn, and whose workings

he testifies with his earliest cries, when, "drowned in tears," he
first beholds the light; for, as the sparks fly upwards, so is man
born to trouble, and woe doth he bring with him into the world,
even thyself, dark one, terrible one, causeless, unbegotten, without a father. Oh, how unfrequently dost thou break down the
barriers which divide thee from the poor soul of man, and over-
cast its sunshine with thy gloomy shadow! In the brightest days
of prosperity—in the midst of health and wealth—how sentient
is the poor human creature of thy neighbourhood! how instinc-
tively aware that the flood-gates of horror may be cast open, and
the dark stream engulf him for ever and ever! Then is it not
lawful for man to exclaim, "Better that I had never been born!"
Fool, for thyself thou wast not born, but to fulfil the inscrutable
decrees of thy Creator; and how dost thou know that this dark
principle is not, after all, thy best friend; that it is not that which
tempers the whole mass of thy corruption? It may be, for what
thou knowest, the mother of wisdom, and of great works; it is
the dread of the horror of the night that makes the pilgrim hasten
on his way. When thou feelest it nigh, let thy safety word be
"Onward"; if thou tarry, thou art overwhelmed. Courage!
build great works—'tis urging thee—it is ever nearest the favourites of God—the fool knows little of it. Thou wouldst be joyous,
wouldst thou? then be a fool. What great work was ever the
result of joy, the puny one? Who have been the wise ones, the
mighty ones, the conquering ones of this earth? the joyous? I
believe not. The fool is happy, or comparatively so—certainly
the least sorrowful, but he is still a fool; and whose notes are
sweetest, those of the nightingale, or of the silly lark?

.   .   .   .

"What ails you, my child?" said a mother to her son, as he
lay on a couch under the influence of the dreadful one; "what
ails you? you seem afraid!"

Boy. And so I am; a dreadful fear is upon me.

Mother. But of what; there is no one can harm you; of what
are you apprehensive?

Boy. Of nothing that I can express; I know not what I am
afraid of, but afraid I am.

Mother. Perhaps you see sights and visions; I knew a lady
once who was continually thinking that she saw an armed man
threaten her, but it was only an imagination, a phantom of the
brain.

Boy. No armed man threatens me; and 'tis not a thing like
that would cause me any fear. Did an armed man threaten me,

I would get up and fight him ; weak as I am, I would wish for nothing better, for then, perhaps, I should lose this fear ; mine is a dread of I know not what, and there the horror lies.

Mother. Your forehead is cool, and your speech collected. Do you know where you are ?

Boy. I know where I am, and I see things just as they are ; you are beside me, and upon the table there is a book which was written by a Florentine ; all this I see, and that there is no ground for being afraid. I am, moreover, quite cool, and feel no pain—but, but——

And then there was a burst of " *gemiti, sospiri ed alti guai* ". Alas, alas, poor child of clay ! as the sparks fly upward, so wast thou born to sorrow—Onward ! [1]

[1] *MS. note :* " Written in 1843 ".

CHAPTER XIX.

It has been said by this or that writer, I scarcely know by whom, that, in proportion as we grow old, and our time becomes short, the swifter does it pass, until at last, as we approach the borders of the grave, it assumes all the speed and impetuosity of a river about to precipitate itself into an abyss ; this is doubtless the case, provided we can carry to the grave those pleasant thoughts and delusions which alone render life agreeable, and to which even to the very last we would gladly cling ; but what becomes of the swiftness of time, when the mind sees the vanity of human pursuits ? which is sure to be the case when its fondest, dearest hopes have been blighted at the very moment when the harvest was deemed secure. What becomes from that moment, I repeat, of the shortness of time ? I put not the question to those who have never known that trial ; they are satisfied with themselves and all around them, with what they have done and yet hope to do ; some carry their delusions with them to the borders of the grave, ay, to the very moment when they fall into it ; a beautiful golden cloud surrounds them to the last, and such talk of the shortness of time ; through the medium of that cloud the world has ever been a pleasant world to them ; their only regret is that they are so soon to quit it ; but oh, ye dear deluded hearts, it is not every one who is so fortunate !

To the generality of mankind there is no period like youth. The generality are far from fortunate ; but the period of youth, even to the least so, offers moments of considerable happiness, for they are not only disposed, but able to enjoy most things within their reach. With what trifles at that period are we content ; the things from which in after-life we should turn away in disdain please us then, for we are in the midst of a golden cloud, and everything seems decked with a golden hue. Never during any portion of my life did time flow on more speedily than during the two or three years immediately succeeding the period to which we arrived in the preceding chapter. Since then it has flagged often enough ; sometimes it has seemed to stand entirely still ; and the

(113)

reader may easily judge how it fares at the present, from the
circumstance of my taking pen in hand, and endeavouring to
write down the passages of my life—a last resource with most
people. But at the period to which I allude I was just, as I may
say, entering upon life; I had adopted a profession, and—to keep
up my character, simultaneously with that profession—the study
of a new language; I speedily became a proficient in the one, but
ever remained a novice in the other: a novice in the law, but a
perfect master in the Welsh tongue.

Yes! very pleasant times were those, when within the womb
of a lofty deal desk, behind which I sat for some eight hours
every day, transcribing (when I imagined eyes were upon me)
documents of every description in every possible hand, Blackstone
kept company with Ab Gwilym—the polished English lawyer of
the last century, who wrote long and prosy chapters on the rights of
things—with a certain wild Welshman, who some four hundred years
before that time indited immortal cowydds and odes to the wives
of Cambrian chieftains—more particularly to one Morfydd, the
wife of a certain hunchbacked dignitary called by the poet facetiously Bwa Bach—generally terminating with the modest request
of a little private parlance beneath the green wood bough, with no
other witness than the eos, or nightingale, a request which, if the
poet himself may be believed—rather a doubtful point—was
seldom, very seldom, denied. And by what strange chance had
Ab Gwilym and Blackstone, two personages so exceedingly
different, been thus brought together? From what the reader
already knows of me, he may be quite prepared to find me
reading the former; but what could have induced me to take up
Blackstone, or rather the law?

I have ever loved to be as explicit as possible; on which
account, perhaps, I never attained to any proficiency in the law,
the essence of which is said to be ambiguity; most questions may
be answered in a few words, and this among the rest, though
connected with the law. My parents deemed it necessary that I
should adopt some profession, they named the law; the law was
as agreeable to me as any other profession within my reach, so I
adopted the law, and the consequence was, that Blackstone, probably for the first time, found himself in company with Ab Gwilym.
By adopting the law I had not ceased to be Lavengro.

So I sat behind a desk many hours in the day, ostensibly
engaged in transcribing documents of various kinds. The scene of
my labours was a strange old house, occupying one side of a long
and narrow court, into which, however, the greater number of the

RACKHAM'S OFFICES, TUCK'S COURT, ST GILES', NORWICH.

[*See page 114.*

WILLIAM TAYLOR OF NORWICH (BORN 1765, DIED 1836).

[See page 146.

windows looked not, but into an extensive garden, filled with
fruit trees, in the rear of a large, handsome house, belonging to a
highly respectable gentleman, who, *moyennant un douceur con-
sidérable*, had consented to instruct my father's youngest son in
the mysteries of glorious English law.   Ah ! would that I could
describe the good gentleman in the manner which he deserves ;
he has long since sunk to his place in a respectable vault, in the
aisle of a very respectable church, whilst an exceedingly respectable marble slab against the neighbouring wall tells on a Sunday
some eye wandering from its prayer-book that his dust lies below ;
to secure such respectabilities in death, he passed a most respectable life.   Let no one sneer, he accomplished much ; his life was
peaceful, so was his death.   Are these trifles? I wish I could
describe him, for I loved the man, and with reason, for he was
ever kind to me, to whom kindness has not always been shown ;
and he was, moreover, a choice specimen of a class which no
longer exists—a gentleman lawyer of the old school.   I would
fain describe him, but figures with which he has nought to do
press forward and keep him from my mind's eye ; there they pass,
Spaniard and Moor, Gypsy, Turk, and livid Jew.   But who is
that ? what that thick pursy man in the loose, snuff-coloured greatcoat, with the white stockings, drab breeches, and silver buckles
on his shoes? that man with the bull neck, and singular head,
immense in the lower part, especially about the jaws, but tapering
upward like a pear ; the man with the bushy brows, small grey
eyes, replete with cat-like expression, whose grizzled hair is cut
close, and whose ear-lobes are pierced with small golden rings?
Oh ! that is not my dear old master, but a widely different personage. *Bon jour, Monsieur Vidocq ! expressions de ma part à
Monsieur le Baron Taylor.*[1]   But here comes at last my veritable
old master !
    A more respectable-looking individual was never seen ; he
really looked what he was, a gentleman of the law—there was
nothing of the pettifogger about him.   Somewhat under the middle
size, and somewhat rotund in person, he was always dressed in a
full suit of black, never worn long enough to become threadbare.
His face was rubicund, and not without keenness ; but the most
remarkable thing about him was the crown of his head, which was
bald, and shone like polished ivory, nothing more white, smooth,
and lustrous.   Some people have said that he wore false calves,
probably because his black silk stockings never exhibited a
wrinkle ; they might just as well have said that he waddled,

[1] *MS.,* " à Monsieur Peyrecourt " or " Pierrecourt ".

because his shoes creaked; for these last, which were always
without a speck, and polished as his crown, though of a different
hue, did creak, as he walked rather slowly. I cannot say that I
ever saw him walk fast.

He had a handsome practice, and might have died a very
rich man, much richer than he did, had he not been in the habit
of giving rather expensive dinners to certain great people, who
gave him nothing in return, except their company; I could never
discover his reasons for doing so, as he always appeared to me a
remarkably quiet man, by nature averse to noise and bustle; but
in all dispositions there are anomalies. I have already said that
he lived in a handsome house, and I may as well here add that
he had a very handsome wife, who both dressed and talked exceedingly well.

So I sat behind the deal desk, engaged in copying documents
of various kinds; and in the apartment in which I sat, and in the
adjoining ones, there were others, some of whom likewise copied
documents, while some were engaged in the yet more difficult
task of drawing them up; and some of these, sons of nobody,
were paid for the work they did, whilst others, like myself,
sons of somebody, paid for being permitted to work, which
as our principal observed, was but reasonable, forasmuch as we
not unfrequently utterly spoiled the greater part of the work
intrusted to our hands.

There was one part of the day when I generally found myself
quite alone, I mean at the hour when the rest went home to their
principal meal; I, being the youngest, was left to take care of the
premises, to answer the bell, and so forth, till relieved, which was
seldom before the expiration of an hour and a half, when I myself went home; this period, however, was anything but disagreeable to me, for it was then that I did what best pleased me, and,
leaving off copying the documents, I sometimes indulged in a fit
of musing, my chin resting on both my hands, and my elbows
planted on the desk; or, opening the desk aforesaid, I would take
out one of the books contained within it, and the book which I
took out was almost invariably, not Blackstone, but Ab Gwilym.

Ah, that Ab Gwilym! I am much indebted to him, and it were
ungrateful on my part not to devote a few lines to him and his
songs in this my history. Start not, reader, I am not going to
trouble you with a poetical dissertation; no, no! I know my duty
too well to introduce anything of the kind; but I, who imagine I
know several things, and amongst others the workings of your
mind at this moment, have an idea that you are anxious to learn

a little, a very little, more about Ab Gwilym than I have hitherto
told you, the two or three words that I have dropped having
awakened within you a languid kind of curiosity. I have no
hesitation in saying that he makes one of the some half-dozen
really great poets whose verses, in whatever language they wrote,
exist at the present day, and are more or less known. It matters
little how I first became acquainted with the writings of this man,
and how the short thick volume, stuffed full with his immortal
imaginings, first came into my hands. I was studying Welsh,
and I fell in with Ab Gwilym by no very strange chance. But
before I say more about Ab Gwilym, I must be permitted—I
really must—to say a word or two about the language in which
he wrote, that same " Sweet Welsh ". If I remember right, I
found the language a difficult one ; in mastering it, however, I
derived unexpected assistance from what of Irish remained in
my head, and I soon found that they were cognate dialects,
springing from some old tongue which itself, perhaps, had sprung
from one much older. And here I cannot help observing
cursorily that I every now and then, whilst studying this Welsh,
generally supposed to be the original tongue of Britain, encountered words which, according to the lexicographers, were
venerable words, highly expressive, showing the wonderful power
and originality of the Welsh, in which, however, they were no
longer used in common discourse, but were relics, precious relics,
of the first speech of Britain, perhaps of the world ; with which
words, however, I was already well acquainted, and which I had
picked up, not in learned books, classic books, and in tongues of
old renown, but whilst listening to Mr. Petulengro and Tawno
Chikno talking over their every-day affairs in the language of
the tents ; which circumstance did not fail to give rise to deep
reflection in those moments when, planting my elbows on the
deal desk, I rested my chin upon my hands. But it is probable
that I should have abandoned the pursuit of the Welsh language,
after obtaining a very superficial acquaintance with it, had it not
been for Ab Gwilym.

A strange songster was that who, pretending to be captivated
by every woman he saw, was, in reality, in love with nature
alone—wild, beautiful, solitary nature—her mountains and cascades, her forests and streams, her birds, fishes, and wild animals.
Go to, Ab Gwilym, with thy pseudo-amatory odes, to Morfydd,
or this or that other lady, fair or ugly ; little didst thou care for
any of them, Dame Nature was thy love, however thou mayest
seek to disguise the truth. Yes, yes, send thy love-message to

Morfydd, the fair wanton. By whom dost thou send it, I would
know? by the salmon, forsooth, which haunts the rushing stream!
the glorious salmon which bounds and gambols in the flashing
water, and whose ways and circumstances thou so well describest
—see, there he hurries upwards through the flashing water.
Halloo! what a glimpse of glory—but where is Morfydd the
while? What, another message to the wife of Bwa Bach? Ay,
truly; and by whom?—the wind! the swift wind, the rider of
the world, whose course is not to be stayed; who gallops o'er the
mountain, and, when he comes to broadest river, asks neither for
boat nor ferry; who has described the wind so well—his speed
and power? But where is Morfydd? And now thou art awaiting
Morfydd, the wanton, the wife of the Bwa Bach; thou art awaiting
her beneath the tall trees, amidst the underwood; but she comes
not; no Morfydd is there. Quite right, Ab Gwilym; what wantest
thou with Morfydd? But another form is nigh at hand, that of
red Reynard, who, seated upon his chine at the mouth of his
cave, looks very composedly at thee; thou startest, bendest thy
bow, thy cross-bow, intending to hit Reynard with the bolt just
about the jaw; but the bow breaks, Reynard barks and dis-
appears into his cave, which by thine own account reaches hell—
and then thou ravest at the misfortune of thy bow and the non-
appearance of Morfydd, and abusest Reynard. Go to, thou
carest neither for thy bow nor for Morfydd, thou merely seekest
an opportunity to speak of Reynard; and who has described him
like thee? the brute with the sharp shrill cry, the black reverse of
melody, whose face sometimes wears a smile like the devil's in the
Evangile. But now thou art actually with Morfydd; yes, she has
stolen from the dwelling of the Bwa Bach and has met thee
beneath those rocks—she is actually with thee, Ab Gwilym; but
she is not long with thee, for a storm comes on, and thunder
shatters the rocks—Morfydd flees! Quite right, Ab Gwilym;
thou hadst no need of her, a better theme for song is the voice of
the Lord—the rock shatterer—than the frail wife of the Bwa
Bach. Go to, Ab Gwilym, thou wast a wiser and a better man
than thou wouldst fain have had people believe.

But enough of thee and thy songs! Those times passed
rapidly away; with Ab Gwilym in my hand, I was in the midst
of enchanted ground, in which I experienced sensations akin to
those I had felt of yore whilst spelling my way through the
wonderful book—the delight of my childhood. I say akin, for
perhaps only once in our lives do we experience unmixed wonder
and delight; and these I had already known.

[It was my own fault if I did not acquire considerable knowledge of life and character, in the place to which my kind parents
had sent me. I performed the tasks that were allotted to me in
the profession I had embraced, if not very scrupulously, yet,
perhaps as well as could be expected in one who was occupied
by many and busy thoughts of his own. I copied what was set
before me, and admitted those who knocked at the door of the
sanctuary of law and conveyancing, performing the latter office
indeed from choice, long after it had ceased to be part of my
duty by the arrival of another, and of course a junior, pupil.

I scarcely know what induced me to take pleasure in this
task, yet there can be no doubt that I did take pleasure in it,
otherwise I should scarcely have performed it so readily. It has
been said, I believe, that whatever we do *con amore*, we are sure
to do well, and I dare say that, as a general rule, this may
hold good. One thing is certain, that with whatever satisfaction
to myself I performed the task, I was not equally fortunate in
pleasing my employer, who complained of my want of discrimination and yet, strange as it may seem, this last is a quality upon
which I not only particularly valued myself at the time, but still
do in a high degree. I made a point never to admit any persons
without subjecting them to the rigorous investigation of the pair
of eyes that providence had been pleased to place in my head.
To those who pleased me not, I was little better than a Cerberus
whom it was very difficult to pass; whilst to others, I was all
easiness and condescension, ushering them straight to the sanctum
sanctorum, in which, behind a desk covered with letters and
papers, stood—for he never sat down to his desk—the respectable
individual whose lawful commands to obey and whose secrets to
keep I had pledged myself by certain articles duly stamped and
signed.

"This will never do," said he to me one day; "you will
make me a bankrupt, unless you alter your conduct. There is
scarcely one of my respectable clients but complains of your
incivility. I speak to you, my poor boy, as much on your own
account as on mine. I quite tremble for you. Are you aware of
the solecisms you commit? Only yesterday you turned Sir
Edward from the door, and immediately after you admitted
Parkinson the poet! What an insult to a gentleman to be turned
from the door, and a strolling vagabond to be admitted before
his eyes!"

" I can't help it," said I ; " I used my best powers of discrimination; I looked both full in the face, and the one struck me as

being an honest man, whilst the other had the very look of a
slave driver."

"In the face? Bless me! But you looked at their dress, I
suppose? You looked at Sir Edward's dress?"

"No," said I, "I merely looked at his countenance."

"Which you thought looked like that of a slave driver. Well,
he's been in the Indies, where he made his fortune; so, perhaps,
you may not be so far out. However, be more cautious in future;
look less at people's countenances and more at their——I dare
say you understand me: admit every decent person, and if you
turn away anybody, pray let it be the poet Parkinson . . ."

Keeping the admonition of my principal in view, I admitted
without word or comment, provided the possessors had a decent
coat to their backs, all kinds of countenances—honest countenances, dishonest countenances, and those which were neither.
Amongst all these, some of which belonged to naval and military
officers, notaries public, magistrates, bailiffs, and young ecclesi-
astics—the latter with spotless neck-cloths and close-shaven chins
—there were three countenances which particularly pleased me:
the first being that of an ancient earl, who wore a pig-tail, and
the back of whose coat was white with powder; the second,
that of a yeoman ninety years old and worth £90,000, who,
dressed in an entire suit of whitish corduroy, sometimes slowly
trotted up the court on a tall heavy steed, which seemed by no
means unused to the plough. The third was that of the poet
Parkinson.

I am not quite sure that I remember the business which
brought this last individual so frequently to our office, for he paid
us a great many visits.

I am inclined to believe, however, that he generally carried
in his pocket a bundle of printed poems of his own composition,
on the sale of which he principally depended for his subsistence.
He was a man of a singular, though to me by no means unpleasant
countenance; he wore an old hat and a snuff-coloured greatcoat,
and invariably carried in his hand a stout cudgel like a man much
in the habit of walking, which he probably was, from the circumstance of his being generally covered with dust in summer, and in
winter splashed with mud from head to foot.

"You cannot see the principal to day, Mr. Parkinson," said I
to him once, as unannounced he entered the room where I sat
alone; "he is gone out and will not return for some time."

"Well, that's unfortunate, for I want to consult him on some
particular business."

"What business is it? Perhaps I can be of service to you. Does it relate to the common law?"

" I suppose so, for I am told it is a common assault; but I had better wait till the gentleman comes home. You are rather too young; and besides I have other matters to consult him about; I have two or three papers in my pocket . . ."

" You cannot see him to-day," said I; " but you were talking of an assault. Has any one been beating you?"

" Not exactly; I got into a bit of a ruffle, and am threatened with an action."

" Oh! so you have been beating somebody."

" And if I did, how could I help it? I'll tell you how it happened. I have a gift of making verses, as perhaps you know—in fact, everybody knows. When I had sowed my little trifle of corn in the bit of ground that my father left me, having nothing better to do, I sat down and wrote a set of lines to my lord, in which I told him what a fine old gentleman he was. Then I took my stick and walked off to ——, where, after a little difficulty, I saw my lord, and read the verses to him which I had made, offering to print them if he thought proper. Well, he was mightily pleased with them, and said they were too good to be printed, and begged that I would do no such thing, which I promised him I would not, and left him, not before, however, he had given me a King James' guinea, which they say is worth two of King George's. Well, I made my bow and went to the village, and in going past the ale-house I thought I would just step in, which I did. The house was full of people, chiefly farmers, and when they saw me they asked me to sit down and take a glass with them, which I did, and being called upon for a song I sang one, and then began talking about myself and how much my lord thought of me, and I repeated the lines which I had written to him, and showed them the James' guinea he had given me. You should have seen the faces they cast upon me at the sight of the gold; they couldn't stand it, for it was a confirmation to their envious hearts of all I had told them. Presently one called me a boasting fool, and getting up said that my lord was a yet greater fool for listening to me, and then added that the lines I had been reading were not of my own making. ' No, you dog,' said he, ' they are not of your own making; you got somebody to make them for you.' Now, I do not mind being called a boaster, nor a dog either, but when he told me that my verses were not my own, I couldn't contain myself, so I told him he lied, whereupon he flung a glass of liquor in my face, and I knocked him down."

"Mr. Parkinson," said I, "are you much in the habit of writing verses to great people?"

"Great and small. I consider nothing too high or too low. I have written verses upon the king, and upon a prize ox; for the first I got nothing, but the owner of the ox at Christmas sent me the better part of the chine."

"In fact, you write on all kinds of subjects."

"And I carry them to the people whom I think they'll please."

"And what subjects please best?"

"Animals; my work chiefly lies in the country, and people in the country prefer their animals to anything else."

"Have you ever written on amatory subjects?"

"When young people are about to be married, I sometimes write in that style; but it doesn't take. People think, perhaps, that I am jesting at them, but no one thinks I am jesting at his horse or his ox when I speak well of them. There was an old lady who had a peacock; I sent her some lines upon the bird; she never forgot it, and when she died she left me the bird stuffed and ten pounds."

"Mr. Parkinson, you put me very much in mind of the Welsh bards."

"The Welsh what?"

"Bards. Did you never hear of them?"

"Can't say that I ever did."

"You do not understand Welsh?"

"I do not."

"Well, provided you did, I should be strongly disposed to imagine that you imitated the Welsh bards."

"I imitate no one," said Mr. Parkinson; "though if you mean by the Welsh bards the singing bards of the country, it is possible we may resemble one another; only I would scorn to imitate anybody, even a bard."

"I was not speaking of birds, but bards—Welsh poets—and it is surprising how much the turn of your genius coincides with theirs. Why, the subjects of hundreds of their compositions are the very subjects which you appear to delight in, and are the most profitable to you—beeves, horses, hawks—which they described to their owners in colours the most glowing and natural, and then begged them as presents. I have even seen in Welsh an ode to a peacock."

"I can't help it," said Parkinson, "and I tell you again that I imitate nobody."

"Do you travel much about?"

" Aye, aye. As soon as I have got my seed into the ground, or my crop into my barn, I lock up my home and set out from house to house and village to village, and many is the time I sit down beneath the hedges and take out my pen and inkhorn. It is owing to that, I suppose, that I have been called the flying poet." . . . [*Wanting.*]

" It appears to me, young man," said Parkinson, " that you are making game of me."

" I should as much scorn to make game of any one, as you would scorn to imitate any one, Mr. Parkinson."

" Well, so much the better for us both. But we'll now talk of my affair. Are you man enough to give me an opinion upon it ? "

" Quite so," said I, " Mr. Parkinson. I understand the case clearly, and I unhesitatingly assert that any action for battery brought against you would be flung out of court, and the bringer of said action be obliged to pay the costs, the original assault having been perpetrated by himself when he flung the liquor in your face ; and to set your mind perfectly at ease I will read to you what Lord Chief Justice Blackstone says upon the subject."

" Thank you," said Parkinson, after I had read him an entire chapter on the rights of persons, expounding as I went along. " I see you understand the subject, and are a respectable young man—which I rather doubted at first from your countenance, which shows the folly of taking against a person for the cast of his face or the glance of his eye. Now, I'll maintain that you are a respectable young man, whoever says to the contrary ; and that some day or other you will be an honour to your profession and a credit to your friends. I like chapter and verse when I ask a question, and you have given me both ; you shall never want my good word ; meanwhile, if there is anything that I can oblige you in——"

" There is, Mr. Parkinson, there is."

" Well, what is it ? "

" It has just occurred to me that you could give me a hint or two at versification. I have just commenced, but I find it no easy matter, the rhymes are particularly perplexing."

" Are you quite serious ? "

" Quite so ; and to convince you, here is an ode of Ab Gwilym which I am translating, but I can get no farther than the first verse."

" Why, that was just my case when I first began," said Parkinson.

"I think I have been tolerably successful in the first verse, and that I have not only gotten the sense of the author, but that alliteration, which, as you may perhaps be aware, is one of the most peculiar features of Welsh poetry. In the ode to which I allude the poet complains of the barbarity of his mistress, Morfydd, and what an unthankful task it is to be the poet of a beauty so proud and disdainful, which sentiment I have partly rendered thus :—

Mine is a task by no means merry,

in which you observe that the first word of the line and the last two commence with the same letter, according to the principle of Welsh prosody. But now cometh the difficulty. What is the rhyme for *merry ?* "

"*Londonderry,*" said the poet without hesitation, "as you will see by the poem which I addressed to Mr. C., the celebrated Whig agriculturist, on its being reported that the king was about to pay him a visit :—

But if in our town he would wish to be merry
Pray don't let him bring with him Lord Londonderry,

which two lines procured me the best friend I ever had in my life."

"They are certainly fine lines," I observed, "and I am not at all surprised that the agriculturist was pleased with them ; but I am afraid that I cannot turn to much account the hint which they convey. How can I possibly introduce Londonderry into my second line ?"

"I see no difficulty," said Parkinson ; "just add :—

I sing proud Mary of Londonderry

to your first line, and I do not see what objection could be made to the couplet, as they call it."

"No farther," said I, "than that she was not of Londonderry, which was not even built at the time she lived."

"Well, have your own way," said Parkinson ; "I see that you have not had the benefit of a classical education."

"What makes you think so ?"

"Why, you never seem to have heard of poetical license."

"I see," said I, "that I must give up alliteration. Alliteration and rhyme together will, I am afraid, be too much for me. Perhaps the couplet had best stand thus :—

I long have had a duty hard,
I long have been fair Morfydd's bard.

"That won't do," said Parkinson.

" Why not?"

" Because 'tis not English. Bard, indeed! I tell you what, young man, you have no talent for poetry; if you had, you would not want my help. No, no; cleave to your own profession and you will be an honour to it, but leave poetry to me. I counsel you as a friend. Good-morning to you."]

CHAPTER XX.

"I AM afraid that I have not acted very wisely in putting this boy of ours to the law," said my father to my mother, as they sat together one summer evening in their little garden, beneath the shade of some tall poplars.

Yes, there sat my father in the garden chair which leaned against the wall of his quiet home, the haven in which he had sought rest, and, praise be to God, found it, after many a year of poorly requited toil; there he sat, with locks of silver gray which set off so nobly his fine bold but benevolent face, his faithful consort at his side, and his trusty dog at his feet—an eccentric animal of the genuine regimental breed, who, born amongst red-coats, had not yet become reconciled to those of any other hue, barking and tearing at them when they drew near the door, but testifying his fond reminiscence of the former by hospitable waggings of the tail whenever a uniform made its appearance—at present a very unfrequent occurrence.

"I am afraid I have not done right in putting him to the law," said my father, resting his chin upon his gold-headed bamboo cane.

"Why, what makes you think so?" said my mother.

"I have been taking my usual evening walk up the road, with the animal here," said my father; "and, as I walked along, I overtook the boy's master, Mr. S——.[1] We shook hands, and after walking a little way farther, we turned back together, talking about this and that; the state of the country, the weather, and the dog, which he greatly admired; for he is a good-natured man, and has a good word for everybody, though the dog all but bit him when he attempted to coax his head; after the dog, we began talking about the boy; it was myself who introduced that subject: I thought it was a good opportunity to learn how he was getting on, so I asked what he thought of my son; he hesitated at first, seeming scarcely to know what to say; at length he came out

[1] *MS.*, "Simpson".

with 'Oh, a very extraordinary youth, a most remarkable youth indeed, captain!' 'Indeed,' said I, 'I am glad to hear it, but I hope you find him steady?' 'Steady, steady,' said he, 'why, yes, he's steady, I cannot say that he is not steady.' 'Come, come,' said I, beginning to be rather uneasy, 'I see plainly that you are not altogether satisfied with him; I was afraid you would not be, for, though he is my own son, I am anything but blind to his imperfections: but do tell me what particular fault you have to find with him; and I will do my best to make him alter his conduct.' 'No fault to find with him, captain, I assure you, no fault whatever; the youth is a remarkable youth, an extraordinary youth, only'—As I told you before, Mr. S—— is the best-natured man in the world, and it was only with the greatest difficulty that I could get him to say a single word to the disadvantage of the boy, for whom he seems to entertain a very great regard. At last I forced the truth from him, and grieved I was to hear it; though I must confess I was somewhat prepared for it. It appears that the lad has a total want of discrimination."

"I don't understand you," said my mother.

"You can understand nothing that would seem for a moment to impugn the conduct of that child. I am not, however, so blind; want of discrimination was the word, and it both sounds well, and is expressive. It appears that, since he has been placed where he is, he has been guilty of the grossest blunders; only the other day, Mr. S—— told me, as he was engaged in close conversation with one of his principal clients, the boy came to tell him that a person wanted particularly to speak with him; and, on going out, he found a lamentable figure with one eye, who came to ask for charity; whom, nevertheless, the lad had ushered into a private room, and installed in an arm-chair, like a justice of the peace, instead of telling him to go about his business—now what did that show, but a total want of discrimination?"

"I wish we may never have anything worse to reproach him with," said my mother.

"I don't know what worse we could reproach him with," said my father: "I mean of course as far as his profession is concerned: discrimination is the very key-stone; if he treated all people alike, he would soon become a beggar himself; there are grades in society as well as in the army; and according to those grades we should fashion our behaviour, else there would instantly be an end of all order and discipline. I am afraid that the child is too condescending to his inferiors, whilst to his superiors he is apt to be unbending enough; I don't believe that would do in the world; I am sure it would not in the army. He told me another anecdote with respect to his behaviour, which shocked me more than the other had done. It appears that his wife, who, by-the-bye, is a very fine woman, and highly fashionable, gave him permission to ask the boy to tea one evening, for she is herself rather partial to the lad; there had been a great dinner party there that day, and there were a great many fashionable people, so the boy went and behaved very well and modestly for some time, and was rather noticed, till, unluckily, a very great gentleman, an archdeacon I think, put some questions to him, and, finding that he understood the languages, began talking to him about the classics. What do you think? the boy had the impertinence to say that the classics were much overvalued, and amongst other things that some horrid fellow or other, some Welshman I think (thank God it was not an Irishman), was a better poet than Ovid; the company were of course horrified; the archdeacon, who is seventy years of age, and has £7000 a year, took snuff and turned away. Mrs. S—— turned up her eyes, Mr. S——, however, told me with his usual good-nature (I suppose to spare my feelings) that he rather enjoyed the thing, and thought it a capital joke."

"I think so too," said my mother.

"I do not," said my father; "that a boy of his years should entertain an opinion of his own—I mean one which militates against all established authority—is astounding; as well might a raw recruit pretend to offer an unfavourable opinion on the manual and platoon exercise; the idea is preposterous; the lad is too independent by half. I never yet knew one of an independent spirit get on in the army; the secret of success in the army is the spirit of subordination."

"Which is a poor spirit after all," said my mother; "but the child is not in the army."

"And it is well for him that he is not," said my father; "but you do not talk wisely, the world is a field of battle, and he who leaves the ranks, what can he expect but to be cut down? I call his present behaviour leaving the ranks, and going vapouring about without orders; his only chance lies in falling in again as quick as possible; does he think he can carry the day by himself? an opinion of his own at these years! I confess I am exceedingly uneasy about the lad."

["I am not," said my mother; "I have no doubt that Providence will take care of him."

"I repeat that I am exceedingly uneasy," said my father; "I

can't help being so, and would give my largest piece of coin to know what kind of part he will play in life."

"Such curiosity is blamable," said my mother, "highly so. Let us leave these things to Providence, and hope for the best; but to wish to pry into the future, which is hidden from us, and wisely too, is mighty wicked. *Tempt not Providence.* I early contracted a dread of that sin. When I was only a child, something occurred connected with diving into the future, which had, I hope, a salutary effect on my subsequent conduct. The fright which I got then, I shall never forget. But it is getting dark, and we had better go into the house."

"We are well enough here," said my father; "go on with your discourse. You were speaking of tempting Providence, and of having been frightened."

"It was a long time ago," said my mother, "when I was quite a child, and I was only a humble assistant in the affair. Your wish to dive into the future brought it to my recollection. It was, perhaps, only a foolish affair after all, and I would rather not talk about it, especially as it is growing dark. We had better go in."

"A tale with any terror in it is all the better for being told in the dark hour," said my father; "you are not afraid, I hope."

"Afraid, indeed! Of what should I be afraid? And yet I know not how it is, I feel a chill, as if something was casting a cold shadow upon me. By-the-bye, I have often heard that child talk of an indescribable fear which sometimes attacks him and which he calls the shadow. I wonder if it at all resembles what I am feeling now!"

"Never mind the child or his shadow," said my father, "but let us hear the story."

"I have no objection to tell it; but perhaps after all it is mere nonsense and will only make you laugh."

"Why, then, so much the better; it will perhaps drive from my head what Mr. Simpson told me, which I certainly considered to be no laughing matter, though you and he did. I would hear the story by all means."

"Well, so you shall. 'Tis said, however, that a superstition lies at the bottom of it, as old as the Danes. So, at least, says the child, who by some means or other has of late become acquainted with their language. He says that of old they worshipped a god whose name was Frey, and that this Frey had a wife."

"Indeed!" said my father, "and who told you this?"

"Why, the child," said my mother hesitatingly; "it was he that told me."

"I am afraid that it will indeed prove a foolish story," said my father; "the child is mixed up with it already."

"He is *not* mixed up with it," said my mother. "What I am about to relate occurred many a long year before he was born. But he is fond of hearing odd tales; and some time ago when he was poorly, I told him this one amongst others, and it was then he made the observation that it is a relic of the worship of the Danes. Truly the child talked both sensibly and learnedly. The Danes, he said, were once a mighty people, and were masters of the land where we at present are; that they had gods of their own, strange and wild like themselves, and that it was their god Frey who gave his name to what we call Friday."

"All this may be true," said my father, "but I should never think of quoting the child as an authority."

"You must not be too hard on him," said my mother. "So this Frey had a wife whose name was Freya, and the child says that the old pagans considered them as the gods of love and marriage, and worshipped them as such; and that all young damsels were in the habit of addressing themselves to Freya in their love adventures, and of requesting her assistance. He told me, and he quite frightened me when he said it, that a certain night ceremony, in which I took part in my early youth, and which is the affair to which I have alluded, was in every point heathenish, being neither more nor less than an invocation to this Freya, the wife of the old pagan god."

"And what ceremony might it be?" demanded my father. "It is getting something dark," he added, glancing around.

"It is so," said my mother; "but these tales, you know, are best suited to the dark hour. The ceremony was rather a singular one; the child, however, explains it rationally enough. He says that this Freya was not only a very comely woman, but also particularly neat in her person, and that she invariably went dressed in snow-white linen."

"And how came the child to know all this?" demanded my father.

"Oh, that's his affair. I am merely repeating what he tells me. He reads strange books and converses with strange people. What he says, however, upon this matter, seems sensible enough. This Freya was fond of snow-white linen."

"And what has that to do with the story?"

"Everything. I have told you that the young maidens were

in the habit of praying to her and requesting her favour and
assistance in their love adventures, which it seems she readily
granted to those whom she took any interest in. Now the
readiest way to secure this interest and to procure her assistance
in any matter of the heart, was to flatter her on the point where
she was the most sensible. Whence the offering."

"And what was the offering?"

"It was once a common belief that the young maiden who
should wash her linen white in pure running water and should
'watch' it whilst drying before a fire from eleven to twelve at
night, would, at the stroke of midnight, see the face of the man
appear before her who was destined to be her husband, and the
child says that this was the '*Wake of Freya*'."

"I have heard of it before," said my father, "but under
another name. So you were engaged in one of these watchings."

"It was no fault of mine," said my mother; "for, as I told
you, I was very young, scarcely ten years of age; but I had a
sister considerably older than myself, a nice girl, but somewhat
giddy and rather unsettled. Perhaps, poor thing, she had some
cause; for a young man to whom she had been betrothed, had
died suddenly, which was of course a terrible disappointment to
her. Well, it is at such times that strange ideas, temptations
perhaps, come into our head. To be brief, she had a mighty
desire to know whether she was doomed to be married or not. I
remember that at that time there were many odd beliefs and
superstitions which have since then died away; for those times
were not like these; there were highwaymen in the land, and
people during the winter evenings used to sit round the fire and
tell wonderful tales of those wild men and their horses; and these
tales they would blend with ghost stories and the like. My sister
was acquainted with all the tales and superstitions afloat and believed
in them. So she determined upon the wake, the night-watch of
Freya, as the child calls it. But with all her curiosity she was a
timid creature, and was afraid to perform the ceremony alone.
So she told me of her plan, and begged me to stand by her.
Now, though I was a child, I had a spirit of my own and likewise
a curiosity; and though I had other sisters, I loved her best of all
of them, so I promised her that I would stand by her. Then we
made our preparations. The first thing we did was to walk over
to the town, which was about three miles distant—the pretty
little rural town which you and the child admire so much, and in
the neighbourhood of which I was born—to purchase the article
we were in need of. After a considerable search we found such

an one as we thought would suit. It was of the best Holland, and I remember that it cost us all the little pocket money we could muster. This we brought home ; and that same night my sister put it on and wore it for that once only. We had washed it in a brook on the other side of the moor. I remember the spot well ; it was in a little pool beneath an old hollow oak. The next night we entered on the ceremony itself.

" It happened to be Saturday, which was lucky for us, as my father that night would be at the town, whither he went every Saturday to sell grain ; for he farmed his own little estate, as you know."

" I remember him well," said my father ; " he preferred ale to wine."

" My father was of the old race," said my mother, " and lived in the days of the highwaymen and their horses, when ' ale was ale,' as he used to say, and ' was good for man and beast '. We knew that on the night in question he would not be home till very late ; so we offered to sit up for him in lieu of the servant, who was glad enough in such weather, and after a hard day's work, to escape to her bed. My mother was indisposed and had retired to rest early. Well do I remember that night ; it was the beginning of December, and the weather for some time past had been piercingly cold. The wind howled through the leafless boughs, and there was every appearance of an early and severe winter, as indeed befel. Long before eleven o'clock all was hushed and quiet within the house, and indeed without (nothing was heard), except the cold wind which howled mournfully in gusts. The house was an old farm-house, and we sat in the large kitchen with its stone floor, awaiting the first stroke of the eleventh hour. It struck at last, and then all pale and trembling we hung the garment to dry before the fire which we had piled up with wood, and set the door ajar, for that was an essential point. The door was lofty and opened upon the farmyard, through which there was a kind of thoroughfare, very seldom used, it is true, and at each end of it there was a gate by which wayfarers occasionally passed to shorten the way. There we sat without speaking a word, shivering with cold and fear, listening to the clock which went slowly, tick, tick, and occasionally starting as the door creaked on its hinges, or a half-burnt billet fell upon the hearth. My sister was ghastly white, as white as the garment which was drying before the fire. And now half an hour had elapsed and it was time to turn. . . . This we did, I and my sister, without saying a word, and then we again sank on our chairs on either side of the fire. I was tired, and as the clock went tick-a-tick, I began to feel myself dozing. I did doze, I believe. All of a sudden I sprang up. The clock was striking one, two, but ere it could give the third chime, mercy upon us! we heard the gate slam to with a tremendous noise. . . ."

" Well, and what happened then ? "

" Happened ! before I could recover myself, my sister had sprung to the door and both locked and bolted it. The next moment she was in convulsions. I scarcely knew what happened ; and yet it appeared to me for a moment that something pressed against the door with a low moaning sound. Whether it was the wind or not, I can't say. I shall never forget that night. About two hours later, my father came home. He had been set upon by a highwayman whom he beat off."

" And what was the result ? "

" The result ? why, my sister was ill for many weeks. Poor thing, she never throve, married poorly, flung herself away."

" I don't see much in the story," said my father ; " I should have laughed at it, only there is one thing I don't like."

" What is that ? "

" Why, the explanation of that strange child. It seems so odd that he should be able to interpret it. The idea came this moment into my head. I daresay it's all nonsense, but, but . . ."

" Oh, I daresay it's nonsense. Let us go in."

" If, after all, it should have been the worship of a demon ! Your sister was punished, you say—she never throve ; now how do we know that you may not be punished too ? That child with his confusion of tongues —— "

" I really think you are too hard upon him. After all, though not, perhaps, all you could wish, he is not a bad child ; he is always ready to read the Bible. Let us go in ; he is in the room above us ; at least he was two hours ago. I left him there bending over his books ; I wonder what he has been doing all this time. Let us go in, and he shall read to us."]

" I am getting old," said my father ; " and I love to hear the Bible read to me, for my own sight is something dim ; yet I do not wish the child to read to me this night, I cannot so soon forget what I have heard ; but I hear my eldest son's voice, he is now entering the gate ; he shall read the Bible to us this night. What say you ? "

CHAPTER XXI.

THE eldest son! The regard and affection which my father entertained for his first-born were natural enough, and appeared to none more so than myself, who cherished the same feelings towards him. What he was as a boy the reader already knows, for the reader has seen him as a boy; fain would I describe him at the time of which I am now speaking, when he had attained the verge of manhood, but the pen fails me, and I attempt not the task; and yet it ought to be an easy one, for how frequently does his form visit my mind's eye in slumber and in wakefulness, in the light of day, and in the night watches; but last night I saw him in his beauty and his strength; he was about to speak, and my ear was on the stretch, when at once I awoke, and there was I alone, and the night storm was howling amidst the branches of the pines which surround my lonely dwelling: "Listen to the moaning of the pine, at whose root thy hut is fastened,"—a saying that, of wild Finland, in which there is wisdom; I listened, and thought of life and death. . . . Of all human beings that I have ever known, that elder brother was the most frank and generous, ay, and the quickest and readiest, and the best adapted to do a great thing needful at the critical time, when the delay of a moment would be fatal. I have known him dash from a steep bank into a stream in his full dress, and pull out a man who was drowning; yet there were twenty others bathing in the water, who might have saved him by putting out a hand, without inconvenience to themselves, which, however, they did not do, but stared with stupid surprise at the drowning one's struggles. Yes, whilst some shouted from the bank to those in the water to save the drowning one, and those in the water did nothing, my brother neither shouted nor stood still, but dashed from the bank and did the one thing needful, which, under such circumstances, not one man in a million would have done. Now, who can wonder that a brave old man should love a son like this, and prefer him to any other?

"My boy, my own boy, you are the very image of myself the day I took off my coat in the park to fight Big Ben," said my father, on meeting his son wet and dripping, immediately after his bold feat. And who cannot excuse the honest pride of the old man —the stout old man ?

Ay, old man, that son was worthy of thee, and thou wast worthy of such a son ; a noble specimen wast thou of those strong single-minded Englishmen, who, without making a parade either of religion or loyalty, feared God and honoured their king, and were not particularly friendly to the French, whose vaunting polls they occasionally broke, as at Minden and Malplaquet, to the confusion vast of the eternal foes of the English land. I, who was so little like thee that thou understoodst me not, and in whom with justice thou didst feel so little pride, had yet perception enough to see all thy worth, and to feel it an honour to be able to call myself thy son ; and if at some no distant time, when the foreign enemy ventures to insult our shore, I be permitted to break some vaunting poll, it will be a triumph to me to think that, if thou hadst lived, thou wouldst have hailed the deed, and mightest yet discover some distant semblance to thyself, the day when thou didst all but vanquish the mighty Brain.

I have already spoken of my brother's taste for painting, and the progress he had made in that beautiful art. It is probable that, if circumstances had not eventually diverted his mind from the pursuit, he would have attained excellence, and left behind him some enduring monument of his powers, for he had an imagination to conceive, and that yet rarer endowment, a hand capable of giving life, body, and reality to the conceptions of his mind ; perhaps he wanted one thing, the want of which is but too often fatal to the sons of genius, and without which genius is little more than a splendid toy in the hands of the possessor—persever-ance, dogged perseverance, in his proper calling ; otherwise, though the grave had closed over him, he might still be living in the admiration of his fellow-creatures. O ye gifted ones, follow your calling, for, however various your talents may be, ye can have but one calling capable of leading ye to eminence and renown ; follow resolutely the one straight path before you, it is that of your good angel, let neither obstacles nor temptations induce ye to leave it ; bound along if you can ; if not on hands and knees follow it, perish in it, if needful ; but ye need not fear that ; no one ever yet died in the true path of his calling before he had attained the pinnacle. Turn into other paths, and for a momentary advantage or gratification ye have sold your inheritance, your immortality. Ye will never be heard of after death.

" My father has given me a hundred and fifty pounds," said

my brother to me one morning, " and something which is better—
his blessing.   I am going to leave you."

" Where are you going ? "

" Where ? to the great city ; to London, to be sure."

" I should like to go with you."

" Pooh," said my brother, " what should you do there ? "   But
don't be discouraged, I daresay a time will come when you too will
go to London."

And, sure enough, so it did, and all but too soon.

" And what do you purpose doing there ? " I demanded.

" Oh, I go to improve myself in art, to place myself under
some master of high name, at least I hope to do so eventually.
I have, however, a plan in my head, which I should wish first to
execute ; indeed, I do not think I can rest till I have done so ;
every one talks so much about Italy, and the wondrous artists
which it has produced, and the wondrous pictures which are to be
found there ; now I wish to see Italy, or rather Rome, the great
city, for I am told that in a certain room there is contained the
grand miracle of art."

" And what do you call it ? "

" The Transfiguration, painted by one Rafael, and it is said to
be the greatest work of the greatest painter which the world has
ever known.   I suppose it is because everybody says so, that I
have such a strange desire to see it.   I have already made myself
well acquainted with its locality, and think that I could almost
find my way to it blindfold.   When I have crossed the Tiber,
which, as you are aware, runs through Rome, I must presently
turn to the right, up a rather shabby street, which communicates
with a large square, the farther end of which is entirely occupied
by the front of an immense church, with a dome, which ascends
almost to the clouds, and this church they call St. Peter's."

" Ay, ay," said I, " I have read about that in Keysler's *Travels.*"

" Before the church, in the square, are two fountains, one on
either side, casting up water in showers ; between them, in the
midst, is an obelisk, brought from Egypt, and covered with
mysterious writing ; on your right rises an edifice, not beautiful
nor grand, but huge and bulky, where lives a strange kind of
priest whom men call the Pope, a very horrible old individual,
who would fain keep Christ in leading-strings, calls the Virgin
Mary the Queen of Heaven, and himself God's Lieutenant-General
upon earth."

" Ay, ay," said I, " I have read of him in Fox's *Book of
Martyrs.*"

" Well, I do not go straight forward up the flight of steps
conducting into the church, but I turn to the right, and, passing
under the piazza, find myself in a court of the huge bulky house ;
and then ascend various staircases, and pass along various corridors
and galleries, all of which I could describe to you, though I have
never seen them ; at last a door is unlocked, and we enter a room
rather high, but not particularly large, communicating with another
room, into which, however, I do not go, though there are noble
things in that second room—immortal things, by immortal artists ;
amongst others, a grand piece of Corregio ; I do not enter it, for
the grand picture of the world is not there : but I stand still
immediately on entering the first room, and I look straight before
me, neither to the right nor left, though there are noble things
both on the right and left, for immediately before me at the
farther end, hanging against the wall, is a picture which arrests
me, and I can see nothing else, for that picture at the farther end
hanging against the wall is the picture of the world . . ."

Yes, go thy way, young enthusiast, and, whether to London
town or to old Rome, may success attend thee ; yet strange fears
assail me and misgivings on thy account.   Thou canst not rest,
thou say'st, till thou hast seen the picture in the chamber at old
Rome hanging over against the wall ; ay, and thus thou dost
exemplify thy weakness—thy strength too, it may be—for the
one idea, fantastic yet lovely, which now possesses thee, could
only have originated in a genial and fervent brain.   Well, go, if
thou must go ; yet it perhaps were better for thee to bide in thy
native land, and there, with fear and trembling, with groanings,
with straining eyeballs, toil, drudge, slave, till thou hast made
excellence thine own ; thou wilt scarcely acquire it by staring at
the picture over against the door in the high chamber of old
Rome.   Seekest thou inspiration ? thou needest it not, thou hast
it already ; and it was never yet found by crossing the sea.   What
hast thou to do with old Rome, and thou an Englishman ?   " Did
thy blood never glow at the mention of thy native land ? " as an
artist merely ?   Yes, I trow, and with reason, for thy native land
need not grudge old Rome her " pictures of the world " ; she has
pictures of her own, " pictures of England " ; and is it a new thing
to toss up caps and shout—England against the world ?   Yes,
against the world in all, in all ; in science and in arms, in minstrel
strain, and not less in the art " which enables the hand to deceive
the intoxicated soul by means of pictures ".*   Seek'st models ? to

* Klopstock

Gainsborough and Hogarth turn, not names of the world, may
be, but English names—and England against the world! A living
master? why, there he comes! thou hast had him long, he has
long guided thy young hand towards the excellence which is yet
far from thee, but which thou canst attain if thou shouldst persist
and wrestle, even as he has done, midst gloom and despondency
—ay, and even contempt; he who now comes up the creaking
stair to thy little studio in the second floor to inspect thy last
effort before thou departest, the little stout man whose face is very
dark, and whose eye is vivacious; that man has attained excellence,
destined some day to be acknowledged, though not till he is cold,
and his mortal part returned to its kindred clay. He has painted,
not pictures of the world, but English pictures, such as Gainsborough himself might have done; beautiful rural pieces, with
trees which might well tempt the wild birds to perch upon them:
thou needest not run to Rome, brother, where lives the old Mario-
later, after pictures of the world, whilst at home there are pictures
of England; nor needest thou even go to London, the big city,
in search of a master, for thou hast one at home in the old East
Anglian town who can instruct thee whilst thou needest instruction. Better stay at home, brother, at least for a season, and toil
and strive 'midst groanings and despondency till thou hast attained
excellence even as he has done—the little dark man with the
brown coat and the top-boots, whose name will one day be considered the chief ornament of the old town, and whose works will
at no distant period rank among the proudest pictures of England
—and England against the world!—thy master, my brother, thy,
at present, all too little considered master—Crome.

CHAPTER XXII.

But to proceed with my own story: I now ceased all at once to take much pleasure in the pursuits which formerly interested me, I yawned over Ab Gwilym; even as I now in my mind's eye perceive the reader yawning over the present pages. What was the cause of this? Constitutional lassitude, or a desire for novelty? Both it is probable had some influence in the matter, but I rather think that the latter feeling was predominant. The parting words of my brother had sunk into my mind. He had talked of travelling in strange regions and seeing strange and wonderful objects, and my imagination fell to work and drew pictures of adventures wild and fantastic, and I thought what a fine thing it must be to travel, and I wished that my father would give me his blessing, and the same sum that he had given my brother, and bid me go forth into the world; always forgetting that I had neither talents nor energies at this period which would enable me to make any successful figure on its stage.

And then I again sought up the book which had so captivated me in my infancy, and I read it through; and I sought up others of a similar character, and in seeking for them I met books also of adventure, but by no means of a harmless description, lives of wicked and lawless men, Murray and Latroon—books of singular power, but of coarse and prurient imagination—books at one time highly in vogue; now deservedly forgotten, and most difficult to be found.

And when I had gone through these books, what was my state of mind? I had derived entertainment from their perusal, but they left me more listless and unsettled than before, and I really knew not what to do to pass my time. My philological studies had become distasteful, and I had never taken any pleasure in the duties of my profession. I sat behind my desk in a state of torpor, my mind almost as blank as the paper before me, on which I rarely traced a line. It was always a relief to hear the bell ring, as it afforded me an opportunity of doing something which I was yet capable of doing, to rise and open the door and stare in the countenances of the visitors. All of a sudden I fell to studying countenances, and soon flattered myself that I had made considerable progress in the science.

"There is no faith in countenances," said some Roman of old; "trust anything but a person's countenance." "Not trust a man's countenance?" say some moderns, "why, it is the only thing in many people that we can trust; on which account they keep it most assiduously out of the way. Trust not a man's words if you please, or you may come to very erroneous conclusions; but at all times place implicit confidence in a man's countenance, in which there is no deceit; and of necessity there can be none. If people would but look each other more in the face, we should have less cause to complain of the deception of the world; nothing so easy as physiognomy nor so useful." Somewhat in this latter strain I thought, at the time of which I am speaking. I am now older, and let us hope, less presumptuous. It is true that in the course of my life I have scarcely ever had occasion to repent placing confidence in individuals whose countenances have prepossessed me in their favour; though to how many I may have been unjust, from whose countenances I may have drawn unfavourable conclusions, is another matter.

But it had been decreed by Fate, which governs our every action, that I was soon to return to my old pursuits. It was written that I should not yet cease to be Lavengro, though I had become, in my own opinion, a kind of Lavater. It is singular enough that my renewed ardour for philology seems to have been brought about indirectly by my physiognomical researches, in which had I not indulged, the event which I am about to relate, as far as connected with myself, might never have occurred. Amongst the various countenances which I admitted during the period of my answering the bell, there were two which particularly pleased me, and which belonged to an elderly yeoman and his wife, whom some little business had brought to our law sanctuary. I believe they experienced from me some kindness and attention, which won the old people's hearts. So, one day, when their little business had been brought to a conclusion, and they chanced to be alone with me, who was seated as usual behind the deal desk in the outer room, the old man with some confusion began to tell me how grateful himself and dame felt for the many attentions I had shown them, and how desirous they were to make me some remuneration. "Of course," said the old man, "we must be cautious what we offer to so fine a young gentleman as yourself; we have, however, something we think will just suit the occasion,

a strange kind of thing which people say is a book, though no one
that my dame or myself have shown it to can make anything out
of it ; so as we are told that you are a fine young gentleman, who
can read all the tongues of the earth and stars, as the Bible says,
we thought, I and my dame, that it would be just the thing you
would like ; and my dame has it now at the bottom of her
basket."

"A book," said I, "how did you come by it ?"

"We live near the sea," said the old man ; "so near that
sometimes our thatch is wet with the spray ; and it may now be a
year ago that there was a fearful storm, and a ship was driven
ashore during the night, and ere the morn was a complete wreck.
When we got up at daylight, there were the poor shivering crew
at our door ; they were foreigners, red-haired men, whose speech
we did not understand ; but we took them in, and warmed them,
and they remained with us three days ; and when they went away
they left behind them this thing, here it is, part of the contents of
a box which was washed ashore."

"And did you learn who they were ?"

"Why, yes ; they made us understand that they were
Danes."

Danes ! thought I, Danes ! and instantaneously, huge and
grizly, appeared to rise up before my vision the skull of the old
pirate Dane, even as I had seen it of yore in the pent-house of the
ancient church to which, with my mother and my brother, I had
wandered on the memorable summer eve.

And now the old man handed me the book ; a strange and
uncouth-looking volume enough. It was not very large, but instead of the usual covering was bound in wood, and was compressed
with strong iron clasps. It was a printed book, but the pages
were not of paper, but vellum, and the characters were black, and
resembled those generally termed Gothic.

"It is certainly a curious book," said I ; "and I should like
to have it, but I can't think of taking it as a gift, I must give you
an equivalent, I never take presents from anybody."

The old man whispered with his dame and chuckled, and then
turned his face to me and said, with another chuckle : "Well, we
have agreed about the price ; but maybe you will not consent."

"I don't know," said I ; "what do you demand ?"

"Why, that you shake me by the hand, and hold out your
cheek to my old dame, she has taken an affection to you."

"I shall be very glad to shake you by the hand," said I, "but
as for the other condition it requires consideration."

"No consideration at all," said the old man, with something like a sigh; "she thinks you like her son, our only child that was lost twenty years ago in the waves of the North Sea."

"Oh, that alters the case altogether," said I, "and of course I can have no objection."

And now, at once, I shook off my listlessness, to enable me to do which nothing could have happened more opportune than the above event. The Danes, the Danes! And I was at last to become acquainted, and in so singular a manner, with the speech of a people which had as far back as I could remember exercised the strongest influence over my imagination, as how should they not!—in infancy there was the summer-eve adventure, to which I often looked back, and always with a kind of strange interest, with respect to those to whom such gigantic and wondrous bones could belong as I had seen on that occasion; and more than this, I had been in Ireland, and there, under peculiar circumstances, this same interest was increased tenfold. I had mingled much whilst there with the genuine Irish—a wild, but kind-hearted race, whose conversation was deeply imbued with traditionary lore, connected with the early history of their own romantic land, and from them I heard enough of the Danes, but nothing commonplace, for they never mentioned them but in terms which tallied well with my own preconceived ideas. For at an early period the Danes had invaded Ireland, and had subdued it, and, though eventually driven out, had left behind them an enduring remembrance in the minds of the people, who loved to speak of their strength and their stature, in evidence of which they would point to the ancient raths or mounds, where the old Danes were buried, and where bones of extraordinary size were occasionally exhumed. And as the Danes surpassed other people in strength, so, according to my narrators, they also excelled all others in wisdom, or rather in *Draoitheac*, or Magic, for they were powerful sorcerers, they said, compared with whom the fairy men of the present day knew nothing at all, at all! and, amongst other wonderful things, they knew how to make strong beer from the heather that grows upon the bogs. Little wonder if the interest, the mysterious interest, which I had early felt about the Danes, was increased tenfold by my sojourn in Ireland.

And now I had in my possession a Danish book, which, from its appearance, might be supposed to have belonged to the very old Danes indeed; but how was I to turn it to any account? I had the book, it is true, but I did not understand the language,

and how was I to overcome that difficulty? hardly by poring over
the book; yet I did pore over the book, daily and nightly, till my
eyes were dim, and it appeared to me every now and then I
encountered words which I understood—English words, though
strangely disguised; and I said to myself, courage! English and
Danish are cognate dialects, a time will come when I shall understand this Danish; and then I pored over the book again, but
with all my poring I could not understand it; and then I became
angry, and I bit my lips till the blood came; and I occasionally
tore a handful from my hair and flung it upon the floor, but that
did not mend the matter, for still I did not understand the book,
which, however, I began to see was written in rhyme—a circumstance rather difficult to discover at first, the arrangement of the
lines not differing from that which is employed in prose; and its
being written in rhyme made me only the more eager to understand it.

But I toiled in vain, for I had neither grammar nor dictionary
of the language; and when I sought for them could procure
neither; and I was much dispirited, till suddenly a bright thought
came into my head, and I said, although I cannot obtain a
dictionary or grammar, I can perhaps obtain a Bible in this
language, and if I can procure a Bible, I can learn the language,
for the Bible in every tongue contains the same thing, and I have
only to compare the words of the Danish Bible with those of
the English, and, if I persevere, I shall in time acquire the
language of the Danes; and I was pleased with the thought,
which I considered to be a bright one, and I no longer bit my
lips, or tore my hair, but took my hat, and, going forth, I flung
my hat into the air.

And when my hat came down, I put it on my head and
commenced running, directing my course to the house of the
Antinomian preacher, who sold books, and whom I knew to
have Bibles in various tongues amongst the number, and I
arrived out of breath, and I found the Antinomian in his little
library, dusting his books; and the Antinomian clergyman was a
tall man of about seventy, who wore a hat with a broad brim and
a shallow crown, and whose manner of speaking was exceedingly
nasal; and when I saw him, I cried, out of breath, "Have you a
Danish Bible?" and he replied, "What do you want it for,
friend?" and I answered, "to learn Danish by;" "and may be
to learn thy duty," replied the Antinomian preacher. "Truly, I
have it not; but, as you are a customer of mine, I will endeavour
to procure you one, and I will write to that laudable society

which men call the Bible Society, an unworthy member of which
I am, and I hope by next week to procure what you desire."

And when I heard these words of the old man, I was very
glad, and my heart yearned towards him, and I would fain enter
into conversation with him; and I said, "Why are you an
Antinomian? For my part, I would rather be a dog than belong
to such a religion." "Nay, friend," said the Antinomian, "thou
forejudgest us; know that those who call us Antinomians call us
so despitefully, we do not acknowledge the designation." "Then
you do not set all law at nought?" said I. "Far be it from
us," said the old man, "we only hope that, being sanctified by
the Spirit from above, we have no need of the law to keep us in
order. Did you ever hear tell of Lodowick Muggleton?" "Not
I." "That is strange; know then that he was the founder of
our poor society, and after him we are frequently, though op-
probriously, termed Muggletonians, for we are Christians. Here
is his book, which, perhaps, you can do no better than purchase,
you are fond of rare books, and this is both curious and rare; I
will sell it cheap. Thank you, and now be gone, I will do all I
can to procure the Bible."

And in this manner I procured the Danish Bible, and I commenced my task; first of all, however, I locked up in a closet the
volume which had excited my curiosity, saying, "Out of this
closet thou comest not till I deem myself competent to read
thee," and then I sat down in right earnest, comparing every line
in the one version with the corresponding one in the other; and
I passed entire nights in this manner, till I was almost blind, and
the task was tedious enough at first, but I quailed not, and soon
began to make progress. And at first I had a misgiving that the
old book might not prove a Danish book, but was soon reassured
by reading many words in the Bible which I remembered to have
seen in the book; and then I went on right merrily, and I found
that the language which I was studying was by no means a
difficult one, and in less than a month I deemed myself able to
read the book.

Anon, I took the book from the closet, and proceeded to make
myself master of its contents; I had some difficulty, for the
language of the book, though in the main the same as the
language of the Bible, differed from it in some points, being
apparently a more ancient dialect; by degrees, however, I overcame this difficulty, and I understood the contents of the book,
and well did they correspond with all those ideas in which I had
indulged connected with the Danes. For the book was a book

of ballads, about the deeds of knights and champions, and men
of huge stature ; ballads which from time immemorial had been
sung in the North, and which some two centuries before the time
of which I am speaking had been collected by one Anders Vedel,
who lived with a certain Tycho Brahe, and assisted him in
making observations upon the heavenly bodies, at a place called
Uranias Castle, on the little island of Hveen, in the Cattegat.

CHAPTER XXIII.

It might be some six months after the events last recorded, that two individuals were seated together in a certain room, in a certain street of the old town which I have so frequently had occasion to mention in the preceding pages ; one of them was an elderly, and the other a very young man, and they sat on either side of the fire-place, beside a table, on which were fruit and wine ; the room was a small one, and in its furniture exhibited nothing remarkable. Over the mantelpiece, however, hung a small picture with naked figures in the foreground, and with much foliage behind. It might not have struck every beholder, for it looked old and smoke-dried ; but a connoisseur, on inspecting it closely, would have pronounced it to be a Judgment of Paris, and a masterpiece of the Flemish School.

The forehead of the elder individual was high, and perhaps appeared more so than it really was, from the hair being carefully brushed back, as if for the purpose of displaying to the best advantage that part of the cranium ; his eyes were large and full, and of a light brown, and might have been called heavy and dull, had they not been occasionally lighted up by a sudden gleam— not so brilliant, however, as that which at every inhalation shone from the bowl of the long clay pipe he was smoking, but which, from a certain sucking sound which about this time began to be heard from the bottom, appeared to be giving notice that it would soon require replenishment from a certain canister, which, together with a lighted taper, stood upon the table beside him.

"You do not smoke?" said he, at length, laying down his pipe, and directing his glance to his companion.

Now there was at least one thing singular connected with this last, namely, the colour of his hair, which, notwithstanding his extreme youth, appeared to be rapidly becoming grey. He had very long limbs, and was apparently tall of stature, in which he differed from his elderly companion, who must have been somewhat below the usual height.

"No, I can't smoke," said the youth in reply to the observation of the other. "I have often tried, but could never succeed to my satisfaction."

"Is it possible to become a good German without smoking?" said the senior, half-speaking to himself.

"I dare say not," said the youth; "but I shan't break my heart on that account."

"As for breaking your heart, of course you would never think of such a thing; he is a fool who breaks his heart on any account; but it is good to be a German, the Germans are the most philosophic people in the world, and the greatest smokers; now I trace their philosophy to their smoking."

"I have heard say their philosophy is all smoke—is that your opinion?"

"Why, no; but smoking has a sedative effect upon the nerves, and enables a man to bear the sorrows of this life (of which every one has his share) not only decently, but dignifiedly. Suicide is not a national habit in Germany as it is in England."

"But that poor creature, Werther, who committed suicide, was a German."

"Werther is a fictitious character, and by no means a felicitous one; I am no admirer either of Werther or his author. But I should say that, if there was a Werther in Germany, he did not smoke. Werther, as you very justly observe, was a poor creature."

"And a very sinful one; I have heard my parents say that suicide is a great crime."

"Broadly, and without qualification, to say that suicide is a crime, is speaking somewhat unphilosophically. No doubt suicide, under many circumstances, is a crime, a very heinous one. When the father of a family, for example, to escape from certain difficulties, commits suicide, he commits a crime; there are those around him who look to him for support, by the law of nature, and he has no right to withdraw himself from those who have a claim upon his exertions; he is a person who decamps with other people's goods as well as his own. Indeed, there can be no crime which is not founded upon the depriving others of something which belongs to them. A man is hanged for setting fire to his house in a crowded city, for he burns at the same time or damages those of other people; but if a man who has a house on a heath sets fire to it, he is not hanged, for he has not damaged or endangered any other individual's property, and the principle of revenge, upon which all punishment is founded, has not been

aroused.   Similar to such a case is that of the man who, without
any family ties, commits suicide ; for example, were I to do the
thing this evening, who would have a right to call me to account ?
I am alone in the world, have no family to support and, so far
from damaging any one, should even benefit my heir by my ac-
celerated death.   However, I am no advocate for suicide under
any circumstances ; there is something undignified in it, unheroic,
un-Germanic.   But if you must commit suicide—and there is no
knowing to what people may be brought—always contrive to do
it as decorously as possible ; the decencies, whether of life or
of death, should never be lost sight of.   I remember a female
Quaker who committed suicide by cutting her throat, but she did
it decorously and decently : kneeling down over a pail, so that
not one drop fell upon the floor, thus exhibiting in her last act
that nice sense of neatness for which Quakers are distinguished.
I have always had a respect for that woman's memory."

And here, filling his pipe from the canister, and lighting it at
the taper, he recommenced smoking calmly and sedately.

" But is not suicide forbidden in the Bible?" the youth
demanded.

"Why, no ; but what though it were !—the Bible is a respectable book, but I should hardly call it one whose philosophy is of
the soundest.   I have said that it is a respectable book ; I mean
respectable from its antiquity, and from containing, as Herder says,
' the earliest records of the human race,' though those records are
far from being dispassionately written, on which account they are
of less value than they otherwise might have been.   There is too
much passion in the Bible, too much violence ; now, to come to
all truth, especially historic truth, requires cool, dispassionate investigation, for which the Jews do not appear to have ever been
famous.   We are ourselves not famous for it, for we are a
passionate people ; the Germans are not—they are not a passionate people—a people celebrated for their oaths : we are.   The
Germans have many excellent historic writers, we—'tis true we
have Gibbon.   You have been reading Gibbon—what do you
think of him ? "

" I think him a very wonderful writer."

" He is a wonderful writer—one *sui generis*—uniting the per-
spicuity of the English—for we are perspicuous—with the cool,
dispassionate reasoning of the Germans.   Gibbon sought after
the truth, found it, and made it clear."

' Then you think Gibbon a truthful writer."

'Why, yes ; who shall convict Gibbon of falsehood ?   Many

people have endeavoured to convict Gibbon of falsehood; they have followed him in his researches, and have never found him once tripping. Oh, he's a wonderful writer! his power of condensation is admirable; the lore of the whole world is to be found in his pages. Sometimes in a single note he has given us the result of the study of years; or, to speak metaphorically, 'he has ransacked a thousand Gulistans, and has condensed all his fragrant booty into a single drop of otto'."

"But was not Gibbon an enemy to the Christian faith?"

"Why, no; he was rather an enemy to priestcraft, so am I; and when I say the philosophy of the Bible is in many respects unsound, I always wish to make an exception in favour of that part of it which contains the life and sayings of Jesus of Bethlehem, to which I must always concede my unqualified admiration—of Jesus, mind you; for with his followers and their dogmas I have nothing to do. Of all historic characters, Jesus is the most beautiful and the most heroic. I have always been a friend to hero-worship, it is the only rational one, and has always been in use amongst civilised people—the worship of spirits is synonymous with barbarism—it is mere fetish; the savages of West Africa are all spirit worshippers. But there is something philosophic in the worship of the heroes of the human race, and the true hero is the benefactor. Brahma, Jupiter, Bacchus, were all benefactors, and, therefore, entitled to the worship of their respective peoples. The Celts worshipped Hesus, who taught them to plough, a highly useful art. We, who have attained a much higher state of civilisation than the Celts ever did, worship Jesus, the first who endeavoured to teach men to behave decently and decorously under all circumstances; who was the foe of vengeance, in which there is something highly indecorous; who had first the courage to lift his voice against that violent dogma, 'an eye for an eye'; who shouted conquer, but conquer with kindness; who said put up the sword, a violent, unphilosophic weapon; and who finally died calmly and decorously in defence of his philosophy. He must be a savage who denies worship to the hero of Golgotha."

"But he was something more than a hero; he was the Son of God, wasn't he?"

The elderly individual made no immediate answer; but, after a few more whiffs from his pipe, exclaimed: "Come, fill your glass! How do you advance with your translation of Tell?"

"It is nearly finished; but I do not think I shall proceed with it; I begin to think the original somewhat dull."

"There you are wrong; it is the masterpiece of Schiller, the first of German poets."

"It may be so," said the youth. "But, pray excuse me, I do not think very highly of German poetry. I have lately been reading Shakespeare, and, when I turn from him to the Germans— even the best of them—they appear mere pigmies. You will pardon the liberty I perhaps take in saying so."

"I like that every one should have an opinion of his own," said the elderly individual; "and, what is more, declare it. Nothing displeases me more than to see people assenting to everything that they hear said; I at once come to the conclusion that they are either hypocrites, or there is nothing in them. But, with respect to Shakespeare, whom I have not read for thirty years, is he not rather given to bombast, 'crackling bombast,' as I think I have said in one of my essays?"

"I daresay he is," said the youth; "but I can't help thinking him the greatest of all poets, not even excepting Homer. I would sooner have written that series of plays, founded on the fortunes of the House of Lancaster, than the *Iliad* itself. The events described are as lofty as those sung by Homer in his great work, and the characters brought upon the stage still more interesting. I think Hotspur as much of a hero as Hector, and young Henry more of a man than Achilles; and then there is the fat knight, the quintessence of fun, wit, and rascality. Falstaff is a creation beyond the genius even of Homer."

"You almost tempt me to read Shakespeare again—but the Germans?"

"I don't admire the Germans," said the youth, somewhat excited. "I don't admire them in any point of view. I have heard my father say that, though good sharpshooters, they can't be much depended upon as soldiers; and that old Sergeant Meredith told him that Minden would never have been won but for the two English regiments, who charged the French with fixed bayonets, and sent them to the right-about in double-quick time. With respect to poetry, setting Shakespeare and the English altogether aside, I think there is another Gothic nation, at least, entitled to dispute with them the palm. Indeed, to my mind, there is more genuine poetry contained in the old Danish book which I came so strangely by, than has been produced in Germany from the period of the Niebelungen Lay to the present."

"Ah, the Kœmpe Viser?" said the elderly individual, breathing forth an immense volume of smoke, which he had been collecting during the declamation of his young companion. "There

are singular things in that book, I must confess; and I thank you
for showing it to me, or rather your attempt at translation.   I was
struck with that ballad of Orm Ungarswayne, who goes by night
to the grave-hill of his father to seek for counsel.   And then,
again, that strange melancholy Swayne Vonved, who roams about
the world propounding people riddles; slaying those who cannot
answer, and rewarding those who can with golden bracelets.
Were it not for the violence, I should say that ballad has a philosophic tendency.   I thank you for making me acquainted with
the book, and I thank the Jew Mousha for making me acquainted
with you."

"That Mousha was a strange customer," said the youth,
collecting himself.

"He *was* a strange customer," said the elder individual,
breathing forth a gentle cloud.   "I love to exercise hospitality to
wandering strangers, especially foreigners; and when he came to
this place, pretending to teach German and Hebrew, I asked him
to dinner.   After the first dinner, he asked me to lend him five
pounds; I *did* lend him five pounds.   After the fifth dinner, he
asked me to lend him fifty pounds; I did *not* lend him the fifty
pounds."

"He was as ignorant of German as of Hebrew," said the
youth; "on which account he was soon glad, I suppose, to
transfer his pupil to some one else."

"He told me," said the elder individual, "that he intended
to leave a town where he did not find sufficient encouragement;
and, at the same time, expressed regret at being obliged to abandon
a certain extraordinary pupil, for whom he had a particular regard.
Now I, who have taught many people German from the love
which I bear to it, and the desire which I feel that it should be
generally diffused, instantly said, that I should be happy to take
his pupil off his hands, and afford him what instruction I could
in German, for, as to Hebrew, I have never taken much interest
in it.   Such was the origin of our acquaintance.   You have been
an apt scholar.   Of late, however, I have seen little of you—what
is the reason?"

The youth made no answer.

"You think, probably, that you have learned all I can teach
you?   Well, perhaps you are right."

"Not so, not so," said the young man eagerly; "before I
knew you I knew nothing, and am still very ignorant; but of late
my father's health has been very much broken, and he requires
attention; his spirits also have become low, which, to tell you the

truth, he attributes to my misconduct. He says that I have imbibed all kinds of strange notions and doctrines, which will, in all probability, prove my ruin, both here and hereafter; which— which ——"

"Ah! I understand," said the elder, with another calm whiff. "I have always had a kind of respect for your father, for there is something remarkable in his appearance, something heroic, and I would fain have cultivated his acquaintance; the feeling, however, has not been reciprocated. I met him, the other day, up the road, with his cane and dog, and saluted him; he did not return my salutation."

"He has certain opinions of his own," said the youth, "which are widely different from those which he has heard that you profess."

"I respect a man for entertaining an opinion of his own," said the elderly individual. "I hold certain opinions; but I should not respect an individual the more for adopting them. All I wish for is tolerance, which I myself endeavour to practise. I have always loved the truth, and sought it; if I have not found it, the greater my misfortune."

"Are you happy?" said the young man.

"Why, no! And, between ourselves, it is that which induces me to doubt sometimes the truth of my opinions. My life, upon the whole, I consider a failure; on which account I would not counsel you, or any one, to follow my example too closely. It is getting late, and you had better be going, especially as your father, you say, is anxious about you. But, as we may never meet again, I think there are three things which I may safely venture to press upon you. The first is, that the decencies and gentlenesses should never be lost sight of, as the practice of the decencies and gentlenesses is at all times compatible with independence of thought and action. The second thing which I would wish to impress upon you is, that there is always some eye upon us; and that it is impossible to keep anything we do from the world, as it will assuredly be divulged by somebody as soon as it is his interest to do so. The third thing which I would wish to press upon you ——"

"Yes," said the youth, eagerly bending forward.

"Is ——" and here the elderly individual laid down his pipe upon the table—"that it will be as well to go on improving yourself in German!"

CHAPTER XXIV.

" Holloa, master ! can you tell us where the fight is likely to be ? "

Such were the words shouted out to me by a short thick fellow in brown top-boots, and bare-headed, who stood, with his hands in his pockets, at the door of a country alehouse as I was passing by.

Now, as I knew nothing about the fight, and as the appearance of the man did not tempt me greatly to enter into conversation with him, I merely answered in the negative and continued my way. *

It was a fine lovely morning in May, the sun shone bright above, and the birds were carolling in the hedgerows. I was wont to be cheerful at such seasons, for, from my earliest recollection, sunshine and the song of birds have been dear to me ; yet, about that period, I was not cheerful, my mind was not at rest ; I was debating within myself, and the debate was dreary and unsatisfactory enough. I sighed, and turning my eyes upward, I ejaculated : " What is truth ? " But suddenly, by a violent effort breaking away from my meditations, I hastened forward ; one mile, two miles, three miles were speedily left behind ; and now I came to a grove of birch and other trees, and opening a gate I passed up a kind of avenue, and soon arriving before a large brick house, of rather antique appearance, knocked at the door.

In this house there lived a gentleman with whom I had business. He was said to be a genuine old English gentleman, and a man of considerable property ; at this time, however, he wanted a thousand pounds, as gentlemen of considerable property every now and then do. I had brought him a thousand pounds in my pocket, for it is astonishing how many eager helpers the rich find, and with what compassion people look upon their distresses. He was said to have good wine in his cellar.

" Is your master at home ? " said I, to a servant who appeared at the door.

" His worship is at home, young man," said the servant, as he looked at my shoes, which bore evidence that I had come walking. "I beg your pardon, sir," he added, as he looked me in the face.

"Ay, ay, servants," thought I, as I followed the man into the house, "always look people in the face when you open the door, and do so before you look at their shoes, or you may mistake the heir of a Prime Minister for a shopkeeper's son."

I found his worship a jolly, red-faced gentleman, of about fifty-five; he was dressed in a green coat, white corduroy breeches, and drab gaiters, and sat on an old-fashioned leather sofa, with two small, thorough-bred, black English terriers, one on each side of him. He had all the appearance of a genuine old English gentleman who kept good wine in his cellar.

"Sir," said I, "I have brought you a thousand pounds;" and I said this after the servant had retired, and the two terriers had ceased their barking, which is natural to all such dogs at the sight of a stranger.

And when the magistrate had received the money, and signed and returned a certain paper which I handed to him, he rubbed his hands, and looking very benignantly at me, exclaimed :—

"And now, young gentleman, that our business is over, perhaps you can tell me where the fight is to take place?"

"I am sorry, sir," said I, "that I can't inform you, but everybody seems to be anxious about it;" and then I told him what had occurred to me on the road with the alehouse keeper.

"I know him," said his worship; "he's a tenant of mine, and a good fellow, somewhat too much in my debt, though. But how is this, young gentleman, you look as if you had been walking; you did not come on foot?"

"Yes, sir, I came on foot."

"On foot! why, it is sixteen miles."

"I shan't be tired when I have walked back."

"You can't ride, I suppose?"

"Better than I can walk."

"Then why do you walk?"

"I have frequently to make journeys connected with my profession; sometimes I walk, sometimes I ride, just as the whim takes me."

"Will you take a glass of wine?"

"Yes."

"That's right; what shall it be?"

"Madeira!"

The magistrate gave a violent slap on his knee; "I like your taste," said he, "I am fond of a glass of Madeira myself, and can give you such a one as you will not drink every day; sit down, young gentleman, you shall have a glass of Madeira, and the best I have."

Thereupon he got up, and, followed by his two terriers, walked slowly out of the room.

I looked round the room, and, seeing nothing which promised me much amusement, I sat down, and fell again into my former train of thought.

" What is truth?" said I.

" Here it is," said the magistrate, returning at the end of a quarter of an hour, followed by the servant with a tray; "here's the true thing, or I am no judge, far less a justice. It has been thirty years in my cellar last Christmas. There," said he to the servant, "put it down, and leave my young friend and me to ourselves. Now, what do you think of it?"

" It is very good," said I.

" Did you ever taste better Madeira?"

" I never before tasted Madeira."

" Then you ask for a wine without knowing what it is?"

" I ask for it, sir, that I may know what it is."

" Well, there is logic in that, as Parr would say; you have heard of Parr?"

" Old Parr?"

" Yes, old Parr, but not that Parr; you mean the English, I the Greek Parr, as people call him."

" I don't know him."

" Perhaps not—rather too young for that, but were you of my age, you might have cause to know him, coming from where you do. He kept school there, I was his first scholar.; he flogged Greek into me till I loved him—and he loved me. He came to see me last year, and sat in that chair; I honour Parr—he knows much, and is a sound man."

" Does he know the truth?"

" Know the truth! he knows what's good, from an oyster to an ostrich—he's not only sound but round."

" Suppose we drink his health?"

" Thank you, boy: here's Parr's health, and Whiter's."

" Who is Whiter?"

" Don't you know Whiter? I thought everybody knew Reverend Whiter, the philologist, though I suppose you scarcely know what that means. A man fond of tongues and languages, quite out of your way—he understands some twenty; what do you say to that?"

"Is he a sound man?"

"Why, as to that, I scarcely know what to say; he has got queer notions in his head—wrote a book to prove that all words came originally from the earth—who knows? Words have roots, and roots live in the earth; but, upon the whole, I should not call him altogether a sound man, though he can talk Greek nearly as fast as Parr."

"Is he a round man?"

"Ay, boy, rounder than Parr; I'll sing you a song, if you like, which will let you into his character :—

'Give me the haunch of a buck to eat, and to drink Madeira old,
And a gentle wife to rest with, and in my arms to fold,
An Arabic book to study, a Norfolk cob to ride,
And a house to live in shaded with trees, and near to a river side;
With such good things around me, and blessed with good health withal,
Though I should live for a hundred years, for death I would not call.'

Here's to Whiter's health—so you know nothing about the fight?"

"No, sir; the truth is, that of late I have been very much occupied with various matters, otherwise I should, perhaps, have been able to afford you some information. Boxing is a noble art."

"Can you box?"

"A little."

"I tell you what, my boy; I honour you, and, provided your education had been a little less limited, I should have been glad to see you here in company with Parr and Whiter; both can box. Boxing is, as you say, a noble art—a truly English art; may I never see the day when Englishmen shall feel ashamed of it, or blacklegs and blackguards bring it into disgrace! I am a magistrate, and, of course, cannot patronise the thing very openly, yet I sometimes see a prize-fight. I saw the Game Chicken beat Gulley."

"Did you ever see Big Ben?"

"No, why do you ask?" But here we heard a noise, like that of a gig driving up to the door, which was immediately succeeded by a violent knocking and ringing, and after a little time, the servant who had admitted me made his appearance in the room.

"Sir," said he, with a certain eagerness of manner, "here are two gentlemen waiting to speak to you."

"Gentlemen waiting to speak to me! who are they?"

"I don't know, sir," said the servant; "but they look like sporting gentlemen, and—and"—here he hesitated; "from a word or two they dropped, I almost think that they come about the fight."

"About the fight," said the magistrate. "No, that can hardly be; however, you had better show them in."

Heavy steps were now heard ascending the stairs, and the servant ushered two men into the apartment. Again there was a barking, but louder than that which had been directed against myself, for here were two intruders; both of them were remarkable looking men, but to the foremost of them the most particular notice may well be accorded: he was a man somewhat under thirty, and nearly six feet in height. He was dressed in a blue coat, white corduroy breeches, fastened below the knee with small golden buttons; on his legs he wore white lamb's-wool stockings, and on his feet shoes reaching to the ankles; round his neck was a handkerchief of the blue and bird's-eye pattern; he wore neither whiskers nor moustaches, and appeared not to delight in hair, that of his head, which was of a light brown, being closely cropped; the forehead was rather high, but somewhat narrow; the face neither broad nor sharp, perhaps rather sharp than broad; the nose was almost delicate; the eyes were grey, with an expression in which there was sternness blended with something approaching to feline; his complexion was exceedingly pale, relieved, however, by certain pockmarks, which here and there studded his countenance; his form was athletic, but lean; his arms long. In the whole appearance of the man there was a blending of the bluff and the sharp. You might have supposed him a bruiser; his dress was that of one in all its minutiæ; something was wanting, however, in his manner—the quietness of the professional man; he rather looked liked one performing the part —well—very well—but still performing a part. His companion! —there, indeed, was the bruiser—no mistake about him: a tall, massive man, with a broad countenance and a flattened nose; dressed like a bruiser, but not like a bruiser going into the ring; he wore white topped boots, and a loose brown jockey coat.

As the first advanced towards the table, behind which the magistrate sat, he doffed a white castor from his head, and made rather a genteel bow; looking at me, who sat somewhat on one side, he gave a kind of nod of recognition.

"May I request to know who you are, gentlemen?" said the magistrate.

"Sir," said the man in a deep, but not unpleasant voice, "allow me to introduce to you my friend, Mr. ——, the celebrated pugilist;" and he motioned with his hand towards the massive man with the flattened nose.

"And your own name, sir?" said the magistrate.

"My name is no matter," said the man; "were I to mention

it to you, it would awaken within you no feeling of interest. It
is neither Kean nor Belcher, and I have as yet done nothing to
distinguish myself like either of those individuals, or even like
my friend here. However, a time may come—we are not yet
buried; and whensoever my hour arrives, I hope I shall prove
myself equal to my destiny, however high—

'Like bird that's bred amongst the Helicons'."

And here a smile half-theatrical passed over his features.

"In what can I oblige you, sir?" said the magistrate.

"Well, sir; the soul of wit is brevity; we want a place for an
approaching combat between my friend here and a brave from
town. Passing by your broad acres this fine morning we saw a
pightle, which we deemed would suit. Lend us that pightle, and
receive our thanks; 'twould be a favour, though not much to
grant: we neither ask for Stonehenge nor for Tempe."

My friend looked somewhat perplexed; after a moment, however, he said, with a firm but gentlemanly air: "Sir, I am sorry
that I cannot comply with your request".

"Not comply!" said the man, his brow becoming dark as
midnight; and with a hoarse and savage tone: "Not comply!
why not?"

"It is impossible, sir; utterly impossible!"

"Why so?"

"I am not compelled to give my reasons to you, sir, nor
to any man."

"Let me beg of you to alter your decision," said the man
in a tone of profound respect.

"Utterly impossible, sir; I am a magistrate."

"Magistrate! then fare ye well, for a green-coated buffer and
a Harmanbeck."

"Sir!" said the magistrate, springing up with a face fiery
with wrath.

But, with a surly nod to me, the man left the apartment;
and in a moment more the heavy footsteps of himself and his
companion were heard descending the staircase.

"Who is that man?" said my friend, turning towards me.

"A sporting gentleman, well known in the place from which
I come."

"He appeared to know you."

"I have occasionally put on the gloves with him."

"What is his name?[1]

[1] *MS.*, "John Thurtell".

CHAPTER XXV.

THERE was one question which I was continually asking myself at this period, and which has more than once met the eyes of the reader who has followed me through the last chapter. " What is truth ? " I had involved myself imperceptibly in a dreary labyrinth of doubt, and, whichever way I turned, no reasonable prospect of extricating myself appeared. The means by which I had brought myself into this situation may be very briefly told; I had inquired into many matters, in order that I might become wise, and I had read and pondered over the words of the wise, so called, till I had made myself master of the sum of human wisdom ; namely, that everything is enigmatical and that man is an enigma to himself; thence the cry of " What is truth ? " I had ceased to believe in the truth of that in which I had hitherto trusted, and yet could find nothing in which I could put any fixed or deliberate belief. I was, indeed, in a labyrinth ! In what did I not doubt ? With respect to crime and virtue I was in doubt ; I doubted that the one was blameable and the other praiseworthy. Are not all things subjected to the law of necessity ? Assuredly ; time and chance govern all things : yet how can this be ? alas !

Then there was myself; for what was I born ? Are not all things born to be forgotten ? That's incomprehensible : yet is it not so ? Those butterflies fall and are forgotten. In what is man better than a butterfly ? All then is born to be forgotten. Ah ! that was a pang indeed ; 'tis at such a moment that a man wishes to die. The wise king of Jerusalem, who sat in his shady arbours beside his sunny fishpools, saying so many fine things, wished to die, when he saw that not only all was vanity, but that he himself was vanity. Will a time come when all will be forgotten that now is beneath the sun ? If so, of what profit is life ?

In truth, it was a sore vexation of spirit to me when I saw, as the wise man saw of old, that whatever I could hope to perform must necessarily be of very temporary duration ; and if so, why do it ? I said to myself, whatever name I can acquire, will it endure for eternity ? scarcely so. A thousand years ? Let me see! What have I done already? I have learnt Welsh, and have translated the songs of Ab Gwilym, some ten thousand lines, into English rhyme; I have also learnt Danish, and have rendered the old book of ballads cast by the tempest upon the beach into corresponding English metre. Good! have I done enough already to secure myself a reputation of a thousand years? No, no! certainly not; I have not the slightest ground for hoping that my translations from the Welsh and Danish will be read at the end of a thousand years. Well, but I am only eighteen, and I have not stated all that I have done; I have learnt many other tongues, and have acquired some knowledge even of Hebrew and Arabic. Should I go on in this way till I am forty, I must then be very learned; and perhaps, among other things, may have translated the Talmud, and some of the great works of the Arabians. Pooh! all this is mere learning and translation, and such will never secure immortality. Translation is at best an echo, and it must be a wonderful echo to be heard after the lapse of a thousand years. No! all I have already done, and all I may yet do in the same way, I may reckon as nothing—mere pastime; something else must be done. I must either write some grand original work, or conquer an empire; the one just as easy as the other. But am I competent to do either? Yes, I think I am, under favourable circumstances. Yes, I think I may promise myself a reputation of a thousand years, if I do but give myself the necessary trouble. Well! but what's a thousand years after all, or twice a thousand years? Woe is me! I may just as well sit still.

"Would I had never been born!" I said to myself; and a thought would occasionally intrude. But was I ever born? Is not all that I see a lie—a deceitful phantom? Is there a world, and earth, and sky? Berkeley's doctrine—Spinosa's doctrine! Dear reader, I had at that time never read either Berkeley or Spinosa. I have still never read them; who are they, men of yesterday? "All is a lie—all a deceitful phantom," are old cries; they come naturally from the mouths of those, who, casting aside that choicest shield against madness, simplicity, would fain be wise as God, and can only know that they are naked. This doubting in the "universal all" is almost coeval with the human race: wisdom, so called, was early sought after. All is a lie—a deceitful phantom—was said when the world was yet young; its surface, save a scanty portion, yet untrodden by human foot, and when the great tortoise yet crawled about. All is a lie, was the doctrine of Buddh; and Buddh lived thirty centuries before the wise king of Jerusalem, who sat in his arbours, beside his sunny fishpools, saying many fine things, and, amongst others, "There is nothing new under the sun!"

One day, whilst I bent my way to the heath of which I have spoken on a former occasion, at the foot of the hills which formed it I came to a place where a wagon was standing, but without horses, the shafts resting on the ground; there was a crowd about it, which extended half-way up the side of the neighbouring hill. The wagon was occupied by some half a dozen men; some sitting, others standing. They were dressed in sober-coloured habiliments of black or brown, cut in plain and rather uncouth fashion, and partially white with dust; their hair was short, and seemed to have been smoothed down by the application of the hand; all were bare-headed—sitting or standing, all were bare-headed. One of them, a tall man, was speaking, as I arrived; ere, however, I could distinguish what he was saying, he left off, and then there was a cry for a hymn "to the glory of God"— that was the word. It was a strange-sounding hymn, as well it might be, for everybody joined in it: there were voices of all kinds, of men, of women, and of children—of those who could sing and of those who could not—a thousand voices all joined, and all joined heartily; no voice of all the multitude was silent save mine. The crowd consisted entirely of the lower classes, labourers, and mechanics, and their wives and children—dusty people, unwashed people, people of no account whatever, and yet they did not look a mob. And when that hymn was over—and here let me observe that, strange as it sounded, I have recalled that hymn to mind, and it has seemed to tingle in my ears on occasions when all that pomp and art could do to enhance religious solemnity was being done—in the Sistine Chapel, what time the papal band was in full play, and the choicest choristers of Italy poured forth their melodious tones in presence of Batuschca and his cardinals—on the ice of the Neva, what time the long train of stately priests, with their noble beards and their flowing robes of crimson and gold, with their ebony and ivory staves, stalked along, chanting their Sclavonian litanies in advance of the mighty Emperor of the North and his Priberjensky guard of giants, towards the orifice through which the river, running below in its swiftness, is to receive the baptismal lymph— when the hymn was over, another man in the wagon proceeded to address the people; he was a much younger man than the last speaker; somewhat square built and about the middle height; his face was rather broad, but expressive of much intelligence, and

with a peculiar calm and serious look; the accent in which he
spoke indicated that he was not of these parts, but from some
distant district. The subject of his address was faith, and how
it could remove mountains. It was a plain address, without any
attempt at ornament, and delivered in a tone which was neither
loud nor vehement. The speaker was evidently not a practised
one—once or twice he hesitated as if for words to express his
meaning, but still he held on, talking of faith, and how it could
remove mountains: "It is the only thing we want, brethren, in
this world; if we have that, we are indeed rich, as it will enable
us to do our duty under all circumstances, and to bear our lot,
however hard it may be—and the lot of all mankind is hard—
the lot of the poor is hard, brethren—and who knows more of the.
poor than I?—a poor man myself, and the son of a poor man:
but are the rich better off? not so, brethren, for God is just.
The rich have their trials too: I am not rich myself, but I have
seen the rich with careworn countenances; I have also seen them
in mad-houses; from which you may learn, brethren, that the lot
of all mankind is hard; that is, till we lay hold of faith, which
makes us comfortable under all circumstances; whether we ride
in gilded chariots or walk bare-footed in quest of bread; whether
we be ignorant, whether we be wise,—for riches and poverty,
ignorance and wisdom, brethren, each brings with it its peculiar
temptations. Well, under all these troubles, the thing which I
would recommend you to seek is one and the same—faith; faith
in our Lord Jesus Christ, who made us and allotted to each his
station. Each has something to do, brethren. Do it, therefore,
but always in faith; without faith we shall find ourselves sometimes at fault; but with faith never—for faith can remove the
difficulty. It will teach us to love life, brethren, when life is
becoming bitter, and to prize the blessings around us; for as every
man has his cares, brethren, so has each man his blessings. It
will likewise teach us not to love life over much, seeing that we
must one day part with it. It will teach us to face death with
resignation, and will preserve us from sinking amidst the swelling
of the river Jordan."

And when he had concluded his address, he said: "Let us
sing a hymn, one composed by Master Charles Wesley—he was
my countryman, brethren.

> ' Jesus, I cast my soul on Thee,
> Mighty and merciful to save;
> Thou shalt to death go down with me,
> And lay me gently in the grave.

This body then shall rest in hope,
This body which the worms destroy ;
For Thou shalt surely raise me up,
To glorious life and endless joy.' "

Farewell, preacher with the plain coat, and the calm, serious
look ! I saw thee once again, and that was lately—only the other
day. It was near a fishing hamlet, by the sea-side, that I saw
the preacher again. He stood on the top of a steep monticle,
used by pilots as a look-out for vessels approaching that coast,
a dangerous one, abounding in rocks and quicksands. There he
stood on the monticle, preaching to weather-worn fishermen and
mariners gathered below upon the sand. "Who is he?" said I
to an old fisherman, who stood beside me with a book of hymns
in his hand; but the old man put his hand to his lips, and that
was the only answer I received. Not a sound was heard but the
voice of the preacher and the roaring of the waves ; but the voice
was heard loud above the roaring of the sea, for the preacher now
spoke with power, and his voice was not that of one who hesitates.
There he stood—no longer a young man, for his black locks were
become gray, even like my own ; but there was the intelligent face,
and the calm, serious look which had struck me of yore. There
stood the preacher, one of those men—and, thank God, their
number is not few—who, animated by the spirit of Christ, amidst
much poverty, and, alas! much contempt, persist in carrying
the light of the Gospel amidst the dark parishes of what, but for
their instrumentality, would scarcely be Christian England. I
would have waited till he had concluded, in order that I might
speak to him and endeavour to bring back the ancient scene to
his recollection, but suddenly a man came hurrying towards the
monticle, mounted on a speedy horse, and holding by the bridle
one yet more speedy, and he whispered to me: "Why loiterest
thou here?—knowest thou not all that is to be done before
midnight?" and he flung me the bridle; and I mounted on the
horse of great speed, and I followed the other, who had already
galloped off. And as I departed, I waved my hand to him on the
monticle, and I shouted, "Farewell, brother! the seed came up at
last, after a long period!" and then I gave the speedy horse his
way, and leaning over the shoulder of the galloping horse, I said:
"Would that my life had been like his—even like that man's !"

I now wandered along the heath, till I came to a place where,
beside a thick furze, sat a man, his eyes fixed intently on the red
ball of the setting sun.

"That's not you, Jasper?"

"Indeed, brother!"

"I've not seen you for years."

"How should you, brother?"

"What brings you here?"

"The fight, brother."

"Where are the tents?"

"On the old spot, brother."

"Any news since we parted?"

"Two deaths, brother."

"Who are dead, Jasper?"

"Father and mother, brother."

"Where did they die?"

"Where they were sent, brother."

"And Mrs. Herne?"

"She's alive, brother."

"Where is she now?"

"In Yorkshire, brother."

"What is your opinion of death, Mr. Petulengro?" said I, as I sat down beside him.

"My opinion of death, brother, is much the same as that in the old song of Pharaoh, which I have heard my grandam sing:—

'Cana marel o manus chivios andé puv,
Ta rovel pa leste o chavo ta romi'.

When a man dies, he is cast into the earth, and his wife and child sorrow over him. If he has neither wife nor child, then his father and mother, I suppose; and if he is quite alone in the world, why, then, he is cast into the earth, and there is an end of the matter."

"And do you think that is the end of a man?"

"There's an end of him, brother, more's the pity."

"Why do you say so?"

"Life is sweet, brother."

"Do you think so?"

"Think so! There's night and day, brother, both sweet things; sun, moon and stars, brother, all sweet things; there's likewise the wind on the heath. Life is very sweet, brother; who would wish to die?"

"I would wish to die ——"

"You talk like a gorgio—which is the same as talking like a fool—were you a Rommany Chal you would talk wiser. Wish to die, indeed! A Rommany Chal would wish to live for ever!"

"In sickness, Jasper?"

"There's the sun and stars, brother."

"In blindness, Jasper?"

"There's the wind on the heath, brother; if I could only feel that, I would gladly live for ever.   Dosta, we'll now go to the tents and put on the gloves; and I'll try to make you feel what a sweet thing it is to be alive, brother!"

CHAPTER XXVI.

How for everything there is a time and a season, and then how does the glory of a thing pass from it, even like the flower of the grass! This is a truism, but it is one of those which are continually forcing themselves upon the mind. Many years have not passed over my head, yet during those which I can call to remembrance, how many things have I seen flourish, pass away, and become forgotten, except by myself, who, in spite of all my endeavours, never can forget anything. I have known the time when a pugilistic encounter between two noted champions was almost considered in the light of a national affair; when tens of thousands of individuals, high and low, meditated and brooded upon it, the first thing in the morning and the last at night, until the great event was decided. But the time is past, and many people will say, thank God that it is; all I have to say is, that the French still live on the other side of the water, and are still casting their eyes hitherward—and that in the days of pugilism it was no vain boast to say, that one Englishman was a match for two of t'other race; at present it would be a vain boast to say so, for these are not the days of pugilism.

But those to which the course of my narrative has carried me were the days of pugilism; it was then at its height, and consequently near its decline, for corruption had crept into the ring; and how many things, states and sects among the rest, owe their decline to this cause! But what a bold and vigorous aspect pugilism wore at that time! and the great battle was just then coming off; the day had been decided upon, and the spot—a convenient distance from the old town; and to the old town were now flocking the bruisers of England, men of tremendous renown. Let no one sneer at the bruisers of England—what were the gladiators of Rome, or the bull-fighters of Spain, in its palmiest days, compared to England's bruisers? Pity that ever corruption should have crept in amongst them—but of that I wish not to talk; let us still hope that a spark of the old religion, of which they were the priests, still lingers in the breasts of Englishmen.

There they come, the bruisers, from far London, or from wherever else they might chance to be at that time, to the great rendezvous in the old city ; some came one way, some another : some of tip-top reputation came with peers in their chariots, for glory and fame are such fair things that even peers are proud to have those invested therewith by their sides ; others came in their own gigs, driving their own bits of blood, and I heard one say : " I have driven through at a heat the whole 111 miles, and only stopped to bait twice ". Oh, the blood-horses of old England ! but they too have had their day—for everything beneath the sun there is a season and a time. But the greater number come just as they can contrive ; on the tops of coaches, for example ; and amongst these there are fellows with dark sallow faces and sharp shining eyes ; and it is these that have planted rottenness in the core of pugilism, for they are Jews, and, true to their kind, have only base lucre in view.

It was fierce old Cobbett, I think, who first said that the Jews first introduced bad faith amongst pugilists. He did not always speak the truth, but at any rate he spoke it when he made that observation. Strange people the Jews—endowed with every gift but one, and that the highest, genius divine,—genius which can alone make of men demigods, and elevate them above earth and what is earthy and what is grovelling ; without which a clever nation—and who more clever than the Jews ?—may have Rambams in plenty, but never a Fielding nor a Shakespeare ; a Rothschild and a Mendoza, yes—but never a Kean nor a Belcher.

So the bruisers of England are come to be present at the grand fight speedily coming off ; there they are met in the precincts of the old town, near the Field of the Chapel, planted with tender saplings at the restoration of sporting Charles, which are now become venerable elms, as high as many a steeple ; there they are met at a fitting rendezvous, where a retired coachman, with one leg, keeps an hotel and a bowling green. I think I now see them upon the bowling-green, the men of renown, amidst hundreds of people with no renown at all, who gaze upon them with timid wonder. Fame, after all, is a glorious thing, though it lasts only for a day. There's Cribb, the champion of England, and perhaps the best man in England ; there he is, with his huge, massive figure, and face wonderfully like that of a lion. There is Belcher, the younger, not the mighty one, who is gone to his place, but the Teucer Belcher, the most scientific pugilist that ever entered a ring, only wanting strength to be, I won't say what. He appears to walk before me now, as he did that evening, with his white hat,

white greatcoat, thin, genteel figure, springy step, and keen, determined eye. Crosses him—what a contrast !—grim, savage Shelton,
who has a civil word for nobody, and a hard blow for anybody—
hard! one blow, given with the proper play of his athletic arm,
will unsense a giant. Yonder individual, who strolls about with
his hands behind him, supporting his brown coat lappets, under-
sized, and who looks anything but what he is, is the king of the
light weights, so called,—Randall! the terrible Randall, who has
Irish blood in his veins ; not the better for that, nor the worse ; and
not far from him is his last antagonist, Ned Turner, who, though
beaten by him, still thinks himself as good a man, in which he is,
perhaps, right, for it was a near thing ; and "a better shentleman,"
in which he is quite right, for he is a Welshman. But how shall
I name them all? they were there by dozens, and all tremendous
in their way. There was Bulldog Hudson and fearless Scroggins,
who beat the conqueror of Sam the Jew. There was Black
Richmond—no, he was not there, but I knew him well ; he was
the most dangerous of blacks, even with a broken thigh. There
was Purcell, who could never conquer till all seemed over with
him. There was—what! shall I name thee last? ay, why not?
I believe that thou art the last of all that strong family still above
the sod, where mayst thou long continue—true piece of English
stuff, Tom of Bedford—sharp as winter, kind as spring.

Hail to thee, Tom of Bedford, or by whatever name it may
please thee to be called, Spring or Winter. Hail to thee, six-foot
Englishman of the brown eye, worthy to have carried a six-foot
bow at Flodden, where England's yeomen triumphed over Scotland's king, his clans and chivalry. Hail to thee, last of England's
bruisers, after all the many victories which thou hast achieved—
true English victories, unbought by yellow gold ; need I recount
them? nay, nay! they are already well known to fame—sufficient
to say that Bristol's Bull and Ireland's Champion were vanquished
by thee, and one mightier still, gold itself, thou didst overcome ;
for gold itself strove in vain to deaden the power of thy arm ; and
thus thou didst proceed till men left off challenging thee, the un-
vanquishable, the incorruptible. 'Tis a treat to see thee, Tom of
Bedford, in thy "public" in Holborn way, whither thou hast
retired with thy well-earned bays. 'Tis Friday night, and nine
by Holborn clock. There sits the yeoman at the end of his long
room, surrounded by his friends : glasses are filled, and a song is
the cry, and a song is sung well suited to the place ; it finds an
echo in every heart—fists are clenched, arms are waved, and the
portraits of the mighty fighting men of yore, Broughton and Slack

and Ben, which adorn the walls, appear to smile grim approbation, whilst many a manly voice joins in the bold chorus :—

" Here's a health to old honest John Bull,
When he's gone we shan't find such another,
And with hearts and with glasses brim full,
We will drink to old England, his mother ".

But the fight! with respect to the fight, what shall I say? Little can be said about it—it was soon over ; some said that the brave from town, who was reputed the best man of the two, and whose form was a perfect model of athletic beauty, allowed himself, for lucre vile, to be vanquished by the massive champion with the flattened nose. One thing is certain, that the former was suddenly seen to sink to the earth before a blow of by no means extraordinary power. Time, time! was called ; but there he lay upon the ground apparently senseless, and from thence he did not lift his head till several seconds after the umpires had declared his adversary victor.

There were shouts ; indeed, there's never a lack of shouts to celebrate a victory, however acquired ; but there was also much grinding of teeth, especially amongst the fighting men from town. "Tom has sold us," said they, "sold us to the yokels ; who would have thought it?" Then there was fresh grinding of teeth, and scowling brows were turned to the heaven ; but what is this? is it possible, does the heaven scowl too? why, only a quarter of an hour ago—but what may not happen in a quarter of an hour? For many weeks the weather had been of the most glorious description, the eventful day, too, had dawned gloriously, and so it had continued till some two hours after noon ; the fight was then over ; and about that time I looked up—what a glorious sky of deep blue, and what a big, fierce sun swimming high above in the midst of that blue ; not a cloud—there had not been one for weeks—not a cloud to be seen, only in the far west, just on the horizon, something like the extremity of a black wing ; that was only a quarter of an hour ago, and now the whole northern side of the heaven is occupied by a huge black cloud, and the sun is only occasionally seen amidst masses of driving vapour ; what a change! but another fight is at hand, and the pugilists are clearing the outer ring ; how their huge whips come crashing upon the heads of the yokels ; blood flows, more blood than in the fight: those blows are given with right good-will, those are not sham blows, whether of whip or fist ; it is with fist that grim Shelton strikes down the big yokel ; he is always dangerous, grim Shelton, but now particularly so, for he has lost

ten pounds betted on the brave who sold himself to the yokels ;
but the outer ring is cleared ; and now the second fight commences ; it is between two champions of less renown than the
others, but is perhaps not the worse on that account.   A tall thin
boy is fighting in the ring with a man somewhat under the middle
size, with a frame of adamant ; that's a gallant boy ! he's a yokel,
but he comes from Brummagem, and he does credit to his extraction ;
but his adversary has a frame of adamant : in what a strange light
they fight, but who can wonder, on looking at that frightful cloud
usurping now one half of heaven, and at the sun struggling with
sulphurous vapour ; the face of the boy, which is turned towards
me, looks horrible in that light, but he is a brave boy, he strikes
his foe on the forehead, and the report of the blow is like the
sound of a hammer against a rock ; but there is a rush and a
roar over head, a wild commotion, the tempest is beginning to
break loose ; there's wind and dust, a crash, rain and hail ; is it
possible to fight amidst such a commotion ? yes ! the fight goes
on ; again the boy strikes the man full on the brow, but it is of
no use striking that man, his frame is of adamant.   " Boy, thy
strength is beginning to give way, and thou art becoming confused ; "
the man now goes to work, amidst rain and hail.   " Boy, thou
wilt not hold out ten minutes longer against rain, hail, and the
blows of such an antagonist."

And now the storm was at its height ; the black thunder-
cloud had broken into many, which assumed the wildest shapes
and the strangest colours, some of them unspeakably glorious ;
the rain poured in a deluge, and more than one water-spout was
seen at no great distance : an immense rabble is hurrying in one
direction ; a multitude of men of all ranks, peers and yokels,
prize-fighters and Jews, and the last came to plunder, and are
now plundering amidst that wild confusion of hail and rain, men
and horses, carts and carriages.   But all hurry in one direction,
through mud and mire ; there's a town only three miles distant,
which is soon reached, and soon filled, it will not contain one-
third of that mighty rabble ; but there's another town farther on
—the good old city is farther on, only twelve miles ; what's that !
who'll stay here ? onward to the old town.

Hurry skurry, a mixed multitude of men and horses, carts
and carriages, all in the direction of the old town ; and, in the
midst of all that mad throng, at a moment when the rain gushes
were coming down with particular fury, and the artillery of the
sky was pealing as I had never heard it peal before, I felt some
one seize me by the arm—I turned round and beheld Mr. Petulengro.

"I can't hear you, Mr. Petulengro," said I; for the thunder drowned the words which he appeared to be uttering.

"Dearginni," I heard Mr. Petulengro say, "it thundereth. I was asking, brother, whether you believe in dukkeripens?"

"I do not, Mr. Petulengro; but this is strange weather to be asking me whether I believe in fortunes."

"Grondinni," said Mr. Petulengro, "it haileth. I believe in dukkeripens, brother."

"And who has more right," said I, "seeing that you live by them? But this tempest is truly horrible."

"Dearginni, grondinni ta villaminni! It thundereth, it haileth, and also flameth," said Mr. Petulengro. "Look up there, brother!"

I looked up. Connected with this tempest there was one feature to which I have already alluded—the wonderful colours of the clouds. Some were of vivid green; others of the brightest orange; others as black as pitch. The gypsy's finger was pointed to a particular part of the sky.

"What do you see there, brother?"

"A strange kind of cloud."

"What does it look like, brother?"

"Something like a stream of blood."

"That cloud foreshoweth a bloody dukkeripen."

"A bloody fortune!" said I. "And whom may it betide?"

"Who knows!" said the gypsy.

Down the way, dashing and splashing and scattering man, horse and cart to the left and right, came an open barouche, drawn by four smoking steeds, with postillions in scarlet jackets, and leather skull-caps. Two forms were conspicuous in it; that of the successful bruiser and of his friend and backer, the sporting gentleman of my acquaintance.

"His!" said the gypsy, pointing to the latter, whose stern features wore a smile of triumph, as, probably recognising me in the crowd, he nodded in the direction of where I stood, as the barouche hurried by.

There went the barouche, dashing through the rain gushes, and in it one whose boast it was that he was equal to "either fortune". Many have heard of that man—many may be desirous of knowing yet more of him. I have nothing to do with that man's after-life—he fulfilled his dukkeripen. "A bad, violent man!" Softly friend; when thou wouldst speak harshly of the dead, remember that thou hast not yet fulfilled thy own dukkeripen!

CHAPTER XXVII.

My father, as I have already informed the reader, had been endowed by nature with great corporeal strength; indeed, I have been assured that, at the period of his prime, his figure had denoted the possession of almost Herculean powers. The strongest forms, however, do not always endure the longest, the very excess of the noble and generous juices which they contain being the cause of their premature decay. But, be that as it may, the health of my father, some few years after his retirement from the service to the quiet of domestic life, underwent a considerable change; his constitution appeared to be breaking up; and he was subject to severe attacks from various disorders, with which, till then, he had been utterly unacquainted. He was, however, wont to rally, more or less, after his illnesses, and might still occasionally be seen taking his walk, with his cane in his hand, and accompanied by his dog, who sympathised entirely with him, pining as he pined, improving as he improved, and never leaving the house save in his company; and in this manner matters went on for a considerable time, no very great apprehension with respect to my father's state being raised either in my mother's breast or my own. But, about six months after the period at which I have arrived in my last chapter, it came to pass that my father experienced a severer attack than on any previous occasion.

He had the best medical advice; but it was easy to see, from the looks of his doctors, that they entertained but slight hopes of his recovery. His sufferings were great, yet he invariably bore them with unshaken fortitude. There was one thing remarkable connected with his illness; notwithstanding its severity, it never confined him to his bed. He was wont to sit in his little parlour, in his easy chair, dressed in a faded regimental coat, his dog at his feet, who would occasionally lift his head from the hearth-rug on which he lay, and look his master wistfully in the face. And thus my father spent the greater part of his time, sometimes in prayer, sometimes in meditation, and sometimes in reading the Scriptures. I frequently sat with him; though, as I entertained a great awe for my father, I used to feel rather ill at ease, when, as sometimes happened, I found myself alone with him.

"I wish to ask you a few questions," said he to me, one day, after my mother had left the room.

"I will answer anything you may please to ask me, my dear father."

"What have you been about lately?"

"I have been occupied as usual, attending at the office at the appointed hours."

"And what do you do there?"

"Whatever I am ordered."

"And nothing else?"

"Oh, yes! sometimes I read a book."

"Connected with your profession?"

"Not always; I have been lately reading Armenian —— "

"What's that?"

"The language of a people whose country is a region on the other side of Asia Minor."

"Well!"

"A region abounding with mountains."

"Well!"

"Amongst which is Mount Ararat."

"Well!"

"Upon which, as the Bible informs us, the ark rested."

"Well!"

"It is the language of the people of those regions."

"So you told me."

"And I have been reading the Bible in their language."

"Well!"

"Or rather, I should say, in the ancient language of these people; from which I am told the modern Armenian differs considerably."

"Well!"

"As much as the Italian from the Latin."

"Well!"

"So I have been reading the Bible in ancient Armenian."

"You told me so before."

"I found it a highly difficult language."

"Yes."

"Differing widely from the languages in general with which I am acquainted."

"Yes."

"Exhibiting, however, some features in common with them."

" Yes."

" And sometimes agreeing remarkably in words with a certain strange wild speech with which I became acquainted ——"

" Irish ? "

" No, father, not Irish—with which I became acquainted by the greatest chance in the world."

" Yes."

" But of which I need say nothing further at present, and which I should not have mentioned but for that fact."

" Well ! "

" Which I consider remarkable."

" Yes."

" The Armenian is copious."

" Is it ? "

" With an alphabet of thirty-nine letters, but it is harsh and guttural."

" Yes."

" Like the language of most mountainous people — the Armenians call it Haik."

" Do they ? "

" And themselves, Haik, also; they are a remarkable people, and, though their original habitation is the Mountain of Ararat, they are to be found, like the Jews, all over the world."

" Well ! "

" Well, father, that's all I can tell you about the Haiks, or Armenians."

" And what does it all amount to ? "

" Very little, father; indeed, there is very little known about the Armenians; their early history, in particular, is involved in considerable mystery."

" And, if you knew all that it was possible to know about them, to what would it amount ? to what earthly purpose could you turn it ? have you acquired any knowledge of your profession ? "

" Very little, father."

" Very little ! Have you acquired all in your power ? "

" I can't say that I have, father."

" And yet it was your duty to have done so. But I see how it is, you have shamefully misused your opportunities; you are like one, who, sent into the field to labour, passes his time in flinging stones at the birds of heaven."

" I would scorn to fling a stone at a bird, father."

" You know what I mean, and all too well, and this attempt to evade deserved reproof by feigned simplicity is quite in character with your general behaviour. I have ever observed about you a want of frankness, which has distressed me; you never speak of what you are about, your hopes, or your projects, but cover yourself with mystery. I never knew till the present moment that you were acquainted with Armenian."

"Because you never asked me, father; there's nothing to conceal in the matter—I will tell you in a moment how I came to learn Armenian. A lady whom I met at one of Mrs. ——'s parties took a fancy to me, and has done me the honour to allow me to go and see her sometimes. She is the widow of a rich clergyman, and on her husband's death came to this place to live bringing her husband's library with her. I soon found my way to it, and examined every book. Her husband must have been a learned man, for amongst much Greek and Hebrew I found several volumes in Armenian, or relating to the language."

"And why did you not tell me of this before?"

"Because you never questioned me; but, I repeat, there is nothing to conceal in the matter. The lady took a fancy to me, and, being fond of the arts, drew my portrait; she said the expression of my countenance put her in mind of Alfieri's Saul."

"And do you still visit her?"

"No, she soon grew tired of me, and told people that she found me very stupid; she gave me the Armenian books, however."

"Saul," said my father, musingly, "Saul, I am afraid she was only too right there; he disobeyed the commands of his master, and brought down on his head the vengeance of Heaven—he became a maniac, prophesied, and flung weapons about him."

"He was, indeed, an awful character—I hope I shan't turn out like him."

"God forbid!" said my father, solemnly; "but in many respects you are headstrong and disobedient like him. I placed you in a profession, and besought you to make yourself master of it, by giving it your undivided attention. This, however, you did not do, you know nothing of it, but tell me that you are acquainted with Armenian; but what I dislike most is your want of candour—you are my son, but I know little of your real history; you may know fifty things for what I am aware; you may know how to shoe a horse, for what I am aware."

"Not only to shoe a horse, father, but to make horse-shoes."

"Perhaps so," said my father; "and it only serves to prove what I was just saying, that I know little about you."

"But you easily may, my dear father; I will tell you anything

that you may wish to know—shall I inform you how I learnt to
make horse-shoes?"

"No," said my father; "as you kept it a secret so long, it
may as well continue so still.   Had you been a frank, open-hearted
boy, like one I could name, you would have told me all about it
of your own accord.   But I now wish to ask you a serious question
—what do you propose to do?"

"To do, father?"

"Yes! the time for which you were articled to your profession
will soon be expired, and I shall be no more."

"Do not talk so, my dear father, I have no doubt that you
will soon be better."

"Do not flatter yourself; I feel that my days are numbered.
I am soon going to my rest, and I have need of rest, for I am
weary.   There, there, don't weep!   Tears will help me as little
as they will you; you have not yet answered my question.   Tell
me what you intend to do?"

"I really do not know what I shall do."

"The military pension which I enjoy will cease with my
life.   The property which I shall leave behind me will be barely
sufficient for the maintenance of your mother respectably.   I
again ask you what you intend to do.   Do you think you can
support yourself by your Armenian or your other acquirements?"

"Alas! I think little at all about it; but I suppose I must
push into the world, and make a good fight, as becomes the son
of him who fought Big Ben: if I can't succeed, and am driven to
the worst, it is but dying——"

"What do you mean by dying?"

"Leaving the world; my loss would scarcely be felt.   I have
never held life in much value, and every one has a right to
dispose as he thinks best of that which is his own."

"Ah! now I understand you; and well I know how and
where you imbibed that horrible doctrine, and many similar ones
which I have heard from your own mouth; but I wish not to
reproach you—I view in your conduct a punishment for my own
sins, and I bow to the will of God.   Few and evil have been my
days upon the earth; little have I done to which I can look back
with satisfaction.   It is true I have served my king fifty years, and
I have fought with—Heaven forgive me, what was I about to say!
—but you mentioned the man's name, and our minds willingly
recall our ancient follies.   Few and evil have been my days upon
earth, I may say with Jacob of old, though I do not mean to say
that my case is so hard as his; he had many undutiful children,

whilst I have only ——— ; but I will not reproach you. I have
also like him a son to whom I can look with hope, who may yet
preserve my name when I am gone, so let me be thankful ; perhaps, after all, I have not lived in vain. Boy, when I am gone,
look up to your brother, and may God bless you both. There,
don't weep ; but take the Bible, and read me something about
the old man and his children."

My brother had now been absent for the space of three years.
At first his letters had been frequent, and from them it appeared
that he was following his profession in London with industry ;
they then became rather rare, and my father did not always
communicate their contents. His last letter, however, had filled
him and our whole little family with joy ; it was dated from Paris,
and the writer was evidently in high spirits. After describing in
eloquent terms the beauties and gaieties of the French capital,
he informed us how he had plenty of money, having copied a
celebrated picture of one of the Italian masters for a Hungarian
nobleman, for which he had received a large sum. " He wishes
me to go with him to Italy," added he, " but I am fond of independence ; and, if ever I visit old Rome, I will have no patrons
near me to distract my attention." But six months had now
elapsed from the date of this letter, and we had heard no further
intelligence of my brother. My father's complaint increased ; the
gout, his principal enemy, occasionally mounted high up in his
system, and we had considerable difficulty in keeping it from the
stomach, where it generally proves fatal. I now devoted almost
the whole of my time to my father, on whom his faithful partner
also lavished every attention and care. I read the Bible to him,
which was his chief delight ; and also occasionally such other
books as I thought might prove entertaining to him. His spirits
were generally rather depressed. The absence of my brother
seemed to prey upon his mind. " I wish he were here," he
would frequently exclaim, " I can't imagine what has become of
him ; I trust, however, he will arrive in time." He still sometimes
rallied, and I took advantage of those moments of comparative
ease to question him upon the events of his early life. My
attentions to him had not passed unnoticed, and he was kind,
fatherly, and unreserved. I had never known my father so
entertaining as at these moments, when his life was but too
evidently drawing to a close. I had no idea that he knew and
had seen so much ; my respect for him increased, and I looked
upon him almost with admiration. His anecdotes were in general
highly curious ; some of them related to people in the highest

stations, and to men whose names were closely connected with some of the brightest glories of our native land.   He had frequently conversed—almost on terms of familiarity—with good old George.   He had known the conqueror of Tippoo Saib; and was the friend of Townshend, who, when Wolfe fell, led the British grenadiers against the shrinking regiments of Montcalm. " Pity," he added, " that when old—old as I am now—he should have driven his own son mad by robbing him of his plighted bride; but so it was; he married his son's bride.   I saw him lead her to the altar; if ever there was an angelic countenance, it was that girl's; she was almost too fair to be one of the daughters of women.   Is there anything, boy, that you would wish to ask me? now is the time."

" Yes, father; there is one about whom I would fain question you."

" Who is it? shall I tell you about Elliot?"

" No, father, not about Elliot; but pray don't be angry; I should like to know something about Big Ben."

"You are a strange lad," said my father; "and, though of late I have begun to entertain a more favourable opinion than heretofore, there is still much about you that I do not understand. Why do you bring up that name?   Don't you know that it is one of my temptations?   You wish to know something about him. Well!   I will oblige you this once, and then farewell to such vanities—something about him.   I will tell you—his—skin when he flung off his clothes—and he had a particular knack in doing so—his skin, when he bared his mighty chest and back for combat; and when he fought, he stood so —— if I remember right—his skin, I say, was brown and dusky as that of a toad. Oh me! I wish my elder son was here."

CHAPTER XXVIII.

At last my brother arrived; he looked pale and unwell; I met him at the door. "You have been long absent!" said I.

"Yes," said he, "perhaps too long; but how is my father?"

"Very poorly," said I, "he has had a fresh attack; but where have you been of late?"

"Far and wide," said my brother; "but I can't tell you anything now, I must go to my father. It was only by chance that I heard of his illness."

"Stay a moment," said I. "Is the world such a fine place as you supposed it to be before you went away?"

"Not quite," said my brother, "not quite; indeed I wish— but ask me no questions now, I must hasten to my father."

There was another question on my tongue, but I forebore; for the eyes of the young man were full of tears. I pointed with my finger, and the young man hastened past me to the arms of his father.

I forebore to ask my brother whether he had been to old Rome.

What passed between my father and brother I do not know; the interview, no doubt, was tender enough, for they tenderly loved each other; but my brother's arrival did not produce the beneficial effect upon my father which I at first hoped it would; it did not even appear to have raised his spirits. He was composed enough, however. "I ought to be grateful," said he; "I wished to see my son, and God has granted me my wish; what more have I to do now than to bless my little family and go?"

My father's end was evidently at hand.

And did I shed no tears? did I breathe no sighs? did I never wring my hands at this period? the reader will perhaps be asking. Whatever I did and thought is best known to God and myself; but it will be as well to observe, that it is possible to feel deeply and yet make no outward sign.

And now for the closing scene.

At the dead hour of night, it might be about two, I was awakened from sleep by a cry which sounded from the room immediately below that in which I slept.   I knew the cry, it was the cry of my mother, and I also knew its import; yet I made no effort to rise, for I was for the moment paralysed.   Again the cry sounded, yet still I lay motionless—the stupidity of horror was upon me.   A third time, and it was then that, by a violent effort bursting the spell which appeared to bind me, I sprang from the bed and rushed downstairs.   My mother was running wildly about the room; she had awoke and found my father senseless in the bed by her side.   I essayed to raise him, and after a few efforts supported him in the bed in a sitting posture.   My brother now rushed in, and snatching up a light that was burning, he held it to my father's face.   "The surgeon, the surgeon!" he cried; then dropping the light, he ran out of the room followed by my mother; I remained alone, supporting the senseless form of my father; the light had been extinguished by the fall, and an almost total darkness reigned in the room.   The form pressed heavily against my bosom—at last methought it moved.   Yes, I was right, there was a heaving of the breast, and then a gasping. Were those words which I heard?   Yes, they were words, low and indistinct at first, and then audible.   The mind of the dying man was reverting to former scenes.   I heard him mention names which I had often heard him mention before.   It was an awful moment; I felt stupefied, but I still contrived to support my dying father.   There was a pause, again my father spoke: I heard him speak of Minden, and of Meredith, the old Minden sergeant, and then he uttered another name, which at one period of his life was much on his lips, the name of —— but this is a solemn moment! There was a deep gasp: I shook, and thought all was over; but I was mistaken—my father moved and revived for a moment; he supported himself in bed without my assistance.   I make no doubt that for a moment he was perfectly sensible, and it was then that, clasping his hands, he uttered another name clearly, distinctly—it was the name of Christ.   With that name upon his lips, the brave old soldier sank back upon my bosom, and, with his hands still clasped, yielded up his soul.

[*End of Vol. I.,* 1851.]

CHAPTER XXIX.

"ONE-AND-NINEPENCE, sir, or the things which you have brought with you will be taken away from you!"

Such were the first words which greeted my ears, one damp, misty morning in March, as I dismounted from the top of a coach in the yard of a London inn.

I turned round, for I felt that the words were addressed to myself. Plenty of people were in the yard—porters, passengers, coachmen, ostlers, and others, who appeared to be intent on anything but myself, with the exception of one individual whose business appeared to lie with me, and who now confronted me at the distance of about two yards.

I looked hard at the man—and a queer kind of individual he was to look at—a rakish figure, about thirty, and of the middle size, dressed in a coat smartly cut, but threadbare, very tight pantaloons of blue stuff, tied at the ankles, dirty white stockings, and thin shoes, like those of a dancing-master; his features were not ugly, but rather haggard, and he appeared to owe his complexion less to nature than carmine; in fact, in every respect, a very queer figure.

"One-and-ninepence, sir, or your things will be taken away from you!" he said, in a kind of lisping tone, coming yet nearer to me.

I still remained staring fixedly at him, but never a word answered. Our eyes met; whereupon he suddenly lost the easy impudent air which he before wore. He glanced, for a moment, at my fist, which I had by this time clenched, and his features became yet more haggard; he faltered; a fresh "one-and-nine-pence" which he was about to utter, died on his lips; he shrank back, disappeared behind a coach, and I saw no more of him.

"One-and-ninepence, or my things will be taken away from me!" said I to myself, musingly, as I followed the porter to whom I had delivered my scanty baggage; "am I to expect many of these greetings in the big world? Well, never mind; I think I know the counter-sign!" And I clenched my fist yet harder than before.

So I followed the porter through the streets of London, to a
lodging which had been prepared for me by an acquaintance.
The morning, as I have before said, was gloomy, and the streets
through which I passed were dank and filthy; the people, also,
looked dank and filthy; and so, probably, did I, for the night
had been rainy, and I had come upwards of a hundred miles on
the top of a coach; my heart had sunk within me by the time we
reached a dark narrow street in which was the lodging.

"Cheer up, young man," said the porter, "we shall have a
fine afternoon!"

And presently I found myself in the lodging which had been
prepared for me. It consisted of a small room, up two pair of
stairs, in which I was to sit, and another still smaller above it, in
which I was to sleep. I remember that I sat down, and looked
disconsolate about me—everything seemed so cold and dingy.
Yet how little is required to make a situation—however cheerless
at first sight—cheerful and comfortable. The people of the
house, who looked kindly upon me, lighted a fire in the dingy
grate; and, then, what a change!—the dingy room seemed dingy
no more! Oh, the luxury of a cheerful fire after a chill night's
journey! I drew near to the blazing grate, rubbed my hands
and felt glad.

And, when I had warmed myself, I turned to the table, on
which, by this time, the people of the house had placed my
breakfast; and I ate and I drank; and, as I ate and drank, I
mused within myself, and my eyes were frequently directed to a
small green box, which constituted part of my luggage, and which,
with the rest of my things, stood in one corner of the room, till at
last, leaving my breakfast unfinished, I rose, and, going to the box,
unlocked it, and took out two or three bundles of papers tied
with red tape, and, placing them on the table, I resumed my seat
and my breakfast, my eyes intently fixed upon the bundles of
papers all the time.

And when I had drained the last cup of tea out of a dingy
teapot, and ate the last slice of the dingy loaf, I untied one of
the bundles, and proceeded to look over the papers, which were
closely written over in a singular hand, and I read for some time,
till at last I said to myself, "It will do.". And then I looked at
the other bundle for some time, without untying it; and at last I
said, "It will do also". And then I turned to the fire, and,
putting my feet against the sides of the grate, I leaned back on
my chair, and, with my eyes upon the fire, fell into deep thought.

And there I continued in thought before the fire, until my

eyes closed, and I fell asleep; which was not to be wondered at,
after the fatigue and cold which I had lately undergone on the
coach-top; and, in my sleep, I imagined myself still there, amidst
darkness and rain, hurrying now over wild heaths, and now along
roads overhung with thick and umbrageous trees, and sometimes
methought I heard the horn of the guard, and sometimes the
voice of the coachman, now chiding, now encouraging his horses,
as they toiled through the deep and miry ways. At length a
tremendous crack of a whip saluted the tympanum of my ear,
and I started up broad awake, nearly oversetting the chair on
which I reclined—and, lo! I was in the dingy room before the
fire, which was by this time half-extinguished. In my dream I
had confounded the noise of the street with those of my night
journey; the crack which had aroused me I soon found proceeded
from the whip of a carter, who, with many oaths, was flogging his
team below the window.

Looking at a clock which stood upon the mantel-piece, I perceived that it was past eleven; whereupon I said to myself, " I am
wasting my time foolishly and unprofitably, forgetting that I am
now in the big world, without anything to depend upon save my
own exertions"; and then I adjusted my dress, and, locking up
the bundle of papers which I had not read, I tied up the other,
and, taking it under my arm, I went down stairs; and, after asking a question or two of the people of the house, I sallied forth
into the street with a determined look, though at heart I felt
somewhat timorous at the idea of venturing out alone into the
mazes of the mighty city, of which I had heard much, but of
which, of my own knowledge, I knew nothing.

I had, however, no great cause for anxiety in the present instance; I easily found my way to the place which I was in quest
of—one of the many new squares on the northern side of the
metropolis, and which was scarcely ten minutes' walk from the
street in which I had taken up my abode. Arriving before the
door of a tolerably large house which bore a certain number, I
stood still for a moment in a kind of trepidation, looking anxiously
at the door; I then slowly passed on till I came to the end of the
square, where I stood still and pondered for awhile. Suddenly,
however, like one who has formed a resolution, I clenched my
right hand, flinging my hat somewhat on one side, and, turning
back with haste to the door before which I had stopped, I sprang
up the steps, and gave a loud rap, ringing at the same time the
bell of the area. After the lapse of a minute the door was
opened by a maid-servant of no very cleanly or prepossessing

appearance, of whom I demanded, in a tone of some *hauteur*, whether the master of the house was at home.   Glancing for a moment at the white paper bundle beneath my arm, the handmaid made no reply in words, but, with a kind of toss of her head, flung the door open, standing on one side as if to let me enter.   I did enter; and the handmaid, having opened another door on the right hand, went in, and said something which I could not hear; after a considerable pause, however, I heard the voice of a man say, " Let him come in "; whereupon the handmaid, coming out, motioned me to enter, and, on my obeying, instantly closed the door behind me.

CHAPTER XXX.

THERE were two individuals in the room in which I now found myself; it was a small study, surrounded with bookcases, the window looking out upon the square. Of these individuals he who appeared to be the principal stood with his back to the fireplace. He was a tall, stout man, about sixty, dressed in a loose morning gown. The expression of his countenance would have been bluff but for a certain sinister glance, and his complexion might have been called rubicund but for a considerable tinge of bilious yellow. He eyed me askance as I entered. The other, a pale, shrivelled-looking person, sat at a table apparently engaged with an account-book; he took no manner of notice of me, never once lifting his eyes from the page before him.

"Well, sir, what is your pleasure?" said the big man, in a rough tone, as I stood there looking at him wistfully—as well I might—for upon that man, at the time of which I am speaking, my principal, I may say my only, hopes rested.

"Sir," said I, "my name is so-and-so, and I am the bearer of a letter to you from Mr. so-and-so, an old friend and correspondent of yours."

The countenance of the big man instantly lost the suspicious and lowering expression which it had hitherto exhibited; he strode forward and, seizing me by the hand, gave me a violent squeeze.

"My dear sir," said he, "I am rejoiced to see you in London. I have been long anxious for the pleasure—we are old friends, though we have never before met. Taggart,"[1] said he to the man who sat at the desk, "this is our excellent correspondent, the friend and pupil of our other excellent correspondent."

The pale, shrivelled-looking man slowly and deliberately raised his head from the account-book, and surveyed me for a moment or two; not the slightest emotion was observable in his countenance. It appeared to me, however, that I could detect a droll twinkle in his eye; his curiosity, if he had any, was soon

[1] *MS.*, "Bartlett".

(185)

gratified ; he made me a kind of bow, pulled out a snuff-box, took
a pinch of snuff, and again bent his head over the page.

"And now, my dear sir," said the big man, "pray sit down,
and tell me the cause of your visit. I hope you intend to remain
here a day or two."

"More than that," said I, "I am come to take up my abode
in London."

"Glad to hear it; and what have you been about of late? got
anything which will suit me? Sir, I admire your style of writing,
and your manner of thinking; and I am much obliged to my
good friend and correspondent for sending me some of your
productions. I inserted them all, and wished there had been
more of them—quite original, sir, quite; took with the public,
especially the essay about the non-existence of anything. I don't
exactly agree with you, though; I have my own peculiar ideas
about matter—as you know, of course, from the book I have
published. Nevertheless, a very pretty piece of speculative
philosophy—no such thing as matter—impossible that there
should be—*ex nihilo*—what is the Greek? I have forgot—very
pretty indeed; very original."

"I am afraid, sir, it was very wrong to write such trash, and
yet more to allow it to be published."

"Trash! not at all; a very pretty piece of speculative philosophy; of course you were wrong in saying there is no world.
The world must exist, to have the shape of a pear; and that the
world is shaped like a pear, and not like an apple, as the fools of
Oxford say, I have satisfactorily proved in my book. Now, if
there were no world, what would become of my system? But
what do you propose to do in London?"

"Here is the letter, sir," said I, "of our good friend, which I
have not yet given to you; I believe it will explain to you the
circumstances under which I come."

He took the letter, and perused it with attention. "Hem!"
said he, with a somewhat altered manner, "my friend tells me that
you are come up to London with the view of turning your literary
talents to account, and desires me to assist you in my capacity of
publisher in bringing forth two or three works which you have
prepared. My good friend is perhaps not aware that for some
time past I have given up publishing—was obliged to do so—had
many severe losses—do nothing at present in that line, save
sending out the Magazine once a month; and, between ourselves,
am thinking of disposing of that—wish to retire—high time at my
age—so you see——"

"I am very sorry, sir, to hear that you cannot assist me" (and I remember that I felt very nervous); "I had hoped——"

"A losing trade, I assure you, sir; literature is a drug. Taggart, what o'clock is it?"

"Well, sir!" said I, rising, "as you cannot assist me, I will now take my leave; I thank you sincerely for your kind reception, and will trouble you no longer."

"Oh, don't go. I wish to have some further conversation with you; and perhaps I may hit upon some plan to benefit you. I honour merit, and always make a point to encourage it when I can; but —— Taggart, go to the bank, and tell them to dishonour the bill twelve months after date for thirty pounds which becomes due to-morrow. I am dissatisfied with that fellow who wrote the fairy tales, and intend to give him all the trouble in my power. Make haste."

Taggart did not appear to be in any particular haste. First of all, he took a pinch of snuff, then, rising from his chair, slowly and deliberately drew his wig, for he wore a wig of a brown colour, rather more over his forehead than it had previously been, buttoned his coat, and, taking his hat, and an umbrella which stood in a corner, made me a low bow, and quitted the room.

"Well, sir, where were we? Oh, I remember, we were talking about merit. Sir, I always wish to encourage merit, especially when it comes so highly recommended as in the present instance. Sir, my good friend and correspondent speaks of you in the highest terms. Sir, I honour my good friend, and have the highest respect for his opinion in all matters connected with literature—rather eccentric though. Sir, my good friend has done my periodical more good and more harm than all the rest of my correspondents. Sir, I shall never forget the sensation caused by the appearance of his article about a certain personage whom he proved—and I think satisfactorily—to have been a legionary soldier—rather startling, was it not? The S——[1] of the world a common soldier, in a marching regiment!—original, but startling; sir, I honour my good friend."

"So you have renounced publishing, sir," said I, "with the exception of the Magazine?"

"Why, yes; except now and then, under the rose; the old coachman, you know, likes to hear the whip. Indeed, at the present moment, I am thinking of starting a Review on an entirely new and original principle; and it just struck me that you might be of high utility in the undertaking—what do you think of the matter?"

[1] *MS.*, "Saviour".

"I should be happy, sir, to render you any assistance, but I am afraid the employment you propose requires other qualifications than I possess; however, I can make the essay. My chief intention in coming to London was to lay before the world what I had prepared; and I had hoped by your assistance ——"

"Ah! I see, ambition! Ambition is a very pretty thing; but, sir, we must walk before we run, according to the old saying— what is that you have got under your arm?"

"One of the works to which I was alluding; the one, indeed, which I am most anxious to lay before the world, as I hope to derive from it both profit and reputation."

"Indeed! what do you call it?"

"Ancient songs of Denmark, heroic and romantic, translated by myself, with notes philological, critical and historical."

"Then, sir, I assure you that your time and labour have been entirely flung away; nobody would read your ballads, if you were to give them to the world to-morrow."

"I am sure, sir, that you would say otherwise if you would permit me to read one to you;" and, without waiting for the answer of the big man, nor indeed so much as looking at him, to see whether he was inclined or not to hear me, I undid my manuscript, and with a voice trembling with eagerness, I read to the following effect :—

> Buckshank bold and Elfinstone,
>   And more than I can mention here,
> They caused to be built so stout a ship,
>   And unto Iceland they would steer.
>
> They launched the ship upon the main,
>   Which bellowed like a wrathful bear;
> Down to the bottom the vessel sank,
>   A laidly Trold has dragged it there.
>
> Down to the bottom sank young Roland,
>   And round about he groped awhile;
> Until he found the path which led
>   Unto the bower of Ellenlyle.

"Stop!" said the publisher; "very pretty, indeed, and very original; beats Scott hollow, and Percy too: but, sir, the day for these things is gone by; nobody at present cares for Percy, nor for Scott, either, save as a novelist; sorry to discourage merit, sir, but what can I do? What else have you got?"

"The songs of Ab Gwilym, the Welsh bard, also translated by myself, with notes critical, philological and historical."

"Pass on—what else?"

"Nothing else," said I, folding up my manuscript with a sigh, "unless it be a romance in the German style; on which, I confess, I set very little value."

"Wild?"

"Yes, sir, very wild."

"Like the Miller of the Black Valley?"

"Yes, sir, very much like the Miller of the Black Valley."

"Well, that's better," said the publisher; "and yet, I don't know, I question whether any one at present cares for the miller himself. No, sir, the time for those things is also gone by; German, at present, is a drug; and, between ourselves, nobody has contributed to make it so more than my good friend and correspondent; but, sir, I see you are a young gentleman of infinite merit, and I always wish to encourage merit. Don't you think you could write a series of evangelical tales?"

"Evangelical tales, sir?"

"Yes, sir, evangelical novels."

"Something in the style of Herder?"

"Herder is a drug, sir; nobody cares for Herder—thanks to my good friend. Sir, I have in yon drawer a hundred pages about Herder, which I dare not insert in my periodical; it would sink it, sir. No, sir, something in the style of the *Dairyman's Daughter.*"

"I never heard of the work till the present moment."

"Then, sir, procure it by all means. Sir, I could afford as much as ten pounds for a well-written tale in the style of the *Dairyman's Daughter;* that is the kind of literature, sir, that sells at the present day! It is not the Miller of the Black Valley— no, sir, nor Herder either, that will suit the present taste; the evangelical body is becoming very strong, sir—the canting scoundrels ——"

"But, sir, surely you would not pander to a scoundrelly taste?"

"Then, sir, I must give up business altogether. Sir, I have a great respect for the goddess Reason—an infinite respect, sir; indeed, in my time, I have made a great many sacrifices for her; but, sir, I cannot altogether ruin myself for the goddess Reason. Sir, I am a friend to Liberty, as is well known; but I must also be a friend to my own family. It is with the view of providing for a son of mine that I am about to start the Review of which I was speaking. He has taken it into his head to marry, sir, and I must do something for him, for he can do but little for himself.

Well, sir, I am a friend to Liberty, as I said before, and likewise a friend to Reason ; but I tell you frankly that the Review which I intend to get up under the rose, and present him with when it is established, will be conducted on Oxford principles." [1]

"Orthodox principles, I suppose you mean, sir?"

"I do, sir; I am no linguist, but I believe the words are synonymous."

Much more conversation passed between us, and it was agreed that I should become a contributor to the Oxford Review. I stipulated, however, that, as I knew little of politics, and cared less, no other articles should be required from me than such as were connected with belles-lettres and philology ; to this the big man readily assented. "Nothing will be required from you," said he, "but what you mention ; and now and then, perhaps, a paper on metaphysics. You understand German, and perhaps it would be desirable that you should review Kant; and in a review of Kant, sir, you could introduce to advantage your peculiar notions about *ex nihilo*." He then reverted to the subject of the *Dairyman's Daughter*, which I promised to take into consideration. As I was going away, he invited me to dine with him on the ensuing Sunday.

"That's a strange man !" said I to myself, after I had left the house, "he is evidently very clever ; but I cannot say that I like him much, with his Oxford Reviews and Dairyman's Daughters. But what can I do? I am almost without a friend in the world. I wish I could find some one who would publish my ballads, or my songs of Ab Gwilym. In spite of what the big man says, I am convinced that, once published, they would bring me much fame and profit. But how is this?—what a beautiful sun !—the porter was right in saying that the day would clear up—I will now go to my dingy lodging, lock up my manuscripts and then take a stroll about the big city."

[1] *MS.*, "High Tory principles".

CHAPTER XXXI.

So I set out on my walk to see the wonders of the big city, and, as chance would have it, I directed my course to the east. The day, as I have already said, had become very fine, so that I saw the great city to advantage, and the wonders thereof, and much I admired all I saw; and, amongst other things, the huge cathedral, standing so proudly on the most commanding ground in the big city; and I looked up to the mighty dome, surmounted by a golden cross, and I said within myself: "That dome must needs be the finest in the world"; and I gazed upon it till my eyes reeled, and my brain became dizzy, and I thought that the dome would fall and crush me; and I shrank within myself, and struck yet deeper into the heart of the big city.

"O Cheapside! Cheapside!" said I, as I advanced up that mighty thoroughfare, "truly thou art a wonderful place for hurry, noise and riches! Men talk of the bazaars of the East—I have never seen them, but I dare say that, compared with thee, they are poor places, silent places, abounding with empty boxes. O thou pride of London's east!—mighty mart of old renown!— for thou art not a place of yesterday: long before the Roses red and white battled in fair England, thou didst exist—a place of throng and bustle—a place of gold and silver, perfumes and fine linen. Centuries ago thou couldst extort the praises even of the fiercest foes of England. Fierce bards of Wales, sworn foes of England, sang thy praises centuries ago; and even the fiercest of them all, Red Julius himself, wild Glendower's bard, had a word of praise for London's "Cheape," for so the bards of Wales styled thee in their flowing odes. Then, if those who were not English, and hated England, and all connected therewith, had yet much to say in thy praise, when thou wast far inferior to what thou art now, why should true-born Englishmen, or those who call themselves so, turn up their noses at thee, and scoff thee at the present day, as I believe they do? But, let others do as they will, I, at least, who am not only an Englishman, but an East Englishman, will not turn up my nose at thee, but will praise and extol thee, calling thee mart of the world—a place of wonder and astonishment!—and, were it right and fitting to wish that anything should

endure for ever, I would say prosperity to Cheapside, throughout
all ages—may it be the world's resort for merchandise, world
without end.

And when I had passed through the Cheape I entered another
street, which led up a kind of ascent, and which proved to be the
street of the Lombards, called so from the name of its founders;
and I walked rapidly up the street of the Lombards, neither
looking to the right nor left, for it had no interest for me, though
I had a kind of consciousness that mighty things were being
transacted behind its walls; but it wanted the throng, bustle and
outward magnificence of the Cheape, and it had never been
spoken of by "ruddy bards!" And, when I had got to the end
of the street of the Lombards, I stood still for some time, deliberating within myself whether I should turn to the right or the
left, or go straight forward, and at last I turned to the right, down
a street of rapid descent, and presently found myself upon a bridge
which traversed the river which runs by the big city.

A strange kind of bridge it was; huge and massive, and
seemingly of great antiquity. It had an arched back, like that of
a hog, a high balustrade, and at either side, at intervals, were
stone bowers bulking over the river, but open on the other side,
and furnished with a semicircular bench. Though the bridge was
wide—very wide—it was all too narrow for the concourse upon it.
Thousands of human beings were pouring over the bridge. But
what chiefly struck my attention was a double row of carts and
wagons, the generality drawn by horses as large as elephants, each
row striving hard in a different direction, and not unfrequently
brought to a standstill. Oh the cracking of whips, the shouts and
oaths of the carters, and the grating of wheels upon the enormous
stones that formed the pavement! In fact, there was a wild
hurly-burly upon the bridge, which nearly deafened me. But, if
upon the bridge there was a confusion, below it there was a confusion ten times confounded. The tide, which was fast ebbing,
obstructed by the immense piers of the old bridge, poured beneath
the arches with a fall of several feet, forming in the river below as
many whirlpools as there were arches. Truly tremendous was the
roar of the descending waters, and the bellow of the tremendous
gulfs, which swallowed them for a time, and then cast them
forth, foaming and frothing from their horrid wombs. Slowly
advancing along the bridge, I came to the highest point, and
there I stood still, close beside one of the stone bowers, in which,
beside a fruitstall, sat an old woman, with a pan of charcoal at
her feet, and a book in her hand, in which she appeared to be
reading intently. There I stood, just above the principal arch,

looking through the balustrade at the scene that presented itself—
and such a scene! Towards the left bank of the river, a forest of
masts, thick and close, as far as the eye could reach; spacious
wharfs, surmounted with gigantic edifices; and, far away, Cæsar's
Castle, with its White Tower. To the right, another forest of
masts, and a maze of buildings, from which, here and there, shot
up to the sky chimneys taller than Cleopatra's Needle, vomit-
ing forth huge wreaths of that black smoke which forms the
canopy—occasionally a gorgeous one—of the more than Babel
city. Stretching before me, the troubled breast of the mighty
river, and, immediately below, the main whirlpool of the Thames
—the Maëlstrom of the bulwarks of the middle arch—a grisly
pool, which, with its superabundance of horror, fascinated me.
Who knows but I should have leapt into its depths?—I have
heard of such things—but for a rather startling occurrence which
broke the spell. As I stood upon the bridge, gazing into the jaws
of the pool, a small boat shot suddenly through the arch beneath
my feet. There were three persons in it; an oarsman in the
middle, whilst a man and a woman sat at the stern. I shall never
forget the thrill of horror which went through me at this sudden
apparition. What!—a boat—a small boat—passing beneath that
arch into yonder roaring gulf! Yes, yes, down through that awful
water-way, with more than the swiftness of an arrow, shot the
boat, or skiff, right into the jaws of the pool. A monstrous
breaker curls over the prow—there is no hope; the boat is
swamped, and all drowned in that strangling vortex. No! the
boat, which appeared to have the buoyancy of a feather, skipped
over the threatening horror, and the next moment was out of
danger, the boatman—a true boatman of Cockaigne that—
elevating one of his sculls in sign of triumph, the man hallooing,
and the woman, a true Englishwoman that—of a certain class—
waving her shawl. Whether any one observed them save myself,
or whether the feat was a common one, I know not; but nobody
appeared to take any notice of them. As for myself, I was so
excited, that I strove to clamber up the balustrade of the bridge,
in order to obtain a better view of the daring adventurers. Before
I could accomplish my design, however, I felt myself seized by the
body, and, turning my head, perceived the old fruit-woman, who
was clinging to me.

"Nay, dear! don't—don't!" said she. "Don't fling yourself
over—perhaps you may have better luck next time!"

"I was not going to fling myself over," said I, dropping from
the balustrade; "how came you to think of such a thing?"

"Why, seeing you clamber up so fiercely, I thought you might have had ill luck, and that you wished to make away with yourself."

"Ill luck," said I, going into the stone bower and sitting down. "What do you mean? ill luck in what?"

"Why, no great harm, dear! cly-faking, perhaps."

"Are you coming over me with dialects," said I, "speaking unto me in fashions I wot nothing of?"

"Nay, dear! don't look so strange with those eyes of your'n, nor talk so strangely; I don't understand you."

"Nor I you; what do you mean by cly-faking?"

"Lor, dear! no harm; only taking a handkerchief now and then."

"Do you take me for a thief?"

"Nay, dear! don't make use of bad language; we never calls them thieves here, but prigs and fakers: to tell you the truth, dear, seeing you spring at that railing put me in mind of my own dear son, who is now at Bot'ny: when he had bad luck, he always used to talk of flinging himself over the bridge; and, sure enough, when the traps were after him, he did fling himself into the river, but that was off the bank; nevertheless, the traps pulled him out, and he is now suffering his sentence; so you see you may speak out, if you have done anything in the harmless line, for I am my son's own mother, I assure you."

"So you think there's no harm in stealing?"

"No harm in the world, dear! Do you think my own child would have been transported for it, if there had been any harm in it? and what's more, would the blessed woman in the book here have written her life as she has done, and given it to the world, if there had been any harm in faking? She, too, was what they call a thief and a cut-purse; ay, and was transported for it, like my dear son; and do you think she would have told the world so, if there had been any harm in the thing? Oh, it is a comfort to me that the blessed woman was transported, and came back—for come back she did, and rich too—for it is an assurance to me that my dear son, who was transported too, will come back like her."

"What was her name?"

"Her name, blessed Mary Flanders."

"Will you let me look at the book?"

"Yes, dear, that I will, if you promise me not to run away with it."

I took the book from her hand; a short thick volume, at least a century old, bound with greasy black leather. I turned the yellow and dog's-eared pages, reading here and there a

sentence. Yes, and no mistake! *His* pen, his style, his spirit
might be observed in every line of the uncouth-looking old
volume—the air, the style, the spirit of the writer of the book
which first taught me to read. I covered my face with my hand,
and thought of my childhood.

"This is a singular book," said I at last; "but it does not
appear to have been written to prove that thieving is no harm,
but rather to show the terrible consequences of crime: it contains
a deep moral."

"A deep what, dear?"

"A —— but no matter, I will give you a crown for this
volume."

"No, dear, I will not sell the volume for a crown."

"I am poor," said I; "but I will give you two silver crowns
for your volume."

"No, dear, I will not sell my volume for two silver crowns;
no, nor for the golden one in the king's tower down there;
without my book I should mope and pine, and perhaps fling
myself into the river; but I am glad you like it, which shows that
I was right about you, after all; you are one of our party, and
you have a flash about that eye of yours which puts me just in
mind of my dear son. No, dear, I won't sell you my book; but,
if you like, you may have a peep into it whenever you come this
way. I shall be glad to see you; you are one of the right sort,
for, if you had been a common one, you would have run away
with the thing; but you scorn such behaviour, and, as you are so
flash of your money, though you say you are poor, you may give
me a tanner to buy a little baccy with; I love baccy, dear, more
by token that it comes from the plantations to which the blessed
woman was sent."

"What's a tanner?" said I.

"Lor! don't you know, dear? Why, a tanner is sixpence;
and, as you were talking just now about crowns, it will be as well
to tell you that those of our trade never calls them crowns, but
bulls; but I am talking nonsense, just as if you did not know all
that already, as well as myself; you are only shamming—I'm no
trap, dear, nor more was the blessed woman in the book. Thank
you, dear—thank you for the tanner; if I don't spend it, I'll keep
it in remembrance of your sweet face. What, you are going?—
well, first let me whisper a word to you. If you have any clies to
sell at any time, I'll buy them of you; all safe with me; I never
'peach, and scorns a trap; so now, dear, God bless you! and
give you good luck. Thank you for your pleasant company, and
thank you for the tanner."

CHAPTER XXXII.

"Tanner!" said I musingly, as I left the bridge; "Tanner! what can the man who cures raw skins by means of a preparation of oak bark and other materials have to do with the name which these fakers, as they call themselves, bestow on the smallest silver coin in these dominions? Tanner! I can't trace the connection between the man of bark and the silver coin, unless journeymen tanners are in the habit of working for sixpence a day. But I have it," I continued, flourishing my hat over my head, "tanner, in this instance, is not an English word." Is it not surprising that the language of Mr. Petulengro and of Tawno Chikno, is continually coming to my assistance whenever I appear to be at a nonplus with respect to the derivation of crabbed words? I have made out crabbed words in Æschylus by means of the speech of Chikno and Petulengro, and even in my Biblical researches I have derived no slight assistance from it. It appears to be a kind of picklock, an open sesame, Tanner—Tawno! the one is but a modification of the other; they were originally identical, and have still much the same signification. Tanner, in the language of the apple-woman, meaneth the smallest of English silver coins; and Tawno, in the language of the Petulengros, though bestowed upon the biggest of the Romans, according to strict interpretation, signifieth a little child.

So I left the bridge, retracing my steps for a considerable way, as I thought I had seen enough in the direction in which I had hitherto been wandering.

[At last I came to a kind of open place from which three large streets branched, and in the middle of the place stood the figure of a man on horseback. It was admirably executed, and I stood still to survey it.

"Is that the statue of Cromwell?" said I to a drayman who was passing by, driving a team of that enormous breed of horses which had struck me on the bridge.

"Who?" said the man in a surly tone, stopping short.

"Cromwell," said I; "did you never hear of Oliver Cromwell?"

"Oh, Oliver," said the drayman, and a fine burst of intelligence lighted up his broad English countenance. "To be sure I have; yes, and read of him too. A fine fellow was Oliver, master, and the poor man's friend. Whether that's his figure, though, I can't say. I hopes it be." Then touching his hat to me, he followed his gigantic team, turning his head to look at the statue as he walked along.

That man had he lived in Oliver's time would have made a capital ironside, especially if mounted on one of those dray horses of his. I remained looking at the statue some time longer. Turning round, I perceived that I was close by a bookseller's shop, into which, after deliberating a moment, I entered. An elderly, good-tempered looking man was standing behind the counter.

"Have you the *Dairyman's Daughter?*" I demanded.

"Just one copy, young gentleman," said the bookseller, rubbing his hands; "you are just in time, if you want one; all the rest are sold."

"What kind of character does it bear?"

"Excellent character, young gentleman; great demand for it; held in much esteem, especially by the Evangelical party."

"Who are the Evangelical party?"

"Excellent people, young gentleman, and excellent customers of mine," rubbing his hands; "but setting that aside," he continued gravely, "religious, good men."

"Not a set of canting scoundrels?"

The bookseller had placed a small book upon the counter; but he now suddenly snatched it up and returned it to the shelf; then looking at me full in the face, he said, quietly: "Young gentleman, I do not wish to be uncivil, but you had better leave the shop."

"I beg your pardon if I have offended you, but I was merely repeating what I had heard."

"Whoever told you so must be either a bad, or a very ignorant, man."

"I wish for the book."

"You shall not have it at any price."

"Why not?"

"I have my reasons," said the bookseller.

"Will you have the kindness," said I, "to tell me whose statue it is which stands there on horseback?"

"Charles the First."

"And where is Cromwell's?"

"You may walk far enough about London, or, indeed, about England, before you will find a statue of Cromwell, young gentleman."

"Well, I could not help thinking that was his."

"How came you to think so?"

"I thought it would be just the place for a statue to the most illustrious Englishman. It is where I would place one were I prime minister."

"Well, I do think that Charles would look better a little farther down, opposite to Whitehall, for example," said the bookseller, rubbing his hands. "Do you really wish to have the book?"

"Very much."

"Well, here it is; no price, young gentleman; no price—can't break my word—give the money, if you like, to the beggars in the street. Cromwell is the first Englishman who endeavoured to put all sects on an equality. Wouldn't do, though—world too fond of humbug—still is. However, good day, young gentleman, and when you are prime minister, do not forget the two statues."]

I should say that I scarcely walked less than thirty miles about the big city on the day of my first arrival. Night came on, but still I was walking about, my eyes wide open, and admiring everything that presented itself to them. Everything was new to me, for everything is different in London from what it is elsewhere —the people, their language, the horses, the *tout ensemble*—even the stones of London are different from others—at least it appeared to me that I had never walked with the same ease and facility on the flag-stones of a country town as on those of London; so I continued roving about till night came on, and then the splendour of some of the shops particularly struck me. "A regular Arabian nights' entertainment!" said I, as I looked into one on Cornhill, gorgeous with precious merchandise, and lighted up with lustres, the rays of which were reflected from a hundred mirrors.

But, notwithstanding the excellence of the London pavement, I began about nine o'clock to feel myself thoroughly tired; painfully and slowly did I drag my feet along. I also felt very much in want of some refreshment, and I remembered that since breakfast I had taken nothing. I was now in the Strand, and, glancing about, I perceived that I was close by an hotel, which bore over the door the somewhat remarkable name of Holy Lands. Without a moment's hesitation I entered a well-lighted passage, and, turning to the left, I found myself in a well-lighted coffee-room, with a well-dressed and frizzled waiter before me. "Bring me some claret," said I, for I was rather faint than hungry, and I felt ashamed to give a humbler order to so well-dressed an individual. The waiter looked at me for a moment; then, making a low bow, he bustled off, and I sat myself down in

the box nearest to the window. Presently the waiter returned,
bearing beneath his left arm a long bottle, and between the
fingers of his right hand two large purple glasses ; placing the
latter on the table, he produced a cork-screw, drew the cork in a
twinkling, set the bottle down before me with a bang, and then,
standing still, appeared to watch my movements. You think I
don't know how to drink a glass of claret, thought I to myself.
I'll soon show you how we drink claret where I come from ; and,
filling one of the glasses to the brim, I flickered it for a moment
between my eyes and the lustre, and then held it to my nose ;
having given that organ full time to test the bouquet of the wine,
I applied the glass to my lips, taking a large mouthful of the
wine, which I swallowed slowly and by degrees, that the palate
might likewise have an opportunity of performing its functions.
A second mouthful I disposed of more summarily ; then, placing
the empty glass upon the table, I fixed my eyes upon the bottle,
and said—nothing ; whereupon the waiter, who had been observing the whole process with considerable attention, made me a
bow yet more low than before, and turning on his heel, retired
with a smart chuck of his head, as much as to say, It is all right ;
the young man is used to claret.

And when the waiter had retired I took a second glass of the
wine, which I found excellent ; and, observing a newspaper lying
near me, I took it up and began perusing it. It has been
observed somewhere that people who are in the habit of reading
newspapers every day are not unfrequently struck with the excellence of style and general talent which they display. Now, if
that be the case, how must I have been surprised, who was
reading a newspaper for the first time, and that one of the best
of the London Journals ! Yes, strange as it may seem, it was
nevertheless true, that, up to the moment of which I am speaking,
I had never read a newspaper of any description. I of course
had frequently seen journals, and even handled them ; but, as
for reading them, what were they to me ?—I cared not for news.
But here I was now with my claret before me, perusing, perhaps,
the best of all the London Journals—it was not the —— and I was
astonished : an entirely new field of literature appeared to be
opened to my view. It was a discovery, but I confess rather an
unpleasant one ; for I said to myself, if literary talent is so very
common in London, that the journals, things which, as their very
name denotes, are ephemeral, are written in a style like the article
I have been perusing, how can I hope to distinguish myself in
this big town, when, for the life of me, I don't think I could

write anything half so clever as what I have been reading. And then I laid down the paper, and fell into deep musing; rousing myself from which, I took a glass of wine, and pouring out another, began musing again. What I have been reading, thought I, is certainly very clever and very talented; but talent and cleverness I think I have heard some one say are very common-place things, only fitted for everyday occasions. I question whether the man who wrote the book I saw this day on the bridge was a clever man; but, after all, was he not something much better? I don't think he could have written this article, but then he wrote the book which I saw on the bridge. Then, if he could not have written the article on which I now hold my forefinger—and I do not believe he could—why should I feel discouraged at the consciousness that I, too, could not write it? I certainly could no more have written the article than he could; but then, like him, though I would not compare myself to the man who wrote the book I saw upon the bridge, I think I could—and here I emptied the glass of claret—write something better.

Thereupon I resumed the newspaper; and, as I was before struck with the fluency of style and the general talent which it displayed, I was now equally so with its common-placeness and want of originality on every subject; and it was evident to me that, whatever advantage these newspaper-writers might have over me in some points, they had never studied the Welsh bards, translated Kæmpe Viser, or been under the pupilage of Mr. Petulengro and Tawno Chikno.

And as I sat conning the newspaper three individuals entered the room, and seated themselves in the box at the farther end of which I was. They were all three very well dressed; two of them elderly gentlemen, the third a young man about my own age, or perhaps a year or two older. They called for coffee; and, after two or three observations, the two eldest commenced a conversation in French, which, however, though they spoke it fluently enough, I perceived at once was not their native language; the young man, however, took no part in their conversation, and when they addressed a portion to him, which indeed was but rarely, merely replied by a monosyllable. I have never been a listener, and I paid but little heed to their discourse, nor indeed to themselves; as I occasionally looked up, however, I could perceive that the features of the young man, who chanced to be seated exactly opposite to me, wore an air of constraint and vexation. This circumstance caused me to observe him more particularly than I otherwise should have done: his features were handsome and prepossessing; he had dark brown hair, and a high-arched forehead. After the lapse of half an hour, the two elder individuals, having finished their coffee, called for the waiter, and then rose as if to depart, the young man, however, still remaining seated in the box. The others, having reached the door, turned round, and, finding that the youth did not follow them, one of them called to him with a tone of some authority; whereupon the young man rose, and, pronouncing half audibly the word "botheration," rose and followed them. I now observed that he was remarkably tall. All three left the house. In about ten minutes, finding nothing more worth reading in the news-paper, I laid it down, and though the claret was not yet exhausted, I was thinking of betaking myself to my lodgings, and was about to call the waiter, when I heard a step in the passage, and in another moment, the tall young man entered the room, advanced to the same box, and, sitting down nearly opposite to me, again pro-nounced to himself, but more audibly than before, the same word.

"A troublesome world this, sir," said I, looking at him.

"Yes," said the young man, looking fixedly at me; "but I am afraid we bring most of our troubles on our own heads—at least I can say so of myself," he added, laughing. Then, after a pause, "I beg pardon," he said, "but am I not addressing one of my own country?"

"Of what country are you?" said I.

"Ireland."

"I am not of your country, sir; but I have an infinite veneration for your country, as Strap said to the French soldier. Will you take a glass of wine?"

"*Ah, de tout mon cœur,* as the parasite said to Gil Blas," cried the young man, laughing. "Here's to our better acquaintance!"

And better acquainted we soon became; and I found that, in making the acquaintance of the young man, I had, indeed, made a valuable acquisition; he was accomplished, highly connected, and bore the name of Francis Ardry.[1] Frank and ardent he was, and in a very little time had told me much that related to himself, and in return I communicated a general outline of my own history; he listened with profound attention, but laughed heartily when I told him some particulars of my visit in the morning to the publisher, whom he had frequently heard of.

We left the house together.

"We shall soon see each other again," said he, as we separated at the door of my lodging.

[1] *MS.,* "*Arden*" throughout.

CHAPTER XXXIII.

On the Sunday I was punctual to my appointment to dine with the publisher. As I hurried along the square in which his house stood, my thoughts were fixed so intently on the great man that I passed by him without seeing him. He had observed me, however, and joined me just as I was about to knock at the door. "Let us take a turn in the square," said he, "we shall not dine for half an hour."

"Well," said he, as we were walking in the square, "what have you been doing since I last saw you?"

"I have been looking about London," said I, "and I have bought the *Dairyman's Daughter;* here it is."

"Pray put it up," said the publisher; "I don't want to look at such trash. Well, do you think you could write anything like it?"

"I do not," said I.

"How is that?" said the publisher, looking at me.

"Because," said I, "the man who wrote it seems to be perfectly well acquainted with his subject; and, moreover, to write from the heart."

"By the subject you mean ——"

"Religion."

"And a'n't you acquainted with religion?"

"Very little."

"I am sorry for that," said the publisher seriously, "for he who sets up for an author ought to be acquainted not only with religion, but religions, and indeed with all subjects, like my good friend in the country. It is well that I have changed my mind about the *Dairyman's Daughter*, or I really don't know whom I could apply to on the subject at the present moment, unless to himself; and after all, I question whether his style is exactly suited for an evangelical novel."

"Then you do not wish for an imitation of the *Dairyman's Daughter?*"

"I do not, sir; I have changed my mind, as I told you

(202)

before; I wish to employ you in another line, but will communicate to you my intentions after dinner."

At dinner, besides the publisher and myself, were present his wife and son, with his newly-married bride; the wife appeared a quiet, respectable woman, and the young people looked very happy and good-natured; not so the publisher, who occasionally eyed both with contempt and dislike. Connected with this dinner there was one thing remarkable; the publisher took no animal food, but contented himself with feeding voraciously on rice and vegetables, prepared in various ways.

"You eat no animal food, sir?" said I.

"I do not, sir," said he; "I have forsworn it upwards of twenty years. In one respect, sir, I am a Brahmin. I abhor taking away life—the brutes have as much right to live as ourselves."

"But," said I, "if the brutes were not killed, there would be such a superabundance of them, that the land would be overrun with them."

"I do not think so, sir; few are killed in India, and yet there is plenty of room."

"But," said I, "Nature intended that they should be destroyed, and the brutes themselves prey upon one another, and it is well for themselves and the world that they do so. What would be the state of things if every insect, bird and worm were left to perish of old age?"

"We will change the subject," said the publisher; "I have never been a friend to unprofitable discussions."

I looked at the publisher with some surprise, I had not been accustomed to be spoken to so magisterially; his countenance was dressed in a portentous frown, and his eye looked more sinister than ever; at that moment he put me in mind of some of those despots of whom I had read in the history of Morocco, whose word was law. He merely wants power, thought I to myself, to be a regular Muley Mehemet; and then I sighed, for I remembered how very much I was in the power of that man.

The dinner over, the publisher nodded to his wife, who departed, followed by her daughter-in-law. The son looked as if he would willingly have attended them; he, however, remained seated; and, a small decanter of wine being placed on the table, the publisher filled two glasses, one of which he handed to myself, and the other to his son, saying: "Suppose you two drink to the success of the Review. I would join you," said he, addressing himself to me, "but I drink no wine; if I am a

Brahmin with respect to meat, I am a Mahometan with respect to wine."

So the son and I drank success to the Review, and then the young man asked me various questions; for example—how I liked London?—Whether I did not think it a very fine place?—Whether I was at the play the night before?—and whether I was in the park that afternoon? He seemed preparing to ask me some more questions; but, receiving a furious look from his father, he became silent, filled himself a glass of wine, drank it off, looked at the table for about a minute, then got up, pushed back his chair, made me a bow, and left the room.

"Is that young gentleman, sir," said I, "well versed in the principles of criticism?"

"He is not, sir," said the publisher; "and, if I place him at the head of the Review ostensibly, I do it merely in the hope of procuring him a maintenance; of the principle of a thing he knows nothing, except that the principle of bread is wheat, and that the principle of that wine is grape. Will you take another glass?"

I looked at the decanter; but not feeling altogether so sure as the publisher's son with respect to the principle of what it contained, I declined taking any more.

"No, sir," said the publisher, adjusting himself in his chair, "he knows nothing about criticism, and will have nothing more to do with the reviewals than carrying about the books to those who have to review them; the real conductor of the Review will be a widely different person, to whom I will, when convenient, introduce you. And now we will talk of the matter which we touched upon before dinner: I told you then that I had changed my mind with respect to you; I have been considering the state of the market, sir, the book market, and I have come to the conclusion that, though you might be profitably employed upon evangelical novels, you could earn more money for me, sir, and consequently for yourself, by a compilation of Newgate lives and trials."

"Newgate lives and trials!"

"Yes, sir," said the publisher, "Newgate lives and trials; and now, sir, I will briefly state to you the services which I expect you to perform, and the terms I am willing to grant. I expect you, sir, to compile six volumes of Newgate lives and trials, each volume to contain by no manner of means less than one thousand pages; the remuneration which you will receive when the work is completed will be fifty pounds, which is likewise intended to cover any expenses you may incur in procuring books, papers and manuscripts necessary for the compilation. Such will be one of your employments, sir,—such the terms. In the second place, you will be expected to make yourself useful in the Review —generally useful, sir—doing whatever is required of you; for it is not customary, at least with me, to permit writers, especially young writers, to choose their subjects. In these two departments, sir, namely, compilation and reviewing, I had yesterday, after due consideration, determined upon employing you. I had intended to employ you no further, sir—at least for the present; but, sir, this morning I received a letter from my valued friend in the country, in which he speaks in terms of strong admiration (I don't overstate) of your German acquirements. Sir, he says that it would be a thousand pities if your knowledge of the German language should be lost to the world, or even permitted to sleep, and he entreats me to think of some plan by which it may be turned to account. Sir, I am at all times willing, if possible, to oblige my worthy friend, and likewise to encourage merit and talent; I have, therefore, determined to employ you in German."

"Sir," said I, rubbing my hands, "you are very kind, and so is our mutual friend; I shall be happy to make myself useful in German; and if you think a good translation from Goethe—his 'Sorrows' for example, or more particularly his 'Faust' ——"

"Sir," said the publisher, "Goethe is a drug; his 'Sorrows' are a drug, so is his 'Faustus,' more especially the last, since that fool —— rendered him into English. No, sir, I do not want you to translate Goethe or anything belonging to him; nor do I want you to translate anything from the German; what I want you to do, is to translate into German. I am willing to encourage merit, sir; and, as my good friend in his last letter has spoken very highly of your German acquirements, I have determined that you shall translate my book of philosophy into German."

"Your book of philosophy into German, sir?"

"Yes, sir; my book of philosophy into German. I am not a drug, sir, in Germany, as Goethe is here, no more is my book. I intend to print the translation at Leipzig, sir; and if it turns out a profitable speculation, as I make no doubt it will, provided the translation be well executed, I will make you some remuneration. Sir, your remuneration will be determined by the success of your translation."

"But, sir ——"

"Sir," said the publisher, interrupting me, "you have heard my intentions; I consider that you ought to feel yourself highly gratified by my intentions towards you; it is not frequently that I deal with a writer, especially a young writer, as I have done with you. And now, sir, permit me to inform you that I wish to be alone. This is Sunday afternoon, sir; I never go to church, but I am in the habit of spending part of every Sunday afternoon alone—profitably, I hope, sir—in musing on the magnificence of nature and the moral dignity of man."

CHAPTER XXXIV.

"What can't be cured must be endured," and "it is hard to kick against the pricks".

At the period to which I have brought my history, I bethought me of the proverbs with which I have headed this chapter, and determined to act up to their spirit. I determined not to fly in the face of the publisher, and to bear—what I could not cure—his arrogance and vanity. At present, at the conclusion of nearly a quarter of a century, I am glad that I came to that determination, which I did my best to carry into effect.

Two or three days after our last interview, the publisher made his appearance in my apartment; he bore two tattered volumes under his arm, which he placed on the table. " I have brought you two volumes of lives, sir," said he, " which I yesterday found in my garret; you will find them of service for your compilation. As I always wish to behave liberally and encourage talent, especially youthful talent, I shall make no charge for them, though I should be justified in so doing, as you are aware that, by our agreement, you are to provide any books and materials which may be necessary. Have you been in quest of any?"

" No," said I, " not yet."

" Then, sir, I would advise you to lose no time in doing so; you must visit all the bookstalls, sir, especially those in the by-streets and blind alleys. It is in such places that you will find the description of literature you are in want of. You must be up and doing, sir; it will not do for an author, especially a young author, to be idle in this town. To-night you will receive my book of philosophy, and likewise books for the Review. And, by-the-bye, sir, it will be as well for you to review my book of philosophy for the Review, the other Reviews not having noticed it. Sir, before translating it, I wish you to review my book of philosophy for the Review."

" I shall be happy to do my best, sir."

" Very good, sir ; I should be unreasonable to expect anything beyond a person's best. And now, sir, if you please, I will

conduct you to the future editor of the Review. As you are to
co-operate, sir, I deem it right to make you acquainted."

The intended editor was a little old man, who sat in a kind of
wooden pavilion in a small garden behind a house in one of the
purlieus of the city, composing tunes upon a piano. The walls
of the pavilion were covered with fiddles of various sizes and
appearances, and a considerable portion of the floor occupied
by a pile of books all of one size. The publisher introduced
him to me as a gentleman scarcely less eminent in literature than
in music, and me to him as an aspirant critic—a young gentleman
scarcely less eminent in philosophy than in philology. The conversation consisted entirely of compliments till just before we
separated, when the future editor inquired of me whether I had
ever read Quintilian ; and, on my replying in the negative, expressed his surprise that any gentleman should aspire to become
a critic who had never read Quintilian, with the comfortable
information, however, that he could supply me with a Quintilian
at half-price, that is, a translation made by himself some years
previously, of which he had, pointing to the heap on the floor,
still a few copies remaining unsold. For some reason or other,
perhaps a poor one, I did not purchase the editor's translation of
Quintilian.

"Sir," said the publisher, as we were returning from our visit
to the editor, "you did right in not purchasing a drug. I am not
prepared, sir, to say that Quintilian is a drug, never having seen
him ; but I am prepared to say that man's translation is a drug,
judging from the heap of rubbish on the floor ; besides, sir, you
will want any loose money you may have to purchase the description of literature which is required for your compilation."

The publisher presently paused before the entrance of a very
forlorn-looking street. "Sir," said he, after looking down it with
attention, "I should not wonder if in that street you find works
connected with the description of literature which is required for
your compilation. It is in streets of this description, sir, and
blind alleys, where such works are to be found. You had better
search that street, sir, whilst I continue my way."

I searched the street to which the publisher had pointed, and,
in the course of the three succeeding days, many others of a
similar kind. I did not find the description of literature alluded
to by the publisher to be a drug, but, on the contrary, both scarce
and dear. I had expended much more than my loose money
long before I could procure materials even for the first volume
of my compilation.

CHAPTER XXXV.

ONE evening I was visited by the tall young gentleman, Francis Ardry, whose acquaintance I had formed at the coffee-house. As it is necessary that the reader should know something more about this young man, who will frequently appear in the course of these pages, I will state in a few words who and what he was. He was born of an ancient Roman Catholic family in Ireland; his parents, whose only child he was, had long been dead. His father, who had survived his mother several years, had been a spendthrift, and at his death had left the family property considerably embarrassed. Happily, however, the son and the estate fell into the hands of careful guardians, near relations of the family, by whom the property was managed to the best advantage, and every means taken to educate the young man in a manner suitable to his expectations. At the age of sixteen he was taken from a celebrated school in England at which he had been placed, and sent to a small French University, in order that he might form an intimate and accurate acquaintance with the grand language of the continent. There he continued three years, at the end of which he went, under the care of a French abbé, to Germany and Italy. It was in this latter country that he first began to cause his guardians serious uneasiness. He was in the hey-day of youth when he visited Italy, and he entered wildly into the various delights of that fascinating region, and, what was worse, falling into the hands of certain sharpers, not Italian, but English, he was fleeced of considerable sums of money. The abbé, who, it seems, was an excellent individual of the old French school, remonstrated with his pupil on his dissipation and extravagance; but, finding his remonstrances vain, very properly informed the guardians of the manner of life of his charge. They were not slow in commanding Francis Ardry home; and, as he was entirely in their power, he was forced to comply. He had been about three months in London when I met him in the coffee-room, and the two elderly gentlemen in his company were his guardians. At this time they were very solicitous that he should choose for

himself a profession, offering to his choice either the army or law
—he was calculated to shine in either of these professions—for,
like many others of his countrymen, he was brave and eloquent ;
but he did not wish to shackle himself with a profession. As,
however, his minority did not terminate till he was three-and-
twenty, of which age he wanted nearly two years, during which
he would be entirely dependent on his guardians, he deemed it
expedient to conceal, to a certain degree, his sentiments, tempor-
ising with the old gentlemen, with whom, notwithstanding his
many irregularities, he was a great favourite, and at whose death
he expected to come into a yet greater property than that which
he inherited from his parents.

Such is a brief account of Francis Ardry—of my friend Francis
Ardry ; for the acquaintance, commenced in the singular manner
with which the reader is acquainted, speedily ripened into a friendship which endured through many long years of separation, and
which still endures certainly on my part, and on his—if he lives ;
but it is many years since I have heard from Francis Ardry.

And yet many people would have thought it impossible for
our friendship to have lasted a week, for in many respects no two
people could be more dissimilar. He was an Irishman, I an
Englishman ; he fiery, enthusiastic and open-hearted, I neither
fiery, enthusiastic nor open-hearted ; he fond of pleasure and
dissipation, I of study and reflection. Yet it is of such dissimilar elements that the most lasting friendships are formed :
we do not like counterparts of ourselves. " Two great talkers will
not travel far together," is a Spanish saying ; I will add, " Nor two
silent people " ; we naturally love our opposites.

So Francis Ardry came to see me, and right glad I was to see
him, for I had just flung my books and papers aside, and was
wishing for a little social converse ; and when we had conversed
for some little time together, Francis Ardry proposed that we
should go to the play to see Kean ; so we went to the play, and
saw—not Kean, who at that time was ashamed to show himself,
but—a man who was not ashamed to show himself, and who
people said was a much better man than Kean—as I have no
doubt he was—though whether he was a better actor I cannot say,
for I never saw Kean.[1]

---

[1] The *MS.* develops this paragraph as follows :—
So Francis Ardry called upon me, and right glad I was that he did so ; and
after we had sat conversing for some time, he said, " Did you ever see Kean ? "
" No," said I, " but I have heard both of him and of Belcher. I should like
to see either, especially the latter. Where are they to be found ? "

Two or three evenings after, Francis Ardry came to see me
again, and again we went out together, and Francis Ardry took
me to—shall I say?—why not?—a gaming-house, where I saw
people playing, and where I saw Francis Ardry play and lose five
guineas, and where I lost nothing, because I did not play, though
I felt somewhat inclined; for a man with a white hat and a sparkling eye held up a box which contained something which rattled,
and asked me to fling the bones. "There is nothing like flinging
the bones!" said he, and then I thought I should like to know
what kind of thing flinging the bones was; I, however, restrained
myself. "There is nothing like flinging the bones!" shouted the
man, as my friend and myself left the room.

Long life and prosperity to Francis Ardry! but for him I should
not have obtained knowledge which I did of the strange and
eccentric places of London. Some of the places to which he took
me were very strange places indeed! but, however strange the

" I know nothing of the latter," said Frank, " but if you wish to see Kean,
you had better come with me where he will appear to-night after a long absence.
The public are anxiously waiting for him, intending to pelt him off the stage."
" And what has he done," said I, " to be pelted off the stage?"
" What is very naughty," said Frank; " breaking one of the commandments."
" And did he break the commandment on the stage?"
" No," said Frank, " I never heard that he broke it on the stage, except in
the way of his profession."
" Then, what have the public to do with the matter?"
" They think they have," said Frank.
And then we went out together to see Shakespeare's " Richard," or rather we
went to see the man who was to personate Shakespeare's " Richard"—and so did
thousands; we did not see him, however. There was a great tumult, I remember,
in the theatre. The man who was to perform the part of Richard, and who it
was said was the best hand for interpreting the character that had ever appeared
on the stage, had a short time before been involved in a disgraceful affair, and
this was to be his first appearance on the stage since the discovery. The consequence was that crowds flocked to the theatre with the firm intention of expressing
their indignation. " We will pelt his eyes out," said a man who sat beside me
in the pit—for we sat in the pit—and who bore the breach of all the commandments in his face. The actor in question, however, who perhaps heard the threats
which were vented against him, very prudently kept out of the way, and the
manager coming forward informed the public that another would perform the
part—whereupon there was a great uproar. " We have been imposed upon,"
said the individual who sat beside me. " I came here for nothing else than to
pelt that scoundrel off the stage." The uproar, however, at length subsided,
and the piece commenced. In a little time there was loud applause. The actor
who had appeared in place of the other was performing. " What do you clap
for?" said I to the individual by my side, who was clapping most of all. " What
do I clap for?" said the man. " Why, to encourage Macready, to be sure.
Don't you see how divinely he acts? why, he beats Kean hollow. Besides this,
he's a moral man, and I like morality." " Do you mean to say," said I, " that
he was never immoral?" " I neither know nor care," said the man; " all I know
is that he has never been found out. It will never do to encourage a public man
who has been found out. No, no! the morality of the stage must be seen after."

places were, I observed that the inhabitants thought there were no places like their several places, and no occupations like their several occupations; and among other strange places to which Francis Ardry conducted me, was a place not far from the abbey church of Westminster.

Before we entered this place our ears were greeted by a confused hubbub of human voices, squealing of rats, barking of dogs, and the cries of various other animals. Here we beheld a kind of cock-pit, around which a great many people, seeming of all ranks, but chiefly of the lower, were gathered, and in it we saw a dog destroy a great many rats in a very small period; and when the dog had destroyed the rats, we saw a fight between a dog and a bear, then a fight between two dogs, then ——

After the diversions of the day were over, my friend introduced me to the genius of the place, a small man of about five feet high, with a very sharp countenance, and dressed in a brown jockey coat, and top boots. "Joey,"[1] said he, "this is a friend of mine." Joey nodded to me with a patronising air. "Glad to see you; sir! —want a dog?"

"No," said I.

"You have got one, then —want to match him?"

"We have a dog at home," said I, "in the country; but I can't say I should like to match him. Indeed, I do not like dog-fighting."

"Not like dog-fighting!" said the man, staring.

"The truth is, Joe, that he is just come to town."

"So I should think; he looks rather green—not like dog-fighting!"

"Nothing like it, is there, Joey?"

"I should think not; what is like it? A time will come, and that speedily, when folks will give up everything else, and follow dog-fighting."

"Do you think so?" said I.

"Think so? Let me ask what there is that a man wouldn't give up for it?"

"Why," said I, modestly, "there's religion."

"Religion! How you talk. Why, there's myself, bred and born an Independent, and intended to be a preacher, didn't I give up religion for dog-fighting? Religion, indeed! If it were not for the rascally law, my pit would fill better on Sundays than any other time. Who would go to church when they could come

MS. "Charlie" and "Charlie's" throughout.

to my pit? Religion! why, the parsons themselves come to my pit; and I have now a letter in my pocket from one of them, asking me to send him a dog."

"Well, then, politics," said I.

"Politics! Why, the gemmen in the House would leave Pitt himself, if he were alive, to come to my pit. There were three of the best of them here to-night, all great horators. Get on with you, what comes next?"

"Why, there's learning and letters."

"Pretty things, truly, to keep people from dog-fighting! Why, there's the young gentlemen from the Abbey School comes here in shoals, leaving books, and letters, and masters too. To tell you the truth, I rather wish they would mind their letters, for a more precious set of young blackguards I never seed. It was only the other day I was thinking of calling in a constable for my own protection, for I thought my pit would have been torn down by them."

Scarcely knowing what to say, I made an observation at random. "You show by your own conduct," said I, "that there are other things worth following besides dog-fighting. You practise rat-catching and badger-baiting as well."

The dog-fancier eyed me with supreme contempt.

"Your friend here," said he, "might well call you a new one. When I talks of dog-fighting, I of course means rat-catching and badger-baiting, ay, and bull-baiting too, just as when I speaks religiously, when I says one I means not one but three. And talking of religion puts me in mind that I have something else to do besides chaffing here, having a batch of dogs to send off by this night's packet to the Pope of Rome."

But at last I had seen enough of what London had to show, whether strange or common-place, so at least I thought, and I ceased to accompany my friend in his rambles about town, and to partake of his adventures. Our friendship, however, still continued unabated, though I saw, in consequence, less of him. I reflected that time was passing on, that the little money I had brought to town was fast consuming, and that I had nothing to depend upon but my own exertions for a fresh supply; and I returned with redoubled application to my pursuits.

CHAPTER XXXVI.

I COMPILED the *Chronicles of Newgate*; I reviewed books for the Review established on an entirely new principle; and I occasionally tried my best to translate into German portions of the publisher's philosophy. In this last task I experienced more than one difficulty. I was a tolerable German scholar, it is true, and I had long been able to translate from German into English with considerable facility; but to translate from a foreign language into your own, is a widely different thing from translating from your own into a foreign language; and, in my first attempt to render the publisher into German, I was conscious of making miserable failures, from pure ignorance of German grammar; however, by the assistance of grammars and dictionaries, and by extreme perseverance, I at length overcame all the difficulties connected with the German language. But alas! another difficulty remained, far greater than any connected with German —a difficulty connected with the language of the publisher—the language which the great man employed in his writings was very hard to understand; I say in his writings, for his colloquial English was plain enough. Though not professing to be a scholar, he was much addicted, when writing, to the use of Greek and Latin terms, not as other people used them, but in a manner of his own, which set the authority of dictionaries at defiance; the consequence was, that I was sometimes utterly at a loss to understand the meaning of the publisher. Many a quarter of an hour did I pass at this period staring at periods of the publisher, and wondering what he could mean, but in vain, till at last, with a shake of the head, I would snatch up the pen, and render the publisher literally into German. Sometimes I was almost tempted to substitute something of my own for what the publisher had written, but my conscience interposed; the awful words *Traduttore traditore* commenced ringing in my ears, and I asked myself whether I should be acting honourably towards the publisher, who had committed to me the delicate task of translating him into German; should I be acting honourably towards him, in making him speak in German in a manner different from that in

(214)

which he expressed himself in English? No, I could not reconcile such conduct with any principle of honour; by substituting something of my own in lieu of these mysterious passages of the publisher, I might be giving a fatal blow to his whole system of philosophy. Besides, when translating into English, had I treated foreign authors in this manner? Had I treated the minstrels of the Kiæmpe Viser in this manner? No. Had I treated Ab Gwilym in this manner? Even when translating his Ode to the Mist, in which he is misty enough, had I attempted to make Ab Gwilym less misty? No; on referring to my translation, I found that Ab Gwilym in my hands was quite as misty as in his own. Then, seeing that I had not ventured to take liberties with people who had never put themselves into my hands for the purpose of being rendered, how could I venture to substitute my own thoughts and ideas for the publisher's, who had put himself into my hands for that purpose? Forbid it every proper feeling! —so I told the Germans in the publisher's own way, the publisher's tale of an apple and a pear.

I at first felt much inclined to be of the publisher's opinion with respect to the theory of the pear. After all, why should the earth be shaped like an apple, and not like a pear?—it would certainly gain in appearance by being shaped like a pear. A pear being a handsomer fruit than an apple, the publisher is probably right, thought I, and I will say that he is right on this point in the notice which I am about to write of his publication for the Review. And yet I don't know, said I, after a long fit of musing —I don't know but what there is more to be said for the Oxford theory. The world may be shaped like a pear, but I don't know that it is; but one thing I know, which is, that it does not taste like a pear; I have always liked pears, but I don't like the world. The world to me tastes much more like an apple, and I have never liked apples. I will uphold the Oxford theory; besides, I am writing in an Oxford Review, and am in duty bound to uphold the Oxford theory. So in my notice I asserted that the world was round; I quoted Scripture, and endeavoured to prove that the world was typified by the apple in Scripture, both as to shape and properties. "An apple is round," said I, "and the world is round; the apple is a sour, disagreeable fruit, and who has tasted much of the world without having his teeth set on edge?" I, however, treated the publisher, upon the whole, in the most urbane and Oxford-like manner; complimenting him upon his style, acknowledging the general soundness of his views, and only differing with him in the affair of the apple and pear.

I did not like reviewing at all—it was not to my taste; it was not in my way; I liked it far less than translating the publisher's philosophy, for that was something in the line of one whom a competent judge had surnamed "Lavengro". I never could understand why reviews were instituted; works of merit do not require to be reviewed, they can speak for themselves, and require no praising; works of no merit at all will die of themselves, they require no killing. The Review to which I was attached was, as has been already intimated, established on an entirely new plan; it professed to review all new publications, which certainly no Review had ever professed to do before, other Reviews never pretending to review more than one-tenth of the current literature of the day. When I say it professed to review all new publications, I should add, which should be sent to it; for, of course, the Review would not acknowledge the existence of publications, the authors of which did not acknowledge the existence of the Review. I don't think, however, that the Review had much cause to complain of being neglected; I have reason to believe that at least nine-tenths of the publications of the day were sent to the Review, and in due time reviewed. I had good opportunity of judging. I was connected with several departments of the Review, though more particularly with the poetical and philosophic ones. An English translation of Kant's philosophy made its appearance on my table the day before its publication. In my notice of this work, I said that the English shortly hoped to give the Germans a *quid pro quo.* I believe at that time authors were much in the habit of publishing at their own expense. All the poetry which I reviewed appeared to be published at the expense of the authors. If I am asked how I comported myself, under all circumstances, as a reviewer, I answer, I did not forget that I was connected with a Review established on Oxford principles, the editor of which had translated Quintilian. All the publications which fell under my notice I treated in a gentlemanly and Oxford-like manner, no personalities—no vituperation—no shabby insinuations; decorum, decorum was the order of the day. Occasionally a word of admonition, but gently expressed, as an Oxford under-graduate might have expressed it, or master of arts. How the authors whose publications were consigned to my colleagues were treated by them I know not; I suppose they were treated in an urbane and Oxford-like manner, but I cannot say; I did not read the reviewals of my colleagues, I did not read my own after they were printed. I did not like reviewing.

Of all my occupations at this period I am free to confess I

liked that of compiling the *Newgate Lives and Trials* the best;
that is, after I had surmounted a kind of prejudice which I
originally entertained. The trials were entertaining enough; but
the lives—how full were they of wild and racy adventures, and in
what racy, genuine language were they told. What struck me
most with respect to these lives was the art which the writers,
whoever they were, possessed of telling a plain story. It is no easy
thing to tell a story plainly and distinctly by mouth; but to tell
one on paper is difficult indeed, so many snares lie in the way.
People are afraid to put down what is common on paper, they
seek to embellish their narratives, as they think, by philosophic
speculations and reflections; they are anxious to shine, and people
who are anxious to shine can never tell a plain story. "So
I went with them to a music booth, where they made me almost
drunk with gin, and began to talk their flash language, which I
did not understand," says, or is made to say, Henry Simms, executed
at Tyburn some seventy years before the time of which I am speaking. I have always looked upon this sentence as a masterpiece
of the narrative style, it is so concise and yet so very clear. As I
gazed on passages like this, and there were many nearly as good
in the *Newgate Lives*, I often sighed that it was not my fortune to
have to render these lives into German rather than the publisher's
philosophy—his tale of an apple and pear.

Mine was an ill-regulated mind at this period. As I read over
the lives of these robbers and pickpockets, strange doubts began
to arise in my mind about virtue and crime. Years before, when
quite a boy, as in one of the early chapters I have hinted, I had
been a necessitarian; I had even written an essay on crime (I have
it now before me, penned in a round, boyish hand), in which I
attempted to prove that there is no such thing as crime or virtue,
all our actions being the result of circumstances or necessity.
These doubts were now again reviving in my mind; I could not
for the life of me imagine how, taking all circumstances into
consideration, these highwaymen, these pickpockets, should have
been anything else than highwaymen and pickpockets; any more
than how, taking all circumstances into consideration, Bishop
Latimer (the reader is aware that I had read Fox's *Book of
Martyrs*) should have been anything else than Bishop Latimer.
I had a very ill-regulated mind at that period.

My own peculiar ideas with respect to everything being a lying
dream began also to revive. Sometimes at midnight, after having
toiled for hours at my occupations, I would fling myself back on
my chair, look about the poor apartment, dimly lighted by an

unsnuffed candle, or upon the heaps of books and papers before me, and exclaim : " Do I exist ?   Do these things, which I think I see about me, exist, or do they not ?   Is not everything a dream —a deceitful dream ?   Is not this apartment a dream—the furniture a dream ?   The publisher a dream—his philosophy a dream ? Am I not myself a dream—dreaming about translating a dream ? I can't see why all should not be a dream ; what's the use of the reality ? "   And then I would pinch myself, and snuff the burdened smoky light.   " I can't see, for the life of me, the use of all this ; therefore, why should I think that it exists ?   If there was a chance, a probability of all this tending to anything, I might believe ; but ——" and then I would stare and think, and after some time shake my head and return again to my occupations for an hour or two ; and then I would perhaps shake, and shiver, and yawn, and look wistfully in the direction of my sleeping apartment ; and then, but not wistfully, at the papers and books before me ; and sometimes I would return to my papers and books ; but oftener I would arise, and, after another yawn and shiver, take my light, and proceed to my sleeping chamber.

They say that light fare begets light dreams ; my fare at that time was light enough, but I had anything but light dreams, for at that period I had all kind of strange and extravagant dreams, and amongst other things I dreamt that the whole world had taken to dog-fighting ; and that I, myself, had taken to dog-fighting, and that in a vast circus I backed an English bulldog against the bloodhound of the Pope of Rome.

CHAPTER XXXVII.

ONE morning I arose somewhat later that usual, having been occupied during the greater part of the night with my literary toil. On descending from my chamber into the sitting-room I found a person seated by the fire, whose glance was directed sideways to the table, on which were the usual preparations for my morning's meal. Forthwith I gave a cry, and sprang forward to embrace the person; for the person by the fire, whose glance was directed to the table, was no one else than my brother.

"And how are things going on at home?" said I to my brother, after we had kissed and embraced. "How is my mother, and how is the dog?"

"My mother, thank God, is tolerably well," said my brother, "but very much given to fits of crying. As for the dog, he is not so well; but we will talk more of these matters anon," said my brother, again glancing at the breakfast things: "I am very hungry, as you may suppose, after having travelled all night."

Thereupon I exerted myself to the best of my ability to perform the duties of hospitality, and I made my brother welcome —I may say more than welcome; and, when the rage of my brother's hunger was somewhat abated, we recommenced talking about the matters of our little family, and my brother told me much about my mother; he spoke of her fits of crying, but said that of late the said fits of crying had much diminished, and she appeared to be taking comfort; and if I am not much mistaken, my brother told me that my mother had of late the prayer-book frequently in her hand, and yet oftener the Bible.

We were silent for a time; at last I opened my mouth and mentioned the dog.

"The dog," said my brother, "is, I am afraid, in a very poor way; ever since the death he has done nothing but pine and take on. A few months ago, you remember, he was as plump and fine as any dog in the town; but at present he is little more than skin and bone. Once we lost him for two days, and never expected to see him again, imagining that some mischance had befallen him; at length I found him—where do you think? Chancing to pass by the churchyard, I found him seated on the grave ! "

"Very strange," said I ; " but let us talk of something else. It was very kind of you to come and see me."

" Oh, as for that matter, I did not come up to see you, though of course I am very glad to see you, having been rather anxious about you, like my mother, who has received only one letter from you since your departure. No, I did not come up on purpose to see you; but on quite a different account. You must know that the corporation of our town have lately elected a new mayor, a person of many qualifications—big and portly, with a voice like Boanerges ; a religious man, the possessor of an immense pew; loyal, so much so that I once heard him say that he would at any time go three miles to hear any one sing 'God save the King'; moreover, a giver of excellent dinners. Such is our present mayor; who, owing to his loyalty, his religion, and a little, perhaps, to his dinners, is a mighty favourite ; so much so that the town is anxious to have his portrait painted in a superior style, so that remote posterity may know what kind of man he was, the colour of his hair, his air and gait. So a committee was formed some time ago, which is still sitting ; that is, they dine with the mayor every day to talk over the subject. A few days since, to my great surprise, they made their appearance in my poor studio, and desired to be favoured with a sight of some of my paintings ; well, I showed them some, and, after looking at them with great attention, they went aside and whispered. 'He'll do,' I heard one say ; 'yes, he'll do,' said another; and then they came to me, and one of them, a little man with a hump on his back, who is a watchmaker, assumed the office of spokesman, and made a long speech (the old town has been always celebrated for orators) in which he told me how much they had been pleased with my productions (the old town has been always celebrated for its artistic taste), and, what do you think? offered me the painting of the mayor's portrait, and a hundred pounds for my trouble.

" Well, of course I was much surprised, and for a minute or two could scarcely speak ; recovering myself, however, I made a speech, not so eloquent as that of the watchmaker, of course, being not so accustomed to speaking; but not so bad either, taking everything into consideration, telling them how flattered I felt by the honour which they had conferred in proposing to me such an undertaking; expressing, however, my fears that I was not competent to the task, and concluding by saying what a pity it was that Crome was dead. 'Crome,' said the little man, 'Crome; yes, he was a clever man, a very clever man in his way; he was good at painting landscapes and farm-houses, but he would not do in the present instance, were he alive. He had no conception of the heroic, sir. We want some person capable of representing our mayor striding under the Norman arch out of the cathedral.' At the mention of the heroic, an idea came at once into my head. 'Oh,' said I, 'if you are in quest of the heroic, I am glad that you came to me; don't mistake me,' I continued, 'I do not mean to say that I could do justice to your subject, though I am fond of the heroic; but I can introduce you to a great master of the heroic, fully competent to do justice to your mayor. Not to me, therefore, be the painting of the picture given, but to a friend of mine, the great master of the heroic, to the best, the strongest, τῷ κρατίστῳ,' I added, for, being amongst orators, I thought a word of Greek would tell."

"Well," said I, "and what did the orators say?"

"They gazed dubiously at me and at one another," said my brother; "at last the watchmaker asked me who this Mr. Christo was; adding, that he had never heard of such a person; that, from my recommendation of him, he had no doubt that he was a very clever man, but that they should like to know something more about him before giving the commission to him. That he had heard of Christie the great auctioneer, who was considered to be an excellent judge of pictures; but he supposed that I scarcely —— Whereupon, interrupting the watchmaker, I told him that I alluded neither to Christo nor to Christie, but to the painter of Lazarus rising from the grave, a painter under whom I had myself studied during some months that I had spent in London, and to whom I was indebted for much connected with the heroic."

"I have heard of him," said the watchmaker, "and his paintings too; but I am afraid that he is not exactly the gentleman by whom our mayor would wish to be painted. I have heard say that he is not a very good friend to Church and State. Come, young man," he added, "it appears to me that you are too modest; I like your style of painting, so do we all, and—why should I mince the matter?—the money is to be collected in the town, why should it go into a stranger's pocket, and be spent in London?"

Thereupon I made them a speech, in which I said that art had nothing to do with Church and State, at least with English

Church and State, which had never encouraged it; and that, though Church and State were doubtless very fine things, a man might be a very good artist who cared not a straw for either. I then made use of some more Greek words, and told them how painting was one of the Nine Muses, and one of the most independent creatures alive, inspiring whom she pleased, and asking leave of nobody; that I should be quite unworthy of the favours of the Muse if, on the present occasion, I did not recommend them a man whom I considered to be a much greater master of the heroic than myself; and that, with regard to the money being spent in the city, I had no doubt that they would not weigh for a moment such a consideration against the chance of getting a true heroic picture for the city. I never talked so well in my life, and said so many flattering things to the hunchback and his friends, that at last they said that I should have my own way; and that if I pleased to go up to London, and bring down the painter of Lazarus to paint the mayor, I might; so they then bade me farewell, and I have come up to London.

"To put a hundred pounds into the hands of——"

"A better man than myself," said my brother, "of course."

"And have you come up at your own expense?"

"Yes," said my brother, "I have come up at my own expense."

I made no answer, but looked in my brother's face. We then returned to the former subjects of conversation, talking of the dead, my mother, and the dog.

After some time my brother said: "I will now go to the painter, and communicate to him the business which has brought me to town; and, if you please, I will take you with me and introduce you to him".[1] Having expressed my willingness, we descended into the street.

---

[1] The *MS.* adds: "'It will, perhaps, be as well, first of all, to go to the exhibition of British art, which is at present open. I hear he has a picture there, which he has just finished. We will look at it, and from that you may form a tolerable estimate of his powers.' Thereupon my brother led the way, and we presently found ourselves in the Gallery of British Art."

CHAPTER XXXVIII.

THE painter of the heroic resided a great way off, at the western end of the town. We had some difficulty in obtaining admission to him, a maid-servant, who opened the door, eyeing us somewhat suspiciously; it was not until my brother had said that he was a friend of the painter that we were permitted to pass the threshold. At length we were shown into the studio, where we found the painter, with an easel and brush, standing before a huge piece of canvas, on which he had lately commenced painting a heroic picture. The painter might be about thirty-five years old; he had a clever, intelligent countenance, with a sharp grey eye; his hair was dark brown, and cut à-la Rafael, as I was subsequently told, that is, there was little before and much behind; he did not wear a neckcloth, but, in its stead, a black riband, so that his neck, which was rather fine, was somewhat exposed; he had a broad, muscular breast, and I make no doubt that he would have been a very fine figure, but unfortunately his legs and thighs were somewhat short. He recognised my brother, and appeared glad to see him.

"What brings you to London?" said he.

Whereupon my brother gave him a brief account of his commission. At the mention of the hundred pounds, I observed the eyes of the painter glisten. "Really," said he, when my brother had concluded, "it was very kind to think of me. I am not very fond of painting portraits; but a mayor is a mayor, and there is something grand in that idea of the Norman arch. I'll go; moreover, I am just at this moment confoundedly in need of money, and when you knocked at the door, I don't mind telling you, I thought it was some dun. I don't know how it is, but in the capital they have no taste for the heroic, they will scarce look at a heroic picture; I am glad to hear that they have better taste in the provinces. I'll go; when shall we set off?"

Thereupon it was arranged between the painter and my brother that they should depart the next day but one; they then began to talk of art. "I'll stick to the heroic," said the painter; "I now and then dabble in the comic, but what I do gives me no pleasure, the comic is so low; there is nothing like the heroic. I am engaged here on a heroic picture," said he, pointing to the canvas; "the subject is 'Pharaoh dismissing Moses from Egypt,' after the last plague—the death of the first-born; it is not far advanced—that finished figure is Moses": they both looked at the canvas, and I, standing behind, took a modest peep. The picture, as the painter said, was not far advanced, the Pharaoh was merely in outline; my eye was, of course, attracted by the finished figure, or rather what the painter had called the finished figure; but, as I gazed upon it, it appeared to me that there was something defective—something unsatisfactory in the figure. I concluded, however, that the painter, notwithstanding what he had said, had omitted to give it the finishing touch. "I intend this to be my best picture," said the painter; "what I want now is a face for Pharaoh; I have long been meditating on a face for Pharaoh." Here, chancing to cast his eye upon my countenance, of whom he had scarcely taken any manner of notice, he remained with his mouth open for some time. "Who is this?" said he at last. "Oh, this is my brother, I forgot to introduce him ——"

We presently afterwards departed; my brother talked much about the painter. "He is a noble fellow," said my brother; "but, like many other noble fellows, has a great many enemies; he is hated by his brethren of the brush—all the land and water-scape painters hate him—but, above all, the race of portrait painters, who are ten times more numerous than the other two sorts, detest him for his heroic tendencies. It will be a kind of triumph to the last, I fear, when they hear he has condescended to paint a portrait; however, that Norman arch will enable him to escape from their malice—that is a capital idea of the watchmaker, that Norman arch."

I spent a happy day with my brother. On the morrow he went again to the painter, with whom he dined; I did not go with him. On his return he said: "The painter has been asking a great many questions about you, and expressed a wish that you would sit to him as Pharaoh; he thinks you would make a capital Pharaoh". "I have no wish to appear on canvas," said I; "moreover, he can find much better Pharaohs than myself; and, if he wants a real Pharaoh, there is a certain Mr. Petulengro." "Petulengro?" said my brother; "a strange kind of fellow came up to me some time ago in our town, and asked me about you; when I inquired his name, he told me Petulengro. No, he will

not do, he is too short; by-the-bye, do you not think that figure
of Moses is somewhat short?" And then it appeared to me that
I had thought the figure of Moses somewhat short, and I told my
brother so. "Ah!" said my brother.

On the morrow my brother departed with the painter for the
old town, and there the painter painted the mayor. I did not see
the picture for a great many years, when, chancing to be at the
old town, I beheld it.

The original mayor was a mighty, portly man, with a bull's
head, black hair, body like that of a dray horse, and legs and
thighs corresponding; a man six foot high at the least. To his
bull's head, black hair and body the painter had done justice;
there was one point, however, in which the portrait did not
correspond with the original—the legs were disproportionably
short, the painter having substituted his own legs for those of the
mayor, which when I perceived I rejoiced that I had not consented
to be painted as Pharaoh, for, if I had, the chances are that he
would have served me in exactly a similar way as he had served
Moses and the mayor.

Short legs in a heroic picture will never do; and, upon the
whole, I think the painter's attempt at the heroic in painting the
mayor of the old town a decided failure. If I am now asked
whether the picture would have been a heroic one provided the
painter had not substituted his own legs for those of the mayor,
I must say, I am afraid not. I have no idea of making heroic
pictures out of English mayors, even with the assistance of
Norman arches; yet I am sure that capital pictures might be
made out of English mayors, not issuing from Norman arches,
but rather from the door of the "Checquers" or the "Brewers
Three". The painter in question had great comic power, which
he scarcely ever cultivated; he would fain be a Rafael, which he
never could be, when he might have been something quite as
good—another Hogarth; the only comic piece which he ever
presented to the world being something little inferior to the best
of that illustrious master. I have often thought what a capital
picture might have been made by my brother's friend, if, instead
of making the mayor issue out of the Norman arch, he had painted
him moving under the sign of the "Checquers," or the "Three
Brewers," with mace—yes, with mace,—the mace appears in the
picture issuing out of the Norman arch behind the mayor,—but
likewise with Snap, and with whiffler, quart pot, and frying pan,
Billy Blind, and Owlenglass, Mr. Petulengro and Pakomovna;
then, had he clapped his own legs upon the mayor, or any one

else in the concourse, what matter? But I repeat that I have no
hope of making heroic pictures out of English mayors, or, indeed,
out of English figures in general. England may be a land of
heroic hearts, but it is not, properly, a land of heroic figures, or
heroic posture-making. Italy —— what was I going to say about
Italy?

CHAPTER XXXIX.

AND now once more to my pursuits, to my *Lives and Trials*. However partial at first I might be to these lives and trials, it was not long before they became regular trials to me, owing to the whims and caprices of the publisher. I had not been long connected with him before I discovered that he was wonderfully fond of interfering with other people's business—at least with the business of those who were under his control. What a life did his unfortunate authors lead ! He had many in his employ toiling at all kinds of subjects—I call them authors because there is something respectable in the term author, though they had little authorship in, and no authority whatever over, the works on which they were engaged. It is true the publisher interfered with some colour of reason, the plan of all and every of the works alluded to having originated with himself; and, be it observed, many of his plans were highly clever and promising, for, as I have already had occasion to say, the publisher in many points was a highly clever and sagacious person ; but he ought to have been contented with planning the works originally, and have left to other people the task of executing them, instead of which he marred everything by his rage for interference. If a book of fairy tales was being compiled, he was sure to introduce some of his philosophy, explaining the fairy tale by some theory of his own. Was a book of anecdotes on hand, it was sure to be half-filled with sayings and doings of himself during the time that he was common councilman of the city of London. Now, however fond the public might be of fairy tales, it by no means relished them in conjunction with the publisher's philosophy ; and however fond of anecdotes in general, or even of the publisher in particular —for indeed there were a great many anecdotes in circulation about him which the public both read and listened to very readily—it took no pleasure in such anecdotes as he was disposed to relate about himself. In the compilation of my *Lives and Trials*, I was exposed to incredible mortification, and ceaseless trouble, from this same rage for interference. It is true he could

not introduce his philosophy into the work, nor was it possible
for him to introduce anecdotes of himself, having never had the
good or evil fortune to be tried at the bar; but he was continually
introducing—what, under a less apathetic government than the
one then being, would have infallibly subjected him, and perhaps
myself, to a trial—his politics; not his Oxford or pseudo politics,
but the politics which he really entertained, and which were of
the most republican and violent kind.   But this was not all;
when about a moiety of the first volume had been printed, he
materially altered the plan of the work; it was no longer to be a
collection of mere Newgate lives and trials, but of lives and trials
of criminals in general, foreign as well as domestic.   In a little
time the work became a wondrous farrago, in which Königs-
mark the robber figured by the side of Sam Lynn, and the
Marchioness de Brinvilliers was placed in contact with a Chinese
outlaw.   What gave me the most trouble and annoyance, was the
publisher's remembering some life or trial, foreign or domestic,
which he wished to be inserted, and which I was forthwith to go
in quest of and purchase at my own expense: some of those
lives and trials were by no means easy to find.   "Where is
Brandt and Struensee?" cries the publisher; "I am sure I don't
know," I replied; whereupon the publisher falls to squealing like
one of Joey's rats.   "Find me up Brandt and Struensee by next
morning, or——" "Have you found Brandt and Struensee?"
cried the publisher, on my appearing before him next morning.
"No," I reply, "I can hear nothing about them;" whereupon
the publisher falls to bellowing like Joey's bull.   By dint of
incredible diligence, I at length discover the dingy volume
containing the lives and trials of the celebrated two who had
brooded treason dangerous to the state of Denmark.   I purchase
the dingy volume, and bring it in triumph to the publisher, the
perspiration running down my brow.   The publisher takes the
dingy volume in his hand, he examines it attentively, then puts
it down; his countenance is calm for a moment, almost benign.
Another moment and there is a gleam in the publisher's sinister
eye; he snatches up the paper containing the names of the
worthies which I have intended shall figure in the forthcoming
volumes—he glances rapidly over it, and his countenance once
more assumes a terrific expression.   "How is this?" he exclaims;
"I can scarcely believe my eyes—the most important life and
trial omitted to be found in the whole criminal record—what
gross, what utter negligence!   Where's the life of Farmer Patch?
where's the trial of Yeoman Patch?"

"What a life! what a dog's life!" I would frequently exclaim, after escaping from the presence of the publisher.

One day, after a scene with the publisher similar to that which I have described above, I found myself about noon at the bottom of Oxford Street, where it forms a right angle with the road which leads or did lead to Tottenham Court. Happening to cast my eyes around, it suddenly occurred to me that something uncommon was expected; people were standing in groups on the pavement— the upstair windows of the houses were thronged with faces, especially those of women, and many of the shops were partly, and not a few entirely closed. What could be the reason of all this? All at once I bethought me that this street of Oxford was no other than the far-famed Tyburn way. Oh, oh, thought I, an execution; some handsome young robber is about to be executed at the farther end; just so, see how earnestly the women are peering; perhaps another Harry Symms—Gentleman Harry as they called him—is about to be carted along this street to Tyburn tree; but then I remembered that Tyburn tree had long since been cut down, and that criminals, whether young or old, good-looking or ugly, were executed before the big stone gaol, which I had looked at with a kind of shudder during my short rambles in the city. What could be the matter? Just then I heard various voices cry "There it comes!" and all heads were turned up Oxford Street, down which a hearse was slowly coming: nearer and nearer it drew; presently it was just opposite the place where I was standing, when, turning to the left, it proceeded slowly along Tottenham Road; immediately behind the hearse were three or four mourning coaches, full of people, some of which, from the partial glimpse which I caught of them, appeared to be foreigners; behind these came a very long train of splendid carriages, all of which, without one exception, were empty.

"Whose body is in that hearse?" said I to a dapper-looking individual seemingly a shopkeeper, who stood beside me on the pavement, looking at the procession.

"The mortal relics of Lord Byron," said the dapper-looking individual, mouthing his words and smirking, "the illustrious poet, which have been just brought from Greece, and are being conveyed to the family vault in ——shire."

"An illustrious poet, was he?" said I.

"Beyond all criticism," said the dapper man; "all we of the rising generation are under incalculable obligation to Byron; I myself, in particular, have reason to say so; in all my correspondence my style is formed on the Byronic model."

I looked at the individual for a moment, who smiled and smirked to himself applause, and then I turned my eyes upon the hearse proceeding slowly up the almost endless street. This man, this Byron, had for many years past been the demigod of England, and his verses the daily food of those who read, from the peer to the draper's assistant; all were admirers, or rather worshippers, of Byron, and all doated on his verses; and then I thought of those who, with genius as high as his, or higher, had lived and died neglected. I thought of Milton abandoned to poverty and blindness; of witty and ingenious Butler consigned to the tender mercies of bailiffs; and starving Otway: they had lived neglected and despised, and, when they died, a few poor mourners only had followed them to the grave; but this Byron had been made a half-god of when living, and now that he was dead he was followed by worshipping crowds, and the very sun seemed to come out on purpose to grace his funeral. And, indeed, the sun, which for many days past had hidden its face in clouds, shone out that morn with wonderful brilliancy, flaming upon the black hearse and its tall ostrich plumes, the mourning coaches, and the long train of aristocratic carriages which followed behind.

"Great poet, sir," said the dapper-looking man, "great poet, but unhappy."

Unhappy? yes, I had heard that he had been unhappy; that he had roamed about a fevered, distempered man, taking pleasure in nothing—that I had heard; but was it true? was he really unhappy? was not this unhappiness assumed, with the view of increasing the interest which the world took in him? and yet who could say? He might be unhappy and with reason. Was he a real poet, after all? might he not doubt himself? might he not have a lurking consciousness that he was undeserving of the homage which he was receiving? that it could not last? that he was rather at the top of fashion than of fame? He was a lordling, a glittering, gorgeous lordling: and he might have had a consciousness that he owed much of his celebrity to being so; he might have felt that he was rather at the top of fashion than of fame. Fashion soon changes, thought I eagerly to myself; a time will come, and that speedily, when he will be no longer in the fashion; when this idiotic admirer of his, who is still grinning at my side, shall have ceased to mould his style on Byron's; and this aristocracy, squirearchy, and what not, who now send their empty carriages to pay respect to the fashionable corpse, shall have transferred their empty worship to some other animate or inanimate thing. Well, perhaps after all it was better to have been mighty Milton in his poverty and blindness—witty and ingenious Butler consigned to the tender mercies of bailiffs, and starving Otway; they might enjoy more real pleasure than this lordling; they must have been aware that the world would one day do them justice—fame after death is better than the top of fashion in life. They have left a fame behind them which shall never die, whilst this lordling—a time will come when he will be out of fashion and forgotten. And yet I don't know; didn't he write "Childe Harold" and that ode? Yes, he wrote "Childe Harold" and that ode. Then a time will scarcely come when he will be forgotten. Lords, squires and cockneys may pass away, but a time will scarcely come when "Childe Harold" and that ode will be forgotten. He was a poet, after all, and he must have known it; a real poet, equal to —— to —— what a destiny! rank, beauty, fashion, immortality—he could not be unhappy; what a difference in the fate of men—I wish I could think he was unhappy.

I turned away.

"Great poet, sir," said the dapper man, turning away too, "but unhappy—fate of genius, sir; I, too, am frequently unhappy."

Hurrying down the street to the right, I encountered Francis Ardry.

"What means the multitude yonder?" he demanded.

"They are looking after the hearse which is carrying the remains of Byron up Tottenham Road."

"I have seen the man," said my friend, as he turned back the way he had come, "so I can dispense with seeing the hearse —I saw the living man at Venice—ah, a great poet."

["I don't think so," said I.

"Hey!" said Francis Ardry.[1]

"A perfumed lordling."

"Ah!"

"With a white hand loaded with gawds."

"Ah!"

"Who wrote verses."

"Ah!"

"Replete with malignity and sensualism."

"Yes!"

"Not half so great a poet as Milton."

"No?"

"Nor Butler."

"No?"

"Nor Otway."

[1] *Arden* throughout the *MS.*

"No?"

"Nor that poor boy Chatterton, who, maddened by rascally patrons and publishers, took poison at last."

"No?" said Francis Ardry.

"Why do you keep saying '*No*'? I tell you that I am no admirer of Byron."

"Well," said Frank, "don't say so to any one else. It will be thought that you are envious of his glory, as indeed I almost think you are."

"Envious of him!" said I; "how should I be envious of him? Besides, the man's dead, and a live dog, you know ——"

"You do not think so," said Frank, "and at this moment I would wager something that you would wish for nothing better than to exchange places with that lordling, as you call him, cold as he is."

"Well, who knows?" said I. "I really think the man is over-valued. There is one thing connected with him which must ever prevent any one of right feelings from esteeming him; I allude to his incessant abuse of his native land, a land, too, which had made him its idol."

"Ah! you are a great patriot, I know," said Frank. "Come, as you are fond of patriots, I will show you the patriot, *par excellence.*"

"If you mean Eolus Jones," said I, "you need not trouble yourself; I have seen him already."

"I don't mean him," said Frank. "By-the-bye, he came to me the other day to condole with me, as he said, on the woes of my bleeding country. Before he left me he made me bleed, for he persuaded me to lend him a guinea. No, I don't mean him, nor any one of his stamp; I mean an Irish patriot, one who thinks he can show his love for his country in no better way than by beating the English."

"Beating the English?" said I; "I should like to see him."

Whereupon taking me by the arm, Francis Ardry conducted me through various alleys, till we came to a long street which seemed to descend towards the south.

"What street is this?" said I, when we had nearly reached the bottom.

"It is no street at all," said my friend; "at least it is not called one in this city of Cockaine; it is a lane, even that of St. Martin; and that church that you see there is devoted to him. It is one of the few fine churches in London. *Malheureusement,*[1] as the French say, it is so choked up by buildings that it is

---

[1] The text is: "*Malheur*, as the French say, *that* it is so choked".

impossible to see it at twenty yards' distance from any side. Whenever I get into Parliament, one of my first motions shall be to remove some twenty score of the aforesaid buildings. But I think we have arrived at the house to which I wished to conduct you."

"Yes, I see, *Portobello.*"

About twenty yards from the church, on the left-hand side of the street or lane, was a mean-looking house having something of the appearance of a fifth-rate inn. Over the door was written in large characters the name of the haven, where the bluff old Vernon achieved his celebrated victory over the whiskered Dons. Entering a passage on one side of which was a bar-room, Ardry enquired of a middle-aged man who stood in it in his shirt-sleeves, whether the captain was at home. Having received for an answer a surly kind of "yes," he motioned me to follow him, and after reaching the end of the passage, which was rather dark, he began to ascend a narrow, winding stair. About half-way up he suddenly stopped, for at that moment a loud, hoarse voice from a room above commenced singing a strange kind of ditty.

"The captain is singing," said Frank, "and, as I live, 'Carolan's Receipt for drinking whisky'. Let us wait a moment till he has done, as he would probably not like to be interrupted in his melody."

CAROLAN'S RECEIPT.

'Whether sick or sound my receipt was the same,
To Stafford I stepp'd and better became;
A visit to Stafford's bounteous hall
Was the best receipt of all, of all.

'Midnight fell round us and drinking found us,
At morn again flow'd his whisky;
By his *in*sight he knew 'twas the only way true
To keep Torlough alive and frisky.

'Now deep healths quaffing, now screeching now laughing,
At my harp-strings tearing, and to madness nearing:
That was the life I led, and which I yet do;
For I will swear it, and to all the world declare it,
If you would fain be happy, you must aye be —— '

"*Fou!*" said Francis Ardry, suddenly pushing open the door of the room from which the voice proceeded; "That's the word, I think, captain."

"By my shoul, Mr. Francis Ardry, you enter with considerable abruptness, sir," said one of two men who were seated smoking at a common deal table, in a large ruinous apartment in which we now found ourselves. "You enter with considerable abruptness, sir," he repeated; "do you know on whom you are intruding?"

"Perfectly well," said Francis; "I am standing in the presence of Torlough O'Donahue, formerly captain in a foreign service, and at present resident in London for the express purpose of beating all the English ——"

"And some of the Irish too, sir, if necessary," said the captain with a menacing look. "I do not like to be broken in upon as if I were a nobody. However, as you are here, I suppose I must abide by it. I am not so little of a gentleman as to be deficient in the rudiments of hospitality. You may both of you sit down and make yourselves aisy."

But this was no such easy matter, the only two chairs in the room being occupied by the captain and the other. I therefore leaned against the door, while Ardry strolled about the apartment.

The captain might be about forty. His head was immensely large, his complexion ruddy, and his features rough, coarse and strongly expressive of sullenness and ill-nature. He was about the middle height, with a frame clumsily made, but denoting considerable strength. He wore a blue coat, the lappets of which were very narrow, but so long that they nearly trailed upon the ground. Yellow leathern breeches unbuttoned at the knee, dazzling white cotton stockings and shoes with buckles, adorned his nether man.

His companion, who was apparently somewhat older than himself, was dressed in a coarse greatcoat and a glazed hat exactly resembling those worn by hackneys. He had a quiet, droll countenance, very much studded with carbuncles, and his nose, which was very long, was of so hooked a description that the point of it nearly entered his mouth.

"Who may this friend of yours be?" said the captain to Ardry, after staring at me.

"A young gentleman much addicted to philosophy, poetry and philology."

"Is he Irish?"

"No, he is English; but I have heard him say that he has a particular veneration for Ireland."

"He has, has he; by my shoul, then, all the better for him. If he had not . . . Can he fight?"

"I think I have heard him say that he can use his fists when necessary."

"He can, can he? by my shoul, I should like to try him. But first of all I have another customer to dispose of. I have just determined to send a challenge to Bishop Sharpe whom these English call the best of their light weights.[1] Perhaps he is, but if I don't——"

" The Bishop is a good man," interrupted his companion of the greatcoat and glazed hat, in a strange croaky tone.

" Is it a good man that you are calling him ? " said the captain. " Well, be it so ; the more merit in my baiting him."

" That's true ; but you have not beat him yet," said his companion.

" Not bate him yet ? Is not there the paper that I am going to write the challenge on ? and is not there the pen and the ink that I am going to write it with ? and is not there yourself, John Turner, my hired servant, that's bound to take him the challenge when 'tis written ? "

" That's true ; here we are all four—pen, ink, paper, and John Turner ; but there's something else wanted to beat Bishop Sharpe."

" What else is wanted ? " shouted the captain.

" Why, to be a better man than he."

" And ain't I that man ? "

" Why, that remains to be seen."

" Ain't I an Irishman ? "

" Yes, I believe you to be an Irishman. No one, to hear you talk, but would think you that, or a Frenchman. I was in conversation with one of that kind the other day. Hearing him talk rather broken, I asked him what countryman he was. ' What countryman are you ? ' said I.—' I ? ' said he, ' I am one Frenchman,' and then he looked at me as if I should sink into the earth under his feet.—' You are not the better for that,' said I ; ' you are not the better for being a Frenchman, I suppose,' said I.—' How ? ' said he ; ' I am of the great nation which has won all the battles in the world.'—' All the battles in the world ? ' said I. ' Did you ever hear of the battle of Waterloo ? ' said I. You should have seen how blue he looked. ' Ah ! you can't get over that,' said I ; ' you can't get over the battle of Waterloo,' said I."

" Is it the battle of Waterloo you are speaking of, you spalpeen ? And to one who was there, an Irish cavalier, fighting in the ranks of the brave French ! By the powers ! if the sacrifice would not be too great, I would break this pipe in your face."

" Why, as to that, two can play at that," said he of the glazed hat, smoking on very composedly. " I remember I once said so to young Cope—you have heard of young Cope. I was vally to young Cope and servant of all work twenty year ago at Brighton.

[1] " Bishop Sharpe," a pugilist of that name and time.

So one morning after I had carried up his boots, he rings the bell as if in a great fury. 'Do you call these boots clean?' said young Cope, as soon as I showed myself at the door. 'Do you call these clean?' said he, flinging one boot at my head, and then the other. 'Two can play at that game,' said I, catching the second boot in my hand, 'two can play at that game,' said I, aiming it at young Cope's head—not that I meant to fling it at young Cope's head, for young Cope was a gentleman; yes, a gentleman, captain, though not Irish, for he paid me my wages."

These last words seemed to have a rather quieting effect upon the captain, who at the commencement of the speech had grasped his pipe somewhat below the bowl and appeared by his glance to be meditating a lunge at the eye of his eccentric servant, who continued smoking and talking with great composure. Suddenly replacing the end of his pipe in his mouth, the man turned to me, and in a tone of great *hauteur* said :—

"So, sir, I am told by your friend there, that you are fond of the humanities."

"Yes," said I, "I am very fond of humanity, and was always a great admirer of the lines of Gay :—

> 'Cowards are cruel, but the brave
> Love mercy and delight to save'."

"By my shoul, sir, it's an ignorant beast I'm thinking ye. It was not *humanity* I was speaking of, but the *humanities*, which have nothing at all to do with it." Then turning to Frank, he demanded, "Was it not yourself, Mr. Francis Ardry, that told me, when you took the liberty of introducing this person to me, that he was addicted to philosophy, prosody, and what not?"

"To be sure I did," said Frank.

"Well, sir, and are not those the humanities, or are you as ignorant as your friend here?"

"You pretend to be a humanist, sir," said he to me, "but I will take the liberty of showing your utter ignorance. Now, sir, do you venture to say that you can answer a question connected with the Irish humanities?"

"I must hear it first," said I.

"You must hear it, must ye? Then you shall hear it to your confusion. A pretty humanist I will show you to be; open your ears, sir!"—

> '*Triuir ata sé air mo bhás*'.[1]

[1] *Three are after my death.*

"Now, sir, what does the poet mean by saying that there are three looking after his death? Whom does he allude to, sir? hey?"

"The devil, the worms, and his children," said I, "who are looking after three things which they can't hope to get before he is dead—the children his property, the worms his body, and the devil his soul, as the man says a little farther on."

The captain looked at me malignantly.

"Now, sir, are you not ashamed of yourself?"

"Wherefore?" said I. "Have I not given the meaning of the poem?"

"You have expounded the elegy, sir, fairly enough; I find no fault with your interpretation. What I mean is this: Are you not ashamed to be denying your country?"

"I never denied my country; I did not even mention it. My friend there told you I was an Englishman, and he spoke the truth."

"Sorrow befall you for saying so," said the captain. "But I see how it is, you have been bought; yes, sir, paid money, to deny your country; but such has ever been the policy of the English; they can't bate us, so they buy us. Now here's myself. No sooner have I sent this challenge to Bishop Sharpe by the hands of my hired servant, than I expect to have a hundred offers to let myself be beat. What is that you say, sir?" said he, addressing his companion who had uttered a kind of inaudible sound—"No hopes of that, did you say? Do you think that I could be bate without allowing myself to be bate? By the powers!—but you are beneath my notice."

"Well, sir," said he, fixing his eyes on me, "though you have cheek enough to deny your own country, I trust you have not enough to deny the merit of the elegy. What do you think of the elegy, sir?"

"I think it very sorry stuff," said I.

"Hear him!" said the captain looking about him. "But he has been bought, paid money, to deny his own country and all that belongs to it. Well, sir, what do you think of Carolan, Carolan the Great? What do you think of his *Receipt*, sir?"

"I think it very sorry stuff, too."

"Very well, sir, very well; but I hope to make you give me a receipt for all this before you leave. One word more. I suppose you'll next deny that we have any poetry or music at all."

" Far be it from me to say any such thing.   There is one song
connected with Ireland which I have always thought very fine, and
likewise the music that accompanies it."

" I am glad to hear it, sir ; there is one piece of Irish poetry
and music which meets your approbation !   Pray name the piece,
sir."

" *Croppies Lie Down !* "

The captain sprang to his feet like one electrified.

" What, sir ? " said he.

" *Croppies Lie Down !* "

The captain dashed his pipe to shivers against the table ; then
tucking up the sleeves of his coat, he advanced to within a yard of
me, and pushing forward his head somewhat in the manner of a
bull-dog when about to make a spring, he said in a tone of
suppressed fury : " I think I have heard of that song before, sir ;
but nobody ever yet cared to sing it to me.   I should admire to
hear from your lips what it is.   Perhaps you will sing me a line or
two."

" With great pleasure," said I :—

> ' There are many brave rivers run into the sea,
> But the best of them all is Boyne water for me ;
> There Croppies were vanquished and terrified fled,
> With Jamie the runagate king at their head.
> When crossing the ford
> In the name of the Lord,
> The conqueror brandished his conquering sword ;
> Then down, down, Croppies lie down ! '

" By the powers ! a very pretty song, and much obliged am I
to ye for singing it, more especially as it gives me an opportunity
of breaking your head, you long-limbed descendant of a Boyne
trooper.   You must deny your country, must ye ? ye dingy
renegade !—the black North, but old Ireland still.   But here's
Connemara for ye—take this—and this——Och, murther !—
What have we got here . . . ? "

" Who and what is this O'Donahue ? " said I to Frank Ardry
after we had descended into the street.

" An ill-tempered Irishman," said Frank, " the most disagreeable animal alive, once a rare bird on the earth.   His father, after
having taught him some Irish and less Latin, together with an
immoderate hatred of the English, sent him abroad at the age of
sixteen to serve the French.   In that service he continued until
the time of the general peace, when he quitted it for the Austrian.

I first became acquainted with him at Vienna, where he bore the rank of captain, but had the character of a notorious gambler. It was owing, I believe, to his gambling practices that he was eventually obliged to leave the Austrian service. He has been in London about six months, where he supports himself as best he can, chiefly, I believe, by means of the gaming-table. His malignity against England has of late amounted almost to insanity, and has been much increased by the perusal of Irish newspapers which abound with invective against England and hyperbolical glorification of Ireland and the Irish. The result is that he has come to the conclusion that the best way for him to take revenge for the injuries of Ireland and to prove the immense superiority of the Irish over the English will be to break the head of Bishop Sharpe in the ring."

"Well," said I, "I do not see why the dispute, if dispute there be, should not be settled in the ring."

"Nor I either," said Frank, "and I could wish my countrymen to choose none other than O'Donahue. With respect to England and Bishop Sharpe . . ."

At that moment a voice sounded close by me: "Coach, your honour, coach? Will carry you anywhere you like." I stopped, and lo the man of the greatcoat and glazed hat stood by my side.

"What do you want?" said I. "Have you brought me any message from your master?"

"Master? What master? Oh! you mean the captain. I left him rubbing his head. No, I don't think you will hear anything from him in a hurry; he has had enough of you. All I wish to know is whether you wish to ride."

"I thought you were the captain's servant."

"Yes, I look after the spavined roan on which he rides about the Park, but he's no master of mine—he doesn't pay me. Who cares? I don't serve him for money. I like to hear his talk about Bishop Sharpe and beating the English—Lord help him! Now, where do you wish to go? Any coach you like—any coachman—and nothing to pay."

"Why do you wish me to ride?" said I.

"Why, for serving out as you did that poor silly captain. I think what he got will satisfy him for a time. No more talk about Bishop Sharpe for a week at least. Come, come along, both of you. The stand is close by, and I'll drive you myself."

"Will you ride?" said I to Francis Ardry.

"No," said Frank.

"Then come alone. Where shall I drive you?"

"To London Bridge."]

CHAPTER XL.

So I went to London Bridge, and again took my station on the spot by the booth where I had stood on the former occasion. The booth, however, was empty; neither the apple-woman nor her stall were to be seen. I looked over the balustrade upon the river; the tide was now, as before, rolling beneath the arch with frightful impetuosity. As I gazed upon the eddies of the whirlpool, I thought within myself how soon human life would become extinct there; a plunge, a convulsive flounder, and all would be over. When I last stood over that abyss I had felt a kind of impulse —a fascination: I had resisted it—I did not plunge into it. At present I felt a kind of impulse to plunge; but the impulse was of a different kind; it proceeded from a loathing of life. I looked wistfully at the eddies—what had I to live for?—what, indeed! I thought of Brandt and Struensee, and Yeoman Patch—should I yield to the impulse—why not? My eyes were fixed on the eddies. All of a sudden I shuddered; I thought I saw heads in the pool; human bodies wallowing confusedly; eyes turned up to heaven with hopeless horror; was that water, or —— Where was the impulse now? I raised my eyes from the pool, I looked no more upon it—I looked forward, far down the stream in the distance. "Ha! what is that? I thought I saw a kind of Fata Morgana, green meadows, waving groves, a rustic home; but in the far distance—I stared—I stared—a Fata Morgana—it was gone ——"

I left the balustrade and walked to the farther end of the bridge, where I stood for some time contemplating the crowd; I then passed over to the other side with the intention of returning home; just half-way over the bridge, in a booth immediately opposite the one in which I had formerly beheld her, sat my friend, the old apple-woman, huddled up behind her stall.

"Well, mother," said I, "how are you?" The old woman lifted her head with a startled look.

"Don't you know me?" said I.

"Yes, I think I do. Ah, yes," said she, as her features

beamed with recollection, " I know you, dear ; you are the young
lad that gave me the tanner.   Well, child, got anything to sell ? "
    " Nothing at all," said I.
    " Bad luck ? "
    " Yes," said I, " bad enough, and ill usage."
    " Ah, I suppose they caught ye ; well, child, never mind,
better luck next time ; I am glad to see you."
    " Thank you," said I, sitting down on the stone bench ; " I
thought you had left the bridge—why have you changed your
side ? "
    The old woman shook.
    " What is the matter with you," said I, " are you ill ? "
    " No, child, no ; only —— "
    " Only what ?   Any bad news of your son ? "
    " No child, no ; nothing about my son.   Only low, child—
every heart has its bitters."
    " That's true," said I ; " well, I don't want to know your
sorrows ; come, where's the book ? "
    The apple-woman shook more violently than before, bent
herself down, and drew her cloak more closely about her than
before.   " Book, child, what book ? "
    " Why, blessed Mary, to be sure."
    " Oh, that ; I ha'n't got it, child—I have lost it, have left it
at home."
    " Lost it," said I ; " left it at home—what do you mean ?
Come, let me have it."
    " I ha'n't got it, child."
    " I believe you have got it under your cloak."
    " Don't tell any one, dear ; don't—don't," and the apple-
woman burst into tears.
    " What's the matter with you ? " said I, staring at her.
    " You want to take my book from me ? "
    " Not I, I care nothing about it ; keep it, if you like, only
tell me what's the matter ? "
    " Why, all about that book."
    " The book ? "
    " Yes, they wanted to take it from me."
    " Who did ? "
    " Why, some wicked boys.   I'll tell you all about it.   Eight
or ten days ago, I sat behind my stall, reading my book ; all of
a sudden I felt it snatched from my hand ; up I started, and see
three rascals of boys grinning at me ; one of them held the book
in his hand.   ' What book is this ? ' said he, grinning at it.

'What do you want with my book?' said I, clutching at it over my stall, 'give me my book.' 'What do you want a book for?' said he, holding it back; 'I have a good mind to fling it into the Thames.' 'Give me my book,' I shrieked; and, snatching at it, I fell over my stall, and all my fruit was scattered about. Off ran the boys—off ran the rascal with my book. Oh dear, I thought I should have died; up I got, however, and ran after them as well as I could. I thought of my fruit; but I thought more of my book. I left my fruit and ran after my book. 'My book! my book!' I shrieked, 'murder! theft! robbery!' I was near being crushed under the wheels of a cart; but I didn't care—I followed the rascals. 'Stop them! stop them!' I ran nearly as fast as they —they couldn't run very fast on account of the crowd. At last some one stopped the rascal, whereupon he turned round, and flinging the book at me, it fell into the mud; well, I picked it up and kissed it, all muddy as it was. 'Has he robbed you?' said the man. 'Robbed me, indeed; why, he had got my book.' 'Oh, your book,' said the man, and laughed, and let the rascal go. Ah, he might laugh, but ——"

"Well, go on."

"My heart beats so. Well, I went back to my booth and picked up my stall and my fruits, what I could find of them. I couldn't keep my stall for two days, I got such a fright, and when I got round I couldn't bide the booth where the thing had happened, so I came over to the other side. Oh, the rascals, if I could but see them hanged."

"For what."

"Why for stealing my book."

"I thought you didn't dislike stealing, that you were ready to buy things—there was your son, you know ——"

"Yes, to be sure."

"He took things."

"To be sure he did."

"But you don't like a thing of yours to be taken."

"No, that's quite a different thing; what's stealing hand-kerchiefs, and that kind of thing, to do with taking my book; there's a wide difference—don't you see?"

"Yes, I see."

"Do you, dear? well, bless your heart, I'm glad you do. Would you like to look at the book?"

"Well, I think I should."

"Honour bright?" said the apple-woman, looking me in the eyes.

"Honour bright," said I, looking the apple-woman in the eyes.

"Well then, dear, here it is," said she, taking it from under her cloak; "read it as long as you like, only get a little farther into the booth. Don't sit so near the edge—you might ——"

I went deep into the booth, and the apple-woman, bringing her chair round, almost confronted me. I commenced reading the book, and was soon engrossed by it; hours passed away, once or twice I lifted up my eyes, the apple-woman was still confronting me: at last my eyes began to ache, whereupon I returned the book to the apple-woman, and giving her another tanner, walked away.

CHAPTER XLI.

Time passed away, and with it the Review, which, contrary to the publisher's expectation, did not prove a successful speculation. About four months after the period of its birth it expired, as all Reviews must for which there is no demand. Authors had ceased to send their publications to it, and, consequently, to purchase it ; for I have already hinted that it was almost entirely supported by authors of a particular class, who expected to see their publications foredoomed to immortality in its pages. The behaviour of these authors towards this unfortunate publication I can attribute to no other cause than to a report which was industriously circulated, namely, that the Review was low, and that to be reviewed in it was an infallible sign that one was a low person, who could be reviewed nowhere else. So authors took fright ; and no wonder, for it will never do for an author to be considered low. Homer himself has never yet entirely recovered from the injury he received by Lord Chesterfield's remark, that the speeches of his heroes were frequently exceedingly low.

So the Review ceased, and the reviewing corps no longer existed as such ; they forthwith returned to their proper avocations —the editor to compose tunes on his piano, and to the task of disposing of the remaining copies of his Quintilian—the inferior members to working for the publisher, being to a man dependants of his ; one, to composing fairy tales ; another, to collecting miracles of Popish saints ; and a third, Newgate lives and trials. Owing to the bad success of the Review, the publisher became more furious than ever. My money was growing short, and I one day asked him to pay me for my labours in the deceased publication.

"Sir," said the publisher, "what do you want the money for ?"

"Merely to live on," I replied ; "it is very difficult to live in this town without money."

"How much money did you bring with you to town?" demanded the publisher.

" Some twenty or thirty pounds," I replied.

" And you have spent it already ? "

" No," said I, " not entirely; but it is fast disappearing."

" Sir," said the publisher, " I believe you to be extravagant; yes, sir, extravagant ! "

" On what grounds do you suppose me to be so ? "

" Sir," said the publisher, " you eat meat."

" Yes," said I, " I eat meat sometimes : what should I eat ? "

" Bread, sir," said the publisher ; " bread and cheese."

" So I do, sir, when I am disposed to indulge ; but I cannot often afford it—it is very expensive to dine on bread and cheese, especially when one is fond of cheese, as I am. My last bread and cheese dinner cost me fourteen pence. There is drink, sir ; with bread and cheese one must drink porter, sir."

" Then, sir, eat bread—bread alone. As good men as yourself have eaten bread alone; they have been glad to get it, sir. If with bread and cheese you must drink porter, sir, with bread alone you can, perhaps, drink water, sir."

However, I got paid at last for my writings in the Review, not, it is true, in the current coin of the realm, but in certain bills ; there were two of them, one payable at twelve, and the other at eighteen months after date. It was a long time before I could turn these bills to any account; at last I found a person who, at a discount of only thirty per cent., consented to cash them ; not, however, without sundry grimaces, and, what was still more galling, holding, more than once, the unfortunate papers high in air between his forefinger and thumb. So ill, indeed, did I like this last action, that I felt much inclined to snatch them away. I restrained myself, however, for I remembered that it was very difficult to live without money, and that, if the present person did not discount the bills, I should probably find no one else that would.

But if the treatment which I had experienced from the publisher, previous to making this demand upon him, was difficult to bear, that which I subsequently underwent was far more so ; his great delight seemed to consist in causing me misery and mortification ; if, on former occasions, he was continually sending me in quest of lives and trials difficult to find, he now was continually demanding lives and trials which it was impossible to find, the personages whom he mentioned never having lived, nor consequently been tried. Moreover, some of my best lives and trials which I had corrected and edited with particular care, and on which I prided myself no little, he caused to be cancelled after

they had passed through the press.   Amongst these was the life
of "Gentleman Harry".   "They are drugs, sir," said the publisher,
"drugs ; that life of Harry Simms has long been the greatest drug
in the calendar—has it not, Taggart?"

Taggart made no answer save by taking a pinch of snuff.
The reader has, I hope, not forgotten Taggart, whom I mentioned
whilst giving an account of my first morning's visit to the publisher.
I beg Taggart's pardon for having been so long silent about him ;
but he was a very silent man—yet there was much in Taggart—
and Taggart had always been civil and kind to me in his peculiar
way.

"Well, young gentleman," said Taggart to me one morning,
when we chanced to be alone a few days after the affair of the
cancelling, "how do you like authorship?"

"I scarcely call authorship the drudgery I am engaged in,"
said I.

"What do you call authorship?" said Taggart.

"I scarcely know," said I ; "that is, I can scarcely express
what I think it."

"Shall I help you out?" said Taggart, turning round his
chair, and looking at me.

"If you like," said I.

"To write something grand," said Taggart, taking snuff; "to
be stared at—lifted on people's shoulders ——"

"Well," said I, "that is something like it."

Taggart took snuff.   "Well," said he, "why don't you write
something grand?"

"I have," said I.

"What?" said Taggart.

"Why," said I, "there are those ballads."

Taggart took snuff.

"And those wonderful versions from Ab Gwilym."

Taggart took snuff again.

"You seem to be very fond of snuff," said I, looking at him
angrily.

Taggart tapped his box.

"Have you taken it long?"

"Three-and-twenty years."

"What snuff do you take?"

"Universal mixture."

"And you find it of use?"

Taggart tapped his box.

"In what respect?" said I.

" In many—there is nothing like it to get a man through ; but for snuff I should scarcely be where I am now."

" Have you been long here ? "

" Three-and-twenty years."

" Dear me," said I ; " and snuff brought you through ? Give me a pinch—pah, I don't like it," and I sneezed.

" Take another pinch," said Taggart.

" No," said I, " I don't like snuff."

" Then you will never do for authorship—at least for this kind."

" So I begin to think—what shall I do ? "

Taggart took snuff.

" You were talking of a great work—what shall it be ? "

Taggart took snuff.

" Do you think I could write one ? "

Taggart uplifted his two forefingers as if to tap, he did not, however.

" It would require time," said I, with half a sigh.

Taggart tapped his box.

" A great deal of time ; I really think that my ballads ——"

Taggart took snuff.

" If published would do me credit. I'll make an effort, and offer them to some other publisher."

Taggart took a double quantity of snuff.

CHAPTER XLII.

OCCASIONALLY I called on Francis Ardry. This young gentleman resided in handsome apartments in the neighbourhood of a fashionable square, kept a livery servant, and upon the whole, lived in very good style. Going to see him one day, between one and two, I was informed by the servant that his master was engaged for the moment, but that, if I pleased to wait a few minutes, I should find him at liberty. Having told the man that I had no objection, he conducted me into a small apartment which served as antechamber to a drawing-room; the door of this last being half-open, I could see Francis Ardry at the farther end, speechifying and gesticulating in a very impressive manner. The servant, in some confusion, was hastening to close the door, but, ere he could effect his purpose, Francis Ardry, who had caught a glimpse of me, exclaimed, "Come in—come in by all means," and then proceeded, as before, speechifying and gesticulating. Filled with some surprise, I obeyed his summons.

On entering the room I perceived another individual to whom Francis Ardry appeared to be addressing himself; this other was a short, spare man of about sixty; his hair was of a badger grey, and his face was covered with wrinkles—without vouchsafing me a look, he kept his eye, which was black and lustrous, fixed full on Francis Ardry, as if paying the deepest attention to his discourse. All of a sudden, however, he cried with a sharp, cracked voice, "that won't do, sir; that won't do—more vehemence—your argument is at present particularly weak; therefore, more vehemence—you must confuse them, stun them, stultify them, sir"; and, at each of these injunctions, he struck the back of his right hand sharply against the palm of the left. "Good, sir—good!" he occasionally uttered, in the same sharp, cracked tone, as the voice of Francis Ardry became more and more vehement. "Infinitely good!" he exclaimed, as Francis Ardry raised his voice to the highest pitch; "and now, sir, abate; let the tempest of vehemence decline—gradually, sir; not too fast. Good, sir—very good!" as the voice of Francis Ardry declined gradually in vehemence. "And now a little pathos, sir—try them with a little pathos. That won't do, sir—that won't do,"—as Francis Ardry made an attempt to become pathetic,—"that will never pass for pathos—with tones and gesture of that description you will never redress the wrongs of your country. Now, sir, observe my gestures, and pay attention to the tone of my voice, sir."

Thereupon, making use of nearly the same terms which Francis Ardry had employed, the individual in black uttered several sentences in tones and with gestures which were intended to express a considerable degree of pathos, though it is possible that some people would have thought both the one and the other highly ludicrous. After a pause, Francis recommenced imitating the tones and the gestures of his monitor in the most admirable manner. Before he had proceeded far, however, he burst into a fit of laughter, in which I should, perhaps, have joined, provided it were ever my wont to laugh. "Ha, ha!" said the other, good humouredly, "you are laughing at me. Well, well, I merely wished to give you a hint; but you saw very well what I meant; upon the whole, I think you improve. But I must now go, having two other pupils to visit before four."

Then taking from the table a kind of three-cornered hat, and a cane headed with amber, he shook Francis Ardry by the hand; and, after glancing at me for a moment, made me a half-bow, attended with a strange grimace, and departed.

"Who is that gentleman?" said I to Francis Ardry as soon as we were alone.

"Oh, that is ——" said Frank smiling, "the gentleman who gives me lessons in elocution."

"And what need have you of elocution?"

"Oh, I merely obey the commands of my guardians," said Francis, "who insist that I should, with the assistance of ——,[1] qualify myself for Parliament; for which they do me the honour to suppose that I have some natural talent. I dare not disobey them, for, at the present moment, I have particular reasons for wishing to keep on good terms with them."

"But," said I, "you are a Roman Catholic, and I thought that persons of your religion were excluded from Parliament?"

"Why, upon that very thing the whole matter hinges; people of our religion are determined to be no longer excluded from Parliament, but to have a share in the government of the nation. Not that I care anything about the matter; I merely obey the

[1] *MS.* (apparently) " L——," but see p. 276.

will of my guardians; my thoughts are fixed on something better than politics."

"I understand you," said I; "dog-fighting—well, I can easily conceive that to some minds dog-fighting ——" [1]

"I was not thinking of dog-fighting," said Francis Ardry, interrupting me.

"Not thinking of dog-fighting!" I ejaculated.

"No," said Francis Ardry, "something higher and much more rational than dog-fighting at present occupies my thoughts."

"Dear me," said I, "I thought I heard you say, that there was nothing like it!"

"Like what?" said Francis Ardry.

"Dog-fighting, to be sure," said I.

"Pooh," said Francis Ardry; "who but the gross and unrefined care anything for dog-fighting? That which at present engages my waking and sleeping thoughts is love—divine love—there is nothing like *that*. Listen to me, I have a secret to confide to you."

And then Francis Ardry proceeded to make me his confidant. It appeared that he had had the good fortune to make the acquaintance of the most delightful young Frenchwoman imaginable, Annette La Noire by name,[2] who had just arrived from her native country with the intention of obtaining the situation of governess in some English family; a position which, on account of her many accomplishments, she was eminently qualified to fill. Francis Ardry had, however, persuaded her to relinquish her intention for the present, on the ground that, until she had become acclimated in England, her health would probably suffer from the confinement inseparable from the occupation in which she was desirous of engaging; he had, moreover—for it appeared that she was the most frank and confiding creature in the world—succeeded in persuading her to permit him to hire for her a very handsome first floor in his own neighbourhood, and to accept a few inconsiderable presents in money and jewellery. "I am looking out for a handsome gig and horse," said Francis Ardry, at the conclusion of his narration; "it were a burning shame that so divine a creature should have to go about a place like London on foot, or in a paltry hackney coach."

"But," said I, "will not the pursuit of politics prevent your devoting much time to this fair lady?"

---

[1] *MS.*, "is quite as rational an amusement as politics".

[2] *Le Noir* in MS. *A*, and in *Rom. Rye*, app.

251

"It will prevent me devoting all my time," said Francis
Ardry, "as I gladly would; but what can I do? My guardians
wish me to qualify myself for a political orator, and I dare not
offend them by a refusal. If I offend my guardians, I should find
it impossible—unless I have recourse to Jews and money-lenders
—to support Annette, present her with articles of dress and
jewellery, and purchase a horse and cabriolet worthy of conveying
her angelic person through the streets of London."

After a pause, in which Francis Ardry appeared lost in
thought, his mind being probably occupied with the subject of
Annette, I broke silence by observing: "So your fellow-religionists
are really going to make a serious attempt to procure their
emancipation?"

"Yes," said Francis Ardry starting from his reverie; "everything has been arranged; even a leader has been chosen, at least
for us of Ireland, upon the whole the most suitable man in the
world for the occasion—a barrister of considerable talent, mighty
voice, and magnificent impudence. With emancipation, liberty
and redress for the wrongs of Ireland in his mouth, he is to
force his way into the British House of Commons, dragging
myself and others behind him—he will succeed, and when he is in
he will cut a figure; I have heard —— himself,[1] who has heard him
speak, say that he will cut a figure."

"And is ——[1] competent to judge?" I demanded.

"Who but he?" said Francis Ardry; "no one questions his
judgment concerning what relates to elocution. His fame on that
point is so well established, that the greatest orators do not
disdain occasionally to consult him; C——[2] himself, as I have
been told, when anxious to produce any particular effect in the
House, is in the habit of calling in ——[1] for consultation."

"As to matter, or manner?" said I.

"Chiefly the latter," said Francis Ardry, "though he is
competent to give advice as to both, for he has been an orator in
his day, and a leader of the people; though he confessed to me
that he was not exactly qualified to play the latter part—'I want
paunch,' said he."

"It is not always indispensable," said I; "there is an orator
in my town, a hunchback and watchmaker, without it, who not
only leads the people, but the mayor too; perhaps he has a
succedaneum in his hunch; but, tell me, is the leader of your
movement in possession of that which wants——?"

[1] *MS.*, "L——," or "T."   [2] *MS.*, "Canning".

"No more deficient in it than in brass," said Francis Ardry.

"Well," said I, "whatever his qualifications may be, I wish him success in the cause which he has taken up—I love religious liberty."

"We shall succeed," said Francis Ardry; "John Bull upon the whole is rather indifferent on the subject, and then we are sure to be backed by the Radical party, who, to gratify their political prejudices, would join with Satan himself."

"There is one thing," said I, "connected with this matter which surprises me—your own lukewarmness. Yes, making every allowance for your natural predilection for dog-fighting, and your present enamoured state of mind, your apathy at the commencement of such a movement is to me unaccountable."

"You would not have cause to complain of my indifference," said Frank, "provided I thought my country would be benefited by this movement; but I happen to know the origin of it. The priests are the originators, 'and what country was ever benefited by a movement which owed its origin to them?' so says Voltaire, a page of whom I occasionally read. By the present move they hope to increase their influence, and to further certain designs which they entertain both with regard to this country and Ireland. I do not speak rashly or unadvisedly. A strange fellow—a half-Italian, half-English priest,—who was recommended to me by my guardians, partly as a spiritual, partly as a temporal guide—has let me into a secret or two; he is fond of a glass of gin and water, and over a glass of gin and water cold, with a lump of sugar in it, he has been more communicative, perhaps, than was altogether prudent. Were I my own master, I would kick him, politics and religious movements, to a considerable distance. And now, if you are going away, do so quickly; I have an appointment with Annette, and must make myself fit to appear before her."

CHAPTER XLIII.

By the month of October I had, in spite of all difficulties and obstacles, accomplished about two-thirds of the principal task which I had undertaken, the compiling of the Newgate lives; I had also made some progress in translating the publisher's philosophy into German. But about this time I began to see very clearly that it was impossible that our connection should prove of long duration; yet, in the event of my leaving the big man, what other resource had I? another publisher? But what had I to offer? There were my ballads, my Ab Gwilym; but then I thought of Taggart and his snuff, his pinch of snuff. However, I determined to see what could be done, so I took my ballads under my arm, and went to various publishers; some took snuff, others did not, but none took my ballads or Ab Gwilym, they would not even look at them. One asked me if I had anything else—he was a snuff-taker—I said yes; and going home returned with my translation of the German novel, to which I have before alluded. After keeping it for a fortnight, he returned it to me on my visiting him, and, taking a pinch of snuff, told me it would not do. There were marks of snuff on the outside of the manuscript, which was a roll of paper bound with red tape, but there were no marks of snuff on the interior of the manuscript, from which I concluded that he had never opened it.

I had often heard of one Glorious John, who lived at the western end of the town; on consulting Taggart, he told me that it was possible that Glorious John would publish my ballads and Ab Gwilym, that is, said he, taking a pinch of snuff, provided you can see him; so I went to the house where Glorious John resided, and a glorious house it was, but I could not see Glorious John. I called a dozen times, but I never could see Glorious John. Twenty years after, by the greatest chance in the world, I saw Glorious John, and sure enough Glorious John published my books, but they were different books from the first; I never offered my ballads or Ab Gwilym to Glorious John. Glorious

John was no snuff-taker. He asked me to dinner, and treated me with superb Rhenish wine. Glorious John is now gone to his rest, but I—what was I going to say?—the world will never forget Glorious John.

So I returned to my last resource for the time then being—to the publisher, persevering doggedly in my labour. One day, on visiting the publisher, I found him stamping with fury upon certain fragments of paper.

"Sir," said he, "you know nothing of German; I have shown your translation of the first chapter of my Philosophy to several Germans: it is utterly unintelligible to them." "Did they see the Philosophy?" I replied. "They did, sir, but they did not profess to understand English." "No more do I," I replied, "if that Philosophy be English."

The publisher was furious—I was silent. For want of a pinch of snuff, I had recourse to something which is no bad substitute for a pinch of snuff to those who can't take it, silent contempt; at first it made the publisher more furious, as perhaps a pinch of snuff would; it, however, eventually calmed him, and he ordered me back to my occupations, in other words, the compilation. To be brief, the compilation was completed, I got paid in the usual manner, and forthwith left him.

He was a clever man, but what a difference in clever men!

CHAPTER XLIV.

It was past mid-winter, and I sat on London Bridge, in company with the old apple-woman: she had just returned to the other side of the bridge to her place in the booth where I had originally found her. This she had done after repeated conversations with me; "she liked the old place best," she said, which she would never have left but for the terror which she experienced when the boys ran away with her book. So I sat with her at the old spot, one afternoon past mid-winter, reading the book, of which I had by this time come to the last pages. I had observed that the old woman for some time past had shown much less anxiety about the book than she had been in the habit of doing. I was, however, not quite prepared for her offering to make me a present of it, which she did that afternoon; when, having finished it, I returned it to her, with many thanks for the pleasure and instruction I had derived from its perusal. "You may keep it, dear," said the old woman, with a sigh; "you may carry it to your lodging, and keep it for your own."

Looking at the old woman with surprise, I exclaimed: "Is it possible that you are willing to part with the book which has been your source of comfort so long?"

Whereupon the old woman entered into a long history, from which I gathered that the book had become distasteful to her; she hardly ever opened it of late, she said, or if she did, it was only to shut it again; also, that other things which she had been fond of, though of a widely different kind, were now distasteful to her. Porter and beef-steaks were no longer grateful to her palate, her present diet chiefly consisting of tea, and bread and butter.

"Ah," said I, "you have been ill, and when people are ill, they seldom like the things which give them pleasure when they are in health." I learned, moreover, that she slept little at night, and had all kinds of strange thoughts; that as she lay awake many things connected with her youth, which she had quite forgotten, came into her mind. There were certain words that came into her mind the night before the last, which were continually humming in her ears: I found that the words were, "Thou shalt not steal".

On inquiring where she had first heard these words, I learned
that she had read them at school, in a book called the primer;
to this school she had been sent by her mother, who was a poor
widow, who followed the trade of apple-selling in the very spot
where her daughter followed it now. It seems that the mother
was a very good kind of woman, but quite ignorant of letters, the
benefit of which she was willing to procure for her child; and
at the school the daughter learned to read, and subsequently
experienced the pleasure and benefit of letters, in being able to
read the book which she found in an obscure closet of her
mother's house, and which had been her principal companion
and comfort for many years of her life.

But, as I have said before, she was now dissatisfied with
the book, and with most other things in which she had taken
pleasure; she dwelt much on the words, "Thou shalt not steal";
she had never stolen things herself, but then she had bought
things which other people had stolen, and which she knew had
been stolen; and her dear son had been a thief, which he perhaps
would not have been but for the example which she set him in
buying things from characters, as she called them, who associated
with her.

On inquiring how she had become acquainted with these
characters, I learned that times had gone hard with her; that she
had married, but her husband had died after a long sickness,
which had reduced them to great distress; that her fruit trade
was not a profitable one, and that she had bought and sold things
which had been stolen to support herself and her son. That for
a long time she supposed there was no harm in doing so, as her
book was full of entertaining tales of stealing; but she now
thought that the book was a bad book, and that learning to read
was a bad thing; her mother had never been able to read, but
had died in peace, though poor.

So here was a woman who attributed the vices and follies of
her life to being able to read; her mother, she said, who could
not read, lived respectably, and died in peace; and what was the
essential difference between the mother and daughter, save that
the latter could read? But for her literature she might in all
probability have lived respectably and honestly, like her mother,
and might eventually have died in peace, which at present she
could scarcely hope to do. Education had failed to produce any
good in this poor woman; on the contrary, there could be little
doubt that she had been injured by it. Then was education a
bad thing? Rousseau was of opinion that it was; but Rousseau

was a Frenchman, at least wrote in French, and I cared not the snap of my fingers for Rousseau. But education has certainly been of benefit in some instances; well, what did that prove, but that partiality existed in the management of the affairs of the world. If education was a benefit to some, why was it not a benefit to others? Could some avoid abusing it, any more than others could avoid turning it to a profitable account? I did not see how they could; this poor simple woman found a book in her mother's closet; a book, which was a capital book for those who could turn it to the account for which it was intended; a book, from the perusal of which I felt myself wiser and better, but which was by no means suited to the intellect of this poor simple woman, who thought that it was written in praise of thieving; yet she found it, she read it, and—and I felt myself getting into a maze; what is right? thought I; what is wrong? Do I exist? Does the world exist? if it does, every action is bound up with necessity.

"Necessity!" I exclaimed, and cracked my finger joints.

"Ah, it is a bad thing," said the old woman.

"What is a bad thing?" said I.

"Why, to be poor, dear."

"You talk like a fool," said I, "riches and poverty are only different forms of necessity."

"You should not call me a fool, dear; you should not call your own mother a fool."

"You are not my mother," said I.

"Not your mother, dear?—no, no more I am; but your calling me fool put me in mind of my dear son, who often used to call me fool—and you just now looked as he sometimes did, with a blob of foam on your lip."

"After all, I don't know that you are not my mother."

"Don't you, dear? I'm glad of it; I wish you would make it out."

"How should I make it out? who can speak from his own knowledge as to the circumstances of his birth? Besides, before attempting to establish our relationship, it would be necessary to prove that such people exist."

"What people, dear?"

"You and I."

"Lord, child, you are mad; that book has made you so."

"Don't abuse it," said I; "the book is an excellent one, that is, provided it exists."

"I wish it did not," said the old woman; "but it sha'n't long;

I'll burn it, or fling it into the river—the voices of night tell me to do so."

"Tell the voices," said I, "that they talk nonsense; the book, if it exists, is a good book, it contains a deep moral; have you read it all?"

"All the funny parts, dear; all about taking things, and the manner it was done; as for the rest, I could not exactly make it out."

"Then the book is not to blame; I repeat that the book is a good book, and contains deep morality, always supposing that there is such a thing as morality, which is the same thing as supposing that there is anything at all."

"Anything at all! Why, a'n't we here on this bridge, in my booth, with my stall and my ——"

"Apples and pears, baked hot, you would say—I don't know; all is a mystery, a deep question. It is a question, and probably always will be, whether there is a world, and consequently apples and pears; and, provided there be a world, whether that world be like an apple or a pear."

"Don't talk so, dear."

"I won't; we will suppose that we all exist—world, ourselves, apples, and pears: so you wish to get rid of the book?"

"Yes, dear, I wish you would take it."

"I have read it, and have no further use for it; I do not need books: in a little time, perhaps, I shall not have a place wherein to deposit myself, far less books."

"Then I will fling it into the river."

"Don't do that; here, give it me. Now what shall I do with it? you were so fond of it."

"I am so no longer."

"But how will you pass your time? what will you read?"

"I wish I had never learned to read, or, if I had, that I had only read the books I saw at school: the primer or the other."

"What was the other?"

"I think they called it the Bible: all about God, and Job, and Jesus."

"Ah, I know it."

"You have read it? is it a nice book—all true?"

"True, true—I don't know what to say; but if the world be true, and not all a lie, a fiction, I don't see why the Bible, as they call it, should not be true. By-the-bye, what do you call Bible in your tongue, or, indeed, book of any kind? as Bible merely means a book."

"What do I call the Bible in my language, dear?"

"Yes, the language of those who bring you things."

"The language of those who *did*, dear; they bring them now no longer. They call me fool, as you did, dear, just now; they call kissing the Bible, which means taking a false oath, smacking calf-skin."

"That's metaphor," said I, "English, but metaphorical; what an odd language! So you would like to have a Bible,—shall I buy you one?"

"I am poor, dear—no money since I left off the other trade."

"Well, then, I'll buy you one."

"No, dear, no; you are poor, and may soon want the money; but if you can take me one conveniently on the sly, you know—I think you may, for, as it is a good book, I suppose there can be no harm in taking it."

"That will never do," said I, "more especially as I should be sure to be caught, not having made taking of things my trade; but I'll tell you what I'll do—try and exchange this book of yours for a Bible; who knows for what great things this same book of yours may serve?"

"Well, dear," said the old woman, "do as you please; I should like to see the—what do you call it?—Bible, and to read it, as you seem to think it true."

"Yes," said I, "seem; that is the way to express yourself in this maze of doubt—I seem to think—these apples and pears seem to be—and here seems to be a gentleman who wants to purchase either one or the other."

A person had stopped before the apple-woman's stall, and was glancing now at the fruit, now at the old woman and myself; he wore a blue mantle, and had a kind of fur cap on his head; he was somewhat above the middle stature; his features were keen, but rather hard; there was a slight obliquity in his vision. Selecting a small apple, he gave the old woman a penny; then, after looking at me scrutinizingly for a moment, he moved from the booth in the direction of Southwark.

"Do you know who that man is?" said I to the old woman.

"No," said she, "except that he is one of my best customers: he frequently stops, takes an apple, and gives me a penny; his is the only piece of money I have taken this blessed day. I don't know him, but he has once or twice sat down in the booth with two strange-looking men—Mulattos, or Lascars, I think they call them."

CHAPTER XLV.

In pursuance of my promise to the old woman, I set about procuring her a Bible with all convenient speed, placing the book
which she had intrusted to me for the purpose of exchange in my
pocket. I went to several shops, and asked if Bibles were to be
had : I found that there were plenty. When, however, I informed
the people that I came to barter, they looked blank, and declined
treating with me, saying that they did not do business in that
way. At last I went into a shop over the window of which I saw
written, " Books bought and exchanged " : there was a smartish
young fellow in the shop, with black hair and whiskers. " You
exchange ? " said I. " Yes," said he, " sometimes, but we prefer
selling ; what book do you want ? " " A Bible," said I. " Ah," said
he, " there's a great demand for Bibles just now ; all kinds of people
are become very pious of late," he added, grinning at me ; " I am
afraid I can't do business with you, more especially as the master
is not at home. What book have you brought ? " Taking the
book out of my pocket, I placed it on the counter. The young
fellow opened the book, and inspecting the title-page, burst into
a loud laugh. " What do you laugh for ? " said I, angrily, and half
clenching my fist. " Laugh ! " said the young fellow ; " laugh !
who could help laughing ? " " I could," said I ; " I see nothing to
laugh at ; I want to exchange this book for a Bible." " You do ? "
said the young fellow ; " well, I daresay there are plenty who would
be willing to exchange, that is, if they dared. I wish master were
at home ; but that would never do, either. Master's a family man,
the Bibles are not mine, and master being a family man, is sharp,
and knows all his stock ; I'd buy it of you, but, to tell you the
truth, I am quite empty here," said he, pointing to his pocket, " so
I am afraid we can't deal."

Whereupon, looking anxiously at the young man, " what am
I to do ? " said I ; " I really want a Bible ".

" Can't you buy one ? " said the young man ; " have you no
money ? "

" Yes," said I, " I have some, but I am merely the agent of
another ; I came to exchange, not to buy ; what am I to do ? "

"I don't know," said the young man, thoughtfully, laying down the book on the counter; "I don't know what you can do; I think you will find some difficulty in this bartering job, the trade are rather precise." All at once he laughed louder than before; suddenly stopping, however, he put on a very grave look. "Take my advice," said he; "there is a firm established in this neighbourhood which scarcely sells any books but Bibles; they are very rich, and pride themselves on selling their books at the lowest possible price; apply to them, who knows but what they will exchange with you?"

Thereupon I demanded with some eagerness of the young man the direction to the place where he thought it possible that I might effect the exchange—which direction the young fellow cheerfully gave me, and, as I turned away, had the civility to wish me success.

I had no difficulty in finding the house to which the young fellow directed me; it was a very large house, situated in a square, and upon the side of the house was written in large letters, "Bibles, and other religious books".

At the door of the house were two or three tumbrils, in the act of being loaded with chests, very much resembling tea-chests; one of the chests falling down, burst, and out flew, not tea, but various books, in a neat, small size, and in neat leather covers; Bibles, said I,—Bibles, doubtless. I was not quite right, nor quite wrong; picking up one of the books, I looked at it for a moment, and found it to be the New Testament. "Come, young lad," said a man who stood by, in the dress of a porter, "put that book down, it is none of yours; if you want a book, go in and deal for one."

Deal, thought I, deal,—the man seems to know what I am coming about,—and going in, I presently found myself in a very large room. Behind a counter two men stood with their backs to a splendid fire, warming themselves, for the weather was cold.

Of these men one was dressed in brown, and the other was dressed in black; both were tall men—he who was dressed in brown was thin, and had a particularly ill-natured countenance; the man dressed in black was bulky, his features were noble, but they were those of a lion.

"What is your business, young man?" said the precise personage, as I stood staring at him and his companion.

"I want a Bible," said I.

"What price, what size?" said the precise-looking man.

"As to size," said I, "I should like to have a large one

—that is, if you can afford me one—I do not come to buy."

"Oh, friend," said the precise-looking man, "if you come here expecting to have a Bible for nothing, you are mistaken—we ——"

"I would scorn to have a Bible for nothing," said I, "or anything else; I came not to beg, but to barter; there is no shame in that, especially in a country like this, where all folks barter."

"Oh, we don't barter," said the precise man, "at least Bibles; you had better depart."

"Stay, brother," said the man with the countenance of a lion, "let us ask a few questions; this may be a very important case; perhaps the young man has had convictions."

"Not I," I exclaimed, "I am convinced of nothing, and with regard to the Bible—I don't believe ——"

"Hey!" said the man with the lion countenance, and there he stopped. But with that "Hey" the walls of the house seemed to shake, the windows rattled, and the porter whom I had seen in front of the house came running up the steps, and looked into the apartment through the glass of the door.

There was silence for about a minute—the same kind of silence which succeeds a clap of thunder.

At last the man with the lion countenance, who had kept his eyes fixed upon me, said calmly: "Were you about to say that you don't believe in the Bible, young man?"

"No more than in anything else," said I; "you were talking of convictions—I have no convictions. It is not easy to believe in the Bible till one is convinced that there is a Bible."

"He seems to be insane," said the prim-looking man, "we had better order the porter to turn him out."

"I am by no means certain," said I, "that the porter could turn me out; always provided there is a porter, and this system of ours be not a lie, and a dream."

"Come," said the lion-looking man, impatiently, "a truce with this nonsense. If the porter cannot turn you out, perhaps some other person can; but to the point—you want a Bible?"

"I do," said I, "but not for myself; I was sent by another person to offer something in exchange for one."

"And who is that person?"

"A poor old woman, who has had what you call convictions, —heard voices, or thought she heard them—I forgot to ask her whether they were loud ones."

"What has she sent to offer in exchange?" said the man, without taking any notice of the concluding part of my speech.

"A book," said I.

"Let me see it."

"Nay, brother," said the precise man, "this will never do; if we once adopt the system of barter, we shall have all the holders of useless rubbish in the town applying to us."

"I wish to see what he has brought," said the other; "perhaps Baxter, or Jewell's Apology, either of which would make a valuable addition to our collection. Well, young man, what's the matter with you?"

I stood like one petrified; I had put my hand into my pocket—the book was gone.

"What's the matter?" repeated the man with the lion countenance, in a voice very much resembling thunder.

"I have it not—I have lost it!"

"A pretty story, truly," said the precise-looking man, "lost it!"

"You had better retire," said the other.

"How shall I appear before the party who intrusted me with the book? She will certainly think that I have purloined it, notwithstanding all I can say; nor, indeed, can I blame her—appearances are certainly against me."

"They are so—you had better retire."

I moved towards the door. "Stay, young man, one word more; there is only one way of proceeding which would induce me to believe that you are sincere."

"What is that?" said I, stopping and looking at him anxiously.

"The purchase of a Bible."

"Purchase!" said I, "purchase! I came not to purchase, but to barter; such was my instruction, and how can I barter if I have lost the book?"

The other made no answer, and turning away I made for the door; all of a sudden I started, and turning round, "Dear me," said I, "it has just come into my head, that if the book was lost by my negligence, as it must have been, I have clearly a right to make it good".

No answer.

"Yes," I repeated, "I have clearly a right to make it good; how glad I am! see the effect of a little reflection. I will purchase a Bible instantly, that is, if I have not lost"—— and with considerable agitation I felt in my pocket.

The prim-looking man smiled : " I suppose," said he, "that he has lost his money as well as book ".

" No," said I, " I have not ; " and pulling out my hand I displayed no less a sum than three half-crowns.

" O, noble goddess of the Mint ! " as Dame Charlotta Nordenflycht, the Swede, said a hundred and fifty years ago, "great is thy power; how energetically the possession of thee speaks in favour of man's character ! "

" Only half a crown for this Bible ? " said I, putting down the money, " it is worth three ; " and bowing to the man of the noble features, I departed with my purchase.

" Queer customer," said the prim-looking man, as I was about to close the door—" don't like him."

" Why, as to that, I scarcely know what to say," said he of the countenance of a lion.

CHAPTER XLVI.

A FEW days after the occurrence of what is recorded in the last chapter, as I was wandering in the City, chance directed my footsteps to an alley leading from one narrow street to another in the neighbourhood of Cheapside. Just before I reached the mouth of the alley, a man in a greatcoat, closely followed by another, passed it; and, at the moment in which they were passing, I observed the man behind snatch something from the pocket of the other; whereupon, darting into the street, I seized the hindermost man by the collar, crying at the same time to the other, "My good friend, this person has just picked your pocket".

The individual whom I addressed, turning round with a start, glanced at me, and then at the person whom I held. London is the place for strange rencounters. It appeared to me that I recognised both individuals—the man whose pocket had been picked and the other; the latter now began to struggle violently; "I have picked no one's pocket," said he. "Rascal," said the other, "you have got my pocket-book in your bosom." "No, I have not," said the other; and struggling more violently than before, the pocket-book dropped from his bosom upon the ground.

The other was now about to lay hands upon the fellow, who was still struggling. "You had better take up your book," said I; "I can hold him." He followed my advice, and, taking up his pocket-book, surveyed my prisoner with a ferocious look, occasionally glaring at me. Yes, I had seen him before—it was the stranger whom I had observed on London Bridge, by the stall of the old apple-woman, with the cap and cloak; but, instead of these, he now wore a hat and greatcoat. "Well," said I, at last, "what am I to do with this gentleman of ours?" nodding to the prisoner, who had now left off struggling. "Shall I let him go?"

"Go!" said the other; "go! The knave—the rascal; let him go, indeed! Not so, he shall go before the Lord Mayor. Bring him along."

"Oh, let me go," said the other: "let me go; this is the first offence, I assure ye—the first time I ever thought to do anything wrong."

"Hold your tongue," said I, "or I shall be angry with you. If I am not very much mistaken, you once attempted to cheat me."

"I never saw you before in all my life," said the fellow, though his countenance seemed to belie his words.

"That is not true," said I; "you are the man who attempted to cheat me of one-and-ninepence in the coach-yard, on the first morning of my arrival in London."

"I don't doubt it," said the other; "a confirmed thief;" and here his tones became peculiarly sharp; "I would fain see him hanged—crucified. Drag him along."

"I am no constable," said I; "you have got your pocket-book—I would rather you would bid me let him go."

"Bid you let him go!" said the other almost furiously, "I command—stay, what was I going to say? I was forgetting myself," he observed more gently; "but he stole my pocket-book; if you did but know what it contained."

"Well," said I, "if it contains anything valuable, be the more thankful that you have recovered it; as for the man, I will help you to take him where you please; but I wish you would let him go."

The stranger hesitated, and there was an extraordinary play of emotion in his features; he looked ferociously at the pick-pocket, and, more than once, somewhat suspiciously at myself; at last his countenance cleared, and, with a good grace, he said, "Well, you have done me a great service, and you have my consent to let him go; but the rascal shall not escape with impunity," he exclaimed suddenly, as I let the man go, and starting forward, before the fellow could escape, he struck him a violent blow on the face. The man staggered, and had nearly fallen; recovering himself, however, he said: "I tell you what, my fellow, if I ever meet you in this street in a dark night, and I have a knife about me, it shall be the worse for you; as for you, young man," said he to me; but, observing that the other was making towards him, he left whatever he was about to say unfinished, and, taking to his heels, was out of sight in a moment.

The stranger and myself walked in the direction of Cheapside, the way in which he had been originally proceeding; he was silent for a few moments, at length he said: "You have really done me a great service, and I should be ungrateful not to acknowledge it. I am a merchant; and a merchant's pocket-

book, as you perhaps know, contains many things of importance;
but young man," he exclaimed, "I think I have seen you before;
I thought so at first, but where I cannot exactly say : where was
it?" I mentioned London Bridge and the old apple-woman.
"Oh," said he, and smiled, and there was something peculiar
in his smile, "I remember now. Do you frequently sit on
London Bridge?" "Occasionally," said I; "that old woman
is an old friend of mine." "Friend?" said the stranger, "I
am glad of it, for I shall know where to find you. At present I
am going to 'Change; time you know is precious to a merchant."
We were by this time close to Cheapside. "Farewell," said he,
"I shall not forget this service. I trust we shall soon meet again."
He then shook me by the hand and went his way.

The next day, as I was seated beside the old woman in the
booth, the stranger again made his appearance, and after a word
or two, sat down beside me; the old woman was sometimes
reading the Bible, which she had already had two or three days
in her possession, and sometimes discoursing with me. Our
discourse rolled chiefly on philological matters.

"What do you call bread in your language?" said I.

"You mean the language of those who bring me things to
buy, or who did; for, as I told you before, I sha'n't buy any
more; it's no language of mine, dear—they call bread pannam
in their language."

"Pannam!" said I, "pannam! evidently connected with, if
not derived from, the Latin panis; even as the word tanner, which
signifieth a sixpence, is connected with, if not derived from, the
Latin tener, which is itself connected with, if not derived from,
tawno or tawner, which, in the language of Mr. Petulengro, signifieth a sucking child. Let me see, what is the term for bread in the
language of Mr. Petulengro? Morro, or manro, as I have sometimes heard it called; is there not some connection between these
words and panis? Yes, I think there is; and I should not
wonder if morro, manro, and panis were connected, perhaps
derived from the same root; but what is that root? I don't know
—I wish I did; though, perhaps, I should not be the happier.
Morro—manro! I rather think morro is the oldest form; it is
easier to say morro than manro. Morro! Irish, aran; Welsh,
bara; English, bread. I can see a resemblance between all the
words, and pannam too; and I rather think that the Petulengrian
word is the elder. How odd it would be if the language of
Mr. Petulengro should eventually turn out to be the mother of all
the languages in the world; yet it is certain that there are some

languages in which the terms for bread have no connection with the word used by Mr. Petulengro, notwithstanding that those languages, in many other points, exhibit a close affinity to the language of the horse-shoe master: for example, bread, in Hebrew, is Laham, which assuredly exhibits little similitude to the word used by the aforesaid Petulengro. In Armenian it is ——"

"Zhats!" said the stranger starting up. "By the Patriarch and the Three Holy Churches, this is wonderful! How came you to know aught of Armenian?"

CHAPTER XLVII.

JUST as I was about to reply to the interrogation of my new-formed acquaintance, a man, with a dusky countenance, probably one of the Lascars, or Mulattos, of whom the old woman had spoken, came up and whispered to him, and with this man he presently departed, not however before he had told me the place of his abode, and requested me to visit him.

After the lapse of a few days, I called at the house which he had indicated. It was situated in a dark and narrow street, in the heart of the city, at no great distance from the Bank. I entered a counting-room, in which a solitary clerk, with a foreign look, was writing. The stranger was not at home; returning the next day, however, I met him at the door as he was about to enter; he shook me warmly by the hand. "I am glad to see you," said he, "follow me, I was just thinking of you." He led me through the counting-room to an apartment up a flight of stairs; before ascending, however, he looked into the book in which the foreign-visaged clerk was writing, and, seemingly not satisfied with the manner in which he was executing his task, he gave him two or three cuffs, telling him at the same time that he deserved crucifixion.

The apartment above stairs, to which he led me, was large, with three windows which opened upon the street. The walls were hung with wired cases, apparently containing books. There was a table and two or three chairs; but the principal article of furniture was a long sofa, extending from the door by which we entered to the farther end of the apartment. Seating himself upon the sofa, my new acquaintance motioned me to a seat beside him, and then, looking me full in the face, repeated his former inquiry. "In the name of all that is wonderful, how came you to know aught of my language?"

"There is nothing wonderful in that," said I; "we are at the commencement of a philological age, every one studies languages: that is, every one who is fit for nothing else; philology being the last resource of dulness and ennui, I have got a little in advance

(269)

of the throng, by mastering the Armenian alphabet; but I fore-
see the time when every unmarriageable miss, and desperate
blockhead, will likewise have acquired the letters of Mesroub,
and will know the term for bread, in Armenian, and perhaps that
for wine,"

"Kini," said my companion; and that and the other word
put me in mind of the duties of hospitality. "Will you eat
bread and drink wine with me?"

"Willingly," said I. Whereupon my companion, unlocking
a closet, produced on a silver salver, a loaf of bread, with a
silver-handled knife, and wine in a silver flask, with cups of the
same metal. "I hope you like my fare," said he, after we had
both eaten and drunk.

"I like your bread," said I, "for it is stale; I like not your
wine, it is sweet, and I hate sweet wine."

"It is wine of Cyprus," said my entertainer; and, when I
found that it was wine of Cyprus, I tasted it again, and the second
taste pleased me much better than the first, notwithstanding that
I still thought it somewhat sweet. "So," said I, after a pause,
looking at my companion, "you are an Armenian."

"Yes," said he, "an Armenian born in London, but not less
an Armenian on that account. My father was a native of Ispahan,
one of the celebrated Armenian colony which was established
there shortly after the time of the dreadful hunger, which drove
the children of Haik in swarms from their original country, and
scattered them over most parts of the eastern and western world.
In Ispahan he passed the greater portion of his life, following
mercantile pursuits with considerable success. Certain enemies,
however, having accused him to the despot of the place, of using
seditious language, he was compelled to flee, leaving most of his
property behind. Travelling in the direction of the west, he
came at last to London, where he established himself, and
where he eventually died, leaving behind a large property and
myself, his only child, the fruit of a marriage with an Armenian
English woman, who did not survive my birth more than
three months."

The Armenian then proceeded to tell me that he had carried
on the business of his father, which seemed to embrace most
matters, from buying silks of Lascars, to speculating in the funds,
and that he had considerably increased the property which his
father had left him. He candidly confessed that he was wonderfully fond of gold, and said there was nothing like it for giving a
person respectability and consideration in the world; to which

assertion I made no answer, being not exactly prepared to contradict it.

And, when he had related to me his history, he expressed a desire to know something more of myself, whereupon I gave him the outline of my history, concluding with saying: "I am now a poor author, or rather a philologist, upon the streets of London, possessed of many tongues, which I find of no use in the world".

"Learning without money is anything but desirable," said the Armenian, "as it unfits a man for humble occupations. It is true that it may occasionally beget him friends; I confess to you that your understanding something of my language weighs more with me than the service you rendered me in rescuing my pocket-book the other day from the claws of that scoundrel whom I yet hope to see hanged, if not crucified, notwithstanding there were in that pocket-book papers and documents of considerable value. Yes, that circumstance makes my heart warm towards you, for I am proud of my language—as I indeed well may be—what a language, noble and energetic! quite original, differing from all others both in words and structure."

"You are mistaken," said I; "many languages resemble the Armenian both in structure and words."

"For example?" said the Armenian.

"For example," said I, "the English."

"The English," said the Armenian; "show me one word in which the English resembles the Armenian."

"You walk on London Bridge," said I.

"Yes," said the Armenian.

"I saw you look over the balustrade the other morning."

"True," said the Armenian.

"Well, what did you see rushing up through the arches with noise and foam?"

"What was it?" said the Armenian. "What was it?—you don't mean the *tide?*"

"Do I not?" said I.

"Well, what has the tide to do with the matter?"

"Much," said I; "what is the tide?"

"The ebb and flow of the sea," said the Armenian.

"The sea itself; what is the Haik word for sea?"

The Armenian gave a strong gasp; then, nodding his head thrice, "you are right," said he, "the English word tide is the Armenian for sea; and now I begin to perceive that there are many English words which are Armenian; there is —— and —— and there again in French there is —— and —— derived from the

Armenian. How strange, how singular—I thank you. It is a proud thing to see that the language of my race has had so much influence over the languages of the world."

I saw that all that related to his race was the weak point of the Armenian. I did not flatter the Armenian with respect to his race or language. "An inconsiderable people," said I, "shrewd and industrious, but still an inconsiderable people. A language bold and expressive, and of some antiquity, derived, though perhaps not immediately, from some much older tongue. I do not think that the Armenian has had any influence over the formation of the languages of the world. I am not much indebted to the Armenian for the solution of any doubts ; whereas to the language of Mr. Petulengro ——"

"I have heard you mention that name before," said the Armenian ; "who is Mr. Petulengro?"

And then I told the Armenian who Mr. Petulengro was. The Armenian spoke contemptuously of Mr. Petulengro and his race. "Don't speak contemptuously of Mr. Petulengro," said I, "nor of anything belonging to him. He is a dark, mysterious personage ; all connected with him is a mystery, especially his language ; but I believe that his language is doomed to solve a great philological problem—Mr. Petulengro ——"

"You appear agitated," said the Armenian ; "take another glass of wine ; you possess a great deal of philological knowledge, but it appears to me that the language of this Petulengro is your foible : but let us change the subject ; I feel much interested in you, and would fain be of service to you. Can you cast accounts?"

I shook my head.

"Keep books?"

"I have an idea that I could write books," said I; "but, as to keeping them ——" and here again I shook my head.

The Armenian was silent some time ; all at once, glancing at one of the wire cases, with which, as I have already said, the walls of the room were hung, he asked me if I was well acquainted with the learning of the Haiks. "The books in these cases," said he, "contain the masterpieces of Haik learning."

"No," said I, "all I know of the learning of the Haiks is their translation of the Bible."

"You have never read Z——?"

"No," said I, "I have never read Z——"

"I have a plan," said the Armenian ; "I think I can employ you agreeably and profitably ; I should like to see Z—— in an

English dress; you shall translate Z—— If you can read the
Scriptures in Armenian, you can translate Z—— He is our
Esop, the most acute and clever of all our moral writers—his
philosophy ——"

"I will have nothing to do with him," said I.

"Wherefore?" said the Armenian.

"There is an old proverb," said I, "that 'a burnt child
avoids the fire'. I have burnt my hands sufficiently with attempting to translate philosophy, to make me cautious of venturing
upon it again;" and then I told the Armenian how I had been
persuaded by the publisher to translate his philosophy into
German, and what sorry thanks I had received; "and who
knows," said I, "but the attempt to translate Armenian philosophy into English might be attended with yet more disagreeable
consequences."

The Armenian smiled. "You would find me very different
from the publisher."

"In many points I have no doubt I should," I replied; "but
at the present moment I feel like a bird which has escaped from
a cage, and, though hungry, feels no disposition to return. Of
what nation is the dark man below stairs, whom I saw writing at
the desk?"

"He is a Moldave," said the Armenian; "the dog (and here
his eyes sparkled) deserves to be crucified, he is continually
making mistakes."

The Armenian again renewed his proposition about Z——,
which I again refused, as I felt but little inclination to place
myself beneath the jurisdiction of a person who was in the habit
of cuffing those whom he employed, when they made mistakes.
I presently took my departure; not, however, before I had
received from the Armenian a pressing invitation to call upon
him whenever I should feel disposed.

CHAPTER XLVIII.

ANXIOUS thoughts frequently disturbed me at this time with respect to what I was to do, and how support myself in the Great City. My future prospects were gloomy enough, and I looked forward and feared; sometimes I felt half disposed to accept the offer of the Armenian, and to commence forthwith, under his superintendence, the translation of the Haik Esop; but the remembrance of the cuffs which I had seen him bestow upon the Moldavian, when glancing over his shoulder into the ledger or whatever it was on which he was employed, immediately drove the inclination from my mind. I could not support the idea of the possibility of his staring over my shoulder upon my translation of the Haik Esop, and, dissatisfied with my attempts, treating me as he had treated the Moldavian clerk; placing myself in a position which exposed me to such treatment, would indeed be plunging into the fire after escaping from the frying pan. The publisher, insolent and overbearing as he was, whatever he might have wished or thought, had never lifted his hand against me, or told me that I merited crucifixion.

What was I to do? turn porter? I was strong; but there was something besides strength required to ply the trade of a porter—a mind of a particularly phlegmatic temperament, which I did not possess. What should I do?—enlist as a soldier? I was tall enough; but something besides height is required to make a man play with credit the part of soldier, I mean a private one—a spirit, if spirit it can be called, which will not only enable a man to submit with patience to insolence and abuse, and even to cuffs and kicks, but occasionally to the lash. I felt that I was not qualified to be a soldier, at least a private one; far better be a drudge to the most ferocious of publishers, editing Newgate lives, and writing in eighteenpenny reviews—better to translate the Haik Esop, under the superintendence of ten Armenians, than be a private soldier in the English service; I did not decide rashly—I knew something of soldiering. What should I do? I thought that I would make a last and desperate attempt to dispose of the ballads and of Ab Gwilym.

I had still an idea that, provided I could persuade any spirited publisher to give these translations to the world, I should acquire both considerable fame and profit; not, perhaps, a world-embracing fame such as Byron's, but a fame not to be sneered at, which would last me a considerable time, and would keep my heart from breaking;—profit, not equal to that which Scott had made by his wondrous novels, but which would prevent me from starving, and enable me to achieve some other literary enterprise. I read and re-read my ballads, and the more I read them the more I was convinced that the public, in the event of their being published, would freely purchase, and hail them with the merited applause. Were not the deeds and adventures wonderful and heart-stirring, from which it is true I could claim no merit, being but the translator; but had I not rendered them into English, with all their original fire? Yes, I was confident I had; and I had no doubt that the public would say so. And then, with respect to Ab Gwilym, had I not done as much justice to him as to the Danish Ballads; not only rendering faithfully his thoughts, imagery and phraseology, but even preserving in my translation the alliterative euphony which constitutes one of the most remarkable features of Welsh prosody? Yes, I had accomplished all this; and I doubted not that the public would receive my translations from Ab Gwilym with quite as much eagerness as my version of the Danish ballads. But I found the publishers as untractable as ever, and to this day the public has never had an opportunity of doing justice to the glowing fire of my ballad versification, and the alliterative euphony of my imitations of Ab Gwilym.

I had not seen Francis Ardry since the day I had seen him taking lessons in elocution. One afternoon, as I was seated at my table, my head resting on my hands, he entered my apartment; sitting down, he inquired of me why I had not been to see him. "I might ask the same question of you," I replied. "Wherefore have you not been to see me?" Whereupon Francis Ardry told me that he had been much engaged in his oratorical exercises, also in escorting the young Frenchwoman about to places of public amusement; he then again questioned me as to the reason of my not having been to see him.

I returned an evasive answer. The truth was, that for some time past my appearance, owing to the state of my finances, had been rather shabby; and I did not wish to expose a fashionable young man like Francis Ardry, who lived in a fashionable neighbourhood, to the imputation of having a shabby acquaintance. I was aware that Francis Ardry was an excellent fellow; but, on that very account, I felt, under existing circumstances, a delicacy in visiting him.

It is very possible that he had an inkling of how matters stood, as he presently began to talk of my affairs and prospects. I told him of my late ill success with the booksellers, and inveighed against their blindness to their own interest in refusing to publish my translations. "The last that I addressed myself to," said I, "told me not to trouble him again, unless I could bring him a decent novel or a tale."

"Well," said Frank, "and why did you not carry him a decent novel or a tale?"

"Because I have neither," said I; "and to write them is, I believe, above my capacity. At present I feel divested of all energy—heartless and almost hopeless."

"I see how it is," said Francis Ardry, "you have overworked yourself, and, worst of all, to no purpose. Take my advice; cast all care aside, and only think of diverting yourself for a month at least."

"Divert myself," said I; "and where am I to find the means?"

"Be that care on my shoulders," said Francis Ardry. "Listen to me—my uncles have been so delighted with the favourable accounts which they have lately received from T—— of my progress in oratory, that, in the warmth of their hearts, they made me a present yesterday of two hundred pounds. This is more money than I want, at least for the present; do me the favour to take half of it as a loan—hear me," said he, observing that I was about to interrupt him, "I have a plan in my head— one of the prettiest in the world. The sister of my charmer is just arrived from France; she cannot speak a word of English; and, as Annette and myself are much engaged in our own matters, we cannot pay her the attention which we should wish, and which she deserves, for she is a truly fascinating creature, although somewhat differing from my charmer, having blue eyes and flaxen hair; whilst Annette, on the contrary —— But I hope you will shortly see Annette. Now my plan is this—Take the money, dress yourself fashionably, and conduct Annette's sister to Bagnigge Wells."

"And what should we do at Bagnigge Wells?"

"Do!" said Francis Ardry. "Dance!"

"But," said I, "I scarcely know anything of dancing."

"Then here's an excellent opportunity of improving yourself. Like most Frenchwomen, she dances divinely; however, if you object to Bagnigge Wells and dancing, go to Brighton, and remain there a month or two, at the end of which time you can return with your mind refreshed and invigorated, and materials, perhaps, for a tale or novel."

"I never heard a more foolish plan," said I, "or one less likely to terminate profitably or satisfactorily. I thank you, however, for your offer, which is, I daresay, well meant. If I am to escape from my cares and troubles, and find my mind refreshed and invigorated, I must adopt other means than conducting a French demoiselle to Brighton or Bagnigge Wells, defraying the expense by borrowing from a friend."

CHAPTER XLIX.

THE Armenian! I frequently saw this individual, availing myself of the permission which he had given me to call upon him. A truly singular personage was he, with his love of amassing money, and his nationality so strong as to be akin to poetry. Many an Armenian I have subsequently known fond of money-getting, and not destitute of national spirit; but never another, who, in the midst of his schemes of lucre, was at all times willing to enter into a conversation on the structure of the Haik language, or who ever offered me money to render into English the fables of Z—— in the hope of astonishing the stock-jobbers of the Exchange with the wisdom of the Haik Esop.

But he was fond of money, very fond. Within a little time I had won his confidence to such a degree that he informed me that the grand wish of his heart was to be possessed of two hundred thousand pounds.

"I think you might satisfy yourself with the half," said I. "One hundred thousand pounds is a large sum."

"You are mistaken," said the Armenian, "a hundred thousand pounds is nothing. My father left me that or more at his death. No; I shall never be satisfied with less than two."

"And what will you do with your riches," said I, "when you have obtained them? Will you sit down and muse upon them, or will you deposit them in a cellar, and go down once a day to stare at them? I have heard say that the fulfilment of one's wishes is invariably the precursor of extreme misery, and forsooth I can scarcely conceive a more horrible state of existence than to be without a hope or wish."

"It is bad enough, I dare say," said the Armenian; "it will, however, be time enough to think of disposing of the money when I have procured it. I still fall short by a vast sum of the two hundred thousand pounds."

I had occasionally much conversation with him on the state and prospects of his nation, especially of that part of it which still continued in the original country of the Haiks—Ararat and its confines, which, it appeared, he had frequently visited. He informed me that since the death of the last Haik monarch, which occurred in the eleventh century, Armenia had been governed both temporally and spiritually by certain personages called patriarchs; their temporal authority, however, was much circumscribed by the Persian and Turk, especially the former, of whom the Armenian spoke with much hatred, whilst their spiritual authority had at various times been considerably undermined by the emissaries of the Papa of Rome, as the Armenian called him.

"The Papa of Rome sent his emissaries at an early period amongst us," said the Armenian, "seducing the minds of weak-headed people, persuading them that the hillocks of Rome are higher than the ridges of Ararat; that the Roman Papa has more to say in heaven than the Armenian patriarch, and that puny Latin is a better language than nervous and sonorous Haik."

"They are both dialects," said I, "of the language of Mr. Petulengro, one of whose race I believe to have been the original founder of Rome; but, with respect to religion, what are the chief points of your faith? you are Christians, I believe."

"Yes," said the Armenian, "we are Christians in our way; we believe in God, the Holy Spirit, and Saviour, though we are not prepared to admit that the last personage is not only himself, but the other two. We believe ——" and then the Armenian told me of several things which the Haiks believed or disbelieved. "But what we find most hard of all to believe," said he, "is that the man of the mole-hills is entitled to our allegiance, he not being a Haik, or understanding the Haik language."

"But, by your own confession," said I, "he has introduced a schism in your nation, and has amongst you many that believe in him."

"It is true," said the Armenian, "that even on the confines of Ararat there are a great number who consider that mountain to be lower than the hillocks of Rome; but the greater number of degenerate Armenians are to be found amongst those who have wandered to the west; most of the Haik churches of the west consider Rome to be higher than Ararat—most of the Armenians of this place hold that dogma; I, however, have always stood firm in the contrary opinion."

"Ha! ha!"—here the Armenian laughed in his peculiar manner—"talking of this matter puts me in mind of an adventure which lately befel me, with one of the emissaries of the Papa of Rome, for the Papa of Rome has at present many emissaries in this country, in order to seduce the people from their own quiet religion to the savage heresy of Rome; this fellow came to me partly in the hope of converting me, but principally to extort money for the purpose of furthering the designs of Rome in this country. I humoured the fellow at first, keeping him in play for nearly a month, deceiving and laughing at him. At last he discovered that he could make nothing of me, and departed with the scowl of Caiaphas, whilst I cried after him : ' The roots of Ararat are *deeper* than those of Rome '."

The Armenian had occasionally reverted to the subject of the translation of the Haik Esop, which he had still a lurking desire that I should execute ; but I had invariably declined the undertaking, without, however, stating my reasons. On one occasion, when we had been conversing on the subject, the Armenian, who had been observing my countenance for some time with much attention, remarked, " Perhaps, after all, you are right, and you might employ your time to better advantage. Literature is a fine thing, especially Haik literature, but neither that nor any other would be likely to serve as a foundation to a man's fortune : and to make a fortune should be the principal aim of every one's life ; therefore listen to me. Accept a seat at the desk opposite to my Moldavian clerk, and receive the rudiments of a merchant's education. You shall be instructed in the Armenian way of doing business—I think you would make an excellent merchant."

" Why do you think so ? "

" Because you have something of the Armenian look."

" I understand you," said I ; " you mean to say that I squint ? "

" Not exactly," said the Armenian, " but there is certainly a kind of irregularity in your features. One eye appears to me larger than the other—never mind, but rather rejoice ; in that irregularity consists your strength. All people with regular features are fools ; it is very hard for them, you'll say, but there is no help : all we can do, who are not in such a predicament, is to pity those who are. Well ! will you accept my offer ? No ! you are a singular individual ; but I must not forget my own concerns. I must now go forth, having an appointment by which I hope to make money."

CHAPTER L.

THE fulfilment of the Armenian's grand wish was nearer at hand than either he or I had anticipated. Partly owing to the success of a bold speculation, in which he had some time previously engaged, and partly owing to the bequest of a large sum of money by one of his nation who died at this period in Paris, he found himself in the possession of a fortune somewhat exceeding two hundred thousand pounds ; this fact he communicated to me one evening about an hour after the close of 'Change, the hour at which I generally called, and at which I mostly found him at home.

" Well," said I, "and what do you intend to do next ? "

" I scarcely know," said the Armenian. " I was thinking of that when you came in. I don't see anything that I can do, save going on in my former course. After all, I was perhaps too moderate in making the possession of two hundred thousand pounds the summit of my ambition ; there are many individuals in this town who possess three times that sum, and are not yet satisfied. No, I think I can do no better than pursue the old career ; who knows but I may make the two hundred thousand three or four ?—there is already a surplus, which is an encouragement ; however, we will consider the matter over a goblet of wine ; I have observed of late that you have become partial to my Cyprus."

And it came to pass that, as we were seated over the Cyprus wine, we heard a knock at the door. " *Adelante !* " cried the Armenian ; whereupon the door opened, and in walked a somewhat extraordinary figure—a man in a long loose tunic of a stuff striped with black and yellow ; breeches of plush velvet, silk stockings, and shoes with silver buckles. On his head he wore a high-peaked hat ; he was tall, had a hooked nose, and in age was about fifty.

"Welcome, Rabbi Manasseh," said the Armenian. " I know your knock—you are welcome ; sit down."

" I am welcome," said Manasseh, sitting down ; " he—he—he ! you know my knock—I bring you money—*bueno !* "

There was something very peculiar in the sound of that *bueno* —I never forgot it.

Thereupon a conversation ensued between Rabbi Manasseh and the Armenian, in a language which I knew to be Spanish, though a peculiar dialect. It related to a mercantile transaction The Rabbi sighed heavily as he delivered to the other a considerable sum of money.

"It is right," said the Armenian, handing a receipt. "It is right; and I am quite satisfied."

"You are satisfied—you have taken money. *Bueno*, I have nothing to say against your being satisfied."

"Come, Rabbi," said the Armenian, "do not despond; it may be your turn next to take money; in the meantime, can't you be persuaded to taste my Cyprus?"

"He—he—he! señor, you know I do not love wine. I love Noah when he is himself; but, as Janus, I love him not. But you are merry, *bueno ;* you have a right to be so."

"Excuse me," said I, "but does Noah ever appear as Janus?"

"He—he—he!" said the Rabbi, "he only appeared as Janus once—*una vez quando estuvo borracho ;* which means ——"

"I understand," said I; "when he was ——" and I drew the side of my right hand sharply across my left wrist.

"Are you one of our people?" said the Rabbi.

"No," said I, "I am one of the Goyim; but I am only half enlightened. Why should Noah be Janus, when he was in that state?"

"He—he—he! you must know that in Lasan akhades wine is janin."

"In Armenian, kini," said I; "in Welsh, gwin; Latin, vinum; but do you think that Janus and janin are one?"

"Do I think? Don't the commentators say so? Does not Master Leo Abarbenel say so in his *Dialogues of Divine Love?*"

"But," said I, "I always thought that Janus was a god of the ancient Romans, who stood in a temple open in time of war, and shut in time of peace ; he was represented with two faces, which —which ——"

"He—he—he!" said the Rabbi, rising from his seat; "he had two faces, had he? And what did those two faces typify? You do not know; no, nor did the Romans who carved him with two faces know why they did so ; for they were only half enlightened, like you and the rest of the Goyim. Yet they were right in carving him with two faces looking from each other—they were right, though they knew not why; there was a tradition among them that the *Janinoso* had two faces, but they knew not that one was for the world which was gone, and the other for the world before him—for the drowned world, and for the present, as

Master Leo Abarbenel says in his *Dialogues of Divine Love.*
He—he—he!" continued the Rabbi, who had by this time
advanced to the door, and, turning round, waved the two forefingers of his right hand in our faces; "the Goyim and Epicouraiyim are clever men, they know how to make money better
than we of Israel.   My good friend there is a clever man, I bring
him money, he never brought me any, *bueno;* I do not blame
him, he knows much, very much; but one thing there is my
friend does not know, nor any of the Epicureans, he does not
know the sacred thing—he has never received the gift of interpretation which God alone gives to the seed—he has his gift, I
have mine—he is satisfied, I don't blame him, *bueno."*
    And with this last word in his mouth, he departed.
    "Is that man a native of Spain?" I demanded.
    "Not a native of Spain," said the Armenian, "though he is
one of those who call themselves Spanish Jews, and who are
to be found scattered throughout Europe, speaking the Spanish
language transmitted to them by their ancestors, who were
expelled from Spain in the time of Ferdinand and Isabella."
    "The Jews are a singular people," said I.
    "A race of cowards and dastards," said the Armenian, "with-
out a home or country; servants to servants; persecuted and
despised by all."
    "And what are the Haiks?" I demanded.
    "Very different from the Jews," replied the Armenian; "the
Haiks have a home—a country, and can occasionally use a good
sword; though it is true they are not what they might be."
    "Then it is a shame that they do not become so," said I;
"but they are too fond of money.   There is yourself, with two
hundred thousand pounds in your pocket, craving for more, whilst
you might be turning your wealth to the service of your country."
    "In what manner?" said the Armenian.
    "I have heard you say that the grand oppressor of your
country is the Persian; why not attempt to free your country
from his oppression—you have two hundred thousand pounds,
and money is the sinew of war?"
    "Would you, then, have me attack the Persian?"
    "I scarcely know what to say; fighting is a rough trade, and
I am by no means certain that you are calculated for the scratch.
It is not every one who has been brought up in the school of Mr.
Petulengro and Tawno Chikno.   All I can say is, that if I were
an Armenian, and had two hundred thousand pounds to back me,
I would attack the Persian."
    "Hem!" said the Armenian,

CHAPTER LI.

ONE morning on getting up I discovered that my whole worldly wealth was reduced to one half-crown—throughout that day I walked about in considerable distress of mind; it was now requisite that I should come to a speedy decision with respect to what I was to do; I had not many alternatives, and, before I had retired to rest on the night of the day in question, I had determined that I could do no better than accept the first proposal of the Armenian, and translate, under his superintendence, the Haik Esop into English.

I reflected, for I made a virtue of necessity, that, after all, such an employment would be an honest and honourable one; honest, inasmuch as by engaging in it I should do harm to nobody; honourable, inasmuch as it was a literary task, which not every one was capable of executing. It was not every one of the booksellers' writers of London who was competent to translate the Haik Esop. I determined to accept the offer of the Armenian.

Once or twice the thought of what I might have to undergo in the translation from certain peculiarities of the Armenian's temper almost unsettled me; but a mechanical diving of my hand into my pocket, and the feeling of the solitary half-crown, confirmed me; after all this was a life of trial and tribulation, and I had read somewhere or other that there was much merit in patience, so I determined to hold fast in my resolution of accepting the offer of the Armenian.

But all of a sudden I remembered that the Armenian appeared to have altered his intentions towards me : he appeared no longer desirous that I should render the Haik Esop into English for the benefit of the stock-jobbers on Exchange, but rather that I should acquire the rudiments of doing business in the Armenian fashion, and accumulate a fortune, which would enable me to make a figure upon 'Change with the best of the stock-jobbers. "Well," thought I, withdrawing my hand from my pocket, whither it had again mechanically dived, "after all, what would the world, what would this city be, without commerce? I believe the world, and particularly this city, would cut a very poor figure without commerce; and then there is something poetical in the idea of doing business after the Armenian fashion, dealing with dark-faced Lascars and Rabbins of the Sephardim. Yes, should the Armenian insist upon it, I will accept a seat at the desk, opposite the Moldavian clerk. I do not like the idea of cuffs similar to those the Armenian bestowed upon the Moldavian clerk; whatever merit there may be in patience, I do not think that my estimation of the merit of patience would be sufficient to induce me to remain quietly sitting under the infliction of cuffs. I think I should, in the event of his cuffing me, knock the Armenian down. Well, I think I have heard it said somewhere, that a knock-down blow is a great cementer of friendship; I think I have heard of two people being better friends than ever after the one had received from the other a knock-down blow."

That night I dreamed I had acquired a colossal fortune, some four hundred thousand pounds, by the Armenian way of doing business, but suddenly awoke in dreadful perplexity as to how I should dispose of it.

About nine o'clock next morning I set off to the house of the Armenian; I had never called upon him so early before, and certainly never with a heart beating with so much eagerness; but the situation of my affairs had become very critical, and I thought that I ought to lose no time in informing the Armenian that I was at length perfectly willing either to translate the Haik Esop under his superintendence, or to accept a seat at the desk opposite to the Moldavian clerk, and acquire the secrets of Armenian commerce. With a quick step I entered the counting-room, where, notwithstanding the earliness of the hour, I found the clerk busied as usual at his desk.

He had always appeared to me a singular being, this same Moldavian clerk. A person of fewer words could scarcely be conceived. Provided his master were at home, he would, on my inquiring, nod his head; and, provided he were not, he would invariably reply with the monosyllable "no," delivered in a strange guttural tone. On the present occasion, being full of eagerness and impatience, I was about to pass by him to the apartment above, without my usual inquiry, when he lifted his head from the ledger in which he was writing, and, laying down his pen, motioned to me with his forefinger, as if to arrest my progress; whereupon I stopped, and, with a palpitating heart, demanded whether the master of the house was at home? The

Moldavian clerk replied with his usual guttural, and, opening his desk ensconced his head therein.

"It does not much matter," said I, "I suppose I shall find him at home after 'Change; it does not much matter, I can return."

I was turning away with the intention of leaving the room; at this moment, however, the head of the Moldavian clerk became visible, and I observed a letter in his hand, which he had inserted in the desk at the same time with his head; this he extended towards me, making at the same time a side-long motion with his head, as much as to say that it contained something which interested me.

I took the letter, and the Moldavian clerk forthwith resumed his occupation. The back of the letter bore my name, written in Armenian characters. With a trembling hand I broke the seal, and, unfolding the letter, I beheld several lines also written in the letters of Mesroub, the Cadmus of the Armenians.

I stared at the lines, and at first could not make out a syllable of their meaning; at last, however, by continued staring, I discovered that, though the letters were Armenian, the words were English; in about ten minutes I had contrived to decipher the sense of the letter; it ran somewhat in this style :—

"MY DEAR FRIEND,—

"The words which you uttered in our last conversation have made a profound impression upon me; I have thought them over day and night, and have come to the conclusion that it is my bounden duty to attack the Persians. When these lines are delivered to you, I shall be on the route to Ararat. A mercantile speculation will be to the world the ostensible motive of my journey, and it is singular enough that one which offers considerable prospect of advantage has just presented itself on the confines of Persia. Think not, however, that motives of lucre would have been sufficiently powerful to tempt me to the East at the present moment. I may speculate, it is true; but I should scarcely have undertaken the journey but for your pungent words inciting me to attack the Persians. Doubt not that I will attack them on the first opportunity. I thank you heartily for putting me in mind of my duty. I have hitherto, to use your own words, been too fond of money-getting, like all my countrymen. I am much indebted to you; farewell! and may every prosperity await you."

For some time after I had deciphered the epistle, I stood as if rooted to the floor. I felt stunned—my last hope was gone;

presently a feeling arose in my mind—a feeling of self-reproach. Whom had I to blame but myself for the departure of the Armenian? Would he have ever thought of attacking the Persians had I not put the idea into his head? he had told me in his epistle that he was indebted to me for the idea. But for that, he might at the present moment have been in London, increasing his fortune by his usual methods, and I might be commencing under his auspices the translation of the Haik Esop, with the promise, no doubt, of a considerable remuneration for my trouble; or I might be taking a seat opposite the Moldavian clerk, and imbibing the first rudiments of doing business after the Armenian fashion, with the comfortable hope of realising, in a short time, a fortune of three or four hundred thousand pounds; but the Armenian was now gone, and farewell to the fine hopes I had founded upon him the day before. What was I to do? I looked wildly around, till my eyes rested on the Moldavian clerk, who was writing away in his ledger with particular vehemence. Not knowing well what to do or to say, I thought I might as well ask the Moldavian clerk when the Armenian had departed, and when he thought he would return. It is true it mattered little to me when he departed seeing that he was gone, and it was evident that he would not be back soon; but I knew not what to do, and in pure helplessness thought I might as well ask; so I went up to the Moldavian clerk and asked him when the Armenian had departed, and whether he had been gone two days or three? Whereupon the Moldavian clerk looking up from his ledger, made certain signs, which I could by no means understand. I stood astonished, but, presently recovering myself, inquired when he considered it probable that the master would return, and whether he thought it would be two months or — my tongue faltered—two years; whereupon the Moldavian clerk made more signs than before, and yet more unintelligible; as I persisted, however, he flung down his pen, and, putting his thumb into his mouth moved it rapidly, causing the nail to sound against the lower jaw; whereupon I saw that he was dumb, and hurried away, for I had always entertained a horror of dumb people, having once heard my mother say, when I was a child, that dumb people were half demoniacs, or little better.

CHAPTER LII.

LEAVING the house of the Armenian, I strolled about for some time ; almost mechanically my feet conducted me to London Bridge, to the booth in which stood the stall of the old apple-woman ; the sound of her voice aroused me, as I sat in a kind of stupor on the stone bench beside her ; she was inquiring what was the matter with me.

At first, I believe, I answered her very incoherently, for I observed alarm beginning to depict itself upon her countenance. Rousing myself, however, I in my turn put a few questions to her upon her present condition and prospects. The old woman's countenance cleared up instantly ; she informed me that she had never been more comfortable in her life ; that her trade, her *honest* trade—laying an emphasis on the word honest—had increased of late wonderfully ; that her health was better, and, above all, that she felt no fear and horror " here," laying her hand on her breast.

On my asking her whether she still heard voices in the night, she told me that she frequently did ; but that the present were mild voices, sweet voices, encouraging voices, very different from the former ones ; that a voice only the night previous, had cried out about " the peace of God," in particularly sweet accents ; a sentence which she remembered to have read in her early youth in the primer, but which she had clean forgotten till the voice the night before brought it to her recollection.

After a pause, the old woman said to me : " I believe, dear, that it is the blessed book you brought me which has wrought this goodly change. How glad I am now that I can read ; but oh what a difference between the book you brought to me and the one you took away. I believe the one you brought is written by the finger of God, and the other by ——"

" Don't abuse the book," said I, " it is an excellent book for those who can understand it ; it was not exactly suited to you, and perhaps it had been better that you had never read it—and yet, who knows ? Peradventure, if you had not read that book, you

(288)

would not have been fitted for the perusal of the one which you say is written by the finger of God;" and, pressing my hand to my head, I fell into a deep fit of musing. "What, after all," thought I, "if there should be more order and system in the working of the moral world than I have thought? Does there not seem in the present instance to be something like the working of a Divine hand? I could not conceive why this woman, better educated than her mother, should have been, as she certainly was, a worse character than her mother. Yet perhaps this woman may be better and happier than her mother ever was; perhaps she is so already—perhaps this world is not a wild, lying dream, as I have occasionally supposed it to be."

But the thought of my own situation did not permit me to abandon myself much longer to these musings. I started up. "Where are you going, child?" said the woman anxiously. "I scarcely know," said I; "anywhere." "Then stay here, child," said she; "I have much to say to you." "No," said I, "I shall be better moving about;" and I was moving away, when it suddenly occurred to me that I might never see this woman again; and turning round I offered her my hand, and bade her good-bye. "Farewell, child," said the old woman, "and God bless you!" I then moved along the bridge until I reached the Southwark side, and, still holding on my course, my mind again became quickly abstracted from all surrounding objects.

At length I found myself in a street or road, with terraces on either side, and seemingly of interminable length, leading, as it would appear, to the south-east. I was walking at a great rate—there were likewise a great number of people, also walking at a great rate; also carts and carriages driving at a great rate; and all, men, carts and carriages, going in the selfsame direction, namely, to the south-east. I stopped for a moment and deliberated whether or not I should proceed. What business had I in that direction? I could not say that I had any particular business in that direction, but what could I do were I to turn back? only walk about well-known streets; and, if I must walk, why not continue in the direction in which I was to see whither the road and its terraces led? I was here in a terra incognita, and an unknown place had always some interest for me; moreover, I had a desire to know whither all this crowd was going, and for what purpose. I thought they could not be going far, as crowds seldom go far, especially at such a rate; so I walked on more lustily than before, passing group after group of the crowd, and almost vieing in speed with some of the carriages, especially the hackney-coaches ; and by dint of walking at this rate, the terraces and houses becoming somewhat less frequent as I advanced, I reached in about three-quarters of an hour a kind of low dingy town, in the neighbourhood of the river ; the streets were swarming with people, and I concluded, from the number of wild-beast shows, caravans, gingerbread stalls, and the like, that a fair was being held. Now, as I had always been partial to fairs, I felt glad that I had fallen in with the crowd which had conducted me to the present one, and, casting away as much as I was able all gloomy thoughts, I did my best to enter into the diversions of the fair ; staring at the wonderful representations of animals on canvas hung up before the shows of wild beasts, which, by-the-bye, are frequently found much more worthy of admiration than the real beasts themselves ; listening to the jokes of the merry-andrews from the platforms in front of the temporary theatres, or admiring the splendid tinsel dresses of the performers who thronged the stages in the intervals of the entertainments ; and in this manner, occasionally gazing and occasionally listening, I passed through the town till I came in front of a large edifice looking full upon the majestic bosom of the Thames.

It was a massive stone edifice, built in an antique style, and black with age, with a broad esplanade between it and the river, on which, mixed with a few people from the fair, I observed moving about a great many individuals in quaint dresses of blue, with strange three-cornered hats on their heads ; most of them were mutilated ; this had a wooden leg—this wanted an arm ; some had but one eye ; and as I gazed upon the edifice, and the singular-looking individuals who moved before it, I guessed where I was. " I am at ——" said I ; " these individuals are battered tars of Old England, and this edifice, once the favourite abode of Glorious Elizabeth, is the refuge which a grateful country has allotted to them. Here they can rest their weary bodies ; at their ease talk over the actions in which they have been injured ; and, with the tear of enthusiasm flowing from their eyes, boast how they have trod the deck of fame with Rodney, or Nelson, or others whose names stand emblazoned in the naval annals of their country."

Turning to the right, I entered a park or wood consisting of enormous trees, occupying the foot, sides, and top of a hill, which rose behind the town ; there were multitudes of people among the trees, diverting themselves in various ways. Coming to the top of the hill, I was presently stopped by a lofty wall, along which I walked, till, coming to a small gate, I passed through and found myself on an extensive green plain, on one side bounded in part by the wall of the park, and on the others, in the distance, by extensive ranges of houses; to the south-east was a lofty eminence, partially clothed with wood. The plain exhibited an animated scene, a kind of continuation of the fair below; there were multitudes of people upon it, many tents, and shows; there was also horse-racing, and much noise and shouting, the sun shining brightly overhead. After gazing at the horse-racing for a little time, feeling myself somewhat tired, I went up to one of the tents, and laid myself down on the grass. There was much noise in the tent. "Who will stand me?" said a voice with a slight tendency to lisp. "Will you, my lord?" "Yes," said another voice. Then there was a sound as of a piece of money banging on a table. "Lost! lost! lost!" cried several voices; and then the banging down of the money, and the "lost! lost! lost!" were frequently repeated; at last the second voice exclaimed: "I will try no more; you have cheated me". "Never cheated any one in my life, my lord—all fair—all chance. Them that finds, wins —them that can't find, loses. Any one else try? Who'll try? Will you, my lord?" and then it appeared that some other lord tried, for I heard more money flung down. Then again the cry of "Lost! lost!"—then again the sound of money, and so on. Once or twice, but not more, I heard "Won! won!" but the predominant cry was "Lost! lost!" At last there was a considerable hubbub, and the words "Cheat!" "Rogue!" and "You filched away the pea!" were used freely by more voices than one, to which the voice with the tendency to lisp replied: "Never filched a pea in my life; would scorn it. Always glad when folks wins; but, as those here don't appear to be civil, nor to wish to play any more, I shall take myself off with my table; so, good-day, gentlemen."

CHAPTER LIII.

PRESENTLY a man emerged from the tent, bearing before him a rather singular table; it appeared to be of white deal, was exceedingly small at the top, and with very long legs. At a few yards from the entrance he paused, and looked round, as if to decide on the direction which he should take; presently, his eye glancing on me as I lay upon the ground, he started, and appeared for a moment inclined to make off as quick as possible, table and all. In a moment, however, he seemed to recover assurance, and, coming up to the place where I was, the long legs of the table projecting before him, he cried: "Glad to see you here, my lord".

"Thank you," said I, "it's a fine day."

"Very fine, my lord; will your lordship play? Them that finds, wins—them that don't find, loses."

"Play at what?" said I.

"Only at the thimble and pea, my lord."

"I never heard of such a game."

"Didn't you? Well, I'll soon teach you," said he, placing the table down. "All you have to do is to put a sovereign down on my table, and to find the pea, which I put under one of my thimbles. If you find it—and it is easy enough to find it—I give you a sovereign besides your own: for them that finds, wins."

"And them that don't find, loses," said I; "no, I don't wish to play."

"Why not, my lord?"

"Why, in the first place, I have no money."

"Oh, you have no money; that of course alters the case. If you have no money, you can't play. Well, I suppose I must be seeing after my customers," said he, glancing over the plain.

"Good-day," said I.

"Good-day," said the man slowly, but without moving, and as if in reflection. After a moment or two, looking at me inquiringly, he added: "Out of employ?"

"Yes," said I, "out of employ."

The man measured me with his eye as I lay on the ground.

At length he said : " May I speak a word or two to you, my lord?"

" As many as you please," said I.

" Then just come a little out of hearing, a little farther on the grass, if you please, my lord."

" Why do you call me my lord?" said I, as I arose and followed him.

" We of the thimble always calls our customers lords," said the man ; " but I won't call you such a foolish name any more ; come along."

The man walked along the plain till he came to the side of a dry pit, when looking round to see that no one was nigh, he laid his table on the grass, and, sitting down with his legs over the side of the pit, he motioned me to do the same.   " So you are in want of employ," said he, after I had sat down beside him.

" Yes," said I, " I am very much in want of employ."

" I think I can find you some."

" What kind?" said I.

" Why," said the man, " I think you would do to be my bonnet."

" Bonnet!" said I, " what is that?"

" Don't you know?   However, no wonder, as you had never heard of the thimble-and-pea game, but I will tell you.   We of the game are very much exposed ; folks when they have lost their money, as those who play with us mostly do, sometimes uses rough language, calls us cheats, and sometimes knocks our hats over our eyes ; and what's more, with a kick under our table, cause the top deals to fly off; this is the third table I have used this day, the other two being broken by uncivil customers : so we of the game generally like to have gentlemen go about with us to take our part, and encourage us, though pretending to know nothing about us ; for example, when the customer says, ' I'm cheated,' the bonnet must say, ' No, you a'n't, it is all right' ; or, when my hat is knocked over my eyes, the bonnet must square, and say, ' I never saw the man before in all my life but I won't see him ill-used' ; and so, when they kicks at the table, the bonnet must say, ' I won't see the table ill-used, such a nice table, too ; besides, I want to play myself;' and then I would say to the bonnet, ' Thank you, my lord, them that finds, wins' ; and then the bonnet plays, and I lets the bonnet win."

" In a word," said I, " the bonnet means the man who covers you, even as the real bonnet covers the head."

"Just so," said the man, "I see you are awake, and would soon make a first-rate bonnet."

"Bonnet," said I, musingly; "bonnet; it is metaphorical."

"Is it?" said the man.

"Yes," said I, "like the cant words ——"

"Bonnet is cant," said the man; "we of the thimble, as well as all clyfakers and the like, understand cant, as, of course, must every bonnet; so, if you are employed by me, you had better learn it as soon as you can, that we may discourse together without being understood by every one. Besides covering his principal, a bonnet must have his eyes about him, for the trade of the pea, though a strictly honest one, is not altogether lawful; so it is the duty of the bonnet, if he sees the constable coming, to say, the gorgio's welling."

"That is not cant," said I, "that is the language of the Rommany Chals."

"Do you know those people?" said the man.

"Perfectly," said I, "and their language too."

"I wish I did," said the man, "I would give ten pounds and more to know the language of the Rommany Chals. There's some of it in the language of the pea and thimble; how it came there I don't know, but so it is. I wish I knew it, but it is difficult. You'll make a capital bonnet; shall we close?"

"What would the wages be?" I demanded.

"Why, to a first-rate bonnet, as I think you would prove, I could afford to give from forty to fifty shillings a week."

"Is it possible?" said I.

"Good wages, a'n't they?" said the man.

"First rate," said I; "bonneting is more profitable than reviewing."

"Anan?" said the man.

"Or translating; I don't think the Armenian would have paid me at that rate for translating his Esop."

"Who is he?" said the man.

"Esop?"

"No, I know what that is, Esop's cant for a hunchback; but t'other?"

"You should know," said I.

"Never saw the man in all my life."

"Yes, you have," said I, "and felt him too; don't you remember the individual from whom you took the pocket-book?"

"Oh, that was he; well, the less said about that matter the better; I have left off that trade, and taken to this, which is a much better. Between ourselves, I am not sorry that I did not carry off that pocket-book; if I had, it might have encouraged me in the trade, in which, had I remained, I might have been lagged, sent abroad, as I had been already imprisoned; so I determined to leave it off at all hazards, though I was hard up, not having a penny in the world."

" And wisely resolved," said I, " it was a bad and dangerous trade; I wonder you should ever have embraced it."

" It is all very well talking," said the man, " but there is a reason for everything; I am the son of a Jewess, by a military officer,"—and then the man told me his story. I shall not repeat the man's story, it was a poor one, a vile one; at last he observed : " So that affair which you know of determined me to leave the filching trade, and take up with a more honest and safe one; so at last I thought of the pea and thimble, but I wanted funds, especially to pay for lessons at the hands of a master, for I knew little about it."

" Well," said I, " how did you get over that difficulty ? "

" Why," said the man, " I thought I should never have got over it. What funds could I raise? I had nothing to sell; the few clothes I had I wanted, for we of the thimble must always appear decent, or nobody would come near us. I was at my wits' end; at last I got over my difficulty in the strangest way in the world."

" What was that ? "

" By an old thing which I had picked up some time before— a book."

" A book ? " said I.

" Yes, which I had taken out of your lordship's pocket one day as you were walking the streets in a great hurry. I thought it was a pocket-book at first, full of bank notes, perhaps," continued he, laughing. " It was well for me, however, that it was not, for I should have soon spent the notes; as it was, I had flung the old thing down with an oath, as soon as I brought it home. When I was so hard up, however, after the affair with that friend of yours, I took it up one day, and thought I might make something by it to support myself a day with. Chance or something else led me into a grand shop; there was a man there who seemed to be the master, talking to a jolly, portly old gentleman, who seemed to be a country squire. Well, I went up to the first, and offered it for sale; he took the book, opened it at the title-page, and then all of a sudden his eyes glistened, and he showed it to the fat, jolly gentleman, and his eyes glistened too, and I heard him say 'How singular!' and then the two talked together in a speech I didn't understand—I rather thought it was French, at any rate it wasn't cant; and presently the first asked me what I would take for the book. Now I am not altogether a fool nor am I blind, and I had narrowly marked all that passed, and it came into my head that now was the time for making a man of myself, at any rate I could lose nothing by a little confidence; so I looked the man boldly in the face, and said: ' I will have five guineas for that book, there a'n't such another in the whole world'. 'Nonsense,' said the first man, ' there are plenty of them, there have been nearly fifty editions to my knowledge; I will give you five shillings.' 'No,' said I, 'I'll not take it, for I don't like to be cheated, so give me my book again; and I attempted to take it away from the fat gentleman's hand. ' Stop,' said the younger man, 'are you sure that you won't take less?' 'Not a farthing,' said I; which was not altogether true, but I said so. 'Well,' said the fat gentleman, ' I will give you what you ask;' and sure enough he presently gave me the money; so I made a bow, and was leaving the shop, when it came into my head that there was something odd in all this, and, as I had got the money in my pocket, I turned back, and, making another bow, said: ' May I be so bold as to ask why you gave me all this money for that 'ere dirty book? When I came into the shop, I should have been glad to get a shilling for it; but I saw you wanted it, and asked five guineas.' Then they looked at one another, and smiled, and shrugged up their shoulders. Then the first man, looking at me, said: ' Friend, you have been a little too sharp for us; however, we can afford to forgive you, as my friend here has long been in quest of this particular book; there are plenty of editions, as I told you, and a common copy is not worth five shillings; but this is a first edition, and a copy of the first edition is worth its weight in gold'."

" So, after all, they outwitted you," I observed.

" Clearly," said the man; " I might have got double the price, had I known the value; but I don't care, much good may it do them, it has done me plenty. By means of it I have got into an honest, respectable trade, in which there's little danger and plenty of profit, and got out of one which would have got me lagged sooner or later."

" But," said I, " you ought to remember that the thing was not yours; you took it from me, who had been requested by a poor old apple-woman to exchange it for a Bible."

" Well," said the man, " did she ever get her Bible?"

"Yes," said I, "she got her Bible."

"Then she has no cause to complain; and, as for you, chance or something else has sent you to me, that I may make you reasonable amends for any loss you may have had. Here am I ready to make you my bonnet, with forty or fifty shillings a week, which you say yourself are capital wages."

"I find no fault with the wages," said I, "but I don't like the employ."

"Not like bonneting," said the man; "ah, I see, you would like to be principal; well, a time may come—those long white fingers of yours would just serve for the business."

"Is it a difficult one?" I demanded.

"Why, it is not very easy: two things are needful—natural talent, and constant practice; but I'll show you a point or two connected with the game;" and, placing his table between his knees as he sat over the side of the pit, he produced three thimbles, and a small brown pellet, something resembling a pea. He moved the thimble and pellet about, now placing it to all appearance under one, and now under another; "Under which is it now?" he said at last. "Under that," said I, pointing to the lowermost of the thimbles, which, as they stood, formed a kind of triangle. "No," said he, "it is not, but lift it up;" and, when I lifted up the thimble, the pellet, in truth, was not under it. "It was under none of them," said he, "it was pressed by my little finger against my palm;" and then he showed me how he did the trick, and asked me if the game was not a funny one; and, on my answering in the affirmative, he said: "I am glad you like it, come along and let us win some money".

Thereupon, getting up, he placed the table before him, and was moving away; observing, however, that I did not stir, he asked me what I was staying for. "Merely for my own pleasure," said I, "I like sitting here very well." "Then you won't close?" said the man. "By no means," I replied, "your proposal does not suit me." "You may be principal in time," said the man. "That makes no difference," said I; and, sitting with my legs over the pit, I forthwith began to decline an Armenian noun. "That a'n't cant," said the man; "no, nor gypsy either. Well, if you won't close, another will, I can't lose any more time," and forthwith he departed.

And after I had declined four Armenian nouns, of different declensions, I rose from the side of the pit, and wandered about amongst the various groups of people scattered over the green. Presently I came to where the man of the thimbles was standing,

with the table before him, and many people about him. " Them
who finds, wins, and them who can't find, loses," he cried.
Various individuals tried to find the pellet, but all were unsuccessful, till at last considerable dissatisfaction was expressed, and the
terms rogue and cheat were lavished upon him. " Never cheated
anybody in all my life," he cried ; and, observing me at hand,
" didn't I play fair, my lord?" he inquired. But I made no
answer. Presently some more played, and he permitted one or
two to win, and the eagerness to play with him became greater.
After I had looked on for some time, I was moving away ; just
then I perceived a short, thick personage, with a staff in his hand,
advancing in a great hurry ; whereupon with a sudden impulse, I
exclaimed :—

> Shoon thimble-engro ;
> Avella gorgio.

The man who was in the midst of his pea-and-thimble process, no
sooner heard the last word of the distich, than he turned an
alarmed look in the direction of where I stood; then, glancing
around, and perceiving the constable, he slipped forthwith his
pellet and thimbles into his pocket, and, lifting up his table, he
cried to the people about him, " Make way ! " and with a motion
of his head to me, as if to follow him, he darted off with a swiftness which the short, pursy constable could by no means rival ;
and whither he went, or what became of him, I know not, inasmuch as I turned away in another direction.

CHAPTER LIV.

AND, as I wandered along the green, I drew near to a place where several men, with a cask beside them, sat carousing in the neighbourhood of a small tent. " Here he comes," said one of them, as I advanced, and standing up he raised his voice and sang :—

> Here the Gypsy gemman see,
> With his Roman jib and his rome and dree—
> Rome and dree, rum and dry
> Rally round the Rommany Rye.

It was Mr. Petulengro, who was here diverting himself with several of his comrades ; they all received me with considerable frankness. " Sit down, brother," said Mr. Petulengro, " and take a cup of good ale."

I sat down. " Your health, gentlemen," said I, as I took the cup which Mr. Petulengro handed to me.

" Aukkǫ tu pios adrey Rommanis. Here is your health in Rommany, brother," said Mr. Petulengro ; who, having refilled the cup, now emptied it at a draught.

" Your health in Rommany, brother," said Tawno Chikno, to whom the cup came next.

" The Rommany Rye," said a third.

" The Gypsy gentleman," exclaimed a fourth, drinking.

And then they all sang in chorus :—

> Here the Gypsy gemman see,
> With his Roman jib and his rome and dree—
> Rome and dree, rum and dry
> Rally round the Rommany Rye.

" And now, brother," said Mr. Petulengro, " seeing that you have drunk and been drunken, you will perhaps tell us where you have been, and what about ? "

" I have been in the Big City," said I, " writing lils."

" How much money have you got in your pocket, brother ? " said Mr. Petulengro.

"Eighteen pence," said I ; "all I have in the world."

"I have been in the Big City, too," said Mr. Petulengro ; "but I have not written lils—I have fought in the ring—I have fifty pounds in my pocket—I have much more in the world. Brother, there is considerable difference between us."

"I would rather be the lil-writer, after all," said the tall, handsome, black man ; "indeed, I would wish for nothing better."

"Why so ?" said Mr. Petulengro.

"Because they have so much to say for themselves," said the black man, "even when dead and gone. When they are laid in the churchyard, it is their own fault if people a'n't talking of them. Who will know, after I am dead, or bitchadey pawdel, that I was once the beauty of the world, or that you, Jasper, were ——"

"The best man in England of my inches. That's true, Tawno—however, here's our brother will perhaps let the world know something about us."

"Not he," said the other, with a sigh ; "he'll have quite enough to do in writing his own lils, and telling the world how handsome and clever he was ; and who can blame him ? Not I. If I could write lils, every word should be about myself and my own tacho Rommanis—my own lawful wedded wife, which is the same thing. I tell you what, brother, I once heard a wise man say in Brummagem, that 'there is nothing like blowing one's own horn,' which I conceive to be much the same thing as writing one's own lil."

After a little more conversation, Mr. Petulengro arose, and motioned me to follow him. "Only eighteen pence in the world, brother !" said he, as we walked together.

"Nothing more, I assure you. How came you to ask me how much money I had ?"

"Because there was something in your look, brother, something very much resembling that which a person showeth who does not carry much money in his pocket. I was looking at my own face this morning in my wife's looking-glass—I did not look as you do, brother."

"I believe your sole motive for inquiring," said I, "was to have an opportunity of venting a foolish boast, and to let me know that you were in possession of fifty pounds."

"What is the use of having money unless you let people know you have it ?" said Mr. Petulengro. "It is not every one can read faces, brother ; and, unless you knew I had money, how could you ask me to lend you any ?"

"I am not going to ask you to lend me any."

"Then you may have it without asking; as I said before, I have fifty pounds, all lawfully earnt money, got by fighting in the ring—I will lend you that, brother."

"You are very kind," said I; "but I will not take it."

"Then the half of it?"

"Nor the half of it; but it is getting towards evening, I must go back to the Great City."

"And what will you do in the Boro Foros?"

"I know not," said I.

"Earn money?"

"If I can."

"And if you can't?"

"Starve!"

"You look ill brother," said Mr. Petulengro.

"I do not feel well; the Great City does not agree with me. Should I be so fortunate as to earn some money, I would leave the Big City, and take to the woods and fields."

"You may do that, brother," said Mr. Petulengro, "whether you have money or not. Our tents and horses are on the other side of yonder wooded hill, come and stay with us; we shall all be glad of your company, but more especially myself and my wife Pakomovna."

"What hill is that?" I demanded.

And then Mr. Petulengro told me the name of the hill. "We shall stay on t'other side of the hill a fortnight," he continued; "and as you are fond of lil writing, you may employ yourself profitably whilst there. You can write the lil of him whose dook gallops down that hill every night, even as the living man was wont to do long ago."

"Who was he?" I demanded.

"Jemmy Abershaw," said Mr. Petulengro; "one of those whom we call Boro-drom-engroes, and the gorgios highwaymen. I once heard a rye say that the life of that man would fetch much money; so come to the other side of the hill, and write the lil in the tent of Jasper and his wife Pakomovna."

At first I felt inclined to accept the invitation of Mr. Petulengro; a little consideration, however, determined me to decline it. I had always been on excellent terms with Mr. Petulengro, but I reflected that people might be excellent friends when they met occasionally in the street, or on the heath, or in the wood; but that these very people when living together in a house, to say nothing of a tent, might quarrel. I reflected, moreover, that Mr. Petulengro had a wife. I had always, it is true, been a great favourite with Mrs. Petulengro, who had frequently been loud in her commendation of the young rye, as she called me, and his turn of conversation ; but this was at a time when I stood in need of nothing, lived under my parents' roof, and only visited at the tents to divert and to be diverted. The times were altered, and I was by no means certain that Mrs. Petulengro, when she should discover that I was in need both of shelter and subsistence, might not alter her opinion both with respect to the individual and what he said—stigmatising my conversation as saucy discourse, and myself as a scurvy companion ; and that she might bring over her husband to her own way of thinking, provided, indeed, he should need any conducting. I therefore, though without declaring my reasons, declined the offer of Mr. Petulengro, and presently, after shaking him by the hand, bent again my course towards the Great City.

I crossed the river at a bridge considerably above that hight of London ; for not being acquainted with the way, I missed the turning which should have brought me to the latter. Suddenly I found myself in a street of which I had some recollection, and mechanically stopped before the window of a shop at which various publications were exposed ; it was that of the bookseller to whom I had last applied in the hope of selling my ballads or Ab Gwilym, and who had given me hopes that in the event of my writing a decent novel, or a tale, he would prove a purchaser. As I stood listlessly looking at the window, and the publications which it contained, I observed a paper affixed to the glass by wafers with something written upon it. I drew yet nearer for the purpose of inspecting it ; the writing was in a fair round hand —"A Novel or Tale is much wanted," was what was written.

CHAPTER LV.

" I MUST do something," said I, as I sat that night in my lonely apartment, with some bread and a pitcher of water before me. Thereupon taking some of the bread, and eating it, I considered what I was to do. "I have no idea what I am to do," said I, as I stretched my hand towards the pitcher, "unless— and here I took a considerable draught—I write a tale or a novel —— That bookseller," I continued, speaking to myself, "is certainly much in need of a tale or novel, otherwise he would not advertise for one. Suppose I write one, I appear to have no other chance of extricating myself from my present difficulties; surely it was Fate that conducted me to his window."

" I will do it," said I, as I struck my hand against the table; " I will do it." Suddenly a heavy cloud of despondency came over me. Could I do it? Had I the imagination requisite to write a tale or a novel? "Yes, yes," said I, as I struck my hand again against the table, " I can manage it; give me fair play, and I can accomplish anything."

But should I have fair play? I must have something to maintain myself with whilst I wrote my tale, and I had but eighteen pence in the world. Would that maintain me whilst I wrote my tale? Yes, I thought it would, provided I ate bread, which did not cost much, and drank water, which cost nothing; it was poor diet, it was true, but better men than myself had written on bread and water; had not the big man told me so, or something to that effect, months before?

It was true there was my lodging to pay for; but up to the present time I owed nothing, and perhaps, by the time the people of the house asked me for money, I should have written a tale or a novel, which would bring me in money; I had paper, pens and ink, and, let me not forget them, I had candles in my closet, all paid for, to light me during my night work. Enough, I would go doggedly to work upon my tale or novel.

But what was the tale or novel to be about? Was it to be a tale of fashionable life, about Sir Harry Somebody, and the Countess

(303)

Something? But I knew nothing about fashionable people, and cared less; therefore how should I attempt to describe fashionable life? What should the tale consist of? The life and adventures of some one. Good—but of whom? Did not Mr. Petulengro mention one Jemmy Abershaw? Yes. Did he not tell me that the life and adventures of Jemmy Abershaw would bring in much money to the writer? Yes, but I knew nothing of that worthy. I heard, it is true, from Mr. Petulengro, that when alive he committed robberies on the hill, on the side of which Mr. Petulengro had pitched his tents, and that his ghost still haunted the hill at midnight; but those were scant materials out of which to write the man's life. It is probable, indeed, that Mr. Petulengro would be able to supply me with further materials if I should apply to him, but I was in a hurry, and could not afford the time which it would be necessary to spend in passing to and from Mr. Petulengro, and consulting him. Moreover, my pride revolted at the idea of being beholden to Mr. Petulengro for the materials of the history. No, I would not write the history of Abershaw. Whose then—Harry Simms? Alas, the life of Harry Simms had been already much better written by himself than I could hope to do it; and, after all, Harry Simms, like Jemmy Abershaw, was merely a robber. Both, though bold and extraordinary men, were merely highwaymen. I questioned whether I could compose a tale likely to excite any particular interest out of the exploits of a mere robber. I want a character for my hero, thought I, something higher than a mere robber; some one like—like Colonel B——. By the way, why should I not write the life and adventures of Colonel B—— of Londonderry, in Ireland?

A truly singular man was this same Colonel B—— of Londonderry, in Ireland; a personage of most strange and incredible feats and daring, who had been a partisan soldier, a bravo—who, assisted by certain discontented troopers, nearly succeeded in stealing the crown and regalia from the Tower of London; who attempted to hang the Duke of Ormond, at Tyburn; and whose strange eventful career did not terminate even with his life, his dead body, on the circulation of an unfounded report that he did not come to his death by fair means, having been exhumed by the mob of his native place, where he had retired to die, and carried in the coffin through the streets.

Of his life I had inserted an account in the *Newgate Lives and Trials;* it was bare and meagre, and written in the stiff, awkward style of the seventeenth century; it had, however, strongly captivated my imagination, and I now thought that out of it something better could be made; that, if I added to the adventures, and purified the style, I might fashion out of it a very decent tale or novel. On a sudden, however, the proverb of mending old garments with new cloth occurred to me. "I am afraid," said I, "any new adventures which I can invent will not fadge well with the old tale; one will but spoil the other." I had better have nothing to do with Colonel B——, thought I, but boldly and independently sit down and write the life of Joseph Sell.

This Joseph Sell, dear reader, was a fictitious personage who had just come into my head. I had never even heard of the name, but just at that moment it happened to come into my head; I would write an entirely fictitious narrative, called the *Life and Adventures of Joseph Sell, the Great Traveller.*

I had better begin at once, thought I; and removing the bread and the jug, which latter was now empty, I seized pen and paper, and forthwith essayed to write the life of Joseph Sell, but soon discovered that it is much easier to resolve upon a thing than to achieve it, or even to commence it; for the life of me I did not know how to begin, and, after trying in vain to write a line, I thought it would be as well to go to bed, and defer my projected undertaking till the morrow.

So I went to bed, but not to sleep. During the greater part of the night I lay awake, musing upon the work which I had determined to execute. For a long time my brain was dry and unproductive; I could form no plan which appeared feasible. At length I felt within my brain a kindly glow; it was the commencement of inspiration; in a few minutes I had formed my plan; I then began to imagine the scenes and the incidents. Scenes and incidents flitted before my mind's eye so plentifully that I knew not how to dispose of them; I was in a regular embarrassment. At length I got out of the difficulty in the easiest manner imaginable, namely, by consigning to the depths of oblivion all the feebler and less stimulant scenes and incidents, and retaining the better and more impressive ones. Before morning I had sketched the whole work on the tablets of my mind, and then resigned myself to sleep in the pleasing conviction that the most difficult part of my undertaking was achieved.

CHAPTER LVI.

Rather late in the morning I awoke; for a few minutes I lay still, perfectly still; my imagination was considerably sobered; the scenes and situations which had pleased me so much over night appeared to me in a far less captivating guise that morning. I felt languid and almost hopeless—the thought, however, of my situation soon roused me—I must make an effort to improve the posture of my affairs; there was no time to be lost; so I sprang out of bed, breakfasted on bread and water, and then sat down doggedly to write the life of Joseph Sell.

It was a great thing to have formed my plan, and to have arranged the scenes in my head, as I had done on the preceding night. The chief thing requisite at present was the mere mechanical act of committing them to paper. This I did not find at first so easy as I could wish—I wanted mechanical skill; but I persevered, and before evening I had written ten pages. I partook of some bread and water; and, before I went to bed that night, I had completed fifteen pages of my life of Joseph Sell.

The next day I resumed my task—I found my power of writing considerably increased; my pen hurried rapidly over the paper—my brain was in a wonderfully teeming state; many scenes and visions which I had not thought of before were evolved, and, as fast as evolved, written down; they seemed to be more pat to my purpose, and more natural to my history, than many others which I had imagined before, and which I made now give place to these newer creations: by about midnight I had added thirty fresh pages to my *Life and Adventures of Joseph Sell*.

The third day arose—it was dark and dreary out of doors, and I passed it drearily enough within; my brain appeared to have lost much of its former glow, and my pen much of its power; I, however, toiled on, but at midnight had only added seven pages to my history of Joseph Sell.

On the fourth day the sun shone brightly—I arose, and, having breakfasted as usual, I fell to work. My brain was this day wonderfully prolific, and my pen never before or since glided so rapidly over the paper; towards night I began to feel strangely about the back part of my head, and my whole system was extraordinarily affected. I likewise occasionally saw double—a tempter now seemed to be at work within me.

"You had better leave off now for a short space," said the tempter, "and go out and drink a pint of beer; you have still one shilling left—if you go on at this rate, you will go mad—go out and spend sixpence, you can afford it, more than half your work is done." I was about to obey the suggestion of the tempter, when the idea struck me that, if I did not complete the work whilst the fit was on me, I should never complete it; so I held on. I am almost afraid to state how many pages I wrote that day of the life of Joseph Sell.

From this time I proceeded in a somewhat more leisurely manner; but, as I drew nearer and nearer to the completion of my task, dreadful fears and despondencies came over me. It will be too late, thought I; by the time I have finished the work, the bookseller will have been supplied with a tale or a novel. Is it probable that, in a town like this, where talent is so abundant —hungry talent too—a bookseller can advertise for a tale or a novel, without being supplied with half a dozen in twenty-four hours? I may as well fling down my pen—I am writing to no purpose. And these thoughts came over my mind so often, that at last, in utter despair, I flung down the pen. Whereupon the tempter within me said: "And, now you have flung down the pen, you may as well fling yourself out of the window; what remains for you to do?" Why, to take it up again, thought I to myself, for I did not like the latter suggestion at all—and then forthwith I resumed the pen, and wrote with greater vigour than before, from about six o'clock in the evening until I could hardly see, when I rested for awhile, when the tempter within me again said, or appeared to say: "All you have been writing is stuff, it will never do—a drug—a mere drug"; and methought these last words were uttered in the gruff tones of the big publisher. "A thing merely to be sneezed at," a voice like that of Taggart added; and then I seemed to hear a sternutation,—as I probably did, for, recovering from a kind of swoon, I found myself shivering with cold. The next day I brought my work to a conclusion.

But the task of revision still remained; for an hour or two I shrank from it, and remained gazing stupidly at the pile of paper which I had written over. I was all but exhausted, and I dreaded, on inspecting the sheets, to find them full of absurdities which I had paid no regard to in the furor of composition. But the task, however trying to my nerves, must be got over ; at last, in a kind of desperation, I entered upon it.   It was far from an easy one ; there were, however, fewer errors and absurdities than I had anticipated.   About twelve o'clock at night I had got over the task of revision.   "To-morrow, for the bookseller," said I, as my head sank on the pillow.   "Oh me!"

CHAPTER LVII.

ON arriving at the bookseller's shop, I cast a nervous look at the window, for the purpose of observing whether the paper had been removed or not. To my great delight the paper was in its place; with a beating heart I entered, there was nobody in the shop; as I stood at the counter, however, deliberating whether or not I should call out, the door of what seemed to be a back-parlour opened, and out came a well-dressed lady-like female, of about thirty, with a good-looking and intelligent countenance. "What is your business, young man?" said she to me, after I had made her a polite bow. "I wish to speak to the gentleman of the house," said I. "My husband is not within at present," she replied; "what is your business?" "I have merely brought something to show him," said I, "but I will call again." "If you are the young gentleman who has been here before," said the lady, "with poems and ballads, as, indeed, I know you are," she added, smiling, "for I have seen you through the glass door, I am afraid it will be useless; that is," she added with another smile, "if you bring us nothing else." "I have not brought you poems and ballads now," said I, "but something widely different; I saw your advertisement for a tale or a novel, and have written something which I think will suit; and here it is," I added, showing the roll of paper which I held in my hand. "Well," said the bookseller's wife, "you may leave it, though I cannot promise you much chance of its being accepted. My husband has already had several offered to him; however, you may leave it; give it me. Are you afraid to entrust it to me?" she demanded somewhat hastily, observing that I hesitated. "Excuse me," said I, "but it is all I have to depend upon in the world; I am chiefly apprehensive that it will not be read." "On that point I can reassure you," said the good lady, smiling, and there was now something sweet in her smile. "I give you my word that it shall be read; come again to-morrow morning at eleven, when, if not approved, it shall be returned to you."

I returned to my lodging, and forthwith betook myself to bed, notwithstanding the earliness of the hour. I felt tolerably tranquil; I had now cast my last stake, and was prepared to abide by the result. Whatever that result might be, I could have nothing to reproach myself with; I had strained all the energies which nature had given me in order to rescue myself from the difficulties which surrounded me. I presently sank into a sleep, which endured during the remainder of the day, and the whole of the succeeding night. I awoke about nine on the morrow, and spent my last threepence on a breakfast somewhat more luxurious than the immediately preceding ones, for one penny of the sum was expended on the purchase of milk.

At the appointed hour I repaired to the house of the bookseller; the bookseller was in his shop. " Ah," said he, as soon as I entered, " I am glad to see you." There was an unwonted heartiness in the bookseller's tones, an unwonted benignity in his face. " So," said he, after a pause, " you have taken my advice, written a book of adventure; nothing like taking the advice, young man, of your superiors in age. Well, I think your book will do, and so does my wife, for whose judgment I have a great regard; as well I may, as she is the daughter of a first-rate novelist, deceased. I think I shall venture on sending your book to the press." " But," said I, " we have not yet agreed upon terms." " Terms, terms," said the bookseller; " ahem! well, there is nothing like coming to terms at once. I will print the book, and give you half the profit when the edition is sold." " That will not do," said I; " I intend shortly to leave London: I must have something at once." " Ah, I see," said the bookseller, " in distress; frequently the case with authors, especially young ones. Well, I don't care if I purchase it of you, but you must be moderate; the public are very fastidious, and the speculation may prove a losing one, after all. Let me see, will five —— hem "—he stopped. I looked the bookseller in the face; there was something peculiar in it. Suddenly it appeared to me as if the voice of him of the thimble sounded in my ear: " Now is your time, ask enough, never such another chance of establishing yourself; respectable trade, pea and thimble ". " Well," said I at last, " I have no objection to take the offer which you were about to make, though I really think five-and-twenty guineas to be scarcely enough, everything considered." " Five-and-twenty guineas! " said the bookseller; " are you—what was I going to say—I never meant to offer half as much—I mean a quarter; I was going to say five guineas—I mean pounds; I will, however, make it up guineas." " That will not do," said I; " but, as I find we shall not deal, return me my manuscript, that I may carry it to some one else." The bookseller looked blank. "Dear me," said he, "I should never have supposed that you would have made any objection to such an offer; I am quite sure that you would have been glad to take five pounds for either of the two huge manuscripts of songs and ballads that you brought me on a former occasion." "Well," said I, "if you will engage to publish either of those two manuscripts, you shall have the present one for five pounds." "God forbid that I should make any such bargain," said the bookseller; "I would publish neither on any account; but, with respect to this last book, I have really an inclination to print it, both for your sake and mine; suppose we say ten pounds." "No," said I, "ten pounds will not do; pray restore me my manuscript." "Stay," said the bookseller, "my wife is in the next room, I will go and consult her." Thereupon he went into his back-room, where I heard him conversing with his wife in a low tone; in about ten minutes he returned. "Young gentleman," said he, "perhaps you will take tea with us this evening, when we will talk further over the matter."

That evening I went and took tea with the bookseller and his wife, both of whom, particularly the latter, overwhelmed me with civility. It was not long before I learned that the work had been already sent to the press, and was intended to stand at the head of a series of entertaining narratives, from which my friends promised themselves considerable profit. The subject of terms was again brought forward. I stood firm to my first demand for a long time; when, however, the bookseller's wife complimented me on my production in the highest terms, and said that she discovered therein the germs of genius, which she made no doubt would some day prove ornamental to my native land, I consented to drop my demand to twenty pounds, stipulating, however, that I should not be troubled with the correction of the work.

Before I departed I received the twenty pounds, and departed with a light heart to my lodgings.

Reader, amidst the difficulties and dangers of this life, should you ever be tempted to despair, call to mind these latter chapters of the life of Lavengro. There are few positions, however difficult, from which dogged resolution and perseverance may not liberate you.

CHAPTER LVIII.

I HAD long ago determined to leave London as soon as the means should be in my power, and, now that they were, I determined to leave the Great City; yet I felt some reluctance to go. I would fain have pursued the career of original authorship which had just opened itself to me, and have written other tales of adventure. The bookseller had given me encouragement enough to do so; he had assured me that he should be always happy to deal with me for an article (that was the word) similar to the one I had brought him, provided my terms were moderate; and the bookseller's wife, by her complimentary language, had given me yet more encouragement. But for some months past I had been far from well, and my original indisposition, brought on partly by the peculiar atmosphere of the Big City, partly by anxiety of mind, had been much increased by the exertions which I had been compelled to make during the last few days. I felt that, were I to remain where I was, I should die, or become a confirmed valetudinarian. I would go forth into the country, travelling on foot, and, by exercise and inhaling pure air, endeavour to recover my health, leaving my subsequent movements to be determined by Providence.

But whither should I bend my course? Once or twice I thought of walking home to the old town, stay some time with my mother and my brother, and enjoy the pleasant walks in the neighbourhood; but, though I wished very much to see my mother and my brother, and felt much disposed to enjoy the said pleasant walks, the old town was not exactly the place to which I wished to go at this present juncture. I was afraid the people would ask, Where are your Northern Ballads? Where are your alliterative translations from Ab Gwilym—of which you were always talking, and with which you promised to astonish the world? Now, in the event of such interrogations, what could I answer? It is true I had compiled *Newgate Lives and Trials*, and had written the life of Joseph Sell, but I was afraid that the people of the old town would scarcely consider these as equiva-

lents for the Northern Ballads and the songs of Ab Gwilym. I
would go forth and wander in any direction but that of the old
town.

But how one's sensibility on any particular point diminishes
with time ! At present, I enter the old town perfectly indifferent
as to what the people may be thinking on the subject of the
songs and ballads. With respect to the people themselves,
whether, like my sensibility, their curiosity has altogether evapor-
ated, or whether, which is at least equally probable, they never
entertained any, one thing is certain, that never in a single
instance have they troubled me with any remarks on the subject
of the songs and ballads.

As it was my intention to travel on foot, with a bundle and
a stick, I despatched my trunk containing some few clothes and
books to the old town. My preparations were soon made ; in
about three days I was in readiness to start.

Before departing, however, I bethought me of my old friend
the apple-woman of London Bridge. Apprehensive that she
might be labouring under the difficulties of poverty, I sent her a
piece of gold by the hands of a young maiden in the house in
which I lived. The latter punctually executed her commission,
but brought me back the piece of gold. The old woman would
not take it ; she did not want it, she said. "Tell the poor thin
lad," she added, "to keep it for himself, he wants it more than I."

Rather late one afternoon I departed from my lodging, with
my stick in one hand and a small bundle in the other, shaping
my course to the south-west. When I first arrived, somewhat
more than a year before, I had entered the city by the north-east.
As I was not going home, I determined to take my departure in
the direction the very opposite to home.

Just as I was about to cross the street called the Haymarket
at the lower part, a cabriolet, drawn by a magnificent animal,
came dashing along at a furious rate ; it stopped close by the
curb-stone where I was, a sudden pull of the reins nearly
bringing the spirited animal upon its haunches. The Jehu who
had accomplished this feat was Francis Ardry. A small beautiful
female, with flashing eyes, dressed in the extremity of fashion,
sat beside him.

"Holloa, friend," said Francis Ardry, "whither bound?"

"I do not know," said I ; "all I can say is, that I am about
to leave London."

"And the means?" said Francis Ardry.

"I have them," said I, with a cheerful smile.

Qui est celui-ci ?" demanded the small female impatiently.

" *C'est —— mon ami le plus intime ;* so you were about to leave London without telling me a word," said Francis Ardry somewhat angrily.

" I intended to have written to you," said I : " what a splendid mare that is ! "

" Is she not ? " said Francis Ardry, who was holding in the mare with difficulty ; " she cost a hundred guineas."

" *Qu'est-ce qu'il dit ?* " demanded his companion.

" *Il dit que le cheval est bien beau.*"

" *Allons, mon ami, il est tard,*" said the beauty, with a scornful toss of her head ; " *allons !* "

" *Encore un moment,*" said Francis Ardry ; "and when shall I see you again ? "

" I scarcely know," I replied : " I never saw a more splendid turn-out."

" *Qu'est-ce qu'il dit ?* " said the lady again.

" *Il dit que tout l'équipage est en assez bon goût.*"

" *Allons, c'est un ours,*" said the lady ; " *le cheval même en a peur,*" added she, as the mare reared up on high.

"Can you find nothing else to admire but the mare and the equipage ? " said Francis Ardry reproachfully, after he had with some difficulty brought the mare to order.

Lifting my hand, in which I held my stick, I took off my hat. " How beautiful ! " said I, looking the lady full in the face.

" *Comment ?* " said the lady inquiringly.

" *Il dit que vous êtes belle comme un ange,*" said Francis Ardry emphatically.

" *Mais à la bonne heure ! arrêtez, mon ami,*" said the lady to Francis Ardry, who was about to drive off; " *je voudrais bien causer un moment avec lui ; arrêtez, il est délicieux. Est-ce bien ainsi que vous traitez vos amis ?* " said she passionately, as Francis Ardry lifted up his whip. " *Bonjour, Monsieur, bonjour,*" said she, thrusting her head from the side and looking back, as Francis Ardry drove off at the rate of thirteen miles an hour.

CHAPTER LIX.

In about two hours I had cleared the Great City, and got beyond the suburban villages, or rather towns, in the direction in which I was travelling ; I was in a broad and excellent road, leading I knew not whither. I now slackened my pace, which had hitherto been great. Presently, coming to a milestone on which was graven nine miles, I rested against it, and looking round towards the vast city, which had long ceased to be visible, I fell into a train of meditation.

I thought of all my ways and doings since the day of my first arrival in that vast city. I had worked and toiled, and, though I had accomplished nothing at all commensurate with the hopes which I had entertained previous to my arrival, I had achieved my own living, preserved my independence, and become indebted to no one. I was now quitting it, poor in purse, it is true, but not wholly empty ; rather ailing, it may be, but not broken in health ; and, with hope within my bosom, had I not cause upon the whole to be thankful ? Perhaps there were some who, arriving at the same time under not more favourable circumstances, had accomplished much more, and whose future was far more hopeful —Good ! But there might be others who, in spite of all their efforts, had been either trodden down in the press, never more to be heard of, or were quitting that mighty town broken in purse, broken in health, and, oh ! with not one dear hope to cheer them. Had I not, upon the whole, abundant cause to be grateful ? Truly, yes !

My meditation over, I left the milestone and proceeded on my way in the same direction as before until the night began to close in. I had always been a good pedestrian ; but now, whether owing to indisposition or to not having for some time past been much in the habit of taking such lengthy walks, I began to feel not a little weary. Just as I was thinking of putting up for the night at the next inn or public-house I should arrive at, I heard what sounded like a coach coming up rapidly behind me. Induced, perhaps, by the weariness which I felt, I stopped and

(315)

looked wistfully in the direction of the sound ; presently up came a coach, seemingly a mail, drawn by four bounding horses—there was no one upon it but the coachman and the guard ; when nearly parallel with me it stopped. "Want to get up?" sounded a voice in the true coachman-like tone—half-querulous, half-authoritative. I hesitated ; I was tired, it is true, but I had left London bound on a pedestrian excursion, and I did not much like the idea of having recourse to a coach after accomplishing so very inconsiderable a distance. "Come, we can't be staying here all night," said the voice, more sharply than before. "I can ride a little way, and get down whenever I like," thought I ; and springing forward I clambered up the coach, and was going to sit down upon the box, next the coachman. "No, no," said the coachman, who was a man about thirty, with a hooked nose and red face, dressed in a fashionably cut greatcoat, with a fashionable black castor on his head. "No, no, keep behind—the box a'n't for the like of you," said he, as he drove off ; "the box is for lords, or gentlemen at least." I made no answer. "D—— that off-hand leader," said the coachman, as the right-hand front horse made a desperate start at something he saw in the road ; and, half rising, he with great dexterity hit with his long whip the off-hand leader a cut on the off cheek. "These seem to be fine horses," said I. The coachman made no answer. "Nearly thorough-bred," I continued ; the coachman drew his breath, with a kind of hissing sound, through his teeth. "Come, young fellow, none of your chaff. Don't you think, because you ride on my mail, I'm going to talk to you about 'orses. I talk to nobody about 'orses except lords." "Well," said I, "I have been called a lord in my time." "It must have been by a thimble-rigger, then," said the coachman, bending back, and half-turning his face round with a broad leer. "You have hit the mark wonderfully," said I. "You coachmen, whatever else you may be, are certainly no fools." "We a'n't, a'n't we?" said the coachman. "There you are right ; and, to show you that you are, I'll now trouble you for your fare. If you have been amongst the thimble-riggers you must be tolerably well cleared out. Where are you going?—to ——? I think I have seen you there. The fare is sixteen shillings. Come, tip us the blunt ; them that has no money can't ride on my mail."

Sixteen shillings was a large sum, and to pay it would make a considerable inroad on my slender finances ; I thought, at first, that I would say I did not want to go so far ; but then the fellow would ask at once where I wanted to go, and I was ashamed to acknowledge my utter ignorance of the road. I determined, therefore, to pay the fare, with a tacit determination not to mount a coach in future without knowing whither I was going. So I paid the man the money, who, turning round, shouted to the guard— " All right, Jem ; got fare to ——," and forthwith whipped on his horses, especially the off-hand leader, for whom he seemed to entertain a particular spite, to greater speed than before—the horses flew.

A young moon gave a feeble light, partially illuminating a line of road which, appearing by no means interesting, I the less regretted having paid my money for the privilege of being hurried along it in the flying vehicle. We frequently changed horses ; and at last my friend the coachman was replaced by another, the very image of himself—hawk nose, red face, with narrow-rimmed hat and fashionable benjamin. After he had driven about fifty yards, the new coachman fell to whipping one of the horses. " D—— this near-hand wheeler," said he, "the brute has got a corn." "Whipping him won't cure him of his corn," said I. "Who told you to speak?" said the driver, with an oath ; " mind your own business ; 'tisn't from the like of you I am to learn to drive 'orses." Presently I fell into a broken kind of slumber. In an hour or two I was aroused by a rough voice— " Got to ——, young man ; get down if you please ". I opened my eyes—there was a dim and indistinct light, like that which precedes dawn ; the coach was standing still in something like a street ; just below me stood the guard. " Do you mean to get down," said he, " or will you keep us here till morning ? other fares want to get up." Scarcely knowing what I did, I took my bundle and stick and descended, whilst two people mounted. " All right, John," said the guard to the coachman, springing up behind ; whereupon off whisked the coach, one or two individuals who were standing by disappeared, and I was left alone.

CHAPTER LX.

AFTER standing still a minute or two, considering what I should do, I moved down what appeared to be the street of a small straggling town; presently I passed by a church, which rose indistinctly on my right hand; anon there was the rustling of foliage and the rushing of waters. I reached a bridge, beneath which a small stream was running in the direction of the south. I stopped and leaned over the parapet, for I have always loved to look upon streams, especially at the still hours. "What stream is this, I wonder?" said I, as I looked down from the parapet into the water, which whirled and gurgled below.

Leaving the bridge, I ascended a gentle acclivity, and presently reached what appeared to be a tract of moory undulating ground. It was now tolerably light, but there was a mist or haze abroad which prevented my seeing objects with much precision. I felt chill in the damp air of the early morn, and walked rapidly forward. In about half an hour I arrived where the road divided into two at an angle or tongue of dark green sward. "To the right or the left?" said I, and forthwith took, without knowing why, the left-hand road, along which I proceeded about a hundred yards, when, in the midst of the tongue of sward formed by the two roads, collaterally with myself, I perceived what I at first conceived to be a small grove of blighted trunks of oaks, barked and grey. I stood still for a moment, and then, turning off the road, advanced slowly towards it over the sward; as I drew nearer, I perceived that the objects which had attracted my curiosity, and which formed a kind of circle, were not trees, but immense upright stones. A thrill pervaded my system; just before me were two, the mightiest of the whole, tall as the stems of proud oaks, supporting on their tops a huge transverse stone, and forming a wonderful doorway. I knew now where I was, and, laying down my stick and bundle, and taking off my hat, I advanced slowly, and cast myself—it was folly, perhaps, but I could not help what I did—cast myself, with my face on the dewy earth, in the middle of the portal of giants, beneath the transverse stone.

[*See page 318.*

STONEHENGE.

[See page 444.

MUMPERS' DINGLE.

The spirit of Stonehenge was strong upon me!

And after I had remained with my face on the ground for some time, I arose, placed my hat on my head, and taking up my stick and bundle, wandered around the wondrous circle, examining each individual stone, from the greatest to the least, and then entering by the great door, seated myself upon an immense broad stone, one side of which was supported by several small ones, and the other slanted upon the earth; and there in deep meditation I sat for an hour or two, till the sun shone in my face above the tall stones of the eastern side.

And as I still sat there, I heard the noise of bells, and presently a large number of sheep came browzing past the circle of stones; two or three entered, and grazed upon what they could find, and soon a man also entered the circle at the northern side.

" Early here, sir," said the man, who was tall, and dressed in a dark green slop, and had all the appearance of a shepherd; " a traveller, I suppose?"

" Yes," said I, " I am a traveller; are these sheep yours?"

" They are, sir; that is, they are my master's. A strange place this, sir," said he, looking at the stones; "ever here before?"

" Never in body, frequently in mind."

" Heard of the stones, I suppose; no wonder—all the people of the plain talk of them."

" What do the people of the plain say of them?"

" Why, they say—How did they ever come here?"

" Do they not suppose them to have been brought?"

' Who should have brought them?"

" I have read that they were brought by many thousand men."

" Where from?"

" Ireland."

" How did they bring them?"

" I don't know."

" And what did they bring them for?"

" To form a temple, perhaps."

" What is that?"

" A place to worship God in."

" A strange place to worship God in."

" Why?"

" It has no roof."

" Yes, it has."

" Where?" said the man looking up.

" What do you see above you?"

" The sky."

" Well ? "

" Well ! "

" Have you anything to say ? "

" How did these stones come here ? "

" Are there other stones like these on the plains ? " said I.

" None ; and yet there are plenty of strange things on these downs."

" What are they ? "

" Strange heaps, and barrows, and great walls of earth built on the tops of hills."

" Do the people of the plain wonder how they came there ? "

" They do not."

" Why ? "

" They were raised by hands."

" And these stones ? "

" How did they ever come here ? "

" I wonder whether they are here ? " said I.

" These stones ? "

" Yes."

" So sure as the world," said the man ; " and, as the world, they will stand as long."

" I wonder whether there is a world."

" What do you mean ? "

" An earth and sea, moon and stars, sheep and men."

" Do you doubt it ? "

" Sometimes."

" I never heard it doubted before."

" It is impossible there should be a world."

" It a'n't possible there shouldn't be a world."

" Just so." At this moment a fine ewe attended by a lamb, rushed into the circle and fondled the knees of the shepherd. " I suppose you would not care to have some milk," said the man.

" Why do you suppose so ? "

" Because, so be, there be no sheep, no milk, you know ; and what there ben't is not worth having."

" You could not have argued better," said I ; " that is, supposing you have argued ; with respect to the milk, you may do as you please."

" Be still, Nanny," said the man ; and producing a tin vessel from his scrip, he milked the ewe into it. " Here is milk of the plains, master," said the man, as he handed the vessel to me.

"Where are those barrows and great walls of earth you were speaking of," said I, after I had drank some of the milk; "are there any near where we are?"

"Not within many miles; the nearest is yonder away," said the shepherd, pointing to the south-east. "It's a grand place, that, but not like this; quite different, and from it you have a sight of the finest spire in the world."

"I must go to it," said I, and I drank the remainder of the milk; "yonder, you say."

"Yes, yonder; but you cannot get to it in that direction, the river lies between."

"What river?"

"The Avon."

"Avon is British," said I.

"Yes," said the man, "we are all British here."

"No, we are not," said I.

"What are we then?"

"English."

"A'n't they one?"

"No."

"Who were the British?"

"The men who are supposed to have worshipped God in this place, and who raised these stones."

"Where are they now?"

"Our forefathers slaughtered them, spilled their blood all about, especially in this neighbourhood, destroyed their pleasant places, and left not, to use their own words, one stone upon another."

"Yes, they did," said the shepherd, looking aloft at the transverse stone.

"And it is well for them they did; whenever that stone, which English hands never raised, is by English hands thrown down, woe, woe, woe to the English race; spare it, English! Hengist spared it!—Here is sixpence."

"I won't have it," said the man.

"Why not?"

"You talk so prettily about these stones; you seem to know all about them."

"I never receive presents; with respect to the stones, I say with yourself, How did they ever come here!"

"How did they ever come here!" said the shepherd.

CHAPTER LXI.

LEAVING the shepherd, I bent my way in the direction pointed out by him as that in which the most remarkable of the strange remains of which he had spoken lay. I proceeded rapidly, making my way over the downs covered with coarse grass and fern; with respect to the river of which he had spoken, I reflected that, either by wading or swimming, I could easily transfer myself and what I bore to the opposite side. On arriving at its banks, I found it a beautiful stream, but shallow, with here and there a deep place, where the water ran dark and still.

Always fond of the pure lymph, I undressed, and plunged into one of these gulfs, from which I emerged, my whole frame in a glow, and tingling with delicious sensations. After conveying my clothes and scanty baggage to the farther side, I dressed, and then with hurried steps bent my course in the direction of some lofty ground; I at length found myself on a high road, leading over wide and arid downs; following the road for some miles without seeing anything remarkable, I supposed at length that I had taken the wrong path, and wended on slowly and disconsolately for some time, till, having nearly surmounted a steep hill, I knew at once, from certain appearances, that I was near the object of my search. Turning to the right near the brow of the hill, I proceeded along a path which brought me to a causeway leading over a deep ravine, and connecting the hill with another which had once formed part of it, for the ravine was evidently the work of art. I passed over the causeway, and found myself in a kind of gateway which admitted me into a square space of many acres, surrounded on all sides by mounds or ramparts of earth. Though I had never been in such a place before, I knew that I stood within the precincts of what had been a Roman encampment, and one probably of the largest size, for many thousand warriors might have found room to perform their evolutions in that space, in which corn was now growing, the green ears waving in the morning wind.

After I had gazed about the space for a time, standing in the gateway formed by the mounds, I clambered up the mound to the left hand, and on the top of that mound I found myself at a great altitude ; beneath, at the distance of a mile, was a fair old city, situated amongst verdant meadows, watered with streams, and from the heart of that old city, from amidst mighty trees, I beheld towering to the sky the finest spire in the world.

After I had looked from the Roman rampart for a long time, I hurried away, and, retracing my steps along the causeway, regained the road, and, passing over the brow of the hill, descended to the city of the spire.

CHAPTER LXII.

AND in the old city I remained two days, passing my time as I best could—inspecting the curiosities of the place, eating and drinking when I felt so disposed, which I frequently did, the digestive organs having assumed a tone to which for many months they had been strangers—enjoying at night balmy sleep in a large bed in a dusky room, at the end of a corridor, in a certain hostelry in which I had taken up my quarters—receiving from the people of the hostelry such civility and condescension as people who travel on foot with bundle and stick, but who nevertheless are perceived to be not altogether destitute of coin, are in the habit of receiving. On the third day, on a fine sunny afternoon, I departed from the city of the spire.

As I was passing through one of the suburbs, I saw, all on a sudden, a respectable-looking female fall down in a fit; several persons hastened to her assistance. "She is dead," said one. "No, she is not," said another. "I am afraid she is," said a third. "Life is very uncertain," said a fourth. "It is Mrs. ——" said a fifth; "let us carry her to her own house." Not being able to render any assistance, I left the poor female in the hands of her townsfolk, and proceeded on my way. I had chosen a road in the direction of the north-west, it led over downs where corn was growing, but where neither tree nor hedge were to be seen; two or three hours' walking brought me to a beautiful valley, abounding with trees of various kinds, with a delightful village at its farthest extremity; passing through it I ascended a lofty acclivity, on the top of which I sat down on a bank, and taking off my hat, permitted a breeze, which swept coolly and refreshingly over the downs, to dry my hair, dripping from the effects of exercise and the heat of the day.

And as I sat there, gazing now at the blue heavens, now at the downs before me, a man came along the road in the direction in which I had hitherto been proceeding: just opposite to me he stopped, and, looking at me, cried: "Am I right for London, master?"

He was dressed like a sailor, and appeared to be between twenty-five and thirty years of age; he had an open manly countenance, and there was a bold and fearless expression in his eye.

"Yes," said I, in reply to his question; "this is one of the ways to London. Do you come from far?"

"From ——," said the man, naming a well-known sea-port.

"Is this the direct road to London from that place?" I demanded.

"No," said the man; "but I had to visit two or three other places on certain commissions I was entrusted with; amongst others to ——, where I had to take a small sum of money. I am rather tired, master; and, if you please, I will sit down beside you."

"You have as much right to sit down here as I have," said I, "the road is free for every one; as for sitting down beside me, you have the look of an honest man, and I have no objection to your company."

"Why, as for being honest, master," said the man, laughing and sitting down by me, "I hav'n't much to say—many is the wild thing I have done when I was younger; however, what is done, is done. To learn, one must live, master; and I have lived long enough to learn the grand point of wisdom."

"What is that?" said I.

"That honesty is the best policy, master."

"You appear to be a sailor," said I, looking at his dress.

"I was not bred a sailor," said the man, "though, when my foot is on the salt water, I can play the part—and play it well too. I am now from a long voyage."

"From America?" said I.

"Farther than that," said the man.

"Have you any objection to tell me?" said I.

"From New South Wales," said the man, looking me full in the face.

"Dear me," said I.

"Why do you say 'Dear me'?" said the man.

"It is a very long way off," said I.

"Was that your reason for saying so?" said the man.

"Not exactly," said I.

"No," said the man, with something of a bitter smile; "it was something else that made you say so; you were thinking of the convicts."

"Well," said I, "what then—you are no convict."

"How do you know?"

"You do not look like one."

"Thank you, master," said the man cheerfully; "and, to a certain extent, you are right—bygones are bygones—I am no longer what I was, nor ever will be again; the truth, however, is the truth—a convict I have been—a convict at Sydney Cove."

"And you have served out the period for which you were sentenced, and are now returned?"

"As to serving out my sentence," replied the man, "I can't say that I did; I was sentenced for fourteen years, and I was in Sydney Cove little more than half that time. The truth is that I did the Government a service. There was a conspiracy amongst some of the convicts to murder and destroy—I overheard and informed the Government; mind one thing, however, I was not concerned in it; those who got it up were no comrades of mine, but a bloody gang of villains. Well, the Government, in consideration of the service I had done them, remitted the remainder of my sentence; and some kind gentlemen interested themselves about me, gave me good books and good advice, and, being satisfied with my conduct, procured me employ in an exploring expedition, by which I earned money. In fact, the being sent to Sydney was the best thing that ever happened to me in all my life."

"And you have now returned to your native country. Longing to see home brought you from New South Wales."

"There you are mistaken," said the man. "Wish to see England again would never have brought me so far; for, to tell you the truth, master, England was a hard mother to me, as she has proved to many. No, a wish to see another kind of mother —a poor old woman whose son I am—has brought me back."

"You have a mother, then?" said I. "Does she reside in London?"

"She used to live in London," said the man; "but I am afraid she is long since dead."

"How did she support herself?" said I.

"Support herself! with difficulty enough; she used to keep a small stall on London Bridge, where she sold fruit; I am afraid she is dead, and that she died perhaps in misery. She was a poor sinful creature; but I loved her, and she loved me. I came all the way back merely for the chance of seeing her."

"Did you ever write to her," said I, "or cause others to write to her?"

"I wrote to her myself," said the man, "about two years ago;

but I never received an answer. I learned to write very tolerably over there, by the assistance of the good people I spoke of. As for reading, I could do that very well before I went—my poor mother taught me to read, out of a book that she was very fond of; a strange book it was, I remember. Poor dear! what I would give only to know that she is alive."

"Life is very uncertain," said I.

"That is true," said the man, with a sigh.

"We are here one moment, and gone the next," I continued. "As I passed through the streets of a neighbouring town, I saw a respectable woman drop down, and people said she was dead. Who knows but that she too had a son coming to see her from a distance, at that very time."

"Who knows, indeed," said the man. "Ah, I am afraid my mother is dead. Well, God's will be done."

"However," said I, "I should not wonder at your finding your mother alive."

"You wouldn't?" said the man, looking at me wistfully.

"I should not wonder at all," said I; "indeed, something within me seems to tell me you will; I should not much mind betting five shillings to five pence that you will see your mother within a week. Now, friend, five shillings to five pence ——"

"Is very considerable odds," said the man, rubbing his hands; "sure you must have good reason to hope, when you are willing to give such odds."

"After all," said I, "it not unfrequently happens that those who lay the long odds lose. Let us hope, however. What do you mean to do in the event of finding your mother alive?"

"I scarcely know," said the man; "I have frequently thought that if I found my mother alive I would attempt to persuade her to accompany me to the country which I have left—it is a better country for a man—that is a free man—to live in than this; however, let me first find my mother—if I could only find my mother!"

"Farewell," said I, rising. "Go your way, and God go with you—I will go mine." "I have but one thing to ask you," said the man. "What is that?" I inquired. "That you would drink with me before we part—you have done me so much good." "How should we drink?" said I; "we are on the top of a hill where there is nothing to drink." "But there is a village below," said the man; "do let us drink before we part." "I have been through that village already," said I, "and I do not like turning back." "Ah," said the man sorrowfully, "you will not drink with me because I told you I was ——" ·

"You are quite mistaken," said I, "I would as soon drink with a convict as with a judge. I am by no means certain that, under the same circumstances, the judge would be one whit better than the convict. Come along! I will go back to oblige you. I have an odd sixpence in my pocket, which I will change, that I may drink with you." So we went down the hill together to the village through which I had already passed, where, finding a public-house, we drank together in true English fashion, after which we parted, the sailor-looking man going his way and I mine.

After walking about a dozen miles, I came to a town, where I rested for the night. The next morning I set out again in the direction of the north-west. I continued journeying for four days, my daily journeys varying from twenty to twenty-five miles. During this time nothing occurred to me worthy of any especial notice. The weather was brilliant, and I rapidly improved both in strength and spirits. On the fifth day, about two o'clock, I arrived at a small town. Feeling hungry, I entered a decent-looking inn. Within a kind of bar I saw a huge, fat, landlord-looking person, with a very pretty, smartly-dressed maiden. Addressing myself to the fat man, "House!" said I, "house! Can I have dinner, house?"

CHAPTER LXIII.

"Young gentleman," said the huge, fat landlord, "you are come at the right time; dinner will be taken up in a few minutes, and such a dinner," he continued, rubbing his hands, "as you will not see every day in these times."

"I am hot and dusty," said I, "and should wish to cool my hands and face."

"Jenny!" said the huge landlord, with the utmost gravity, "show the gentleman into number seven that he may wash his hands and face."

"By no means," said I, "I am a person of primitive habits, and there is nothing like the pump in weather like this."

"Jenny!" said the landlord, with the same gravity as before, "go with the young gentleman to the pump in the back kitchen, and take a clean towel along with you."

Thereupon the rosy-faced clean-looking damsel went to a drawer, and producing a large, thick, but snowy-white towel, she nodded to me to follow her; whereupon I followed Jenny through a long passage into the back kitchen.

And at the end of the back kitchen there stood a pump; and going to it I placed my hands beneath the spout, and said, "Pump, Jenny," and Jenny incontinently, without laying down the towel, pumped with one hand, and I washed and cooled my heated hands.

And, when my hands were washed and cooled, I took off my neckcloth, and unbuttoning my shirt collar, I placed my head beneath the spout of the pump, and I said unto Jenny: "Now, Jenny, lay down the towel, and pump for your life".

Thereupon Jenny, placing the towel on a linen-horse, took the handle of the pump with both hands and pumped over my head as handmaid had never pumped before; so that the water poured in torrents from my head, my face, and my hair down upon the brick floor.

And after the lapse of somewhat more than a minute, I called out with a half-strangled voice, "Hold, Jenny!" and Jenny desisted. I stood for a few moments to recover my breath, then taking the towel which Jenny proffered, I dried composedly my hands and head, my face and hair; then, returning the towel to Jenny, I gave a deep sigh and said: " Surely this is one of the pleasant moments of life ".

Then, having set my dress to rights, and combed my hair with a pocket comb, I followed Jenny, who conducted me back through the long passage, and showed me into a neat, sanded parlour on the ground floor.

I sat down by a window which looked out upon the dusty street; presently in came the handmaid, and commenced laying the table-cloth. " Shall I spread the table for one, sir," said she, " or do you expect anybody to dine with you?"

" I can't say that I expect anybody," said I, laughing inwardly to myself; "however, if you please you can lay for two, so that if any acquaintance of mine should chance to step in, he may find a knife and fork ready for him."

So I sat by the window, sometimes looking out upon the dusty street, and now glancing at certain old-fashioned prints which adorned the wall over against me. I fell into a kind of doze, from which I was almost instantly awakened by the opening of the door. Dinner, thought I; and I sat upright in my chair. No, a man of the middle age, and rather above the middle height dressed in a plain suit of black, made his appearance, and sat down in a chair at some distance from me, but near to the table, and appeared to be lost in thought.

" The weather is very warm, sir," said I.

" Very," said the stranger laconically, looking at me for the first time.

" Would you like to see the newspaper?" said I, taking up one which lay on the window seat.

" I never read newspapers," said the stranger, " nor, indeed ——" Whatever it might be that he had intended to say he left unfinished. Suddenly he walked to the mantelpiece at the farther end of the room, before which he placed himself with his back towards me. There he remained motionless for some time; at length, raising his hand, he touched the corner of the mantelpiece with his finger, advanced towards the chair which he had left, and again seated himself.

" Have you come far?" said he, suddenly looking towards me, and speaking in a frank and open manner, which denoted a wish to enter into conversation. " You do not seem to be of this place."

"I come from some distance," said I; "indeed, I am walking for exercise, which I find as necessary to the mind as the body. I believe that by exercise people would escape much mental misery."

Scarcely had I uttered these words when the stranger laid his hand, with seeming carelessness, upon the table, near one of the glasses; after a moment or two he touched the glass with his finger as if inadvertently, then, glancing furtively at me, he withdrew his hand and looked towards the window.

"Are you from these parts?" said I at last, with apparent carelessness.

"From this vicinity," replied the stranger. "You think, then, that it is as easy to walk off the bad humours of the mind as of the body."

"I, at least, am walking in that hope," said I.

"I wish you may be successful," said the stranger; and here he touched one of the forks which lay on the table near him.

Here the door, which was slightly ajar, was suddenly pushed open with some fracas, and in came the stout landlord, supporting with some difficulty an immense dish, in which was a mighty round mass of smoking meat garnished all round with vegetables; so high was the mass that it probably obstructed his view, for it was not until he had placed it upon the table that he appeared to observe the stranger; he almost started, and quite out of breath exclaimed: "God bless me, your honour; is your honour the acquaintance that the young gentleman was expecting?"

"Is the young gentleman expecting an acquaintance?" said the stranger.

There is nothing like putting a good face upon these matters, thought I to myself; and, getting up, I bowed to the unknown. "Sir," said I, "when I told Jenny that she might lay the table-cloth for two, so that in the event of any acquaintance dropping in he might find a knife and fork ready for him, I was merely jocular, being an entire stranger in these parts, and expecting no one. Fortune, however, it would seem, has been unexpectedly kind to me; I flatter myself, sir, that since you have been in this room I have had the honour of making your acquaintance; and in the strength of that hope I humbly entreat you to honour me with your company to dinner, provided you have not already dined."

The stranger laughed outright.

"Sir," I continued, "the round of beef is a noble one, and seems exceedingly well boiled, and the landlord was just right when he said I should have such a dinner as is not seen every day. A round of beef, at any rate such a round of beef as this, is seldom seen smoking upon the table in these degenerate times. Allow me, sir," said I, observing that the stranger was about to speak, "allow me another remark. I think I saw you just now touch the fork, I venture to hail it as an omen that you will presently seize it and apply it to its proper purpose, and its companion the knife also."

The stranger changed colour, and gazed upon me in silence.

"Do, sir," here put in the landlord; "do, sir, accept the young gentleman's invitation. Your honour has of late been looking poorly, and the young gentleman is a funny young gentleman, and a clever young gentleman; and I think it will do your honour good to have a dinner's chat with the young gentleman."

"It is not my dinner hour," said the stranger; "I dine considerably later; taking anything now would only discompose me; I shall, however, be most happy to sit down with the young gentleman; reach me that paper, and, when the young gentleman has satisfied his appetite, we may perhaps have a little chat together."

The landlord handed the stranger the newspaper, and, bowing, retired with his maid Jenny. I helped myself to a portion of the smoking round, and commenced eating with no little appetite. The stranger appeared to be soon engrossed with the newspaper. We continued thus a considerable time—the one reading and the other dining. Chancing suddenly to cast my eyes upon the stranger, I saw his brow contract; he gave a slight stamp with his foot, and flung the newspaper to the ground, then stooping down he picked it up, first moving his forefinger along the floor, seemingly slightly scratching it with his nail.

"Do you hope, sir," said I, "by that ceremony with the finger to preserve yourself from the evil chance?"

The stranger started; then, after looking at me for some time in silence, he said: "Is it possible that you ——?"

"Ay, ay," said I, helping myself to some more of the round, "I have touched myself in my younger days, both for the evil chance and the good. Can't say, though, that I ever trusted much in the ceremony."

The stranger made no reply, but appeared to be in deep thought; nothing further passed between us until I had concluded the dinner, when I said to him: "I shall now be most happy, sir, to have the pleasure of your conversation over a pint of wine".

The stranger rose; "No, my young friend," said he, smiling,

" that would scarce be fair.   It is my turn now—pray do me the favour to go home with me, and accept what hospitality my poor roof can offer ; to tell you the truth, I wish to have some particular discourse with you which would hardly be possible in this place.   As for wine, I can give you some much better than you can get here ; the landlord is an excellent fellow, but he is an innkeeper, after all.   I am going out for a moment, and will send him in, so that you may settle your account ; I trust you will not refuse me, I only live about two miles from here."

I looked in the face of the stranger—it was a fine intelligent face, with a cast of melancholy in it.   " Sir," said I, " I would go with you though you lived four miles instead of two."

" Who is that gentleman ? " said I to the landlord, after I had settled his bill ; " I am going home with him."

" I wish I were going too," said the fat landlord, laying his hand upon his stomach.   " Young gentleman, I shall be a loser by his honour's taking you away ; but, after all, the truth is the truth—there are few gentlemen in these parts like his honour, either for learning or welcoming his friends.   Young gentleman, I congratulate you."

CHAPTER LXIV.

I FOUND the stranger awaiting me at the door of the inn. "Like yourself, I am fond of walking," said he, "and when any little business calls me to this place I generally come on foot."

We were soon out of the town, and in a very beautiful country. After proceeding some distance on the high road, we turned off, and were presently in one of those mazes of lanes for which England is famous ; the stranger at first seemed inclined to be taciturn ; a few observations, however, which I made, appeared to rouse him, and he soon exhibited not only considerable powers of conversation, but stores of information which surprised me. So pleased did I become with my new acquaintance, that I soon ceased to pay the slightest attention either to place or distance. At length the stranger was silent, and I perceived that we had arrived at a handsome iron gate and a lodge ; the stranger having rung a bell, the gate was opened by an old man, and we proceeded along a gravel path, which in about five minutes brought us to a large brick house, built something in the old French style, having a spacious lawn before it, and immediately in front a pond in which were golden fish, and in the middle a stone swan discharging quantities of water from its bill. We ascended a spacious flight of steps to the door, which was at once flung open, and two servants with powdered hair, and in livery of blue plush, came out and stood one on either side as we passed the threshold. We entered a large hall, and the stranger, taking me by the hand, welcomed me to his poor home, as he called it, and then gave orders to another servant, but out of livery, to show me to an apartment, and give me whatever assistance I might require in my toilette. Notwithstanding the plea as to primitive habits which I had lately made to my other host in the town, I offered no objection to this arrangement, but followed the bowing domestic to a spacious and airy chamber, where he rendered me all those little nameless offices which the somewhat neglected state of my dress required. When everything had been completed to my perfect satisfaction, he told me that if I pleased he would conduct me to the library, where dinner would be speedily served.

In the library I found a table laid for two ; my host was not there, having as I supposed not been quite so speedy with his toilette as his guest.   Left alone, I looked round the apartment with inquiring eyes ; it was long and tolerably lofty, the walls from the top to the bottom were lined with cases containing books of all sizes and bindings ; there was a globe or two, a couch, and an easy chair.   Statues and busts there were none, and only one painting, a portrait, that of my host, but not him of the mansion. Over the mantelpiece, the features staringly like, but so ridiculously exaggerated that they scarcely resembled those of a human being, daubed evidently by the hand of the commonest sign-artist, hung a half-length portrait of him of round of beef celebrity—my sturdy host of the town.

I had been in the library about ten minutes, amusing myself as I best could, when my friend entered ; he seemed to have resumed his taciturnity—scarce a word escaped his lips till dinner was served, when he said, smiling : " I suppose it would be merely a compliment to ask you to partake ? "

" I don't know," said I, seating myself; " your first course consists of troutlets, I am fond of troutlets, and I always like to be companionable."

The dinner was excellent, though I did but little justice to it from the circumstance of having already dined ; the stranger also, though without my excuse, partook but slightly of the good cheer; he still continued taciturn, and appeared lost in thought, and every attempt which I made to induce him to converse was signally unsuccessful.

And now dinner was removed, and we sat over our wine, and I remember that the wine was good, and fully justified the encomiums of my host of the town.   Over the wine I made sure that my entertainer would have loosened the chain which seemed to tie his tongue—but no !   I endeavoured to tempt him by various topics, and talked of geometry and the use of the globes, of the heavenly sphere, and the star Jupiter, which I said I had heard was a very large star, also of the evergreen tree, which, according to Olaus, stood of old before the heathen temple of Upsal, and which I affirmed was a yew—but no, nothing that I said could induce my entertainer to relax his taciturnity.

It grew dark, and I became uncomfortable ; " I must presently be going," I at last exclaimed.

At these words he gave a sudden start ; " Going," said he, " are you not my guest, and an honoured one ? "

" You know best," said I ; " but I was apprehensive I was an intruder ; to several of my questions you have returned no answer."

"Ten thousand pardons!" he exclaimed, seizing me by the hand; "but you cannot go now, I have much to talk to you about—there is one thing in particular ——"

"If it be the evergreen tree at Upsal," said I, interrupting him, "I hold it to have been a yew—what else? The evergreens of the south, as the old bishop observes, will not grow in the north, and a pine was unfitted for such a locality, being a vulgar tree. What else could it have been but the yew—the sacred yew which our ancestors were in the habit of planting in their churchyards? Moreover, I affirm it to have been the yew for the honour of the tree; for I love the yew, and had I home and land, I would have one growing before my front windows."

"You would do right; the yew is indeed a venerable tree, but it is not about the yew."

"The star Jupiter, perhaps?"

"Nor the star Jupiter, nor its moons; an observation which escaped you at the inn has made a considerable impression upon me."

"But I really must take my departure," said I; "the dark hour is at hand."

And as I uttered these last words, the stranger touched rapidly something which lay near him, I forget what it was. It was the first action of the kind which I had observed on his part since we sat down to table.

"You allude to the evil chance," said I; "but it is getting both dark and late."

"I believe we are going to have a storm," said my friend, "but I really hope that you will give me your company for a day or two; I have, as I said before, much to talk to you about."

"Well," said I, "I shall be most happy to be your guest for this night; I am ignorant of the country, and it is not pleasant to travel unknown paths by night—dear me, what a flash of lightning!"

It had become very dark; suddenly a blaze of sheet-lightning illumed the room. By the momentary light I distinctly saw my host touch another object upon the table.

"Will you allow me to ask you a question or two?" said he at last.

"As many as you please," said I; "but shall we not have lights?"

"Not unless you particularly wish it," said my entertainer; "I rather like the dark, and though a storm is evidently at hand, neither thunder not lightning have any terrors for me. It is other things I quake at—I should rather say ideas. Now, permit me to ask you——"

And then my entertainer asked me various questions, to all of which I answered unreservedly; he was then silent for some

time, at last he exclaimed : " I should wish to tell you the history
of my life ; though not an adventurous one, I think it contains
some things which will interest you ".

Without waiting for my reply he began.   Amidst darkness
and gloom, occasionally broken by flashes of lightning, the
stranger related to me, as we sat at the table in the library, his
truly touching history.

" Before proceeding to relate the events of my life, it will not
be amiss to give you some account of my ancestors.   My great-
grandfather on the male side was a silk mercer, in Cheapside, who,
when he died, left his son, who was his only child, a fortune of
one hundred thousand pounds, and a splendid business ; the son,
however, had no inclination for trade, the summit of his ambition
was to be a country gentleman, to found a family, and to pass
the remainder of his days in rural ease and dignity, and all this
he managed to accomplish ; he disposed of his business, purchased a beautiful and extensive estate for four score thousand
pounds, built upon it the mansion to which I had the honour of
welcoming you to-day, married the daughter of a neighbouring
squire, who brought him a fortune of five thousand pounds,
became a magistrate, and only wanted a son and heir to make
him completely happy ; this blessing, it is true, was for a long
time denied him ; it came, however, at last, as is usual, when least
expected.   His lady was brought to bed of my father, and then
who so happy a man as my grandsire ; he gave away two thousand
pounds in charities, and in the joy of his heart made a speech at
the next quarter sessions ; the rest of his life was spent in ease,
tranquillity and rural dignity ; he died of apoplexy on the day that
my father came of age ; perhaps it would be difficult to mention
a man who in all respects was so fortunate as my grandfather ;
his death was sudden, it is true, but I am not one of those who
pray to be delivered from a sudden death.

" I should not call my father a fortunate man ; it is true that
he had the advantage of a first-rate education ; that he made the
grand tour with a private tutor, as was the fashion at that time ;
that he came to a splendid fortune on the very day that he came
of age ; that for many years he tasted all the diversions of the
capital ; that, at last determined to settle, he married the sister of
a baronet, an amiable and accomplished lady, with a large fortune ;
that he had the best stud of hunters in the county, on which,
during the season, he followed the fox gallantly ; had he been a
fortunate man he would never have cursed his fate, as he was
frequently known to do ; ten months after his marriage his horse

fell upon him, and so injured him, that he expired in a few days in great agony. My grandfather was, indeed, a fortunate man; when he died he was followed to the grave by the tears of the poor—my father was not.

"Two remarkable circumstances are connected with my birth —I am a posthumous child, and came into the world some weeks before the usual time, the shock which my mother experienced at my father's death having brought on the pangs of premature labour; both my mother's life and my own were at first despaired of; we both, however, survived the crisis. My mother loved me with the most passionate fondness, and I was brought up in this house under her own eye—I was never sent to school.

"I have already told you that mine is not a tale of adventure; my life has not been one of action, but of wild imaginings and strange sensations; I was born with excessive sensibility, and that has been my bane. I have not been a fortunate man.

"No one is fortunate unless he is happy, and it is impossible for a being constructed like myself to be happy for an hour, or even enjoy peace and tranquillity; most of our pleasures and pains are the effects of imagination, and wherever the sensibility is great, the imagination is great also. No sooner has my imagination raised up an image of pleasure, than it is sure to conjure up one of distress and gloom; these two antagonistic ideas instantly commence a struggle in my mind, and the gloomy one generally, I may say invariably, prevails. How is it possible that I should be a happy man?

"It has invariably been so with me from the earliest period that I can remember; the first playthings that were given me caused me for a few minutes excessive pleasure; they were pretty and glittering; presently, however, I became anxious and perplexed, I wished to know their history, how they were made, and what of—were the materials precious; I was not satisfied with their outward appearance. In less than an hour I had broken the playthings in an attempt to discover what they were made of.

"When I was eight years of age my uncle the baronet, who was also my godfather, sent me a pair or Norway hawks, with directions for managing them; he was a great fowler. Oh, how rejoiced was I with the present which had been made me, my joy lasted for at least five minutes; I would let them breed, I would have a house of hawks; yes, that I would—but—and here came the unpleasant idea—suppose they were to fly away, how very annoying! Ah, but, said hope, there's little fear of that; feed them well and they will never fly away, or if they do they will come back, my uncle says so; so sunshine triumphed for a little time. Then the strangest of all doubts came into my head; I doubted the legality of my tenure of these hawks; how did I come by them? why, my uncle gave them to me, but how did they come into his possession? what right had he to them? after all, they might not be his to give,—I passed a sleepless night. The next morning I found that the man who brought the hawks had not departed. 'How came my uncle by these hawks?' I anxiously inquired. 'They were sent to him from Norway, master, with another pair.' 'And who sent them?' 'That I don't know, master, but I suppose his honour can tell you.' I was even thinking of scrawling a letter to my uncle to make inquiry on this point, but shame restrained me, and I likewise reflected that it would be impossible for him to give my mind entire satisfaction; it is true he could tell who sent him the hawks, but how was he to know how the hawks came into the possession of those who sent them to him, and by what right they possessed them or the parents of the hawks. In a word, I wanted a clear valid title, as lawyers would say, to my hawks, and I believe no title would have satisfied me that did not extend up to the time of the first hawk, that is, prior to Adam; and, could I have obtained such a title, I make no doubt that, young as I was, I should have suspected that it was full of flaws.

"I was now disgusted with the hawks, and no wonder, seeing all the disquietude they had caused me; I soon totally neglected the poor birds, and they would have starved had not some of the servants taken compassion upon them and fed them. My uncle, soon hearing of my neglect, was angry, and took the birds away; he was a very good-natured man, however, and soon sent me a fine pony; at first I was charmed with the pony, soon, however, the same kind of thoughts arose which had disgusted me on a former occasion. How did my uncle become possessed of the pony? This question I asked him the first time I saw him. Oh, he had bought it of a gypsy, that I might learn to ride upon it. A gypsy; I had heard that gypsies were great thieves, and I instantly began to fear that the gypsy had stolen the pony, and it is probable that for this apprehension I had better grounds than for many others. I instantly ceased to set any value upon the pony, but for that reason, perhaps, I turned it to some account; I mounted it, and rode it about, which I don't think I should have done had I looked upon it as a secure possession. Had I looked upon my title as secure, I should have prized it so much that I should scarcely have mounted it for fear of injuring the

animal; but now, caring not a straw for it, I rode it most un-
mercifully, and soon became a capital rider.   This was very selfish
in me, and I tell the fact with shame.   I was punished, however,
as I deserved; the pony had a spirit of its own, and, moreover, it
had belonged to gypsies; once, as I was riding it furiously over
the lawn, applying both whip and spur, it suddenly lifted up its
heels, and flung me at least five yards over its head.   I received
some desperate contusions, and was taken up for dead; it was
many months before I perfectly recovered.

   " But it is time for me to come to the touching part of my
story.   There was one thing that I loved better than the choicest
gift which could be bestowed upon me, better than life itself
—my mother; at length she became unwell, and the thought
that I might possibly lose her now rushed into my mind for the
first time; it was terrible, and caused me unspeakable misery, I
may say horror.   My mother became worse, and I was not allowed
to enter her apartment, lest by my frantic exclamations of grief I
might aggravate her disorder.   I rested neither day nor night, but
roamed about the house like one distracted.   Suddenly I found
myself doing that which even at the time struck me as being highly
singular; I found myself touching particular objects that were near
me, and to which my fingers seemed to be attracted by an irresistible
impulse.   It was now the table or the chair that I was compelled
to touch; now the bell-rope; now the handle of the door; now
I would touch the wall, and the next moment stooping down, I
would place the point of my finger upon the floor: and so I continued to do day after day; frequently I would struggle to resist
the impulse, but invariably in vain.   I have even rushed away
from the object, but I was sure to return, the impulse was too
strong to be resisted: I quickly hurried back, compelled by the
feeling within me to touch the object.   Now, I need not tell you
that what impelled me to these actions was the desire to prevent
my mother's death; whenever I touched any particular object, it
was with the view of baffling the evil chance, as you would call it
—in this instance my mother's death.

   " A favourable crisis occurred in my mother's complaint, and she
recovered; this crisis took place about six o'clock in the morning;
almost simultaneously with it there happened to myself a rather
remarkable circumstance connected with the nervous feeling
which was rioting in my system.   I was lying in bed in a kind of
uneasy doze, the only kind of rest which my anxiety, on account
of my mother, permitted me at this time to take, when all at once
I sprang up as if electrified, the mysterious impulse was upon

me, and it urged me to go without delay, and climb a stately elm behind the house, and touch the topmost branch ; otherwise—you know the rest—the evil chance would prevail. Accustomed for some time as I had been, under this impulse, to perform extravagant actions, I confess to you that the difficulty and peril of such a feat startled me ; I reasoned against the feeling, and strove more strenuously than I had ever done before ; I even made a solemn vow not to give way to the temptation, but I believe nothing less than chains, and those strong ones, could have restrained me. The demoniac influence, for I can call it nothing else, at length prevailed ; it compelled me to rise, to dress myself, to descend the stairs, to unbolt the door, and to go forth ; it drove me to the foot of the tree, and it compelled me to climb the trunk ; this was a tremendous task, and I only accomplished it after repeated falls and trials. When I had got amongst the branches, I rested for a time, and then set about accomplishing the remainder of the ascent ; this for some time was not so difficult, for I was now amongst the branches ; as I approached the top, however, the difficulty became greater, and likewise the danger ; but I was a light boy, and almost as nimble as a squirrel, and, moreover, the nervous feeling was within me, impelling me upward. It was only by means of a spring, however, that I was enabled to touch the top of the tree ; I sprang, touched the top of the tree, and fell a distance of at least twenty feet, amongst the branches ; had I fallen to the bottom I must have been killed, but I fell into the middle of the tree, and presently found myself astride upon one of the boughs ; scratched and bruised all over, I reached the ground, and regained my chamber unobserved ; I flung myself on my bed quite exhausted ; presently they came to tell me that my mother was better—they found me in the state which I have described, and in a fever besides. The favourable crisis must have occurred just about the time that I performed the magic touch ; it certainly was a curious coincidence, yet I was not weak enough, even though a child, to suppose that I had baffled the evil chance by my daring feat.

"Indeed, all the time that I was performing these strange feats, I knew them to be highly absurd, yet the impulse to perform them was irresistible—a mysterious dread hanging over me till I had given way to it ; even at that early period I frequently used to reason within myself as to what could be the cause of my propensity to touch, but of course I could come to no satisfactory conclusion respecting it ; being heartily ashamed of the practice, I never spoke of it to any one, and was at all times highly solicitous that no one should observe my weakness."

CHAPTER LXV.

AFTER a short pause my host resumed his narration. "Though I was never sent to school, my education was not neglected on that account; I had tutors in various branches of knowledge, under whom I made a tolerable progress; by the time I was eighteen I was able to read most of the Greek and Latin authors with facility; I was likewise, to a certain degree, a mathematician.

"I cannot say that I took much pleasure in my studies; my chief aim in endeavouring to accomplish my tasks was to give pleasure to my beloved parent, who watched my progress with anxiety truly maternal. My life at this period may be summed up in a few words; I pursued my studies, roamed about the woods, walked the green lanes occasionally, cast my fly in a trout stream, and sometimes, but not often, rode a hunting with my uncle.

"A considerable part of my time was devoted to my mother, conversing with her and reading to her; youthful companions I had none, and as to my mother, she lived in the greatest retirement, devoting herself to the superintendence of my education, and the practice of acts of charity; nothing could be more innocent than this mode of life, and some people say that in innocence there is happiness, yet I can't say that I was happy. A continual dread overshadowed my mind, it was the dread of my mother's death. Her constitution had never been strong, and it had been considerably shaken by her last illness; this I knew, and this I saw—for the eyes of fear are marvellously keen. Well, things went on in this way till I had come of age; my tutors were then dismissed, and my uncle the baronet took me in hand, telling my mother that it was high time for him to exert his authority; that I must see something of the world, for that, if I remained much longer with her, I should be ruined. 'You must consign him to me,' said he, 'and I will introduce him to the world.' My mother sighed and consented; so my uncle the baronet introduced me to the world, took me to horse races and to London, and endeavoured to make a man of me according to his idea of the term, and in part succeeded.　I became moderately dissipated—I say moderately, for dissipation had but little zest for me.

"In this manner four years passed over.　It happened that I was in London in the height of the season with my uncle, at his house; one morning he summoned me into the parlour, he was standing before the fire, and looked very serious.　'I have had a letter,' said he; 'your mother is very ill.'　I staggered, and touched the nearest object to me; nothing was said for two or three minutes, and then my uncle put his lips to my ear and whispered something.　I fell down senseless.　My mother was —— I remember nothing for a long time—for two years I was out of my mind; at the end of this time I recovered, or partly so. My uncle the baronet was very kind to me; he advised me to travel, he offered to go with me.　I told him he was very kind, but I would rather go by myself.　So I went abroad, and saw, amongst other things, Rome and the Pyramids.　By frequent change of scene my mind became not happy, but tolerably tranquil. I continued abroad some years, when, becoming tired of travelling, I came home, found my uncle the baronet alive, hearty, and unmarried, as he still is.　He received me very kindly, took me to Newmarket, and said that he hoped by this time I was become quite a man of the world; by his advice I took a house in town, in which I lived during the season.　In summer I strolled from one watering-place to another; and, in order to pass the time, I became very dissipated.

"At last I became as tired of dissipation as I had previously been of travelling, and I determined to retire to the country, and live on my paternal estate; this resolution I was not slow in putting into effect; I sold my house in town, repaired and re-furnished my country house, and for at least ten years, lived a regular country life; I gave dinner parties, prosecuted poachers, was charitable to the poor, and now and then went into my library; during this time I was seldom or never visited by the magic impulse, the reason being, that there was nothing in the wide world for which I cared sufficiently to move a finger to preserve it. When the ten years, however, were nearly ended, I started out of bed one morning in a fit of horror, exclaiming, 'Mercy, mercy! what will become of me?　I am afraid I shall go mad.　I have lived thirty-five years and upwards without doing anything; shall I pass through life in this manner?　Horror!'　And then in rapid succession I touched three different objects.

"I dressed myself and went down, determining to set about something; but what was I to do?—there was the difficulty.　I ate no breakfast, but walked about the room in a state of distraction; at last I thought that the easiest way to do something was to get into Parliament, there would be no difficulty in that. I had plenty of money, and could buy a seat: but what was I to do in Parliament? Speak, of course—but could I speak? 'I'll try at once,' said I, and forthwith I rushed into the largest dining-room, and, locking the door, I commenced speaking; 'Mr. Speaker,' said I, and then I went on speaking for about ten minutes as I best could, and then I left off, for I was talking nonsense. No, I was not formed for Parliament; I could do nothing there. What—what was I to do?

"Many, many times I thought this question over, but was unable to solve it; a fear now stole over me that I was unfit for anything in the world, save the lazy life of vegetation which I had for many years been leading; yet, if that were the case, thought I, why the craving within me to distinguish myself? Surely it does not occur fortuitously, but is intended to rouse and call into exercise certain latent powers that I possess? and then with infinite eagerness I set about attempting to discover these latent powers. I tried an infinity of pursuits, botany and geology amongst the rest, but in vain; I was fitted for none of them. I became very sorrowful and despondent, and at one time I had almost resolved to plunge again into the whirlpool of dissipation; it was a dreadful resource, it was true, but what better could I do?

"But I was not doomed to return to the dissipation of the world. One morning a young nobleman, who had for some time past shown a wish to cultivate my acquaintance, came to me in a considerable hurry. 'I am come to beg an important favour of you,' said he; 'one of the county memberships is vacant—I intend to become a candidate; what I want immediately is a spirited address to the electors. I have been endeavouring to frame one all the morning, but in vain; I have, therefore, recourse to you as a person of infinite genius; pray, my dear friend, concoct me one by the morning.' 'What you require of me,' I replied, 'is impossible; I have not the gift of words; did I possess it I would stand for the county myself, but I can't speak. Only the other day I attempted to make a speech, but left off suddenly, utterly ashamed, although I was quite alone, of the nonsense I was uttering.' 'It is not a speech that I want,' said my friend, 'I can talk for three hours without hesitating, but I want an address to circulate through the county, and I find myself utterly incompetent to put one together; do oblige me by writing one for me, I know you can; and, if at any time you want a person to

speak for you, you may command me not for three but for six
hours.   Good morning; to-morrow I will breakfast with you.'   In
the morning he came again.   'Well,' said he, 'what success?'
'Very poor,' said I; 'but judge for yourself;' and I put into
his hand a manuscript of several pages.   My friend read it through
with considerable attention.   'I congratulate you,' said he, 'and
likewise myself; I was not mistaken in my opinion of you; the
address is too long by at least two-thirds, or I should rather say it
is longer by two-thirds than addresses generally are; but it will
do—I will not curtail it of a word.   I shall win my election.'
And in truth he did win his election; and it was not only his
own but the general opinion that he owed it to the address.

"But, however that might be, I had, by writing the address,
at last discovered what had so long eluded my search—what I
was able to do.   I, who had neither the nerve nor the command
of speech necessary to constitute the orator—who had not the
power of patient research required by those who would investigate
the secrets of nature, had, nevertheless, a ready pen and teeming
imagination.   This discovery decided my fate—from that moment
I became an author."

CHAPTER LXVI.

"An author," said I, addressing my host; "is it possible that I am under the roof of an author?"

"Yes," said my host, sighing, "my name is so and so, and I am the author of so and so; it is more than probable that you have heard both of my name and works. I will not detain you much longer with my history; the night is advancing, and the storm appears to be upon the increase. My life since the period of my becoming an author may be summed briefly as an almost uninterrupted series of doubts, anxieties and trepidations. I see clearly that it is not good to love anything immoderately in this world, but it has been my misfortune to love immoderately everything on which I have set my heart. This is not good, I repeat— but where is the remedy? The ancients were always in the habit of saying, 'Practise moderation,' but the ancients appear to have considered only one portion of the subject. It is very possible to practice moderation in some things, in drink and the like—to restrain the appetites—but can a man restrain the affections of his mind, and tell them, so far you shall go, and no farther? Alas, no! for the mind is a subtle principle, and cannot be confined. The winds may be imprisoned; Homer says that Odysseus carried certain winds in his ship, confined in leathern bags, but Homer never speaks of confining the affections. It were but right that those who exhort us against inordinate affections, and setting our hearts too much upon the world and its vanities, would tell us how to avoid doing so.

"I need scarcely tell you, that no sooner did I become an author, than I gave myself up immoderately to my vocation. It became my idol, and, as a necessary consequence, it has proved a source of misery and disquietude to me, instead of pleasure and blessing. I had trouble enough in writing my first work, and I was not long in discovering that it was one thing to write a stirring and spirited address to a set of county electors, and another widely different to produce a work at all calculated to make an impression upon the great world. I felt, however, that I was in my proper

(346)

sphere, and by dint of unwearied diligence and exertion I succeeded
in evolving from the depths of my agitated breast a work which,
though it did not exactly please me, I thought would serve to
make an experiment upon the public; so I laid it before the
public, and the reception which it met with was far beyond my
wildest expectations. The public were delighted with it, but
what were my feelings? Anything, alas! but those of delight.
No sooner did the public express its satisfaction at the result of
my endeavours, than my perverse imagination began to conceive
a thousand chimerical doubts; forthwith I sat down to analyse it;
and my worst enemy, and all people have their enemies, especially
authors—my worst enemy could not have discovered or sought
to discover a tenth part of the faults which I, the author and
creator of the unfortunate production, found or sought to find in
it. It has been said that love makes us blind to the faults of the
loved object—common love does, perhaps—the love of a father
to his child, or that of a lover to his mistress, but not the inordinate love of an author to his works, at least not the love which one
like myself bears to his works: to be brief, I discovered a thousand
faults in my work, which neither public nor critics discovered.
However, I was beginning to get over this misery, and to forgive
my work all its imperfections, when—and I shake when I mention
it—the same kind of idea which perplexed me with regard to the
hawks and the gypsy pony rushed into my mind, and I forthwith
commenced touching the objects around me, in order to baffle the
evil chance, as you call it; it was neither more nor less than a
doubt of the legality of my claim to the thoughts, expressions and
situations contained in the book; that is, to all that constituted
the book. How did I get them? How did they come into my
mind? Did I invent them? Did they originate with myself?
Are they my own, or are they some other body's? You see into
what difficulty I had got; I won't trouble you by relating all that
I endured at that time, but will merely say that after eating my
own heart, as the Italians say, and touching every object that
came in my way for six months, I at length flung my book, I
mean the copy of it which I possessed, into the fire, and began
another.

" But it was all in vain; I laboured at this other, finished it,
and gave it to the world; and no sooner had I done so, than the
same thought was busy in my brain, poisoning all the pleasure
which I should otherwise have derived from my work. How did
I get all the matter which composed it? Out of my own mind,
unquestionably; but how did it come there—was it the indigenous

growth of the mind? And then I would sit down and ponder over the various scenes and adventures in my book, endeavouring to ascertain how I came originally to devise them, and by dint of reflecting I remembered that to a single word in conversation, or some simple accident in a street, or on a road, I was indebted for some of the happiest portions of my work; they were but tiny seeds, it is true, which in the soil of my imagination had subsequently become stately trees, but I reflected that without them no stately trees would have been produced, and that, consequently, only a part in the merit of these compositions which charmed the world—for they did charm the world—was due to myself. Thus, a dead fly was in my phial, poisoning all the pleasure which I should otherwise have derived from the result of my brain sweat. 'How hard!' I would exclaim, looking up to the sky, 'how hard! I am like Virgil's sheep, bearing fleeces not for themselves.' But, not to tire you, it fared with my second work as it did with my first; I flung it aside and, in order to forget it, I began a third, on which I am now occupied; but the difficulty of writing it is immense, my extreme desire to be original sadly cramping the powers of my mind; my fastidiousness being so great that I invariably reject whatever ideas I do not think to be legitimately my own. But there is one circumstance to which I cannot help alluding here, as it serves to show what miseries this love of originality must needs bring upon an author. I am constantly discovering that, however original I may wish to be, I am continually producing the same things which other people say or write. Whenever, after producing something which gives me perfect satisfaction, and which has cost me perhaps days and nights of brooding, I chance to take up a book for the sake of a little relaxation, a book which I never saw before, I am sure to find in it something more or less resembling some part of what I have been just composing. You will easily conceive the distress which then comes over me; 'tis then that I am almost tempted to execrate the chance which, by discovering my latent powers, induced me to adopt a profession of such anxiety and misery.

"For some time past I have given up reading almost entirely, owing to the dread which I entertain of lighting upon something similar to what I myself have written. I scarcely ever transgress without having almost instant reason to repent. To-day, when I took up the newspaper, I saw in a speech of the Duke of Rhododendron, at an agricultural dinner, the very same ideas, and almost the same expressions which I had put into the mouth of an imaginary personage of mine, on a widely different occasion;

you saw how I dashed the newspaper down—you saw how I touched the floor; the touch was to baffle the evil chance, to prevent the critics detecting any similarity between the speech of the Duke of Rhododendron at the agricultural dinner, and the speech of my personage. My sensibility on the subject of my writings is so great, that sometimes a chance word is sufficient to unman me, I apply it to them in a superstitious sense; for example, when you said some time ago that the dark hour was coming on, I applied it to my works—it appeared to bode them evil fortune; you saw how I touched, it was to baffle the evil chance; but I do not confine myself to touching when the fear of the evil chance is upon me. To baffle it I occasionally perform actions which must appear highly incomprehensible; I have been known, when riding in company with other people, to leave the direct road, and make a long circuit by a miry lane to the place to which we were going. I have also been seen attempting to ride across a morass, where I had no business whatever, and in which my horse finally sank up to its saddle-girths, and was only extricated by the help of a multitude of hands. I have, of course, frequently been asked the reason for such conduct, to which I have invariably returned no answer, for I scorn duplicity; whereupon people have looked mysteriously, and sometimes put their fingers to their foreheads. 'And yet it can't be,' I once heard an old gentleman say; 'don't we know what he is capable of?' and the old man was right; I merely did these things to avoid the evil chance, impelled by the strange feeling within me; and this evil chance is invariably connected with my writings, the only things at present which render life valuable to me. If I touch various objects, and ride into miry places, it is to baffle any mischance befalling me as an author, to prevent my books getting into disrepute; in nine cases out of ten to prevent any expressions, thoughts or situations in any work which I am writing from resembling the thoughts, expressions and situations of other authors, for my great wish, as I told you before, is to be original.

"I have now related my history, and have revealed to you the secrets of my inmost bosom. I should certainly not have spoken so unreservedly as I have done, had I not discovered in you a kindred spirit. I have long wished for an opportunity of discoursing on the point which forms the peculiar feature of my history with a being who could understand me; and truly it was a lucky chance which brought you to these parts; you who seem to be acquainted with all things strange and singular, and who are as well acquainted with the subject of the magic touch as with all that relates to the star Jupiter, or the mysterious tree at Upsal."

Such was the story which my host related to me in the library, amidst the darkness, occasionally broken by flashes of lightning. Both of us remained silent for some time after it was concluded.

"It is a singular story," said I, at last, "though I confess that I was prepared for some part of it. Will you permit me to ask you a question?"

"Certainly," said my host.

"Did you never speak in public?" said I.

"Never."

"And when you made this speech of yours in the dining-room, commencing with Mr. Speaker, no one was present?"

"None in the world, I double-locked the door; what do you mean?"

"An idea came into my head—dear me, how the rain is pouring—but, with respect to your present troubles and anxieties, would it not be wise, seeing that authorship causes you so much trouble and anxiety, to give it up altogether?"

"Were you an author yourself," replied my host, "you would not talk in this manner; once an author, ever an author—besides, what could I do? return to my former state of vegetation? no, much as I endure, I do not wish that; besides, every now and then my reason tells me that these troubles and anxieties of mine are utterly without foundation; that whatever I write is the legitimate growth of my own mind, and that it is the height of folly to afflict myself at any chance resemblance between my own thoughts and those of other writers, such resemblance being inevitable from the fact of our common human origin. In short ——"

"I understand you," said I; "notwithstanding your troubles and anxieties you find life very tolerable; has your originality ever been called in question?"

"On the contrary, every one declares that originality constitutes the most remarkable feature of my writings; the man has some faults, they say, but want of originality is certainly not one of them. He is quite different from others; a certain newspaper, it is true, the ——[1] I think, once insinuated that in a certain work of mine I had taken a hint or two from the writings of a couple of authors which it mentioned; it happened, however, that I had never even read one syllable of the writings of either, and of one of them had never even heard the name; so much for the discrimination of the —— By-the-bye, what a rascally newspaper that is!"

"A very rascally newspaper," said I.

[1] *MS.*, " The Times ".

CHAPTER LXVII.

DURING the greater part of that night my slumbers were disturbed by strange dreams. Amongst other things, I fancied that I was my host; my head appeared to be teeming with wild thoughts and imaginations, out of which I was endeavouring to frame a book. And now the book was finished and given to the world, and the world shouted; and all eyes were turned upon me, and I shrunk from the eyes of the world. And, when I got into retired places, I touched various objects in order to baffle the evil chance. In short, during the whole night, I was acting over the story which I had heard before I went to bed.

At about eight o'clock I awoke. The storm had long since passed away, and the morning was bright and shining; my couch was so soft and luxurious that I felt loth to quit it, so I lay some time, my eyes wandering about the magnificent room to which fortune had conducted me in so singular a manner; at last I heaved a sigh; I was thinking of my own homeless condition, and imagining where I should find myself on the following morning. Unwilling, however, to indulge in melancholy thoughts, I sprang out of bed and proceeded to dress myself, and, whilst dressing, I felt an irresistible inclination to touch the bed-post.

I finished dressing and left the room, feeling compelled, however, as I left it, to touch the lintel of the door. Is it possible, thought I, that from what I have lately heard the long-forgotten influence should have possessed me again? but I will not give way to it; so I hurried down stairs, resisting as I went a certain inclination which I occasionally felt to touch the rail of the bannister. I was presently upon the gravel walk before the house: it was indeed a glorious morning. I stood for some time observing the golden fish disporting in the waters of the pond, and then strolled about amongst the noble trees of the park; the beauty and freshness of the morning—for the air had been considerably cooled by the late storm—soon enabled me to cast away the gloomy ideas which had previously taken possession of my mind, and, after a stroll of about half an hour, I returned towards the house in high spirits. It is true that once I felt very much inclined to go and touch the leaves of a flowery shrub which I saw at some distance, and had even moved two or three paces towards it; but, bethinking myself, I manfully resisted the temptation. " Begone ! " I exclaimed, " ye sorceries, in which I formerly trusted—begone for ever vagaries which I had almost forgotten ; good luck is not to be obtained, or bad averted, by magic touches ; besides, two wizards in one parish would be too much, in all conscience."

I returned to the house, and entered the library ; breakfast was laid on the table, and my friend was standing before the portrait which I have already said hung above the mantelpiece ; so intently was he occupied in gazing at it that he did not hear me enter, nor was aware of my presence till I advanced close to him and spoke, when he turned round, and shook me by the hand.

" What can possibly have induced you to hang that portrait up in your library ? it is a staring likeness, it is true, but it appears to me a wretched daub."

" Daub as you call it," said my friend, smiling, " I would not part with it for the best piece of Raphael. For many a happy thought I am indebted to that picture—it is my principal source of inspiration ; when my imagination flags, as of course it occasionally does, I stare upon those features, and forthwith strange ideas of fun and drollery begin to flow into my mind ; these I round, amplify, or combine into goodly creations, and bring forth as I find an opportunity. It is true that I am occasionally tormented by the thought that, by doing this, I am committing plagiarism ; though in that case, all thoughts must be plagiarisms, all that we think being the result of what we hear, see or feel. What can I do ? I must derive my thoughts from some source or other ; and, after all, it is better to plagiarise from the features of my landlord than from the works of Butler and Cervantes. My works, as you are aware, are of a serio-comic character. My neighbours are of opinion that I am a great reader, and so I am, but only of those features—my real library is that picture."

" But how did you obtain it ? "

" Some years ago a travelling painter came into this neighbourhood, and my jolly host, at the request of his wife, consented to sit for his portrait ; she highly admired the picture, but she soon died, and then my fat friend, who is of an affectionate disposition, said he could not bear the sight of it, as it put him in mind of his poor wife. I purchased it of him for five pounds— I would not take five thousand for it ; when you called that picture a daub, you did not see all the poetry of it."

We sat down to breakfast; my entertainer appeared to be in much better spirits than on the preceding day; I did not observe him touch once; ere breakfast was over a servant entered—"The Reverend Mr. Platitude, sir," said he.

A shade of dissatisfaction came over the countenance of my host. "What does the silly pestilent fellow mean by coming here?" said he, half to himself; "let him come in," said he to the servant.

The servant went out, and in a moment reappeared, introducing the Reverend Mr. Platitude. The Reverend Mr. Platitude, having what is vulgarly called a game leg, came shambling into the room; he was about thirty years of age, and about five feet three inches high; his face was of the colour of pepper, and nearly as rugged as a nutmeg grater; his hair was black; with his eyes he squinted, and grinned with his lips, which were very much apart, disclosing two very irregular rows of teeth; he was dressed in the true Levitical fashion, in a suit of spotless black, and a neckerchief of spotless white.

The Reverend Mr. Platitude advanced winking and grinning to my entertainer, who received him politely but with evident coldness; nothing daunted, however, the Reverend Mr. Platitude took a seat by the table, and, being asked to take a cup of coffee, winked, grinned and consented.

In company I am occasionally subject to fits of what is generally called absence; my mind takes flight and returns to former scenes, or presses forward into the future. One of these fits of absence came over me at this time—I looked at the Reverend Mr. Platitude for a moment, heard a word or two that proceeded from his mouth, and saying to myself, "You are no man for me," fell into a fit of musing—into the same train of thought as in the morning, no very pleasant one—I was thinking of the future.

I continued in my reverie for some time, and probably should have continued longer, had I not been suddenly aroused by the voice of Mr. Platitude raised to a very high key. "Yes, my dear sir," said he, "it is but too true; I have it on good authority—a gone church—a lost church—a ruined church—a demolished church is the Church of England. Toleration to Dissenters! oh, monstrous!"

"I suppose," said my host, "that the repeal of the Test Acts will be merely a precursor of the emancipation of the Papists?"

"Of the Catholics," said the Reverend Mr. Platitude. "Ahem. There was a time, as I believe you are aware, my dear sir, when I was as much opposed to the emancipation of the Catholics as it

was possible for any one to be; but I was prejudiced, my dear
sir, labouring under a cloud of most unfortunate prejudice; but
I thank my Maker I am so no longer.   I have travelled, as you
are aware.   It is only by travelling that one can rub off prejudices; I think you will agree with me there.   I am speaking
to a traveller.   I left behind all my prejudices in Italy.   The
Catholics are at least our fellow-Christians.   I thank Heaven
that I am no longer an enemy to Catholic emancipation."

"And yet you would not tolerate Dissenters?"

"Dissenters, my dear sir; I hope you would not class such a
set as the Dissenters with Catholics?"

"Perhaps it would be unjust," said my host, "though to
which of the two parties is another thing; but permit me to ask
you a question: Does it not smack somewhat of paradox to talk
of Catholics, whilst you admit there are Dissenters?   If there are
Dissenters, how should there be Catholics?"

"It is not my fault that there are Dissenters," said the
Reverend Mr. Platitude; "if I had my will I would neither
admit there were any, nor permit any to be."

"Of course you would admit there were such as long as they
existed; but how would you get rid of them?"

"I would have the Church exert its authority."

"What do you mean by exerting its authority?"

"I would not have the Church bear the sword in vain."

"What, the sword of St. Peter?   You remember what the
founder of the religion which you profess said about the sword,
'He who striketh with it ——'   I think those who have called
themselves the Church have had enough of the sword.   Two can
play with the sword, Mr. Platitude.   The Church of Rome tried
the sword with the Lutherans: how did it fare with the Church
of Rome?   The Church of England tried the sword, Mr.
Platitude, with the Puritans: how did it fare with Laud and
Charles?"

"Oh, as for the Church of England," said Mr. Platitude, "I
have little to say.   Thank God I left all my Church of England
prejudices in Italy.   Had the Church of England known its true
interests, it would long ago have sought a reconciliation with its
illustrious mother.   If the Church of England had not been in
some degree a schismatic church, it would not have fared so ill
at the time of which you are speaking; the rest of the Church
would have come to its assistance.   The Irish would have helped
it, so would the French, so would the Portuguese.   Disunion has
always been the bane of the Church."

Once more I fell into a reverie. My mind now reverted to the past; methought I was in a small, comfortable room wainscoted with oak; I was seated on one side of a fireplace, close by a table on which were wine and fruit; on the other side of the fire sat a man in a plain suit of brown, with the hair combed back from his somewhat high forehead; he had a pipe in his mouth, which for some time he smoked gravely and placidly, without saying a word; at length, after drawing at the pipe for some time rather vigorously, he removed it from his mouth, and emitting an accumulated cloud of smoke, he exclaimed in a slow and measured tone: "As I was telling you just now, my good chap, I have always been an enemy to humbug".

When I awoke from my reverie the Reverend Mr. Platitude was quitting the apartment.

"Who is that person?" said I to my entertainer, as the door closed behind him.

"Who is he?" said my host; "why, the Rev. Mr. Platitude."

"Does he reside in this neighbourhood?"

"He holds a living about three miles from here; his history, as far as I am acquainted with it, is as follows: His father was a respectable tanner in the neighbouring town, who, wishing to make his son a gentleman, sent him to college. Having never been at college myself, I cannot say whether he took the wisest course; I believe it is more easy to unmake than to make a gentleman; I have known many gentlemanly youths go to college, and return anything but what they went. Young Mr. Platitude did not go to college a gentleman, but neither did he return one; he went to college an ass, and returned a prig; to his original folly was superadded a vast quantity of conceit. He told his father that he had adopted high principles, and was determined to discountenance everything low and mean; advised him to eschew trade, and to purchase him a living. The old man retired from business, purchased his son a living, and shortly after died, leaving him what remained of his fortune. The first thing the Reverend Mr. Platitude did after his father's decease, was to send his mother and sister into Wales to live upon a small annuity, assigning as a reason that he was averse to anything low and that they talked ungrammatically. Wishing to shine in the pulpit, he now preached high sermons, as he called them, interspersed with scraps of learning. His sermons did not, however, procure him much popularity; on the contrary, his church soon became nearly deserted, the greater part of his flock going over to certain dissenting preachers, who had shortly

before made their appearance in the neighbourhood.   Mr. Platitude was filled with wrath, and abused Dissenters in most un-
measured terms.   Coming in contact with some of the preachers
at a public meeting, he was rash enough to enter into argument
with them.   Poor Platitude ! he had better have been quiet, he
appeared like a child, a very infant in their grasp ; he attempted
to take shelter under his college learning, but found, to his
dismay, that his opponents knew more Greek and Latin than
himself.   These illiterate boors, as he had supposed them, caught
him at once in a false concord, and Mr. Platitude had to slink
home overwhelmed with shame.   To avenge himself he applied
to the ecclesiastical court, but was told that the Dissenters could
not be put down by the present ecclesiastical law.   He found
the Church of England, to use his own expression, a poor,
powerless, restricted Church.   He now thought to improve his
consequence by marriage, and made up to a rich and beautiful
young lady in the neighbourhood ; the damsel measured him from
head to foot with a pair of very sharp eyes, dropped a curtsey, and
refused him.   Mr. Platitude, finding England a very stupid place,
determined to travel ; he went to Italy ; how he passed his time
there he knows best, to other people it is a matter of little
importance.   At the end of two years he returned with a real or
assumed contempt for everything English, and especially for the
Church to which he belongs, and out of which he is supported.
He forthwith gave out that he had left behind him all his Church
of England prejudices, and, as a proof thereof, spoke against
sacerdotal wedlock and the toleration of schismatics.   In an evil
hour for myself he was introduced to me by a clergyman of my
acquaintance, and from that time I have been pestered, as I was
this morning, at least once a week.   I seldom enter into any
discussion with him, but fix my eyes on the portrait over the
mantelpiece, and endeavour to conjure up some comic idea or
situation, whilst he goes on talking tomfoolery by the hour about
Church authority, schismatics, and the unlawfulness of sacerdotal
wedlock ; occasionally he brings with him a strange kind of
being, whose acquaintance he says he made in Italy.   I believe
he is some sharking priest, who has come over to proselytize and
plunder.   This being has some powers of conversation and some
learning, but carries the countenance of an arch villain ;
Platitude is evidently his tool.''

" Of what religion are you ? " said I to my host.

"That of the Vicar of Wakefield—good, quiet, Church of
England, which would live and let live, practises charity, and rails

at no one; where the priest is the husband of one wife, takes
care of his family and his parish—such is the religion for me,
though I confess I have hitherto thought too little of religious
matters. When, however, I have completed this plaguy work on
which I am engaged, I hope to be able to devote more attention
to them."

After some further conversation, the subjects being, if I remember right, college education, priggism, church authority,
tomfoolery, and the like, I rose and said to my host, " I must
now leave you ".

" Whither are you going ? "

" I do not know."

" Stay here, then—you shall be welcome as many days,
months, and years as you please to stay."

" Do you think I would hang upon another man? No, not
if he were Emperor of all the Chinas. I will now make my
preparations, and then bid you farewell."

I retired to my apartment and collected the handful of things
which I carried with me on my travels.

" I will walk a little way with you," said my friend on my
return.

He walked with me to the park gate ; neither of us said anything by the way. When we had come upon the road, I said :
" Farewell now ; I will not permit you to give yourself any
further trouble on my account. Receive my best thanks for your
kindness ; before we part, however, I should wish to ask you a
question. Do you think you shall ever grow tired of authorship ? "

" I have my fears," said my friend, advancing his hand to one
of the iron bars of the gate.

" Don't touch," said I, " it is a bad habit. I have but one
word to add : should you ever grow tired of authorship follow
your first idea of getting into Parliament; you have words enough
at command ; perhaps you want manner and method ; but, in
that case, you must apply to a teacher, you must take lessons of
a master of elocution."

" That would never do ! " said my host; " I know myself too
well to think of applying for assistance to any one. Were I to
become a parliamentary orator, I should wish to be an original
one, even if not above mediocrity. What pleasure should I take
in any speech I might make, however original as to thought, provided the gestures I employed and the very modulation of my
voice were not my own? Take lessons, indeed ! why, the fellow
who taught me, the professor, might be standing in the gallery

whilst I spoke; and, at the best parts of my speech, might say to himself: 'That gesture is mine—that modulation is mine'. I could not bear the thought of such a thing."

"Farewell," said I, "and may you prosper. I have nothing more to say."

I departed. At the distance of twenty yards I turned round suddenly; my friend was just withdrawing his finger from the bar of the gate.

"He has been touching," said I, as I proceeded on my way; "I wonder what was the evil chance he wished to baffle."

[End of Vol. II., 1851.]

CHAPTER LXVIII.

AFTER walking some time, I found myself on the great road, at the same spot where I had turned aside the day before with my new-made acquaintance, in the direction of his house. I now continued my journey as before, towards the north. The weather, though beautiful, was much cooler than it had been for some time past; I walked at a great rate, with a springing and elastic step. In about two hours I came to where a kind of cottage stood a little way back from the road, with a huge oak before it, under the shade of which stood a little pony and cart, which seemed to contain various articles. I was going past, when I saw scrawled over the door of the cottage, " Good beer sold here "; upon which, feeling myself all of a sudden very thirsty, I determined to go in and taste the beverage.

I entered a well-sanded kitchen, and seated myself on a bench, on one side of a long white table ; the other side, which was nearest to the wall, was occupied by a party, or rather family, consisting of a grimy-looking man, somewhat under the middle size, dressed in faded velveteens, and wearing a leather apron—a rather pretty-looking woman, but sun-burnt, and meanly dressed, and two ragged children, a boy and girl, about four or five years old. The man sat with his eyes fixed upon the table, supporting his chin with both his hands ; the woman, who was next to him, sat quite still, save that occasionally she turned a glance upon her husband with eyes that appeared to have been lately crying. The children had none of the vivacity so general at their age. A more disconsolate family I had never seen ; a mug, which, when filled, might contain half a pint, stood empty before them ; a very disconsolate party indeed.

" House ! " said I ; " House ! " and then as nobody appeared, I cried again as loud as I could, " House ! do you hear me, House ! "

" What's your pleasure, young man ? " said an elderly woman, who now made her appearance from a side apartment.

" To taste your ale," said I.

(359)

"How much?" said the woman, stretching out her hand towards the empty mug upon the table.

"The largest measure-full in your house," said I, putting back her hand gently. "This is not the season for half-pint mugs."

"As you will, young man," said the landlady, and presently brought in an earthen pitcher which might contain about three pints, and which foamed and frothed withal.

"Will this pay for it?" said I, putting down sixpence.

"I have to return you a penny," said the landlady, putting her hand into her pocket.

"I want no change," said I, flourishing my hand with an air.

"As you please, young gentleman," said the landlady, and then making a kind of curtsey, she again retired to the side apartment.

"Here is your health, sir," said I to the grimy-looking man, as I raised the pitcher to my lips.

The tinker, for such I supposed him to be, without altering his posture, raised his eyes, looked at me for a moment, gave a slight nod, and then once more fixed his eyes upon the table. I took a draught of the ale, which I found excellent; "won't you drink?" said I, holding the pitcher to the tinker.

The man again lifted his eyes, looked at me, and then at the pitcher, and then at me again. I thought at one time that he was about to shake his head in sign of refusal, but no, he looked once more at the pitcher, and the temptation was too strong. Slowly removing his head from his arms, he took the pitcher, sighed, nodded, and drank a tolerable quantity, and then set the pitcher down before me upon the table.

"You had better mend your draught," said I to the tinker; "it is a sad heart that never rejoices."

"That's true," said the tinker, and again raising the pitcher to his lips, he mended his draught as I had bidden him, drinking a larger quantity than before.

"Pass it to your wife," said I.

The poor woman took the pitcher from the man's hand; before, however, raising it to her lips, she looked at the children. True mother's heart, thought I to myself, and taking the half-pint mug, I made her fill it, and then held it to the children, causing each to take a draught. The woman wiped her eyes with the corner of her gown before she raised the pitcher and drank to my health.

In about five minutes none of the family looked half so disconsolate as before, and the tinker and I were in deep discourse.

Oh, genial and gladdening is the power of good ale, the true and proper drink of Englishmen. He is not deserving of the name of Englishman who speaketh against ale, that is good ale, like that which has just made merry the hearts of this poor family ; and yet there are beings, calling themselves Englishmen, who say that it is a sin to drink a cup of ale, and who, on coming to this passage will be tempted to fling down the book and exclaim : " The man is evidently a bad man, for behold, by his own confession, he is not only fond of ale himself, but is in the habit of tempting other people with it ". Alas! alas! what a number of silly individuals there are in this world ; I wonder what they would have had me do in this instance—given the afflicted family a cup of cold water? go to! They could have found water in the road, for there was a pellucid spring only a few yards distant from the house, as they were well aware—but they wanted not water ; what should I have given them? meat and bread? go to! They were not hungry ; there was stifled sobbing in their bosoms, and the first mouthful of strong meat would have choked them. What should I have given them? Money ! what right had I to insult them by offering them money? Advice ! words, words, words ; friends, there is a time for everything ; there is a time for a cup of cold water ; there is a time for strong meat and bread ; there is a time for advice, and there is a time for ale ; and I have generally found that the time for advice is after a cup of ale—I do not say many cups ; the tongue then speaketh more smoothly, and the ear listeneth more benignantly ; but why do I attempt to reason with you? do I not know you for conceited creatures, with one idea— and that a foolish one—a crotchet, for the sake of which ye would sacrifice anything, religion if required—country? There, fling down my book, I do not wish ye to walk any farther in my company, unless you cast your nonsense away, which ye will never do, for it is the breath of your nostrils ; fling down my book, it was not written to support a crotchet, for know one thing, my good people, I have invariably been an enemy to humbug.

"Well," said the tinker, after we had discoursed some time, " I little thought when I first saw you, that you were of my own trade."

Myself.—Nor am I, at least not exactly. There is not much difference, 'tis true, between a tinker and a smith.

Tinker.—You are a whitesmith, then ?

Myself.—Not I, I'd scorn to be anything so mean ; no, friend, black's the colour ; I am a brother of the horseshoe. Success to the hammer and tongs.

Tinker.—Well, I shouldn't have thought you were a blacksmith by your hands.

Myself.—I have seen them, however, as black as yours. The truth is, I have not worked for many a day.

Tinker.—Where did you serve first?

Myself.—In Ireland.

Tinker.—That's a good way off, isn't it?

Myself.—Not very far; over those mountains to the left, and the run of salt water that lies behind them, there's Ireland.

Tinker.—It's a fine thing to be a scholar.

Myself.—Not half so fine as to be a tinker.

Tinker.—How you talk!

Myself.—Nothing but the truth; what can be better than to be one's own master? Now, a tinker is his own master, a scholar is not. Let us suppose the best of scholars, a schoolmaster, for example, for I suppose you will admit that no one can be higher in scholarship than a schoolmaster; do you call his a pleasant life? I don't; we should call him a school-slave, rather than a schoolmaster. Only conceive him in blessed weather like this, in his close school, teaching children to write in copy-books, " Evil communication corrupts good manners," or " You cannot touch pitch without defilement," or to spell out of Abedariums, or to read out of Jack Smith, or Sandford and Merton. Only conceive him, I say, drudging in such guise from morning till night, without any rational enjoyment but to beat the children. Would you compare such a dog's life as that with your own—the happiest under heaven—true Eden life, as the Germans would say,—pitching your tent under the pleasant hedge-row, listening to the song of the feathered tribes, collecting all the leaky kettles in the neighbourhood, soldering and joining, earning your honest bread by the wholesome sweat of your brow—making ten holes—hey, what's this? what's the man crying for?

Suddenly the tinker had covered his face with his hands, and begun to sob and moan like a man in the deepest distress; the breast of his wife was heaved with emotion; even the children were agitated, the youngest began to roar.

Myself.—What's the matter with you; what are you all crying about?

Tinker (uncovering his face).—Lord, why to hear you talk; isn't that enough to make anybody cry—even the poor babes? Yes, you said right, 'tis life in the garden of Eden—the tinker's; I see so now that I'm about to give it up.

Myself.—Give it up! you must not think of such a thing.

Tinker.—No, I can't bear to think of it, and yet I must; what's to be done? How hard to be frightened to death, to be driven off the roads.

Myself.—Who has driven you off the roads?

Tinker.—Who! the Flaming Tinman.

Myself.—Who is he?

Tinker.—The biggest rogue in England, and the cruellest, or he wouldn't have served me as he has done—I'll tell you all about it. I was born upon the roads, and so was my father before me, and my mother too; and I worked with them as long as they lived, as a dutiful child, for I have nothing to reproach myself with on their account; and when my father died I took up the business, and went his beat, and supported my mother for the little time she lived; and when she died I married this young woman, who was not born upon the roads, but was a small tradesman's daughter, at Glo'ster. She had a kindness for me, and, notwithstanding her friends were against the match, she married the poor tinker, and came to live with him upon the roads. Well, young man, for six or seven years I was the happiest fellow breathing, living just the life you described just now—respected by everybody in this beat; when in an evil hour comes this Black Jack, this flaming tinman, into these parts, driven as they say out of Yorkshire—for no good, you may be sure. Now, there is no beat will support two tinkers, as you doubtless know; mine was a good one, but it would not support the flying tinker and myself, though if it would have supported twenty it would have been all the same to the flying villain, who'll brook no one but himself; so he presently finds me out, and offers to fight me for the beat. Now, being bred upon the roads, I can fight a little, that is with anything like my match, but I was not going to fight him, who happens to be twice my size, and so I told him; whereupon he knocks me down, and would have done me further mischief had not some men been nigh and prevented him; so he threatened to cut my throat, and went his way. Well, I did not like such usage at all, and was woundily frightened, and tried to keep as much out of his way as possible, going anywhere but where I thought I was likely to meet him; and sure enough for several months I contrived to keep out of his way. At last somebody told me he was gone back to Yorkshire, whereupon I was glad at heart, and ventured to show myself, going here and there as I did before. Well, young man, it was yesterday that I and mine set ourselves down in a lane, about five miles from here, and lighted our fire, and had our

dinner, and after dinner I sat down to mend three kettles and a
frying pan which the people in the neighbourhood had given me
to mend—for, as I told you before, I have a good connection,
owing to my honesty. Well, as I sat there hard at work, happy
as the day's long, and thinking of anything but what was to
happen, who should come up but this Black Jack, this king of the
tinkers, rattling along in his cart, with his wife, that they call Grey
Moll, by his side—for the villain has got a wife, and a maid-
servant too ; the last I never saw, but they that has, says that she
is as big as a house, and young, and well to look at, which can't
be all said of Moll, who, though she's big enough in all conscience,
is neither young nor handsome. Well, no sooner does he see me
and mine, than giving the reins to Grey Moll, he springs out of
his cart, and comes straight at me ; not a word did he say, but
on he comes straight at me like a wild bull. I am a quiet man,
young fellow, but I saw now that quietness would be of no use,
so I sprang up upon my legs, and being bred upon the roads, and
able to fight a little, I squared as he came running in upon me,
and had a round or two with him. Lord bless you, young man,
it was like a fly fighting with an elephant—one of those big beasts
the show-folks carry about. I had not a chance with the fellow,
he knocked me here, he knocked me there, knocked me into the
hedge, and knocked me out again. I was at my last shifts, and
my poor wife saw it. Now, my poor wife, though she is as gentle
as a pigeon, has yet a spirit of her own, and though she wasn't
bred upon the roads, can scratch a little, so when she saw me at
my last shifts, she flew at the villain—she couldn't bear to see her
partner murdered—and she scratched the villain's face. Lord
bless you, young man, she had better have been quiet : Grey
Moll no sooner saw what she was about, than springing out of the
cart, where she had sat all along perfectly quiet, save a little
whooping and screeching to encourage her blade—Grey Moll, I
say (my flesh creeps when I think of it—for I am a kind husband,
and love my poor wife) ——

Myself.—Take another draught of the ale ; you look frightened,
and it will do you good. Stout liquor makes stout heart, as the
man says in the play.

Tinker.—That's true, young man ; here's to you—where was
I ? Grey Moll no sooner saw what my wife was about, than
springing out of the cart, she flew at my poor wife, clawed off her
bonnet in a moment, and seized hold of her hair. Lord bless
you, young man, my poor wife, in the hands of Grey Moll, was
nothing better than a pigeon in the claws of a buzzard hawk, or I

in the hands of the Flaming Tinman, which when I saw, my heart
was fit to burst, and I determined to give up everything—every
thing to save my poor wife out of Grey Moll's claws. "Hold!"
I shouted. "Hold, both of you—Jack, Moll. Hold, both of
you, for God's sake, and I'll do what you will : give up trade and
business, connection, bread, and everything, never more travel the
roads, and go down on my knees to you in the bargain." Well,
this had some effect : Moll let go my wife, and the Blazing Tinman
stopped for a moment ; it was only for a moment, however, that
he left off—all of a sudden he hit me a blow which sent me against
a tree ; and what did the villian then ? why the flying villain seized
me by the throat, and almost throttled me, roaring—what do you
think, young man, that the flaming villain roared out ?

Myself.—I really don't know—something horrible, I suppose.

Tinker.—Horrible, indeed ; you may well say horrible, young
man ; neither more nor less than the Bible—"a Bible, a Bible!"
roared the Blazing Tinman ; and he pressed my throat so hard
against the tree that my senses began to dwaul away—a Bible, a
Bible, still ringing in my ears. Now, young man, my poor wife is
a Christian woman, and, though she travels the roads, carries a
Bible with her at the bottom of her sack, with which sometimes
she teaches the children to read—it was the only thing she brought
with her from the place of her kith and kin, save her own body
and the clothes on her back ; so my poor wife, half-distracted,
runs to her sack, pulls out the Bible, and puts it into the hand of
the Blazing Tinman, who then thrusts the end of it into my mouth
with such fury that it made my lips bleed, and broke short one
of my teeth which happened to be decayed. "Swear," said
he, "swear you mumping villain, take your Bible oath that you
will quit and give up the beat altogether, or I'll"—and then the
hard-hearted villain made me swear by the Bible, and my own
damnation, half-throttled as I was—to—to—I can't go on ——

Myself. Take another draught   stout liquor ——

Tinker.—I can't, young man, my heart's too full, and what's
more, the pitcher is empty.

Myself.—And so he swore you, I suppose, on the Bible, to
quit the roads ?

Tinker.—You are right, he did so, the gypsy villain.

Myself.—Gypsy ! Is he a gypsy ?

Tinker.—Not exactly ; what they call a half and half. His
father was a gypsy, and his mother, like mine, one who walked
the roads.

Myself.—Is he of the Smiths—the Petulengres ?

Tinker.—I say, young man, you know a thing or two ; one would think, to hear you talk, you had been bred upon the roads. I thought none but those bred upon the roads knew anything of that name—Petulengres ! No, not he, he fights the Petulengres whenever he meets them ; he likes nobody but himself, and wants to be king of the roads. I believe he is a Boss, or a —— at any rate he's a bad one, as I know to my cost.

Myself.—And what are you going to do ?

Tinker.—Do ! you may well ask that ; I don't know what to do. My poor wife and I have been talking of that all the morn- ing, over that half-pint mug of beer ; we can't determine on what's to be done. All we know is, that we must quit the roads. The villain swore that the next time he saw us on the roads he'd cut all our throats, and seize our horse and bit of a cart that are now standing out there under the tree.

Myself.—And what do you mean to do with your horse and cart ?

Tinker.—Another question ! What shall we do with our cart and pony ? they are of no use to us now. Stay on the roads I will not, both for my oath's sake and my own. If we had a trifle of money, we were thinking of going to Bristol, where I might get up a little business, but we have none ; our last three farthings we spent about the mug of beer.

Myself.—But why don't you sell your horse and cart ?

Tinker.—Sell them ? And who would buy them, unless some one who wished to set up in my line ; but there's no beat, and what's the use of the horse and cart and the few tools without the beat ?

Myself.—I'm half-inclined to buy your cart and pony, and your beat too.

Tinker.—You ! How came you to think of such a thing ?

Myself.—Why, like yourself, I hardly know what to do. I want a home and work. As for a home, I suppose I can contrive to make a home out of your tent and cart ; and as for work, I must learn to be a tinker, it would not be hard for one of my trade to learn to tinker ; what better can I do ? Would you have me go to Chester and work there now ? I don't like the thoughts of it. If I go to Chester and work there, I can't be my own man ; I must work under a master, and perhaps he and I should quarrel, and when I quarrel I am apt to hit folks, and those that hit folks are sometimes sent to prison ; I don't like the thought either of going to Chester or to Chester prison. What do you think I could earn at Chester ?

Tinker.—A matter of eleven shillings a week, if anybody would employ you, which I don't think they would with those hands of yours. But whether they would or not, if you are of a quarrelsome nature, you must not go to Chester; you would be in the castle in no time. I don't know how to advise you. As for selling you my stock, I'd see you farther first, for your own sake.

Myself.—Why?

Tinker.—Why! you would get your head knocked off. Suppose you were to meet him?

Myself.—Pooh, don't be afraid on my account; if I were to meet him I could easily manage him one way or other. I know all kinds of strange words and names, and, as I told you before, I sometimes hit people when they put me out.

Here the tinker's wife, who for some minutes past had been listening attentively to our discourse, interposed, saying, in a low, soft tone: "I really don't see, John, why you shouldn't sell the young man the things, seeing that he wishes for them, and is so confident; you have told him plainly how matters stand, and if anything ill should befall him, people couldn't lay the blame on you; but I don't think any ill will befall him, and who knows but God has sent him to our assistance in time of need."

"I'll hear of no such thing," said the tinker; "I have drunk at the young man's expense, and though he says he's quarrelsome, I would not wish to sit in pleasanter company. A pretty fellow I should be, now, if I were to let him follow his own will. If he once sets up on my beat, he's a lost man, his ribs will be stove in, and his head knocked off his shoulders. There, you are crying, but you shan't have your will, though; I won't be the young man's destruction —— If, indeed, I thought he could manage the tinker—but he never can; he says he can hit, but it's no use hitting the tinker;—crying still! you are enough to drive one mad. I say, young man, I believe you understand a thing or two; just now you were talking of knowing hard words and names—I don't wish to send you to your mischief—you say you know hard words and names, let us see. Only on one condition I'll sell you the pony and things; as for the beat it's gone, isn't mine—sworn away by my own mouth. Tell me what's my name; if you can't, may I ——"

Myself.—Don't swear, it's a bad habit, neither pleasant nor profitable. Your name is Slingsby—Jack Slingsby. There, don't stare, there's nothing in my telling you your name: I've been in these parts before, at least not very far from here. Ten years ago, when I was little more than a child, I was about twenty miles

from here in a post-chaise at the door of an inn, and as I looked
from the window of the chaise, I saw you standing by a gutter,
with a big tin ladle in your hand, and somebody called you Jack
Slingsby. I never forget anything I hear or see ; I can't, I wish
I could. So there's nothing strange in my knowing your name ;
indeed, there's nothing strange in anything, provided you examine
it to the bottom. Now, what am I to give you for the things ?

I paid Slingsby five pounds ten shillings for his stock in trade,
cart, and pony—purchased sundry provisions of the landlady, also
a wagoner's frock, which had belonged to a certain son of hers,
deceased, gave my little animal a feed of corn, and prepared to
depart.

"God bless you, young man," said Slingsby, shaking me by
the hand, "you are the best friend I've had for many a day : I
have but one thing to tell you : " Don't cross that fellow's path if
you can help it ; and stay—should the pony refuse to go, just
touch him so, and he'll fly like the wind."

CHAPTER LXIX.

It was two or three hours past noon when I took my departure from the place of the last adventure, walking by the side of my little cart; the pony, invigorated by the corn, to which he was probably not much accustomed, proceeded right gallantly; so far from having to hasten him forward by the particular application which the tinker had pointed out to me, I had rather to repress his eagerness, being, though an excellent pedestrian, not unfrequently left behind. The country through which I passed was beautiful and interesting, but solitary: few habitations appeared. As it was quite a matter of indifference to me in what direction I went, the whole world being before me, I allowed the pony to decide upon the matter; it was not long before he left the high road, being probably no friend to public places. I followed him I knew not whither, but, from subsequent observation, have reason to suppose that our course was in a north-west direction. At length night came upon us, and a cold wind sprang up, which was succeeded by a drizzling rain.

I had originally intended to pass the night in the cart, or to pitch my little tent on some convenient spot by the road's side; but, owing to the alteration in the weather, I thought that it would be advisable to take up my quarters in any hedge alehouse at which I might arrive. To tell the truth, I was not very sorry to have an excuse to pass the night once more beneath a roof. I had determined to live quite independent, but I had never before passed a night by myself abroad, and felt a little apprehensive at the idea; I hoped, however, on the morrow, to be a little more prepared for the step, so I determined for one night—only for one night longer—to sleep like a Christian; but human determinations are not always put into effect, such a thing as opportunity is frequently wanting, such was the case here. I went on for a considerable time, in expectation of coming to some rustic hostelry, but nothing of the kind presented itself to my eyes; the country in which I now was seemed almost uninhabited, not a house of any kind was to be seen—at least I saw none—though it is true

houses might be near without my seeing them, owing to the
darkness of the night, for neither moon nor star was abroad. I
heard, occasionally, the bark of dogs; but the sound appeared to
come from an immense distance. The rain still fell, and the
ground beneath my feet was wet and miry; in short, it was a
night in which even a tramper by profession would feel more
comfortable in being housed than abroad. I followed in the rear
of the cart, the pony still proceeding at a sturdy pace, till
methought I heard other hoofs than those of my own nag; I
listened for a moment, and distinctly heard the sound of hoofs
approaching at a great rate, and evidently from the quarter
towards which I and my little caravan were moving. We were in
a dark lane—so dark that it was impossible for me to see my own
hand. Apprehensive that some accident might occur, I ran
forward, and, seizing the pony by the bridle, drew him as near as
I could to the hedge. On came the hoofs—trot, trot, trot; and
evidently more than those of one horse; their speed as they
advanced appeared to slacken—it was only, however, for a
moment. I heard a voice cry, "Push on, this is a desperate
robbing place, never mind the dark"; and the hoofs came on
quicker than before. "Stop!" said I, at the top of my voice;
"stop! or ——" Before I could finish what I was about to say
there was a stumble, a heavy fall, a cry, and a groan, and putting
out my foot I felt what I conjectured to be the head of a horse
stretched upon the road. "Lord have mercy upon us! what's
the matter?" exclaimed a voice. "Spare my life," cried another
voice, apparently from the ground; "only spare my life, and take
all I have." "Where are you, Master Wise?" cried the other
voice. "Help! here, Master Bat," cried the voice from the
ground, "help me up or I shall be murdered." "Why, what's
the matter?" said Bat. "Some one has knocked me down,
and is robbing me," said the voice from the ground. "Help!
murder!" cried Bat; and, regardless of the entreaties of the
man on the ground that he would stay and help him up, he urged
his horse forward and galloped away as fast as he could. I
remained for some time quiet, listening to various groans and
exclamations uttered by the person on the ground; at length I
said, "Holloa! are you hurt?" "Spare my life, and take all I
have!" said the voice from the ground. "Have they not done
robbing you yet?" said I; "when they have finished let me
know, and I will come and help you." "Who is that?" said
the voice; "pray come and help me, and do me no mischief."
"You were saying that some one was robbing you," said I;

"don't think I shall come till he is gone away." "Then you ben't he?" said the voice. "Ar'n't you robbed?" said I. "Can't say I be," said the voice; "not yet at any rate; but who are you? I don't know you." "A traveller whom you and your partner were going to run over in this dark lane; you almost frightened me out of my senses." "Frightened!" said the voice, in a louder tone; "frightened! oh!" and thereupon I heard somebody getting upon his legs. This accomplished, the individual proceeded to attend to his horse, and with a little difficulty raised him upon his legs also. "Ar'n't you hurt?" said I. "Hurt!" said the voice; "not I; don't think it, whatever the horse may be. I tell you what, my fellow, I thought you were a robber, and now I find you are not; I have a good mind ——" "To do what?" "To serve you out; ar'n't you ashamed ——?" "At what?" said I; "not to have robbed you? Shall I set about it now?" "Ha, ha!" said the man, dropping the bullying tone which he had assumed; "you are joking—robbing! who talks of robbing? I wonder how my horse's knees are; not much hurt, I think—only mired." The man, whoever he was, then got upon his horse; and, after moving him about a little, said, "Good-night, friend; where are you?" "Here I am," said I, "just behind you." "You are, are you? Take that." I know not what he did, but probably pricking his horse with the spur the animal kicked out violently; one of his heels struck me on the shoulder, but luckily missed my face; I fell back with the violence of the blow, whilst the fellow scampered off at a great rate. Stopping at some distance, he loaded me with abuse, and then, continuing his way at a rapid trot, I heard no more of him.

"What a difference!" said I, getting up; "last night I was *fêted* in the hall of a rich genius, and to-night I am knocked down and mired in a dark lane by the heel of Master Wise's horse—I wonder who gave him that name? And yet he was wise enough to wreak his revenge upon me, and I was not wise enough to keep out of his way. Well, I am not much hurt, so it is of little consequence."

I now bethought me that, as I had a carriage of my own, I might as well make use of it; I therefore got into the cart, and, taking the reins in my hand, gave an encouraging cry to the pony, whereupon the sturdy little animal started again at as brisk a pace as if he had not already come many a long mile. I lay half-reclining in the cart, holding the reins lazily, and allowing the animal to go just where he pleased, often wondering where he would conduct me. At length I felt drowsy, and my head sank upon my breast; I soon aroused myself, but it was only to doze again; this occurred several times. Opening my eyes after a doze somewhat longer than the others, I found that the drizzling rain had ceased, a corner of the moon was apparent in the heavens, casting a faint light; I looked around for a moment or two, but my eyes and brain were heavy with slumber, and I could scarcely distinguish where we were. I had a kind of dim consciousness that we were traversing an uninclosed country—perhaps a heath; I thought, however, that I saw certain large black objects looming in the distance, which I had a confused idea might be woods or plantations; the pony still moved at his usual pace. I did not find the jolting of the cart at all disagreeable; on the contrary, it had quite a somniferous effect upon me. Again my eyes closed; I opened them once more, but with less perception in them than before, looked forward, and, muttering something about woodlands, I placed myself in an easier posture than I had hitherto done, and fairly fell asleep.

How long I continued in that state I am unable to say, but I believe for a considerable time; I was suddenly awakened by the ceasing of the jolting to which I had become accustomed, and of which I was perfectly sensible in my sleep. I started up and looked around me, the moon was still shining, and the face of the heaven was studded with stars; I found myself amidst a maze of bushes of various kinds, but principally hazel and holly, through which was a path or driftway with grass growing on either side, upon which the pony was already diligently browsing. I conjectured that this place had been one of the haunts of his former master, and, on dismounting and looking about, was strengthened in that opinion by finding a spot under an ash tree which, from its burnt and blackened appearance, seemed to have been frequently used as a fireplace. I will take up my quarters here, thought I; it is an excellent spot for me to commence my new profession in; I was quite right to trust myself to the guidance of the pony. Unharnessing the animal without delay, I permitted him to browse at free will on the grass, convinced that he would not wander far from a place to which he was so much attached; I then pitched the little tent close beside the ash tree to which I have alluded, and conveyed two or three articles into it, and instantly felt that I had commenced housekeeping for the first time in my life. Housekeeping, however, without a fire is a very sorry affair, something like the housekeeping of children in their toy houses; of this I was the more sensible from feeling very cold and shivering, owing to my late exposure to the rain, and sleeping in the night air. Collecting, therefore, all the dry sticks and furze I could find, I placed them upon the fireplace, adding certain chips and a billet which I found in the cart, it having apparently been the habit of Slingsby to carry with him a small store of fuel. Having then struck a spark in a tinder-box and lighted a match, I set fire to the combustible heap, and was not slow in raising a cheerful blaze ; I then drew my cart near the fire, and, seating myself on one of the shafts, hung over the warmth with feelings of intense pleasure and satisfaction. Having continued in this posture for a considerable time, I turned my eyes to the heaven in the direction of a particular star ; I, however, could not find the star; nor indeed many of the starry train, the greater number having fled, from which circumstance, and from the appearance of the sky, I concluded that morning was nigh. About this time I again began to feel drowsy; I therefore arose, and having prepared for myself a kind of couch in the tent, I flung myself upon it and went to sleep.

I will not say that I was awakened in the morning by the carolling of birds, as I perhaps might if I were writing a novel ; I awoke because, to use vulgar language, I had slept my sleep out, not because the birds were carolling around me in numbers, as they had probably been for hours without my hearing them. I got up and left my tent ; the morning was yet more bright than that of the preceding day. Impelled by curiosity, I walked about, endeavouring to ascertain to what place chance, or rather the pony, had brought me ; following the driftway for some time, amidst bushes and stunted trees, I came to a grove of dark pines, through which it appeared to lead ; I tracked it a few hundred yards, but seeing nothing but trees, and the way being wet and sloughy, owing to the recent rain, I returned on my steps, and, pursuing the path in another direction, came to a sandy road leading over a common, doubtless the one I had traversed the preceding night. My curiosity satisfied, I returned to my little encampment, and on the way beheld a small footpath on the left winding through the bushes, which had before escaped my observation. Having reached my tent and cart, I breakfasted on some of the provisions which I had procured the day before, and then proceeded to take a regular account of the stock formerly possessed by Slingsby the tinker, but now become my own by right of lawful purchase.

Besides the pony, the cart, and the tent, I found I was possessed of a mattress stuffed with straw on which to lie, and a blanket to cover me, the last quite clean and nearly new ; then

there was a frying-pan and a kettle, the first for cooking any food
which required cooking, and the second for heating any water
which I might wish to heat.   I likewise found an earthen teapot
and two or three cups; of the first I should rather say I found
the remains, it being broken in three parts, no doubt since it came
into my possession, which would have precluded the possibility of
my asking anybody to tea for the present, should anybody visit
me, even supposing I had tea and sugar, which was not the case.
I then overhauled what might more strictly be called the stock in
trade; this consisted of various tools, an iron ladle, a chafing pan
and small bellows, sundry pans and kettles, the latter being of tin,
with the exception of one which was of copper, all in a state of
considerable dilapidation—if I may use the term; of these first
Slingsby had spoken in particular, advising me to mend them as
soon as possible, and to endeavour to sell them, in order that I
might have the satisfaction of receiving some return upon the
outlay which I had made.   There was likewise a small quantity
of block tin, sheet tin, and solder.   "This Slingsby," said I, "is
certainly a very honest man, he has sold me more than my
money's worth; I believe, however, there is something more in
the cart."   Thereupon I rumaged the farther end of the cart, and,
amidst a quantity of straw, I found a small anvil and bellows of
that kind which are used in forges, and two hammers such as
smiths use, one great, and the other small.

The sight of these last articles caused me no little surprise,
as no word which had escaped from the mouth of Slingsby had
given me reason to suppose that he had ever followed the occupation of a smith; yet, if he had not, how did he come by them?
I sat down upon the shaft, and pondered the question deliberately
in my mind; at length I concluded that he had come by them
by one of those numerous casualties which occur upon the roads,
of which I, being a young hand upon the roads, must have a very
imperfect conception; honestly, of course—for I scouted the idea
that Slingsby would have stolen this blacksmith's gear—for I had
the highest opinion of his honesty, which opinion I still retain at
the present day, which is upwards of twenty years from the time
of which I am speaking, during the whole of which period I have
neither seen the poor fellow, nor received any intelligence of him.

CHAPTER LXX.

I PASSED the greater part of the day in endeavouring to teach myself the mysteries of my new profession. I cannot say that I was very successful, but the time passed agreeably, and was therefore not ill spent. Towards evening I flung my work aside, took some refreshment, and afterwards a walk.

This time I turned up the small footpath, of which I have already spoken. It led in a zigzag manner through thickets of hazel, elder and sweet briar; after following its windings for somewhat better than a furlong, I heard a gentle sound of water, and presently came to a small rill, which ran directly across the path. I was rejoiced at the sight, for I had already experienced the want of water, which I yet knew must be nigh at hand, as I was in a place to all appearance occasionally frequented by wandering people, who I was aware never take up their quarters in places where water is difficult to be obtained. Forthwith I stretched myself on the ground, and took a long and delicious draught of the crystal stream, and then, seating myself in a bush, I continued for some time gazing on the water as it purled tinkling away in its channel through an opening in the hazels, and should have probably continued much longer had not the thought that I had left my property unprotected compelled me to rise and return to my encampment.

Night came on, and a beautiful night it was; up rose the moon, and innumerable stars decked the firmament of heaven. I sat on the shaft, my eyes turned upwards. I had found it: there it was twinkling millions of miles above me, mightiest star of the system to which we belong: of all stars, the one which has the most interest for me—the star Jupiter.

Why have I always taken an interest in thee, O Jupiter? I know nothing about thee, save what every child knows, that thou art a big star, whose only light is derived from moons. And is not that knowledge enough to make me feel an interest in thee? Ay, truly, I never look at thee without wondering what is going on in thee; what is life in Jupiter? That there is life in Jupiter

who can doubt ?   There is life in our own little star, therefore
there must be life in Jupiter, which is not a little star.   But how
different must life be in Jupiter from what it is in our own little
star !   Life here is life beneath the dear sun—life in Jupiter
is life beneath moons—four moons—no single moon is able to
illumine that vast bulk.   All know what life is in our own little
star ; it is anything but a routine of happiness here, where the
dear sun rises to us every day : then how sad and moping must
life be in mighty Jupiter, on which no sun ever shines, and which
is never lighted save by pale moonbeams !   The thought that
there is more sadness and melancholy in Jupiter than in this
world of ours, where, alas ! there is but too much, has always
made me take a melancholy interest in that huge, distant star.

Two or three days passed by in much the same manner as the
first.   During the morning I worked upon my kettles, and employed the remaining part of the day as I best could.   The whole
of this time I only saw two individuals, rustics, who passed by
my encampment without vouchsafing me a glance ; they probably considered themselves my superiors, as perhaps they were.

One very brilliant morning, as I sat at work in very good
spirits, for by this time I had actually mended in a very creditable
way, as I imagined, two kettles and a frying-pan, I heard a voice
which seemed to proceed from the path leading to the rivulet ;
at first it sounded from a considerable distance, but drew nearer
by degrees.   I soon remarked that the tones were exceedingly
sharp and shrill, with yet something of childhood in them.   Once
or twice I distinguished certain words in the song which the voice
was singing ; the words were—but no, I thought again I was
probably mistaken—and then the voice ceased for a time ; presently I heard it again, close to the entrance of the footpath ; in
another moment I heard it in the lane or glade in which stood
my tent, where it abruptly stopped, but not before I had heard
the very words which I at first thought I had distinguished.

I turned my head ; at the entrance of the footpath, which
might be about thirty yards from the place where I was sitting,
I perceived the figure of a young girl ; her face was turned
towards me, and she appeared to be scanning me and my encampment ; after a little time she looked in the other direction,
only for a moment, however ; probably observing nothing in
that quarter, she again looked towards me, and almost immediately stepped forward ; and, as she advanced, sang the song
which I had heard in the wood, the first words of which were
those which I have already alluded to :—

> The Rommany chi
> And the Rommany chal,
> Shall jaw tasaulor
> To drab the bawlor,
> And dook the gry
> Of the farming rye.

A very pretty song, thought I, falling again hard to work upon my kettle ; a very pretty song, which bodes the farmers much good. Let them look to their cattle.

"All alone here, brother?" said a voice close by me, in sharp but not disagreeable tones.

I made no answer, but continued my work, click, click, with the gravity which became one of my profession. I allowed at least half a minute to elapse before I even lifted up my eyes.

A girl of about thirteen was standing before me ; her features were very pretty, but with a peculiar expression ; her complexion was a clear olive, and her jet black hair hung back upon her shoulders. She was rather scantily dressed, and her arms and feet were bare ; round her neck, however, was a handsome string of corals, with ornaments of gold : in her hand she held a bulrush.

"All alone here, brother?" said the girl, as I looked up ; "all alone here, in the lane ; where are your wife and children?"

"Why do you call me brother?" said I ; "I am no brother of yours. Do you take me for one of your people? I am no gypsy ; not I, indeed!"

"Don't be afraid, brother, you are no Roman—Roman indeed, you are not handsome enough to be a Roman ; not black enough, tinker though you be. If I called you brother, it was because I didn't know what else to call you. Marry, come up, brother, I should be sorry to have you for a brother."

"Then you don't like me?"

"Neither like you, nor dislike you, brother ; what will you have for that kekaubi?"

"What's the use of talking to me in that unchristian way ; what do you mean, young gentlewoman?"

"Lord, brother, what a fool you are ; every tinker knows what a kekaubi is. I was asking you what you would have for that kettle."

"Three-and-sixpence, young gentlewoman ; isn't it well mended?"

"Well mended! I could have done it better myself ; three-and-sixpence! it's only fit to be played at football with."

"I will take no less for it, young gentlewoman ; it has caused me a world of trouble."

"I never saw a worse mended kettle. I say, brother, your hair is white."

" 'Tis nature; your hair is black; nature, nothing but nature."

"I am young, brother; my hair is black—that's nature: you are young, brother; your hair is white—that's not nature."

"I can't help it if it be not, but it is nature after all; did you never see grey hair on the young?"

"Never! I have heard it is true of a grey lad, and a bad one he was. Oh, so bad."

"Sit down on the grass, and tell me all about it, sister; do to oblige me, pretty sister."

"Hey, brother, you don't speak as you did—you don't speak like a gorgio, you speak like one of us, you call me sister."

"As you call me brother; I am not an uncivil person after all, sister."

"I say, brother, tell me one thing, and look me in the face—there—do you speak Rommany?"

"Rommany! Rommany! what is Rommany?"

"What is Rommany? our language, to be sure; tell me, brother, only one thing, you don't speak Rommany?"

"You say it."

"I don't say it, I wish to know. Do you speak Rommany?"

"Do you mean thieves' slang—cant? no, I don't speak cant, I don't like it, I only know a few words; they call a sixpence a tanner, don't they?"

"I don't know," said the girl, sitting down on the ground, "I was almost thinking—well, never mind, you don't know Rommany. I say, brother, I think I should like to have the kekaubi."

"I thought you said it was badly mended?"

"Yes, yes, brother, but ——"

"I thought you said it was only fit to be played at football with?"

"Yes, yes, brother, but ——"

"What will you give for it?"

"Brother, I am the poor person's child, I will give you sixpence for the kekaubi."

"Poor person's child; how came you by that necklace?"

"Be civil, brother; am I to have the kekaubi?"

"Not for sixpence; isn't the kettle nicely mended?"

"I never saw a nicer mended kettle, brother; am I to have the kekaubi, brother?"

"You like me then?"

"I don't dislike you—I dislike no one; there's only one, and him I don't dislike, him I hate."

"Who is he?"

"I scarcely know, I never saw him, but 'tis no affair of yours, you don't speak Rommany; you will let me have the kekaubi, pretty brother?"

"You may have it, but not for sixpence, I'll give it to you."

"Parraco tute, that is, I thank you, brother; the rikkeni kekaubi is now mine. O, rare! I thank you kindly, brother."

Starting up, she flung the bulrush aside which she had hitherto held in her hand, and seizing the kettle, she looked at it for a moment, and then began a kind of dance, flourishing the kettle over her head the while, and singing—

> The Rommany chi
> And the Rommany chal,
> Shall jaw tasaulor
> To drab the bawlor,
> And dook the gry
> Of the farming rye.

"Good-bye, brother, I must be going."

"Good-bye, sister; why do you sing that wicked song?"

"Wicked song, hey, brother! you don't understand the song!"

"Ha, ha! gypsy daughter," said I, starting up and clapping my hands, "I don't understand Rommany, don't I? You shall see; here's the answer to your gillie—

> "The Rommany chi
> And the Rommany chal
> Love Luripen
> And dukkeripen,
> And hokkeripen,
> And every pen
> But Lachipen
> And tatchipen."

The girl, who had given a slight start when I began, remained for some time after I had concluded the song, standing motionless as a statue, with the kettle in her hand. At length she came towards me, and stared me full in the face. "Grey, tall, and talks Rommany," said she to herself. In her countenance there was an expression which I had not seen before—an expression which struck me as being composed of fear, curiosity and the deepest hate. It was momentary, however, and was succeeded by one smiling, frank, and open. "Ha, ha, brother," said she, "well, I like you all the better for talking Rommany; it is a

sweet language, isn't it? especially as you sing it. How did you
pick it up? But you picked it up upon the roads, no doubt?
Ha, it was funny in you to pretend not to know it, and you so
flush with it all the time; it was not kind in you, however, to
frighten the poor person's child so by screaming out, but it was
kind in you to give the rikkeni kekaubi to the child of the poor
person. She will be grateful to you; she will bring you her little
dog to show you, her pretty juggal; the poor person's child will
come and see you again; you are not going away to-day, I hope,
or to-morrow, pretty brother, grey-hair'd brother—you are not
going away to-morrow, I hope?"

"Nor the next day," said I, "only to take a stroll to see if I
can sell a kettle; good-bye, little sister, Rommany sister, dingy
sister."

"Good-bye, tall brother," said the girl, as she departed,
singing:—

The Rommany chi, etc.

"There's something about that girl that I don't understand,"
said I to myself; "something mysterious. However, it is nothing
to me, she knows not who I am, and if she did, what then?"

Late that evening as I sat on the shaft of my cart in deep
meditation, with my arms folded, I thought I heard a rustling in
the bushes over against me. I turned my eyes in that direction,
but saw nothing. "Some bird," said I; "an owl, perhaps;"
and once more I fell into meditation; my mind wandered from
one thing to another—musing now on the structure of the Roman
tongue—now on the rise and fall of the Persian power—and now
on the powers vested in recorders at quarter sessions. I was
thinking what a fine thing it must be to be a recorder of the peace,
when lifting up my eyes, I saw right opposite, not a culprit at the
bar, but, staring at me through a gap in the bush, a face wild and
strange, half-covered with grey hair; I only saw it a moment, the
next it had disappeared.

CHAPTER LXXI.

THE next day at an early hour I harnessed my little pony, and, putting my things in my cart, I went on my projected stroll. Crossing the moor, I arrived in about an hour at a small village, from which, after a short stay, I proceeded to another, and from thence to a third. I found that the name of Slingsby was well known in these parts.

" If you are a friend of Slingsby you must be an honest lad," said an ancient crone; " you shall never want for work whilst I can give it you. Here, take my kettle, the bottom came out this morning, and lend me that of yours till you bring it back. I'm not afraid to trust you—not I. Don't hurry yourself, young man ; if you don't come back for a fortnight I shan't have the worse opinion of you."

I returned to my quarters at evening, tired but rejoiced at heart ; I had work before me for several days, having collected various kekaubies which required mending, in place of those which I left behind—those which I had been employed upon during the last few days. I found all quiet in the lane or glade, and, un-harnessing my little horse, I once more pitched my tent in the old spot beneath the ash, lighted my fire, ate my frugal meal, and then, after looking for some time at the heavenly bodies, and more particularly at the star Jupiter, I entered my tent, lay down upon my pallet, and went to sleep.

Nothing occurred on the following day which requires any particular notice, nor indeed on the one succeeding that. It was about noon on the third day that I sat beneath the shade of the ash tree ; I was not at work, for the weather was particularly hot, and I felt but little inclination to make any exertion. Leaning my back against the tree, I was not long in falling into a slumber. I particularly remember that slumber of mine beneath the ash tree, for it was about the sweetest that I ever enjoyed ; how long I continued in it I do not know ; I could almost have wished that it had lasted to the present time. All of a sudden it appeared to me that a voice cried in my ear, " Danger ! danger ! danger ! "

Nothing seemingly could be more distinct than the words which
I heard; then an uneasy sensation came over me, which I strove
to get rid of, and at last succeeded, for I awoke. The gypsy girl
was standing just opposite to me, with her eyes fixed upon my
countenance; a singular kind of little dog stood beside her.

" Ha ! " said I, " was it you that cried danger? What danger
is there? "

" Danger, brother, there is no danger; what danger should
there be. I called to my little dog, but that was in the wood; my
little dog's name is not danger, but stranger; what danger should
there be, brother? "

"What, indeed, except in sleeping beneath a tree; what is
that you have got in your hand ? "

" Something for you," said the girl, sitting down and proceeding to untie a white napkin; "a pretty manricli, so sweet, so nice;
when I went home to my people I told my grandbebee how kind
you had been to the poor person's child, and when my grandbebee
saw the kekaubi, she said : ' Hir mi devlis, it won't do for the
poor people to be ungrateful; by my God, I will bake a cake for
the young harko mescro '."

" But there are two cakes."

" Yes, brother, two cakes, both for you; my grandbebee
meant them both for you—but list, brother, I will have one of
them for bringing them. I know you will give me one, pretty
brother, grey-haired brother—which shall I have, brother? "

In the napkin were two round cakes, seemingly made of rich
and costly compounds, and precisely similar in form, each weigh-
ing about half a pound.

" Which shall I have, brother? " said the gypsy girl.

" Whichever you please."

" No, brother, no, the cakes are yours, not mine, it is for you
to say."

" Well, then, give me the one nearest you, and take the
other."

" Yes, brother, yes," said the girl; and taking the cakes, she
flung them into the air two or three times, catching them as they
fell, and singing the while. " Pretty brother, grey-haired brother
—here, brother," said she, " here is your cake, this other is
mine."

" Are you sure," said I, taking the cake, " that this is the one
I chose? "

" Quite sure, brother; but if you like you can have mine;
there's no difference; however—shall I eat? "

"Yes, sister, eat."

"See, brother, I do; now, brother, eat, pretty brother, grey-haired brother."

"I am not hungry."

"Not hungry! well, what then—what has being hungry to do with the matter? It is my grandbebee's cake which was sent because you were kind to the poor person's child; eat, brother, eat, and we shall be like the children in the wood that the gorgios speak of."

"The children in the wood had nothing to eat."

"Yes, they had hips and haws; we have better. Eat, brother."

"See, sister, I do," and I ate a piece of the cake.

"Well, brother, how do you like it?" said the girl, looking fixedly at me.

"It is very rich and sweet, and yet there is something strange about it; I don't think I shall eat any more."

"Fie, brother, fie, to find fault with the poor person's cake; see, I have nearly eaten mine."

"That's a pretty little dog."

"Is it not, brother? that's my juggal, my little sister, as I call her."

"Come here, Juggal," said I to the animal.

"What do you want with my juggal?" said the girl.

"Only to give her a piece of cake," said I, offering the dog a piece which I had just broken off.

"What do you mean?" said the girl, snatching the dog away; "my grandbebee's cake is not for dogs."

"Why, I just now saw you give the animal a piece of yours."

"You lie, brother, you saw no such thing; but I see how it is, you wish to affront the poor person's child. I shall go to my house."

"Keep still, and don't be angry; see, I have eaten the piece which I offered the dog. I meant no offence. It is a sweet cake after all."

"Isn't it, brother? I am glad you like it. Offence! brother, no offence at all! I am so glad you like my grandbebee's cake, but she will be wanting me at home. Eat one piece more of grandbebee's cake and I will go."

"I am not hungry, I will put the rest by."

"One piece more before I go, handsome brother, grey-haired brother."

"I will not eat any more, I have already eaten more than I wished to oblige you; if you must go, good-day to you."

The girl rose upon her feet, looked hard at me, then at the remainder of the cake which I held in my hand, and then at me again, and then stood for a moment or two, as if in deep thought ; presently an air of satisfaction came over her countenance, she smiled and said : " Well, brother, well, do as you please ; I merely wished you to eat because you have been so kind to the poor person's child.   She loves you so, that she could have wished to have seen you eat it all ; good-bye, brother, I daresay when I am gone you will eat some more of it, and if you don't I daresay you have eaten enough to—to—show your love for us.   After all, it was a poor person's cake, a Rommany manricli, and all you gorgios are somewhat gorgious.   Farewell, brother, pretty brother, grey-haired brother.   Come, juggal."

I remained under the ash tree seated on the grass for a minute or two, and endeavoured to resume the occupation in which I had been engaged before I fell asleep, but I felt no inclination for labour.   I then thought I would sleep again, and once more reclined against the tree, and slumbered for some little time, but my sleep was more agitated than before.   Something appeared to bear heavy on my breast.   I struggled in my sleep, fell on the grass, and awoke ; my temples were throbbing, there was a burning in my eyes, and my mouth felt parched ; the oppression about the chest which I had felt in my sleep still continued.   " I must shake off these feelings," said I, "and get upon my legs."   I walked rapidly up and down upon the green sward ; at length, feeling my thirst increase, I directed my steps down the narrow path to the spring which ran amidst the bushes ; arriving there, I knelt down and drank of the water, but on lifting up my head I felt thirstier than before ; again I drank, but with like results ; I was about to drink for the third time, when I felt a dreadful qualm which instantly robbed me of nearly all my strength.   What can be the matter with me, thought I ; but I suppose I have made myself ill by drinking cold water.   I got up and made the best of my way back to my tent ; before I reached it the qualm had seized me again, and I was deadly sick.   I flung myself on my pallet ; qualm succeeded qualm, but in the intervals my mouth was dry and burning, and I felt a frantic desire to drink, but no water was at hand, and to reach the spring once more was impossible : the qualms continued, deadly pains shot through my whole frame ; I could bear my agonies no longer, and I fell into a trance or swoon.   How long I continued therein I know not ; on recovering, however, I felt somewhat better, and attempted to lift my head off my couch ; the next moment, however, the qualms and pains returned, if possible, with greater violence than before. I am dying, thought I, like a dog, without any help; and then methought I heard a sound at a distance like people singing, and then once more I relapsed into my swoon.

I revived just as a heavy blow sounded upon the canvas of the tent. I started, but my condition did not permit me to rise; again the same kind of blow sounded upon the canvas; I thought for a moment of crying out and requesting assistance, but an inexplicable something chained my tongue, and now I heard a whisper on the outside of the tent. " He does not move, bebee," said a voice which I knew. " I should not wonder if it has done for him already; however, strike again with your ran; " and then there was another blow, after which another voice cried aloud in a strange tone: " Is the gentleman of the house asleep, or is he taking his dinner? " I remained quite silent and motionless, and in another moment the voice continued: " What, no answer? what can the gentleman of the house be about that he makes no answer? Perhaps the gentleman of the house may be darning his stockings? " Thereupon a face peered into the door of the tent, at the farther extremity of which I was stretched. It was that of a woman, but owing to the posture in which she stood, with her back to the light, and partly owing to a large straw bonnet, I could distinguish but very little of the features of her countenance. I had, however, recognised her voice; it was that of my old acquaintance, Mrs. Herne. " Ho, ho, sir! " said she, " here you are. Come here, Leonora," said she to the gypsy girl, who pressed in at the other side of the door; " here is the gentleman, not asleep, but only stretched out after dinner. Sit down on your ham, child, at the door; I shall do the same. There—you have seen me before, sir, have you not? "

" The gentleman makes no answer, bebee; perhaps he does not know you."

" I have known him of old, Leonora," said Mrs. Herne; " and, to tell you the truth, though I spoke to him just now, I expected no answer."

" It's a way he has, bebee, I suppose? "

" Yes, child, it's a way he has."

" Take off your bonnet, bebee; perhaps he cannot see your face."

" I do not think that will be of much use, child; however, I will take off my bonnet—there—and shake out my hair—there—you have seen this hair before, sir, and this face —— "

" No answer, bebee."

"Though the one was not quite so grey, nor the other so wrinkled."

"How came they so, bebee?"

"All along of this gorgio, child."

"The gentleman in the house, you mean, bebee."

"Yes, child, the gentleman in the house. God grant that I may preserve my temper. Do you know, sir, my name? My name is Herne, which signifies a hairy individual, though neither grey-haired nor wrinkled. It is not the nature of the Hernes to be grey or wrinkled, even when they are old, and I am not old."

"How old are you, bebee?"

"Sixty-five years, child—an inconsiderable number. My mother was a hundred and one—a considerable age—when she died, yet she had not one grey hair, and not more than six wrinkles—an inconsiderable number."

"She had no griefs, bebee?"

"Plenty, child, but not like mine."

"Not quite so hard to bear, bebee?"

"No, child; my head wanders when I think of them. After the death of my husband, who came to his end untimeously, I went to live with a daughter of mine, married out among certain Romans who walk about the eastern counties, and with whom for some time I found a home and pleasant society, for they lived right Romanly, which gave my heart considerable satisfaction, who am a Roman born, and hope to die so. When I say right Romanly, I mean that they kept to themselves, and were not much given to blabbing about their private matters in promiscuous company. Well, things went on in this way for some time, when one day my son-in-law brings home a young gorgio of singular and outrageous ugliness, and without much preamble, says to me and mine, 'This is my pal, a'n't he a beauty? fall down and worship him'. 'Hold,' said I, 'I for one will never consent to such foolishness.'"

"That was right, bebee, I think I should have done the same."

"I think you would, child; but what was the profit of it? The whole party makes an almighty of this gorgio, lets him into their ways, says prayers of his making, till things come to such a pass that my own daughter says to me: 'I shall buy myself a veil and fan, and treat myself to a play and sacrament'. 'Don't,' says I; says she, 'I should like for once in my life to be courtesied to as a Christian gentlewoman'."

"Very foolish of her, bebee."

" Wasn't it, child ? Where was I ? At the fan and sacrament ; with a heavy heart I put seven score miles between us,
came back to the hairy ones, and found them over-given to gorgious
companions ; said I, ' foolish manners is catching, all this comes
of that there gorgio'.   Answers the child Leonora, ' Take comfort,
bebee, I hate the gorgios as much as you do '." ⋅

" And I say so again, bebee, as much or more."

" Time flows on, I engage in many matters, in most miscarry.
Am sent to prison ; says I to myself, I am become foolish.   Am
turned out of prison, and go back to the hairy ones, who receive
me not over courteously; says I, for their unkindness, and my
own foolishness, all the thanks to that gorgio.   Answers to me
the child, ' I wish I could set eyes upon him, bebee'."

" I did so, bebee ; go on."

" How shall I know him, bebee ? " says the child.   ' Young
and grey, tall, and speaks Romanly.'   Runs to me the child, and
says, 'I've found him, bebee'.   ' Where, child ? ' says I.   ' Come
with me, bebee,' says the child.   ' That's he,' says I, as I looked
at my gentleman through the hedge."

" Ha, ha ! bebee, and here he lies, poisoned like a hog."

" You have taken drows, sir," said Mrs. Herne ; " do you
hear, sir ? drows ; tip him a stave, child, of the song of poison."
And thereupon the girl clapped her hands, and sang—

> The Rommany churl
> And the Rommany girl,
> To-morrow shall hie
> To poison the sty,
> And bewitch on the mead
> The farmer's steed.

" Do you hear that, sir ? " said Mrs. Herne ; " the child has
tipped you a stave of the song of poison : that is, she has sung it
Christianly, though perhaps you would like to hear it Romanly ;
you were always fond of what was Roman.   Tip it him Romanly,
child."

" He has heard it Romanly already, bebee ; 'twas by that I
found him out, as I told you."

" Halloo, sir, are you sleeping ? you have taken drows ; the
gentleman makes no answer.   God give me patience ! "

" And what if he doesn't, bebee ; isn't he poisoned like a hog?
Gentleman ! indeed, why call him gentleman? If he ever was one
he's broke, and is now a tinker, a worker of blue metal."

" That's his way, child, to-day a tinker, to-morrow something
else ; and as for being drabbed, I don't know what to say about it."

"Not drabbed! what do you mean, bebee? but look there, bebee; ha, ha, look at the gentleman's motions."

"He is sick, child, sure enough. Ho, ho! sir, you have taken drows; what, another throe! writhe, sir, writhe, the hog died by the drow of gypsies; I saw him stretched at evening. That's yourself, sir. There is no hope, sir, no help, you have taken drow; shall I tell you your fortune, sir, your dukkerin? God bless you, pretty gentleman, much trouble will you have to suffer, and much water to cross; but never mind, pretty gentleman, you shall be fortunate at the end, and those who hate shall take off their hats to you."

"Hey, bebee!" cried the girl; "what is this? what do you mean? you have blessed the gorgio!"

"Blessed him! no, sure; what did I say? Oh, I remember, I'm mad; well, I can't help it, I said what the dukkerin dook told me; woe's me; he'll get up yet."

"Nonsense, bebee! Look at his motions, he's drabbed, spite of dukkerin."

"Don't say so, child; he's sick, 'tis true, but don't laugh at dukkerin, only folks do that that know no better. I, for one, will never laugh at the dukkerin dook. Sick again; I wish he was gone."

"He'll soon be gone, bebee; let's leave him. He's as good as gone; look there, he's dead."

"No, he's not, he'll get up—I feel it; can't we hasten him?"

"Hasten him! yes, to be sure; set the dog upon him. Here, juggal, look in there, my dog."

The dog made its appearance at the door of the tent, and began to bark and tear up the ground.

"At him, juggal, at him; he wished to poison, to drab you. Halloo!"

The dog barked violently, and seemed about to spring at my face, but retreated.

"The dog won't fly at him, child; he flashed at the dog with his eye, and scared him. He'll get up."

"Nonsense, bebee! you make me angry; how should he get up?"

"The dook tells me so, and, what's more, I had a dream. I thought I was at York, standing amidst a crowd to see a man hung, and the crowd shouted, 'There he comes!' and I looked, and lo! it was the tinker; before I could cry with joy I was whisked away, and I found myself in Ely's big church, which was chock full of people to hear the dean preach, and all eyes were turned to the big pulpit; and presently I heard them say, ' There he mounts!' and I looked up to the big pulpit, and, lo! the tinker was in the pulpit, and he raised his arm and began to preach. Anon, I found myself at York again, just as the drop fell, and I looked up, and I saw, not the tinker, but my own self hanging in the air."

"You are going mad, bebee; if you want to hasten him, take your stick and poke him in the eye."

"That will be of no use, child, the dukkerin tells me so; but I will try what I can do. Halloo, tinker! you must introduce yourself into a quiet family, and raise confusion—must you? You must steal its language, and, what was never done before, write it down Christianly—must you? Take that—and that;" and she stabbed violently with her stick towards the end of the tent.

"That's right, bebee, you struck his face; now, once more, and let it be in the eye. Stay, what's that? get up, bebee."

"What's the matter, child?"

"Some one is coming, come away."

"Let me make sure of him, child; he'll be up yet." And thereupon Mrs. Herne, rising, leaned forward into the tent, and supporting herself against the pole, took aim in the direction of the farther end. "I will thrust out his eye," said she; and, lunging with her stick, she would probably have accomplished her purpose had not at that moment the pole of the tent given way, whereupon she fell to the ground, the canvas falling upon her and her intended victim.

"Here's a pretty affair, bebee," screamed the girl.

"He'll get up yet," said Mrs. Herne, from beneath the canvas.

"Get up!—get up yourself; where are you? where is your —— Here, there, bebee, here's the door; there, make haste, they are coming."

"He'll get up yet," said Mrs. Herne, recovering her breath; "the dook tells me so."

"Never mind him or the dook; he is drabbed; come away, or we shall be grabbed—both of us."

"One more blow, I know where his head lies."

"You are mad, bebee; leave the fellow—gorgio avella."

And thereupon the females hurried away.

A vehicle of some kind was evidently drawing nigh; in a little time it came alongside of the place where lay the fallen tent, and stopped suddenly. There was a silence for a moment, and then a parley ensued between two voices, one of which was that of a woman. It was not in English, but in a deep guttural tongue.

"*Peth yw hono sydd yn gorwedd yna ar y ddaear?*" said a masculine voice.

"*Yn wirionedd*—I do not know what it can be," said the female voice, in the same tongue.

"Here is a cart, and there are tools; but what is that on the ground?"

"Something moves beneath it; and what was that—a groan?"

"Shall I get down?"

"Of course, Peter, some one may want your help."

"Then I will get down, though I do not like this place, it is frequented by Egyptians, and I do not like their yellow faces, nor their clibberty clabber, as Master Ellis Wyn says. Now, I am down. It is a tent, Winifred, and see, here is a boy beneath it. Merciful father! what a face!"

A middle-aged man, with a strongly marked and serious countenance, dressed in sober-coloured habiliments, had lifted up the stifling folds of the tent and was bending over me. "Can you speak, my lad?" said he in English, "what is the matter with you? If you could but tell me, I could perhaps help you ——" "What is it that you say? I can't hear you. I will kneel down;" and he flung himself on the ground, and placed his ear close to my mouth. "Now speak if you can. Hey! what! no, sure, God forbid!" then starting up, he cried to a female who sat in the cart, anxiously looking on—*Gwenwyn! Gwenwyn! yw y gwas wedi ei gwenwynaw.* The oil! Winifred, the oil!"

CHAPTER LXXII.

THE oil, which the strangers compelled me to take, produced the desired effect, though, during at least two hours, it was very doubtful whether or not my life would be saved. At the end of that period the man said, that with the blessing of God, he would answer for my life. He then demanded whether I thought I could bear to be removed from the place in which we were? "for I like it not," he continued, "as something within me tells me that it is not good for any of us to be here". I told him, as well as I was able, that I, too, should be glad to leave the place; whereupon, after collecting my things, he harnessed my pony, and, with the assistance of the woman, he contrived to place me in the cart; he then gave me a draught out of a small phial, and we set forward at a slow pace, the man walking by the side of the cart in which I lay. It is probable that the draught consisted of a strong opiate, for after swallowing it I fell into a deep slumber; on my awaking, I found that the shadows of night had enveloped the earth—we were still moving on. Shortly, however, after descending a declivity, we turned into a lane, at the entrance of which was a gate. This lane conducted to a meadow, through the middle of which ran a small brook; it stood between two rising grounds, that on the left, which was on the farther side of the water, was covered with wood, whilst the one on the right, which was not so high, was crowned with the white walls of what appeared to be a farm-house.

Advancing along the meadow, we presently came to a place where grew three immense oaks, almost on the side of the brook, over which they flung their arms, so as to shade it as with a canopy; the ground beneath was bare of grass, and nearly as hard and smooth as the floor of a barn. Having led his own cart on one side of the midmost tree, and my own on the other, the stranger said to me: "This is the spot where my wife and myself generally tarry in the summer season, when we come into these parts. We are about to pass the night here. I suppose you will have no objection to do the same? Indeed, I do not see what

(391)

else you could do under present circumstances." After receiving my answer, in which I, of course, expressed my readiness to assent to his proposal, he proceeded to unharness his horse, and, feeling myself much better, I got down, and began to make the necessary preparations for passing the night beneath the oak.

Whilst thus engaged, I felt myself touched on the shoulder, and, looking round, perceived the woman, whom the stranger called Winifred, standing close to me. The moon was shining brightly upon her, and I observed that she was very good-looking, with a composed, yet cheerful expression of countenance; her dress was plain and primitive, very much resembling that of a Quaker. She held a straw bonnet in her hand. "I am glad to see thee moving about, young man," said she, in a soft, placid tone; "I could scarcely have expected it. Thou must be wondrous strong; many, after what thou hast suffered, would not have stood on their feet for weeks and months. What do I say?— Peter, my husband, who is skilled in medicine, just now told me that not one in five hundred would have survived what thou hast this day undergone; but allow me to ask thee one thing, Hast thou returned thanks to God for thy deliverance?" I made no answer, and the woman, after a pause, said: "Excuse me, young man, but do you know anything of God?" "Very little," I replied, "but I should say He must be a wondrous strong person, if He made all those big bright things up above there, to say nothing of the ground on which we stand, which bears beings like these oaks, each of which is fifty times as strong as myself, and will live twenty times as long." The woman was silent for some moments, and then said: "I scarcely know in what spirit thy words are uttered. If thou art serious, however, I would caution thee against supposing that the power of God is more manifested in these trees, or even in those bright stars above us, than in thyself—they are things of time, but thou art a being destined to an eternity; it depends upon thyself whether thy eternity shall be one of joy or sorrow."

Here she was interrupted by the man, who exclaimed from the other side of the tree: "Winifred, it is getting late, you had better go up to the house on the hill to inform our friends of our arrival, or they will have retired for the night". "True," said Winifred, and forthwith wended her way to the house in question, returning shortly with another woman, whom the man, speaking in the same language which I had heard him first use, greeted by the name of Mary; the woman replied in the same tongue, but almost immediately said, in English: "We hoped to have heard you speak to night, Peter, but we cannot expect that now, seeing that it is so late, owing to your having been detained by the way, as Winifred tells me; nothing remains for you to do now but to sup—to-morrow, with God's will, we shall hear you". "And to-night, also, with God's will, provided you be so disposed. Let those of your family come hither." "They will be hither presently," said Mary, "for knowing that thou art arrived, they will, of course, come and bid thee welcome." And scarcely had she spoke, when I beheld a party of people descending the moon-lit side of the hill. They soon arrived at the place where we were; they might amount in all to twelve individuals. The principal person was a tall, athletic man, of about forty, dressed like a plain country farmer; this was, I soon found, the husband of Mary; the rest of the group consisted of the children of these two, and their domestic servants. One after another they all shook Peter by the hand, men and women, boys and girls, and expressed their joy at seeing him. After which, he said: "Now, friends, if you please, I will speak a few words to you". A stool was then brought him from the cart, which he stepped on, and the people arranging themselves round him, some standing, some seated on the ground, he forthwith began to address them in a clear, distinct voice; and the subject of his discourse was the necessity, in all human beings, of a change of heart.

The preacher was better than his promise, for, instead of speaking a few words, he preached for at least three-quarters of an hour; none of the audience, however, showed the slightest symptom of weariness; on the contrary, the hope of each individual appeared to hang upon the words which proceeded from his mouth. At the conclusion of the sermon or discourse, the whole assembly again shook Peter by the hand, and returned to their house, the mistress of the family saying, as she departed: "I shall soon be back, Peter, I go but to make arrangements for the supper of thyself and company"; and, in effect, she presently returned, attended by a young woman, who bore a tray in her hands. "Set it down, Jessy," said the mistress to the girl, "and then betake thyself to thy rest; I shall remain here for a little time to talk with my friends." The girl departed, and the preacher and the two females placed themselves on the ground about the tray. The man gave thanks, and himself and his wife appeared to be about to eat, when the latter suddenly placed her hand upon his arm, and said something to him in a low voice, whereupon he exclaimed, "Ay, truly, we were both forgetful"; and then getting up, he came towards me, who stood a little way off, leaning against the wheel of my cart; and, taking me by the hand, he said: "Pardon us, young man, we were both so engaged in our own creature-comforts that we forgot thee, but it is not too late to repair our fault; wilt thou not join us, and taste our bread and milk?" "I cannot eat," I replied, "but I think I could drink a little milk;" whereupon he led me to the rest, and seating me by his side, he poured some milk into a horn cup, saying: "'*Croesaw*'. That," added he with a smile, "is Welsh for welcome."

The fare upon the tray was of the simplest description, consisting of bread, cheese, milk and curds. My two friends partook with a good appetite. "Mary," said the preacher, addressing himself to the woman of the house, "every time I come to visit thee, I find thee less inclined to speak Welsh. I suppose, in a little time, thou wilt entirely have forgotten it; hast thou taught it to any of thy children?" "The two eldest understand a few words," said the woman, "but my husband does not wish them to learn it; he says sometimes, jocularly, that though it pleased him to marry a Welsh wife, it does not please him to have Welsh children. 'Who,' I have heard him say, 'would be a Welshman, if he could be an Englishman?'" "I for one," said the preacher, somewhat hastily; "not to be king of all England would I give up my birthright as a Welshman. Your husband is an excellent person, Mary, but I am afraid he is somewhat prejudiced." "You do him justice, Peter, in saying that he is an excellent person," said the woman; "as to being prejudiced, I scarcely know what to say, but he thinks that two languages in the same kingdom are almost as bad as two kings." "That's no bad observation," said the preacher, "and it is generally the case; yet, thank God, the Welsh and English go on very well, side by side, and I hope will do so till the Almighty calls all men to their long account." "They jog on very well now," said the woman; "but I have heard my husband say that it was not always so, and that the Welsh, in old times, were a violent and ferocious people, for that once they hanged the mayor of Chester." "Ha, ha!" said the preacher, and his eyes flashed in the moonlight; "he told you that, did he?" "Yes," said Mary; "once, when the mayor of Chester, with some of his people, was present at one of the fairs over the border, a quarrel arose between the Welsh and English, and the Welsh beat the English and hanged the mayor." "Your husband is a clever man," said Peter, "and knows a great deal; did he tell you the name of the leader of the Welsh? No? then I will: the leader of the Welsh on that occasion was —— He

was a powerful chieftain, and there was an old feud between him
and the men of Chester.   Afterwards, when two hundred of the
men of Chester invaded his country to take revenge for their
mayor, he enticed them into a tower, set fire to it, and burnt
them all.   That —— was a very fine, noble—God forgive me,
what was I about to say !—a very bad, violent man ; but, Mary,
this is very carnal and unprofitable conversation, and in holding
it we set a very bad example to the young man here—let us
change the subject."

They then began to talk on religious matters.   At length
Mary departed to her abode, and the preacher and his wife
retired to their tilted cart.

" Poor fellow, he seems to be almost brutally ignorant," said
Peter, addressing his wife in their native language, after they had
bidden me farewell for the night.

" I am afraid he is," said Winifred ; "yet my heart warms to
the poor lad, he seems so forlorn."

CHAPTER LXXIII.

I SLEPT soundly during that night, partly owing to the influence of the opiate. Early in the morning I was awakened by the voices of Peter and his wife, who were singing a morning hymn in their own language. Both subsequently prayed long and fervently. I lay still till their devotions were completed, and then left my tent. "Good-morning," said Peter, "how dost thou feel?" "Much better," said I, "than I could have expected." "I am glad of it," said Peter. "Art thou hungry? yonder comes our breakfast," pointing to the same young woman I had seen the preceding night, who was again descending the hill, bearing the tray upon her head.

"What dost thou intend to do, young man, this day?" said Peter, when we had about half finished breakfast. "Do," said I, "as I do other days, what I can." "And dost thou pass this day as thou dost other days?" said Peter. "Why not?" said I; "what is there in this day different from the rest? it seems to be of the same colour as yesterday." "Art thou aware," said the wife interposing, "what day it is? that it is Sabbath? that it is Sunday?" "No," said I, "I did not know that it was Sunday." "And how did that happen?" said Winifred with a sigh. "To tell you the truth," said I, "I live very much alone, and pay very little heed to the passing of time." "And yet of what infinite importance is time," said Winifred. "Art thou not aware that every year brings thee nearer to thy end?" "I do not think," said I, "that I am so near my end as I was yesterday." "Yes thou art," said the woman; "thou wast not doomed to die yesterday; an invisible hand was watching over thee yesterday; but thy day will come, therefore improve the time; be grateful that thou wast saved yesterday; and, oh! reflect on one thing; if thou hadst died yesterday, where wouldst thou have been now?" "Cast into the earth, perhaps," said I. "I have heard Mr. Petulengro say that to be cast into the earth is the natural end of man." "Who is Mr. Petulengro?" said Peter, interrupting his wife, as she was about to speak. "Master of the horse-shoe," said I, "and, according to his own account, king of Egypt." "I understand," said Peter, "head of some family of wandering Egyptians—they are a race utterly godless. Art thou of them?—but no, thou art not, thou hast not their yellow blood. I suppose thou belongest to the family of wandering artisans called —— I do not like you the worse for belonging to them. A mighty speaker of old sprang up from amidst that family." "Who was he?" said I. "John Bunyan," replied Peter, reverently, "and the mention of his name reminds me that I have to preach this day; wilt thou go and hear? the distance is not great, only half a mile." "No," said I, "I will not go and hear." "Wherefore?" said Peter. "I belong to the church," said I, "and not to the congregations." "Oh! the pride of that church," said Peter, addressing his wife in their own tongue, "exemplified even in the lowest and most ignorant of its members." "Then thou, doubtless, meanest to go to church," said Peter, again addressing me; "there is a church on the other side of that wooded hill." "No," said I, "I do not mean to go to church." "May I ask thee wherefore?" said Peter. "Because," said I, "I prefer remaining beneath the shade of these trees, listening to the sound of the leaves, and the tinkling of the waters."

"Then thou intendest to remain here?" said Peter, looking fixedly at me. "If I do not intrude," said I; "but if I do, I will wander away; I wish to be beholden to nobody—perhaps you wish me to go?" "On the contrary," said Peter, "I wish you to stay. I begin to see something in thee which has much interest for me; but we must now bid thee farewell for the rest of the day, the time is drawing nigh for us to repair to the place of preaching; before we leave thee alone, however, I should wish to ask thee a question: Didst thou seek thy own destruction yesterday, and didst thou wilfully take that poison?" "No," said I; "had I known there had been poison in the cake, I certainly should not have taken it." "And who gave it thee?" said Peter. "An enemy of mine," I replied. "Who is thy enemy?" "An Egyptian sorceress and poisonmonger." "Thy enemy is a female. I fear thou hadst given her cause to hate thee—of what did she complain?" "That I had stolen the tongue out of her head." "I do not understand thee—is she young?" "About sixty-five."

Here Winifred interposed. "Thou didst call her just now by hard names, young man," said she; "I trust thou dost bear no malice against her." "No," said I, "I bear no malice against her." "Thou art not wishing to deliver her into the hand of what is called justice?" "By no means," said I; "I have lived long enough upon the roads not to cry out for the constable when my finger is broken. I consider this poisoning as an accident of the roads; one of those to which those who travel are occasionally subject." "In short, thou forgivest thine adversary?" "Both now and for ever," said I. "Truly," said Winifred, "the spirit which the young man displayeth pleases me much: I should be loth that he left us yet. I have no doubt that, with the blessing of God, and a little of thy exhortation, he will turn out a true Christian before he leaveth us." "My exhortation!" said Peter, and a dark shade passed over his countenance; "thou forgettest what I am—I—I—but I am forgetting myself; the Lord's will be done; and now put away the things, for I perceive that our friends are coming to attend us to the place of meeting."

Again the family which I had seen the night before descended the hill from their abode. They were now dressed in their Sunday's best. The master of the house led the way. They presently joined us, when a quiet, sober greeting ensued on each side. After a little time Peter shook me by the hand and bade me farewell till the evening; Winifred did the same, adding, that she hoped I should be visited by sweet and holy thoughts. The whole party then moved off in the direction by which we had come the preceding night, Peter and the master leading the way, followed by Winifred and the mistress of the family. As I gazed on their departing forms, I felt almost inclined to follow them to their place of worship. I did not stir, however, but remained leaning against my oak with my hands behind me.

And after a time I sat me down at the foot of the oak with my face turned towards the water, and, folding my hands, I fell into deep meditation. I thought on the early Sabbaths of my life, and the manner in which I was wont to pass them. How carefully I said my prayers when I got up on the Sabbath morn, and how carefully I combed my hair and brushed my clothes in order that I might do credit to the Sabbath day. I thought of the old church at pretty D——, the dignified rector, and yet more dignified clerk. I thought of England's grand Liturgy, and Tate and Brady's sonorous minstrelsy. I thought of the Holy Book, portions of which I was in the habit of reading between service. I thought, too, of the evening walk which I sometimes took in fine weather like the present, with my mother and brother —a quiet, sober walk, during which I would not break into a run, even to chase a butterfly, or yet more a honey-bee, being fully convinced of the dread importance of the day which God had hallowed. And how glad I was when I had got over the Sabbath day without having done anything to profane it. And how soundly I slept on the Sabbath night after the toil of being very good throughout the day.

And when I had mused on those times a long while, I sighed and said to myself, I am much altered since then; am I altered for the better? And then I looked at my hands and my apparel, and sighed again. I was not wont of yore to appear thus on the Sabbath day.

For a long time I continued in a state of deep meditation, till at last I lifted up my eyes to the sun, which, as usual during that glorious summer, was shining in unclouded majesty; and then I lowered them to the sparkling water, in which hundreds of the finny brood were disporting themselves, and then I thought what a fine thing it was to be a fish on such a fine summer day, and I wished myself a fish, or at least amongst the fishes; and then I looked at my hands again, and then, bending over the water, I looked at my face in the crystal mirror, and started when I saw it, for it looked squalid and miserable.

Forthwith I started up, and said to myself, I should like to bathe and cleanse myself from the squalor produced by my late hard life and by Mrs. Herne's drow. I wonder if there is any harm in bathing on the Sabbath day. I will ask Winifred when she comes home; in the meantime I will bathe, provided I can find a fitting place.

But the brook, though a very delightful place for fish to disport in, was shallow, and by no means adapted for the recreation of so large a being as myself; it was, moreover, exposed, though I saw nobody at hand, nor heard a single human voice or sound. Following the winding of the brook I left the meadow, and, passing through two or three thickets, came to a place where between lofty banks the water ran deep and dark, and there I bathed, imbibing new tone and vigour into my languid and exhausted frame.

Having put on my clothes, I returned by the way I had come to my vehicle beneath the oak tree. From thence, for want of something better to do, I strolled up the hill, on the top of which stood the farm-house; it was a large and commodious building built principally of stone, and seeming of some antiquity, with a porch, on either side of which was an oaken bench. On the right was seated a young woman with a book in her hand, the same who had brought the tray to my friends and myself.

"Good-day," said I, "pretty damsel, sitting in the farm porch."

"Good-day," said the girl, looking at me for a moment, and then fixing her eyes on her book.

"That's a nice book you are reading," said I.

The girl looked at me with surprise. "How do you know what book it is?" said she.

"How do I know—never mind; but a nice book it is—no love, no fortune-telling in it."

The girl looked at me half offended. "Fortune-telling!" said she, "I should think not. But you know nothing about it;" and she bent her head once more over the book.

"I tell you what, young person," said I, "I know all about that book; what will you wager that I do not?"

"I never wager," said the girl.

"Shall I tell you the name of it," said I, "O daughter of the dairy?"

The girl half started. "I should never have thought," said she, half timidly, "that you could have guessed it."

"I did not guess it," said I, "I knew it; and meet and proper it is that you should read it."

"Why so?" said the girl.

"Can the daughter of the dairy read a more fitting book than the *Dairyman's Daughter?*"

"Where do you come from?" said the girl.

"Out of the water," said I. "Don't start, I have been bathing; are you fond of the water?"

"No," said the girl, heaving a sigh; "I am not fond of the water, that is, of the sea;" and here she sighed again.

"The sea is a wide gulf," said I, "and frequently separates hearts."

The girl sobbed.

"Why are you alone here?" said I.

"I take my turn with the rest," said the girl, "to keep at home on Sunday."

"And you are ——" said I.

"The master's niece!" said the girl. "How came you to know it? But why did you not go with the rest and with your friends?"

"Who are those you call my friends?" said I.

"Peter and his wife."

"And who are they?" said I.

"Do you not know?" said the girl; "you came with them."

" 'They found me ill by the way," said I ; " and they relieved me : I know nothing about them."

" I thought you knew everything," said the girl.

" There are two or three things which I do not know, and this is one of them.   Who are they ? "

" Did you never hear of the great Welsh preacher, Peter Williams ? "

" Never," said I.

" Well," said the girl, " this is he, and Winifred is his wife, and a nice person she is.   Some people say, indeed, that she is as good a preacher as her husband, though of that matter I can say nothing, having never heard her preach.   So these two wander over all Wales and the greater part of England, comforting the hearts of the people with their doctrine, and doing all the good they can.   They frequently come here, for the mistress is a Welsh woman, and an old friend of both, and then they take up their abode in the cart beneath the old oaks down there by the stream."

" And what is their reason for doing so ? " said I ; " would it not be more comfortable to sleep beneath a roof ? "

" I know not their reasons," said the girl, " but so it is ; they never sleep beneath a roof unless the weather is very severe.   I once heard the mistress say that Peter had something heavy upon his mind ; perhaps that is the cause.   If he is unhappy, all I can say is, that I wish him otherwise, for he is a good man and a kind ——"

" Thank you," said I, " I will now depart."

" Hem ! " said the girl, " I was wishing —— "

" What ? to ask me a question ? "

" Not exactly ; but you seem to know everything ; you mentioned, I think, fortune-telling."

" Do you wish me to tell your fortune ? "

" By no means ; but I have a friend at a distance at sea, and I should wish to know —— "

" When he will come back ?   I have told you already there are two or three things which I do not know—this is another of them.   However, I should not be surprised if he were to come back some of these days ; I would, if I were in his place.   In the meantime be patient, attend to the dairy, and read the *Dairyman's Daughter* when you have nothing better to do."

It was late in the evening when the party of the morning returned.   The farmer and his family repaired at once to their abode, and my two friends joined me beneath the tree.   Peter sat down at the foot of the oak, and said nothing.   Supper was brought by a servant, not the damsel of the porch.   We sat round the tray, Peter said grace, but scarcely anything else ; he appeared sad and dejected, his wife looked anxiously upon him.   I was as silent as my friends ; after a little time we retired to our separate places of rest.

About midnight I was awakened by a noise ; I started up and listened ; it appeared to me that I heard voices and groans.   In a moment I had issued from my tent—all was silent—but the next moment I again heard groans and voices ; they proceeded from the tilted cart where Peter and his wife lay ; I drew near, again there was a pause, and then I heard the voice of Peter, in an accent of extreme anguish, exclaim : " *Pechod Ysprydd Glan—O pechod Ysprydd Glan !*" and then he uttered a deep groan. Anon, I heard the voice of Winifred, and never shall I forget the sweetness and gentleness of the tones of her voice in the stillness of that night.   I did not understand all she said—she spoke in her native language, and I was some way apart ; she appeared to endeavour to console her husband, but he seemed to refuse all comfort, and, with many groans, repeated—"*Pechod Ysprydd Glan—O pechod Ysprydd Glan !*"   I felt I had no right to pry into their afflictions, and retired.

Now, "*pechod Ysprydd Glan,*" interpreted, is the sin against the Holy Ghost.

CHAPTER LXXIV.

PETER and his wife did not proceed on any expedition during the following day. The former strolled gloomily about the fields, and the latter passed many hours in the farm-house. Towards evening, without saying a word to either, I departed with my vehicle, and finding my way to a small town at some distance, I laid in a store of various articles, with which I returned. It was night, and my two friends were seated beneath the oak ; they had just completed their frugal supper. "We waited for thee some time," said Winifred, " but finding that thou didst not come, we began without thee ; but sit down, I pray thee, there is still enough for thee." "I will sit down," said I, "but I require no supper, for I have eaten where I have been." Nothing more particular occurred at the time. Next morning the kind pair invited me to share their breakfast. "I will not share your breakfast," said I. "Wherefore not?" said Winifred anxiously. "Because," said I, "it is not proper that I be beholden to you for meat and drink." "But we are beholden to other people," said Winifred. "Yes," said I, "but you preach to them, and give them ghostly advice, which considerably alters the matter ; not that I would receive anything from them, if I preached to them six times a day." "Thou art not fond of receiving favours, then, young man," said Winifred. "I am not," said I. "And of conferring favours?" "Nothing affords me greater pleasure," said I, "than to confer favours." "What a disposition!" said Winifred, holding up her hands ; "and this is pride, genuine pride—that feeling which the world agrees to call so noble. Oh, how mean a thing is pride! never before did I see all the meanness of what is called pride!"

"But how wilt thou live, friend?" said Peter ; "dost thou not intend to eat?" "When I went out last night," said I, "I laid in a provision." "Thou hast laid in a provision!" said Peter, " pray let us see it. Really, friend," said he, after I had produced it, " thou must drive a thriving trade ; here are provisions enough to last three people for several days. Here are butter and eggs, here is tea, here is sugar, and there is a flitch. I hope thou wilt

(403)

let us partake of some of thy fare." "I should be very happy
if you would," said I. "Doubt not but we shall," said Peter;
"Winifred shall have some of thy flitch cooked for dinner. In
the meantime, sit down, young man, and breakfast at our expense
—we will dine at thine."

On the evening of that day, Peter and myself sat alone beneath
the oak. We fell into conversation ; Peter was at first melancholy,
but he soon became more cheerful, fluent and entertaining. I
spoke but little, but I observed that sometimes what I said
surprised the good Methodist. We had been silent some time.
At length, lifting up my eyes to the broad and leafy canopy of the
trees, I said, having nothing better to remark, "What a noble
tree ! I wonder if the fairies ever dance beneath it ? "

"Fairies !" said Peter, "fairies ! how came you, young man,
to know anything about the fair family ? "

"I am an Englishman," said I, "and of course know
something about fairies ; England was once a famous place for
them."

"Was once, I grant you," said Peter, "but is so no longer.
I have travelled for years about England, and never heard them
mentioned before; the belief in them has died away, and even
their name seems to be forgotten. If you had said you were a
Welshman, I should not have been surprised. The Welsh have
much to say of the *Tylwyth Teg*, or fair family, and many believe
in them."

"And do you believe in them ? " said I.

"I scarcely know what to say. Wise and good men have
been of opinion that they are nothing but devils, who, under the
form of pretty and amiable spirits, would fain allure poor human
beings ; I see nothing irrational in the supposition."

" Do you believe in devils, then ? "

" Do I believe in devils, young man !" said Peter, and his
frame was shaken as if by convulsions. "If I do not believe in
devils, why am I here at the present moment ? "

" You know best," said I ; " but I don't believe that fairies are
devils, and I don't wish to hear them insulted. What learned
men have said they are devils ? "

" Many have said it, young man, and, amongst others, Master
Ellis Wyn, in that wonderful book of his, the *Bardd Cwsg*."

"The *Bardd Cwsg*," said I ; "what kind of book is that ? I
have never heard of that book before."

"Heard of it before ; I suppose not; how should you have
heard of it before ! By-the-bye, can you read ? "

"Very tolerably," said I ; "so there are fairies in this book. What do you call it—the *Bardd Cwsg* ? "

"Yes, the *Bardd Cwsg*. You pronounce Welsh very fairly; have you ever been in Wales? "

"Never," said I.

"Not been in Wales; then, of course, you don't understand Welsh; but we were talking of the *Bardd Cwsg*—yes, there are fairies in the *Bardd Cwsg*—the author of it, Master Ellis Wyn, was carried away in his sleep by them over mountains and valleys, rivers and great waters, incurring mighty perils at their hands, till he was rescued from them by an angel of the Most High, who subsequently showed him many wonderful things."

"I beg your pardon," said I, "but what were those wonderful things? "

"I see, young man," said Peter, smiling, "that you are not without curiosity; but I can easily pardon anyone for being curious about the wonders contained in the book of Master Ellis Wyn. The angel showed him the course of this world, its pomps and vanities, its cruelty and its pride, its crimes and deceits. On another occasion, the angel showed him Death in his nether palace, surrounded by his grisly ministers, and by those who are continually falling victims to his power. And, on a third occasion, the state of the condemned in their place of everlasting torment."

"But this was all in his sleep," said I, "was it not? "

"Yes," said Peter, "in his sleep; and on that account the book is called *Gweledigaethau y Bardd Cwsg*, or, Visions of the Sleeping Bard."

"I do not care for wonders which occur in sleep," said I. "I prefer real ones; and perhaps, notwithstanding what he says, the man had no visions at all—they are probably of his own invention."

"They are substantially true, young man," said Peter; "like the dreams of Bunyan, they are founded on three tremendous facts, Sin, Death, and Hell; and like his they have done incalculable good, at least in my own country, in the language in which they are written. Many a guilty conscience has the *Bardd Cwsg* aroused with its dreadful sights, its strong sighs, its puffs of smoke from the pit, and its showers of sparks from the mouth of the yet lower gulf of [the deep] Unknown. Were it not for the *Bardd Cwsg* perhaps I might not be here."

"I would sooner hear your own tale," said I, "than all the visions of the *Bardd Cwsg*."

Peter shook, bent his form nearly double, and covered his face with his hands. I sat still and motionless, with my eyes fixed upon him. Presently Winifred descended the hill, and joined us. "What is the matter?" said she, looking at her husband, who still remained in the posture I have described. He made no answer; whereupon, laying her hand gently on his shoulder, she said, in the peculiar soft and tender tone which I had heard her use on a former occasion, "Take comfort, Peter; what has happened now to afflict thee?" Peter removed his hands from his face. "The old pain, the old pain," said he; "I was talking with this young man, and he would fain know what brought me here, he would fain hear my tale, Winifred—my sin: *O pechod Ysprydd Glan! O pechod Ysprydd Glan!*" and the poor man fell into a more fearful agony than before. Tears trickled down Winifred's face; I saw them trickling by the moonlight, as she gazed upon the writhing form of her afflicted husband. I arose from my seat; "I am the cause of all this," said I, "by my folly and imprudence, and it is thus I have returned your kindness and hospitality; I will depart from you and wander my way." I was retiring, but Peter sprang up and detained me. "Go not," said he, "you were not in fault; if there be any fault in the case, it was mine; if I suffer, I am but paying the penalty of my own iniquity;" he then paused, and appeared to be considering: at length he said, "Many things which thou hast seen and heard connected with me require explanation; thou wishest to know my tale, I will tell it thee, but not now, not to-night; I am too much shaken".

Two evenings later, when we were again seated beneath the oak, Peter took the hand of his wife in his own, and then, in tones broken and almost inarticulate, commenced telling me his tale—the tale of the *Pechod Ysprydd Glan.*

CHAPTER LXXV.

"I was born in the heart of North Wales, the son of a respectable farmer, and am the youngest of seven brothers.

"My father was a member of the Church of England, and was what is generally called a serious man. He went to church regularly, and read the Bible every Sunday evening; in his moments of leisure he was fond of holding religious discourse both with his family and his neighbours.

"One autumn afternoon, on a week day, my father sat with one of his neighbours taking a cup of ale by the oak table in our stone kitchen. I sat near them, and listened to their discourse. I was at that time seven years of age. They were talking of religious matters. 'It is a hard matter to get to heaven,' said my father. 'Exceedingly so,' said the other. 'However, I don't despond, none need despair of getting to heaven, save those who have committed the sin against the Holy Ghost.'

"'Ah!' said my father, 'thank God I never committed that —how awful must be the state of a person who has committed the sin against the Holy Ghost! I can scarcely think of it without my hair standing on end;' and then my father and his friend began talking of the nature of the sin against the Holy Ghost, and I heard them say what it was, as I sat with greedy ears listening to their discourse.

"I lay awake the greater part of the night musing upon what I had heard. I kept wondering to myself what must be the state of a person who had committed the sin against the Holy Ghost, and how he must feel. Once or twice I felt a strong inclination to commit it—a strange kind of fear, however, prevented me; at last I determined not to commit it, and having said my prayers, I fell asleep.

"When I awoke in the morning the first thing I thought of was the mysterious sin, and a voice within me seemed to say, 'Commit it'; and I felt a strong temptation to do so, even stronger than in the night. I was just about to yield, when the same dread, of which I have already spoken, came over me, and,

(407)

springing out of bed, I went down on my knees. I slept in a small room alone, to which I ascended by a wooden stair, open to the sky. I have often thought since that it is not a good thing for children to sleep alone.

"After breakfast I went to school, and endeavoured to employ myself upon my tasks, but all in vain; I could think of nothing but the sin against the Holy Ghost; my eyes, instead of being fixed upon my book, wandered in vacancy. My master observed my inattention, and chid me. The time came for saying my task, and I had not acquired it. My master reproached me, and, yet more, he beat me; I felt shame and anger, and I went home with a full determination to commit the sin against the Holy Ghost.

" But when I got home my father ordered me to do something connected with the farm, so that I was compelled to exert myself; I was occupied till night, and was so busy that I almost forgot the sin and my late resolution. My work completed, I took my supper, and went to my room; I began my prayers, and, when they were ended, I thought of the sin, but the temptation was slight; I felt very tired, and was presently asleep.

" Thus, you see, I had plenty of time allotted me by a gracious and kind God to reflect on what I was about to do. He did not permit the enemy of souls to take me by surprise, and to hurry me at once into the commission of· that which was to be my ruin here and hereafter. Whatever I did was of my own free will, after I had had time to reflect. Thus God is justified; He had no hand in my destruction, but, on the contrary, He did all that was compatible with justice to prevent it. I hasten to the fatal moment. Awaking in the night, I determined that nothing should prevent my committing the sin. Arising from my bed, I went out upon the wooden gallery, and having stood for a few moments looking at the stars, with which the heavens were thickly strewn, I laid myself down, and supporting my face with my hand, I murmured out words of horror— words not to be repeated—and in this manner I committed the sin against the Holy Ghost.

" When the words were uttered I sat up upon the topmost step of the gallery; for some time I felt stunned in somewhat the same manner as I once subsequently felt after being stung by an adder. I soon arose, however, and retired to my bed, where, notwithstanding what I had done, I was not slow in falling asleep.

" I awoke several times during the night, each time with the dim idea that something strange and monstrous had occurred, but presently I fell asleep again ; in the morning I awoke with the same vague feeling, but presently recollection returned, and I remembered that I had committed the sin against the Holy Ghost. I lay musing for some time on what I had done, and I felt rather stunned, as before ; at last I arose and got out of bed, dressed myself, and then went down on my knees, and was about to pray from the force of mechanical habit ; before I said a word, however, I recollected myself, and got up again. What was the use of praying ? I thought ; I had committed the sin against the Holy Ghost.

" I went to school, but sat stupefied. I was again chidden, again beaten by my master. I felt no anger this time, and scarcely heeded the strokes. I looked, however, at my master's face, and thought to myself, you are beating me for being idle, as you suppose ; poor man, what would you do if you knew I had committed the sin against the Holy Ghost ?

" Days and weeks passed by. I had once been cheerful, and fond of the society of children of my own age ; but I was now reserved and gloomy. It seemed to me that a gulf separated me from all my fellow-creatures. I used to look at my brothers and schoolfellows, and think how different I was from them ; they had not done what I had. I seemed, in my own eyes, a lone, monstrous being, and yet, strange to say, I felt a kind of pride in being so. I was unhappy, but I frequently thought to myself, I have done what no one else would dare to do ; there was something grand in the idea ; I had yet to learn the horror of my condition.

" Time passed on, and I began to think less of what I had done ; I began once more to take pleasure in my childish sports ; I was active, and excelled at football and the like all the lads of my age. I likewise began, what I had never done before, to take pleasure in the exercises of the school. I made great progress in Welsh and English grammar, and learnt to construe Latin. My master no longer chid or beat me, but one day told my father that he had no doubt that one day I should be an honour to Wales.

" Shortly after this my father fell sick ; the progress of the disorder was rapid ; feeling his end approaching, he called his children before him. After tenderly embracing us, he said : 'God bless you, my children ; I am going from you, but take comfort, I trust that we shall all meet again in heaven '.

" As he uttered these last words, horror took entire possession

of me.   Meet my father in heaven—how could I ever hope to
meet him there?   I looked wildly at my brethren and at my
mother; they were all bathed in tears, but how I envied them!
They might hope to meet my father in heaven, but how different
were they from me—they had never committed the unpardonable
sin.

"In a few days my father died; he left his family in comfortable circumstances, at least such as would be considered so in
Wales, where the wants of the people are few.   My elder brother
carried on the farm for the benefit of my mother and us all.   In
course of time my brothers were put out to various trades.   I
still remained at school, but without being a source of expense to
my relations, as I was by this time able to assist my master in
the business of the school.

"I was diligent both in self-improvement and in the instruction
of others; nevertheless, a horrible weight pressed upon my breast;
I knew I was a lost being; that for me there was no hope; that,
though all others might be saved, I must of necessity be lost: I
had committed the unpardonable sin, for which I was doomed to
eternal punishment, in the flaming gulf, as soon as life was over!—
and how long could I hope to live? perhaps fifty years, at the
end of which I must go to my place; and then I would count
the months and the days, nay, even the hours which yet intervened between me and my doom.   Sometimes I would comfort
myself with the idea that a long time would elapse before my
time would be out; but then again I thought that, however long
the term might be, it must be out at last; and then I would fall
into an agony, during which I would almost wish that the term
were out, and that I were in my place; the horrors of which I
thought could scarcely be worse than what I then endured.

"There was one thought about this time which caused me
unutterable grief and shame, perhaps more shame than grief.   It
was that my father, who was gone to heaven, and was there daily
holding communion with his God, was by this time aware of my
crime.   I imagined him looking down from the clouds upon his
wretched son, with a countenance of inexpressible horror.   When
this idea was upon me, I would often rush to some secret place
to hide myself—to some thicket, where I would cast myself on the
ground, and thrust my head into a thick bush, in order to escape
from the horror-struck glance of my father above in the clouds;
and there I would continue groaning till the agony had, in some
degree, passed away.

"The wretchedness of my state increasing daily, it at last

became apparent to the master of the school, who questioned me earnestly and affectionately. I, however, gave him no satisfactory answer, being apprehensive that, if I unbosomed myself, I should become as much an object of horror to him as I had long been to myself. At length he suspected that I was unsettled in my intellects; and, fearing probably the ill effect of my presence upon his scholars, he advised me to go home—which I was glad to do, as I felt myself every day becoming less qualified for the duties of the office which I had undertaken.

"So I returned home to my mother and my brother, who received me with the greatest kindness and affection. I now determined to devote myself to husbandry, and assist my brother in the business of the farm. I was still, however, very much distressed. One fine morning, however, as I was at work in the field, and the birds were carolling around me, a ray of hope began to break upon my poor dark soul. I looked at the earth, and looked at the sky, and felt as I had not done for many a year; presently a delicious feeling stole over me. I was beginning to enjoy existence. I shall never forget that hour. I flung myself on the soil, and kissed it; then, springing up with a sudden impulse, I rushed into the depths of a neighbouring wood, and, falling upon my knees, did what I had not done for a long time— prayed to God.

"A change, an entire change, seemed to have come over me. I was no longer gloomy and despairing, but gay and happy. My slumbers were light and easy; not disturbed, as before, by frightful dreams. I arose with the lark, and like him uttered a cheerful song of praise to God, frequently and earnestly, and was particularly cautious not to do anything which I considered might cause His displeasure.

"At church I was constant, and when there listened with deepest attention to every word which proceeded from the mouth of the minister. In a little time it appeared to me that I had become a good, very good young man. At times the recollection of the sin would return, and I would feel a momentary chill; but the thought quickly vanished, and I again felt happy and secure.

"One Sunday morning, after I had said my prayers, I felt particularly joyous. I thought of the innocent and virtuous life I was leading; and when the recollection of the sin intruded for a moment, I said, 'I am sure God will never utterly cast away so good a creature as myself'. I went to church, and was as usual attentive. The subject of the sermon was on the duty of searching the Scriptures: all I knew of them was from the

Liturgy. I now, however, determined to read them, and perfect the good work which I had begun. My father's Bible was upon the shelf, and on that evening I took it with me to my chamber. I placed it on the table, and sat down. My heart was filled with pleasing anticipation. I opened the book at random, and began to read; the first passage on which my eyes lighted was the following :—

" ' He who committeth the sin against the Holy Ghost shall not be forgiven, either in this world or the next '."

Here Peter was seized with convulsive tremors. Winifred sobbed violently. I got up, and went away. Returning in about a quarter of an hour, I found him more calm; he motioned me to sit down; and, after a short pause, continued his narration.

CHAPTER LXXVI.

" WHERE was I, young man? Oh, I remember, at the fatal passage which removed all hope. I will not dwell on what I felt. I closed my eyes, and wished that I might be dreaming; but it was no dream, but a terrific reality. I will not dwell on that period, I should only shock you. I could not bear my feelings; so, bidding my friends a hasty farewell, I abandoned myself to horror and despair, and ran wild through Wales, climbing mountains and wading streams.

" Climbing mountains and wading streams, I ran wild about; I was burnt by the sun, drenched by the rain, and had frequently at night no other covering than the sky, or the humid roof of some cave. But nothing seemed to affect my constitution; probably the fire which burned within me counteracted what I suffered from without. During the space of three years I scarcely knew what befel me; my life was a dream—a wild, horrible dream; more than once I believe I was in the hands of robbers, and once in the hands of gypsies. I liked the last description of people least of all; I could not abide their yellow faces, or their ceaseless clabber. Escaping from these beings whose countenances and godless discourse brought to my mind the demons of the deep Unknown, I still ran wild through Wales, I know not how long. On one occasion, coming in some degree to my recollection, I felt myself quite unable to bear the horrors of my situation; looking round I found myself near the sea; instantly the idea came into my head that I would cast myself into it, and thus anticipate my final doom. I hesitated a moment, but a voice within me seemed to tell me that I could do no better; the sea was near, and I could not swim, so I determined to fling myself into the sea. As I was running along at great speed, in the direction of a lofty rock, which beetled over the waters, I suddenly felt myself seized by the coat. I strove to tear myself away, but in vain; looking round, I perceived a venerable, hale old man, who had hold of me. 'Let me go!' said I fiercely. 'I will not let thee go,' said the old man; and now, instead of with one, he grappled me

with both hands. ' In whose name dost thou detain me ? ' said I,
scarcely knowing what I said. ' In the name of my Master, who
made thee and yonder sea, and has said to the sea, so far shalt
thou come, and no farther, and to thee, thou shalt do no murder.'
' Has not a man a right to do what he pleases with his own ? '
said I. ' He has,' said the old man, ' but thy life is not thy own ;
thou art accountable for it to thy God. Nay, I will not let thee
go,' he continued, as I again struggled ; ' if thou struggle with me
the whole day I will not let thee go, as Charles Wesley says in
his *Wrestlings of Jacob ;* and see, it is of no use struggling, for
I am, in the strength of my Master, stronger than thou ; ' and,
indeed, all of a sudden I had become very weak and exhausted ;
whereupon the old man, beholding my situation, took me by the
arm and led me gently to a neighbouring town, which stood
behind a hill, and which I had not before observed ; presently he
opened the door of a respectable-looking house, which stood
beside a large building having the appearance of a chapel, and
conducted me into a small room, with a great many books in it.
Having caused me to sit down, he stood looking at me for some
time, occasionally heaving a sigh. I was, indeed, haggard and
forlorn. ' Who art thou ? ' he said at last. ' A miserable man,'
I replied. ' What makes thee miserable ? ' said the old man.
' A hideous crime,' I replied. ' I can find no rest ; like Cain, I
wander here and there.' The old man turned pale. ' Hast thou
taken another's life ? ' said he ; ' if so, I advise thee to surrender
thyself to the magistrate ; thou canst do no better ; thy doing so
will be the best proof of thy repentance ; and though there be no
hope for thee in this world there may be much in the next.' ' No,'
said I, ' I have never taken another's life.' ' What then, another's
goods ? If so, restore them seven-fold if possible : or, if it be
not in thy power, and thy conscience accuse thee, surrender thyself
to the magistrate, and make the only satisfaction thou art able.'
' I have taken no one's goods,' said I. ' Of what art thou guilty,
then ? ' said he. ' Art thou a drunkard ? a profligate ? ' ' Alas, no,'
said I ; ' I am neither of these ; would that I were no worse ! '

    " Thereupon the old man looked steadfastly at me for some
time ; then, after appearing to reflect, he said : ' Young man, I
have a great desire to know your name '. ' What matters it to
you what is my name ? ' said I ; ' you know nothing of me.'
' Perhaps you are mistaken,' said the old man, looking kindly
at me ; ' but at all events tell me your name.' I hesitated a
moment, and then told him who I was, whereupon he exclaimed
with much emotion, ' I thought so ; how wonderful are the ways

of Providence ! I have heard of thee, young man, and know thy
mother well. Only a month ago, when upon a journey, I experienced much kindness from her. She was speaking to me of her
lost child, with tears ; she told me that you were one of the best of
sons, but that some strange idea appeared to have occupied your
mind. Despair not, my son. If thou hast been afflicted, I doubt
not but that thy affliction will eventually turn out to thy benefit ; I
doubt not but that thou wilt be preserved, as an example of the
great mercy of God. I will now kneel down and pray for thee,
my son.'

    " He knelt down, and prayed long and fervently. I remained
standing for some time ; at length I knelt down likewise. I
scarcely knew what he was saying, but when he concluded I said
' Amen '.

    " And when we had risen from our knees, the old man left me
for a short time, and on his return led me into another room,
where were two females ; one was an elderly person, the wife of
the old man, the other was a young woman of very prepossessing
appearance (hang not down thy head, Winifred), who I soon
found was a distant relation of the old man. Both received me
with great kindness, the old man having doubtless previously told
them who I was.

    " I staid several days in the good man's house. I had still
the greater portion of a small sum which I happened to have
about me when I departed on my dolorous wandering, and with
this I purchased clothes, and altered my appearance considerably.
On the evening of the second day, my friend said : ' I am going
to preach, perhaps you will come and hear me'. I consented,
and we all went, not to a church, but to the large building next
the house ; for the old man, though a clergyman, was not of the
established persuasion, and there the old man mounted a pulpit,
and began to preach. ' Come unto Me, all ye that labour and
are heavy laden,' etc., etc., was his text. His sermon was long,
but I still bear the greater portion of it in my mind.

    " The substance of it was that Jesus was at all times ready to
take upon Himself the burden of our sins, provided we came to
Him with a humble and contrite spirit, and begged His help.
This doctrine was new to me ; I had often been at church, but
had never heard it preached before, at least so distinctly. When
he said that all men might be saved, I shook, for I expected he
would add, all except those who had committed the mysterious
sin ; but no, all men were to be saved who with a humble and
contrite spirit would come to Jesus, cast themselves at the foot

of His cross, and accept pardon through the merits of His blood-shedding alone. ' Therefore, my friends,' said he, in conclusion, ' despair not—however guilty you may be, despair not—however desperate your condition may seem,' said he, fixing his eyes upon me, ' despair not. There is nothing more foolish and more wicked than despair; overweening confidence is not more foolish than despair; both are the favourite weapons of the enemy of souls.'

" This discourse gave rise in my mind to no slight perplexity. I had read in the Scriptures that he who committeth a certain sin shall never be forgiven, and that there is no hope for him either in this world or the next. And here was a man, a good man certainly, and one who, of necessity, was thoroughly acquainted with the Scriptures, who told me that any one might be forgiven, however wicked, who would only trust in Christ and in the merits of His blood-shedding. Did I believe in Christ? Ay, truly. Was I willing to be saved by Christ? Ay, truly. Did I trust in Christ? I trusted that Christ would save every one but myself. And why not myself? simply because the Scriptures had told me that he who has committed the sin against the Holy Ghost can never be saved, and I had committed the sin against the Holy Ghost—perhaps the only one who ever had committed it. How could I hope? The Scriptures could not lie, and yet here was this good old man, profoundly versed in the Scriptures, who bade me hope; would he lie? No. But did the old man know my case? Ah, no, he did not know my case! but yet he had bid me hope, whatever I had done, provided I would go to Jesus. But how could I think of going to Jesus, when the Scriptures told me plainly that all would be useless? I was perplexed, and yet a ray of hope began to dawn in my soul. I thought of consulting the good man, but I was afraid he would drive away the small glimmer. I was afraid he would say, ' Oh, yes, every one is to be saved, except a wretch like you; I was not aware before that there was anything so horrible—begone!' Once or twice the old man questioned me on the subject of my misery, but I evaded him; once, indeed, when he looked particularly benevolent, I think I should have unbosomed myself to him, but we were interrupted. He never pressed me much; perhaps he was delicate in probing my mind, as we were then of different persuasions. Hence he advised me to seek the advice of some powerful minister in my own church; there were many such in it, he said.

" I staid several days in the family, during which time I more than once heard my venerable friend preach; each time he preached he exhorted his hearers not to despair. The whole family were kind to me; his wife frequently discoursed with me, and also the young person to whom I have already alluded. It appeared to me that the latter took a peculiar interest in my fate.

"At last my friend said to me: 'It is now time thou shouldst return to thy mother and thy brother'. So I arose, and departed to my mother and my brother; and at my departure my old friend gave me his blessing, and his wife and the young person shed tears, the last especially. And when my mother saw me, she shed tears, and fell on my neck and kissed me, and my brother took me by the hand and bade me welcome; and when our first emotions were subsided, my mother said: 'I trust thou art come in a lucky hour. A few weeks ago my cousin (whose favourite thou always wast) died and left thee his heir—left thee the goodly farm in which he lived. I trust, my son, that thou wilt now settle, and be a comfort to me in my old days.' And I answered: 'I will, if so please the Lord'; and I said to myself, 'God grant that this bequest be a token of the Lord's favour'.

"And in a few days I departed to take possession of my farm; it was about twenty miles from my mother's house, in a beautiful but rather wild district; I arrived at the fall of the leaf. All day long I busied myself with my farm, and thus kept my mind employed. At night, however, I felt rather solitary, and I frequently wished for a companion. Each night and morning I prayed fervently unto the Lord; for His hand had been very heavy upon me, and I feared Him.

"There was one thing connected with my new abode, which gave me considerable uneasiness—the want of spiritual instruction. There was a church, indeed, close at hand, in which service was occasionally performed, but in so hurried and heartless a manner that I derived little benefit from it. The clergyman to whom the benefice belonged was a valetudinarian, who passed his time in London, or at some watering-place, entrusting the care of his flock to the curate of a distant parish, who gave himself very little trouble about the matter. Now, I wanted every Sunday to hear from the pulpit words of consolation and encouragement, similar to those which I had heard uttered from the pulpit by my good and venerable friend, but I was debarred from this privilege. At length, one day being in conversation with one of my labourers, a staid and serious man, I spoke to him of the matter which lay heavy upon my mind; whereupon, looking me wistfully in the face, he said : ' Master, the want of religious instruction in my church was what drove me to the Methodists '. ' The Methodists,' said I ; ' are there any in these parts ? ' ' There is a chapel,' said he, ' only half a mile distant, at which there are two services every Sunday, and other two during the week.' Now, it happened that my venerable friend was of the Methodist persuasion, and when I heard the poor man talk in this manner, I said to him : ' May I go with you next Sunday ? ' ' Why not ? ' said he ; so I went with the labourer on the ensuing Sabbath to the meeting of the Methodists.

" I liked the preaching which I heard at the chapel very well, though it was not quite so comfortable as that of my old friend, the preacher being in some respects a different kind of man. It, however, did me good, and I went again, and continued to do so, though I did not become a regular member of the body at that time.

" I had now the benefit of religious instruction, and also to a certain extent of religious fellowship, for the preacher and various members of his flock frequently came to see me. They were honest, plain men, not exactly of the description which I wished for, but still good sort of people, and I was glad to see them. Once on a time, when some of them were with me, one of them inquired whether I was fervent in prayer. ' Very fervent,' said I. ' And do you read the Scriptures often ? ' said he. ' No,' said I. ' Why not ? ' said he. ' Because I am afraid to see there my own condemnation.' They looked at each other, and said nothing at the time. On leaving me, however, they all advised me to read the Scriptures with fervency and prayer.

" As I had told these honest people, I shrank from searching the Scriptures ; the remembrance of the fatal passage was still too vivid in my mind to permit me. I did not wish to see my condemnation repeated, but I was very fervent in prayer, and almost hoped that God would yet forgive me by virtue of the blood-shedding of the Lamb. Time passed on, my affairs prospered, and I enjoyed a certain portion of tranquillity. Occasionally, when I had nothing else to do, I renewed my studies. Many is the book I read, especially in my native language, for I was always fond of my native language, and proud of being a Welshman. Amongst the books I read were the odes of the great Ab Gwilym, whom thou, friend, hast never heard of ; no, nor any of thy countrymen, for you are an ignorant race, you Saxons, at least with respect to all that relates to Wales and Welshmen. I likewise read the book of Master Ellis Wyn. The latter work possessed a singular fascination for me, on account of its wonderful delineations of the torments of the nether world.

"But man does not love to be alone; indeed, the Scripture says that it is not good for man to be alone. I occupied my body with the pursuits of husbandry, and I improved my mind with the perusal of good and wise books; but, as I have already said, I frequently sighed for a companion with whom I could exchange ideas, and who could take an interest in my pursuits; the want of such a one I more particularly felt in the long winter evenings. It was then that the image of the young person whom I had seen in the house of the preacher frequently rose up distinctly before my mind's eye, decked with quiet graces—hang not down your head, Winifred—and I thought that of all the women in the world I should wish her to be my partner, and then I considered whether it would be possible to obtain her. I am ready to acknowledge, friend, that it was both selfish and wicked in me to wish to fetter any human being to a lost creature like myself, conscious of having committed a crime for which the Scriptures told me there is no pardon. I had, indeed, a long struggle as to whether I should make the attempt or not—selfishness, however, prevailed. I will not detain your attention with relating all that occurred at this period—suffice it to say that I made my suit and was successful; it is true that the old man, who was her guardian, hesitated, and asked several questions respecting my state of mind. I am afraid that I partly deceived him, perhaps he partly deceived himself; he was pleased that I had adopted his profession—we are all weak creatures. With respect to the young person, she did not ask many questions; and I soon found that I had won her heart. To be brief, I married her; and here she is, the truest wife that ever man had, and the kindest. Kind I may well call her, seeing that she shrinks not from me, who so cruelly deceived her, in not telling her at first what I was. I married her, friend, and brought her home to my little possession, where we passed our time very agreeably. Our affairs prospered, our garners were full, and there was coin in our purse. I worked in the field; Winifred busied herself with the dairy. At night I frequently read books to her, books of my own country, friend; I likewise read to her songs of my own, holy songs and carols which she admired, and which yourself would perhaps admire, could you understand them; but I repeat, you Saxons are an ignorant people with respect to us, and a perverse, inasmuch as you despise Welsh without understanding it. Every night I prayed fervently, and my wife admired my gift of prayer.

"One night, after I had been reading to my wife a portion of Ellis Wyn, my wife said: 'This is a wonderful book, and containing much true and pleasant doctrine; but how is it that you, who are so fond of good books, and good things in general, never read the Bible? You read me the book of Master Ellis Wyn, you read me sweet songs of your own composition, you edify me with your gift of prayer, but yet you never read the Bible.' And when I heard her mention the Bible I shook, for I thought of my own condemnation. However, I dearly loved my wife, and as she pressed me, I commenced on that very night reading the Bible. All went on smoothly for a long time; for months and months I did not find the fatal passage, so that I almost thought that I had imagined it. My affairs prospered much the while, so that I was almost happy, taking pleasure in everything around me,—in my wife, in my farm, my books and compositions, and the Welsh language; till one night, as I was reading the Bible, feeling particularly comfortable, a thought having just come into my head that I would print some of my compositions, and purchase a particular field of a neighbour—oh, God—God! I came to the fatal passage.

"Friend, friend, what shall I say? I rushed out. My wife followed me, asking me what was the matter. I could only answer with groans—for three days and three nights I did little else than groan. Oh, the kindness and solicitude of my wife! 'What is the matter, husband, dear husband?' she was continually saying. I became at last more calm. My wife still persisted in asking me the cause of my late paroxysm. It is hard to keep a secret from a wife, especially such a wife as mine, so I told my wife the tale, as we sat one night—it was a mid-winter night—over the dying brands of our hearth, after the family had retired to rest, her hand locked in mine, even as it is now.

"I thought she would have shrunk from me with horror; but she did not; her hand, it is true, trembled once or twice; but that was all. At last she gave mine a gentle pressure; and, looking up in my face, she said—what do you think my wife said, young man?"

"It is impossible for me to guess," said I.

"'Let us go to rest, my love; your fears are all groundless.'"

CHAPTER LXXVII.

" And so I still say," said Winifred, sobbing. " Let us retire to rest, dear husband; your fears are groundless. I had hoped long since that your affliction would have passed away, and I still hope that it eventually will; so take heart, Peter, and let us retire to rest, for it is getting late."

" Rest !" said Peter; "there is no rest for the wicked !"

" We are all wicked," said Winifred; "but you are afraid of a shadow. How often have I told you that the sin of your heart is not the sin against the Holy Ghost: the sin of your heart is its natural pride, of which you are scarcely aware, to keep down which God in His mercy permitted you to be terrified with the idea of having committed a sin which you never committed."

" Then you will still maintain," said Peter, "that I never committed the sin against the Holy Spirit ?"

" I will," said Winifred; "you never committed it. How should a child seven years old commit a sin like that ?"

" Have I not read my own condemnation?" said Peter. " Did not the first words which I read in the Holy Scripture condemn me? ' He who committeth the sin against the Holy Ghost shall never enter into the kingdom of God.' "

" You never committed it," said Winifred.

" But the words ! the words ! the words !" said Peter.

" The words are true words," said Winifred, sobbing; "but they were not meant for you, but for those who have broken their profession, who, having embraced the cross, have receded from their Master."

" And what sayest thou to the effect which the words produced upon me?" said Peter. "Did they not cause me to run wild through Wales for years, like Merddin Wyllt of yore? Thinkest thou that I opened the book at that particular passage by chance ?"

" No," said Winifred, " not by chance; it was the hand of God directed you, doubtless for some wise purpose. You had become satisfied with yourself. The Lord wished to rouse thee from thy state of carnal security, and therefore directed your eyes to that fearful passage."

" Does the Lord then carry out His designs by means of guile ?" said Peter, with a groan. "Is not the Lord true?

(421)

Would the Lord impress upon me that I had committed a sin of which I am guiltless? Hush, Winifred! hush! thou knowest that I have committed the sin."

"Thou hast not committed it," said Winifred, sobbing yet more violently. "Were they my last words, I would persist that thou hast not committed it, though, perhaps, thou wouldst, but for this chastening; it was not to convince thee that thou hast committed the sin, but rather to prevent thee from committing it, that the Lord brought that passage before thy eyes. He is not to blame, if thou art wilfully blind to the truth and wisdom of His ways."

"I see thou wouldst comfort me," said Peter, "as thou hast often before attempted to do. I would fain ask the young man his opinion."

"I have not yet heard the whole of your history," said I.

"My story is nearly told," said Peter; "a few words will complete it. My wife endeavoured to console and reassure me, using the arguments which you have just heard her use, and many others, but in vain. Peace nor comfort came to my breast. I was rapidly falling into the depths of despair, when one day Winifred said to me: 'I see thou wilt be lost if we remain here. One resource only remains. Thou must go forth, my husband, into the wide world, and to comfort thee I will go with thee.' 'And what can I do in the wide world?' said I, despondingly. 'Much,' replied Winifred, 'if you will but exert yourself; much good canst thou do with the blessing of God.' Many things of the same kind she said to me; and at last I arose from the earth to which God had smitten me, and disposed of my property in the best way I could, and went into the world. We did all the good we were able, visiting the sick, ministering to the sick, and praying with the sick. At last I became celebrated as the possessor of a great gift of prayer. And people urged me to preach, and Winifred urged me too, and at last I consented, and I preached. I—I—outcast Peter, became the preacher, Peter Williams. I, the lost one, attempted to show others the right road. And in this way I have gone on for thirteen years, preaching and teaching, visiting the sick, and ministering to them, with Winifred by my side hearkening me on. Occasionally I am visited with fits of indescribable agony, generally on the night before the Sabbath; for I then ask myself, how dare I, the outcast, attempt to preach the word of God? Young man, my tale is told; you seem in thought!"

"I am thinking of London Bridge," said I.

"Of London Bridge!" said Peter and his wife.

"Yes," said I, "of London Bridge. I am indebted for much

wisdom to London Bridge; it was there that I completed my studies. But to the point. I was once reading on London Bridge a book which an ancient gentlewoman, who kept the bridge, was in the habit of lending me; and there I found written, 'Each one carries in his breast the recollection of some sin which presses heavy upon him. O! if men could but look into each other's hearts, what blackness would they find there!'"

"That's true," said Peter. "What is the name of the book?"

"*The Life of Blessed Mary Flanders.*"

"Some popish saint, I suppose," said Peter.

"As much of a saint, I dare say," said I, "as most popish ones; but you interrupted me. One part of your narrative brought the passage which I have quoted into my mind. You said that after you had committed this same sin of yours you were in the habit, at school, of looking upon your schoolfellows with a kind of gloomy superiority, considering yourself a lone, monstrous being who had committed a sin far above the daring of any of them. Are you sure that many others of your schoolfellows were not looking upon you and the others with much the same eyes with which you were looking upon them?"

"How!" said Peter, "dost thou think that they had divined my secret?"

"Not they," said I; "they were, I dare say, thinking too much of themselves and of their own concerns to have divined any secrets of yours. All I mean to say is, they had probably secrets of their own, and who knows that the secret sin of more than one of them was not the very sin which caused you so much misery?"

"Dost thou then imagine," said Peter, "the sin against the Holy Ghost to be so common an occurrence?"

"As you have described it," said I, "of very common occurrence, especially amongst children, who are, indeed, the only beings likely to commit it."

"Truly," said Winifred, "the young man talks wisely."

Peter was silent for some moments, and appeared to be reflecting; at last, suddenly raising his head, he looked me full in the face, and, grasping my hand with vehemence, he said: "Tell me, young man, only one thing, hast thou, too, committed the sin against the Holy Ghost?"

"I am neither Papist nor Methodist," said I, "but of the Church, and, being so, confess myself to no one, but keep my own counsel; I will tell thee, however, had I committed, at the same age, twenty such sins as that which you committed, I should feel no uneasiness at these years—but I am sleepy, and must go to rest."

"God bless thee, young man," said Winifred.

CHAPTER LXXVIII.

BEFORE I sank to rest I heard Winifred and her husband conversing in the place where I had left them; both their voices were low and calm. I soon fell asleep, and slumbered for some time. On my awakening I again heard them conversing, but they were now in their cart; still the voices of both were calm. I heard no passionate bursts of wild despair on the part of the man. Methought I occasionally heard the word *Pechod* proceeding from the lips of each, but with no particular emphasis. I supposed they were talking of the innate sin of both their hearts.

"I wish that man were happy," said I to myself, "were it only for his wife's sake, and yet he deserves to be happy for his own."

The next day Peter was very cheerful, more cheerful than I had ever seen him. At breakfast his conversation was animated, and he smiled repeatedly. I looked at him with the greatest interest, and the eyes of his wife were almost constantly fixed upon him. A shade of gloom would occasionally come over his countenance, but it almost instantly disappeared; perhaps it proceeded more from habit than anything else. After breakfast he took his Welsh Bible and sat down beneath a tree. His eyes were soon fixed intently on the volume; now and then he would call his wife, show her some passage, and appeared to consult with her. The day passed quickly and comfortably.

"Your husband seems much better," said I, at evening fall, to Winifred, as we chanced to be alone.

"He does," said Winifred; "and that on the day of the week when he was wont to appear most melancholy, for to-morrow is the Sabbath. He now no longer looks forward to the Sabbath with dread, but appears to reckon on it. What a happy change! and to think that this change should have been produced by a few words, seemingly careless ones, proceeding from the mouth of one who is almost a stranger to him. Truly, it is wonderful."

"To whom do you allude," said I, "and to what words?"

"To yourself, and to the words which came from your lips last night, after you had heard my poor husband's history. Those strange words, drawn out with so much seeming indifference, have produced in my husband the blessed effect which you have

(424)

observed. They have altered the current of his ideas. He no
longer thinks himself the only being in the world doomed to
destruction,—the only being capable of committing the never-to-
be-forgiven sin. Your supposition that that which harrowed his
soul is of frequent occurrence amongst children, has tranquillised
him ; the mist which hung over his mind has cleared away, and
he begins to see the groundlessness of his apprehensions. The
Lord has permitted him to be chastened for a season, but his
lamp will only burn the brighter for what he has undergone."

Sunday came, fine and glorious as the last. Again my friends
and myself breakfasted together, again the good family of the
house on the hill above, headed by the respectable master,
descended to the meadow. Peter and his wife were ready to
receive them. Again Peter placed himself at the side of the
honest farmer, and Winifred by the side of her friend. "Wilt
thou not come?" said Peter, looking towards me with a face in
which there was much emotion. "Wilt thou not come?" said Winifred, with a face beaming with kindness. But I made no answer,
and presently the party moved away, in the same manner in which
it had moved on the preceding Sabbath, and I was again left alone.

The hours of the Sabbath passed slowly away. I sat gazing at
the sky, the trees and the water. At last I strolled up to the
house and sat down in the porch. It was empty; there was no
modest maiden there, as on the preceding Sabbath. The damsel
of the book had accompanied the rest. I had seen her in the
procession, and the house appeared quite deserted. The owners
had probably left it to my custody, so I sat down in the porch,
quite alone. The hours of the Sabbath passed heavily away.

At last evening came, and with it the party of the morning.
I was now at my place beneath the oak. I went forward to meet
them. Peter and his wife received me with a calm and quiet
greeting, and passed forward. The rest of the party had broke
into groups. There was a kind of excitement amongst them, and
much eager whispering. I went to one of the groups ; the young
girl of whom I have spoken more than once, was speaking : "Such
a sermon," said she, "it has never been our lot to hear ; Peter never
before spoke as he has done this day—he was always a powerful
preacher ; but oh, the unction of the discourse of this morning, and
yet more of that of the afternoon, which was the continuation of it."
"What was the subject?" said I, interrupting her. "Ah! you
should have been there, young man, to have heard it ; it would have
made a lasting impression upon you. I was bathed in tears all the
time ; those who heard it will never forget the preaching of the good
Peter Williams on the Power, Providence and Goodness of God."

CHAPTER LXXIX.

On the morrow I said to my friends: "I am about to depart; farewell!" "Depart!" said Peter and his wife simultaneously, "whither wouldst thou go?" "I can't stay here all my days," I replied. "Of course not," said Peter, "but we had no idea of losing thee so soon: we had almost hoped that thou wouldst join us, become one of us. We are under infinite obligations to thee." "You mean I am under infinite obligations to you," said I. "Did you not save my life?" "Perhaps so, under God," said Peter; "and what hast thou not done for me? Art thou aware that, under God, thou hast preserved my soul from despair? But, independent of that, we like thy company, and feel a deep interest in thee, and would fain teach thee the way that is right. Hearken, to-morrow we go into Wales; go with us." "I have no wish to go into Wales," said I. "Why not?" said Peter with animation. "Wales is a goodly country; as the Scripture says—a land of brooks of water, of fountains and depths, that spring out of valleys and hills, a land whose stones are iron, and out of whose hills thou mayest dig lead."

"I daresay it is a very fine country," said I, "but I have no wish to go there just now; my destiny seems to point in another direction, to say nothing of my trade." "Thou dost right to say nothing of thy trade," said Peter, smiling, "for thou seemest to care nothing about it; which has led Winifred and myself to suspect that thou art not altogether what thou seemest; but, setting that aside, we should be most happy if thou wouldst go with us into Wales." "I cannot promise to go with you into Wales," said I; "but, as you depart to-morrow, I will stay with you through the day, and on the morrow accompany you part of the way." "Do," said Peter. "I have many people to see to-day, and so has Winifred; but we will both endeavour to have some serious discourse with thee, which, perhaps, will turn to thy profit in the end."

In the course of the day the good Peter came to me, as I was seated beneath the oak, and, placing himself by me, commenced addressing me in the following manner:—

"I have no doubt, my young friend, that you are willing to

admit, that the most important thing which a human being possesses is his soul; it is of infinitely more importance than the body, which is a frail substance, and cannot last for many years; but not so the soul, which, by its nature, is imperishable. To one of two mansions the soul is destined to depart, after its separation from the body, to heaven or hell: to the halls of eternal bliss, where God and His holy angels dwell, or to the place of endless misery, inhabited by Satan and his grisly companions. My friend, if the joys of heaven are great, unutterably great, so are the torments of hell unutterably so. I wish not to speak of them, I wish not to terrify your imagination with the torments of hell; indeed, I like not to think of them; but it is necessary to speak of them sometimes, and to think of them sometimes, lest you should sink into a state of carnal security. Authors, friend, and learned men are not altogether agreed as to the particulars of hell. They all agree, however, in considering it a place of exceeding horror. Master Ellis Wyn, who by-the-bye was a Churchman, calls it, amongst other things, a place of strong sighs, and of flaming sparks. Master Rees Pritchard, who was not only a Churchman, but Vicar of Llandovery, and flourished about two hundred years ago—I wish many like him flourished now—speaking of hell, in his collection of sweet hymns, called the *Welshman's Candle*, observes:—

" ' The pool is continually blazing; it is very deep, without any known bottom, and the walls are so high, that there is neither hope nor possibility of escaping over them '.

" But, as I told you just now, I have no great pleasure in talking of hell. No, friend, no; I would sooner talk of the other place, and of the goodness and hospitality of God amongst His saints above."

And then the excellent man began to dilate upon the joys of heaven, and the goodness and hospitality of God in the mansions above, explaining to me, in the clearest way, how I might get there.

And when he had finished what he had to say, he left me, whereupon Winifred drew nigh, and sitting down by me, began to address me. "I do not think," said she, "from what I have observed of thee, that thou wouldst wish to be ungrateful, and yet, is not thy whole life a series of ingratitude, and to whom?—to thy Maker. Has He not endowed thee with a goodly and healthy form, and senses which enable thee to enjoy the delights of His beautiful universe—the work of His hands? Canst thou not enjoy, even to rapture, the brightness of the sun, the perfume of the meads, and the song of the dear birds, which inhabit among the trees? Yes, thou canst; for I have seen thee, and observed thee doing so. Yet, during the whole time that I have known thee, I have not heard proceed from thy lips one single word of praise or thanksgiving to ——"

And in this manner the admirable woman proceeded for a considerable time, and to all her discourse I listened with attention; and when she had concluded I took her hand and said, " I thank you," and that was all.

On the next day everything was ready for our departure. The good family of the house came to bid us farewell. There were shaking of hands, and kisses, as on the night of our arrival.

And as I stood somewhat apart, the young girl of whom I have spoken so often came up to me, and, holding out her hand, said : " Farewell, young man, wherever thou goest ". Then, after looking around her, she said : " It was all true you told me. Yesterday I received a letter from him thou wottest of, he is coming soon. God bless you, young man ; who would have thought thou knewest so much ! "

So after we had taken our farewell of the good family, we departed, proceeding in the direction of Wales. Peter was very cheerful, and enlivened the way with godly discourse and spiritual hymns, some of which were in the Welsh language. At length I said : " It is a pity that you did not continue in the Church ; you have a turn for Psalmody, and I have heard of a man becoming a bishop, by means of a less qualification ".

" Very probably," said Peter ; " more the pity. But I have told you the reason of my forsaking it. Frequently, when I went to the church door, I found it barred, and the priest absent ; what was I to do ? My heart was bursting for want of some religious help and comfort; what could I do ! as good Master Rees Pritchard observes in his *Candle for Welshmen :*—

" ' It is a doleful thing to see little children burning on the hot coals for want of help, but yet more doleful to see a flock of souls falling into the burning lake for want of a priest '."

" The Church of England is a fine church," said I ; " I would not advise any one to speak ill of the Church of England before me."

" I have nothing to say against the church," said Peter ; " all I wish is that it would fling itself a little more open, and that its priests would a little more bestir themselves ; in a word, that it would shoulder the cross and become a missionary church."

" It is too proud for that," said Winifred.

" You are much more of a Methodist," said I, " than your husband. But tell me," said I, addressing myself to Peter, " do you not differ from the church in some points of doctrine ? I, of course, as a true member of the church, am quite ignorant of the peculiar opinions of wandering sectaries."

"Oh, the pride of that church!" said Winifred half to herself; "wandering sectaries!"

"We differ in no points of doctrine," said Peter; "we believe all the church believes, though we are not so fond of vain and superfluous ceremonies, snow-white neckcloths and surplices, as the church is. We likewise think that there is no harm in a sermon by the road-side, or in holding free discourse with a beggar beneath a hedge, or a tinker," he added, smiling; "it was those superfluous ceremonies, those surplices and white neckcloths, and, above all, the necessity of strictly regulating his words and conversation, which drove John Wesley out of the church, and sent him wandering up and down as you see me, poor Welsh Peter, do."

Nothing further passed for some time; we were now drawing near the hills: at last I said: "You must have met with a great many strange adventures since you took up this course of life?"

"Many," said Peter, "it has been my lot to meet with, but none more strange than one which occurred to me only a few weeks ago. You were asking me, not long since, whether I believed in devils? Ay, truly, young man; and I believe that the abyss and the yet deeper unknown do not contain them all; some walk about upon the green earth. So it happened, some weeks ago, that I was exercising my ministry, about forty miles from here. I was alone, Winifred, being slightly indisposed, staying for a few days at the house of an acquaintance; I had finished afternoon's worship—the people had dispersed, and I was sitting solitary by my cart under some green trees in a quiet, retired place; suddenly a voice said to me: 'Good evening, Pastor'; I looked up, and before me stood a man, at least the appearance of a man, dressed in a black suit of rather a singular fashion. He was about my own age, or somewhat older. As I looked upon him, it appeared to me that I had seen him twice before whilst preaching. I replied to his salutation, and perceiving that he looked somewhat fatigued, I took out a stool from the cart, and asked him to sit down. We began to discourse; I at first supposed that he might be one of ourselves, some wandering minister; but I was soon undeceived. Neither his language nor his ideas were those of any one of our body. He spoke on all kinds of matters with much fluency, till at last he mentioned my preaching, complimenting me on my powers. I replied, as well I might, that I could claim no merit of my own, and that if I spoke with any effect, it was only by the grace of God. As I uttered these last words, a horrible kind of sneer came over his

countenance, which made me shudder, for there was something
diabolical in it.   I said little more, but listened attentively to
his discourse.   At last he said that I was engaged in a paltry
cause, quite unworthy of one of my powers.   'How can that
be,' said I, 'even if I possessed all the powers in the world, seeing
that I am engaged in the cause of our Lord Jesus?'

"The same kind of sneer again came on his countenance, but
he almost instantly observed that if I chose to forsake this same
miserable cause, from which nothing but contempt and privation
were to be expected, he would enlist me into another, from which
I might expect both profit and renown.   An idea now came into
my head, and I told him firmly, that if he wished me to forsake
my present profession and become a member of the Church of
England, I must absolutely decline; that I had no ill-will against
that church, but I thought I could do most good in my present
position, which I would not forsake to be Archbishop of Canterbury.   Thereupon he burst into a strange laughter, and went
away, repeating to himself, 'Church of England! Archbishop
of Canterbury!'   A few days after, when I was once more in a
solitary place, he again appeared before me, and asked me
whether I had thought over his words, and whether I was willing
to enlist under the banners of his master, adding, that he was
eager to secure me, as he conceived that I might be highly useful
to the cause.   I then asked him who his master was; he hesitated
for a moment, and then answered, 'The Roman Pontiff'.   'If it
be he,' said I, 'I can have nothing to do with him; I will serve
no one who is an enemy of Christ.'   Thereupon he drew near to
me and told me not to talk so much like a simpleton; that as for
Christ, it was probable that no such person ever existed, but that
if He ever did, He was the greatest impostor the world ever saw.
How long he continued in this way I know not, for I now considered that an evil spirit was before me, and shrank within myself,
shivering in every limb; when I recovered myself and looked
about me, he was gone.   Two days after, he again stood before
me, in the same place, and about the same hour, renewing his
propositions, and speaking more horribly than before.   I made him
no answer, whereupon he continued; but suddenly hearing a
noise behind him, he looked round and beheld Winifred, who
had returned to me on the morning of that day.   'Who are you?'
said he fiercely.   'This man's wife,' said she, calmly fixing her
eyes upon him.   'Begone from him, unhappy one, thou temptest
him in vain.'   He made no answer, but stood as if transfixed;
at length recovering himself, he departed, muttering 'Wife! Wife!
If the fool has a wife, he will never do for us.'"

CHAPTER LXXX.

WE were now drawing very near the hills, and Peter said, "If you are to go into Wales, you must presently decide, for we are close upon the border".

" Which is the border ? " said I.

" Yon small brook," said Peter, " into which the man on horseback, who is coming towards us, is now entering."

" I see it," said I, " and the man ; he stops in the middle of it, as if to water his steed."

We proceeded till we had nearly reached the brook. " Well," said Peter, "will you go into Wales ? "

" What should I do in Wales ? " I demanded.

" Do ! " said Peter, smiling, " learn Welsh."

I stopped my little pony. " Then I need not go into Wales ; I already know Welsh."

" Know Welsh ! " said Peter, staring at me.

" Know Welsh ! " said Winifred, stopping her cart.

" How and when did you learn it ? " said Peter.

" From books, in my boyhood."

" Read Welsh ! " said Peter, " is it possible ? "

" Read Welsh ! " said Winifred, " is it possible ? "

" Well, I hope you will come with us," said Peter.

" Come with us, young man," said Winifred ; " let me, on the other side of the brook, welcome you into Wales."

" Thank you both," said I, " but I will not come."

" Wherefore ? " exclaimed both simultaneously.

" Because it is neither fit nor proper that I cross into Wales at this time, and in this manner. When I go into Wales, I should wish to go in a new suit of superfine black, with hat and beaver, mounted on a powerful steed, black and glossy, like that which bore Greduv to the fight of Catraeth. I should wish, moreover, to see the Welshmen assembled on the border ready to welcome me with pipe and fiddle, and much whooping and shouting, and to attend me to Wrexham, or even as far as Machynllaith, where I should wish to be invited to a dinner at which all the bards

(431)

should be present, and to be seated at the right hand of the president, who, when the cloth was removed, should arise, and, amidst cries of silence, exclaim — 'Brethren and Welshmen, allow me to propose the health of my most respectable friend the translator of the odes of the great Ab Gwilym, the pride and glory of Wales '."

"How!" said Peter; "hast thou translated the works of the mighty Dafydd?"

"With notes critical, historical and explanatory."

"Come with us, friend," said Peter. "I cannot promise such a dinner as thou wishest, but neither pipe nor fiddle shall be wanting."

"Come with us, young man," said Winifred, "even as thou art, and the daughters of Wales shall bid thee welcome."

"I will not go with you," said I. "Dost thou see that man in the ford?"

"Who is staring at us so, and whose horse has not yet done drinking? Of course I see him."

"I shall turn back with him. God bless you!"

"Go back with him not," said Peter, "he is one of those whom I like not, one of the clibberty-clabber, as Master Ellis Wyn observes—turn not with that man."

"Go not back with him," said Winifred. "If thou goest with that man, thou wilt soon forget all our profitable counsels; come with us."

"I cannot; I have much to say to him. Kosko Divvus, Mr. Petulengro."

"Kosko Divvus, Pal," said Mr. Petulengro, riding through the water; "are you turning back?"

I turned back with Mr. Petulengro.

Peter came running after me: "One moment, young man, who and what are you?"

"I must answer in the words of Taliesin," said I; "none can say with positiveness whether I be fish or flesh, least of all myself. God bless you both!"

"Take this," said Peter; and he thrust his Welsh Bible into my hand.

CHAPTER LXXXI.

So I turned back with Mr. Petulengro. We travelled for some time in silence; at last we fell into discourse. "You have been in Wales, Mr. Petulengro?"

"Ay, truly, brother."

"What have you been doing there?"

"Assisting at a funeral."

"At whose funeral?"

"Mrs. Hearne's, brother."

"Is she dead, then?"

"As a nail, brother."

"How did she die?"

"By hanging, brother."

"I am lost in astonishment," said I; whereupon Mr. Petulengro, lifting his sinister leg over the neck of his steed, and adjusting himself sideways in the saddle, replied with great deliberation :—

"Two days ago, I happened to be at a fair not very far from here; I was all alone by myself, for our party were upwards of forty miles off, when who should come up but a chap that I knew, a relation, or rather, a connection of mine—one of those Hearnes. 'Ar'n't you going to the funeral?' said he; and then, brother, there passed between him and me, in the way of questioning and answering, much the same as has just now passed between I and you; but when he mentioned hanging, I thought I could do no less· than ask who hanged her, which you forgot to do. 'Who hanged her?' said I; and then the man told me that she had done it herself—been her own hinjiri; and then I thought to myself what a sin and shame it would be if I did not go to the funeral, seeing that she was my own mother-in-law. I would have brought my wife, and, indeed, the whole of our party, but there was no time for that; they were too far off, and the dead was to be buried early the next morning, so I went with the man, and he led me into Wales, where his party had lately retired, and when there, through many wild and desolate places

(433)

to their encampment, and there I found the Hearnes, and the dead body—the last laid out on a mattress, in a tent, dressed Romaneskoenæs, in a red cloak and big bonnet of black beaver. I must say for the Hearnes that they took the matter very coolly : some were eating, others drinking, and some were talking about their small affairs ; there was one, however, who did not take the matter so coolly, but took on enough for the whole family, sitting beside the dead woman, tearing her hair, and re- fusing to take either meat or drink ; it was the child Leonora. I arrived at nightfall, and the burying was not to take place till the morning, which I was rather sorry for, as I am not very fond of them Hearnes, who are not very fond of anybody. They never asked me to eat or drink, notwithstanding I had married into the family ; one of them, however, came up and offered to fight me for five shillings ; had it not been for them, I should have come back as empty as I went—he didn't stand up five minutes. Brother, I passed the night as well as I could, beneath a tree, for the tents were full, and not over clean ; I slept little, and had my eyes about me, for I knew the kind of people I was among.

"Early in the morning the funeral took place. The body was placed not in a coffin but on a bier, and carried not to a churchyard but to a deep dell close by ; and there it was buried beneath a rock, dressed just as I have told you ; and this was done by the bidding of Leonora, who had heard her bebee say that she wished to be buried, not in gorgious fashion, but like a Roman woman of the old blood, the kosko puro rati, brother. When it was over, and we had got back to the encampment, I prepared to be going. Before mounting my gry, however, I be- thought me to ask what could have induced the dead woman to make away with herself, a thing so uncommon amongst Romanies ; whereupon one squinted with his eyes, a second spirted saliver into the air, and a third said that he neither knew nor cared ; she was a good riddance, having more than once been nearly the ruin of them all, from the quantity of brimstone she carried about her. One, however, I suppose, rather ashamed of the way in which they had treated me, said at last, that if I wanted to know all about the matter, none could tell me better than the child, who was in all her secrets, and was not a little like her ; so I looked about for the child, but could find her nowhere. At last the same man told me that he shouldn't wonder if I found her at the grave ; so I went back to the grave, and sure enough there I found the child, Leonora, seated on the ground above the body, crying and taking on ; so I spoke kindly to her, and said, how came all this,

Leonora? tell me all about it.   It was a long time before
I could get any answer; at last she opened her mouth, and spoke,
and these were the words she said : ' It was all along of your pal';
and then she told me all about the matter.   How Mrs. Hearne
could not abide you, which I knew before, and that she had sworn
your destruction, which I did not know before.   And then she
told me how she found you living in the wood by yourself, and
how you were enticed to eat a poisoned cake; and she told me
many other things that you wot of, and she told me what perhaps
you don't wot, namely, that finding you had been removed, she,
the child, had tracked you a long way, and found you at last well
and hearty, and no ways affected by the poison, and heard you,
as she stood concealed, disputing about religion with a Welsh
Methody.   Well, brother, she told me all this; and, moreover,
that when Mrs. Hearne heard of it, she said that a dream of hers
had come to pass.   I don't know what it was, but something
about herself, a tinker, and a dean ; and then she added, that it
was all up with her, and that she must take a long journey.   Well,
brother, that same night Leonora, waking from her sleep in the
tent, where Mrs. Hearne and she were wont to sleep, missed her
bebee, and, becoming alarmed, went in search of her, and at last
found her hanging from a branch ; and when the child had got
so far, she took on violently, and I could not get another word
from her ; so I left her, and here I am."

"And I am glad to see you, Mr. Petulengro ; but this is sad
news which you tell me about Mrs. Hearne."

"Somewhat dreary, brother; yet, perhaps, after all, it is a
good thing that she is removed ; she carried so much Devil's
tinder about with her, as the man said."

"I am sorry for her," said I ; "more especially as I am the
cause of her death—though the innocent one."

"She could not bide you, brother, that's certain ; but that is
no reason "—said Mr. Petulengro, balancing himself upon the
saddle—" that is no reason why she should prepare drow to take
away your essence of life, and, when disappointed, to hang herself upon a tree : if she was dissatisfied with you, she might have
flown at you, and scratched your face ; or, if she did not judge
herself your match, she might have put down five shillings for a
turn-up between you and some one she thought could beat you
—myself, for example, and so the matter might have ended comfortably ; but she was always too fond of covert ways, drows and
brimstones.   This is not the first poisoning affair she has been
engaged in."

" You allude to drabbing bawlor."

" Bah ! " said Mr. Petulengro ; " there's no harm in that. No, no ! she has cast drows in her time for other guess things than bawlor ; both Gorgios and Romans have tasted of them, and died. Did you never hear of the poisoned plum pudding ? "

" Never."

" Then I will tell you about it. It happened about six years ago, a few months after she had quitted us—she had gone first among her own people, as she called them ; but there was another small party of Romans, with whom she soon became very intimate. It so happened that this small party got into trouble ; whether it was about a horse or an ass, or passing bad money, no matter to you and me, who had no hand in the business ; three or four of them were taken and lodged in —— Castle, and amongst them was a woman ; but the sherengro, or principal man of the party, and who it seems had most hand in the affair, was still at large. All of a sudden a rumour was spread abroad that the woman was about to play false, and to peach the rest. Said the principal man, when he heard it, ' If she does, I am nashkado '. Mrs. Hearne was then on a visit to the party, and when she heard the principal man take on so, she said : ' But I suppose you know what to do ? ' ' I do not,' said he. ' Then hir mi devlis,' said she, ' you are a fool. But leave the matter to me, I know how to dispose of her in Roman fashion.' Why she wanted to in-terfere in the matter, brother, I don't know, unless it was from pure brimstoneness of disposition—she had no hand in the matter which had brought the party into trouble, she was only on a visit, and it had happened before she came ; but she was always ready to give dangerous advice. Well, brother, the principal man listened to what she had to say, and let her do what she would ; and she made a pudding, a very nice one, no doubt—for, besides plums, she put in drows and all the Roman condiments that she knew of ; and she gave it to the principal man, and the principal man put it into a basket and directed it to the woman in —— Castle, and the woman in the castle took it and ——"

" Ate of it," said I, " just like my case ? "

" Quite different, brother ; she took it, it is true, but instead of giving way to her appetite as you might have done, she put it before the rest whom she was going to impeach—perhaps she wished to see how they liked it before she tasted it herself— and all the rest were poisoned, and one died, and there was a precious outcry, and the woman cried loudest of all ; and she said : ' It was my death was sought for ; I know the man, and I'll be revenged,' and then the Poknees spoke to her and said, ' Where can we find him?' and she said, ' I am awake to his motions; three weeks from hence, the night before the full moon, at such and such an hour, he will pass down such a lane with such a man '."

"Well," said I, " and what did the Poknees do?"

" Do, brother, sent for a plastramengro from Bow Street, quite secretly, and told him what the woman had said; and the night before the full moon, the plastramengro went to the place which the juwa had pointed out, all alone, brother; and, in order that he might not be too late, he went two hours before his time. I know the place well, brother, where the plastramengro placed himself behind a thick holly tree, at the end of a lane, where a gate leads into various fields, through which there is a path for carts and horses. The lane is called the dark lane by the Gorgios, being much shaded by trees; so the plastramengro placed himself in the dark lane behind the holly tree; it was a cold February night, dreary, though; the wind blew in gusts, and the moon had not yet risen, and the plastramengro waited behind a tree till he was tired, and thought he might as well sit down; so he sat down and was not long in falling to sleep, and there he slept for some hours; and when he awoke, the moon had risen, and was shining bright, so that there was a kind of moonlight even in the dark lane; and the plastramengro pulled out his watch, and contrived to make out that it was just two hours beyond the time when the men should have passed by. Brother, I do not know what the plastramengro thought of himself, but I know, brother, what I should have thought of myself in his situation. I should have thought, brother, that I was a drowsy scoppelo, and that I had let the fellow pass by whilst I was sleeping behind a bush. As it turned out, however, his going to sleep did no harm, but quite the contrary; just as he was going away, he heard a gate slam in the direction of the fields, and then he heard the low stumping of horses, as if on soft ground, for the path in those fields is generally soft, and at that time it had been lately ploughed up. Well, brother, presently he saw two men on horseback coming towards the lane through the field behind the gate; the man who rode foremost was a tall, big fellow, the very man he was in quest of: the other was a smaller chap, not so small either, but a light, wiry fellow, and a proper master of his hands when he sees occasion for using them. Well, brother, the foremost man came to the gate, reached at the hank, undid it, and rode through, holding it open for the other. Before, however, the other could follow into the lane, out bolted the plastramengro from behind the tree, kicked the gate too with his foot, and, seizing the big man on horseback, 'You are my prisoner,' said he.   I am of opinion, brother, that the plastramengro, notwithstanding he went to sleep, must have been a regular fine fellow."

"I am entirely of your opinion," said I ; "but what happened then ?"

"Why, brother, the Rommany chal, after he had somewhat recovered from his surprise, for it is rather uncomfortable to be laid hold of at night-time, and told you are a prisoner ; more especially when you happen to have two or three things on your mind, which, if proved against you, would carry you to the nashky. The Rommany chal, I say, clubbed his whip, and aimed a blow at the plastramengro, which, if it had hit him on the skull, as was intended, would very likely have cracked it.   The plastramengro, however, received it partly on his staff, so that it did him no particular damage.   Whereupon seeing what kind of customer he had to deal with, he dropped his staff, and seized the chal with both his hands, who forthwith spurred his horse, hoping by doing so, either to break away from him, or fling him down ; but it would not do—the plastramengro held on like a bulldog, so that the Rommany chal, to escape being hauled to the ground, suddenly flung himself off the saddle, and then happened in that lane, close by the gate, such a struggle between those two—the chal and the runner—as I suppose will never happen again.   But you must have heard of it ; every one has heard of it ; every one has heard of the fight between the Bow street engro and the Rommany chal."

"I never heard of it till now."

"All England rung of it, brother.   There never was a better match than between those two.   The runner was somewhat the stronger of the two—all these engroes are strong fellows—and a great deal cooler, for all of that sort are wondrous cool people— he had, however, to do with one who knew full well how to take his own part.   The chal fought the engro, brother, in the old Roman fashion.   He bit, he kicked, and screamed like a wild cat of Benygant ; casting foam from his mouth, and fire from his eyes.   Sometimes he was beneath the engro's legs, and sometimes he was upon his shoulders.   What the engro found the most difficult, was to get a firm hold of the chal, for no sooner did he seize the chal by any part of his wearing apparel, than the chal either tore himself away, or contrived to slip out of it ; so that in a little time the chal was three parts naked ; and as for holding him by

1825.] SATISFACTION.

the body, it was out of the question, for he was as slippery as an eel. At last the engro seized the chal by the Belcher's handker-chief, which he wore in a knot round his neck, and do whatever the chal could, he could not free himself; and when the engro saw that, it gave him fresh heart, no doubt; 'It's of no use,' said he; 'you had better give in; hold out your hands for the darbies, or I will throttle you'."

"And what did the other fellow do, who came with the chal?" said I.

"I sat still on my horse, brother."

"You?" said I. "Were you the man?"

"I was he, brother."

"And why did you not help your comrade?"

"I have fought in the ring, brother."

"And what had fighting in the ring to do with fighting in the lane?"

"You mean not fighting. A great deal, brother; it taught me to prize fair play. When I fought Staffordshire Dick, t'other side of London, I was alone, brother. Not a Rommany chal to back me, and he had all his brother pals about him; but they gave me fair play, brother; and I beat Staffordshire Dick, which I couldn't have done had they put one finger on his side the scale; for he was as good a man as myself, or nearly so. Now, brother, had I but bent a finger in favour of the Rommany chal the plastramengro would never have come alive out of the lane; but I did not, for I thought to myself fair play is a precious stone; so you see, brother ——"

"That you are quite right, Mr. Petulengro; I see that clearly; and now, pray proceed with your narration; it is both moral and entertaining."

But Mr. Petulengro did not proceed with his narration, neither did he proceed upon his way; he had stopped his horse, and his eyes were intently fixed on a broad strip of grass beneath some lofty trees, on the left side of the road. It was a pleasant enough spot, and seemed to invite wayfaring people, such as we were, to rest from the fatigues of the road, and the heat and vehemence of the sun. After examining it for a considerable time, Mr. Petulengro said : " I say, brother, that would be a nice place for a tuzzle ! "

"I daresay it would," said I, "if two people were inclined to fight."

"The ground is smooth," said Mr. Petulengro; "without holes or ruts, and the trees cast much shade, I don't think,

brother, that we could find a better place," said Mr. Petulengro,
springing from his horse.

"But you and I don't want to fight!"

"Speak for yourself, brother," said Mr. Petulengro. "However, I will tell you how the matter stands. There is a point at
present between us. There can be no doubt that you are the
cause of Mrs. Hearne's death, innocently, you will say, but still
the cause. Now, I shouldn't like it to be known that I went up
and down the country with a pal who was the cause of my mother-
in-law's death—that's to say, unless he gave me satisfaction. Now,
if I and my pal have a tuzzle, he gives me satisfaction; and if he
knocks my eyes out, which I know you can't do, it makes no
difference at all, he gives me satisfaction; and he who says to
the contrary, knows nothing of gypsy law, and is a dinelo into
the bargain."

"But we have no gloves!"

"Gloves!" said Mr. Petulengro contemptuously, "gloves!
I tell you what, brother, I always thought you were a better hand
at the gloves than the naked fist; and, to tell you the truth, besides taking satisfaction for Mrs. Hearne's death, I wish to see
what you can do with your morleys; so now is your time, brother,
and this is your place, grass and shade, no ruts or holes; come
on, brother, or I shall think you what I should not like to call
you."

CHAPTER LXXXII.

AND when I heard Mr. Petulengro talk in this manner, which I had never heard him do before, and which I can only account for by his being fasting and ill-tempered, I had of course no other alternative than to accept his challenge; so I put myself into a posture which I deemed the best both for offence and defence, and the tuzzle commenced; and when it had endured for about half an hour, Mr. Petulengro said: " Brother, there is much blood on your face, you had better wipe it off"; and when I had wiped it off, and again resumed my former attitude, Mr. Petulengro said: " I think enough has been done, brother, in the affair of the old woman; I have, moreover, tried what you are able to do, and find you as I thought, less apt with the naked morleys than the stuffed gloves; nay, brother, put your hands down; I'm satisfied; blood has heen shed, which is all that can be reasonably expected for an old woman, who carried so much brimstone about her as Mrs. Hearne ".

So the struggle ended, and we resumed our route, Mr. Petulengro sitting sideways upon his horse as before, and I driving my little pony-cart; and when we had proceeded about three miles, we came to a small public-house, which bore the sign of the Silent Woman, where we stopped to refresh our cattle and ourselves; and as we sat over our bread and ale, it came to pass that Mr. Petulengro asked me various questions, and amongst others, how I intended to dispose of myself; I told him that I did not know; whereupon with considerable frankness, he invited me to his camp, and told me that if I chose to settle down amongst them, and become a Rommany chal, I should have his wife's sister, Ursula, who was still unmarried, and occasionally talked of me.

I declined his offer, assigning as a reason the recent death of Mrs. Hearne, of which I was the cause, although innocent. " A pretty life I should lead with those two," said I, " when they came to know it." " Pooh," said Mr. Petulengro, " they will never know it. I shan't blab, and as for Leonora, that girl has a

head on her shoulders." "Unlike the woman in the sign," said
I, "whose head is cut off. You speak nonsense, Mr. Petulengro;
as long as a woman has a head on her shoulders she'll talk,—but,
leaving women out of the case, it is impossible to keep anything
a secret; an old master of mine told me so long ago. I have
moreover another reason for declining your offer. I am at
present not disposed for society. I am become fond of solitude.
I wish I could find some quiet place to which I could retire to
hold communion with my own thoughts, and practise, if I thought
fit, either of my trades." "What trades?" said Mr. Petulengro.
"Why, the one which I have lately been engaged in, or my
original one, which I confess I should like better, that of a
kaulomescro." "Ah, I have frequently heard you talk of making
horse-shoes," said Mr. Petulengro. "I, however, never saw you
make one, and no one else that I am aware. I don't believe—
come, brother, don't be angry, it's quite possible that you may
have done things which neither I nor any one else has seen you
do, and that such things may some day or other come to light, as
you say nothing can be kept secret. Be that, however, as it may,
pay the reckoning and let us be going; I think I can advise you
to just such a kind of place as you seem to want."

     "And how do you know that I have got wherewithal to pay
the reckoning?" I demanded. "Brother," said Mr. Petulengro,
"I was just now looking in your face, which exhibited the very
look of a person conscious of the possession of property; there
was nothing hungry or sneaking in it. Pay the reckoning,
brother."

     And when we were once more upon the road Mr. Petulengro
began to talk of the place which he conceived would serve me as
a retreat under present circumstances. "I tell you frankly,
brother, that it is a queer kind of place, and I am not very fond
of pitching my tent in it, it is so surprisingly dreary. It is a deep
dingle in the midst of a large field, on an estate about which there
has been a lawsuit for some years past. I daresay you will be
quiet enough, for the nearest town is five miles distant, and there
are only a few huts and hedge public-houses in the neighbourhood.
Brother, I am fond of solitude myself, but not that kind of
solitude; I like a quiet heath, where I can pitch my house, but I
always like to have a gay, stirring place not far off, where the
women can pen dukkerin, and I myself can sell or buy a horse,
if needful—such a place as the Chong Gav. I never feel so
merry as when there, brother, or on the heath above it, where I
taught you Rommany."

Shortly after this discourse we reached a milestone, and a few yards from the milestone, on the left hand, was a cross-road. Thereupon Mr. Petulengro said : " Brother, my path lies to the left ; if you choose to go with me to my camp, good, if not, Chal Devlehi ". But I again refused Mr. Petulengro's invitation, and, shaking him by the hand, proceeded forward alone, and about ten miles farther on I reached the town of which he had spoken, and following certain directions which he had given, discovered, though not without sóme difficulty, the dingle which he had mentioned. It was a deep hollow in the midst of a wide field, the shelving sides were overgrown with trees and bushes, a belt of sallows surrounded it on the top, a steep winding path led down into the depths, practicable, however, for a light cart, like mine ; at the bottom was an open space, and there I pitched my tent, and there I contrived to put up my forge. " I will here ply the trade of kaulomescro," said I.

CHAPTER LXXXIII.

It has always struck me that there is something highly poetical about a forge. I am not singular in this opinion: various individuals have assured me that they can never pass by one, even in the midst of a crowded town, without experiencing sensations which they can scarcely define, but which are highly pleasurable. I have a decided *penchant* for forges, especially rural ones, placed in some quaint, quiet spot—a dingle, for example, which is a poetical place, or at a meeting of four roads, which is still more so; for how many a superstition—and superstition is the soul of poetry—is connected with these cross-roads! I love to light upon such a one, especially after nightfall, as everything about a forge tells to most advantage at night; the hammer sounds more solemnly in the stillness; the glowing particles scattered by the strokes sparkle with more effect in the darkness, whilst the sooty visage of the sastramescro, half in shadow, and half-illumed by the red and partial blaze of the forge, looks more mysterious and strange. On such occasions I draw in my horse's rein, and, seated in the saddle, endeavour to associate with the picture before me—in itself a picture of romance—whatever of the wild and wonderful I have read of in books, or have seen with my own eyes in connection with forges.

I believe the life of any blacksmith, especially a rural one, would afford materials for a highly poetical history. I do not speak unadvisedly, having the honour to be free of the forge, and therefore fully competent to give an opinion as to what might be made out of the forge by some dextrous hand. Certainly, the strangest and most entertaining life ever written is that of a blacksmith of the olden north, a certain Volundr, or Velint, who lived in woods and thickets, made keen swords, so keen, indeed, that if placed in a running stream, they would fairly divide an object, however slight, which was borne against them by the water, and who eventually married a king's daughter, by whom he had a son, who was as bold a knight as his father was a cunning blacksmith. I never see a forge at night, when seated on the back of my horse at the bottom of a dark lane, but I somehow or other associate it with the exploits of this extraordinary fellow, with many other extraordinary things, amongst which, as I have hinted before, are particular passages of my own life, one or two of which I shall perhaps relate to the reader.

I never associate Vulcan and his Cyclops with the idea of a forge. These gentry would be the very last people in the world to flit across my mind whilst gazing at the forge from the bottom of the dark lane. The truth is, they are highly unpoetical fellows, as well they may be, connected as they are with Grecian mythology. At the very mention of their names the forge burns dull and dim, as if snow-balls had been suddenly flung into it; the only remedy is to ply the bellows, an operation which I now hasten to perform.

I am in the dingle making a horse-shoe. Having no other horses on whose hoofs I could exercise my art, I made my first essay on those of my own horse, if that could be called horse which horse was none, being only a pony. Perhaps if I had sought all England, I should scarcely have found an animal more in need of the kind offices of the smith. On three of his feet there were no shoes at all, and on the fourth only a remnant of one, on which account his hoofs were sadly broken and lacerated by his late journeys over the hard and flinty roads. "You belonged to a tinker before," said I, addressing the animal, "but now you belong to a smith. It is said that the household of the shoemaker invariably go worse shod than that of any other craft. That may be the case of those who make shoes of leather, but it sha'n't be said of the household of him who makes shoes of iron; at any rate, it sha'n't be said of mine. I tell you what, my gry, whilst you continue with me, you shall both be better shod, and better fed, than you were with your last master."

I am in the dingle making a petul; and I must here observe, that whilst I am making a horse-shoe, the reader need not be surprised if I speak occasionally in the language of the lord of the horse-shoe—Mr. Petulengro. I have for some time past been plying the peshota, or bellows, endeavouring to raise up the yag, or fire, in my primitive forge. The angar, or coals, are now burning fiercely, casting forth sparks and long vagescoe chipes, or tongues of flame; a small bar of sastra, or iron, is lying in the fire, to the length of ten or twelve inches, and so far it is hot, very hot, exceeding hot, brother. And now you see me, prala, snatch the bar of iron, and place the heated end of it upon the covantza, or anvil, and forthwith I commence cooring the sastra as hard as if I had been just engaged by a master at the rate of dui caulor, or two shillings a day, brother; and when I have beaten the iron till it is nearly cool, and my arm tired, I place it again in the angar, and begin again to rouse the fire with the pudamengro, which signifies the blowing thing, and is another and more common word for bellows, and whilst thus employed I sing a gypsy song, the sound of which is wonderfully in unison with the hoarse moaning of the pudamengro, and ere the song is finished, the iron is again hot and malleable. Behold, I place it once more on the covantza, and recommence hammering; and now I am somewhat at fault; I am in want of assistance; I want you, brother, or some one else, to take the bar out of my hand and support it upon the covantza, whilst I, applying a chinomescro, or kind of chisel, to the heated iron, cut off with a lusty stroke or two of the shukaro baro, or big hammer, as much as is required for the petul. But having no one to help me, I go on hammering till I have fairly knocked off as much as I want, and then I place the piece in the fire, and again apply the bellows, and take up the song where I left it off; and when I have finished the song, I take out the iron, but this time with my plaistra, or pincers, and then I recommence hammering, turning the iron round and round with my pincers: and now I bend the iron, and lo, and behold, it has assumed something the outline of a petul.

I am not going to enter into further details with respect to the process—it was rather a wearisome one. I had to contend with various disadvantages; my forge was a rude one, my tools might have been better; I was in want of one or two highly necessary implements, but, above all, manual dexterity. Though free of the forge, I had not practised the albeytarian art for very many years, never since—but stay, it is not my intention to tell the reader, at least in this place, how and when I became a blacksmith. There was one thing, however, which stood me in good stead in my labour, the same thing which through life has ever been of incalculable utility to me, and has not unfrequently supplied the place of friends, money, and many other things of almost equal importance—iron perseverance, without which all the advantages of time and circumstance are of very little avail in any undertaking. I was determined to make a horse-shoe, and a good one, in spite of every obstacle—ay, in spite of dukkerin. At the end of four days, during which I had fashioned and refashioned the thing at least fifty times, I had made a petul such as no master of the craft need have been ashamed of; with the second shoe I had less difficulty, and, by the time I had made the fourth, I would have scorned to take off my hat to the best smith in Cheshire.

But I had not yet shod my little gry; this I proceeded now to do. After having first well pared the hoofs with my churi, I applied each petul hot, glowing hot to the pindro. Oh, how the hoofs hissed; and, oh, the pleasant, pungent odour which diffused itself through the dingle, an odour good for an ailing spirit.

I shod the little horse bravely—merely pricked him once, slightly, with a cafi, for doing which, I remember, he kicked me down; I was not disconcerted, however, but, getting up, promised to be more cautious in future; and having finished the operation, I filed the hoof well with the rin baro; then dismissed him to graze amongst the trees, and, putting my smaller tools into the muchtar, I sat down on my stone, and, supporting my arm upon my knee, leaned my head upon my hand. Heaviness had come over me.

CHAPTER LXXXIV.

HEAVINESS had suddenly come over me, heaviness of heart, and of body also. I had accomplished the task which I had imposed upon myself, and now that nothing more remained to do, my energies suddenly deserted me, and I felt without strength, and without hope. Several causes, perhaps, co-operated to bring about the state in which I then felt myself. It is not improbable that my energies had been overstrained during the work, the progress of which I have attempted to describe; and every one is aware that the results of overstrained energies are feebleness and lassitude—want of nourishment might likewise have something to do with it. During my sojourn in the dingle, my food had been of the simplest and most unsatisfying description, by no means calculated to support the exertion which the labour I had been engaged upon required; it had consisted of coarse oaten cakes, and hard cheese, and for beverage I had been indebted to a neighbouring pit, in which, in the heat of the day, I frequently saw, not golden or silver fish, but frogs and eftes swimming about. I am, however, inclined to believe that Mrs. Hearne's cake had quite as much to do with the matter as insufficient nourishment. I had never entirely recovered from the effects of its poison, but had occasionally, especially at night, been visited by a grinding pain in the stomach, and my whole body had been suffused with cold sweat; and indeed these memorials of the drow have never entirely disappeared—even at the present time they display themselves in my system, especially after much fatigue of body and excitement of mind. So there I sat in the dingle upon my stone, nerveless and hopeless, by whatever cause or causes that state had been produced —there I sat with my head leaning upon my hand, and so I continued a long, long time. At last I lifted my head from my hand, and began to cast anxious, unquiet looks about the dingle—the entire hollow was now enveloped in deep shade— I cast my eyes up; there was a golden gleam on the tops of the trees which grew towards the upper parts of the dingle, but lower

(448)

down all was gloom and twilight, yet, when I first sat down on my stone, the sun was right above the dingle, illuminating all its depths by the rays which it cast perpendicularly down, so I must have sat a long, long time upon my stone. And now, once more, I rested my head upon my hand, but almost instantly lifted it again in a kind of fear, and began looking at the objects before me, the forge, the tools, the branches of the trees, endeavouring to follow their rows, till they were lost in the darkness of the dingle; and now I found my right hand grasping convulsively the three forefingers of the left, first collectively, and then successively, wringing them till the joints cracked; then I became quiet, but not for long.

Suddenly I started up, and could scarcely repress the shriek which was rising to my lips. Was it possible? Yes, all too certain; the evil one was upon me; the inscrutable horror which I had felt in my boyhood had once more taken possession of me. I had thought that it had forsaken me; that it would never visit me again; that I had outgrown it; that I might almost bid defiance to it; and I had even begun to think of it without horror, as we are in the habit of doing of horrors of which we conceive we run no danger; and, lo! when least thought of, it had seized me again. Every moment I felt it gathering force, and making me more wholly its own. What should I do?— resist, of course; and I did resist. I grasped, I tore, and strove to fling it from me; but of what avail were my efforts? I could only have got rid of it by getting rid of myself: it was part of myself, or rather it was all myself. I rushed amongst the trees, and struck at them with my bare fists, and dashed my head against them, but I felt no pain. How could I feel pain with that horror upon me! and then I flung myself on the ground, gnawed the earth and swallowed it; and then I looked round; it was almost total darkness in the dingle, and the darkness added to my horror. I could no longer stay there; up I rose from the ground, and attempted to escape; at the bottom of the winding path which led up the acclivity I fell over something which was lying on the ground; the something moved, and gave a kind of whine. It was my little horse, which had made that place its lair; my little horse, my only companion and friend in that now awful solitude. I reached the mouth of the dingle; the sun was just sinking in the far west, behind me; the fields were flooded with his last gleams. How beautiful everything looked in the last gleams of the sun! I felt relieved for a moment; I was no longer in the horrid dingle; in another minute the sun was gone, and a big cloud occupied the place where he had been; in a little time it was almost as dark as it had previously been in the open part of the dingle. My horror increased; what was I to do?—it was of no use fighting against the horror, that I saw; the more I fought against it, the stronger it became. What should I do: say my prayers? Ah! why not? So I knelt down under the hedge, and said, "Our Father"; but that was of no use; and now I could no longer repress cries; the horror was too great to be borne. What should I do: run to the nearest town or village, and request the assistance of my fellow-men? No! that I was ashamed to do; notwithstanding the horror was upon me, I was ashamed to do that. I knew they would consider me a maniac, if I went screaming amongst them; and I did not wish to be considered a maniac. Moreover, I knew that I was not a maniac, for I possessed all my reasoning powers, only the horror was upon me—the screaming horror! But how were indifferent people to distinguish between madness and this screaming horror? So I thought and reasoned; and at last I determined not to go amongst my fellow-men whatever the result might be. I went to the mouth of the dingle, and there placing myself on my knees, I again said the Lord's Prayer; but it was of no use; praying seemed to have no effect over the horror; the unutterable fear appeared rather to increase than diminish; and I again uttered wild cries, so loud that I was apprehensive they would be heard by some chance passenger on the neighbouring road; I, therefore, went deeper into the dingle; I sat down with my back against a thorn bush; the thorns entered my flesh, and when I felt them I pressed harder against the bush; I thought the pain of the flesh might in some degree counteract the mental agony; presently I felt them no longer; the power of the mental horror was so great that it was impossible, with that upon me, to feel any pain from the thorns. I continued in this posture a long time, undergoing what I cannot describe, and would not attempt if I were able. Several times I was on the point of starting up and rushing anywhere; but I restrained myself, for I knew I could not escape from myself, so why should I not remain in the dingle? so I thought and said to myself, for my reasoning powers were still uninjured. At last it appeared to me that the horror was not so strong, not quite so strong upon me. Was it possible that it was relaxing its grasp, releasing its prey? O what a mercy! but it could not be—and yet I looked up to heaven, and clasped my hands, and said, "Our Father". I said no more, I was too agitated; and now I was almost sure that the horror had done its worst.

After a little time I arose, and staggered down yet farther into the dingle. I again found my little horse on the same spot as before; I put my hand to his mouth, he licked my hand. I flung myself down by him and put my arms round his neck; the creature whinned, and appeared to sympathise with me; what a comfort to have any one, even a dumb brute, to sympathise with me at such a moment! I clung to my little horse as if for safety and protection. I laid my head on his neck, and felt almost calm; presently the fear returned, but not so wild as before; it subsided, came again, again subsided; then drowsiness came over me, and at last I fell asleep, my head supported on the neck of the little horse. I awoke; it was dark, dark night—not a star was to be seen—but I felt no fear, the horror had left me. I arose from the side of the little horse, and went into my tent, lay down, and again went to sleep.

I awoke in the morning weak and sore, and shuddering at the remembrance of what I had gone through on the preceding day; the sun was shining brightly, but it had not yet risen high enough to show its head above the trees which fenced the eastern side of the dingle, on which account the dingle was wet and dank from the dews of the night. I kindled my fire, and, after sitting by it for some time to warm my frame, I took some of the coarse food which I have already mentioned; notwithstanding my late struggle and the coarseness of the fare, I ate with appetite. My provisions had by this time been very much diminished, and I saw that it would be speedily necessary, in the event of my continuing to reside in the dingle, to lay in a fresh store. After my meal I went to the pit and filled a can with water, which I brought to the dingle, and then again sat down on my stone. I considered what I should next do; it was necessary to do something, or my life in this solitude would be insupportable. What should I do? rouse up my forge and fashion a horse-shoe? but I wanted nerve and heart for such an employment; moreover, I had no motive for fatiguing myself in this manner; my own horse was shod, no other was at hand, and it is hard to work for the sake of working. What should I do? read? Yes, but I had no other book than the Bible which the Welsh Methodist had given me; well, why not read the Bible? I was once fond of reading the Bible; ay, but those days were long gone by. However, I did not see what else I could well do on the present occasion; so I determined to read the Bible; it was in Welsh—at any rate it might amuse me; so I took the Bible out of the sack in which it was lying in the cart,and began to read at the place where I chanced to open it.

I opened it at that part where the history of Saul commences. At first I read with indifference; but after some time my attention was riveted, and no wonder; I had come to the visitations of Saul—those dark moments of his when he did and said such unaccount-able things; it almost appeared to me that I was reading of myself; I, too, had my visitations, dark as ever his were. Oh, how I sympathised with Saul, the tall, dark man! I had read his life before, but it had made no impression on me; it had never occurred to me that I was like him, but I now sympathised with Saul, for my own dark hour was but recently passed, and, perhaps, would soon return again; the dark hour came frequently on Saul.

Time wore away; I finished the book of Saul, and, closing the volume, returned it to its place. I then returned to my seat on the stone, and thought of what I had read, and what I had lately undergone. All at once I thought I felt well-known sensa-tions, a cramping of the breast, and a tingling of the soles of the feet; they were what I had felt on the preceding day—they were the forerunners of the fear. I sat motionless on my stone: the sensations passed away, and the fear came not. Darkness was now coming again over the earth; the dingle was again in deep shade; I roused the fire with the breath of the bellows, and sat looking at the cheerful glow; it was cheering and comforting. My little horse came now and lay down on the ground beside the forge; I was not quite deserted. I again ate some of the coarse food, and drank plentifully of the water which I had fetched in the morning. I then put fresh fuel on the fire, and sat for a long time looking on the blaze; I then went into my tent.

I awoke, on my own calculation, about midnight—it was pitch dark, and there was much fear upon me.

CHAPTER LXXXV.

Two mornings after the period to which I have brought the reader in the preceding chapter, I sat by my fire at the bottom of the dingle. I had just breakfasted, and had finished the last morsel of food which I had brought with me to that solitude.

"What shall I now do?" said I to myself; "shall I continue here, or decamp? This is a sad, lonely spot; perhaps I had better quit it; but whither should I go? the wide world is before me, but what can I do therein? I have been in the world already without much success. No, I had better remain here; the place is lonely, it is true, but here I am free and independent, and can do what I please; but I can't remain here without food. Well, I will find my way to the nearest town, lay in a fresh supply of provision, and come back, turning my back upon the world, which has turned its back upon me. I don't see why I should not write a little sometimes; I have pens and an ink-horn, and for a writing-desk I can place the Bible on my knee. I shouldn't wonder if I could write a capital satire on the world on the back of that Bible; but first of all I must think of supplying myself with food."

I rose up from the stone on which I was seated, determining to go to the nearest town with my little horse and cart, and procure what I wanted. The nearest town, according to my best calculation, lay about five miles distant; I had no doubt, however, that by using ordinary diligence I should be back before evening. In order to go lighter, I determined to leave my tent standing as it was, and all the things which I had purchased of the tinker, just as they were. "I need not be apprehensive on their account," said I to myself; "nobody will come here to meddle with them; the great recommendation of this place is its perfect solitude; I daresay that I could live here six months without seeing a single human visage. I will now harness my little gry and be off to the town."

At a whistle which I gave, the little gry, which was feeding on the bank near the uppermost part of the dingle, came running to

me : for by this time he had become so accustomed to me, that
he would obey my call for all the world as if he had been one of
the canine species.   " Now," said I to him, " we are going to the
town to buy bread for myself, and oats for you.   I am in a hurry
to be back ; therefore, I pray you to do your best, and to draw
me and the cart to the town with all possible speed, and to bring
us back ; if you do your best, I promise you oats on your return.
You know the meaning of oats, Ambrol ? "

Ambrol whinnied as if to let me know that he understood me
perfectly well, as indeed he well might, as I had never once fed
him during the time he had been in my possession without saying
the word in question to him.   Now, ambrol, in the Gypsy tongue,
signifieth a *pear.*

So I caparisoned Ambrol, and then, going to the cart, I removed two or three things from out it into the tent ; I then
lifted up the shafts, and was just going to call to the pony to come
and be fastened to them, when I thought I heard a noise.

I stood stock still supporting the shaft of the little cart in my
hand, and bending the right side of my face slightly towards the
ground ; but I could hear nothing.   The noise which I thought I
had heard was not one of those sounds which I was accustomed
to hear in that solitude : the note of a bird, or the rustling of a
bough ; it was—there I heard it again, a sound very much resembling the grating of a wheel amongst gravel.   Could it proceed
from the road ?   Oh no, the road was too far distant for me to
hear the noise of anything moving along it.   Again I listened,
and now I distinctly heard the sound of wheels, which seemed to
be approaching ·the dingle ; nearer and nearer they drew, and
presently the sound of wheels was blended with the murmur of
voices.   Anon I heard a boisterous shout, which seemed to proceed from the entrance of the dingle.   " Here are folks at hand,"
said I, letting the shaft of the cart fall to the ground, " is it possible
that they can be coming here ? "

My doubts on that point, if I entertained any, were soon dis-
pelled ; the wheels, which had ceased moving for a moment or
two, were once again in motion, and were now evidently moving
down the winding path which led to my retreat.   Leaving my
cart, I came forward and placed myself near the entrance of the
open space, with my eyes fixed on the path down which my
unexpected, and I may say unwelcome, visitors were coming.
Presently I heard a stamping or sliding, as if of a horse in some
difficulty ; and then a loud curse, and the next moment appeared
a man and a horse and cart ; the former holding the head of the

horse up to prevent him from falling, of which he was in danger, owing to the precipitous nature of the path. Whilst thus occupied, the head of the man was averted from me. When, however, he had reached the bottom of the descent, he turned his head, and perceiving me, as I stood bareheaded, without either coat or waist-coat, about two yards from him, he gave a sudden start, so violent, that the backward motion of his hand had nearly flung the horse upon his haunches.

"Why don't you move forward?" said a voice from behind, apparently that of a female, "you are stopping up the way, and we shall be all down upon one another;" and I saw the head of another horse overtopping the back of the cart.

"Why don't you move forward, Jack?" said another voice, also of a female, yet higher up the path.

The man stirred not, but remained staring at me in the posture which he had assumed on first perceiving me, his body very much drawn back, his left foot far in advance of his right, and with his right hand still grasping the halter of the horse, which gave way more and more, till it was clean down on his haunches.

"What's the matter?" said the voice which I had last heard.

"Get back with you, Belle, Moll," said the man, still staring at me, "here's something not over-canny or comfortable."

"What is it?" said the same voice; "let me pass, Moll, and I'll soon clear the way," and I heard a kind of rushing down the path.

"You need not be afraid," said I, addressing myself to the man, "I mean you no harm; I am a wanderer like yourself—come here to seek for shelter—you need not be afraid; I am a Roman chabo by matriculation—one of the right sort, and no mis-take. Good-day to ye, brother; I bid ye welcome."

The man eyed me suspiciously for a moment, then turning to his horse with a loud curse, he pulled him up from his haunches, and led him and the cart farther down to one side of the dingle, muttering as he passed me, "afraid. Hm!"

I do not remember ever to have seen a more ruffianly-looking fellow; he was about six feet high, with an immensely athletic frame; his face was black and bluff, and sported an immense pair of whiskers, but with here and there a grey hair, for his age could not be much under fifty. He wore a faded blue frock-coat, corduroys, and highlows; on his black head was a kind of red nightcap; round his bull neck a Barcelona handkerchief—I did not like the look of the man at all.

"Afraid," growled the fellow, proceeding to unharness his horse; "that was the word, I think."

But other figures were now already upon the scene. Dashing past the other horse and cart, which by this time had reached the bottom of the pass, appeared an exceedingly tall woman, or rather girl, for she could scarcely have been above eighteen; she was dressed in a tight bodice, and a blue stuff gown; hat, bonnet or cap she had none, and her hair, which was flaxen, hung down on her shoulders unconfined; her complexion was fair, and her features handsome, with a determined but open expression. She was followed by another female, about forty, stout and vulgar-looking, at whom I scarcely glanced, my whole attention being absorbed by the tall girl.

"What's the matter, Jack?" said the latter, looking at the man.

"Only afraid, that's all," said the man, still proceeding with his work.

"Afraid at what—at that lad? why, he looks like a ghost. I would engage to thrash him with one hand."

"You might beat me with no hands at all," said I, "fair damsel, only by looking at me; I never saw such a face and figure, both regal. Why, you look like Ingeborg, Queen of Norway; she had twelve brothers, you know, and could lick them all, though they were heroes:—

> ' On Dovrefeld in Norway,
> Were once together seen,
> The twelve heroic brothers
> Of Ingeborg the queen.' "

"None of your chaffing, young fellow," said the tall girl, " or I will give you what shall make you wipe your face; be civil, or you will rue it."

"Well, perhaps I was a peg too high," said I; " I ask your pardon—here's something a bit lower:—

> 'As I was jawing to the gav yeck divvus
> I met on the drom miro Rommany chi—' "

"None of your Rommany chies, young fellow," said the tall girl, looking more menacingly than before and clenching her fist, "you had better be civil, I am none of your chies; and though I keep company with gypsies, or, to speak more proper, half and halfs, I would have you to know that I come of Christian blood and parents, and was born in the great house of Long Melford."

"I have no doubt," said I, "that it was a great house;

judging from your size, I shouldn't wonder if you were born in a church."

" Stay, Belle," said the man, putting himself before the young virago, who was about to rush upon me, " my turn is first; " then, advancing to me in a menacing attitude, he said, with a look of deep malignity, " Afraid was the word, wasn't it ? "

" It was," said I, " but I think I wronged you ; I should have said, aghast, you exhibited every symptom of one labouring under uncontrollable fear."

The fellow stared at me with a look of stupid ferocity, and appeared to be hesitating whether to strike or not ; ere he could make up his mind, the tall girl started forward, crying, " He's chaffing, let me at him " ; and, before I could put myself on my guard, she struck me a blow on the face which had nearly brought me to the ground.

" Enough," said I, putting my hand to my cheek ; " you have now performed your promise, and made me wipe my face ; now be pacified, and tell me fairly the grounds of this quarrel."

" Grounds ! " said the fellow ; " didn't you say I was afraid ? and if you hadn't, who gave you leave to camp on my ground ? "

" Is it your ground ? " said I.

" A pretty question," said the fellow ; " as if all the world didn't know that. Do you know who I am ? "

" I guess I do," said I ; " unless I am much mistaken, you are he whom folks call the ' Flaming Tinman '. To tell you the truth, I'm glad we have met, for I wished to see you. These are your two wives, I suppose ; I greet them. There's no harm done —there's room enough here for all of us—we shall soon be good friends, I dare say ; and when we are a little better acquainted, I'll tell you my history."

" Well, if that doesn't beat all," said the fellow.

" I don't think he's chaffing now," said the girl, whose anger seemed to have subsided on a sudden ; " the young man speaks civil enough."

" Civil," said the fellow with an oath ; " but that's just like you ; with you it is a blow, and all over. Civil ! I suppose you would have him stay here, and get into all my secrets, and hear all I may have to say to my two morts."

" Two morts ! " said the girl, kindling up, " where are they ? Speak for one, and no more. I am no mort of yours, whatever some one else may be. I tell you one thing, Black John, or Anselo, for t'other an't your name, the same thing I told the young man here : be civil, or you will rue it."

The fellow looked at the girl furiously, but his glance soon quailed before hers ; he withdrew his eyes, and cast them on my little horse, which was feeding amongst the trees. "What's this?" said he, rushing forward and seizing the animal. "Why, as I am alive, this is the horse of that mumping villain Slingsby."

"It's his no longer ; I bought it and paid for it."

"It's mine now," said the fellow ; "I swore I would seize it the next time I found it on my beat ; ay, and beat the master too."

"I am not Slingsby."

"All's one for that."

"You don't say you will beat me?"

"Afraid was the word."

"I'm sick and feeble."

"Hold up your fists."

"Won't the horse satisfy you?"

"Horse nor bellows either."

"No mercy, then."

"Here's at you."

"Mind your eyes, Jack. There, you've got it. I thought so," shouted the girl, as the fellow staggered back from a sharp blow in the eye. "I thought he was chaffing at you all along."

"Never mind, Anselo. You know what to do—go in," said the vulgar woman, who had hitherto not spoken a word, but who now came forward with all the look of a fury ; "go in apopli ; you'll smash ten like he."

The Flaming Tinman took her advice, and came in, bent on smashing, but stopped short on receiving a left-handed blow on the nose.

"You'll never beat the Flaming Tinman in that way," said the girl, looking at me doubtfully.

And so I began to think myself, when, in the twinkling of an eye, the Flaming Tinman disengaging himself of his frock-coat, and, dashing off his red night-cap, came rushing in more desperately than ever. To a flush hit which he received in the mouth he paid as little attention as a wild bull would have done ; in a moment his arms were around me, and in another, he had hurled me down, falling heavily upon me. The fellow's strength appeared to be tremendous.

"Pay him off now," said the vulgar woman. The Flaming Tinman made no reply, but planting his knee on my breast, seized my throat with two huge horny hands. I gave myself up for dead, and probably should have been so in another minute

but for the tall girl, who caught hold of the handkerchief which
the fellow wore round his neck with a grasp nearly as powerful as
that with which he pressed my throat.

"Do you call that fair play?" said she.

"Hands off, Belle," said the other woman; "do you call it
fair play to interfere? hands off, or I'll be down upon you myself."

But Belle paid no heed to the injunction, and tugged so hard
at the handkerchief that the Flaming Tinman was nearly
throttled; suddenly relinquishing his hold of me, he started on
his feet, and aimed a blow at my fair preserver, who avoided it,
but said coolly:—

"Finish t'other business first, and then I'm your woman
whenever you like; but finish it fairly—no foul play when I'm
by—I'll be the boy's second, and Moll can pick you up when he
happens to knock you down."

The battle during the next ten minutes raged with considerable fury; but it so happened that during this time I was never
able to knock the Flaming Tinman down, but on the contrary
received six knock-down blows myself. "I can never stand
this," said I, as I sat on the knee of Belle, "I am afraid I must
give in; the Flaming Tinman hits very hard," and I spat out a
mouthful of blood.

"Sure enough you'll never beat the Flaming Tinman in the
way you fight—it's of no use flipping at the Flaming Tinman
with your left hand; why don't you use your right?"

"Because I'm not handy with it," said I; and then getting
up, I once more confronted the Flaming Tinman, and struck him
six blows for his one, but they were all left-handed blows, and the
blow which the Flaming Tinman gave me knocked me off my
legs.

"Now, will you use Long Melford?" said Belle, picking me
up.

"I don't know what you mean by Long Melford," said I,
gasping for breath.

"Why, this long right of yours," said Belle, feeling my right
arm—"if you do, I shouldn't wonder if you yet stand a chance."

And now the Flaming Tinman was once more ready, much
more ready than myself. I, however, rose from my second's
knee as well as my weakness would permit me; on he came,
striking left and right, appearing almost as fresh as to wind
and spirit as when he first commenced the combat, though his
eyes were considerably swelled, and his nether lip was cut in two;
on he came, striking left and right, and I did not like his blows

at all, or even the wind of them, which was anything but agreeable, and I gave way before him. At last he aimed a blow which, had it taken full effect, would doubtless have ended the battle, but owing to his slipping, the fist only grazed my left shoulder, and came with terrific force against a tree, close to which I had been driven; before the Tinman could recover himself, I collected all my strength, and struck him beneath the ear, and then fell to the ground completely exhausted, and it so happened that the blow which I struck the tinker beneath the ear was a right-handed blow.

"Hurrah for Long Melford!" I heard Belle exclaim; "there is nothing like Long Melford for shortness all the world over."

At these words I turned round my head as I lay, and perceived the Flaming Tinman stretched upon the ground apparently senseless. "He is dead," said the vulgar woman, as she vainly endeavoured to raise him up; "he is dead; the best man in all the north country, killed in this fashion, by a boy." Alarmed at these words, I made shift to get on my feet; and, with the assistance of the woman, placed my fallen adversary in a sitting posture. I put my hand to his heart, and felt a slight pulsation. "He's not dead," said I, "only stunned; if he were let blood, he would recover presently." I produced a penknife which I had in my pocket, and, baring the arm of the Tinman, was about to make the necessary incision, when the woman gave me a violent blow, and, pushing me aside, exclaimed: "I'll tear the eyes out of your head, if you offer to touch him. Do you want to complete your work, and murder him outright, now he's asleep? you have had enough of his blood already." "You are mad," said I, "I only seek to do him service. Well, if you won't let him be blooded, fetch some water and fling it in his face, you know where the pit is."

"A pretty manœuvre," said the woman; "leave my husband in the hands of you and that limmer, who has never been true to us; I should find him strangled or his throat cut when I came back." "Do you go," said I, to the tall girl, "take the can and fetch some water from the pit." "You had better go yourself," said the girl, wiping a tear as she looked on the yet senseless form of the tinker; "you had better go yourself, if you think water will do him good." I had by this time somewhat recovered my exhausted powers, and, taking the can, I bent my steps as fast as I could to the pit; arriving there, I lay down on the brink, took a long draught, and then plunged my head into the water; after which I filled the can, and bent my way back to the dingle.

Before I could reach the path which led down into its depths, I had to pass some way along its side; I had arrived at a part immediately over the scene of the last encounter, where the bank, overgrown with trees, sloped precipitously down. Here I heard a loud sound of voices in the dingle; I stopped, and laying hold of a tree, leaned over the bank and listened. The two women appeared to be in hot dispute in the dingle. "It was all owing to you, you limmer," said the vulgar woman to the other; "had you not interfered, the old man would soon have settled the boy."

"I'm for fair play and Long Melford," said the other. "If your old man, as you call him, could have settled the boy fairly, he might, for all I should have cared, but no foul work for me; and as for sticking the boy with our gulleys when he comes back, as you proposed, I am not so fond of your old man or you that I should oblige you in it, to my soul's destruction." "Hold your tongue, or I'll ——"; I listened no farther, but hastened as fast as I could to the dingle. My adversary had just begun to show signs of animation; the vulgar woman was still supporting him, and occasionally cast glances of anger at the tall girl who was walking slowly up and down. I lost no time in dashing the greater part of the water into the Tinman's face, whereupon he sneezed, moved his hands, and presently looked round him. At first his looks were dull and heavy, and without any intelligence at all; he soon, however, began to recollect himself, and to be conscious of his situation; he cast a scowling glance at me, then one of the deepest malignity at the tall girl, who was still walking about without taking much notice of what was going forward. At last he looked at his right hand, which had evidently suffered from the blow against the tree, and a half-stifled curse escaped his lips. The vulgar woman now said something to him in a low tone, whereupon he looked at her for a moment, and then got upon his legs. Again the vulgar woman said something to him; her looks were furious, and she appeared to be urging him on to attempt something. I observed that she had a clasped knife in her hand. The fellow remained standing for some time as if hesitating what to do; at last he looked at his hand, and, shaking his head, said something to the woman which I did not understand. The tall girl, however, appeared to overhear him, and, probably repeating his words, said : "No, it won't do; you are right there, and now hear what I have to say,—let bygones be bygones, and let us all shake hands, and camp here, as the young man was saying just now". The man looked at her, and then, without any reply, went to his horse, which was lying down among the trees, and kicking it up, led it to the cart, to which he forthwith began to harness it. The other cart and horse had remained standing motionless during the whole affair which I have been recounting, at the bottom of the pass. The woman now took the horse by the head, and leading it with the cart into the open part of the dingle turned both round, and then led them back, till the horse and cart had mounted a little way up the assent; she then stood still and appeared to be expecting the man. During this proceeding Belle had stood looking on without saying anything; at last, perceiving that the man had harnessed his horse to the other cart, and that both he and the woman were about to take their departure, she said: "You are not going, are you?" Receiving no answer, she continued: "I tell you what, both of you, Black John, and you Moll, his mort, this is not treating me over civilly, —however, I am ready to put up with it, and to go with you if you like, for I bear no malice. I'm sorry for what has happened, but you have only yourselves to thank for it. Now, shall I go with you, only tell me?" The man made no manner of reply, but flogged his horse. The woman, however, whose passions were probably under less control, replied, with a screeching tone: "Stay where you are, you jade, and may the curse of Judas cling to you,—stay with the bit of a mullo whom you helped, and my only hope is that he may gulley you before he comes to be —— Have you with us, indeed! after what's past, no, nor nothing belonging to you. Fetch down your mailla go-cart and live here with your chabo." She then whipped on the horse, and ascended the pass, followed by the man. The carts were light, and they were not long in ascending the winding path. I followed to see that they took their departure. Arriving at the top, I found near the entrance a small donkey cart, which I concluded belonged to the girl. The tinker and his mort were already at some distance; I stood looking after them for a little time, then taking the donkey by the reins I led it with the cart to the bottom of the dingle. Arrived there, I found Belle seated on the stone by the fireplace. Her hair was all dishevelled, and she was in tears.

"They were bad people," said she, "and I did not like them, but they were my only acquaintance in the wide world."

CHAPTER LXXXVI.

In the evening of that same day the tall girl and I sat at tea by the fire, at the bottom of the dingle; the girl on a small stool, and myself, as usual, upon my stone.

The water which served for the tea had been taken from a spring of pellucid water in the neighbourhood, which I had not had the good fortune to discover, though it was well known to my companion, and to the wandering people who frequented the dingle.

"This tea is very good," said I, "but I cannot enjoy it as much as if I were well: I feel very sadly."

"How else should you feel," said the girl, "after fighting with the Flaming Tinman? All I wonder at is that you can feel at all! As for the tea, it ought to be good, seeing that it cost me ten shillings a pound."

"That's a great deal for a person in your station to pay."

"In my station! I'd have you to know, young man—however, I haven't the heart to quarrel with you, you look so ill; and after all, it is a good sum for one to pay who travels the roads; but if I must have tea, I like to have the best; and tea I must have, for I am used to it, though I can't help thinking that it sometimes fills my head with strange fancies—what some folks call vapours, making me weep and cry."

"Dear me," said I, "I should never have thought that one of your size and fierceness would weep and cry!"

"My size and fierceness! I tell you what, young man, you are not over civil this evening; but you are ill, as I said before, and I sha'n't take much notice of your language, at least for the present; as for my size, I am not so much bigger than yourself; and as for being fierce, you should be the last one to fling that at me. It is well for you that I can be fierce sometimes. If I hadn't taken your part against Blazing Bosville, you wouldn't be now taking tea with me."

"It is true that you struck me in the face first; but we'll let that pass. So that man's name is Bosville; what's your own?"

(463)

" Isopel Berners."

" How did you get that name ? "

" I say, young man, you seem fond of asking questions ! will you have another cup of tea ? "

" I was just going to ask for another."

" Well, then, here it is, and much good may it do you ; as for my name, I got it from my mother."

" Your mother's name, then, was Isopel ? "

" Isopel Berners."

" But had you never a father ? "

" Yes, I had a father," said the girl, sighing, "but I don't bear his name."

" Is it the fashion, then, in your country for children to bear their mother's name ? "

" If you ask such questions, young man, I shall be angry with you. I have told you my name, and whether my father's or mother's, I am not ashamed of it."

" It is a noble name."

" There you are right, young man. The chaplain in the great house where I was born, told me it was a noble name ; it was odd enough, he said, that the only three noble names in the county were to be found in the great house ; mine was one ; the other two were Devereux and Bohun."

" What do you mean by the great house ? "

" The workhouse."

" Is it possible that you were born there ? "

" Yes, young man ; and as you now speak softly and kindly, I will tell you my whole tale. My father was an officer of the sea, and was killed at sea as he was coming home to marry my mother, Isopel Berners. He had been acquainted with her, and had left her ; but after a few months he wrote her a letter, to say that he had no rest, and that he repented, and that as soon as his ship came to port he would do her all the reparation in his power. Well, young man, the very day before they reached port they met the enemy, and there was a fight, and my father was killed, after he had struck down six of the enemy's crew on their own deck ; for my father was a big man, as I have heard, and knew tolerably well how to use his hands. And when my mother heard the news, she became half distracted, and ran away into the fields and forests, totally neglecting her business, for she was a small milliner ; and so she ran demented about the meads and forests for a long time, now sitting under a tree, and now by the side of a river—at last she flung herself into some water, and

would have been drowned, had not some one been at hand and
rescued her, whereupon she was conveyed to the great house,
lest she should attempt to do herself further mischief, for she
had neither friends nor parents—and there she died three months
after, having first brought me into the world.   She was a sweet,
pretty creature, I'm told, but hardly fit for this world, being
neither large, nor fierce, nor able to take her own part.   So I
was born and bred in the great house, where I learnt to read
and sew, to fear God, and to take my own part.   When I
was fourteen I was put out to service to a small farmer and his
wife, with whom, however, I did not stay long, for I was half
starved, and otherwise ill-treated, especially by my mistress, who
one day attempting to knock me down with a besom, I knocked
her down with my fist, and went back to the great house."

    " And how did they receive you in the great house ? "

    " Not very kindly, young man—on the contrary, I was put
into a dark room, where I was kept a fortnight on bread and
water ; I did not much care, however, being glad to have got
back to the great house at any rate, the place where I was born,
and where my poor mother died, and in the great house I continued two years longer, reading and sewing, fearing God, and
taking my own part when necessary.   At the end of the two
years I was again put out to service, but this time to a rich
farmer and his wife, with whom, however, I did not live long,
less time, I believe, than with the poor ones, being obliged to
leave for ——"

    " Knocking your mistress down ? "

    " No, young man, knocking my master down, who conducted
himself improperly towards me.   This time I did not go back to
the great house, having a misgiving that they would not receive
me, so I turned my back to the great house where I was born,
and where my poor mother died, and wandered for several days,
I know not whither, supporting myself on a few halfpence which
I chanced to have in my pocket.   It happened one day, as I sat
under a hedge crying, having spent my last farthing, that a
comfortable-looking elderly woman came up in a cart, and seeing
the state in which I was, she stopped and asked what was the
matter with me ; I told her some part of my story, whereupon
she said : ' Cheer up, my dear, if you like you shall go with me,
and wait upon me '.   Of course I wanted little persuasion, so I
got into the cart and went with her.   She took me to London
and various other places, and I soon found that she was a
travelling woman, who went about the country with silks and

linen. I was of great use to her, more especially in those places
where we met evil company. Once, as we were coming from
Dover, we were met by two sailors, who stopped our cart, and
would have robbed and stripped us. ' Let me get down,' said I ;
so I got down, and fought with them both, till they turned round
and ran away.   Two years I lived with the old gentlewoman who
was very kind to me, almost as kind as a mother ; at last she fell
sick at a place in Lincolnshire, and after a few days died, leaving
me her cart and stock in trade, praying me only to see her
decently buried, which I did, giving her a funeral fit for a gentlewoman.   After which I travelled the country melancholy enough
for want of company, but so far fortunate, that I could take my
own part when anybody was uncivil to me.   At last, passing
through the valley of Todmorden, I formed the acquaintance of
Blazing Bosville and his wife, with whom I occasionally took
journeys for company's sake, for it is melancholy to travel about
alone, even when one can take one's own part.   I soon found
they were evil people ; but, upon the whole, they treated me
civilly, and I sometimes lent them a little money, so that we got
on tolerably well together.   He and I, it is true, had once a
dispute, and nearly came to blows, for once, when we were alone,
he wanted me to marry him, promising if I would, to turn off
Grey Moll, or if I liked it better, to make her wait upon me as
a maid-servant ; I never liked him much, but from that hour less
than ever.   Of the two, I believe Grey Moll to be the best, for
she is at any rate true and faithful to him, and I like truth and
constancy, don't you, young man ? "

"Yes," said I, "they are very nice things. I feel very
strangely."

" How do you feel, young man ? "

" Very much afraid."

" Afraid, at what ? At the Flaming Tinman ? Don't be
afraid of him.   He won't come back, and if he did, he shouldn't
touch you in this state.   I'd fight him for you, but he won't
come back, so you needn't be afraid of him."

" I'm not afraid of the Flaming Tinman."

" What, then, are you afraid of ? "

" The evil one."

" The evil one," said the girl, " where is he ? "

" Coming upon me."

" Never heed," said the girl, " I'll stand by you."

CHAPTER LXXXVII.

THE kitchen of the public-house was a large one, and many people were drinking in it; there was a confused hubbub of voices.

I sat down on a bench behind a deal table, of which there were three or four in the kitchen; presently a bulky man, in a green coat, of the Newmarket cut, and without a hat, entered, and observing me, came up, and in rather a gruff tone cried : " Want anything, young fellow ? "

" Bring me a jug of ale," said I, " if you are the master, as I suppose you are, by that same coat of yours, and your having no hat on your head."

" Don't be saucy, young fellow," said the landlord, for such he was, " don't be saucy, or ——" Whatever he intended to say, he left unsaid, for fixing his eyes upon one of my hands, which I had placed by chance upon the table, he became suddenly still.

This was my left hand, which was raw and swollen, from the blows dealt on a certain hard skull in a recent combat. " What do you mean by staring at my hand so ? " said I, withdrawing it from the table.

" No offence, young man, no offence," said the landlord, in a quite altered tone ; " but the sight of your hand ——," then observing that our conversation began to attract the notice of the guests in the kitchen, he interrupted himself, saying in an under tone : " But mum's the word for the present, I will go and fetch the ale."

In about a minute he returned, with a jug of ale foaming high. " Here's your health," said he, blowing off the foam, and drinking ; but perceiving that I looked rather dissatisfied, he murmured : " All's right, I glory in you ; but mum's the word." Then placing the jug on the table, he gave me a confidential nod, and swaggered out of the room.

What can the silly, impertinent fellow mean, thought I ; but the ale was now before me, and I hastened to drink, for my weakness was great, and my mind was full of dark thoughts, the

(467)

remains of the indescribable horror of the preceding night. It may kill me, thought I, as I drank deep, but who cares, anything is better than what I have suffered. I drank deep, and then leaned back against the wall; it appeared as if a vapour was stealing up into my brain, gentle and benign, soothing and stilling the horror and the fear; higher and higher it mounted, and I felt nearly overcome; but the sensation was delicious, compared with that I had lately experienced, and now I felt myself nodding; and bending down I laid my head on the table on my folded hands.

And in that attitude I remained some time, perfectly unconscious. At length, by degrees, perception returned, and I lifted up my head. I felt somewhat dizzy and bewildered, but the dark shadow had withdrawn itself from me. And now, once more, I drank of the jug; this second draught did not produce an overpowering effect upon me—it revived and strengthened me. I felt a new man.

I looked around me: the kitchen had been deserted by the greater part of the guests; besides myself, only four remained; these were seated at the farther end. One was haranguing fiercely and eagerly; he was abusing England, and praising America. At last he exclaimed: "So when I gets to New York, I will toss up my hat, and damn the King".

That man must be a Radical, thought I.

CHAPTER LXXXVIII.

THE individual whom I supposed to be a radical, after a short pause, again uplifted his voice : he was rather a strong-built fellow of about thirty, with an ill-favoured countenance, a white hat on his head, a snuff-coloured coat on his back, and, when he was not speaking, a pipe in his mouth. " Who would live in such a country as England ? " he shouted.

" There is no country like America," said his nearest neighbour, a man also in a white hat, and of a very ill-favoured countenance, " there is no country like America," said he, withdrawing a pipe from his mouth ; " I think I shall "—and here he took a draught from a jug, the contents of which he appeared to have in common with the other,—" go to America one of these days myself."

" Poor old England is not such a bad country, after all," said a third, a simple-looking man in a labouring dress, who sat smoking a pipe without anything before him. " If there was but a little more work to be got, I should have nothing to say against her. I hope, however ——"

" You hope, who cares what you hope ? " interrupted the first, in a savage tone ; " you are one of those sneaking hounds who are satisfied with dog's wages, a bit of bread and a kick. Work, indeed ! who, with the spirit of a man, would work for a country where there is neither liberty of speech, nor of action ? a land full of beggarly aristocracy, hungry borough-mongers, insolent parsons, and ' their —— wives and daughters,' as William Cobbett says, in his *Register.*"

" Ah, the Church of England has been a source of incalculable mischief to these realms," said another.

The person who uttered these words sat rather aloof from the rest ; he was dressed in a long black surtout. I could not see much of his face, partly owing to his keeping it very much directed to the ground, and partly owing to a large slouched hat, which he wore ; I observed, however, that his hair was of a reddish tinge. On the table near him was a glass and spoon,

"You are quite right," said the first, alluding to what this last had said, "the Church of England has done incalculable mischief here. I value no religion three halfpence, for I believe in none; but the one that I hate most is the Church of England; so when I get to New York, after I have shown the fine fellows on the quay a spice of me, by —— the King, I'll toss up my hat again, and —— the Church of England too."

"And suppose the people of New York should clap you in the stocks?" said I.

These words drew upon me the attention of the whole four. The radical and his companion stared at me ferociously; the man in black gave me a peculiar glance from under his slouched hat; the simple-looking man in the labouring dress laughed.

"What are you laughing at, you fool?" said the radical, turning and looking at the other, who appeared to be afraid of him, "hold your noise; and a pretty fellow, you," said he, looking at me, "to come here, and speak against the great American nation."

"I speak against the great American nation?" said I, "I rather paid them a compliment."

"By supposing they would put me in the stocks. Well, I call it abusing them, to suppose they would do any such thing— stocks, indeed!—there are no stocks in all the land. Put me in the stocks? why, the President will come down to the quay, and ask me to dinner, as soon as he hears what I have said about the King and the Church."

"I shouldn't wonder," said I, "if you go to America, you will say of the President and country what now you say of the King and Church, and cry out for somebody to send you back to England."

The radical dashed his pipe to pieces against the table. "I tell you what, young fellow, you are a spy of the aristocracy, sent here to kick up a disturbance."

"Kicking up a disturbance," said I, "is rather inconsistent with the office of spy. If I were a spy, I should hold my head down, and say nothing."

The man in black partially raised his [head and gave me another peculiar glance.

"Well, if you ar'n't sent to spy, you are sent to bully, to prevent people speaking, and to run down the great American nation; but you sha'n't bully me. I say down with the aristocracy, the beggarly aristocracy. Come, what have you to say to that?"

"Nothing," said I.

" Nothing ! " repeated the radical.

" No," said I, " down with them as soon as you can."

" As soon as I can ! I wish I could. But I can down with a bully of theirs. Come, will you fight for them ? "

" No," said I.

" You won't ? "

" No," said I ; " though from what I have seen of them I should say they are tolerably able to fight for themselves."

" You won't fight for them," said the radical, triumphantly ; " I thought so ; all bullies, especially those of the aristocracy, are cowards. Here, landlord," said he, raising his voice, and striking against the table with the jug, " some more ale—he won't fight for his friends."

" A white feather," said his companion.

" He ! he ! " tittered the man in black.

" Landlord, landlord," shouted the radical, striking the table with the jug louder than before. " Who called ? " said the land-lord, coming in at last. " Fill this jug again," said the other, " and be quick about it." " Does any one else want anything ? " said the landlord. " Yes," said the man in black ; " you may bring me another glass of gin and water." " Cold ? " said the landlord. " Yes," said the man in black, " with a lump of sugar in it."

" Gin and water cold, with a lump of sugar in it," said I, and struck the table with my fist.

" Take some ? " said the landlord, inquiringly.

" No," said I, " only something came into my head."

" He's mad," said the man in black.

" Not he," said the radical. " He's only shamming ; he knows his master is here, and therefore has recourse to these manœuvres, but it won't do. Come, landlord, what are you staring at ? · Why don't you obey your orders ? Keeping your customers waiting in this manner is not the way to increase your business."

The landlord looked at the radical and then at me. At last, taking the jug and glass, he left the apartment, and presently returned with each filled with its respective liquor. He placed the jug with the beer before the radical, and the glass with the gin and water before the man in black, and then, with a wink to me, he sauntered out.

" Here is your health, sir," said the man of the snuff-coloured coat, addressing himself to the man in black, " I honour you for what you said about the Church of England. Every one who speaks against the Church of England has my warm heart. Down with it, I say, and may the stones of it be used for mending the roads, as my friend William says in his *Register.*"

The man in black, with a courteous nod of his head, drank to the man in the snuff-coloured coat.   "With respect to the steeples," said he, "I am not altogether of your opinion ; they might be turned to better account than to serve to mend the roads ; they might still be used as places of worship, but not for the worship of the Church of England.   I have no fault to find with the steeples, it is the church itself which I am compelled to arraign ; but it will not stand long, the respectable part of its ministers are already leaving it.   It is a bad church, a persecuting church."

"Whom does it persecute ?" said I.

The man in black glanced at me slightly, and then replied slowly, "the Catholics".

"And do those whom you call Catholics never persecute ?" said I.

"Never," said the man in black.

"Did you ever read Fox's *Book of Martyrs ?*" said I.

"He ! he ! tittered the man in black, "there is not a word of truth in Fox's *Book of Martyrs.*"

"Ten times more than in the *Flos Sanctorum,*" said I.

The man in black looked at me, but made no answer.

"And what say you to the Massacre of the Albigenses and the Vaudois, 'whose bones lie scattered on the cold Alp,' or the Revocation of the Edict of Nantes ?"

The man in black made no answer.

"Go to," said I, "it is because the Church of England is not a persecuting church, that those whom you call the respectable part are leaving her ; it is because they can't do with the poor Dissenters what Simon de Montfort did with the Albigenses, and the cruel Piedmontese with the Vaudois, that they turn to bloody Rome ; the Pope will no doubt welcome them, for the Pope, do you see, being very much in want, will welcome ——"

"Hollo !" said the radical, interfering, "What are you saying about the Pope ?   I say hurrah for the Pope ! I value no religion three halfpence, as I said before, but if I were to adopt any, it should be the Popish, as it's called, because I conceives the Popish to be the grand enemy of the Church of England, of the beggarly aristocracy, and the borough-monger system, so I won't hear the Pope abused while I am by.   Come, don't look fierce.   You won't fight, you know, I have proved it ; but I will give you another chance—I will fight for the Pope, will you fight against him ?"

"Oh dear me, yes," said I, getting up and stepping forward. "I am a quiet, peaceable young man, and, being so, am always ready to fight against the Pope—the enemy of all peace and quiet. To refuse fighting for the aristocracy is a widely different thing from refusing to fight against the Pope—so come on, if you are disposed to fight for him. To the Pope broken bells, to Saint James broken shells. No Popish vile oppression, but the Protestant succession. Confusion to the Groyne, hurrah for the Boyne, for the army at Clonmel, and the Protestant young gentlemen who live there as well."

"An Orangeman," said the man in black.

"Not a Platitude," said I.

The man in black gave a slight start.

"Amongst that family," said I, "no doubt something may be done, but amongst the Methodist preachers I should conceive that the success would not be great."

The man in black sat quite still.

"Especially amongst those who have wives," I added.

The man in black stretched his hand towards his gin and water.

"However," said I, "we shall see what the grand movement will bring about, and the results of the lessons in elocution."

The man in black lifted the glass up to his mouth, and in doing so, let the spoon fall.

"But what has this to do with the main question?" said I: "I am waiting here to fight against the Pope."

"Come, Hunter," said the companion of the man in the snuff-coloured coat, "get up, and fight for the Pope."

"I don't care for the young fellow," said the man in the snuff-coloured coat.

"I know you don't," said the other, "so get up, and serve him out."

"I could serve out three like him," said the man in the snuff-coloured coat.

"So much the better for you," said the other, "the present work will be all the easier for you, get up, and serve him out at once."

The man in the snuff-coloured coat did not stir.

"Who shows the white feather now?" said the simple-looking man.

"He! he! he!" tittered the man in black.

"Who told you to interfere?" said the radical, turning ferociously towards the simple-looking man; "say another word, and I'll —— And you ! " said he, addressing himself to the man in black, " a pretty fellow you to turn against me, after I had taken your part. I tell you what, you may fight for yourself. I'll see you and your Pope in the pit of Eldon, before I fight for either of you, so make the most of it."

" Then you won't fight ? " said I.

" Not for the Pope," said the radical; " I'll see the Pope ——"

" Dear me ! " said I, " not fight for the Pope, whose religion you would turn to, if you were inclined for any. I see how it is, you are not fond of fighting; but I'll give you another chance— you were abusing the Church of England just now. I'll fight for it—will you fight against it ? "

" Come, Hunter," said the other, " get up, and fight against the Church of England."

" I have no particular quarrel against the Church of England," said the man in the snuff-coloured coat, " my quarrel is with the aristocracy. If I said anything against the church, it was merely for a bit of corollary, as Master William Cobbett would say ; the quarrel with the church belongs to this fellow in black ; so let him carry it on. However," he continued suddenly, " I won't slink from the matter either ; it shall never be said by the fine fellows on the quay of New York, that I wouldn't fight against the Church of England. So down with the beggarly aristocracy, the church, and the Pope, to the bottom of the pit of Eldon, and may the Pope fall first, and the others upon him."

Thereupon, dashing his hat on the table, he placed himself in an attitude of offence, and rushed forward. He was, as I have said before, a powerful fellow, and might have proved a dangerous antagonist, more especially to myself, who, after my recent encounter with the Flaming Tinman, and my wrestlings with the evil one, was in anything but fighting order. Any collision, how- ever, was prevented by the landlord, who, suddenly appearing, thrust himself between us. " There shall be no fighting here," said he, " no one shall fight in this house, except it be with myself; so if you two have anything to say to each other, you had better go into the field behind the house. But, you fool," said he, pushing Hunter violently on the breast, " do you know whom you are going to tackle with ? this is the young chap that beat Blazing Bosville, only as late as yesterday, in Mumpers' Dingle. Grey Moll told me all about it last night, when she came for some brandy for her husband, who, she said, had been half killed ; and she described the young man to me so closely, that I knew him at once, that is, as soon as I saw how his left hand was bruised, for she told me he was a left-hand hitter. Ar'n't it all true, young man? Ar'n't you he that beat Flaming Bosville in Mumpers' Dingle?" "I never beat Flaming Bosville," said I, "he beat himself. Had he not struck his hand against a tree, I shouldn't be here at the present moment." "Here! here!" said the landlord, "now that's just as it should be; I like a modest man, for, as the parson says, nothing sits better upon a young man than modesty. I remember, when I was young, fighting with Tom of Hopton, the best man that ever pulled off coat in England. I remember, too, that I won the battle; for I happened to hit Tom of Hopton, in the mark, as he was coming in, so that he lost his wind, and falling squelch on the ground, do ye see, he lost the battle, though I am free to confess that he was a better man than myself; indeed, the best man that ever fought in England; yet still I won the battle, as every customer of mine, and everybody within twelve miles round, has heard over and over again. Now, Mr. Hunter, I have one thing to say, if you choose to go into the field behind the house, and fight the young man, you can. I'll back him for ten pounds; but no fighting in my kitchen—because why? I keeps a decent kind of an establishment."

"I have no wish to fight the young man," said Hunter; "more especially as he has nothing to say for the aristocracy. If he chose to fight for them, indeed—but he won't, I know; for I see he's a decent, respectable young man; and, after all, fighting is a blackguard way of settling a dispute; so I have no wish to fight; however, there is one thing I'll do," said he, uplifting his fist, "I'll fight this fellow in black here for half a crown, or for nothing, if he pleases; it was he that got up the last dispute between me and the young man, with his Pope and his nonsense; so I will fight him for anything he pleases, and perhaps the young man will be my second; whilst you ——"

"Come, doctor," said the landlord, "or whatsoever you be, will you go into the field with Hunter? I'll second you, only you must back yourself. I'll lay five pounds on Hunter, if you are inclined to back yourself; and will help you to win it as far, do you see, as a second can; because why? I always likes to do the fair thing."

"Oh! I have no wish to fight," said the man in black hastily; "fighting is not my trade. If I have given any offence, I beg anybody's pardon."

"Landlord," said I, "what have I to pay?"

"Nothing at all," said the landlord; "glad to see you. This

is the first time that you have been at my house, and I never charge
new customers, at least customers such as you, anything for the
first draught. You'll come again, I dare say ; shall always be
glad to see you. I won't take it," said he, as I put sixpence on
the table ; " I won't take it."

" Yes, you shall," said I ; " but not in payment for anything
I have had myself : it shall serve to pay for a jug of ale for that
gentleman," said I, pointing to the simple-looking individual ;
" he is smoking a poor pipe. I do not mean to say that a pipe is
a bad thing ; but a pipe without ale, do you see ——"

" Bravo ! " said the landlord, " that's just the conduct I like."

" Bravo ! " said Hunter. " I shall be happy to drink with the
young man whenever I meet him at New York, where, do you
see, things are better managed than here."

" If I have given offence to anybody, " said the man in black,
" I repeat that I ask pardon,—more especially to the young
gentleman, who was perfectly right to stand up for his religion,
just as I—not that I am of any particular religion, no more than
this honest gentleman here," bowing to Hunter ; " but I happen
to know something of the Catholics—several excellent friends
of mine are Catholics—and of a surety the Catholic religion is an
ancient religion, and a widely extended religion, though it certainly
is not a universal religion, but it has of late made considerable
progress, even amongst those nations who have been particularly
opposed to it—amongst the Prussians and the Dutch, for example,
to say nothing of the English ; and then, in the East, amongst the
Persians, amongst the Armenians ——"

" The Armenians," said I ; " oh dear me, the Armenians ——"

" Have you anything to say about those people, sir ? " said
the man in black, lifting up his glass to his mouth.

" I have nothing further to say," said I, " than that the roots
of Ararat are occasionally found to be deeper than those of Rome."

" There's half a crown broke," said the landlord, as the man
in black let fall the glass, which was broken to pieces on the floor.
" You will pay me the damage, friend, before you leave this kitchen.
I like to see people drink freely in my kitchen, but not too freely,
and I hate breakages ; because why ? I keeps a decent kind of an
establishment."

CHAPTER LXXXIX.

THE public-house where the scenes which I have attempted to describe in the preceding chapters took place, was at the distance of about two miles from the dingle. The sun was sinking in the west by the time I returned to the latter spot. I found Belle seated by a fire, over which her kettle was suspended. During my absence she had prepared herself a kind of tent, consisting of large hoops covered over with tarpaulin, quite impenetrable to rain, however violent. " I am glad you are returned," said she, as soon as she perceived me; "I began to be anxious about you. Did you take my advice?"

" Yes," said I; "I went to the public-house and drank ale as you advised me; it cheered, strengthened, and drove away the horror from my mind—I am much beholden to you."

" I knew it would do you good," said Belle; "I remembered that when the poor woman in the great house were afflicted with hysterics and fearful imaginings, the surgeon, who was a good, kind man, used to say : ' Ale, give them ale, and let it be strong '."

" He was no advocate for tea, then?" said I.

" He had no objection to tea; but he used to say, ' Everything in its season '. Shall we take ours now—I have waited for you."

" I have no objection," said I; "I feel rather heated, and at present should prefer tea to ale—' Everything in its season,' as the surgeon said."

Thereupon Belle prepared tea, and, as we were taking it, she said : " What did you see and hear at the public-house?"

" Really," said I, "you appear to have your full portion of curiosity; what matters it to you what I saw and heard at the public-house?"

" It matters very little to me," said Belle; "I merely inquired of you, for the sake of a little conversation—you were silent, and it is uncomfortable for two people to sit together without opening their lips—at least I think so."

" One only feels uncomfortable," said I, " in being silent,

(477)

when one happens to be thinking of the individual with whom one is in company. To tell you the truth, I was not thinking of my companion, but of certain company with whom I had been at the public-house."

"Really, young man," said Belle, "you are not over complimentary ; but who may this wonderful company have been—some young ——?" and here Belle stopped.

"No," said I, "there was no young person—if person you were going to say. There was a big portly landlord, whom I dare say you have seen ; a noisy savage radical, who wanted at first to fasten upon me a quarrel about America, but who subsequently drew in his horns ; then there was a strange fellow, a prowling priest, I believe, whom I have frequently heard of, who at first seemed disposed to side with the radical against me, and afterwards with me against the radical. There, you know my company, and what took place."

"Was there no one else?" said Belle.

"You are mighty curious," said I. "No, none else, except a poor, simple mechanic, and some common company, who soon went away."

Belle looked at me for a moment, and then appeared to be lost in thought—"America?" said she, musingly—"America?"

"What of America?" said I.

"I have heard that it is a mighty country."

"I dare say it is," said I ; "I have heard my father say that the Americans are first-rate marksmen."

"I heard nothing about that," said Belle ; "what I heard was, that it is a great and goodly land, where people can walk about without jostling, and where the industrious can always find bread ; I have frequently thought of going thither."

"Well," said I, "the radical in the public-house will perhaps be glad of your company thither ; he is as great an admirer of America as yourself, though I believe on different grounds."

"I shall go by myself," said Belle, "unless—unless that should happen which is not likely—I am not fond of radicals no more than I am of scoffers and mockers."

"Do you mean to say that I am a scoffer and mocker?"

"I don't wish to say you are," said Belle ; "but some of your words sound strangely like scoffing and mocking. I have now one thing to beg, which is, that if you have anything to say against America, you would speak it out boldly."

"What should I have to say against America? I never was there."

" Many people speak against America who never were there."

" Many people speak in praise of America who never were there; but with respect to myself, I have not spoken for or against America."

" If you liked America you would speak in its praise."

" By the same rule, if I disliked America I should speak against it."

" I can't speak with you," said Belle; " but I see you dislike the country."

" The country ! "

" Well, the people—don't you ? "

" I do."

" Why do you dislike them ? "

" Why, I have heard my father say that the American marksmen, led on by a chap of the name of Washington, sent the English to the right-about in double-quick time."

" And that is your reason for disliking the Americans ? "

" Yes," said I, " that is my reason for disliking them."

" Will you take another cup of tea ? " said Belle.

I took another cup; we were again silent.   " It is rather uncomfortable," said I, at last, " for people to sit together without having anything to say."

" Were you thinking of your company ? " said Belle.

" What company ? " said I.

" The present company."

" The present company ! oh, ah !—I remember that I said one only feels uncomfortable in being silent with a companion, when one happens to be thinking of the companion.   Well, I had been thinking of you the last two or three minutes, and had just come to the conclusion, that to prevent us both feeling occasionally uncomfortably towards each other, having nothing to say, it would be as well to have a standing subject, on which to employ our tongues.   Belle, I have determined to give you lessons in Armenian."

" What is Armenian ? "

" Did you ever hear of Ararat ? "

" Yes, that was the place where the ark rested; I have heard the chaplain in the great house talk of it; besides, I have read of it in the Bible."

" Well, Armenian is the speech of people of that place, and I should like to teach it you."

" To prevent —— "

" Ay, ay, to prevent our occasionally feeling uncomfortable

together. Your acquiring it besides might prove of ulterior advantage to us both; for example, suppose you and I were in promiscuous company, at Court, for example, and you had something to communicate to me which you did not wish any one else to be acquainted with, how safely you might communicate it to me in Armenian."

"Would not the language of the roads do as well?" said Belle.

"In some places it would," said I, "but not at Court, owing to its resemblance to thieves' slang. There is Hebrew, again, which I was thinking of teaching you, till the idea of being presented at Court made me abandon it, from the probability of our being understood, in the event of our speaking it, by at least half a dozen people in our vicinity. There is Latin, it is true, or Greek, which we might speak aloud at Court with perfect confidence of safety, but upon the whole I should prefer teaching you Armenian, not because it would be a safer language to hold communication with at Court, but because, not being very well grounded in it myself, I am apprehensive that its words and forms may escape from my recollection, unless I have sometimes occasion to call them forth."

"I am afraid we shall have to part company before I have learnt it," said Belle; "in the meantime, if I wish to say anything to you in private, somebody being by, shall I speak in the language of the roads?"

"If no roadster is nigh, you may," said I, "and I will do my best to understand you. Belle, I will now give you a lesson in Armenian."

"I suppose you mean no harm," said Belle.

"Not in the least; I merely propose the thing to prevent our occasionally feeling uncomfortable together. Let us begin."

"Stop till I have removed the tea-things," said Belle; and, getting up, she removed them to her own encampment.

"I am ready," said Belle, returning, and taking her former seat, "to join with you in anything which will serve to pass away the time agreeably, provided there is no harm in it."

"Belle," said I, "I have determined to commence the course of Armenian lessons by teaching you the numerals; but, before I do that, it will be as well to tell you that the Armenian language is called Haik."

"I am sure that word will hang upon my memory," said Belle.

"Why hang upon it?"

" Because the old woman in the great house used to call so
the chimney-hook, on which they hung the kettle ; in like manner,
on the hake of my memory I will hang your hake."

" Good ! " said I, " you will make an apt scholar ; but, mind,
that I did not say hake, but haik ; the words are, however, very
much alike ; and, as you observe, upon your hake you may hang
my haik.   We will now proceed to the numerals."

" What are numerals ? " said Belle.

" Numbers.   I will say the Haikan numbers up to ten.   There,
have you heard them ? "—" Yes."   " Well, try and repeat them."

" I only remember number one," said Belle, "and that
because it is *me*."

" I will repeat them again," said I, " and pay greater attention.
Now, try again."

" *Me, jergo, earache.*"

" I neither said *jergo* nor *earache*.   I said *yergou* and *yerek*.
Belle, I am afraid I shall have some difficulty with you as a
scholar."

Belle made no answer.   Her eyes were turned in the direction
of the winding path, which led from the bottom of the hollow
where we were seated, to the plain above.   " Gorgio shunella,"
she said, at length, in a low voice.

" Pure Rommany," said I ; " where ? " I added in a whisper.

" Dovey odoi," said Belle, nodding with her head towards the
path.

" I will soon see who it is," said I ; and starting up, I rushed
towards the pathway, intending to lay violent hands on any one
I might find lurking in its windings.   Before, however, I had
reached its commencement, a man, somewhat above the middle
height, advanced from it into the dingle, in whom I recognised
the man in black whom I had seen in the public-house.

CHAPTER XC.

The man in black and myself stood opposite to each other for a minute or two in silence; I will not say that we confronted each other that time, for the man in black, after a furtive glance, did not look me in the face, but kept his eyes fixed, apparently on the leaves of a bunch of ground nuts which were growing at my feet. At length, looking around the dingle, he exclaimed: "*Buona Sera*, I hope I don't intrude".

"You have as much right here," said I, "as I or my companion; but you had no right to stand listening to our conversation."

" I was not listening," said the man, " I was hesitating whether to advance or retire ; and if I heard some of your conversation, the fault was not mine."

" I do not see why you should have hesitated if your intentions were good," said I.

" I think the kind of place in which I found myself might excuse some hesitation," said the man in black, looking around ; "moreover, from what I had seen of your demeanour at the public-house, I was rather apprehensive that the reception I might experience at your hands might be more rough than agreeable."

" And what may have been your motive for coming to this place ? " said I.

" *Per far visita à sua signoria, ecco il motivo.*"

" Why do you speak to me in that gibberish ? " said I ; " do you think I understand it ? "

" It is not Armenian," said the man in black ; " but it might serve in a place like this, for the breathing of a little secret communication, were any common roadster near at hand. It would not do at Court, it is true, being the language of singing women, and the like ; but we are not at Court—when we are, I can perhaps summon up a little indifferent Latin, if I have anything private to communicate to the learned Professor."

And at the conclusion of this speech the man in black lifted up his head, and, for some moments, looked me in the face.

(482)

The muscles of his own seemed to be slightly convulsed, and his mouth opened in a singular manner.

"I see," said I, "that for some time you were standing near me and my companion, in the mean act of listening."

"Not at all," said the man in black; "I heard from the steep bank above that to which I have now alluded, whilst I was puzzling myself to find the path which leads to your retreat. I made, indeed, nearly the compass of the whole thicket before I found it."

"And how did you know that I was here?" I demanded.

"The landlord of the public-house, with whom I had some conversation concerning you, informed me that he had no doubt I should find you in this place, to which he gave me instructions not very clear. But now I am here, I crave permission to remain a little time, in order that I may hold some communion with you."

"Well," said I, "since you are come, you are welcome, please to step this way."

Thereupon I conducted the man in black to the fireplace where Belle was standing, who had risen from her stool on my springing up to go in quest of the stranger. The man in black looked at her with evident curiosity, then making her rather a graceful bow, "Lovely virgin," said he, stretching out his hand, "allow me to salute your fingers".

"I am not in the habit of shaking hands with strangers," said Belle.

"I did not presume to request to shake hands with you," said the man in black, "I merely wished to be permitted to salute with my lips the extremity of your two forefingers."

"I never permit anything of the kind," said Belle; "I do not approve of such unmanly ways, they are only befitting those who lurk in corners or behind trees, listening to the conversation of people who would fain be private."

"Do you take me for a listener, then?" said the man in black.

"Ay, indeed I do," said Belle; "the young man may receive your excuses, and put confidence in them if he please, but for my part I neither admit them, nor believe them;" and thereupon flinging her long hair back, which was hanging over her cheeks, she seated herself on her stool.

"Come, Belle," said I, "I have bidden the gentleman welcome; I beseech you, therefore, to make him welcome; he is a stranger, where we are at home, therefore, even did we wish him away, we are bound to treat him kindly."

" That's not English doctrine," said the man in black.

" I thought the English prided themselves on their hospitality," said I.

" They do so," said the man in black ; " they are proud of showing hospitality to people above them, that is, to those who do not want it, but of the hospitality which you were now describing, and which is Arabian, they know nothing. No Englishman will tolerate another in his house, from whom he does not expect advantage of some kind, and to those from whom he does, he can be civil enough. An Englishman thinks that, because he is in his own house, he has a right to be boorish and brutal to any one who is disagreeable to him, as all those are who are really in want of assistance. Should a hunted fugitive rush into an Englishman's house, beseeching protection, and appealing to the master's feelings of hospitality, the Englishman would knock him down in the passage."

" You are too general," said I, " in your strictures ; Lord ———,[1] the unpopular Tory minister, was once chased through the streets of London by a mob, and, being in danger of his life, took shelter in the shop of a Whig linen-draper, declaring his own unpopular name, and appealing to the linen-draper's feelings of hospitality ; whereupon, the linen-draper, utterly forgetful of all party rancour, nobly responded to the appeal, and telling his wife to conduct his lordship upstairs, jumped over the counter with his ell in his hand, and placing himself with half a dozen of his assistants at the door of his *boutique*, manfully confronted the mob, telling them that he would allow himself to be torn to a thousand pieces, ere he would permit them to injure a hair of his lordship's head ; what do you think of that ? "

" He ! he ! he ! " tittered the man in black.

" Well," said I, " I am afraid your own practice is not very different from that which you have been just now describing ; you sided with the radical in the public-house against me, as long as you thought him the most powerful, and then turned against him, when you saw he was cowed. What have you to say to that ? "

" Oh ! when one is in Rome, I mean England, one must do as they do in England, I was merely conforming to the custom of the country, he ! he ! but I beg your pardon here, as I did in the public-house. I made a mistake."

" Well," said I, " we will drop the matter, but pray seat yourself on that stone, and I will sit down on the grass near you."

---

[1] *MS.*, " Lord A[berdeen]"

The man in black, after proffering two or three excuses for occupying what he supposed to be my seat, sat down upon the stone, and I squatted down gypsy fashion, just opposite to him, Belle sitting on her stool at a slight distance on my right. After a time I addressed him thus: "Am I to reckon this a mere visit of ceremony? Should it prove so, it will be, I believe, the first visit of the kind ever paid me."

"Will you permit me to ask," said the man in black—"the weather is very warm," said he, interrupting himself, and taking off his hat.

I now observed that he was partly bald, his red hair having died away from the fore part of his crown; his forehead was high, his eyebrows scanty, his eyes grey and sly, with a downward tendency, his nose was slightly aquiline, his mouth rather large— a kind of sneering smile played continually on his lips, his complexion was somewhat rubicund.

"A bad countenance," said Belle, in the language of the roads, observing that my eyes were fixed on his face.

"Does not my countenance please you, fair damsel?" said the man in black, resuming his hat and speaking in a peculiarly gentle voice. "How," said I, "do you understand the language of the roads?"

"As little as I do Armenian," said the man in black; "but I understand look and tone."

"So do I, perhaps," retorted Belle; "and, to tell you the truth, I like your tone as little as your face."

"For shame," said I; "have you forgot what I was saying just now about the duties of hospitality? You have not yet answered my question," said I, addressing myself to the man, "with respect to your visit."

"Will you permit me to ask who you are?"

"Do you see the place where I live?" said I.

"I do," said the man in black, looking around.

"Do you know the name of this place?"

"I was told it was Mumpers', or Gypsies' Dingle," said the man in black.

"Good," said I; "and this forge and tent, what do they look like?"

"Like the forge and tent of a wandering Zigan; I have seen the like in Italy."

"Good," said I; they belong to me."

"Are you, then, a Gypsy?" said the man in black.

"What else should I be?"

"But you seem to have been acquainted with various individuals with whom I have likewise had acquaintance; and you have even alluded to matters, and even words, which have passed between me and them."

"Do you know how Gypsies live?" said I.

"By hammering old iron, I believe, and telling fortunes."

"Well," said I, "there's my forge, and yonder is some iron, though not old, and by your own confession I am a soothsayer."

"But how did you come by your knowledge?"

"Oh," said I, "if you want me to reveal the secrets of my trade, I have, of course, nothing further to say. Go to the scarlet dyer, and ask him how he dyes cloth."

"Why scarlet?" said the man in black. "Is it because Gypsies blush like scarlet."

"Gypsies never blush," said I; "but Gypsies' cloaks are scarlet."

"I should almost take you for a Gypsy," said the man in black, "but for ——"

"For what?" said I.

"But for that same lesson in Armenian, and your general knowledge of languages; as for your manners and appearance I will say nothing," said the man in black, with a titter.

"And why should not a Gypsy possess a knowledge of languages?" said I.

"Because the Gypsy race is perfectly illiterate," said the man in black; "they are possessed, it is true, of a knavish acuteness; and are particularly noted for giving subtle and evasive answers—and in your answers, I confess, you remind me of them; but that one of the race should acquire a learned language like the Armenian, and have a general knowledge of literature, is a thing *che io non credo afatto.*"

"What do you take me for?" said I.

"Why," said the man in black, "I should consider you to be a philologist, who, for some purpose, has taken up a Gypsy life; but I confess to you that your way of answering questions is far too acute for a philologist."

"And why should not a philologist be able to answer questions acutely?" said I.

"Because the philological race is the most stupid under Heaven," said the man in black; "they are possessed, it is true, of a certain faculty for picking up words, and a memory for retaining them; but that any one of the sect should be able to give a rational answer, to say nothing of an acute one, on any subject

—even though the subject were philology—is a thing of which I have no idea."

" But you found me giving a lesson in Armenian to this hand-maid?"

" I believe I did," said the man in black.

" And you heard me give what you are disposed to call acute answers to the questions you asked me?"

" I believe I did," said the man in black."

" And would any one but a philologist think of giving a lesson in Armenian to a handmaid in a dingle?"

" I should think not," said the man in black.

" Well, then, don't you see that it is possible for a philologist to give not only a rational, but an acute answer?"

" I really don't know," said the man in black.

" What's the matter with you?" said I.

" Merely puzzled," said the man in black.

" Puzzled?"

" Yes."

" Really puzzled?"

" Yes."

" Remain so."

" Well," said the man in black, rising, " puzzled or not, I will no longer tresspass upon your and this young lady's retirement ; only allow me, before I go, to apologise for my intrusion."

" No apology is necessary," said I ; " will you please to take anything before you go? I think this young lady, at my request, would contrive to make you a cup of tea."

" Tea!" said the man in black—" he! he! I don't drink tea ; I don't like it—if, indeed, you had," and here he stopped.

" There's nothing like gin and water, is there?" said I, " but I am sorry to say I have none."

" Gin and water," said the man in black, " how do you know that I am fond of gin and water?"

" Did I not see you drinking some at the public-house?"

" You did," said the man in black, " and I remember, that when I called for some, you repeated my words—permit me to ask, is gin and water an unusual drink in England?"

" It is not usually drunk cold, and with a lump of sugar," said I.

" And did you know who I was by my calling for it so?"

" Gypsies have various ways of obtaining information," said I.

" With all your knowledge," said the man in black, " you do not appear to have known that I was coming to visit you"

"Gypsies do not pretend to know anything which relates to themselves," said I; "but I advise you, if you ever come again, to come openly."

"Have I your permission to come again?" said the man in black."

"Come when you please; this dingle is as free for you as me."

"I will visit you again," said the man in black—"till then, *addio.*"

"Belle," said I, after the man in black had departed, "we did not treat that man very hospitably; he left us without having eaten or drunk at our expense."

"You offered him some tea," said Belle, "which, as it is mine, I should have grudged him, for I like him not."

"Our liking or disliking him had nothing to do with the matter, he was our visitor and ought not to have been permitted to depart dry; living as we do in this desert, we ought always to be prepared to administer to the wants of our visitors. Belle, do you know where to procure any good Hollands?"

"I think I do," said Belle, "but ——"

"I will have no 'buts'. Belle, I expect that with as little delay as possible, you procure, at my expense, the best Hollands you can find."

CHAPTER XCI.

TIME passed on, and Belle and I lived in the dingle; when I say lived, the reader must not imagine that we were always there. She went out upon her pursuits, and I went out where inclination led me; but my excursions were very short ones, and hers occasionally occupied whole days and nights. If I am asked how we passed the time when we were together in the dingle, I would answer that we passed the time very tolerably, all things considered; we conversed together, and when tired of conversing I would sometimes give Belle a lesson in Armenian; her progress was not particularly brilliant, but upon the whole satisfactory; in about a fortnight she had hung up 100 Haikan numerals upon the hake of her memory. I found her conversation highly entertaining; she had seen much of England and Wales, and had been acquainted with some of the most remarkable characters who travelled the roads at that period; and let me be permitted to say that many remarkable characters have travelled the roads of England, of whom fame has never said a word. I loved to hear her anecdotes of these people; some of whom I found had occasionally attempted to lay violent hands either upon her person or effects, and had invariably been humbled by her without the assistance of either justice or constable. I could clearly see, however, that she was rather tired of England, and wished for a change of scene; she was particularly fond of talking of America, to which country her aspirations chiefly tended. She had heard much of America, which had excited her imagination; for at that time America was much talked of, on roads and in homesteads, at least so said Belle, who had good opportunities of knowing, and most people allowed that it was a good country for adventurous English. The people who chiefly spoke against it, as she informed me, were soldiers disbanded upon pensions, the sextons of village churches, and excisemen. Belle had a craving desire to visit that country, and to wander with cart and little animal amongst its forests; when I would occasionally object, that she would be exposed to danger from strange and perverse customers, she said that she had not wandered the roads of England so long and alone, to be afraid of anything which might befall in America ; and that she hoped, with God's favour, to be able to take her own part, and to give to perverse customers as good as they might bring. She had a dauntless heart that same Belle. Such was the staple of Belle's conversation. As for mine, I would endeavour to entertain her with strange dreams of adventure, in which I figured in opaque forests, strangling wild beasts, or discovering and plundering the hordes of dragons ; and sometimes I would narrate to her other things far more genuine —how I had tamed savage mares, wrestled with Satan, and had dealings with ferocious publishers. Belle had a kind heart, and would weep at the accounts I gave her of my early wrest- lings with the dark monarch. She would sigh, too, as I recounted the many slights and degradations I had received at the hands of ferocious publishers ; but she had the curiosity of a woman ; and once, when I talked to her of the triumphs which I had achieved over unbroken mares, she lifted up her head and questioned me as to the secret of the virtue which I possessed over the aforesaid animals ; whereupon I sternly reprimanded, and forthwith commanded her to repeat the Armenian numerals ; and, on her demurring, I made use of words, to escape which she was glad to comply, saying the Armenian numerals from one to a hundred, which numerals, as a punishment for her curiosity, I made her repeat three times, loading her with the bitterest re- proaches whenever she committed the slightest error, either in accent or pronunciation, which reproaches she appeared to bear with the greatest patience. And now I have given a very fair account of the manner in which Isopel Berners and myself passed our time in the dingle.

CHAPTER XCII.

AMONGST other excursions, I went several times to the public-house, to which I introduced the reader in a former chapter. I had experienced such beneficial effects from the ale I had drunk on that occasion, that I wished to put its virtue to a frequent test; nor did the ale on subsequent trials belie the good opinion which I had at first formed of it. After each visit which I made to the public-house, I found my frame stronger, and my mind more cheerful than they had previously been. The landlord appeared at all times glad to see me, and insisted that I should sit within the bar, where, leaving his other guests to be attended to by a niece of his who officiated as his house-keeper, he would sit beside me and talk of matters concerning "the ring," indulging himself with a cigar and a glass of sherry, which he told me was his favourite wine, whilst I drank my ale. "I loves the conversation of all you coves of the ring," said he once, "which is natural, seeing as how I have fought in a ring myself. Ah, there is nothing like the ring; I wish I was not rather too old to go again into it. I often think I should like to have another rally—one more rally, and then—but there's a time for all things—youth will be served, every dog has his day, and mine has been a fine one—let me be content. After beating Tom of Hopton, there was not much more to be done in the way of reputation; I have long sat in my bar the wonder and glory of this here neighbourhood. I'm content, as far as reputation goes; I only wish money would come in a little faster; however, the next main of cocks will bring me in something handsome—comes off next Wednesday at —— have ventured ten five-pound notes— shouldn't say ventured either—run no risk at all, because why? I know my birds." About ten days after this harangue, I called again at about three o'clock one afternoon. The landlord was seated on a bench by a table in the common room, which was entirely empty; he was neither smoking nor drinking, but sat with his arms folded, and his head hanging down over his breast. At the sound of my step he looked up; "Ah," said he, "I am glad you are come, I was just thinking about you ". " Thank you," said I ; " it was very kind of you, especially at a time like this, when your mind must be full of your good fortune. Allow me to congratulate you on the sums of money you won by the main of cocks at —— I hope you brought it all safe home." " Safe home," said the landlord ; " I brought myself safe home, and that was all; came home without a shilling, regularly done, cleaned out." " I am sorry for that," said I ; " but after you had won the money, you ought to have been satisfied, and not risked it again—how did you lose it ? I hope not by the pea and thimble." " Pea and thimble," said the landlord, " not I ; those confounded cocks left me nothing to lose by the pea and thimble." " Dear me," said I ; " I thought that you knew your birds." " Well, so I did," said the landlord ; " I knew the birds to be good birds, and so they proved, and would have won if better birds had not been brought against them, of which I knew nothing, and so do you see I am done, regularly done." " Well," said I, " don't be cast down ; there is one thing of which the cocks by their misfortune cannot deprive you—your reputation ; make the most of that, give up cock-fighting, and be content with the custom of your house, of which you will always have plenty, as long as you are the wonder and glory of the neighbourhood."

The landlord struck the table before him violently with his fist. " Confound my reputation ! " said he. " No reputation that I have will be satisfaction to my brewer for the seventy pounds I owe him. Reputation won't pass for the current coin of this here realm ; and let me tell you, that if it a'n't backed by some of it, it a'n't a bit better than rotten cabbage, as I have found. Only three weeks since I was, as I told you, the wonder and glory of the neighbourhood ; and people used to come and look at me, and worship me, but as soon as it began to be whispered about that I owed money to the brewer, they presently left off all that kind of thing ; and now, during the last three days, since the tale of my misfortune with the cocks has got wind, almost everbody has left off coming to the house, and the few who does, merely comes to insult and flout me. It was only last night that fellow, Hunter, called me an old fool in my own kitchen here. He wouldn't have called me a fool a fortnight ago ; 'twas I called him fool then, and last night he called me old fool ; what do you think of that ? the man that beat Tom of Hopton, to be called, not only a fool, but an old fool ; and I hadn't heart, with one blow of this here fist into his face, to send his head ringing against the wall; for when a man's pocket is low, do you see, his heart a'n't much higher; but it is of no use talking, something must be done. I was thinking of you just as you came in, for you are just the person that can help me."

"If you mean," said I, "to ask me to lend you the money which you want, it will be to no purpose, as I have very little of my own, just enough for my own occasions; it is true, if you desired it, I would be your intercessor with the person to whom you owe the money, though I should hardly imagine that anything I could say ——" " You are right there," said the landlord; " much the brewer would care for anything you could say on my behalf—your going would be the very way to do me up entirely. A pretty opinion he would have of the state of my affairs if I were to send him such a 'cessor as you, and as for your lending me money, don't think I was ever fool enough to suppose either that you had any, or if you had that you would be fool enough to lend me any. No, no, the coves of the ring knows better; I have been in the ring myself, and knows what fighting a cove is, and though I was fool enough to back those birds, I was never quite fool enough to lend anybody money. What I am about to propose is something very different from going to my landlord, or lending any capital; something which, though it will put money into my pocket, will likewise put something handsome into your own. I want to get up a fight in this here neighbourhood, which would be sure to bring plenty of people to my house, for a week before and after it takes place, and as people can't come without drinking, I think I could, during one fortnight, get off for the brewer all the sour and unsaleable liquids he now has, which people wouldn't drink at any other time, and by that means, do you see, liquidate my debt; then, by means of betting, making first all right, do you see, I have no doubt that I could put something handsome into my pocket and yours, for I should wish you to be the fighting man, as I think I can depend upon you." "You really must excuse me," said I, "I have no wish to figure as a pugilist, besides there is such a difference in our ages; you may be the stronger man of the two, and perhaps the hardest hitter, but I am in much better condition, am more active on my legs, so that I am almost sure I should have the advantage, for, as you very properly observed, 'Youth will be served'." "Oh, I didn't mean to fight," said the landlord; "I think I could beat you if I were to train a little; but in the fight I propose I looks more to the main chance than anything else. I question whether half so many people could be brought together if you were to fight with me as the person I have in view, or whether there would be half such opportunities for betting, for I am a man, do you see, the person I wants you to fight with is not a man, but the young woman you keeps company with."

"The young woman I keep company with," said I; "pray what do you mean?"

"We will go into the bar, and have something," said the landlord, getting up. "My niece is out, and there is no one in the house, so we can talk the matter over quietly." Thereupon I followed him into the bar, where, having drawn me a jug of ale, helped himself as usual to a glass of sherry, and lighted a cigar, he proceeded to explain himself farther. "What I wants is to get up a fight between a man and a woman; there never has yet been such a thing in the ring, and the mere noise of the matter would bring thousands of people together, quite enough to drink out—for the thing should be close to my house—all the brewer's stock of liquids, both good and bad." "But," said I, "you were the other day boasting of the respectability of your house; do you think that a fight between a man and a woman close to your establishment would add to its respectability?" "Confound the respectability of my house," said the landlord, "will the respectability of my house pay the brewer, or keep the roof over my head? No, no! when respectability won't keep a man, do you see, the best thing is to let it go and wander. Only let me have my own way, and both the brewer, myself, and every one of us, will be satisfied. And then the betting—what a deal we may make by the betting—and that we shall have all to ourselves, you, I, and the young woman; the brewer will have no hand in that. I can manage to raise ten pounds, and if by flashing that about, I don't manage to make a hundred, call me horse." "But, suppose," said I, "the party should lose, on whom you sport your money, even as the birds did?" "We must first make all right," said the landlord, "as I told you before; the birds were irrational beings, and therefore couldn't come to an understanding with the others, as you and the young woman can. The birds fought fair; but I intend you and the young woman should fight cross." "What do you mean by cross?" said I. "Come, come," said the landlord, "don't attempt to gammon me; you in the ring, and pretend not to know what fighting cross is. That won't do, my fine fellow; but as no one is near us, I will speak out. I intend that you and the young woman should understand one another and agree beforehand which should be beat; and if you take my advice you will determine between you that the young woman shall be beat, as I am sure that the odds will run high upon her, her character as a fist woman being spread far and wide, so that all the flats who think it will be all right, will back her, as I myself would, if I thought it would be a fair thing." "Then," said I, "you would not have us fight fair." "By no means," said the landlord, "because why? I conceives that a cross is a certainty to those who are in it, whereas by the fair thing one may lose all he has." "But," said I, "you said the other day, that you liked the fair thing." "That was by way of gammon," said the landlord; "just, do you see, as a Parliament cove might say speechifying from a barrel to a set of flats, whom he means to sell. Come, what do you think of the plan?"

"It is a very ingenious one," said I.

"A'n't it," said the landlord. "The folks in this neighbourhood are beginning to call me old fool, but if they don't call me something else, when they sees me friends with the brewer, and money in my pocket, my name is not Catchpole. Come, drink your ale, and go home to the young gentlewoman."

"I am going," said I, rising from my seat, after finishing the remainder of the ale.

"Do you think she'll have any objection?" said the landlord.

"To do what?" said I.

"Why, to fight cross."

"Yes, I do," said I.

"But you will do your best to persuade her?"

"No, I will not," said I.

"Are you fool enough to wish to fight fair?"

"No," said I, "I am wise enough to wish not to fight at all."

"And how's my brewer to be paid?" said the landlord.

"I really don't know," said I.

"I'll change my religion," said the landlord.

CHAPTER XCIII.

ONE evening Belle and myself received another visit from the man in black. After a little conversation of not much importance, I asked him whether he would not take some refreshment, assuring him that I was now in possession of some very excellent Hollands which, with a glass, a jug of water, and a lump of sugar, were heartily at his service ; he accepted my offer, and Belle going with a jug to the spring, from which she was in the habit of procuring water for tea, speedily returned with it full of the clear, delicious water of which I have already spoken. Having placed the jug by the side of the man in black, she brought him a glass and spoon, and a tea-cup, the latter containing various lumps of snowy-white sugar : in the meantime I had produced a bottle of the stronger liquid. The man in black helped himself to some water, and likewise to some Hollands, the proportion of water being about two-thirds ; then adding a lump of sugar, he stirred the whole up, tasted it, and said that it was good.

"This is one of the good things of life," he added, after a short pause.

"What are the others ? " I demanded.

"There is Malvoisia sack," said the man in black, "and partridge, and beccafico."

"And what do you say to high mass ? " said I.

"High mass ! " said the man in black ; "however," he continued, after a pause, "I will be frank with you ; I came to be so ; I may have heard high mass on a time, and said it too, but as for any predilection for it, I assure you I have no more than for a long High Church sermon."

"You speak à la Margutte ? " said I.

"Margutte ! " said the man in black, musingly, "Margutte ? "

"You have read Pulci, I suppose ? " said I.

"Yes, yes," said the man in black, laughing ; "I remember."

"He might be rendered into English," said I, "something in this style :—

> " To which Margutte answered with a sneer,
> I like the blue no better than the black,
> My faith consists alone in savoury cheer,
> In roasted capons, and in potent sack ;
> But above all, in famous gin and clear,
> Which often lays the Briton on his back,
> With lump of sugar, and with lympth from well,
> I drink it, and defy the fiends of hell."

" He ! he ! he ! " said the man in black ; " that is more than Mezzofante could have done for a stanza of Byron."

" A clever man," said I.

" Who ? " said the man in black.

" Mezzofante di Bologna."

" He ! he ! he ! " said the man in black ; " now I know that you are not a Gypsy, at least a soothsayer ; no soothsayer would have said that ——"

" Why," said I, " does he not understand five-and-twenty tongues ? "

" Oh, yes," said the man in black ; " and five-and-twenty added to them ; but—he ! he ! he ! it was principally from him who is certainly the greatest of philologists that I formed my opinion of the sect."

" You ought to speak of him with more respect," said I ; " I have heard say that he has done good service to your see."

" Oh, yes," said the man in black ; " he has done good service to our see, that is, in his way ; when the neophytes of the propaganda are to be examined in the several tongues in which they are destined to preach, he is appointed to question them, the questions being first written down for him, or else, he ! he ! he ! Of course you know Napoleon's estimate of Mezzofante ; he sent for the linguist from motives of curiosity, and after some discourse with him, told him that he might depart ; then turning to some of his generals, he observed : '*Nous avons eu ici un exemple qu'un homme peut avoir beaucoup de paroles avec bien peu d'esprit*'."

" You are ungrateful to him," said I ; " well, perhaps, when he is dead and gone you will do him justice."

" True," said the man in black ; " when he is dead and gone we intend to erect him a statue of wood, on the left-hand side of the door of the Vatican library."

" Of wood ? " said I.

" He was the son of a carpenter, you know," said the man in black ; " the figure will be of wood, for no other reason, I assure you ; he ! he ! "

" You should place another statue on the right."

"Perhaps we shall," said the man in black; "but we know of no one amongst the philologists of Italy, nor, indeed, of the other countries, inhabited by the faithful, worthy to sit parallel in effigy with our illustrissimo; when, indeed, we have conquered these regions of the perfidious by bringing the inhabitants thereof to the true faith, I have no doubt that we shall be able to select one worthy to bear him company, one whose statue shall be placed on the right hand of the library, in testimony of our joy at his conversion; for, as you know, 'There is more joy,' etc."

"Wood?" said I.

"I hope not," said the man in black; "no, if I be consulted as to the material for the statue, I should strongly recommend bronze."

And when the man in black had said this, he emptied his second tumbler of its contents, and prepared himself another.

CHAPTER XCIV.

"So you hope to bring these regions again beneath the banner of the Roman See?" said I, after the man in black had prepared the beverage, and tasted it.

" Hope," said the man in black ; " how can we fail?   Is not the Church of these regions going to lose its prerogative ?"

" Its prerogative ?"

" Yes ; those who should be the guardians of the religion of England are about to grant Papists emancipation and to remove the disabilities from Dissenters, which will allow the Holy Father to play his own game in England."

On my inquiring how the Holy Father intended to play his game, the man in black gave me to understand that he intended for the present to cover the land with temples, in which the religion of Protestants would be continually scoffed at and reviled.

On my observing that such behaviour would savour strongly of ingratitude, the man in black gave me to understand that if I entertained the idea that the See of Rome was ever influenced in its actions by any feeling of gratitude I was much mistaken, assuring me that if the See of Rome in any encounter should chance to be disarmed and its adversary, from a feeling of magnanimity, should restore the sword which had been knocked out of its hand, the See of Rome always endeavoured on the first opportunity to plunge the said sword into its adversary's bosom,— conduct which the man in black seemed to think was very wise, and which he assured me had already enabled it to get rid of a great many troublesome adversaries, and would, he had no doubt, enable it to get rid of a great many more.

On my attempting to argue against the propriety of such behaviour, the man in black cut the matter short, by saying, that if one party was a fool he saw no reason why the other should imitate it in its folly.

After musing a little while I told him that emancipation had not yet passed through the legislature, and that perhaps it never would, reminding him that there was often many a slip between the cup and the lip ; to which observation the man in black agreed, assuring me, however, that there was no doubt that

(499)

emancipation would be carried, inasmuch as there was a very loud cry at present in the land ; a cry of " tolerance," which had almost frightened the Government out of its wits ; who, to get rid of the cry, was going to grant all that was asked in the way of toleration, instead of telling the people to " Hold their nonsense," and cutting them down, provided they continued bawling longer.

I questioned the man in black with respect to the origin of this cry ; but he said to trace it to its origin would require a long history ; that, at any rate, such a cry was in existence, the chief raisers of it being certain of the nobility, called Whigs, who hoped by means of it to get into power, and to turn out certain ancient adversaries of theirs called Tories, who were for letting things remain in *statu quo ;* that these Whigs were backed by a party amongst the people called Radicals, a specimen of whom I had seen in the public-house ; a set of fellows who were always in the habit of bawling against those in place ; " and so," he added, " by means of these parties, and the hubbub which the papists and other smaller sects are making, a general emancipation will be carried, and the Church of England humbled, which is the principal thing which the See of Rome cares for."

On my telling the man in black that I believed that even among the high dignitaries of the English Church there were many who wished to grant perfect freedom to religions of all descriptions, he said : " He was aware that such was the fact, and that such a wish was anything but wise, inasmuch as if they had any regard for the religion they professed, they ought to stand by it through thick and thin, proclaiming it to be the only true one, and denouncing all others, in an alliterative style, as dangerous and damnable ; whereas by their present conduct, they were bringing their religion into contempt with the people at large, who would never continue long attached to a church, the ministers of which did not stand up for it, and likewise cause their own brethren, who had a clearer notion of things, to be ashamed of belonging to it. I speak advisedly," said he, in continuation, " there is one Platitude."

" And I hope there is only one," said I ; " you surely would not adduce the likes and dislikes of that poor silly fellow as the criterions of the opinions of any party ? "

" You know him ? " said the man in black ; " nay, I heard you mention him in the public-house ; the fellow is not very wise, I admit, but he has sense enough to know that unless a church can make people hold their tongues when it thinks fit, it is scarcely deserving the name of a church ; no, I think that the

fellow is not such a very bad stick, and that upon the whole he
is, or rather was, an advantageous specimen of the High Church
English clergy, who, for the most part, so far from troubling their
heads about persecuting people, only think of securing their tithes,
eating their heavy dinners, puffing out their cheeks with importance on country justice benches, and occasionally exhibiting
their conceited wives, hoyden daughters, and gawky sons at
country balls, whereas Platitude ——"

"Stop," said I; "you said in the public-house that the
Church of England was a persecuting church, and here in the
dingle you have confessed that one section of it is willing to grant
perfect freedom to the exercise of all religions, and the other
only thinks of leading an easy life."

"Saying a thing in the public-house is a widely different thing
from saying it in the dingle," said the man in black; "had the
Church of England been a persecuting church, it would not
stand in the position in which it stands at present; it might, with
its opportunities, have spread itself over the greater part of the
world. I was about to observe, that instead of practising the
indolent habits of his High Church brethren, Platitude would
be working for his money, preaching the proper use of fire and
faggot, or rather of the halter and the whipping-post, encouraging
mobs to attack the houses of Dissenters, employing spies to collect
the scandal of neighbourhoods, in order that he might use it for
sacerdotal purposes, and, in fact, endeavouring to turn an English
parish into something like a Jesuit benefice in the south of France."

"He tried that game," said I, "and the parish said, ' Pooh,
pooh,' and, for the most part, went over to the Dissenters."

"Very true," said the man in black, taking a sip at his glass,
"but why were the Dissenters allowed to preach? why were they
not beaten on the lips till they spat out blood, with a dislodged
tooth or two? Why, but because the authority of the Church of
England has, by its own fault, become so circumscribed that Mr.
Platitude was not able to send a host of beadles and sbirri to their
chapel to bring them to reason, on which account Mr. Platitude
is very properly ashamed of his church, and is thinking of uniting
himself with one which possesses more vigour and authority."

"It may have vigour and authority," said I, "in foreign
lands, but in these kingdoms the day for practising its atrocities
is gone by. It is at present almost below contempt, and is obliged
to sue for grace *in formâ pauperis.*"

"Very true," said the man in black, "but let it once obtain
emancipation, and it will cast its slough, put on its fine clothes,

and make converts by thousands. ' What a fine church,' they'll say ; ' with what authority it speaks—no doubts, no hesitation, no sticking at trifles.' What a contrast to the sleepy English Church ! they'll go over to it by millions, till it preponderates here over every other, when it will of course be voted the dominant one ; and then—and then ——" and here the man in black drank a considerable quantity of gin and water.

" What then ? " said I.

" What then ? " said the man in black, " why, she will be true to herself. Let Dissenters, whether they be Church of England, as perhaps they may still call themselves, Methodist or Presbyterian, presume to grumble, and there shall be bruising of lips in pulpits, tying up to whipping-posts, cutting off ears and noses— he ! he ! the farce of King Log has been acted long enough; the time for Queen Stork's tragedy is drawing nigh ; " and the man in black sipped his gin and water in a very exulting manner.

" And this is the church which, according to your assertion in the public-house, never persecutes ? "

" I have already given you an answer," said the man in black, " with respect to the matter of the public-house ; it is one of the happy privileges of those who belong to my church to deny in the public-house what they admit in the dingle ; we have high warranty for such double speaking. Did not the foundation stone of our church, Saint Peter, deny in the public-house what he had previously professed in the valley ? "

" And do you think," said I, " that the people of England, who have shown aversion to anything in the shape of intolerance, will permit such barbarities as you have described ? "

" Let them become Papists," said the man in black ; " only let the majority become Papists, and you will see."

" They will never become so," said I ; " the good sense of the people of England will never permit them to commit such an absurdity."

" The good sense of the people of England ? " said the man in black, filling himself another glass.

" Yes," said I ; " the good sense of not only the upper, but the middle and lower classes."

" And of what description of people are the upper class ? " said the man in black, putting a lump of sugar into his gin and water.

" Very fine people," said I, " monstrously fine people ; so, at least, they are generally believed to be."

" He ! he ! " said the man in black ; " only those think them so who don't know them. The male part of the upper class are in youth a set of heartless profligates; in old age, a parcel of poor, shaking, nervous paillards. The female part, worthy to be the sisters and wives of such wretches, unmarried, full of cold vice, kept under by vanity and ambition, but which, after marriage, they seek not to restrain; in old age, abandoned to vapours and horrors, do you think that such beings will afford any obstacle to the progress of the church in these regions, as soon as her movements are unfettered?"

"I cannot give an opinion; I know nothing of them, except from a distance. But what think you of the middle classes?"

"Their chief characteristic," said the man in black, "is a rage for grandeur and gentility; and that same rage makes us quite sure of them in the long run. Everything that's lofty meets their unqualified approbation; whilst everything humble, or, as they call it, 'low,' is scouted by them. They begin to have a vague idea that the religion which they have hitherto professed is low; at any rate that it is not the religion of the mighty ones of the earth, of the great kings and emperors whose shoes they have a vast inclination to kiss, nor was used by the grand personages of whom they have read in their novels and romances, their Ivanhoes, their Marmions, and their Ladies of the Lake."

"Do you think that the writings of Scott have had any influence in modifying their religious opinions?"

"Most certainly I do," said the man in black. "The writings of that man have made them greater fools than they were before. All their conversation now is about gallant knights, princesses and cavaliers, with which his pages are stuffed—all of whom were Papists, or very High Church, which is nearly the same thing; and they are beginning to think that the religion of such nice sweet-scented gentry must be something very superfine. Why, I know at Birmingham the daughter of an ironmonger, who screeches to the piano the Lady of the Lake's hymn to the Virgin Mary, always weeps when Mary Queen of Scots is mentioned, and fasts on the anniversary of the death of that very wise martyr, Charles the First. Why, I would engage to convert such an idiot to popery in a week, were it worth my trouble. *O Cavaliere Gualtiero, avete fatto molto in favore della Santa Sede!*"

"If he has," said I, "he has done it unwittingly; I never heard before that he was a favourer of the popish delusion."

"Only in theory," said the man in black. "Trust any of the clan MacSycophant for interfering openly and boldly in favour of any cause on which the sun does not shine benignantly. Popery is at present, as you say, suing for grace in these regions *in formâ pauperis;* but let royalty once take it up, let old gouty George once patronise it, and I would consent to drink puddle-water, if the very next time the canny Scot was admitted to the royal symposium he did not say: 'By my faith, yere Majesty, I have always thought, at the bottom of my heart, that popery, as ill-scrapit tongues ca' it, was a very grand religion; I shall be proud to follow your Majesty's example in adopting it'."

"I doubt not," said I, "that both gouty George and his devoted servant will be mouldering in their tombs long before royalty in England thinks about adopting popery."

"We can wait," said the man in black; "in these days of rampant gentility, there will be no want of kings nor of Scots about them."

"But not Walters," said I.

"Our work has been already tolerably well done by one," said the man in black; "but if we wanted literature we should never lack in these regions hosts of literary men of some kind or other to eulogise us, provided our religion were in the fashion, and our popish nobles chose, and they always do our bidding, to admit the canaille to their tables, their kitchen tables. As for literature in general," said he, "the Santa Sede is not particularly partial to it, it may be employed both ways. In Italy, in particular, it has discovered that literary men are not always disposed to be lick-spittles."

"For example, Dante," said I.

"Yes," said the man in black. "A dangerous personage; that poem of his cuts both ways; and then there was Pulci, that Morgante of his cuts both ways, or rather one way, and that sheer against us; and then there was Aretino, who dealt so hard with the *poveri frati;* all writers, at least Italian ones, are not lick-spittles. And then in Spain, 'tis true, Lope de Vega and Calderon were most inordinate lick-spittles; the *Principe Constante* of the last is a curiosity in its way; and then the *Mary Stuart* of Lope; I think I shall recommend the perusal of that work to the Birmingham ironmonger's daughter; she has been lately thinking of adding 'a slight knowledge of the magneeficent language of the Peninsula' to the rest of her accomplishments, he! he! he! but then there was Cervantes, starving, but straight; he deals us some hard knocks in that second part of his Quixote; then there was some of the writers of the picaresque novels. No; all literary men are not lick-spittles, whether in Italy or Spain, or, indeed, upon the Continent; it is only in England that all ——"

"Come," said I, "mind what you are about to say of English literary men."

"Why should I mind?" said the man in black, "there are
no literary men here. I have heard of literary men living in
garrets, but not in dingles, whatever philologists may do ; I may,
therefore, speak out freely. It is only in England that literary
men are invariably lick-spittles ; on which account, perhaps, they
are so despised, even by those who benefit by their dirty services.
Look at your fashionable novel writers, he ! he ! and above all at
your newspaper editors, ho ! ho !"

"You will, of course, except the editors of the —— from your
censure of the last class?" said I.

"Them !" said the man in black ; "why, they might serve as
models in the dirty trade to all the rest who practise it. See how
they bepraise their patrons, the grand Whig nobility, who hope,
by raising the cry of liberalism, and by putting themselves at the
head of the populace, to come into power shortly. I don't wish
to be hard, at present, upon those Whigs," he continued, "for
they are playing our game ; but a time will come when, not wanting them, we will kick them to a considerable distance : and then,
when toleration is no longer the cry, and the Whigs are no longer
backed by the populace, see whether the editors of the —— will
stand by them ; they will prove themselves as expert lick-spittles
of despotism as of liberalism. Don't think they will always
bespatter the Tories and Austria."

" Well," said I, " I am sorry to find that you entertain so low
an opinion of the spirit of English literary men ; we will now
return, if you please, to the subject of the middle classes ; I think
your strictures upon them in general are rather too sweeping—they
are not altogether the foolish people which you have described.
Look, for example, at that very powerful and numerous body the
Dissenters, the descendants of those sturdy Patriots who hurled
Charles the Simple from his throne."

" There are some sturdy fellows amongst them, I do not deny,"
said the man in black, "especially amongst the preachers, clever
withal—two or three of that class nearly drove Mr. Platitude mad,
as perhaps you are aware, but they are not very numerous ; and
the old sturdy sort of preachers are fast dropping off, and, as we
observe with pleasure, are generally succeeded by frothy coxcombs,
whom it would not be very difficult to gain over. But what we
most rely upon as an instrument to bring the Dissenters over to
us is the mania for gentility, which amongst them has of late become as great, and more ridiculous, than amongst the middle classes
belonging to the Church of England. All the plain and simple
fashions of their forefathers they are either about to abandon, or

have already done so.   Look at the most part of their chapels, no
longer modest brick edifices, situated in quiet and retired streets,
but lunatic-looking erections, in what the simpletons call the
modern Gothic taste, of Portland stone, with a cross upon the top,
and the site generally the most conspicuous that can be found ;
and look at the manner in which they educate their children, I
mean those that are wealthy.   They do not even wish them to be
Dissenters, ' the sweet dears shall enjoy the advantages of good
society, of which their parents were debarred '.   So the girls are
sent to tip-top boarding-schools, where amongst other trash they
read *Rokeby,* and are taught to sing snatches from that high-flying
ditty the ' Cavalier ——'

> ' Would you match the base Skippon, and Massey, and Brown,
> With the barons of England, who fight for the crown ? '

he ! he ! their own names.   Whilst the lads are sent to those
hot-beds of pride and folly—colleges, whence they return with
a greater contempt for everything ' low,' and especially for their
own pedigree, than they went with.   I tell you, friend, the
children of Dissenters, if not their parents, are going over to the
church, as you call it, and the church is going over to Rome."

    " I do not see the justice of that latter assertion at all," said
I ; " some of the Dissenters' children may be coming over to the
Church of England, and yet the Church of England be very far
from going over to Rome."

    " In the high road for it, I assure you," said the man in
black, " part of it is going to abandon, the rest to lose, their prerogative, and when a church no longer retains its prerogative, it
speedily loses its own respect, and that of others."

    " Well," said I, " if the higher classes have all the vices and
follies which you represent, on which point I can say nothing, as
I have never mixed with them ; and even supposing the middle
classes are the foolish beings you would fain make them, and
which I do not believe them as a body to be, you would still find
some resistance amongst the lower classes ; I have a considerable
respect for their good sense and independence of character, but
pray let me hear your opinion of them."

    " As for the lower classes," said the man in black, " I believe
them to be the most brutal wretches in the world, the most addicted
to foul feeding, foul language, and foul vices of every kind ; wretches
who have neither love for country, religion, nor anything save their
own vile selves.   You surely do not think that they would oppose a
change of religion? why, there is not one of them but would hurrah for

the Pope, or Mahomet, for the sake of a hearty gorge and a drunken bout, like those which they are treated with at election contests."

" Has your church any followers amongst them ?" said I.

" Wherever there happens to be a Romish family of consider-able possessions," said the man in black, " our church is sure to have followers of the lower class, who have come over in the hope of getting something in the shape of dole or donation. As, how-ever, the Romish is not yet the dominant religion, and the clergy of the English establishment have some patronage to bestow, the churches are not quite deserted by the lower classes ; yet were the Romish to become the established religion, they would, to a certainty, all go over to it ; you can scarcely imagine what a self-interested set they are—for example, the landlord of that public-house in which I first met you, having lost a sum of money upon a cock-fight, and his affairs in consequence being in a bad condition, is on the eve of coming over to us, in the hope that two old Popish females of property, whom I confess, will advance a sum of money to set him up again in the world."

" And what could have put such an idea into the poor fellow's head ?" said I.

" Oh ! he and I have had some conversation upon the state of his affairs," said the man in black ; " I think he might make a rather useful convert in these parts, provided things take a certain turn, as they doubtless will. It is no bad thing to have a fighting fellow, who keeps a public-house, belonging to one's religion. He has been occasionally employed as a bully at elections by the Tory party, and he may serve us in the same capacity. The fellow comes of a good stock ; I heard him say that his father headed the High Church mob, who sacked and burnt Priestley's house at Birmingham towards the end of the last century."

" A disgraceful affair," said I.

" What do you mean by a disgraceful affair ?" said the man in black. " I assure you that nothing has occurred for the last fifty years which has given the High Church party so much credit in the eyes of Rome as that ; we did not imagine that the fellows had so much energy. Had they followed up that affair by twenty others of a similar kind, they would by this time have had everything in their own power ; but they did not, and, as a necessary conse-quence, they are reduced to almost nothing."

" I suppose," said I, " that your church would have acted very differently in its place."

" It has always done so," said the man in black, coolly sipping. " Our church has always armed the brute population against the genius and intellect of a country, provided that same intellect and genius were not willing to become its instruments and eulogists; and provided we once obtain a firm hold here again, we would not fail to do so. We would occasionally stuff the beastly rabble with horseflesh and bitter ale, and then halloo them on against all those who were obnoxious to us."

"Horseflesh and bitter ale!" I replied.

"Yes," said the man in black; "horseflesh and bitter ale, the favourite delicacies of their Saxon ancestors, who were always ready to do our bidding after a liberal allowance of such cheer. There is a tradition in our church, that before the Northumbrian rabble, at the instigation of Austin, attacked and massacred the presbyterian monks of Bangor, they had been allowed a good gorge of horseflesh and bitter ale. He! he! he!" continued the man in black, "what a fine spectacle to see such a mob, headed by a fellow like our friend, the landlord, sack the house of another Priestley!"

"Then you don't deny that we have had a Priestley," said I, "and admit the possibility of our having another? You were lately observing that all English literary men were sycophants?"

"Lick-spittles," said the man in black; "yes, I admit that you have had a Priestley, but he was a Dissenter of the old sort; you have had him, and perhaps may have another."

"Perhaps we may," said I. "But with respect to the lower classes, have you mixed much with them?"

"I have mixed with all classes," said the man in black, "and with the lower not less than the upper and middle, they are much as I have described them; and of the three, the lower are the worst. I never knew one of them that possessed the slightest principle, no, not —— It is true, there was one fellow whom I once met, who ——, but it is a long story, and the affair happened abroad."

"I ought to know something of the English people," he continued, after a moment's pause; "I have been many years amongst them labouring in the cause of the church."

"Your see must have had great confidence in your powers, when it selected you to labour for it in these parts?" said I.

"They chose me," said the man in black, "principally because being of British extraction and education, I could speak the English language and bear a glass of something strong. It is the opinion of my see, that it would hardly do to send a missionary into a country like this who is not well versed in English; a country where they think, so far from understanding any language besides his own, scarcely one individual in ten speaks his own intelligibly; or an ascetic person, where as they say, high and low, male and female, are, at some period of their lives, fond of a renovating glass, as it is styled, in other words, of tippling."

"Your see appears to entertain a very strange opinion of the English," said I.

"Not altogether an unjust one," said the man in black, lifting the glass to his mouth.

"Well," said I, "it is certainly very kind on its part to wish to bring back such a set of beings beneath its wing."

"Why, as to the kindness of my see," said the man in black, "I have not much to say ; my see has generally in what it does a tolerably good motive ; these heretics possess in plenty what my see has a great hankering for, and can turn to a good account—money !"

"The founder of the Christian religion cared nothing for money," said I.

"What have we to do with what the founder of the Christian religion cared for ? " said the man in black ; "how could our temples be built, and our priests supported without money ? but you are unwise to reproach us with a desire of obtaining money ; you forget that your own church, if the Church of England be your own church, as I suppose it is, from the willingness which you displayed in the public-house to fight for it, is equally avaricious ; look at your greedy Bishops, and your corpulent Rectors ; do they imitate Christ in His disregard for money ? Go to ! you might as well tell me that they imitate Christ in His meekness and humility."

"Well," said I, "whatever their faults may be, you can't say that they go to Rome for money."

The man in black made no direct answer, but appeared by the motion of his lips to be repeating something to himself.

"I see your glass is again empty," said I ; "perhaps you will replenish it."

The man in black arose from his seat, adjusted his habiliments, which were rather in disorder, and placed upon his head his hat, which he had laid aside, then, looking at me, who was still lying on the ground, he said : "I might, perhaps, take another glass, though I believe I have had quite as much as I can well bear ; but I do not wish to hear you utter anything more this evening after that last observation of yours—it is quite original ; I will meditate upon it on my pillow this night after having said an ave and a pater—go to Rome for money !" He then made Belle a low bow, slightly motioned to me with his hand as if bidding farewell, and then left the dingle with rather uneven steps.

"Go to Rome for money," I heard him say as he ascended the winding path, "he ! he ! he !   Go to Rome for money, ho ! ho ! ho !"

CHAPTER XCV.

NEARLY three days elapsed without anything of particular moment occurring. Belle drove the little cart containing her merchandise about the neighbourhood, returning to the dingle towards the evening. As for myself, I kept within my wooded retreat, working during the periods of her absence leisurely at my forge. Having observed that the quadruped which my companion drove was as much in need of shoes as my own had been some time previously, I had determined to provide it with a set, and during the aforesaid periods occupied myself in preparing them. As I was employed three mornings and afternoons about them, I am sure that the reader will agree that I worked leisurely, or rather lazily. On the third day Belle arrived somewhat later than usual; I was lying on my back at the bottom of the dingle, employed in tossing up the shoes, which I had produced, and catching them as they fell, some being always in the air mounting or descending, somewhat after the fashion of the waters of a fountain.

"Why have you been absent so long?" said I to Belle, "it must be long past four by the day."

"I have been almost killed by the heat," said Belle; "I was never out in a more sultry day—the poor donkey, too, could scarcely move along."

"He shall have fresh shoes," said I, continuing my exercise; "here they are, quite ready; to-morrow I will tack them on."

"And why are you playing with them in that manner?" said Belle.

"Partly in triumph at having made them, and partly to show that I can do something besides making them; it is not every one who, after having made a set of horse-shoes, can keep them going up and down in the air, without letting one fall."

"One has now fallen on your chin," said Belle.

"And another on my cheek," said I, getting up; "it is time to discontinue the game, for the last shoe drew blood."

Belle went to her own little encampment; and as for myself, after having flung the donkey's shoes into my tent, I put some fresh wood on the fire, which was nearly out, and hung the kettle over it. I then issued forth from the dingle, and strolled round the wood that surrounded it; for a long time I was busied in meditation, looking at the ground, striking with my foot, half unconsciously, the tufts of grass and thistles that I met in my way. After some time, I lifted up my eyes to the sky, at first vacantly, and then with more attention, turning my head in all directions for a minute or two; after which I returned to the dingle. Isopel was seated near the fire, over which the kettle was now hung; she had changed her dress—no signs of the dust and fatigue of her late excursion remained; she had just added to the fire a small billet of wood, two or three of which I had left beside it; the fire cracked, and a sweet odour filled the dingle.

"I am fond of sitting by a wood fire," said Belle, "when abroad, whether it be hot or cold; I love to see the flames dart out of the wood; but what kind is this, and where did you get it?"

"It is ash," said I, "green ash. Somewhat less than a week ago, whilst I was wandering along the road by the side of a wood, I came to a place where some peasants were engaged in cutting up and clearing away a confused mass of fallen timber: a mighty-aged oak had given way the night before, and in its fall had shivered some smaller trees; the upper part of the oak, and the fragments of the rest, lay across the road. I purchased, for a trifle, a bundle or two, and the wood on the fire is part of it—ash, green ash."

"That makes good the old rhyme," said Belle, "which I have heard sung by the old woman in the great house:—

'Ash, when green,
Is fire for a queen.'"

"And on fairer form of queen, ash fire never shone," said I, "than on thine, O beauteous queen of the dingle."

"I am half disposed to be angry with you, young man," said Belle.

"And why not entirely?" said I.

Belle made no reply.

"Shall I tell you?" I demanded. "You had no objection to the first part of the speech, but you did not like being called queen of the dingle. Well, if I had the power, I would make you queen of something better than the dingle—Queen of China. Come, let us have tea."

"Something less would content me," said Belle, sighing, as she rose to prepare our evening meal.

So we took tea together, Belle and I. " How delicious tea is after a hot summer's day, and a long walk," said she.

" I dare say it is most refreshing then," said I; " but I have heard people say that they most enjoy it on a cold winter's night, when the kettle is hissing on the fire, and their children playing on the hearth."

Belle sighed. " Where does tea come from ? " she presently demanded.

" From China," said I; " I just now mentioned it, and the mention of it put me in mind of tea."

" What kind of country is China ? "

" I know very little about it; all I know is, that it is a very large country far to the East, but scarcely large enough to contain its inhabitants, who are so numerous, that though China does not cover one-ninth part of the world, its inhabitants amount to one-third of the population of the world."

" And do they talk as we do ? "

" Oh no ! I know nothing of their language ; but I have heard that it is quite different from all others, and so difficult that none but the cleverest people amongst foreigners can master it, on which account, perhaps, only the French pretend to know anything about it."

" Are the French so very clever, then ? " said Belle.

" They say there are no people like them, at least in Europe. But talking of Chinese reminds me that I have not for some time past given you a lesson in Armenian. The word for tea in Armenian is—by-the-bye, what is the Armenian word for tea ? "

" That's your affair, not mine," said Belle ; " it seems hard that the master should ask the scholar."

" Well," said I, " whatever the word may be in Armenian, it is a noun ; and as we have never yet declined an Armenian noun together, we may as well take this opportunity of declining one. Belle, there are ten declensions in Armenian ! "

" What's a declension ? "

" The way of declining a noun."

" Then, in the civilest way imaginable, I decline the noun. Is that a declension ? "

" You should never play on words ; to do so is low, vulgar, smelling of the pothouse, the workhouse. Belle, I insist on your declining an Armenian noun."

" I have done so already," said Belle.

" If you go on in this way," said I, " I shall decline taking any more tea with you. Will you decline an Armenian noun ? "

" I don't like the language," said Belle. " If you must teach
me languages, why not teach me French or Chinese ? "

" I know nothing of Chinese ; and as for French, none but a
Frenchman is clever enough to speak it—to say nothing of teaching ; no, we will stick to Armenian, unless, indeed, you would
prefer Welsh ! "

" Welsh, I have heard, is vulgar," said Belle ; " so, if I must
learn one of the two, I will prefer Armenian, which I never heard
of till you mentioned it to me ; though of the two, I really think
Welsh sounds best."

" The Armenian noun," said I, " which I propose for your
declension this night, is . . . which signifieth Master."

" I neither like the word nor the sound," said Belle.

" I can't help that," said I ; " it is the word I choose ; Master,
with all its variations, being the first noun, the sound of which I
would have you learn from my lips.   Come, let us begin—

" A master . . . Of a master, etc.   Repeat—"

" I am not much used to say the word," said Belle.   " But,
to oblige you, I will decline it as you wish ; " and thereupon
Belle declined master in Armenian.

" You have declined the noun very well," said I ; " that is in
the singular number ; we will now go to the plural."

" What is the plural ? " said Belle.

" That which implies more than one, for example, masters ;
you shall now go through masters in Armenian."

" Never," said Belle, " never ; it is bad to have one master,
but more I would never bear, whether in Armenian or English."

" You do not understand," said I ; " I merely want you to
decline masters in Armenian."

" I do decline them ; I will have nothing to do with them,
nor with master either ; I was wrong to—— What sound is
that ? "

" I did not hear it, but I daresay it is thunder ; in Armenian ——"

" Never mind what it is in Armenian ; but why do you think
it is thunder ? "

" Ere I returned from my stroll, I looked up into the heavens,
and by their appearance I judged that a storm was nigh at hand."

" And why did you not tell me so ? "

" You never asked me about the state of the atmosphere, and
I am not in the habit of giving my opinion to people on any
subject, unless questioned.   But, setting that aside, can you blame
me for not troubling you with forebodings about storm and

tempest, which might·have prevented the pleasure you promised
yourself in drinking tea, or perhaps a lesson in Armenian, though
you pretend to dislike the latter."

"My dislike is not pretended," said Belle; "I hate the sound
of it, but I love my tea, and it was kind of you not to wish to cast
a cloud over my little pleasures; the thunder came quite time
enough to interrupt it without being anticipated—there is another
peal—I will clear away, and see that my tent is in a condition to
resist the storm, and I think you had better bestir yourself."

Isopel departed, and I remained seated on my stone, as
nothing belonging to myself required any particular attention; in
about a quarter of an hour she returned, and seated herself upon
her stool.

"How dark the place is become since I left you," said she;
"just as if night were just at hand."

"Look up at the sky," said I, "and you will not wonder; it
is all of a deep olive. The wind is beginning to rise; hark how
it moans among the branches; and see how their tops are bending—it brings dust on its wings—I felt some fall on my face; and
what is this, a drop of rain?"

"We shall have plenty anon," said Belle; "do you hear? it
already begins to hiss upon the embers; that fire of ours will soon
be extinguished."

"It is not probable that we shall want it," said I, "but we
had better seek shelter; let us go into my tent."

"Go in," said Belle, "but you go in alone; as for me, I will
seek my own."

"You are right," said I, "to be afraid of me; I have taught
you to decline master in Armenian."

"You almost tempt me," said Belle, "to make you decline
mistress in English."

"To make matters short," said I, "I decline a mistress."

"What do you mean?" said Belle angrily.

"I have merely done what you wished me," said I, "and in
your own style; there is no other way of declining anything in
English, for in English there are no declensions."

"The rain is increasing," said Belle.

"It is so," said I; "I shall go to my tent; you may come,
if you please; I do assure you I am not afraid of you."

"Nor I of you," said Belle; "so I will come. Why should
I be afraid? I can take my own part; that is ——"

We went into the tent and sat down, and now the rain began
to pour with vehemence. "I hope we shall not be flooded in

this hollow," said I to Belle. "There is no fear of that," said Belle; "the wandering people, amongst other names, call it the dry hollow. I believe there is a passage somewhere or other by which the wet is carried off. There must be a cloud right above us, it is so dark. Oh! what a flash!"

"And what a peal," said I; "that is what the Hebrews call *Koul Adonai*—the voice of the Lord. Are you afraid?"

"No," said Belle, "I rather like to hear it."

"You are right," said I; "I am fond of the sound of thunder myself. There is nothing like it; *Koul Adonai behadar;* the voice of the Lord is a glorious voice, as the prayer-book version hath it."

"There is something awful in it," said Belle; "and then the lightning, the whole dingle is now in a blaze."

"'The voice of the Lord maketh the hinds to calve, and discovereth the thick bushes.' As you say, there is something awful in thunder."

"There are all kinds of noises above us," said Belle; "surely I heard the crashing of a tree?"

"'The voice of the Lord breaketh the cedar trees,'" said I, "but what you hear is caused by a convulsion of the air; during a thunderstorm there are occasionally all kinds of aërial noises. Ab Gwilym, who, next to King David, has best described a thunderstorm, speaks of these aërial noises in the following manner :—

> 'Astonied now I stand at strains,
> As of ten thousand clanking chains;
> And once, methought, that overthrown,
> The welkin's oaks came whelming down;
> Upon my head up starts my hair:
> Why hunt abroad the hounds of air?
> What cursed hag is screeching high,
> Whilst crash goes all her crockery?'

You would hardly believe, Belle, that though I offered at least ten thousand lines nearly as good as those to the booksellers in London, the simpletons were so blind to their interest as to refuse purchasing them."

"I don't wonder at it," said Belle, "especially if such dreadful expressions frequently occur as that towards the end; surely that was the crash of a tree?"

"Ah!" said I, "there falls the cedar tree—I mean the sallow; one of the tall trees on the outside of the dingle has been snapped short."

"What a pity," said Belle, "that the fine old oak, which you

saw the peasants cutting up, gave way the other night, when
scarcely a breath of air was stirring; how much better to have
fallen in a storm like this, the fiercest I remember."

"I don't think so," said I; "after braving a thousand tem-
pests, it was meeter for it to fall of itself than to be vanquished
at last. But to return to Ab Gwilym's poetry, he was above
culling dainty words, and spoke boldly his mind on all subjects.
Enraged with the thunder for parting him and Morfydd, he says,
at the conclusion of his ode :—

> ' My curse, O Thunder, cling to thee,
> For parting my dear pearl and me '."

"You and I shall part; that is, I shall go to my tent if you
persist in repeating from him. The man must have been a
savage. A poor wood-pigeon has fallen dead."

"Yes," said I, "there he lies just outside the tent; often
have I listened to his note when alone in this wilderness. So
you do not like Ab Gwilym; what say you to old Göthe :—

> ' Mist shrouds the night, and rack;
> Hear, in the woods, what an awful crack!
> Wildly the owls are flitting,
> Hark to the pillars splitting
> Of palaces verdant ever,
> The branches quiver and sever,
> The mighty stems are creaking,
> The poor roots breaking and shrieking,
> In wild mixt ruin down dashing,
> O'er one another they're crashing;
> Whilst 'midst the rocks so hoary,
> Whirlwinds hurry and worry.
> Hear'st not, sister ——' "

"Hark!" said Belle, "hark!"

> " ' Hear'st not, sister, a chorus
> Of voices —— ? ' "

"No," said Belle, "but I hear a voice."

CHAPTER XCVI.

I LISTENED attentively, but I could hear nothing but the loud clashing of branches, the pattering of rain, and the muttered growl of thunder. I was about to tell Belle that she must have been mistaken, when I heard a shout, indistinct it is true, owing to the noises aforesaid, from some part of the field above the dingle. "I will soon see what's the matter," said I to Belle, starting up. "I will go, too," said the girl. "Stay where you are," said I; "if I need you, I will call;" and, without waiting for any answer, I hurried to the mouth of the dingle. I was about a few yards only from the top of the ascent, when I beheld a blaze of light, from whence I knew not; the next moment there was a loud crash, and I appeared involved in a cloud of sulphurous smoke. "Lord have mercy upon us," I heard a voice say, and methought I heard the plunging and struggling of horses. I had stopped short on hearing the crash, for I was half stunned; but I now hurried forward, and in a moment stood upon the plain. Here I was instantly aware of the cause of the crash and the smoke. One of those balls, generally called fireballs, had fallen from the clouds, and was burning on the plain at a short distance; and the voice which I had heard, and the plunging, were as easily accounted for. Near the left-hand corner of the grove which surrounded the dingle, and about ten yards from the fire-ball, I perceived a chaise, with a postillion on the box, who was making efforts, apparently useless, to control his horses, which were kicking and plunging in the highest degree of excitement. I instantly ran towards the chaise, in order to offer what help was in my power. "Help me," said the poor fellow, as I drew nigh; but, before I could reach the horses, they had turned rapidly round, one of the fore-wheels flew from its axle-tree, the chaise was overset, and the postillion flung violently from his seat upon the field. The horses now became more furious than before, kicking desperately, and endeavouring to disengage themselves from the fallen chaise. As I was hesitating whether to run to the assistance of the postillion, or endeavour to disengage

(517)

the animals, I heard the voice of Belle exclaiming : "See to the horses, I will look after the man". She had, it seems, been alarmed by the crash which accompanied the fire-bolt, and had hurried up to learn the cause. I forthwith seized the horses by the heads, and used all the means I possessed to soothe and pacify them, employing every gentle modulation of which my voice was capable. Belle, in the meantime, had raised up the man, who was much stunned by his fall ; but presently recovering his recollection to a certain degree, he came limping to me, holding his hand to his right thigh. "The first thing that must now be done," said I, "is to free these horses from the traces ; can you undertake to do so?" "I think I can," said the man, looking at me somewhat stupidly. "I will help," said Belle, and without loss of time laid hold of one of the traces. The man, after a short pause, also set to work, and in a few minutes the horses were extricated. "Now," said I to the man, "what is next to be done?" "I don't know," said he ; "indeed, I scarcely know anything ; I have been so frightened by this horrible storm, and so shaken by my fall." "I think," said I, "that the storm is passing away, so cast your fears away too ; and as for your fall, you must bear it as lightly as you can. I will tie the horses amongst those trees, and then we will all betake us to the hollow below." "And what's to become of my chaise?" said the postillion, looking ruefully on the fallen vehicle. "Let us leave the chaise for the present," said I ; "we can be of no use to it." "I don't like to leave my chaise lying on the ground in this weather," said the man ; "I love my chaise, and him whom it belongs to." "You are quite right to be fond of yourself," said I, "on which account I advise you to seek shelter from the rain as soon as possible." "I was not talking of myself," said the man, "but my master, to whom the chaise belongs." "I thought you called the chaise yours," said I. "That's my way of speaking," said the man ; "but the chaise is my master's, and a better master does not live. Don't you think we could manage to raise up the chaise?" "And what is to become of the horses?" said I. "I love my horses well enough," said the man ; "but they will take less harm than the chaise. We two can never lift up that chaise." "But we three can," said Belle ; "at least, I think so ; and I know where to find two poles which will assist us." "You had better go to the tent," said I, "you will be wet through." "I care not for a little wetting," said Belle ; "moreover, I have more gowns than one—see you after the horses." Thereupon, I led the horses past the mouth of the dingle, to a place where a gap in the hedge afforded admission to the copse or plantation, on the southern side. Forcing them through the gap, I led them to a spot amidst the trees, which I deemed would afford them the most convenient place for standing; then, darting down into the dingle, I brought up a rope, and also the halter of my own nag, and with these fastened them each to a separate tree in the best manner I could. This done, I returned to the chaise and the postillion. In a minute or two Belle arrived with two poles, which, it seems, had long been lying, overgrown with brushwood, in a ditch or hollow behind the plantation. With these both she and I set to work in endeavouring to raise the fallen chaise from the ground.

We experienced considerable difficulty in this undertaking; at length, with the assistance of the postillion, we saw our efforts crowned with success—the chaise was lifted up, and stood upright on three wheels.

"We may leave it here in safety," said I, "for it will hardly move away on three wheels, even supposing it could run by itself; I am afraid there is work here for a wheelwright, in which case I cannot assist you; if you were in need of a blacksmith it would be otherwise." "I don't think either the wheel or the axle is hurt," said the postillion, who had been handling both; "it is only the linch-pin having dropped out that caused the wheel to fly off; if I could but find the linch-pin! though, perhaps, it fell out a mile away." "Very likely," said I; "but never mind the linch-pin, I can make you one, or something that will serve: but I can't stay here any longer, I am going to my place below with this young gentlewoman, and you had better follow us." "I am ready," said the man; and after lifting up the wheel and propping it against the chaise, he went with us, slightly limping, and with his hand pressed to his thigh.

As we were descending the narrow path, Belle leading the way, and myself the last of the party, the postillion suddenly stopped short, and looked about him. "Why do you stop?" said I. "I don't wish to offend you," said the man; "but this seems to be a strange place you are leading me into; I hope you and the young gentlewoman, as you call her, don't mean me any harm—you seemed in a great hurry to bring me here." "We wished to get you out of the rain," said I, "and ourselves too; that is, if we can, which I rather doubt, for the canvas of a tent is slight shelter in such a rain; but what harm should we wish to do you?" "You may think I have money," said the man, "and I have some, but only thirty shillings, and for a sum like that it would be hardly worth while to ——" "Would it not?" said

I; "thirty shillings, after all, are thirty shillings, and for what I know, half a dozen throats may have been cut in this place for that sum at the rate of five shillings each; moreover, there are the horses, which would serve to establish this young gentlewoman and myself in housekeeping, provided we were thinking of such a thing." "Then I suppose I have fallen into pretty hands," said the man, putting himself in a posture of defence; "but I'll show no craven heart; and if you attempt to lay hands on me, I'll try to pay you in your own coin. I'm rather lamed in the leg, but I can still use my fists; so come on both of you, man and woman, if woman this be, though she looks more like a grenadier."

"Let me hear no more of this nonsense," said Belle; "if you are afraid, you can go back to your chaise—we only seek to do you a kindness."

"Why, he was just now talking of cutting throats," said the man. "You brought it on yourself," said Belle; "you suspected us, and he wished to pass a joke upon you; he would not hurt a hair of your head, were your coach laden with gold, nor would I." "Well," said the man, "I was wrong—here's my hand to both of you," shaking us by the hands; "I'll go with you where you please, but I thought this a strange, lonesome place, though I ought not much to mind strange, lonesome places, having been in plenty of such when I was a servant in Italy, without coming to any harm—come, let us move on, for 'tis a shame to keep you two in the rain."

So we descended the path which led into the depths of the dingle; at the bottom I conducted the postillion to my tent, which, though the rain dripped and trickled through it, afforded some shelter; there I bade him sit down on the log of wood, while I placed myself as usual on my stone. Belle in the meantime had repaired to her own place of abode. After a little time, I produced a bottle of the cordial of which I have previously had occasion to speak, and made my guest take a considerable draught. I then offered him some bread and cheese, which he accepted with thanks. In about an hour the rain had much abated: "What do you now propose to do?" said I. "I scarcely know," said the man; "I suppose I must endeavour to put on the wheel with your help." "How far are you from your home?" I demanded. "Upwards of thirty miles," said the man; "my master keeps an inn on the great north road, and from thence I started early this morning with a family which I conveyed across the country to a hall at some distance from here. On my return I was beset by the thunderstorm, which frightened the horses, who dragged the chaise off the road to the field above, and overset it as you saw. I had proposed to pass the night at an inn about twelve miles from here on my way back, though how I am to get there to-night I scarcely know, even if we can put on the wheel, for, to tell you the truth, I am shaken by my fall, and the smoulder and smoke of that fire-ball have rather bewildered my head ; I am, moreover, not much acquainted with the way."

"The best thing you can do," said I, "is to pass the night here ; I will presently light a fire, and endeavour to make you comfortable—in the morning we will see to your wheel." "Well," said the man, " I shall be glad to pass the night here, provided I do not intrude, but I must see to the horses." Thereupon I conducted the man to the place where the horses were tied. "The trees drip very much upon them," said the man, " and it will not do for them to remain here all night ; they will be better out on the field picking the grass, but first of all they must have a good feed of corn ; " thereupon he went to his chaise, from which he presently brought two small bags, partly filled with corn ; into them he inserted the mouths of the horses, tying them over their heads. " Here we will leave them for a time," said the man ; " when I think they have had enough, I will come back, tie their fore-legs, and let them pick about."

CHAPTER XCVII.

It might be about ten o'clock at night. Belle, the postillion, and myself, sat just within the tent, by a fire of charcoal which I had kindled in the chafing-pan. The man had removed the harness from his horses, and, after tethering their legs, had left them for the night in the field above, to regale themselves on what grass they could find. The rain had long since entirely ceased, and the moon and stars shone bright in the firmament, up to which, putting aside the canvas, I occasionally looked from the depths of the dingle. Large drops of water, however, falling now and then upon the tent from the neighbouring trees, would have served, could we have forgotten it, to remind us of the recent storm, and also a certain chilliness in the atmosphere, unusual to the season, proceeding from the moisture with which the ground was saturated ; yet these circumstances only served to make our party enjoy the charcoal fire the more. There we sat bending over it : Belle, with her long beautiful hair streaming over her magnificent shoulders ; the postillion smoking his pipe, in his shirt-sleeves and waistcoat, having flung aside his great-coat, which had sustained a thorough wetting; and I without my wagoner's slop, of which, it being in the same plight, I had also divested myself.

The new comer was a well-made fellow of about thirty, with an open and agreeable countenance. I found him very well informed for a man in his station, and with some pretensions to humour. After we had discoursed for some time on indifferent subjects, the postillion, who had exhausted his pipe, took it from his mouth, and, knocking out the ashes upon the ground, exclaimed : " I little thought, when I got up in the morning, that I should spend the night in such agreeable company, and after such a fright ".

" Well," said I, " I am glad that your opinion of us has improved; it is not long since you seemed to hold us in rather a suspicious light."

" And no wonder," said the man, " seeing the place you were taking me to. I was not a little, but very much afraid of ye both ; and so I continued for some time, though, not to show a craven heart, I pretended to be quite satisfied; but I see I was altogether mistaken about ye. I thought you vagrant Gypsy folks and trampers; but now —— "

" Vagrant Gypsy folks and trampers," said I; " and what are we but people of that stamp? "

" Oh," said the postillion, " if you wish to be thought such, I am far too civil a person to contradict you, especially after your kindness to me, but —— "

" But! " said I; " what do you mean by but? I would have you to know that I am proud of being a travelling blacksmith: look at these donkey-shoes, I finished them this day."

The postillion took the shoes and examined them. " So you made these shoes? " he cried at last.

" To be sure I did; do you doubt it? "

" Not in the least," said the man.

" Ah! ah! " said I, " I thought I should bring you back to your original opinion. I am, then, a vagrant Gypsy body, a tramper, a wandering blacksmith."

" Not a blacksmith, whatever else you may be," said the postillion laughing.

" Then how do you account for my making those shoes? "

" By your not being a blacksmith," said the postillion; " no blacksmith would have made shoes in that manner. Besides, what did you mean just now by saying you had finished these shoes to-day? a real blacksmith would have flung off three or four sets of donkey shoes in one morning, but you, I will be sworn, have been hammering at these for days, and they do you credit, but why? because you are no blacksmith; no, friend, your shoes may do for this young gentlewoman's animal, but I shouldn't like to have my horses shod by you, unless at a great pinch indeed."

" Then," said I, " for what do you take me? "

" Why, for some runaway young gentleman," said the postillion. " No offence, I hope? "

" None at all; no one is offended at being taken or mistaken for a young gentleman, whether runaway or not; but from whence do you suppose I have run away? "

" Why, from college," said the man: " no offence? "

" None whatever; and what induced me to run away from college? "

" A love affair, I'll be sworn," said the postillion. " You had become acquainted with this young gentlewoman, so she and you —— "

" Mind how you get on, friend," said Belle, in a deep serious tone.

" Pray proceed," said I ; " I dare say you mean no offence."

" None in the world," said the postillion ; " all I was going to say was that you agreed to run away together, you from college, and she from boarding-school. Well, there's nothing to be ashamed of in a matter like that, such things are done every day by young folks in high life."

" Are you offended ? " said I to Belle.

Belle made no answer ; but, placing her elbows on her knees, buried her face in her hands.

" So we ran away together ? " said I.

" Ay, ay," said the postillion, " to Gretna Green, though I can't say that I drove ye, though I have driven many a pair."

" And from Gretna Green we came here ? "

" I'll be bound you did," said the man, " till you could arrange matters at home."

" And the horse-shoes ? " said I.

" The donkey-shoes, you mean," answered the postillion ; " why, I suppose you persuaded the blacksmith who married you to give you, before you left, a few lessons in his trade."

" And we intend to stay here till we have arranged matters at home ? "

" Ay, ay," said the postillion, " till the old people are pacified and they send you letters directed to the next post town, to be left till called for, beginning with, ' Dear children,' and enclosing you each a cheque for one hundred pounds, when you will leave this place, and go home in a coach like gentlefolks, to visit your governors ; I should like nothing better than to have the driving of you : and then there will be a grand meeting of the two families, and after a few reproaches, the old people will agree to do something handsome for the poor thoughtless things ; so you will have a genteel house taken for you, and an annuity allowed you. You won't get much the first year, five hundred at the most, in order that the old folks may let you feel that they are not altogether satisfied with you, and that you are yet entirely in their power ; but the second, if you don't get a cool thousand, may I catch cold, especially should young madam here present a son and heir for the old people to fondle, destined one day to become sole heir of the two illustrious houses, and then all the grand folks in the neighbourhood, who have, bless their prudent hearts ! kept rather aloof from you till then, for fear you should want anything from them—I say, all the carriage people in the neighbourhood, when they see how swimmingly matters are going on, will come in shoals to visit you."

" Really," said I, " you are getting on swimmingly."

" Oh," said the postillion, " I was not a gentleman's servant nine years without learning the ways of gentry, and being able to know gentry when I see them."

" And what do you say to all this? " I demanded of Belle.

" Stop a moment," interposed the postillion, " I have one more word to say : and when you are surrounded by your comforts, keeping your nice little barouche and pair, your coachman and livery servant, and visited by all the carriage people in the neighbourhood—to say nothing of the time when you come to the family estates on the death of the old people—I shouldn't wonder if now and then you look back with longing and regret to the days when you lived in the damp, dripping dingle, had no better equipage than a pony or donkey-cart, and saw no better company than a tramper or Gypsy, except once, when a poor postillion was glad to seat himself at your charcoal fire."

" Pray," said I, " did you ever take lessons in elocution? "

" Not directly," said the postillion ; " but my old master who was in Parliament, did, and so did his son, who was intended to be an orator. A great professor used to come and give them lessons, and I used to stand and listen, by which means I picked up a considerable quantity of what is called rhetoric. In what I last said, I was aiming at what I have heard him frequently endeavouring to teach my governors as a thing indispensably necessary in all oratory, a graceful pere—pere—peregrination."

" Peroration, perhaps? "

" Just so," said the postillion ; " and now I am sure I am not mistaken about you; you have taken lessons yourself, at first hand, in the college vacations, and a promising pupil you were, I make no doubt. Well, your friends will be all the happier to get you back. Has your governor much borough interest? "

" I ask you once more," said I, addressing myself to Belle, " what do you think of the history which this good man has made for us ? "

" What should I think of it," said Belle, still keeping her face buried in her hands, " but that it is mere nonsense? "

" Nonsense! " said the postillion.

" Yes," said the girl, " and you know it."

" May my leg always ache, if I do," said the postillion, patting his leg with his hand ; " will you persuade me that this young man has never been at college? "

" I have never been at college, but ——"

" Ay, ay," said the postillion ; " but ——"

" I have been to the best schools in Britain, to say nothing of a celebrated one in Ireland."

"Well, then, it comes to the same thing," said the postillion; " or perhaps you know more than if you had been at college — and your governor?"

" My governor, as you call him," said I, "is dead."

" And his borough interest?"

" My father had no borough interest," said I; " had he possessed any, he would perhaps not have died as he did, honourably poor."

" No, no," said the postillion; "if he had had borough interest, he wouldn't have been poor, nor honourable, though perhaps a right honourable. However, with your grand education and genteel manners, you made all right at last by persuading this noble young gentlewoman to run away from boarding-school with you."

" I was never at boarding-school," said Belle, " unless you call——"

" Ay, ay," said the postillion, " boarding-school is vulgar, I know : I beg your pardon, I ought to have called it academy, or by some other much finer name—you were in something much greater than a boarding-school."

" There you are right," said Belle, lifting up her head and looking the postillion full in the face by the light of the charcoal fire ; " for I was bred in the workhouse."

" Wooh !" said the postillion.

" It is true that I am of good ——"

" Ay, ay," said the postillion, "let us hear ——"

" Of good blood," continued Belle; " my name is Berners, Isopel Berners, though my parents were unfortunate. Indeed, with respect to blood, I believe I am of better blood than the young man."

" There you are mistaken," said I; " by my father's side I am of Cornish blood, and by my mother's of brave French Protestant extraction. Now, with respect to the blood of my father—and to be descended well on the father's side is the principal thing—it is the best blood in the world, for the Cornish blood, as the proverb says ——"

" I don't care what the proverb says," said Belle; " I say my blood is the best—my name is Berners, Isopel Berners—it was my mother's name, and is better, I am sure, than any you bear, whatever that may be ; and though you say that the descent on the father's side is the principal thing—and I know why you say so," she added with some excitement—"I say that descent on the mother's side is of most account, because the mother ——"

"Just come from Gretna Green, and already quarrelling," said the postillion.

"We do not come from Gretna Green," said Belle.

"Ah, I had forgot," said the postillion, "none but great people go to Gretna Green. Well, then, from church, and already quarrelling about family, just like two great people."

"We have never been to church," said Belle, "and, to prevent any more guessing on your part, it will be as well for me to tell you, friend, that I am nothing to the young man, and he, of course, nothing to me. I am a poor travelling girl, born in a workhouse: journeying on my occasions with certain companions, I came to this hollow, where my company quarrelled with the young man, who had settled down here, as he had a right to do, if he pleased ; and not being able to drive him out, they went away after quarrelling with me, too, for not choosing to side with them ; so I stayed here along with the young man, there being room for us both, and the place being as free to me as to him."

"And, in order that you may be no longer puzzled with respect to myself," said I, "I will give you a brief outline of my history. I am the son of honourable parents, who gave me a first-rate education, as far as literature and languages went, with which education I endeavoured, on the death of my father, to advance myself to wealth and reputation in the big city; but failing in the attempt, I conceived a disgust for the busy world, and determined to retire from it. After wandering about for some time, and meeting with various adventures, in one of which I contrived to obtain a pony, cart and certain tools, used by smiths and tinkers, I came to this place, where I amused myself with making horse-shoes, or rather pony-shoes, having acquired the art of wielding the hammer and tongs from a strange kind of smith—not him of Gretna Green—whom I knew in my childhood. And here I lived, doing harm to no one, quite lonely and solitary, till one fine morning the premises were visited by this young gentlewoman and her companions. She did herself anything but justice when she said that her companions quarrelled with her because she would not side with them against me ; they quarrelled with her, because she came most heroically to my assistance as I was on the point of being murdered ; and she forgot to tell you, that after they had abandoned her she stood by me in the dark hour, comforting and cheering me, when unspeakable dread, to which I am occasionally subject, took possession of my mind. She says she is nothing to me, even as I am nothing to her. I am of course nothing to her, but she is mistaken in thinking she is nothing to me. I entertain the highest regard and admiration for her, being convinced that I might search the whole world in vain for a nature more heroic and devoted."

"And for my part," said Belle, with a sob, "a more quiet, agreeable partner in a place like this I would not wish to have; it is true he has strange ways, and frequently puts words into my mouth very difficult to utter; but—but ——" and here she buried her face once more in her hands.

"Well," said the postillion, "I have been mistaken about you; that is, not altogether, but in part. You are not rich folks, it seems, but you are not common people, and that I could have sworn. What I call a shame is, that some people I have known are not in your place and you in theirs—you with their estates and borough interest, they in this dingle with these carts and animals; but there is no help for these things. Were I the great Mumbo Jumbo above, I would endeavour to manage matters better; but being a simple postillion, glad to earn three shillings a day, I can't be expected to do much."

"Who is Mumbo Jumbo?" said I.

"Ah!" said the postillion, "I see there may be a thing or two I know better than yourself. Mumbo Jumbo is a god of the black coast, to which people go for ivory and gold."

"Were you ever there?" I demanded.

"No," said the postillion, "but I heard plenty of Mumbo Jumbo when I was a boy."

"I wish you would tell us something about yourself. I believe that your own real history would prove quite as entertaining, if not more, than that which you imagined about us."

"I am rather tired," said the postillion, "and my leg is rather troublesome. I should be glad to try to sleep upon one of your blankets. However, as you wish to hear something about me, I shall be happy to oblige you; but your fire is rather low, and this place is chilly."

Thereupon I arose, and put fresh charcoal on the pan; then taking it outside the tent, with a kind of fan which I had fashioned, I fanned the coals into a red glow, and continued doing so until the greater part of the noxious gas, which the coals are in the habit of exhaling, was exhausted. I then brought it into the tent and reseated myself, scattering over the coals a small portion of sugar. "No bad smell," said the postillion; "but upon the whole I think I like the smell of tobacco better; and with your permission I will once more light my pipe."

Thereupon he relighted his pipe; and after taking two or three whiffs, began in the following manner.

CHAPTER XCVIII.

" I AM a poor postillion, as you see ; yet, as I have seen a thing or two, and heard a thing or two of what is going on in the world, perhaps what I have to tell you connected with myself may not prove altogether uninteresting. Now, my friends, this manner of opening a story is what the man who taught rhetoric would call a hex—hex ——"

" Exordium," said I.

" Just so," said the postillion ; " I treated you to a per—per—peroration some time ago, so that I have contrived to put the cart before the horse, as the Irish orators frequently do in the honourable House, in whose speeches, especially those who have taken lessons in rhetoric, the per—per—what's the word?—frequently goes before the exordium.

" I was born in the neighbouring county ; my father was land-steward to a squire of about a thousand a year. My father had two sons, of whom I am the youngest by some years. My elder brother was of a spirited, roving disposition, and for fear that he should turn out what is generally termed ungain, my father determined to send him to sea : so once upon a time, when my brother was about fifteen, he took him to the great sea-port of the county, where he apprenticed him to a captain of one of the ships which trade to the high Barbary coast. Fine ships they were, I have heard say, more than thirty in number, and all belonging to a wonderful great gentleman, who had once been a parish boy, but had contrived to make an immense fortune by trading to that coast for gold dust, ivory and other strange articles ; and for doing so, I mean for making a fortune, had been made a knight baronet. So my brother went to the high Barbary shore, on board the fine vessel, and in about a year returned and came to visit us ; he repeated the voyage several times, always coming to see his parents on his return. Strange stories he used to tell us of what he had been witness to on the high Barbary coast, both off shore and on. He said that the fine vessel in which he sailed was nothing better than a painted hell ;

(529)

that the captain was a veritable fiend, whose grand delight was
in tormenting his men, especially when they were sick, as they
frequently were, there being always fever on the high Barbary
coast; and that though the captain was occasionally sick himself,
his being so made no difference, or rather it did make a difference, though for the worse, he being when sick always more
inveterate and malignant than at other times.   He said that
once, when he himself was sick, his captain had pitched his face
all over, which exploit was much applauded by the other high
Barbary captains; all of whom, from what my brother said,
appeared to be of much the same disposition as my brother's
captain, taking wonderful delight in tormenting the crews, and
doing all manner of terrible things.   My brother frequently said
that nothing whatever prevented him from running away from his
ship, and never returning, but the hope he entertained of one day
being captain himself, and able to torment people in his turn,
which he solemnly vowed he would do, as a kind of compensa-
tion for what he himself had undergone.   And if things were
going on in a strange way off the high Barbary shore amongst
those who came there to trade, they were going on in a way yet
stranger with the people who lived upon it.

   " Oh, the strange ways of the black men who lived on that
shore, of which my brother used to tell us at home; selling their
sons, daughters and servants for slaves, and the prisoners taken
in battle, to the Spanish captains, to be carried to Havannah, and
when there, sold at a profit, the idea of which, my brother said,
went to the hearts of our own captains, who used to say what a
hard thing it was that free-born Englishmen could not have a
hand in the traffic, seeing that it was forbidden by the laws of
their country; talking fondly of the good old times when their
forefathers used to carry slaves to Jamaica and Barbadoes,
realising immense profit, besides the pleasure of hearing their
shrieks on the voyage; and then the superstitions of the blacks,
which my brother used to talk of; their sharks' teeth, their wisps
of fowls' feathers, their half-baked pots, full of burnt bones, of
which they used to make what they called fetish; and bow down
to, and ask favours of, and then, perhaps, abuse and strike,
provided the senseless rubbish did not give them what they
asked for; and then, above all, Mumbo Jumbo, the grand fetish
master, who lived somewhere in the woods, and who used to
come out every now and then with his fetish companions; a
monstrous figure, all wound round with leaves and branches, so
as to be quite indistinguishable, and, seating himself on the high

seat in the villages, receive homage from the people, and also gifts and offerings, the most valuable of which were pretty damsels, and then betake himself back again, with his followers into the woods. Oh, the tales that my brother used to tell us of the high Barbary shore! Poor fellow! what became of him I can't say; the last time he came back from a voyage, he told us that his captain, as soon as he had brought his vessel to port, and settled with his owner, drowned himself off the quay in a fit of the horrors, which it seems high Barbary captains, after a certain number of years, are much subject to. After staying about a month with us, he went to sea again, with another captain; and bad as the old one had been, it appears the new one was worse, for, unable to bear his treatment, my brother left his ship off the high Barbary shore, and ran away up the country. Some of his comrades, whom we afterwards saw, said that there were various reports about him on the shore; one that he had taken on with Mumbo Jumbo, and was serving him in his house in the woods, in the capacity of swash-buckler, or life-guardsman; another, that he was gone in quest of a mighty city in the heart of the negro country; another, that in swimming a stream he had been devoured by an alligator. Now, these two last reports were bad enough; the idea of their flesh and blood being bit asunder by a ravenous fish, was sad enough to my poor parents; and not very comfortable was the thought of his sweltering over the hot sands in quest of the negro city; but the idea of their son, their eldest child, serving Mumbo Jumbo as swash-buckler, was worst of all, and caused my poor parents to shed many a scalding tear.

  " I stayed at home with my parents until I was about eighteen, assisting my father in various ways. I then went to live at the squire's, partly as groom, partly as footman. After living in the country some time, I attended the family in a trip of six weeks, which they made to London. Whilst there, happening to have some words with an old ill-tempered coachman, who had been for a great many years in the family, my master advised me to leave, offering to recommend me to a family of his acquaintance who were in need of a footman. I was glad to accept his offer, and in a few days went to my new place. My new master was one of the great gentry, a baronet in Parliament, and possessed of an estate of about twenty thousand a year; his family consisted of his lady, a son, a fine young man, just coming of age, and two very sweet, amiable daughters. I liked this place much better than my first, there was so much more pleasant noise and bustle—so much more grand company—and so many more opportunities of im-

proving myself.   Oh, how I liked to see the grand coaches drive
up to the door, with the grand company; and though, amidst
that company, there were some who did not look very grand,
there were others, and not a few, who did.   Some of the ladies
quite captivated me; there was the Marchioness of —— in
particular.   This young lady puts me much in mind of her; it is
true, the Marchioness, as I saw her then, was about fifteen years
older than this young gentlewoman is now, and not so tall by
some inches, but she had the very same hair, and much the same
neck and shoulders—no offence, I hope?   And then some of the
young gentlemen, with their cool, haughty, care-for-nothing looks,
struck me as being very fine fellows.   There was one in particular,
whom I frequently used to stare at, not altogether unlike some
one I have seen hereabouts—he had a slight cast in his eye, and
—— but I won't enter into every particular.   And then the
footmen!   Oh, how those footmen helped to improve me with
their conversation.   Many of them could converse much more
glibly than their masters, and appeared to have much better taste.
At any rate, they seldom approved of what their masters did.   I
remember being once with one in the gallery of the play-house,
when something of Shakspeare's was being performed; some one
in the first tier of boxes was applauding very loudly.   ' That's
my fool of a governor,' said he; 'he is weak enough to like
Shakspeare—I don't—he's so confoundedly low, but he won't last
long—going down.   Shakspeare culminated '—I think that was
the word—'culminated some time ago.'

"And then the professor of elocution, of whom my governors
used to take lessons, and of which lessons I had my share, by
listening behind the door; but for that professor of elocution I
should not be able to round my periods—an expression of his—
in the manner I do.

"After I had been three years at this place my mistress died.
Her death, however, made no great alteration in my way of
living, the family spending their winters in London, and their
summers at their old seat in S—— as before.   At last, the young
ladies, who had not yet got husbands, which was strange enough,
seeing, as I told you before, they were very amiable, proposed to
our governor a travelling expedition abròad.   The old baronet
consented, though young master was much against it, saying,
they would all be much better at home.   As the girls persisted,
however, he at last withdrew his opposition, and even promised
to follow them, as soon as his parliamentary duties would permit,
for he was just got into Parliament; and, like most other young

members, thought that nothing could be done in the House without him.   So the old gentleman and the two young ladies set off, taking me with them, and a couple of ladies' maids to wait upon them.   First of all, we went to Paris, where we continued three months, the old baronet and the ladies going to see the various sights of the city and the neighbourhood, and I attending them. They soon got tired of sight-seeing, and of Paris too ; and so did I.   However, they still continued there, in order, I believe, that the young ladies might lay in a store of French finery.   I should have passed my idle time at Paris, of which I had plenty after the sight-seeing was over, very unpleasantly, but for Black Jack. Eh! did you never hear of Black Jack? Ah! if you had ever been an English servant in Paris, you would have known Black Jack ; not an English gentleman's servant who has been at Paris for this last ten years but knows Black Jack and his ordinary. A strange fellow he was—of what country no one could exactly say—for as for judging from speech, that was impossible, Jack speaking all languages equally ill.   Some said he came direct from Satan's kitchen, and that when he gives up keeping ordinary, he will return there again, though the generally received opinion at Paris was, that he was at one time butler to King Pharaoh, and that, after lying asleep for four thousand years in a place called the Kattycombs, he was awaked by the sound of Nelson's canon, at the battle of the Nile ; and going to the shore took on with the admiral, and became, in course of time, ship steward ; and that after Nelson's death, he was captured by the French, on board one of whose vessels he served in a somewhat similar capacity till the peace, when he came to Paris, and set up an ordinary for servants, sticking the name of Katcomb over the door, in allusion to the place where he had his long sleep.   But, whatever his origin was, Jack kept his own counsel, and appeared to care nothing for what people said about him, or called him. Yes, I forgot, there was one name he would not be called, and that was Portuguese.   I once saw Black Jack knock down a coachman, six foot high, who called him black-faced Portuguese. 'Any name but dat, you shab,' said Black Jack, who was a little round fellow, of about five feet two ; ' I would not stand to be called Portuguese by Nelson himself.'   Jack was rather fond of talking about Nelson, and hearing people talking about him, so that it is not improbable that he may have sailed with him ; and with respect to his having been King Pharaoh's butler, all I have to say is, I am not disposed to give the downright lie to the report.   Jack was always ready to do a kind turn to a poor servant out of place, and has often been known to assist such as were in prison, which charitable disposition he perhaps acquired from having lost a good place himself, having seen the inside of a prison, and known the want of a meal's victuals, all which trials King Pharaoh's butler underwent, so he may have been that butler; at any rate, I have known positive conclusions come to, on no better premises, if indeed as good.   As for the story of his coming direct from Satan's kitchen, I place no confidence in it at all, as Black Jack had nothing of Satan about him, but blackness, on which account he was called Black Jack.   Nor am I disposed to give credit to a report that his hatred of the Portuguese arose from some ill treatment which he had once experienced when on shore, at Lisbon, from certain gentlewomen of the place, but rather conclude that it arose from an opinion he entertained that the Portuguese never paid their debts, one of the ambassadors of that nation, whose house he had served, having left Paris several thousand francs in his debt.   This is all that I have to say about Black Jack, without whose funny jokes, and good ordinary, I should have passed my time in Paris in a very disconsolate manner.

" After we had been at Paris between two and three months, we left it in the direction of Italy, which country the family had a great desire to see.   After travelling a great many days in a thing which, though called a diligence, did not exhibit much diligence, we came to a great big town, seated around a nasty saltwater basin, connected by a narrow passage with the sea.   Here we were to embark; and so we did as soon as possible, glad enough to get away; at least I was, and so I make no doubt were the rest; for such a place for bad smells I never was in.   It seems all the drains and sewers of the place run into that same salt basin, voiding into it all their impurities, which, not being able to escape into the sea in any considerable quantity, owing to the narrowness of the entrance, there accumulate, filling the whole atmosphere with these same outrageous scents, on which account the town is a famous lodging-house of the plague.   The ship in which we embarked was bound for a place in Italy called Naples, where we were to stay some time.   The voyage was rather a lazy one, the ship not being moved by steam; for at the time of which I am speaking, some five years ago, steamships were not so plentiful as now.   There were only two passengers in the grand cabin, where my governor and his daughters were, an Italian lady and a priest.   Of the lady I have not much to say; she appeared to be a quiet respectable person enough, and after our arrival at Naples, I neither saw nor heard anything more of her; but of the priest I shall have a good deal to say in the sequel (that, by-the-bye, is a word I learnt from the professor of rhetoric), and it would have been well for our family had they never met him.

"On the third day of the voyage the priest came to me, who was rather unwell with sea-sickness, which he, of course, felt nothing of, that kind of people being never affected like others. He was a finish-looking man of about forty-five, but had something strange in his eyes, which I have since thought denoted that all was not right in a certain place called the heart. After a few words of condolence, in a broken kind of English, he asked me various questions about our family; and I, won by his seeming kindness, told him all I knew about them, of which communicativeness I afterwards very much repented. As soon as he had got out of me all he desired, he left me; and I observed that during the rest of the voyage he was wonderfully attentive to our governor, and yet more to the young ladies. Both, however, kept him rather at a distance; the young ladies were reserved, and once or twice I heard our governor cursing him between his teeth for a sharking priest. The priest, however, was not disconcerted, and continued his attentions, which in a little time produced an effect, so that, by the time we landed at Naples, our great folks had conceived a kind of liking for the man, and when they took their leave invited him to visit them, which he promised to do. We hired a grand house or palace at Naples; it belonged to a poor kind of prince, who was glad enough to let it to our governor, and also his servants and carriages; and glad enough were the poor servants, for they got from us what they never got from the prince—plenty of meat and money—and glad enough, I make no doubt, were the horses for the provender we gave them; and I daresay the coaches were not sorry to be cleaned and furbished up. Well, we went out and came in; going to see the sights, and returning. Amongst other things we saw was the burning mountain, and the tomb of a certain sorcerer called Virgilio, who made witch rhymes, by which he could raise the dead. Plenty of people came to see us, both English and Italians, and amongst the rest the priest. He did not come amongst the first, but allowed us to settle and become a little quiet before he showed himself; and after a day or two he paid us another visit, then another, till at last his visits were daily.

"I did not like that Jack Priest; so I kept my eye upon all his motions. Lord! how that Jack Priest did curry favour with our governor and the two young ladies; and he curried, and curried, till he had got himself into favour with the governor, and more especially with the two young ladies, of whom their father was doatingly fond.   At last the ladies took lessons in Italian of the priest, a language in which he was said to be a grand proficient, and of which they had hitherto known but very little; and from that time his influence over them, and consequently over the old governor, increased, till the tables were turned, and he no longer curried favour with them, but they with him; yes, as true as my leg aches, the young ladies curried, and the old governor curried favour with that same priest; when he was with them, they seemed almost to hang on his lips, that is, the young ladies; and as for the old governor, he never contradicted him, and when the fellow was absent, which, by-the-bye was not often, it was ' Father so-and-so said this, and Father so-and-so said that; Father so-and-so thinks we should do so-and-so, or that we should not do so-and-so '.   I at first thought that he must have given them something, some philtre or the like ; but one of the English maid-servants, who had a kind of respect for me, and who saw much more behind the scenes than I did, informed me that he was continually instilling strange notions into their heads, striving, by every possible method, to make them despise the religion of their own land, and take up that of the foreign country in which they were.   And sure enough, in a little time, the girls had altogether left off going to an English chapel, and were continually visiting places of Italian worship. The old governor, it is true, still went to his church, but he appeared to be hesitating between two opinions ; and once when he was at dinner he said to two or three English friends, that since he had become better acquainted with it, he had conceived a much more favourable opinion of the Catholic religion than he had previously entertained.   In a word, the priest ruled the house, and everything was done according to his will and pleasure ; by degrees he persuaded the young ladies to drop their English acquaintances, whose place he supplied with Italians, chiefly females.   My poor old governor would not have had a person to speak to, for he never could learn the language, but for two or three Englishmen who used to come occasionally and take a bottle with him, in a summer-house, whose company he could not be persuaded to resign, notwithstanding the entreaties of his daughters, instigated by the priest, whose grand endeavour seemed to be to render the minds of all three foolish, for his own ends.   And if he was busy above stairs with the governor, there was another busy below with us poor English servants, a kind of subordinate priest, a low Italian ; as he could speak no language but his own, he was continually jabbering to us in that, and by hearing him the maids and myself contrived to pick up a good deal of the language, so that we understood most that was said, and could speak it very fairly ; and the themes of his jabber were the beauty and virtues of one whom he called Holy Mary, and the power and grandeur of one whom he called the Holy Father ; and he told us that we should shortly have an opportunity of seeing the Holy Father, who could do anything he liked with Holy Mary : in the meantime we had plenty of opportunities of seeing Holy Mary, for in every church, chapel and convent to which we were taken, there was an image of Holy Mary, who, if the images were dressed at all in her fashion, must have been very fond of short petticoats and tinsel, and who, if those said figures at all resembled her in face, could scarcely have been half as handsome as either of my two fellow-servants, not to speak of the young ladies.

"Now it happened that one of the female servants was much taken with what she saw and heard, and gave herself up entirely to the will of the subordinate, who had quite as much dominion over her as his superior had over the ladies ; the other maid, however, the one who had a kind of respect for me, was not so easily besotted ; she used to laugh at what she saw, and at what the fellow told her, and from her I learnt that amongst other things intended by these priestly confederates was robbery ; she said that the poor old governor had already been persuaded by his daughters to put more than a thousand pounds into the superior priest's hands for purposes of charity and religion, as was said, and that the subordinate one had already inveigled her fellow-servant out of every penny which she had saved from her wages, and had endeavoured likewise to obtain what money she herself had, but in vain. With respect to myself, the fellow shortly after made an attempt towards obtaining a hundred crowns, of which, by some means, he knew me to be in possession, telling me what a meritorious thing it was to give one's superfluities for the purposes of religion. ' That is true,' said I, ' and if, after my return to my native country, I find I have anything which I don't want myself, I will employ it in helping to build a Methodist chapel.'

"By the time that the three months were expired for which we had hired the palace of the needy Prince, the old governor began to talk of returning to England, at least of leaving Italy.

I believe he had become frightened at the calls which were
continually being made upon him for money; for after all, you
know, if there is a sensitive part of a man's wearing apparel, it is
his breeches pocket; but the young ladies could not think of
leaving dear Italy and the dear priest; and then they had seen
nothing of the country, they had only seen Naples; before leaving dear Italia they must see more of the country and the cities;
above all, they must see a place which they called the Eternal
City, or by some similar nonsensical name; and they persisted
so that the poor governor permitted them, as usual, to have their
way; and it was decided what route they should take, that is, the
priest was kind enough to decide for them; and was also kind
enough to promise to go with them part of the route, as far as a
place where there was a wonderful figure of Holy Mary, which
the priest said it was highly necessary for them to see before
visiting the Eternal City; so we left Naples in hired carriages,
driven by fellows they call *veturini*, cheating, drunken dogs, I
remember they were.   Besides our own family there was the
priest and his subordinate, and a couple of hired lackeys.   We
were several days upon the journey, travelling through a very wild
country, which the ladies pretended to be delighted with, and
which the governor cursed on account of the badness of the
roads; and when we came to any particularly wild spot we used
to stop, in order to enjoy the scenery, as the ladies said; and
then we would spread a horse-cloth on the ground, and eat bread
and cheese, and drink wine of the country; and some of the
holes and corners in which we bivouacked, as the ladies called it,
were something like this place where we are now, so that when I
came down here it put me in mind of them.   At last we arrived
at the place where was the holy image.

   " We went to the house or chapel in which the holy image
was kept, a frightful, ugly black figure of Holy Mary, dressed in
her usual way; and after we had stared at the figure, and some
of our party had bowed down to it, we were shown a great many
things which were called holy relics, which consisted of thumb-
nails and fore-nails and toe-nails, and hair and teeth, and a
feather or two, a mighty thigh-bone, but whether of a man or a
camel, I can't say; all of which things I was told, if properly
touched and handled, had mighty power to cure all kinds of
disorders; and as we went from the holy house, we saw a man in
a state of great excitement; he was foaming at the mouth, and
cursing the holy image and all its household, because, after he
had worshipped it and made offerings to it, and besought it to

assist him in a game of chance which he was about to play, it had
left him in the lurch, allowing him to lose all his money ; and
when I thought of all the rubbish I had seen, and the purposes
which it was applied to, in conjunction with the rage of the losing
gamester at the deaf and dumb image, I could not help comparing the whole with what my poor brother used to tell me of the
superstitious practices of the blacks on the high Barbary shore,
and their occasional rage and fury at the things they worshipped ;
and I said to myself, if all this here doesn't smell of fetish may I
smell fetid.

"At this place the priest left us, returning to Naples with his
subordinate, on some particular business, I suppose. It was,
however, agreed that he should visit us at the Holy City. We
did not go direct to the Holy City, but bent our course to two or
three other cities which the family were desirous of seeing, but as
nothing occurred to us in these places of any particular interest,
I shall take the liberty of passing them by in silence. At length
we arrived at the Eternal City ; an immense city it was, looking
as if it had stood for a long time, and would stand for a long
time still ; compared with it, London would look like a mere
assemblage of bee-skeps ; however, give me the bee-skeps with
their merry hum and bustle, and life and honey, rather than that
huge town, which looked like a sepulchre, where there was no
life, no busy hum, no bees, but a scanty, sallow population, inter-
mixed with black priests, white priests, grey priests ; and though
I don't say there was no honey in the place, for I believe there
was, I am ready to take my Bible oath that it was not made
there, and that the priests kept it all for themselves."

CHAPTER XCIX.

"The day after our arrival," continued the postillion, "I was sent, under the guidance of a lackey of the place, with a letter, which the priest, when he left, had given us for a friend of his in the Eternal City. We went to a large house, and on ringing, were admitted by a porter into a cloister, where I saw some ill-looking, shabby young fellows walking about, who spoke English to one another. To one of these the porter delivered the letter, and the young fellow going away, presently returned and told me to follow him; he led me into a large room, where, behind a table, on which were various papers, and a thing, which they call in that country a crucifix, sat a man in a kind of priestly dress. The lad having opened the door for me, shut it behind me, and went away. The man behind the table was so engaged in reading the letter which I had brought, that at first he took no notice of me; he had red hair, a kind of half-English countenance, and was seemingly about five-and-thirty. After a little time he laid the letter down, appeared to consider a moment, and then opened his mouth with a strange laugh, not a loud laugh, for I heard nothing but a kind of hissing deep down the throat; all of a sudden, however, perceiving me, he gave a slight start, but instantly recovering himself, he inquired in English concerning the health of the family, and where we lived; on my delivering him a card, he bade me inform my master and the ladies that in the course of the day he would do himself the honour of waiting upon them. He then arose and opened the door for me to depart; the man was perfectly civil and courteous, but I did not like that strange laugh of his, after having read the letter. He was as good as his word, and that same day paid us a visit. It was now arranged that we should pass the winter in Rome, to my great annoyance, for I wished to return to my native land, being heartily tired of everything connected with Italy. I was not, however, without hope that our young master would shortly arrive, when I trusted that matters, as far as the family were concerned, would be put on a better footing. In a few days our new acquaintance, who, it seems, was a mongrel Englishman,

(540)

had procured a house for our accommodation; it was large enough, but not near so pleasant as that we had at Naples, which was light and airy, with a large garden. This was a dark, gloomy structure in a narrow street, with a frowning church beside it; it was not far from the place where our new friend lived, and its being so was probably the reason why he selected it. It was furnished partly with articles which we bought, and partly with those which we hired. We lived something in the same way as at Naples; but though I did not much like Naples, I yet liked it better than this place, which was so gloomy. Our new acquaintance made himself as agreeable as he could, conducting the ladies to churches and convents, and frequently passing the afternoon drinking with the governor, who was fond of a glass of brandy and water and a cigar, as the new acquaintance also was —no, I remember, he was fond of gin and water, and did not smoke. I don't think he had so much influence over the young ladies as the other priest, which was, perhaps, owing to his not being so good-looking; but I am sure he had more influence with the governor, owing, doubtless, to his bearing him company in drinking mixed liquors, which the other priest did not do.

" He was a strange fellow, that same new acquaintance of ours, and unlike all the priests I saw in that country, and I saw plenty of various nations—they were always upon their guard, and had their features and voice modulated; but this man was subject to fits of absence, during which he would frequently mutter to himself; then, though he was perfectly civil to everybody, as far as words went, I observed that he entertained a thorough contempt for most people, especially for those whom he was making dupes. I have observed him whilst drinking with our governor, when the old man's head was turned, look at him with an air which seemed to say, ' What a thundering old fool you are!' and at our young ladies, when their backs were turned, with a glance which said distinctly enough, ' You precious pair of ninnyhammers'; and then his laugh—he had two kinds of laughs—one which you could hear, and another which you could only see. I have seen him laugh at our governor and the young ladies, when their heads were turned away, but I heard no sound. My mother had a sandy cat, which sometimes used to open its mouth wide with a mew which nobody could hear, and the silent laugh of that red-haired priest used to put me wonderfully in mind of the silent mew of my mother's sandy-red cat. And then the other laugh, which you could hear; what a strange laugh that was, never loud, yes, I have heard it tolerably loud. He once

passed near me, after having taken leave of a silly English fellow
—a limping parson of the name of Platitude, who they said was
thinking of turning Papist, and was much in his company ; I was
standing behind the pillar of a piazza, and as he passed he was
laughing heartily. Oh, he was a strange fellow, that same red-
haired acquaintance of ours !

" After we had been at Rome about six weeks, our old friend
the priest of Naples arrived, but without his subordinate, for
whose services he now perhaps thought that he had no occasion.
I believe he found matters in our family wearing almost as
favourable an aspect as he could desire : with what he had
previously taught them and shown them at Naples and elsewhere,
and with what the red-haired confederate had taught them and
shown them at Rome, the poor young ladies had become quite
handmaids of superstition, so that they, especially the youngest,
were prepared to bow down to anything, and kiss anything however vile and ugly, provided a priest commanded them ; and as
for the old governor, what with the influence which his daughters
exerted, and what with the ascendancy which the red-haired man
had obtained over him, he dared not say his purse, far less his
soul, was his own. Only think of an Englishman not being
master of his own purse. My acquaintance, the lady's maid,
assured me, that to her certain knowledge, he had disbursed to
the red-haired man, for purposes of charity, as it was said, at
least one thousand pounds during the five weeks we had been at
Rome. She also told me that things would shortly be brought
to a conclusion, and so indeed they were, though in a different
manner from what she and I and some other people imagined ;
that there was to be a grand festival, and a mass, at which we
were to be present, after which the family were to be presented
to the Holy Father, for so those two priestly sharks had managed
it ; and then —— she said she was certain that the two ladies,
and perhaps the old governor, would forsake the religion of their
native land, taking up with that of these foreign regions, for so
my fellow-servant expressed it, and that perhaps attempts might
be made to induce us poor English servants to take up with the
foreign religion, that is, herself and me, for as for our fellow-
servant, the other maid, she wanted no inducing, being disposed
body and soul to go over to it. Whereupon, I swore with an
oath that nothing should induce me to take up with the foreign
religion ; and the poor maid, my fellow-servant, bursting into
tears, said that for her part she would sooner die than have
anything to do with it ; thereupon we shook hands and agreed

to stand by and countenance one another: and moreover, provided our governors were fools enough to go over to the religion
of these here foreigners, we would not wait to be asked to do the
like, but leave them at once, and make the best of our way home,
even if we were forced to beg on the road.

"At last the day of the grand festival came, and we were all
to go to the big church to hear the mass. Now it happened
that for some time past I had been much afflicted with melancholy, especially when I got up of a morning, produced by the
strange manner in which I saw things going on in our family;
and to dispel it in some degree, I had been in the habit of
taking a dram before breakfast. On the morning in question,
feeling particularly low-spirited when I thought of the foolish
step our governor would probably take before evening, I took two
drams before breakfast; and after breakfast, feeling my melancholy
still continuing, I took another, which produced a slight effect
upon my head, though I am convinced nobody observed it.

"Away we drove to the big church; it was a dark, misty day,
I remember, and very cold, so that if anybody had noticed my
being slightly in liquor, I could have excused myself by saying
that I had merely taken a glass to fortify my constitution against
the weather; and of one thing I am certain, which is, that such
an excuse would have stood me in stead with our governor, who
looked, I thought, as if he had taken one too; but I may be
mistaken, and why should I notice him, seeing that he took no
notice of me: so away we drove to the big church, to which all
the population of the place appeared to be moving.

"On arriving there we dismounted, and the two priests who
were with us led the family in, whilst I followed at a little distance,
but quickly lost them amidst the throng of people. I made my
way, however, though in what direction I knew not, except it
was one in which everybody seemed striving, and by dint of
elbowing and pushing, I at last got to a place which looked like
the aisle of a cathedral, where the people stood in two rows, a
space between being kept open by certain strangely-dressed men
who moved up and down with rods in their hands; all were
looking to the upper end of this place or aisle; and at the upper
end, separated from the people by palings like those of an altar,
sat in magnificent-looking stalls, on the right and the left, various
wonderful-looking individuals in scarlet dresses. At the farther
end was what appeared to be an altar, on the left hand was a
pulpit, and on the right a stall higher than any of the rest, where
was a figure whom I could scarcely see.

" I can't pretend to describe what I saw exactly, for my head, which was at first rather flurried, had become more so from the efforts which I had made to get through the crowd ; also from certain singing which proceeded from I know not where, and above all from the bursts of an organ which were occasionally so loud that I thought the roof, which was painted with wondrous colours, would come toppling down on those below. So there stood I, a poor English servant, in that outlandish place, in the midst of that foreign crowd, looking at that outlandish sight, hearing those outlandish sounds, and occasionally glancing at our party, which, by this time, I distinguished at the opposite side to where I stood, but much nearer the place where the red figures sat. Yes, there stood our poor governor, and the sweet young ladies, and I thought they never looked so handsome before, and close by them were the sharking priests, and not far from them was that idiotical parson Platitude, winking and grinning, and occasionally lifting up his hands as if in ecstasy at what he saw and heard, so that he drew upon himself the notice of the congregation.

" And now an individual mounted the pulpit, and began to preach in a language which I did not understand, but which I believe to be Latin, addressing himself seemingly to the figure in the stall ; and when he had ceased, there was more singing, more organ playing, and then two men in robes brought forth two things which they held up ; and then the people bowed their heads, and our poor governor bowed his head, and the sweet young ladies bowed their heads, and the sharking priests, whilst the idiotical parson Platitude tried to fling himself down ; and then there were various evolutions withinside the pale, and the scarlet figures got up and sat down, and this kind of thing continued for some time ; at length the figure which I had seen in the principal stall came forth and advanced towards the people ; an awful figure he was, a huge old man with a sugar-loaf hat, with a sulphur-coloured dress, and holding a crook in his hand like that of a shepherd ; and as he advanced the people fell on their knees, our poor old governor amongst them ; the sweet young ladies, the sharking priests, the idiotical parson Platitude all fell on their knees, and somebody or other tried to pull me on my knees, but by this time I had become outrageous ; all that my poor brother used to tell me of the superstitions of the high Barbary shore rushed into my mind, and I thought they were acting them over here ; above all, the idea that the sweet young ladies, to say nothing of my poor old governor, were, after the conclusion of all this mummery, going to deliver themselves up body and soul into the power of that horrid-looking old man, maddened me, and, rushing forward into the open space, I confronted the horrible-looking old figure with the sugar-loaf hat, the sulphur-coloured garments, and shepherd's crook, and shaking my fist at his nose, I bellowed out in English :—

"' I don't care for you, old Mumbo Jumbo, though you have fetish!

" I can scarcely tell you what occurred for some time. I have a dim recollection that hands were laid upon me, and that I struck out violently left and right. On coming to myself, I was seated on a stone bench in a large room, something like a guard-room, in the custody of certain fellows dressed like Merry Andrews; they were bluff, good-looking, wholesome fellows, very different from the sallow Italians; they were looking at me attentively, and occasionally talking to each other in a language which sounded very like the cracking of walnuts in the mouth, very different from cooing Italian. At last one of them asked me in Italian what had ailed me, to which I replied, in an incoherent manner, something about Mumbo Jumbo; whereupon the fellow, one of the bluffest of the lot, a jovial, rosy-faced rascal, lifted up his right hand, placing it in such a manner that the lips were between the forefinger and thumb, then lifting up his right foot and drawing back his head, he sucked in his breath with a hissing sound, as if to imitate one drinking a hearty draught, and then slapped me on the shoulder, saying something which sounded like goot wine, goot companion, whereupon they all laughed, exclaiming, ya, ya, goot companion. And now hurried into the room our poor old governor, with the red-haired priest; the first asked what could have induced me to behave in such a manner in such a place, to which I replied that I was not going to bow down to Mumbo Jumbo, whatever other people might do. Whereupon my master said he believed I was mad, and the priest said he believed I was drunk; to which I answered that I was neither so mad nor drunk but I could distinguish how the wind lay. Whereupon they left me, and in a little time I was told by the bluff-looking Merry Andrews I was at liberty to depart. I believe the priest, in order to please my governor, interceded for me in high quarters.

" But one good resulted from this affair; there was no presentation of our family to the Holy Father, for old Mumbo was so frightened by my outrageous looks that he was laid up for a week, as I was afterwards informed.

" I went home, and had scarcely been there half an hour

when I was sent for by the governor, who again referred to the scene in church, said that he could not tolerate such scandalous behaviour, and that unless I promised to be more circumspect in future, he should be compelled to discharge me. I said that if he was scandalised at my behaviour in the church, I was more scandalised at all I saw going on in the family, which was governed by two rascally priests, who, not content with plundering him, appeared bent on hurrying the souls of us all to destruction; and that with respect to discharging me, he could do so that moment, as I wished to go. I believe his own reason told him that I was right, for he made no direct answer; but, after looking on the ground for some time, he told me to leave him. As he did not tell me to leave the house, I went to my room intending to lie down for an hour or two; but scarcely was I there when the door opened, and in came the red-haired priest. He showed himself, as he always did, perfectly civil, asked me how I was, took a chair and sat down. After a hem or two he entered into a long conversation on the excellence of what he called the Catholic religion; told me that he hoped I would not set myself against the light, and likewise against my interest; for that the family were about to embrace the Catholic religion, and would make it worth my while to follow their example. I told him that the family might do what they pleased, but that I would never forsake the religion of my country for any consideration whatever; that I was nothing but a poor servant, but I was not to be bought by base gold. ' I admire your honourable feelings,' said he; ' you shall have no gold; and as I see you are a fellow of spirit, and do not like being a servant, for which I commend you, I can promise you something better. I have a good deal of influence in this place, and if you will not set your face against the light, but embrace the Catholic religion, I will undertake to make your fortune. You remember those fine fellows to-day who took you into custody, they are the guards of his Holiness. I have no doubt that I have interest enough to procure your enrolment amongst them.' ' What,' said I, ' become swash-buckler to Mumbo Jumbo up here! May I —— '—and here I swore—' if I do. The mere possibility of one of their children being swash-buckler to Mumbo Jumbo on the high Barbary shore has always been a source of heart-breaking to my poor parents. What, then, would they not undergo if they knew for certain that their other child was swash-buckler to Mumbo Jumbo up here?' Thereupon he asked me, even as you did some time ago, what I meant by Mumbo Jumbo? And I told him all I had heard about the Mumbo Jumbo of the high Barbary shore; telling him that I had no doubt that the old fellow up here was his brother, or nearly related to him. The man with the red hair listened with the greatest attention to all I said, and when I had concluded, he got up, nodded to me, and moved to the door; ere he reached the door I saw his shoulders shaking, and as he closed it behind him I heard him distinctly laughing, to the tune of—he! he! he!

"But now matters began to mend. That same evening my young master unexpectedly arrived. I believe he soon perceived that something extraordinary had been going on in the family. He was for some time closeted with the governor, with whom, I believe, he had a dispute; for my fellow-servant, the ladies' maid, informed me that she heard high words.

"Rather late at night the young gentleman sent for me into his room, and asked me various questions with respect to what had been going on, and my behaviour in the church, of which he had heard something. I told him all I knew with respect to the intrigues of the two priests in the family, and gave him a circumstantial account of all that had occurred in the church, adding that, under similar circumstances, I was ready to play the same part over again. Instead of blaming me, he commended my behaviour, told me I was a fine fellow, and said he hoped that if he wanted my assistance, I would stand by him: this I promised to do. Before I left him, he entreated me to inform him the very next time I saw the priests entering the house.

"The next morning, as I was in the court-yard, where I had placed myself to watch, I saw the two enter and make their way up a private stair to the young ladies' apartment; they were attended by a man dressed something like a priest, who bore a large box; I instantly ran to relate what I had seen to my young master. I found him shaving. 'I will just finish what I am about,' said he, 'and then wait upon these gentlemen.' He finished what he was about with great deliberation, then taking a horsewhip, and bidding me follow him, he proceeded at once to the door of his sisters' apartment: finding it fastened, he burst it open at once with his foot and entered, followed by myself. There we beheld the two unfortunate young ladies down on their knees before a large female doll, dressed up, as usual, in rags and tinsel; the two priests were standing near, one on either side, with their hands uplifted, whilst the fellow who brought the trumpery stood a little way down the private stair, the door of which stood open; without a moment's hesitation, my young master rushed forward, gave the image a cut or two with his horsewhip, then flying at the priests, he gave them a sound flogging, kicked them down the private stair, and spurned the man, box and image after them; then locking the door, he gave his sisters a fine sermon, in which he represented to them their folly in worshipping a silly wooden graven image, which, though it had eyes, could see not; though it had ears, could hear not; though it had hands, could not help itself; and though it had feet, could not move about unless it were carried. Oh, it was a fine sermon that my young master preached, and sorry I am that the Father of the Fetish, old Mumbo, did not hear it. The elder sister looked ashamed, but the youngest, who was very weak, did nothing but wring her hands, weep and bewail the injury which had been done to the dear image. The young man, however, without paying much regard to either of them went to his father, with whom he had a long conversation, which terminated in the old governor giving orders for preparations to be made for the family's leaving Rome and returning to England. I believe that the old governor was glad of his son's arrival, and rejoiced at the idea of getting away from Italy, where he had been so plundered and imposed upon. The priests, however, made another attempt upon the poor young ladies. By the connivance of the female servant who was in their interest, they found their way once more into their apartment, bringing with them the fetish image, whose body they partly stripped, exhibiting upon it certain sanguine marks which they had daubed upon it with red paint, but which they said were the result of the lashes which it had received from the horsewhip. The youngest girl believed all they said, and kissed and embraced the dear image; but the eldest, whose eyes had been opened by her brother, to whom she was much attached, behaved with proper dignity; for, going to the door, she called the female servant who had a respect for me, and in her presence reproached the two deceivers for their various impudent cheats, and especially for this their last attempt at imposition; adding, that if they did not forthwith withdraw and rid her sister and herself of their presence, she would send word by her maid to her brother, who would presently take effectual means to expel them. They took the hint and departed, and we saw no more of them.

"At the end of three days we departed from Rome, but the maid whom the priests had cajoled remained behind, and it is probable that the youngest of our ladies would have done the same thing if she could have had her own will, for she was continually raving about her image, and saying, she should wish to live with it in a convent; but we watched the poor thing, and got her on board ship. Oh, glad was I to leave that fetish country, and old Mumbo behind me!"

CHAPTER C

" WE arrived in England, and went to our country seat, but the peace and tranquillity of the family had been marred, and I no longer found my place the pleasant one which it had formerly been ; there was nothing but gloom in the house, for the youngest daughter exhibited signs of lunacy, and was obliged to be kept under confinement. The next season I attended my master, his son and eldest daughter to London, as I had previously done. There I left them, for hearing that a young baronet, an acquaintance of the family, wanted a servant, I applied for the place, with the consent of my masters, both of whom gave me a strong recommendation, and being approved of, I went to live with him.

" My new master was what is called a sporting character, very fond of the turf, upon which he was not very fortunate. He was frequently very much in want of money, and my wages were anything but regularly paid ; nevertheless, I liked him very much, for he treated me more like a friend than a domestic, continually consulting me as to his affairs. At length he was brought nearly to his last shifts, by backing the favourite at the Derby, which favourite turned out a regular brute, being found nowhere at the rush. Whereupon, he and I had a solemn consultation over fourteen glasses of brandy and water, and as many cigars— I mean, between us—as to what was to be done. He wished to start a coach, in which event he was to be driver and I guard. He was quite competent to drive a coach, being a first-rate whip, and I dare say I should have made a first-rate guard ; but to start a coach requires money, and we neither of us believed that anybody would trust us with vehicles and horses, so that idea was laid aside. We then debated as to whether or not he should go into the Church ; but to go into the Church—at any rate to become a dean or bishop, which would have been our aim—it is necessary for a man to possess some education ; and my master, although he had been at the best school in England, that is, the most expensive, and also at College, was almost totally illiterate, so we let the Church scheme follow that of the coach. At last, bethinking me that he was tolerably glib at the tongue, as most people are who are addicted to the turf, also a great master of slang, remembering also that he had a crabbed old uncle, who had some borough interest, I proposed that he should get into the House, promising in one fortnight to qualify him to make a figure in it, by certain lessons which I would give him. He consented ; and during the next fortnight I did little else than give him lessons in elocution, following to a tittle the method of the great professor, which I had picked up listening behind the door. At the end of that period, we paid a visit to his relation, an old gouty Tory, who, at first, received us very coolly. My master, however, by flattering a predilection of his for Billy Pitt, soon won his affections so much that he promised to bring him into Parliament, and in less than a month was as good as his word. My master, partly by his own qualifications, and partly by the assistance which he had derived, and still occasionally derived, from me, cut a wonderful figure in the House, and was speedily considered one of the most promising speakers ; he was always a good hand at promising. He is at present, I believe, a Cabinet minister.

"But as he got up in the world, he began to look down on me. I believe he was ashamed of the obligation under which he lay to me ; and at last, requiring no further hints as to oratory from a poor servant like me, he took an opportunity of quarrelling with me and discharging me. However, as he had still some grace, he recommended me to a gentleman with whom, since he had attached himself to politics, he had formed an acquaintance, the editor of a grand Tory Review. I lost caste terribly amongst the servants for entering the service of a person connected with a profession so mean as literature ; and it was proposed at the Servants' Club, in Park Lane, to eject me from that society. The proposition, however, was not carried into effect, and I was permitted to show myself among them, though few condescended to take much notice of me. My master was one of the best men in the world, but also one of the most sensitive. On his veracity being impugned by the editor of a newspaper, he called him out, and shot him through the arm. Though servants are seldom admirers of their masters, I was a great admirer of mine, and eager to follow his example. The day after the encounter, on my veracity being impugned by the servant of Lord C—— in something I said in praise of my master, I determined to call him out, so I went into another room and wrote a challenge. But whom should I send it by? Several servants to whom I applied refused to be the bearers of it; they said I had lost caste, and they could not think of going out with me. At length the servant of the Duke of B—— consented to take it; but he made me to understand that, though he went out with me, he did so merely because he despised the Whiggish principles of Lord C——'s servant, and that if I thought he intended to associate with me, I should be mistaken. Politics, I must tell you, at that time ran as high amongst the servants as the gentlemen, the servants, however, being almost invariably opposed to the politics of their respective masters, though both parties agreed in one point, the scouting of everything low and literary, though I think, of the two, the liberal or reform party were the most inveterate. So he took my challenge, which was accepted; we went out, Lord C——'s servant being seconded by a reformado footman from the Palace. We fired three times without effect; but this affair lost me my place, my master on hearing it forthwith discharged me; he was, as I have said before, very sensitive, and he said this duel of mine was a parody of his own. Being, however, one of the best men in the world, on his discharging me he made me a donation of twenty pounds.

"And it was well that he made me this present, for without it I should have been penniless, having contracted rather expensive habits during the time that I lived with the young baronet. I now determined to visit my parents, whom I had not seen for years. I found them in good health, and, after staying with them for two months, I returned again in the direction of town, walking in order to see the country. On the second day of my journey, not being used to such fatigue, I fell ill at a great inn on the north road, and there I continued for some weeks till I recovered, but by that time my money was entirely spent. By living at the inn I had contracted an acquaintance with the master and the people, and become accustomed to inn life. As I thought that I might find some difficulty in procuring any desirable situation in London, owing to my late connection with literature, I determined to remain where I was, provided my services would be accepted. I offered them to the master, who, finding I knew something of horses, engaged me as a postillion. I have remained there since. You have now heard my story.

"Stay, you sha'n't say that I told my tale without a per— peroration. What shall it be? Oh, I remember something which will serve for one. As I was driving my chaise some weeks ago, on my return from L——, I saw standing at the gate of an avenue, which led up to an old mansion, a figure which I thought I recognised. I looked at it attentively, and the figure, as I passed, looked at me ; whether it remembered me I do not know, but I recognised the face it showed me full well.

"If it was not the identical face of the red-haired priest whom I had seen at Rome, may I catch cold !

"Young gentleman, I will now take a spell on your blanket— young lady, good-night."

[End of Vol. III., 1851.]

THE EDITOR'S POSTSCRIPT.

Lavengro and *The Romany Rye* (properly *Romanó Rái*) were terms applied to George Borrow in his youth by the Norfolk Gypsy, Ambrose Smith, better known in these volumes as Jasper Petulengro. The names signify respectively "Philologist" and "the Gypsy Gentleman". The two works thus entitled constitute a more or less exact autobiography of the writer of them, from the date of his birth to the end of August, 1825. The author himself confesses in his Preface that "the time embraces nearly the first quarter of the present century".

Lavengro was written at Oulton, in Suffolk, slowly and at intervals, between the years 1842 and 1851. The MSS. exist in three varieties: 1. The primitive draft of a portion, found scattered through sundry notebooks and on isolated scraps of paper, as described in the letter to Dawson Turner (*Life*, i., p. 394). 2. The definitive autograph text in one thick quarto volume. 3. The transcript for the printers, made by Mrs. Borrow, in one large folio volume, interlarded with the author's additions and corrections.

The text of the present edition reproduces with fidelity the first issue of 1851. Occasionally a verbal alteration, introduced by the author himself into his second edition of 1872, has been adopted in this, whenever it seemed to improve the reading. In general, however, that reprint was in many respects a defective one. Not only words, but even whole sentences, which had escaped the printers, remained undetected by the editor, and, as a consequence, were lost to later impressions, based, as they all have been, on that issue. We should have preferred to alter, quietly and without remark, certain errors in the text, as we did in the documents published in the *Life;* but save in a single instance, we have left such inaccuracies intact, reserving all corrections for the place where we might be supposed to exercise a free hand.[1]

---

[1] The one sole emendation consists in substituting the masc. *cheval* for the fem. *jument*, on p. 314. *Le* jument est *beau* was a solecism that could not longer be tolerated.

The insertion, with brackets of course, of the promised inedited episodes, caused in two cases some embarrassment. In removing them from the final form of his MS., Mr. Borrow closed up the gap with a few fitting lines which concealed the withdrawal. These words had to be suppressed on the restoration of the passages.

The insertions will be met with as follows :—

The Poet Parkinson, pp. 119-25.

The Wake of Freya, pp. 128-33.

Cromwell's Statue and the *Dairyman's Daughter*, pp. 196-98.

Portobello or the Irish Patriot, pp. 231-39.

Thomas d'Éterville, in the *Notes*, pp. 558-59.

Thus we have made a full statement as regards the text of the present reprint. Any one who takes up this edition will discover no visible name, or preface, or introduction, save only those of George Borrow, from the title to the close. The book is, therefore, "all Borrow," and we have sought to render the helping hand as inconspicuous as possible. Should, however, the prejudiced stumble at the *Notes*, we can say in the language of the fairy smith of Loughmore: *is agad an t-leigheas*, you have the remedy in your own power.

Speaking of the *Notes*, they have been drawn up on the unimpeachable testimony of contemporaneous record. Especially have we sought the works which Mr. Borrow was accustomed to read in his younger days, and at times with curious results. A list of these is given at the close of *The Romany Rye*, and is referred to in these notes as " Bibliography " for the sake of concision. What is not here explained can be easily looked up in our *Life, Writings, and Correspondence of George Borrow*, London, 1899, which of itself furnishes a sufficient and unalterable exhibition of the facts concerning the man and his work.

W. I. KNAPP.

HIGH ST., OXFORD,
November, 1899.

NOTES TO *LAVENGRO,*

WITH

CORRECTIONS, IDENTIFICATIONS AND TRANSLATIONS.

Page 1. **East D——** : East Dereham, a small town in Norfolk, 16 miles W. of Norwich, and 102 N.E. of London. Here Capt. Thomas Borrow, the father of George, was often stationed from 1792 to 1812.—1. **East Anglia** : This Anglo-Saxon kingdom comprised the present counties of Norfolk, Suffolk and Cambridge.—1. **Tredinnock**, read *Trethinnick :* Parish of St. Cleer, Cornwall.—2. **Big Ben** : Benjamin Brain or Bryan was born in 1753. Some of his most severe "battles" were fought between 1780 and 1790—one on the 30th of August in the latter year, with Hooper at Newbury, Berks. A few days after this exploit, he picked a quarrel with Sergeant Borrow of the Coldstream Guards, which resulted in the Hyde Park encounter. Some four months later, *i.e.*, 17th January, 1791, the decisive fight for the championship came off between Brain and Johnson. It was an appalling spectacle, and struck dumb with horror, even in that day, the witnesses to the dreadful conflict. Big Ben was the victor, and remained champion of England from that date until his death *three years* (not "four months") later—8th April, 1794. "Lavengro," carried away by the enthusiasm of early reminiscence, allowed himself to declare that his father read the Bible to Brain in his latter moments. But in 1794 Thomas Borrow was busy recruiting soldiers in Norfolk, one hundred miles from the scene of the dying pugilist. However, the error was probably one of date merely, and during the year 1791 Thomas doubtless read the Bible to him in London, since we learn from Pierce Egan that " Ben derived great consolation from hearing the Bible read, and generally solicited those of his acquaintance who called upon him to read a chapter to him ".[1]—3. **Captain** : The West Norfolk Militia was raised in 1759 by the third Earl of Orford. He died in December, 1791, when the regiment was *reorganised* (not "raised") under the new Colonel, the Hon. Horatio Walpole, subsequently the sixth Earl of Orford. Thus in February, 1792, Thomas was transferred from the Guards to be Sergeant-major in the W.N.M., and stationed at East Dereham. He married the following year, became Quarter-master (with the rank of Ensign) in 1795, and Adjutant (Lieutenant) in February, 1798. This his final promotion doubtless gave him the *honorary* rank of Captain, since in the *Monthly Army List* for 1804 we read : "Adjutant, Thomas Borrow, *Capt.*". But a letter before me dated 18th April, 1799, from his Major, is officially addressed to him as "Lieut. Borrow, Adjutant," etc., etc.—3. **Petrement** : Our author knew very well that his mother's maiden name was Ann *Perfrement*, pronounced and written *Parfrement* at the present day by those of the family we have met. The correct spelling is found on the tombstone

[1] *Boxiana*, ii., 497.

of her sister, Sarah, at Dereham (1817), and on that of her brother, Samuel, at Salthouse near Holt (1864).—3. **Castle of De Burgh**: A fanciful Borrovian epithet applied to Norwich Castle. Nor did the exiles *build* the Church of St. Mary-the-Less, in Queen Street, Norwich; it was a distinct parish church long before Elizabeth's reign, and in her time the parish was consolidated with the neighbouring one of St. George's, Tombland, while the church became municipal property. But the French exiles of the Edict of 1685 *did* worship there, even as did the Dutch refugees from Alva's persecution a century before (1565-70).—4. **Middle Age**: Borrow's father was thirty-four, and his mother twenty-one, at the date of their marriage. John was born seven years after the marriage, and George ten. The mother was, then, thirty-one at George's birth.—4. **Bishop Hopkins**: Sermons.—4. **Angola**: More correctly *Angora.*—5. **Foreign grave**: Lieut. John Thomas Borrow died at Guanajuato, Mexico, 22nd November, 1833.

Pages **12-13**. **"Snorro"** Sturleson: Poet and historian of Iceland (1178-1241). Harald (not *Harold*) III., called "Haardraade". Battle of Stamford Bridge, A.D. 1066, same year as Norman Conquest. See Mallet's *Northern Antiquities*, pp. 168-71 and 194; Snorro's *Heimskringla*, ii., p. 164, and his *Chronica*, 1633, p. 381, for the quotation; also *Bibliog.* at end of *Romany Rye.*—13. **Winchester**: Rather *Winchelsea*, according to the Regimental Records.—14. **A gallant frigate**: A reminiscence of Norman Cross gossip in 1810-11. "Ninety-eight French prisoners, the crew of a large French privateer of eighteen guns called the *Contre-Amiral Magon*, and commanded by the notorious Blackman, were captured 16th October, 1804, by Capt. Hancock of the *Cruiser* sloop, and brought into Yarmouth. They marched into Norwich, 26th November, and the next morning proceeded under guard on their way to Norman Cross barracks"—*Norwich Papers*, 1804.—15. **Lady Bountiful**: Dame Eleanor Fenn (1743-1813).—15. **Bard**: William Cowper (1731-1800).—16. **Some Saint**: Withburga, daughter of Anna, king of the East Angles, was the "saint" and the "daughter" at the same time.—19. **Hunchbacked rhymer**: Alexander Pope.—20. **Properties** of God, read *attributes.*—20. **Rector**: The Rev. F. J. H. Wollaston.—20. **Philoh**: James Philo (1745-1829).—21. **Tolerism**, read *toleration.*—24. **Mere**: Whittlesea Mere, long since drained.—31. **Bengui**: See the vocabulary at the end for all Gypsy words in this volume.—34. **Jasper**: The change from *Ambrose* to Jasper was made in pencil in Mrs. Borrow's transcript at the last moment in 1849, before handing it to the printers.—38. **Three years**: Included in the subsequent narrative, *not* excluded from it as his Norwich school days (1814-15, 1816-18) were. They extend from July, 1811, to April, 1813—from Norman Cross to Edinburgh. The chronology, according to the Regimental Records, was as follows: George was at East Dereham from 22nd July to 18th November, 1811, at J. S. Buck's ("*Dr. B.'s*") school; 30th November, 1811, to February, 1812, at Colchester; 28th February to 5th March, 1812, at Harwich; 15th to 19th March, at Leicester; 21st to 30th March, at Melton Mowbray; 2nd to 25th April, at Leicester again; 28th April to 3rd May, at Tamworth (*Lavengro*, pp. 367-68); 8th to 26th May, at Macclesfield; 28th May to 2nd August, at Stockport; 3rd to 23rd August, at Ashton; 24th August to 15th December, at Huddersfield (*W. W.*, p. 64, and *Lavengro*, pp. 39-41); 16th December, 1812, to 19th March, 1813, at Sheffield; 20th and 21st March, 1813, at Leeds; 22nd March, at Wetherby; 23rd March, Boroughbridge; 24th March, Allerton; 25th March, Darlington; 26th March, Durham (*W. W.*, pp. 258-59); 27th and 28th March, Newcastle; 29th March, Morpeth; 30th March, Alnwick; 3rd and 4th April, at Berwick-upon-Tweed; 6th April, 1813, Edinburgh Castle.—38. **Lilly**: See *Bibliog.*

Page 42. **Bank of a river**: The Tweed. The scene here described occurred on a Sunday, 4th April, 1813, near Berwick, where they " arrived the preceding night " (p. 44).—42. **Elvir Hill**: See Borrow's *Romantic Ballads*, Norwich, 1826, pp. 111-14. This piece entitled " Elvir Hill," one of the old Danish ballads of Vedel's collection, 1591, represents the dangers attending a youth who " rested " his " head upon Elvir Hill's side " where he was so charmed in his sleep by a brace of seductive fairies, that

> " If my good luck had not managed it so
> That the cock crew out then in the distance,
> I should have been murder'd by them on the Hill,
> Without power to offer resistance.

> " 'Tis therefore I counsel each young Danish swain
> Who may ride in the forest so dreary,
> Ne'er to lay down upon lone Elvir Hill
> Though he chance to be ever so weary."

43. Skaldaglam: The *barditus* of Tacitus, or the " din " made by the Norse " bards " (skalds) on shields and with shouts as they rushed into battle. It is not in Molbech, but Snorro frequently uses it in his *Chronica*, 1633.—**43. Kalevala**: Title of the great Finnish epic, of which the hero is Woinomöinen. —**43. Polak**: Polander or Pole.—**43. Magyar** (pron. *Mädjr*): Hungarian.— **43. Batuscha**: An erratum of the author for his *Batuschca* (161)—better *Batyushca*, " father Tsar "—but generally applied by Borrow to his friend the *Pope*.—**45 to 55**: See *Life*, i., pp. 39-43.—**46. Bui hin Digri**: The Jomsburg Viking, A.D. 994. See Borrow's *Romantic Ballads*, p. 136, and *Once A Week*, ix., p. 686. The account is given in Snorro's *Chronica*, 1633, p. 136 (see *Bibliog.*), but a more accessible version of it is found in Mallet's *Northern Antiquities* (Bohn's ed.), pp. 144-45.—**46. Horunga Vog**, read *Hjörúnga Vágr* in Icelandic, or *Vaag* in Danish. In *Romany Rye* (p. 359) it is Englished as " Horinger Bay ".—**50. Hickathrift**: A Norfolk worthy of the eleventh century, whose prodigious exploits with the axle of his cart as an offensive weapon, and the wheel as a shield, are handed down in the chap-books of the last three centuries. See p. 63 ; also *Bibliog.* at the end of *Romany Rye*.—**51. Elzigood**: William E., of Heigham, Norwich, enlisted October, 1789, became Drum-major in the regiment, 22nd October, 1802 ; called facetiously or maliciously *Else-than-gude* on p. 54.—**55. O'Hanlon**: Redmond O'Hanlon (d. 1681), a proprietor of Ulster, dispossessed under the Cromwellian settlement, and afterwards leader of a band of outlaws.—**56. Disbanded**: The W.N.M. regiment left Edinburgh in July, 1814, and was disembodied at Norwich, 19th July. It was again called out, 10th July, 1815, and sent to Ireland. John Borrow was appointed Ensign, 29th May, 1815, and Lieutenant, 13th December of the same year. The regiment sailed from Harwich (" port in Essex ") 31st August, reaching Cork harbour (" the cove ") about 9th September, 1815. **63. Wight Wallace** (story book of): See *Bibliog.*
Page 63. **Shorsha**: The Irish for *George*, properly written *Seors*, but the author usually wrote his Irish by sound.—**64. Saggart**, read *sagart* : (Lat. *sacerdos*), a priest.—**64. Finn-ma-Coul**: In Irish Fionn-mac-Cumhail, the father of Ossian.—**64. Brian Boroo**: In Irish, Brian Boroimhe, a king of Ireland (926-1014).—**65. Saggarting**: Studying with reference to the priest-hood.—**65. Mavourneen**: Properly *mo mhuirnin*, my darling.—**65. Hanam**

mon Dioul: Wrongly given for *M'anam o'n Diabhal* [God preserve] my soul
from the devil! See *Romany Rye*, p. 286, where it is quite correct—*from sound.*
—**66. Christmas over**: 1816. Regiment quartered at Templemore. John,
now a lieutenant (not "ensign"), is sent with a detachment to Loughmore,
three miles away. Sergeant Bagg, promoted to that rank, 10th July, 1815,
accompanies him.—**66. Mountain**: Called locally, "Devil's *Bit*," and not
Devil's *Hill* or *Mt.*, as in the text.—**68. Fine old language** (add: *which*):

> "*A labhair Padric 'nninsè Fail na Riogh*
> *'San faighe caomhsin Colum naomhtha 'n I.*"
> (which) "Patrick spoke in Innisfail to heathen chiefs of old,
> And Columb, the mild prophet saint, spoke in his island-hold."

So Borrow gives the Irish and his version in *Romantic Ballads*, p. viii. The Erse
lines were taken from Lhuyd's *Archæologia Britannica*, Oxford, 1707, sign. *d.*
—**69. The Castle**: Loughmore Castle.—**71. Figure of a man**: Jerry Grant
the Irish outlaw. See the *Newgate Calendars* subsequent to 1840—Pelhan.
Griffith, etc.—**72 and 83.** "**Sas**" and "**Sassanach**," of course mean Englishman or English (Saxon).—**74. Clergyman of the parish**: The Rev. Patrick
Kennedy, vicar of Loughmore. His name is also on the list of subscribers
to the *Romantic Ballads*, Norwich, 1826, as *J.* Kennedy, by mistake.—**76.
Swanton Morley**: A village near East Dereham.—**82. Arrigod yuit** (Irish),
read *airgiod dhuit*: Have you any money?—**82. Tabhair chugam** (pron.
tower khoogam): Give (it) to me.—**83. Is agam an't leigeas** (read *an t-
-leigheas*): I have the remedy.—**83. Another word**: *deaghbhlasda*: See
Romany Rye, p. 266, and *Notes and Queries*, 5th May, 1855, p. 339, article
by George Métivier.

   Page **84. Old city**: Norwich. The regiment having returned to
head-quarters, 11th May, 1816, was mustered out 17th June. The author
describes the city from the "ruined wall" of the old Priory on the hill to
the east.—**85. The Norman Bridge**: is Bishop's Bridge.—**85. Sword
of Cordova**, in Guild Hall, is a mistake for the sword of the Spanish
General Don Xavier Winthuysen.—**90. Vone banished priest**: Rev.
Thomas d'Éterville. The *MS.* gives the following inedited account of
D'Éterville. I omit the oft-recurring expletive *sacré* (accursed):—

   [*Myself.* Were you not yourself forced to flee from your country?

   D'Éterville. That's very true. . . . I became one vagabond—nothing
better, I assure you, my dear; had you seen me, you would have said so.
I arrive at Douvres; no welcome. I walk to Canterbury and knock at the
door of one *auberge.* The landlord opens. "What do you here?" he says;
"who are you?" "Vone exiled priest," I reply. "Get you gone, sirrah!"
he says; "we have beggars enough of our own," and he slams the door in
my face. *Ma foi, il faisoit bien*, for my toe was sticking through my shoe.

   Myself. But you are no longer a vagabond, and your toe does not stick
through your shoe now.

   D'Éterville. No, thank God, the times are changed. I walked and
walked, till I came here, where I became one *philologue* and taught tongues
—French and Italian. I found good friends here, those of my religion.
"He very good man," they say; "one banished priest; we must help him."
I am no longer a vagabond—ride a good horse when I go to visit pupils in
the country—stop at *auberge*—landlord comes to the door: "What do you
please to want, sir?" "Only to bait my horse, that is all." *Eh bien*, landlord very polite; he not call me vagabond; I carry pistols in my pocket.

   Myself. I know you do; I have often seen them. But why do you carry
pistols?

D'Éterville. I ride along the road from the distant village. I have been to visit my pupil whom I instruct in philology. My pupil has paid me my bill, and I carry in my purse the fruits of my philology. I come to one dark spot. Suddenly my bridle is seized, and one tall robber stands at my horse's head with a very clumsy club in his hand. " Stand, rascal," says he ; "your life or your purse! " "Very good, sir," I respond ; "there you have it.' So I put my hand, not into my pocket, but into my holster ; I draw out, not my purse, but my weapon, and—bang! I shoot the English robber through the head.

Myself. It is a bad thing to shed blood ; I should be loth to shoot a robber to save a purse.

D'Eterville. Que tu es bête ! mon ami. Am I to be robbed of the fruits of my philology, made in foreign land, by one English robber ? Shall I become once more one vagabond as of old ? one exiled priest turned from people's doors, my shoe broken, toe sticking through it, like that bad poet who put the Pope in hell ? Bah, bah !

By degrees D'Eterville acquired a considerable fortune for one in his station. Some people go so far as to say that it was principally made by an extensive contraband trade in which he was engaged. Be this as it may, some twenty years from the time of which I am speaking, he departed this life, and shortly before his death his fellow-religionists, who knew him to be wealthy, persuaded him to make a will, by which he bequeathed all his property to certain popish establishments in England. In his last hours, however, he repented, destroyed his first will, and made another, in which he left all he had to certain of his relations in his native country ;—" for," said he, "they think me one fool, but I will show them that they are mistaken. I came to this land one banished priest, where I made one small fortune ; and now I am dying, to whom should I leave the fruits of my philology but to my blood-relations ? In God's name, let me sign. Monsieur Boileau left the fruits of his verses to his niece ; *eh bien,* I will bequeath the fruits of my philology to my niece and nephew. There, there ! thanks be to God, it is done ! They take me for a fool; I am no fool. Leave to the Pope the fruits of my philology ! Bah, bah ! I do no such thing. I do like Monsieur Boileau."]

Page **93.** Earl's Home : Earlham Hall, the residence of Joseph John Gurney (1788-1847), the Norwich banker and famous Quaker. The " tall figure " mentioned on the next page was Mr. Gurney, then twenty-eight years of age.—**95. Only read Greek** : This is a mistake. Mr. Gurney was an early student of Italian. See Braithwaite's *Life,* i., pp. 25 and 49. —**Zohar** : Very correct. Braithwaite, i., p. 37.—**Abarbenel,** read Abarbanel or Abrabanel : A Spanish Jew driven from Spain in 1492. See p. 282.—**97. Castle Hill** : Norwich.—**97. Fair of horses** : Tombland Fair, held on Maundy Thursday every year.—**100. Heath** : Mousehold Heath, near Norwich. See also pp. 106, 161, etc.—**112.** " **Gemiti, sospiri ed alti guai** " (compare Dante, *Inf.,* iii., 8 : " *Quivi sospiri, pianti, e alti guai* ") : Groans, sighs, and deep lamentations.—**114. Ab Gwilym** : See *Bibliog.* at the end of *Romany Rye.*—**114. Cowydd** : A species of Welsh poetry.—**114. Eos** (W.) : Nightingale.—**114. Narrow Court** : Tuck's Court, St. Giles, Norwich.—**115. Old master** : William Simpson of the law firm of Simpson & Rackham, Norwich.—**115. Bon jour** : read *Bonjour* . . .*! bien des choses de ma part à Monsieur Peyrecourt* or *Pierrecourt* ". " Expressions " in this sense (kind regards) is the Spanish *expresiones,* disguised as French.—**118. Bwa Bach** : The " little hunchback ". See p. 114.—**119 to 125. Parkinson the poet** :

This character, who appears for the first time among the inedited episodes of *Lavengro*, was a real one, although his true name (Parkerson) is given somewhat veiled, as usual with Mr. Borrow. He seems to have been the poet-laureate of farmers, corn-merchants, drovers and publicans, selling his muse to the highest bidder, at first in printed sheets of eight pages, and subsequently gathered into pamphlets of thirty or more pages which he offered for one or two shillings each. They were printed by R. Walker, " near the Duke's Palace, Norwich," and sold by " Lane and Walker, St. Andrew's ". They are without date, but cannot range far from 1818. Here are some specimens of his style : " The Norwich Corn Mart. By J. Parkerson, Junior."

> *At one o'clock the busy scene begin,*
> *Quick to the hall they all are posting in ;*
> *The cautious merchant takes his stand,*
> *The farmer shows the produce of his land,*

etc., for sixty-six lines. " On Mr. L . . . taking leave of his wife and children, who was sentenced to transportation for fourteen years " (!):—

> *Hannah, farewell, I'm bound to go,*
> *To taste the bitter draught of woe,*

134 lines. " A Description of the Pine-Apple at Trowse " :—

> *Both Beauty and Art have exerted their skill,*
> *You will find on a spot near the brow of a hill ;*
> *The hill is near Norwich and call'd Bracondale,*
> *I stept into Vince's myself to regale,*

etc., four pages of that.—**124. Mr. C.**: Thomas William Coke, Esq., of Holkham, Earl of Leicester in 1837, and died in 1842.

Pages **128-133. The Wake of Freya**: This incident must have occurred to Mrs. Borrow at her home, Dumpling Green, East Dereham, on a Friday night, 5th December, 1783, when she was twelve (not " *ten* ") years old. Her eldest sister, Elizabeth, would be in her seventeenth year. *Friday* was then, as now, market day at Dereham. The place was the Blyth farm about one and a half miles (not " *three* ") from " pretty D ". The superstition referred to in this episode is, or was, a very common one in Norfolk, and even other countries. See the *Norfolk Chronicle* for 14th May, 1791 ; Glyde's *Norfolk Garland*, pp. 13-14, and George Borrow in the *Quarterly Review* for January, 1861, p. 62.—**130. Freya**: The Venus of the North was the *sister* of Frey, according to Mallet (p. 94), and the original sources.—**136. To London**: Crome (John's teacher) died at Norwich, 22nd April, 1821 ; but John could not leave until after the Regimental Training, which closed that year on 26th June ; hence his departure may be set down for the last of June, 1821.—**136. Rafael**: Note spelling here (also pp. 223 and 225) and *Raphael* on p. 352.— **137. Corregio**, read *Correggio*.—**139. Murray** and **Latroon**, the Scotch outlaw and the " English Rogue ". See *Bibliog.* at the end of *Romany Rye*.—**142.** " **Draoitheac**," magic, read *draoidheachd* (Ir.).—**144. Muggle- tonians**: Evidently a Borrovian slip here. See *Notes and Queries* for 3rd April, 1852, p. 320.—**145. Vedel**: Anders Sörensen Vedel, first collector of the *Kiæmpeviser*, or Heroic Ballads of the Danes, Copenh., 1591.—**146. Chapter xxiii.**: Interview between William Taylor (21 King Street, Norwich) and George Borrow.—**151. Orm Ungarswayne**: "Orm the youthful Swain," *Romantic Ballads*, p. 86. But see the Danish ballad "Birting" in Borrow's *Targum*, St. Petersb., 1835, pp. 59-61, commencing :—

> " It was late at evening tide,
> Sinks the day-star in the wave,
> When alone Orm Ungarswayne
> Rode to seek his father's grave ".

—**151. Swayne Vonved**: See this piece in *Romantic Ballads*, pp. 61-81.— **151. Mousha**, read *Muça*, in Arabic or *Moshé* in Hebrew; both represent our *Moses*. But the Jew's name was *Levi*, according to the *MS*.—**153. The Fight**: Between Painter and Oliver, near North Walsham, 17th July, 1820. This chapter xxiv. relates the author's call on Mr. Petre of Westwick House, which must have been after 20th May, when it was decided that the " battle " should take place within twenty miles of Norwich.—**155. Parr**: There were *two* Parrs, one, Thomas, called " English " or " Old " Parr (1483-1635) who lived 152 years, and Samuel, called the " Greek " Parr (1747-1825,) who had been Head Master of the Norwich Grammar School from 1778 to 1785. This Dr. Samuel Parr was the one referred to by Mr. Petre.—**155. Whiter**: Rev. Walter Whiter, author of the *Commentary on Shakespeare*, Lond. 1794, and *Etymologicum Magnum*, Camb., 1800, 4to; enlarged ed., Camb., 1822-25, 3 vols. 4to.—**156. Game Chicken**: Henry Pierce, nicknamed Game Chicken, beat Gulley, 8th October, 1805 (Egan's *Boxiana*, i., p. 145).—**156. Sporting Gentlemen**: John Thurtell and Edward Painter (" Ned Flatnose "). —**158. Harmanbeck**: Slang for *constable*—word taken from the *English Rogue*.—**161. Batuschca** (read *Bátyooshca*): See p. 43.—**161. Priberjensky**, read *Préobrazhenski* : Crack regiment of the Russian Imperial Guard, so called from the barracks situated near the Church of the Transfiguration (*Préobrazhenïe*).

Page **166. The Fight of 1820**, chapter xxvi. We will here give a condensed portion of a chapter which we suppressed from the *Life*.

On the 20th of May, 1820, an eager crowd might have been seen pressing up to a card displayed in the Castle Tavern, Norwich. The card was signed *T. C.* and *T. Belcher;* but every one knew that the initials stood for the Champion of England, Thomas Cribb. The purport of the notice was that Edward Painter of Norwich was to fight Thomas Oliver of London for a purse of 100 guineas, on Monday, the 17th of July, in a field within twenty miles of the city.

A few days after this announcement, George Borrow was charged by his principals to convey a sum of money to a country gentleman by the name of John Berney Petre, Esq., J.P., residing at Westwick House, some thirteen and a half miles distant on the North Walsham road. The gentleman was just settling the transfer of his inheritance, his father having died eight months before. Borrow walked the entire distance, and while he tarried with the magistrate, the interview took place between him and Thurtell who desired to secure a field for the fight. Mr. Petre could not accommodate them, and they drove on to North Walsham. There they found the " pightle " which suited them in the vicinity of that town, on the road leading to Happisburgh (Hazebro).

Norwich began to fill on Saturday, the 15th of July, as the stage-coaches rolled in by the London (now Ipswich) and Newmarket roads. The Inn

562   *NOTES.*

attached to the Bowling Green on Chapel-Field, then kept by the famous one-legged ex-coachman Dan Gurney (p. 167), was the favourite resort of the "great men" of the day. Belcher, not old Belcher of 1791, but the "Teucer" Belcher, and Cribb, the champion of England, slept at the Castle Tavern, which like Janus had two faces—backed on the Meadows and fronted on White-Lion. The Norfolk in St. Giles and the Angel on the "Walk," housed other varieties of the sporting world.

At an early hour on Monday, the 17th, the roads were alive with pedestrians, equestrians, Jews, Gentiles and Gypsies, in coaches, barouches and vehicles of every sort. From Norwich they streamed down Tombland into Magdalen street and road, out on the Coltishall highway, and thence—sixteen and one half miles in all—to North Walsham and the field. One ancient MacGowan (the Scotch for Petulengro) stood on Coltishall bridge and counted 2050 carriages as they swept past. More than 25,000 men and thieves gathered in concentric circles about the stand.

I do not propose to attempt the description of this celebrated *pugna* or "battle with the fists". Those who crave such diversions will find this one portrayed fittingly in the newspapers of the time. The closing passage of one of them has always seemed to me to be a masterpiece of grim brutality : " Oliver's nob was exchequered, and he fell by heavy right-handed blows on his ears and temple. When on his second's knee, his head dangled about like a poppy after a shower."

A second fight, this time between Sampson, called the "Birmingham boy," and Martin the "baker," lost much of its interest by reason of the storm described in *Lavengro*. "During the contest," says the *Norfolk Chronicle*, "a most tremendous black cloud informed the spectators that a rare sousing was in preparation for them." And the *Mercury* states that "the heavy rain drenched the field, and most betook themselves to a retreat, but the rats were all drinkled". Thus the "cloud" was no fiction, by which the Gypsy foretold the dreadful fate awaiting John Thurtell before Hertford gaol, 9th January, 1824. Ned Painter never fought again. He was landlord of the White Hart Inn from 1823 to 1835. The present proprietor still shows his portrait there, with the above fact duly inscribed on the back of the frame.

Page **168. Public:** The Castle Tavern, Holborn, kept by Tom Belcher—the " Daffy Club ".—**169. " Here's a health to old honest John Bull : "** The verses were taken from a rare old volume entitled : *The Norwich Minstrel*, p. 30. (See *Bibliog.*) :—

"HONEST JOHN BULL."

"Here's a health to 'Old honest John Bull';
    When he's gone we shan't find such another ;
With hearts and with glasses brim full,
    We'll drink to 'Britannia, his mother';
For she gave him a good education,
    Bade him keep to his God and his King,
Be loyal and true to the nation,
    And then to get merry and sing.

"For John is a good-natured fellow,
    Industrious, honest and brave ;
Not afraid of his betters when mellow,
    For betters he knows he must have.

There must be fine lords and fine ladies,
 There must be some little, some great;
Their wealth the support of our trade is,
 Our trade the support of the State.

" Some were born for the court and the city,
 And some for the village and cot;
For it would be a dolorous ditty,
 If we were born ' equal in lot '.
If our ships had no pilots to steer,
 What would come of poor Jack on the shrouds ?
Or our troops no commanders to fear,
 They would soon be arm'd robbers in crowds.

" The plough and the loom would stand still,
 If we were made gentlefolks all ;
If clodhoppers—who then would fill
 The parliament, pulpit or hall ?
' Rights of Man ' makes a very fine sound,
 ' Equal riches ' a plausible tale ;
Whose labourers would then till the ground ?
 All would drink, but who'd brew the ale ?

" Half naked and starv'd, in the streets
 We should wander about, *sans culottes ;*
Would Liberty find us in meats,
 Or Equality lengthen our coats ?
That knaves are for levelling, don't wonder,
 We may easily guess at their views ;
Pray, who'd gain the most by the plunder ?
 Why, they that have nothing to lose.

" Then away with this nonsense and stuff,
 Full of treason, confusion and blood ;
Every Briton has freedom enough
 To be happy as long as he's good.
To be rul'd by a glorious king,
 To be govern'd by jury and laws ;
Then let us be happy and sing,
 ' This, this, is true Liberty's cause '."

Page 174. **Haik**, read *Haïk :* Armenian.—178. **Conqueror of Tippoo
Sahib** : General Harris (1791).—181. **March** : The exact date was discovered by me in private letters in Norwich. See *Life*, i., p. 91. George
left Norwich on the evening of 1st April, 1824, and consequently reached
London early on the morning of 2nd April.—182. **Lodging** : No. 16 Mill-
man Street, Bedford Row.—185. **The publisher** : Sir Richard Phillips.—
185. **Mr. so-and-so** : Taylor of Norwich.—186. **The Magazine** :
The Monthly Magazine ; or, British Register.—187. **The Oxford Review** : *The Universal Review ; or, Chronicle of the Literature of all
Nations.* No. 1, March, 1824, to No. 6, January, 1825. See also pp. 190,
203 and ff.—191. **Red Julius**, called elsewhere by Borrow *Iolo Goch :* A
Welsh bard of the fifteenth century.—193. **Cæsar's Castle** : The Tower
of London.—194 and 423. **Blessed Mary Flanders** : Defoe's *Moll
Flanders.* See *Bibliog.* at the end of *Romany Rye.*—197. **Bookseller's**

shop: The shop was a depository of the Religious Tract Society, the publishers of Legh Richmond's *Annals of the Poor*, of which the first section was the *Dairyman's Daughter* (pp. 101).—203. **Newly married** : Richard, Jr., m. Feb., 1823.—204. **"Newgate Lives"** : The true title was : *Celebrated Trials, and Remarkable Cases of Criminal Jurisprudence, from the earliest records to the year 1825*, Lond., 1825 (February), 6 vols. 8vo.—205. **Translator of "Faustus"** : *Faust, a Drama by Goethe, and Schiller's Song of the Bell ; translated by Lord Francis Leveson Gower*, Lond., J. Murray, 1823, 8vo ; 2nd ed., enlarged, *ibid.*, 1825, 2 vols. 8vo.—208. **Translator of Quintilian**: I doubt whether this was John Carey, LL.D. (1756-1826), who published an edition of Quintilian, 1822, but no *translation*. My information is positive that it was Wm. Gifford, translator of Juvenal, 1802, 3rd ed. 1817. —215. **Oxford**: This constant satirising of the great English university in connection with the publisher's theory, doubtless grew out of a series of articles printed in the Magazine during the years '23 and '24, and which may be summarised by this notice in vol. lvi., p. 349: "In a few days will appear a series of Dialogues between an Oxford Tutor and a Disciple of the new Commonsense Philosophy; in which the mechanical principles of matter and motion will be accurately contrasted with the theories of occult powers which are at present cherished by the Universities and Royal Associations throughout Europe ".—220. **Churchyard**: St. Giles churchyard where Capt. Borrow was buried on the 4th of March previous.—220. **A New Mayor**: Inexact. Robert Hawkes was mayor of Norwich in 1822. Therefore he was now *ex*-mayor—220. **Man with a Hump**: Thomas Osborn Springfield, was not a watchmaker so far as is known in Norwich, but " carried on the wholesale silk business, having almost a monopoly of the market " (Bayne's *Norwich*, p. 588).—221. **Painter of the heroic**: Benjamin Robert Haydon (1785-1846).—224. **Norman Arch**: The grand entrance and exit to the Norwich Cathedral, west side.—225. **Snap**: The Snap-Dragon of Norwich is the *Tarasque* of the south of France, and the *Tarasca* of Corpus day in Spain. It represents a Dragon or monster with hideous jaws, supported by men concealed, all but their legs, within its capacious belly, and carried about in civic processions prior to the year 1835 ; even now it is seen on Guy Fawkes' day, the 5th of November.—**Whiffler**: An official character of the old Norwich Corporation, strangely uniformed and accoutred, who headed the annual procession on Guildhall day, flourishing a sword in a marvellous manner. All this was abolished on the passage of the Municipal Reform Act in 1835. As a consequence, says a contemporaneous writer, "the Aldermen left off wearing their scarlet gowns, *Snap* was laid up on a shelf in the 'Sword Room' in the Guildhall, and the *Whifflers* no longer danced at the head of the procession in their picturesque costume. It was a pretty sight, and their skill in flourishing their short swords was marvellous to behold." See *Romany Rye*, pp. 349-50.—**Billy Blind** and **Owlenglass** (Till Eulenspiegel) : See *Bibliography*.—228. **Brandt and Struensee**: For High-Treason in Denmark, 1772. See *Celebrated Trials*, iv., p. 465 ; and for Richard Patch (" yeoman Patch "), 1805, vol. v., p. 584. —229. **Lord Byron**: The remains of the poet lay in state from Friday 9th July, 1824, in Sir Edward Knatchbull's house, Great George Street, to Monday the 12th when they were conveyed to Hucknall-Torkard in Nottinghamshire. On that day (12th July) Borrow witnessed the procession as described in the text.—233. **Carolan's Receipt**: Torlough (*i.e.*, Charles) O'Carolan, the celebrated Irish harper and bard, was born at Nobber, Co. Meath, in 1670, and died in 1738. See Alfred Webb's *Compendium of*

Irish Biography, Dublin, 1878, p. 372; J. C. Walker's *Irish Bards*, 1786, App., pp. 86-87, and *Dict. of Nat. Biog.*, xli., p. 343. The " Receipt " in *Irish* is in Walker, and at the end of Vallancey's Irish Grammar, second ed., Dublin, 1781.[1] Here is the translation given in Walker :—

" When by sickness or sorrow assail'd,
To the mansion of Stafford I hie'd ;
His advice or his cordial ne'er fail'd
To relieve me—nor e'er was denied.

" At midnight our glasses went round,
In the morning a cup he would send ;
By the force of his wit he has found
That my life did on drinking depend.

" With the spirit of Whiskey inspir'd,
By my Harp e'en the pow'r is confess'd ;
'Tis then that my genius is fir'd,
'Tis then I sing sweetest and best.

" Ye friends and ye neighbours draw near,
Attend to the close of my song ;
Remember, if life you hold dear,
That drinking your life will prolong."

Curiously enough among the subscribers to the *Romantic Ballads*, Norwich, 1826, we find these names : (p. 185) " F. Arden, Esq., London, five copies," " T. G. O'Donnahoo, Esq., London, five copies ; " (p. 187) " Mr. J. Turner, London ".

Page **244. The Review**: The Review actually ceased January, 1825, with its sixth number.—**268. Laham** : In Heb. bread is *lèhem ;* but our author probably wrote it by sound. *Z'hats* is the acc. of *hats*, the Arm. for bread ; for as Borrow's source, old Villotte (1714), says : " *Accusativus præfigit nominativo literam z* ".—**270** and **286. Mesroub,** read *Miesrob,* who, about A.D. 450 introduced the Armenian alphabet. **271. Sea** in Arm. is *dzow*. See *Romany Rye*, p. 356—**281. Adelánte** (Span.) : Come in.—**281. Bueno** (Span.) : Good. This sound of the word *bueno*, heard in 1825 from the Jew Manasseh, was brought to Borrow's memory in 1836 when he met the Jew Abarbanel on the roads in Spain. See *B. in S.*, p. 65, sm. ed. — **282. Una vez,** etc. (Span.) : On one occasion when he was intoxicated.—**282. Goyim** (Heb.) : Nations, Gentiles.—**282. Lasan akhades,** read *Lâshôn haqqôdesh :* Sacred language, *i.e.,* Hebrew.—**282. Janin** : Wine in Heb. is *yáyin* (not *yânin*), but our author quoted correctly from the *Dialoghi di Amore composti per Leone Medico*, Vinegia, 1541, and the Span. ed. (which I use) : *Los Dialogos de Amor de mestre Leon Abarbanel medico y Filosofo excelente*, Venetia, 1568, sm. 4to (Bodleian). The passage is : " And he (Noah), after the flood, was called *Janus* on account of his invention of wine, for *Janin* in Hebrew signifies wine, and he is represented with two faces

[1] Beginning—
" *Mas tinn no slán atharlaigheas féin,*
Do ghluáis me trá, agus bfhéirde mé,
Air cuáirt an Seóin le sócal dfhághail,
An Stafartach saimh, nach gnáth gan chéill."

turned in opposite directions, because he saw before the flood and after it ".[1]
G. B. always writes Abarbenel for Abarbanel. His true name was Leo
Abrabanel.—**282. Janinoso** (Judæo-Span.) meaning *vinosus*, intoxicated.—
283. Epicouraiyim: Christians, as below, the "Epicureans," for so the
rabbis of the East call us in the West—properly, "unbelievers". But
Borrow's form is not found in Buxtorf (1869)—read אפיקורוסין *Epikûrôsîn*
and (pop.) *Epikûrin*.—**285. Sephardim**: Spanish and Portuguese Jews, as the
Ashkenazim are the German Jews.—**290 to 301. I am at . . .** : Green-
wich, Blackheath and Shooter's Hill (301).—**304. Colonel B. . . .**: Col.
Blood. See *Celebrated Trials*, vol. ii., pp. 248-354: "Thomas Blood, generally called Colonel Blood, who stole the crown from the Tower of London,
1671".—**317. Got fare to . . .** , read Amesbury, Wilts.—**323. City of
the Spire**: Salisbury.—**325. From . . .** , read Bristol.—**330. Stranger**:
Could not be William Beckford (1759-1844) of Fonthill Park, three miles
from Hinton, a dozen or fifteen miles from Salisbury. Besides the place
was sold in 1822 and George Mortimer occupied it in 1825. Borrow had
been walking *five* days in a N.W. direction from Salisbury, and all his
narrative harmonises with the places and dates that bring him to Horn-
castle in August, 1825.—**362. Abedariums**, read *abecedariums*.—**363.
Flaming Tinman**: He is also called by Borrow, Blazing Tinman, Flying
Tinker, Blazing Bosville or Boswell, and finally Anselo Herne, his true
clan-name.—**367. Ten years ago**, *i.e.*, thirteen, when he was at Tamworth in April or May, 1812.—**377. The Romany chi**, etc.: See p. 387
for the translation.—**379. Answer to the gillie**: The Rommany churl and
the Rommany girl love thieving and spaeing and lying and everything but
honesty and truth.—**390. Peth yw**, etc. (W.): What is that lying there on the
ground? *Yn wirionedd*, in truth, surely.—**390. Gwenwyn**: Poison! Poison!
the lad has been poisoned! - **394. Hanged the mayor**: The suppressed
name of the Welshman and the whole account of the affair is given in *Wild
Wales*, p. 7 (chapter iii).—**404. Bardd Cwsg**: The Sleeping Bard, by
Ellis Wynn. See *Bibliog.*—**421. Merddin Wyllt** (*Myrddin*): *i.e.*, Wild
Merlin, called the Wizard.—**423. Found written**: See *Moll Flanders*
by Defoe, p. 188, ed. 1722: "Oh! what a felicity is it to mankind," *said I*,
"that they cannot see into the hearts of one another!" I have carefully
re-read the whole volume of *Moll Flanders*, and find no such passages as
those referred to here, save the one above. Hence, we may justly infer
that Borrow quoted the *spirit*, rather than the words, of his author. See
Romany Rye, pp. 305-6.—**431. Catraeth**, read *Cattraeth*. The reference is to
Aneurin's book, the *Gododin*, or Battle of Cattraeth. See *Bibliog.*—**432.
Fish or flesh**: See Borrow's *Targum*, St. Petersb., 1835, p. 76, under the
"History of Taliesin," ending:—

> "I saw the end with horror
> Of Sodom and Gomorrah!
> And with this very eye
> Have seen the [Trinity];
> I till the judgment day
> Upon the earth shall stray:
> *None knows for certainty*
> *Whether fish or flesh I be.*"

[1] "El qual (Noé) despues del diluuio, por su inuencion del uino, fue lhamado
Iano, porque Ianin en ebràico quiere dezir uino, y lo pintan con dos caras boltadas,
porque tuuo uista antes del diluuio y despues" (*Foja* 71, *verso*).

The original Welsh of the "Hanes Taliesin" is in the *Gorchestion Beirdd Cymru*, 1773—*Bibliog.* at the end of *Romany Rye.*—432. **Take this** : This Bible, with Peter Williams' name in it, was sold in London in 1886 out of Geo. Borrow's collection.—443. **Mumpers' Dingle** : Near Willenhall, Staffordshire. The place is properly *Momber* or *Monmer Lane*, and is now occupied by the "Monmer Lane Ironworks," hence totally obliterated.—444. **Volundr** (*Völundr*) : The Wayland Smith of Northern legends. See in the *Bibliog.* under "Wayland Smith," and Mallet, p. 570.—456. **Ingeborg** : The lines are from the *Romantic Ballads* of 1826, p. 58, entitled the "Heroes of Dovrefeld. From the old Danish."—456. "**As I was jawing** : " Text and translation of the whole eight lines are found on pp. 182-83 of the *Lavo-Lil*, 1874 :—

> *As I to the town was going one day*
> *My Roman lass I met by the way.*

The *MS.* is somewhat different—"Rommany" instead of *Roman*, and the last line, "If you will share my lot with me ".—469. **The man in black** : This priest seems to have been a Fraser of Lovat. See *Romany Rye*, p. 25, and "Arbuthnot" in the *Bibliog.*—481. **Armenian** : It must be remembered that Borrow's Armenian was limited to the Introduction, Grammar and Lat.-Arm. Dict. of the Jesuit Joseph Villotte, 1714, fol., which he picked up at Norwich in 1822-23 as he tells us on p. 175, and *Romany Rye*, p. 92. Hence all his examples are taken from that book—*mi*, one ; *yergou*, two ; *yerek*, three, and those in *Romany Rye.*— 482. **Buona sera** (It.) : Good evening.—482. **Per far visita**, etc. : To pay your lordship a call, that is my motive.—486. **Che io non**, etc., read *ch' io*, etc. : That I do not believe at all.—488. **Addio** : Farewell.—497. **Pulci** : See the *Bibliog.* This version is rather free and *local*. Here is the original (canto xviii., f. 97, ed. 1546) :—

> *Rispose allhor Margutte : " A dirtel tosto,*
> *Io non credo piu al nero ch' a l'azzurro,*
> *Ma nel cappone, o lesso, o, vuogli, arrosto,*
> *E credo alcuna volta anco nel burro,*
> *Nella cervogia, e, quando io n'ho, nel mosto,*
> *E molto piu nell' aspro che il mangurro,*
> *Ma sopra tutto nel buon vino ho fede,*
> *E credo che sia salvo chi gli crede."*

503. **O Cavaliere**, etc. : Oh, Sir Walter, ye have wrought much in behalf of the Holy See !—504. **Poveri frati** : Poor friars !—508. **One fellow I met** : See the postillion's story on pp. 536-48.—513. **Master** in Arm. is *d'yèr ;* of a master, *d'yearn ;* pl., *d'yeark.*—515. **Koul Adonai**, read *Kôl A.* The next quotation is from part of verse 4 of the xxixth Psalm, which he gives according to the prayer-book version.

LIST OF GYPSY WORDS IN *LAVENGRO*.

Adrey, in.
Ambról, pear.
Andé, in, into.
André, in, within.
Angár, charcoal, coals.
Apopli, again.
Aukko, here is.
Ava, yes.
Ávali, yes.
Avella, comes, is coming.

Baró, large, big.
Bawlor, swine.
Bebee (aunt), grandmother.
Bengui, devil.
Bitchadey, pl. sent.
Bitchadey pawdel (p. 300), an error for *bitchadó pawdel*, sing.
Boró, great.
Borodromengro, highwayman.
Boro foros, London.

Cafi, horse-shoe nail.
Cana, when.
Caulor, shillings.
Chabé, pl. of
Chabó, child, lad, Gypsy.
Chachipen, truth.
Chal, lad, Gypsy.
Chal Devlehi, go with God, farewell.
Chavó, *i.q. chabó.*
Chi, girl, lass, Gypsy.
Chinomescro, chisel.
Chipes, pl. tongues.
Chive, to throw; pass (bad money).
Chivios, he or it is cast.
Chong, hill.
Chong gav, Norwich.
Churi, knife.
Coor, to strike, hammer.
Cooromengro, boxer.
Covantza, anvil.

Dearginni (Hung. G.), it thunders.
Dinelo, a fool, silly.
Divvus, day.
Dloovu, money (for *lovo*).

Dook, to bewitch, to spirit away.
Dook, spirit, soul, divining spirit, demon, ghost.
Dosta, enough.
Dovey odoi, that there, up yonder.
Drab, herb, poison.
Drab, to poison.
Drom, road, way.
Drow (often pl.), drugs; poison.
Dui, two.
Dukker*in* (the *in* is Eng. "ing"), any one's fortune, or fortunes, fate, fortune-telling.
Dukker*in* dook, the fortune-telling or divining spirit or demon.
Dukkeripen, fortune-telling.
Duvel, God.
Duvelskoe, divine.

Engro (mere *ending*), Borrovian for "master," "fellow," "chap".
Foros, city, town.

Gav, village, town.
Gillie, song, ditty.
Gorgio, non-gypsy, stranger, somebody, police. G. avella, some one is coming. G. shunella, some one is listening. G.'s welling, the police are about.
Gorgious, adj. formed from *gorgio.*
Grandbebee, see *bebee.*
Grondinni (*Roumanian* G.), it hails.
Gry, horse, pony.

Harkomescro, tinker.
Hinjiri, executioner.
Hir mi Devlis, by my G——.
Hokkeripen, falsehood.

Jaw, to go. **Jaw-ing,** going.
Jib, tongue, language.
Juggal, dog.
Juwa, woman.

Kauley, f. of
Kaulo, black, dark.

(568)

Kaulomescro, blacksmith.
Kaured, stole.
Kekaubi, kettle.
Ker, house.
Kosko, good.
Kral or Krallis, king.

Lachipen, honesty.
Lavengro, "word-master," "philologist".
Leste, him.
Lil, book.
Loovu, coin, money.
Lundra, London.
Luripen, theft, robbery.

Mailla, donkey.
Manricli, cake.
Manro, bread.
Manus, man.
Marel (read *merel*), dies.
Men, we.
Mensar (read *mensa*), with us.
Miro, my.
Morro, bread.
Muchtar, tool-box.

Nashkado, lost, hanged.
Nashky, gallows.

O, the.
Odoi, there ; dovey o., yonder.

Pa, over, for.
Pal, brother, friend, mate.
Palor, brothers.
Parraco, I thank.
Pawdel, on the other side, across; bitchadey p., transported.
Pen, to say, to tell ; penning, telling.
Peshota, pl. bellows.
Petul, horse-shoe.
Petulengro, smith.
Pindro, hoof, foot.
Pios, health (in toasting).
Plaistra, pincers.
Plastramengro, runner, detective.
Poknees, magistrate.
Prala (*voc.*). brother.
Pudamengro, blower, bellows.
Puró, old, ancient.
Puv, earth, ground.

Ran, stick, cane.

Rati, blood, stock.
Rikkení, f. of
Rikkenó, pretty, fine.
Rin, file.
Rom, husband ; Gypsy.
Roman, Borrovian for Gypsy.
Romaneskoenæs, in Gypsy fashion.
Romanly (Bor.), in Gypsy, G.-like.
Romanó, Gypsy.
Rome and dree (Rom andré ?) Gypsy at heart.
Romí, wife.
Rommanis, in Gypsy.
Rommany, Gypsy.
Rommany Chal, Eng. Gypsy.
Rommany Chi, f. Eng. Gypsy-girl.
Rovel, weeps.
Rye, gentleman ; farming r., farmer.

Sap, snake.
Sapengro, snake-catcher.
Sastra, iron.
Sastramescro, worker in iron, smith.
Scoppelo, ninny.
Sherengro, head man.
Shoon, to hear, to listen.
Shukaro, hammer.
Shunella, is listening.
Si, is, are.
Sore, all (who).

Ta, and.
Tacho rommanis, faithful wife.
Tan; tent.
Tasaulor (ta-sorlo), to-morrow.
Tatchipen, truth.
Tawno Chickno, "Shorty".
Tu, thy.
Tute, thee.

Vagescoe chipes, tongues of fire.
Villaminni (Hung. G.), it lightens.

Wafodo, bad, false.
Welling (corruption of *avella*), coming. G.'s welling, "the hawks are abroad"
Wesh, forest.

Yag, fire.
Yeck, one.

Zigañ (*Slavic*), Gypsy.
Zingaro (*Italian*), Gypsy.

823.8 Borrow, George Henry
BOR   Lavengro

DATE DUE

~~FEB 10 1996~~		
FEB 27 1996		
MAR 11 1996		
MAY 23 1996		

1. Materials checked out from the library may be for two weeks and renewed for another two weeks, unless otherwise specified.

2. A fine of five cents a day will be charged for any library materials kept past the due date. No book will be issued to any person incurring such a fine until paid.

3. Library materials must be returned to the library in as good condition as when taken.

4. Patrons must pay for lost or mutilated books, records, or magazines.

5. Each borrower is held responsible for all books drawn on his card and for all fines accruing on the same.

DEMCO